Date: 03/26/21

GRA MORIOKA V.1-3
Morioka, Hiroyuki,
Crest of the stars /

CREST OF THE STARS

THE IMPERIAL PRINCESS

CREST OF THE STARS

2

A WAR MOST MODEST

CREST OF THE STARS

THE RETURN TO STRANGE SKIES

CREST OF THE STARS

AUTHOR: HIROYUKI MORIOKA
ILLUSTRATOR: TOSHIHIRO ONO

Crest of the Stars: Collector's Edition
by Hiroyuki Morioka

Translated by Giuseppe di Martino
Edited by Brandon Koepp

Copyright © Hiroyuki Morioka 1996
Illustrations by Toshihiro Ono

Crest of the Stars Volume 1: The Imperial Princess
Crest of the Stars Volume 2: A Modest War
Crest of the Stars Volume 3: Return to a Strange World

First published in Japan in 1996 by Hayakawa Publishing Corporation
English translation rights arranged with Hayakawa Publishing Corporation

Find more books like this one at www.j-novel.club!

President and Publisher: Samuel Pinansky
Managing Editor: Aimee Zink

ISBN: 978-1-7183-5070-0
Printed in Korea
First Printing: March 2020
10 9 8 7 6 5 4 3 2 1

TABLE OF CONTENTS

CREST 1 OF THE STARS
THE IMPERIAL PRINCESS

AUTHOR: HIROYUKI MORIOKA

ILLUSTRATOR: TOSHIHIRO ONO

TABLE OF CONTENTS

Translator's Notes

Hello, readers. Your humble translator here! And I do mean humble. This has very much been a team effort, in multiple ways—from the work that fans put in (and have put in over the decades) to make this fantastic series more accessible to English-speaking audiences, to the invaluable assistance of my editor and the crew at J-Novel Club.

Thank you for picking this up. Whether this is your first time exploring the Seikai universe, or you're a veteran who can parse the particulars of various classes of starships, we'll make sure you won't regret it.

If you're wondering what the word "Seikai" refers to, it means "realm of the stars" (as in the cosmos), and it forms part of the title of each book in this ongoing masterwork. Comprised of three volumes in total, "Crest of the Stars" forms the epic primer to the story proper, named "Banner of the Stars" (which is in its sixth installment as of the time this is published). If you stick with Lafier and Jint, you can count on the adventure of a lifetime—courtesy, naturally, of the brilliant mind of one Mr. MORIOKA Hiroyuki.

Now, onto the behind-the-scenes. How exactly is this juicy steak getting cooked?

Main Translation Policies

- **Accuracy.** As little information omitted as possible.
- **Legibility.** Where the original text is changed, it's to make the reading experience smoother while conserving the sentiment and spirit of the source.

- **Accessibility.** No confusion as to what is meant, and no need to constantly consult the glossary at the back. There is also a language overview primer included for the curious.

The Language of the Abh

Disclaimer: There are multiple factors that constrain how certain a given transliteration of Baronh can be. For one, while MORIOKA has provided some significant supplementary information, there is no all-encompassing language compendium. I have honored the efforts of fans who have extrapolated from the known spelling conventions in compiling Baronh spellings where they don't clash with the *furigana* pronunciation guides already present over vocabulary in the text. However, said *furigana* is itself tricky to transliterate into English (since there are many sounds that exist in Baronh that don't in Japanese). In other words, some translator discretion was necessary.

As you've seen for yourself, Baronh is near ubiquitous in the books. In order to keep from interrupting the action with the same distracting definitions over and over again, most times a given Baronh word crops up beyond its initial appearance, it has been replaced by its English-meaning-counterpart in **bold**.

The only thing that doesn't follow Baronh spelling conventions is *character names*, which have been kept as accessible as possible, with pronunciations spelled out at points to cover all bases. For example, Lafier's name is actually spelled "Lamhirh" (with "mh" pronounced as "f" and "rh" as a rolling "r"), but her name was often rendered as "Lafiel" in prior translations, and "Lamhirh" would be tough for unacquainted readers to parse. Moreover, I think names come with more transliteration wiggle room than vocabulary, much like how the Japanese name しんいちろう can be rendered as "Shin'icihirō" or as "Shinichirou," among other ways. Names will be shown in their actual Baronh spelling when: a) belted out in long monikers (e.g., *Ablïarsec Néïc Dubreuscr [Bœrh Parhynr] Lamhirh*), so as to preserve some of the formal, stuffy feeling of them; b) when first introduced; c) when the accessibility-spelling looks a little silly (e.g., *Dusanh* vs. Doosanyuh).

It's important to note that accessibility spellings of proper nouns are *not* the IPA pronunciations (which are difficult to convey in phonetically-spelled English, and impossible in most cases to know for sure anyway), but rather useful approximations.

In addition, I've taken it upon myself to coin some neologisms to match Seikai-only terms. Some examples you might have noticed include **starpilot** and **compucrystals**. Personally, I reckon the retro-futurist feel of these does a decent job of conveying the plot's semi-pulpy atmosphere. Some of the other terms I came up with to mitigate potential reader confusion (e.g., making the rank of *bhodac* into "grandee" as opposed to "prince" because that might lead readers to think Jint is royalty as opposed to nobility [incidentally, where Jint's status as heir to his countdom is brought up, he has been called a "noble prince" and not just a "prince"]). To slay another elephant in the room for Seikai fans, it's "Jint," not "Jinto"—or his name isn't *Linn Ssynec Raucr (Ïarlucec Dreur Haïder) Ghintec*!

Please forgive my indulgent pontificating; it's just that I've become a diehard fan of the Seikai series in the process of working on it! Hope I'll catch you in *Banner of the Stars*, where I'll no doubt drone on even more in the Translator's Note section!

Still exploring the vast reaches of the inhabited universe, and of the thesaurus,

Giuseppe di Martino

Welcome to the Abh Empire

…Or as they would say in their native tongue of *Baronh*, the great and indefatigable *Bar Frybarec!*

"Bar fry-ba-rec?"

Nope, it's actually pronounced "Bar Fryoobar!" Some quick points!

- It's spelled "Abh" but pronounced "Ahv!" "Bh" is a "v" sound! Keep your eye out for other two-letter combinations that use the letter "h" to make for a single sound!

    For Example: Rébh (a passenger ship) is pronounced "REV." Meanwhile, the word *onh* (idiot) is pronounced "OHNYUH," because *nh* makes a "nyuh" sound.

- You'll see a lot of "-c" and "–ec" at the ends of Baronh nouns. These are silent!

    For Example: Lonidec (a base) is pronounced "LOHNEED."

- When "c" isn't silent, it's ALWAYS a hard "c" (like a "k")!

    For Example: Cénh (a trainee pupil) is pronounced "KENYUH."

- You'll also see a lot of "ai"s that represent "eh" sounds (or close enough), as well as "au"s that make "oh" sounds.

    For Example: Arnaigh (an orbital tower) is pronounced "ARNEHZH." Meanwhile, *baurh* (zero) is "BORR."

- "Eu" is akin to a "yoo" sound.

    For Example: Reucec (gentry) is "RYOOK."

- There are some spelling exceptions.

    For Example: It's spelled *Aïbss* (surface-dwelling "Lander" human) but pronounced "AEEP."

We're sure you'll pick it up as you go!

14

NOTE: The *actual* phonology is more varied, and these pronunciation guides are handy *approximations*. The way these words are spelled is based on Baronh's own baked-in system of Romanization/transliteration (the script is in fact written in glyphs called "Ath").

ALSO NOTE: After the first appearance of the majority of Baronh vocabulary, if they appear again, they will be replaced by their English equivalent in **bold**.

The language is just another aspect of what makes this magnificent space empire and its culture so fascinating! And we're confident that you'll know your *froch* from your *frocragh* in no time! Now to pull the curtain on a saga that will rattle the very cosmos!

Foreword

The figure that is depicted in this crest is called a "Gaftnochec," (or, when written phonetically, a "GAHFTNOHSH"). It is a dragon of aberrant form, as it sports eight heads. This mythical beast had long been forgotten. However, a certain empire chose it to adorn the design of its crest, and so the "Gaftnochec" became the most prominent of all the imaginary creatures humanity has conceived.

That was by simple dint of the fact that the empire comprised a nation of enormity unparalleled in human history. The race that built the empire is named the Abh (pronounced "AHV"). Perhaps they ought to be called what they, in their pride, call themselves — the Kin of the Stars.

In any case, let us return our attention to the Gaftnochec. After all, there are countless texts on the subject of that race.

Roberto Lopez, *The Cryptids That Inhabited Earth*

Characters

Jint (or "*Ghintec*" in Abh writing)
...... Son of the President of the Planetary Government of Martin

Lafier (or "*Lamhirh*" in Abh writing)
...... Trainee Starpilot aboard the patrol ship *Gothelauth*

Hecto-Commander Lecsh ("*Laicch*")
...... Ship Commander of the *Gothelauth*

Deca-Commander Rayria (or "*Rairïac*")
...... Vice Commander of the *Gothelauth*

Clowar (or "*Clüarh*")
...... Ruler of the Febdash Barony

Sroof (or "*Srumh*")
...... Klowal's father and former Baron of Febdash

Sehrnye (or "*Sérnaïc*")
...... Servant vassal of the Febdash Barony

Que Durin
...... Jint's friend from his time on the planet Delktu

Prologue

The night sky was nigh cloudless. Staring up at the heavens on a night like this evoked the sensation they might just suck up its hapless spectators.

Between the stars, a satellite glided slowly — a satellite that wasn't present near the planet Martin 30 days prior. It gazed down menacingly, as though upon a planet of prisoners, illuminating with its phosphorescent glow. One might have wondered whether the moon they said orbited Earth shone like that, too.

That pinprick of light that just passed underneath it must have been an Abh spaceship: the real, true oppressors of the 10 million citizens of Martin.

Actually, there wasn't merely a single point of light. There were, in fact, dozens. No matter where in the night sky one planted their eyes, at least one of them came into view.

Even now, another flock emerged from beyond the Exotic Jungle that plunged ever deeper into the pitch dark, not unlike the bugs of Martin that gathered, teeming to frolic. The points of light were especially numerous near that giant sphere wrapped in a faint light. Careful observation revealed that the lights were moving in and out of the sphere.

The lights painted long luminescent streaks behind them, sliding across the celestial expanse with a speed that proved they couldn't be stars. There were even those that dipped close enough to the surface that one could ascertain their shape, if only dimly. It was like something out of a dream. Jint ought to have resented them, but he could only stare, transfixed.

Jint Lynn was eight years of age then. According to the standard calendar insisted upon by a subset of adherents of the old nostalgic Earth ways, he was 10. By either reckoning, he was a child. Though it was well past a child's bedtime, Jint stared up at this unfamiliar night sky from the hybrid-functionality structure's rooftop park.

In the distant past, before Jint was born, the only star system humanity inhabited was what was called the "Solar System."

A research vessel named the "Oort Cloud" that was deployed by a certain nation discovered a wondrous elementary particle in a sector 0.3 light-years away from the sun. Its mass was 1,000 times greater than a proton's. It would have been a huge anomaly had that been all, yet its baffling characteristics proved numerous.

For one, each released around 500 megawatts. No one could point to where that energy came from. Some put forward the so-called "White Hole Theory" to explain it; others theorized it was due to parallel dimensions, hyperspace, or subspace — whatever the term for it, they claimed one or more holes must have opened up in the barrier that divides this universe from alternate ones. All of those ideas were nothing more than speculation: hypotheses at best.

In any event, the particle was given the name "yuanon," and research commenced. That research's primary aim was not to determine the particle's true nature; rather, it sought to secure methods of *utilizing* it.

Humanity had, at that juncture, already obtained nuclear fusion, so they did not usually worry about their source of power on land, but the depths of space were another matter entirely. Before any prospect of efficient interstellar travel could be entertained, the issue of mass differentials lay before them. If someone attempted to travel to the next star over within their lifetime, it would require an amount of fuel many hundreds of times heavier than the combined weight of the ship and its load.

That was the principle set in stone by physics. A fuel-on-board nuclear fusion propulsion model would never be suitable for practical use. Even the Bussard Ramscoop Propulsion Method, which had a fair amount of hope placed in it, was ultimately considered impossible due to the density of interstellar matter. Nor, indeed, was matter-antimatter annihilation-propulsion then within reach, and even if it had been, it wouldn't solve the mass problem.

On the other hand, if yuanons could be made the spaceship's energy source, then differentials of mass could be disregarded without concern. After all, fuel would no longer be necessary. For that reason, the yuanon-propulsion spaceship was engineered.

Its basic structure was cylindrical; at the core of the cylinder lay a magnetic trap that held in yuanons. The cylinder's interior was lined with a high-temperature superconducting substance which reflected the charged particles emitted by yuanons. A portion of the electromagnetic waves were then absorbed, with the surplus energy radiating into the vacuum through a heat sink. Meanwhile, electrically neutral particles could be absorbed by the material inserted between the inner tubes and the overall structure.

When a pilot wished to accelerate with full power, they could close a number of the tubes and funnel the rushing torrent of energy in a single direction. If they didn't want to accelerate, they could keep more tubes open to emit equal amounts of energy in both directions. Adjusting the rate of acceleration was as simple as opening and closing the tubes' apertures.

Despite the multitude of technical and economic barriers, rampant overpopulation and the strife it caused would mark the final stages of the era and lend strongly to the realization of yuanon propulsion.

A survey into nearby star systems had already been completed by unmanned nuclear fusion-propelled ships. As a result, atmospheres containing free oxygen were found to be rare in this galaxy. It was not enough for the planet to have the right level of gravity and distance from its sun; other factors such as the initial conditions of the star system's formation and its rock composition ratios also came into play. Earthlike planets were the exception among exceptions. That meant that the number of planets on which carbon-based lifeforms could live was low.

Regardless, that was not an insurmountable problem for the Star System Emigration Plan, since the pressure caused by the ever-burgeoning population spurred humanity to outfit themselves with terraforming technology, implementing trial runs on bodies such as Mars and Venus. After that, it became apparent that all they had to do was apply the technology (to which they'd already grown accustomed) to other star systems. Nor was there any need to worry their heads over ethical issues regarding extraterrestrial lifeforms.

Thus, the first yuanon-propelled spaceship, dubbed "the Pioneer," was constructed. The Pioneer's mission was to carry the personnel and materials necessary to open a colonial hub-point. Once laser-propeller bases were set up, people and objects could then be ferried through light-sail-propelled spaceships, mitigating overreliance on precious yuanon-propelled ships.

Whenever humanity would find a planet that even remotely resembled their old home, they would move in on it. They expanded their domain by terraforming planets that resembled Venus or Mars as well. This was achieved by increasing the density of otherwise overly thin atmospheres to breathable concentrations, or else by trapping and thinning excess parts of high-pressure atmospheres. Atmospheric remodeling, soil production, ecosystem construction...

As they expanded their domain, a new type of yuanon was discovered, unlocking the potential for a groundbreaking interstellar emigration ship. Its construction was undertaken not only within the Solar System, but also in other settled star systems.

The ancestors of the inhabitants of the planet Martin came on an interstellar immigration vessel built in the Solar System named "the Leif Erikson." During this era, the scarcity of yuanons slightly dropped, such that instead of opening a colonial hub, it became possible to introduce yuanon-propelled starships throughout all corners of the emigration program. In the case of the Leif Erikson, it was subsumed into the mission of surveying and selecting places to reside during its preliminary stage. In other words, to board the Leif Erikson was to be sent away, the call to "go live somewhere, anywhere else" ringing in its wake.

Indeed, there were cases where people were merely sent on ships as nuisances to get rid of. But the passengers and crew of the Leif Erikson harbored a peculiar desire. They were thoroughly fixated on a planet wrapped in an atmosphere containing large amounts of oxygen. They thought that there must be an exotic ecosystem out there somewhere, and for countless generations they searched far and wide, until finally, they found a blue planet orbiting a G-type star.

The star (and its system) were named after their first captain, Hyde, while the planet with the oxygenic atmosphere was named after their captain at the time of discovery. Although there was no intelligent life on the planet Martin, a plethora of bizarre flora and fauna did thrive there. The population of the settlers that came aboard the Leif Erikson, who were careful not to disrupt the alien ecosystem there, slowly increased over time.

Following the completion of the settlement process, the Leif Erikson, the interstellar immigration vessel whose duty was now over, was moored in continuous orbit around Martin in commemoration.

On Day 57 of the first season of the 172nd year of their Post-Landing Calendar, the Leif Erikson exploded without warning. In its aftermath lingered the phosphorescent satellite. Although a "satellite" by name, it did not constitute any solid matter, as it was a mere clump of gas. More accurately, it was a unique, formless, spherical pocket of space — in truth, a collective mass of completely transformed yuanons, the yuanons that were once captive within the Leif Erikson. Such was the true nature of Martin's portentous new "moon," which had not yet been given a name.

A single spaceship appeared from out of the explosion. That ship refused all communication, but, interestingly, it circled Martin three times before turning its back on the planet's uneasy populace and quickly returning through the dimly glowing spherical pocket of space.

People made moves to look into the space-sphere, the parting gift left by the mysterious spaceship. However, before the government could appropriate the necessary funding, any opportunity to investigate was dashed, alongside any point of conducting one.

On Day 81 of that very same season and year, a large fleet suddenly made its appearance from within the space-sphere. This time, it was they who wished to communicate. They'd most likely analyzed the radio waves from 24 days prior, determined that Martinese had its roots in the tongue of "English," and set their translation device accordingly. It was not so difficult for Martin to decipher that ancient language, and so there was no language barrier for their first contact.

They called themselves "Abh" (pronounced "AHV"): that was the name of their race. They had blue hair, but their faces and figures were decidedly human, and they were all outwardly youthful and beautiful. They attested thus: "We may look a little different, but we too are children of Earth." It was just that their genes had been slightly modified.

The Abh were said to rule 1,500 human-populated star systems and over 20,000 partly populated star systems. The official title of their system of government (that is to say, their nation) was the *Frybarec Glœr Gor Bari* (Humankind Empire of Abh), though it was often called the *Bar Frybarec* (Abh Empire) for short.

The star system's administration promptly called for talks to enter into a friendly accord. Yet Commander-in-Chief *Abliarsec*, leader of the invasion armada, rejected the offer.

"Sadly," said Abliar, "I cannot do that. My duty is not to forge an alliance for the sake of the Empire; it is to add another world to the Empire's dominion."

Given that these were not unarmed ships, but a deployed armada, there were people who suspected they intended to invade, but even they were not immune from the shock. No one could have imagined they'd be hit with such a direct, unabashed declaration. Was it not a matter of reason to start things off with peaceful negotiation? Even if it would turn into intimidation and browbeating more or less immediately.

It was useless to insist on talking to a diplomat as opposed to a soldier:

"I am not just a soldier," the Commander-in-Chief replied. "I am also a diplomat. In fact, to tell you the truth, I am also Crown Prince. My will is the Empire's will, at least with regards to how you shall be dealt with. I understand your concerns, so I shall deign to explain what it will be like to be a subject of the Empire. I cannot, however, agree to hold negotiations. We have already recognized this planet as belonging to the Empire."

Naturally, an explanation was in order. It was not only government officials, but also the common citizenry who keenly needed one. As such, the video image of the Fleet Commander speaking from the flagship was relayed in real time. It was only then that the people saw what their assailants looked like for the first time.

Pointed ears poked through dark, navy blue locks that draped down to his waist area. That, combined with the coronet of delicate make upon his head, conjured up the image of a fairy out of a children's fable more than a stereotypical *invader*. His face white as fresh snow, he seemed a youth of around 25, and a handsome one. The expression on his countenance, which could be mistaken for a comely lady's, was listless, languid. It spoke volumes of how tedious he found the task of conquering the Hyde Star System.

"Now then, I shall outline the terms between the Empire and your surface world," said the Crown Prince of the Abh, his voice loud and clear. The words, spoken in Baronh (the language of the Abh), continued to be translated into Ancient English, which was in turn translated into Modern Martinese by their own automatic translator.

"First of all, a noble shall be appointed to your star system. In light of this star system's special nature, Her Majesty the Empress will be your governing lady, at least for the time being. Naturally, Her Majesty has other duties to which she must attend, and as such, a magistrate will be dispatched. We believe overworld governance to be a labor far removed from the realm of the elegant, and so long as the landworld populace can look after themselves, lords and magistrates will seldom interfere in any of your more trifling matters. Needless to say, those principles apply to all of you as well."

"Now, kindly put forward your representative. That individual will become your negotiator with your lord or magistrate, as well as with the Empire. It matters not to us what title you bestow upon the office. You may call them 'President,' or 'Chief,' or 'Presiding Chair,' or even 'Emperor.' If you would like to hold onto the illusion that you are a sovereign nation, you may call them 'Foreign Minister.' All the same, the title will appear in imperial documents as 'Landworld Territorial Representative.'"

"It goes without saying, but you are free to choose how you select them. Please use any method you like — elections, hereditary succession, nominations, drawing lots. However, in order to be a Territorial Representative, do be aware that it is necessary to receive the approval of your lord. This will essentially amount to a formality, but veto rights will be exercised against those who would flagrantly advocate secession from the Empire."

"Your lord will not claim any right to levy taxes. Instead, the Empire recognizes the exclusive right to trade with other star systems. The profits so acquired will sustain your lord's livelihood. In some cases, we may invest in your planet, or other planets in your system. In addition, in order to safeguard your assets, it may prove necessary to post an independent garrison, separate and distinct from your autonomous governing body. That being said, it would be in accordance with a pact reached by you with your lord, and you will retain plenty of room for negotiation."

"Roughly speaking, the Empire will only compel you to obey two dictates."

"Firstly, construction of spaceships capable of interstellar navigation shall be forbidden. This is because once you are under imperial control, you, too, will quickly learn how to overcome the light-speed barrier. Such a development is inevitable, but see to it that you do not entertain the notion of actually applying that knowledge. We do not generally permit vessels that navigate to other systems across space. At the risk of repeating myself: Inter-system trade is a privilege enjoyed by your lord, and one protected by imperial patronage. Depending on whether your lord gives the nod, you may be allowed to possess spaceships should they keep their travels within your star system. However, we will not recognize any right to arm those ships."

"Secondly, we shall be putting into place a recruitment office for the Imperial Star Forces. We dispatch soldiers to carry out official duties and maintain security, and the soldiers stationed on your planet's surface will be there for those purposes only. Inferring from your population, these will not exceed 100 in number. As long as your autonomous government is alive and well, I promise that we will not press upon you any additional troops without your consent. Furthermore, there will be no draft, nor any conscription. Surface people are free to choose to join the Star Forces if they so desire. However, we must add that any attempt to interfere with an individual's free will to volunteer for military service is forbidden."

"Now, as for your social status, you are all considered 'landworld citizens.' If, however, you enlist in the Star Forces or become a vassal of your lord, and decide of your own volition to work for the Empire, you will then become a citizen not of your territory but of the Empire and its nation, thereby relinquishing any ties with your territory's local government in favor of obtaining the Empire's patronage. That is what it means to be a subject of the Empire."

"In any case, dramatic change will be coming to your daily lives. That change will not be effected by any tyranny on the part of your lord, but rather by the goods that will become available from other systems. We do not expect any loyalty to the Empire or Her Majesty, so once you become accustomed to these unfamiliar novelty goods, your conscious awareness of your subjection to the Empire as 'landworld citizens' will largely fade."

"Now, I have reached the end of my speech."

"From now on, a subordinate will answer any questions you may have in my stead. Please choose how you will come under the Empire's rule: peacefully, or by outcome of war. Personally, I have deemed the bio-resources of this planet a valuable commodity, but I caution you not to make any unfounded assumptions that we will therefore hesitate to burn you off the surface of your planet. Happily for us, your metropolis is quite conspicuous. It would be more than feasible for us to destroy it without causing much harm to the surrounding nature."

"Now then, you are free to vex my subordinates with an endless *font* of questions, but their patience is limited, so we cannot humor your questions indefinitely. Your deadline to reply is precisely three rotations from now."

Among other imperial subjects, the address was more respectful than most anticipated, but the people of the city who watched the broadcast were incensed. Though polite on a surface level, no care had been taken to word things so as to gain their good will. After all, the rank arrogance was there for all to hear. There was no sign of any consideration that there was even a possibility they could be rebuffed.

The ire of the politicians and the senior bureaucrats was especially intense. The positions that they'd jostled so hard to seize had been described by that young Abh noble as "a labor far removed from the realm of the elegant"! Besides, what proof did they have that he was telling the truth? For all they knew, the Abh Commander-in-Chief could be lying, and subjects of the Empire were victims of repression. In fact, it would be crazy to honestly believe that a bunch of people who had come out of nowhere to all but attack them were actually sincere.

Naturally, bureaucrats and representatives of the city's inhabitants did go on to pepper the officers with endless questions through the communication circuits, gaining a lot of information in the process. However, the time they were given to analyze that information was far too short. Attempting to determine the authenticity of their answers was an exercise in despair. A group of experienced court attorneys joined the lawmakers in questioning the Abh officers, but they failed to find any points of contradiction. Though, even if the information they were given had been full of lies, the administration of the Hyde Star System had little choice regardless.

The planet Martin housed an anti-space defense system. Since they had also come here from the reaches of space, it was rather easy to predict there would one day be an incursion from that very same space. There was no need to envisage an extrastellar intelligence, either. The possibility their very own fellow humans, violent and ill-mannered, would come for them was already there. Yet allocating the necessary defense funding was easier said than done.

The heads of several different administrations zealously tackled this issue, but all they had were 10 grounded anti-space lasers and 20 anti-space missiles. They boasted no spacefaring army, and it fell on a department within the Ministry of Facilities to maintain and inspect those anti-space weapons. In times of emergency, the weapons' launch controls were supposed to be overseen by a part-time general in an underground control room.

The only other arm of military power the star system's government had access to was the police force that was equipped to, at best, tamp down on a large-scale riot. To say facing off against the firepower of a space armada would place too heavy a burden on them would be an understatement.

Despite that, there was a faction in Parliament that wanted war. They reasoned that the giant fleet could be a bluff, and that, even if they were no match for them in the theater of space, there was hope for victory on the surface. They also reasoned that all other considerations aside, this was a matter of honor. Would it really be fine with the people to simply submit without even attempting to fight?

Of course, there were equally staunch people who thought those arguments were shallow-minded, and as such they dug themselves deeper and deeper in the debates. Discussion went from the clash of lofty concepts and philosophies, to the flinging of personal invective.

However, their session could hardly go on forever. After all was said and done, their deadline loomed in three short days. A day on Martin lasted two hours longer than a day on humanity's ancestral homeworld, but they had to reach a consensus of opinions, and urgently. Unfortunately, Parliament wasn't accustomed to issuing a decision with any swiftness. Reluctantly, they entrusted the decision to the head of government.

The head of government at that time was Rock Lynn — Jint Lynn's father.

President Lynn shared his thoughts with only a handful of others, and whipped up support. Some vigorously opposed him, but he succeeded in laying a gag order on them. With the deadline approaching, President Lynn stood before the transmission equipment of his presidential residence with his reply prepared...

"So that's where you were," said a familiar voice from behind him. "I was looking for you."

"Ah, right," replied Jint.

There stood a tall, slim, middle-aged man. It was Till Corint, President Lynn's private secretary. He had served in that role since Lynn was a member of Parliament, and had known him since before Jint was born.

Jint, for his part, had known about him since he was a child. He more than merely *knew* him, though. He had practically been raised as his own flesh and blood.

Jint never knew his mother. She had been a mine supervisor, dying in an accident before her only son had even learned to crawl. Rock Lynn had felt uneasy about the prospect of raising his son as a single father, and he had his hands full with his political responsibilities, so he asked Till, whom he found so dependable, as well as his wife Lina, to bring up Jint. The Corints were fond of one another, but by happenstance were without child, so they were actually grateful when they took up Rock's request. Jint believed himself to be Till's son until primary school, and the affection he felt for that secretary was deeper than what he felt for his real father. The person he loved the most in the world, however, was Lina Corint.

The sharp features of Till's dark-skinned face were overcast by a sullen shadow.

"I'm sorry," Jint apologized. He thought he'd be scolded for being outside in the dead of night — and a particularly *dangerous* night at that, given the situation. "I'll go back to my room right now!"

"That's all right. Just come with me." Till grasped his hand with enough force to nearly tear it off and stomped off.

Fear dawned on Jint at the sight of Till's unusual, alarming behavior. "Where're we going?"

"The Presidential Residence."

"The Presidential Residence?"

The City of Crandon, the sole city on all of Martin and home to its humans, was composed of three hybrid-functionality structures. They had been given exceedingly practical names, devoid of sentiment: "Omni I," "Omni II," and "Omni III." Jint lived in Omni III with the Corints, while the Presidential Residence was in Omni I.

"What're we going there for?" Going to the Presidential Residence meant seeing his father. What business did his father have with him during such a pivotal time? To say nothing of Till Corint, who, as the secretary of the head of government, should have had more vital work than picking up an eight-year-old boy.

"Just come!" Till turned his back and strode on.

"Wait! Hold on!" Till's strides, which were long even for an adult, forced the adolescent boy to trot to keep up with him. Normally, he'd slow his pace for Jint; what on earth had happened?

Till didn't so much as turn his head. "We have no time, hurry up."

Finally, they had arrived at the elevator-box.

"Hey, are you mad at me about something? I'll say I'm sorry, so please…"

Till didn't answer back. His frustration evident, he just poked at the elevator-box's wall with his index and middle fingers, waiting for it to open up.

Finally, the elevator-box doors opened. No one was in it. Jint had never been so frightened by the idea of being alone with Till.

"Take us to the Nexus Floor," Till told the computer that directed the elevator.

The doors closed and, when the elevator began to lower, Jint felt he couldn't keep quiet for even a second longer. "Hey, do you think we can win?"

"We'll neither win nor lose. There won't be a war to win," he grumbled in reply.

"So we gave up?"

Till glared at the boy. "That's right. Your father chose to surrender. He didn't just 'surrender,' though — he sold us out."

"He sold us out? What do you mean?"

"The bastard made a deal. A dirty, rotten deal," spat Till bluntly.

"A deal?"

"Stop repeating me like a damn parrot!"

"I… I'm sorry." The boy ducked his head.

"Don't get me wrong; I was against war, too. It really doesn't look like we could win. But to make a deal like that!? Dammit, I've lost all respect for Rock!"

Jint grew sad. He'd been secretly proud that he had two fathers. And yet, here was the father who raised him cursing out the father who sired him. His eyes filled with tears.

The father that raised him flashed a guilty expression upon seeing the boy start sobbing convulsively. "I'm sorry. It's not remotely your fault, but I…"

"Tell me what's going on! I've got no idea…"

"Nor would you." Till ruffled his short black hair. "Like I said before, Rock struck a deal. What he did will be announced all too soon. There's no doubt he'll be the object of the scorn of all who live on Martin. There will even be quite a few who will think that if they can't lay their hands on him, they can at least pummel his family members. That's the reason I'm taking you to the Presidential Residence, where there's strict security."

"You mean I'll get beaten up by a mob?" Jint quivered.

"It's not out of the question." Till nodded in cruel confirmation. "Even if it doesn't come to that, they'll heap harassment on you. Verbal abuse. Throwing things. Maybe you'll get a smoke candle tossed into your room."

When Till referred to Jint's room, the first thing that popped in his mind was Lina Corint. "Then what's Lina gonna do? Tons of people know I live in your house!"

"I've already contacted her. She's a grown-up; she can take care of herself."

"You mean she's gone to a safe place before us?" He couldn't believe Lina would run away without him.

"Yep." Till read Jint's expression. "She was worried about you, you know. I calmed her down by telling her I'd go look for you."

"Okay." But something wasn't sitting right with him. After all, there would have been no guarantee Till would actually find him. Lina would have wanted to search for Jint, too. That's what the Lina that Jint knew would have done.

The elevator reached the Nexus Floor on Tier 3, and its doors opened. Each morose for different reasons, the two stepped out onto the Nexus Floor. Countless elevator-tubes were lined up on this floor, running up and down the hybrid-functionality building. They were reminiscent of the pillars holding up the heavy roof of an ancient temple. Unmanned taxi-boxes rushed around between the tubes.

A taxi-box detected the elevator-doors opening and stopped in front of them. With just his right arm, Till prompted Jint to get on. Jint tried to settle his nerves, but he couldn't regain his composure.

"The Presidential Residence. Hurry," Till murmured tersely to the taxi-box. Afterwards, he crossed his arms, and remained silent.

Jint wondered what exactly the "deal" entailed. The mood that hung in the air made it exceedingly difficult to probe Till, but he gathered up all the courage in his small frame and asked: "C'mon, tell me about the deal."

"It's confidential. It's being kept under wraps from the general public until the official announcement."

"From me, too?" he hazarded to ask, timidly.

The secretary snorted in response. "Capitalizing on your *new privileges* already, I see!"

"What do you mean...?"

"Switch on the holo. The announcement will be on in no time." Jint did as he was told and switched on the taxi-box's attached holovision. The stereoscopic holovision video played above the manual driving apparatus.

"For now, the Abh fleet hasn't made any moves," said the tiny, translucent figure. "Reports have come in that there has been some kind of back-and-forth between President Lynn and the invaders. According to information obtained from a certain source, it is said that our surrender to the Empire has been confirmed. Even so, we cannot but continue to hope that those reports are mistaken, and that our leaders will make decisions with honor. In addition, we received notice that there will be a, quote, 'statement of grave significance' delivered at the Presidential Residence at precisely 25 o'clock. 90 seconds remain."

They were a long 90 seconds — a minute and a half he wanted to elapse quickly, but that he also wanted to stretch on forever. Jint was running out of patience as he anxiously stared at the 3-dimensional video, glancing occasionally at the man beside him.

Till was as still as a statue. He didn't give the hologram so much as a peek, instead fixing his line of sight straight ahead.

The taxi-box exited the hybrid-functionality structure and ran through the Liaison Tube suspended in the Exotic Jungle.

Finally, the time came.

The video had already shifted to displaying an empty podium. Then, a handsome-looking spokesman appeared to take the podium. "I will deliver the statement."

Jint gulped from the tension, and gazed at the spokesman's mouth.

"Today, at 23:52, Rock Lynn, President of the Government of the Hyde Star System, expressed to Crown Prince and Imperial Fleet Commander *Abliarsec Neïc Lamsarr Dusanh*, His Highness King of Barkeh, his intention to cede the Hyde Star System's autonomy. Starting today, we are a part of the Humankind Empire of Abh."

Though the holographic projection didn't display them, Jint could hear the clamor of the press corps that had been intently watching the spokesman. There was no shock, no anger in that tumult of voices. There was only resignation. He even heard someone mutter an "I knew it."

Jint glanced at Till, thinking: *See, it couldn't be that bad, right?*

"There's more," said Till.

"However, the President felt that he'd like for the citizens of the Hyde Star System to be the ones to operate the paths to other systems, and as such suggested a compromise. That is to say, a proposal to install a citizen of this system as our 'lord.'"

"You mean that's possible!?" someone gasped.

"There will be time for questions later. Please maintain order," the spokesman said, parrying with ease. "However, I will make an exception in this case and answer. Given the terms they reached, it was indeed possible. In exchange for the codes necessary to disable our anti-space defense system, our new ruler acceded to conditions more favorable for us."

"Then who's this new 'lord'?"

"I told you, you may ask questions later. The initial idea was to select our lord by means of an election. Unfortunately, however, the positions of imperial nobility aren't swayed by electoral results. Nobles aren't generally familiar with the electoral system to begin with!" the spokesman said, attempting a chuckle and botching it.

Even through the airwaves, viewers picked up on the increasingly murderous current in that room.

"Who's our lord!?" Same question, different voice.

"You did watch Commander Abliar's explanation regarding the Empire and Star System, did you not? He may be our 'lord' in a technical sense, but he'll be more akin to the owner of a space trade company. Owners of corporations aren't chosen through elections; it's mostly hereditary in practice, so…"

"Who's our lord!? Dammit, I know, everyone here knows, and you better believe everyone watching knows! We just want to hear you say it, loud and clear! Tell us, what's the name of our new *lord and master*?"

Even Jint had caught on, however much he didn't want to believe it. "It can't be… he's lying…" He looked to Till's eyes for salvation. And yet, he sat there expressionless, his lips shut. Jint turned back to the broadcast, to find the spokesman staring up. He'd been driven into a corner.

"Very well. It's as you've all probably surmised. Rock Lynn will be making our star system his territory." The outcry that ensued could only be described as unmitigated rage.

"That was it. That was the deal," said Till. "Just so he could rise in status to a noble, he handed our only weapon over to our invaders. I had no idea those Abhs had feared our anti-space defense system so much. Maybe we could have put up a real fight after all."

"B-But…" Jint tried his level best to defend his father's honor. "He tried to get them to let us vote for who'd be lord at first! Which means—"

"I wouldn't know!" Till ground his back teeth. "I only caught wind of his 'idea' after it was all over. After the defense systems had been disabled, after the Lynn family would join the ranks of imperial nobility. I don't care what terms he initially proposed. That weasel didn't bother consulting me, his own secretary, beforehand, and he apparently didn't think he had much use for me, either. He must have thought all I could do was bring his kid someplace safe. And here I thought we were best friends!"

"Ah..." Now an additional reason Till was so mad was made clear. Till saw what he did as a *personal* betrayal as well.

"All of you, calm down!" the spokesman on the holovision shrieked. "If you would just think it through rationally, you would understand that this is our best course of action. President Lynn will pay the utmost consideration to all of our government's demands. In truth, as long as he doesn't violate the orders of the Empire, he intends to follow the will of the star system's government — the government of the people. I hope you realize that that wouldn't be something we could hope of someone born a noble of the Empire. We can expect the maximum level of freedom afforded to any star system under the Empire's control."

"Malarkey!"

"How can we take you at your word!?" Some questions could be heard through the jeering outbursts.

"Where is President, ahem, Lord Lynn currently?"

"Yeah, where is that lout!?"

"Errr..." The spokesman had reached a state of stammering previously unthinkable given his job performance up until that moment. "In order to iron out the particulars and to formally receive his peerage at the Empire's capital, he headed to an Abh fleet flagship. He embarked on an Abh landing ship on the French Prairie, and he's currently aboard."

"So he scarpered off!"

"Must be why he put off the announcement for so long."

"Wonder if he'll be back?"

"Oh he'll be back, surrounded by imperial guards."

"No, even if he wanted to return, there's no way he could. You think the Empire'd make him a noble that easily? Heh, looks like he himself got duped. Serves him right!"

"Everyone, please!" But the spokesman was waging a one-man battle. "Please, you must understand, the President made the decisions he made with the happiness of every citizen in mind, not for personal profit—"

Jint couldn't take any more. He switched off the holovision.

"And that's how it is," said Till. "This makes you the next in line for the lordship, you know. Oh my, how crass of me to address you in such a vulgar fashion. You are our 'Noble Prince,' after all. I humbly beseech you, if you would be so magnanimous, forgive me my lapse in manners, Your Excellency."

Jint tried to convince himself that it was all in good humor, but there wasn't a shred of levity on Till's face.

"Stop it, Till..." Jint struggled to hold in the tears. "Why are you talking to me like that... It's not fair... "

"I know it's not." Till kept staring straight ahead. "I know I'm treating you horribly. It's just, I can't get over it. Son of a... It may not look it, but I'm trying my hardest not to yell. Dammit, damn it all..."

The taxi-box entered Omni I's Nexus Floor. The elevator for the Presidential Residence would be arriving soon.

"There's only one thing I want to know..."

"What?" Till looked his way.

"When you told Lina to run..." Suddenly, he lost the desire to finish asking the question. But there was no getting around it; he had to hear the answer. "...Did you tell her about the deal, too?"

"...No. It was being kept under wraps from the general public." That moment's hesitation mercilessly exposed his lie.

"I see..." Jint could virtually hear the rattling as the world with which he was so intimately familiar — the world he loved — collapsed around him.

Chapter 1: Delktu Spaceport

The hustle and bustle hit his ears the instant he stepped off the *dobroriac* (elevator-tube) leading away from the planet's surface. Jint stood still and looked around the waiting-plaza.

Is this *what this place looked like?* Jint tried to recall what it had been like, back then.

It was his second time arriving at a *bidautec* (spaceport). The first time was seven years ago, when he'd arrived at this very **spaceport** on the planet Delktu from Martin (or *Martinh*, as the Abh pronounce it).

His memories of that time, however, were quite fuzzy. He was sure he must have passed through here while he was following that stewardess on the *rébisadh* (cargo passenger ship), though.

All around the circular floor shot elevator-tubes connecting to various places within the port, and at the center lay the elevator-tube leading back to the surface (the tube was also used for cargo). The sight reminded him of the Nexus Floor in the hybrid-functionality building in which he was born and raised.

The difference was that this place was a space for endless carousing. People, self-propelled vending machines, and more were milling around all the countless tables and seats. Of course, there were also people seated on those chairs, many tucking into the food and drink they'd purchased off the vending machines passing by, all while chatting cheerfully in a variety of languages.

The informational broadcast rose in volume so as not to be drowned out by the background music.

"The Lengarf Glorn, the *rébh* (passenger ship) headed toward the *Laicerhynh Estatr* (Duchy of Estoht), is scheduled for a 17:30 departure. Customers who have not yet completed their check-in procedures, we urge you to do so soon, before proceeding to **Elevator-Tube** 17…" Either Delktunians knew how to kill time, or this was the norm across most of the spaceports of the *Frybarec* (Empire).

Other passengers darted around Jint in annoyance. Realizing he had become an obstacle in their path, Jint started walking, too. The *dagboch* (automated luggage) zoomed after him. Gravity here was maintained to be equal to that of Delktu's surface.

The hundred or so people who'd departed the surface aboard the elevator-tube got swallowed by the bustle, and in mere moments, Jint was all by himself. Not that he hadn't felt alone even inside the tube. As a whole, Delktunians were friendly, but when it came to *him*, no one initiated any conversation. For instance, a group of three had been laughing and chatting until they caught sight of Jint, after which they quickly cleared out to the side. When Jint passed into view, the atmosphere around them grew tense.

Oh well, I guess only real weirdos would want to chat it up with somebody dressed like me.

The *sormh* (jumpsuit) he was wearing underneath was more than fine. It was the fashion of the day, after all.

The *daüch* (long robe), on the other hand! Why in blazes did he need to parade around in a *daüch!?* It was absurd. The robe lacked sleeves, while its shoulders hung over each of his own in a V-shape. Held in place by the *ctarœbh* (bandolier sash) tied around his waist, it widened from there until it reached his feet. It was a stark white, while its hem and collar bore thick bordering.

The *datycirh* (compucrystals) inlaid in his *creunoc* (wristgear) were green, identifying his family status as a newly ascended noble.

In addition, an elegant *almfac* (circlet) adorned his head. It was made to match Jint's status, though he didn't know that. As it was vouched for by the *Gar Scass* (Institute of Imperial Crests), one could only assume it was a good match for him.

This was the standard outfit among *rüé simh* (imperial nobility).

In fact, this was the first day he'd ever put on the appearance of a noble. Granted, upon inspecting his reflection in the mirror, it wasn't as bad as he'd expected. If one didn't pay too much mind to how his shoulders were broader than a typical Abh's, the look was tolerable, if only barely.

That being said, it was not at all common for a noble to be alone in a civilian spaceport, and his brown hair instantly gave him away as not being Abh.

"We thank all currently disembarking patrons for riding with the passenger ship Sellef Niziel. Welcome to the *Dreuhynh Bhorlacr* (the Countdom of Vorlash)! The next **elevator-tube** will be departing for the surface in three minutes. The *baüriac* (ferry shuttle) for the planet Gyuxath will be…"

These announcements were also broadcast twice: The first time in Delktunian, and the second in Baronh.

Sure enough, there was a crowd that had just disembarked the Sellef Niziel, but they didn't seem to have any desire to get right on the elevator-tube. By all appearances, they instead planned to hold their first drinking party on Delktu at this geosynchronous orbital spaceport. They bought food and drink from the vending machines and spread them out on the tables.

Passengers who would soon be leaving this star system also drank together, and with great gusto. Jint wondered how many people passed out drunk and let their ships slip away each day.

He couldn't blame them. Almost all of them were immigrants, and for them, this was the one and only time they'd ever travel through space. Small wonder, then, that they'd want to cut loose.

"Hey! Lynn Jint!"

Jint thought he must be hearing things. Unlike on Martin, on Delktu an individual's family name came before their given name, so "Lynn Jint" was most definitely his name.

Not expecting much, Jint searched for the source of that voice. If he hadn't been hearing things, he was sure to have simply heard someone wrong; failing that, there was somebody else with the same name.

So he thought, but when he made out a strapping young man occupying a round table for four by himself, he started beaming with a joy he couldn't see coming.

"Que Durin!" Jint called his friend's name as he came to the table half-running. "What're you doing in a place like this?"

"What am I doing? What else could I be doing here, ya blockhead? I'm here to see you off, dude. *Duh*."

"I see! Thank you, man."

"Or is the presence of a little urchin come to see you off *bothersome* to Mr. Fancy-shmancy Noble?"

Jint laughed. "I said 'thank you,' didn't I? Dumbass. You do know what the words 'thank' and 'you' mean, right?"

"I do when they're *pronounced right*, ya phony immigrant. I'm surprised your accent never slipped out. Well, whatever, just sit down, would ya? I'm tired of waiting for you. Wasn't it supposed to be an 18 o'clock departure? I wanted to see you off before you boarded, but I got here too early."

"You should've sent me a message. I would've met up with you." Jint plopped onto a seat and took a look around expectantly.

"Ah, yeah." Durin looked a little shamefaced. "I'm the only one who's here to see you off. The others aren't coming."

"...Oh." He tried to conceal his disappointment, but he wasn't very successful.

"To tell you the truth, I was a little uneasy myself. I was afraid you might just ignore me when I called you over."

"What're you talking about?" Jint objected placidly. "C'mon, man, we're *minchiu* mates and everything. I wouldn't ignore you."

"Yeah, and we never had another player as terrible as you," Durin replied. But then, suddenly, his expression turned gloomy.

"Don't blame them, all right? We were all shocked. I mean, we knew you were going to an Abh school, but we never dreamed you were so... *high-status...*"

"It's fine," said Jint. "I was probably in the wrong for keeping mum. But would you have honestly let me be your friend if I'd told you I was a **noble**?"

"No." Durin shook his head. "It'd be pretty hard to imagine."

"Yeah."

"*Minchiu*" was the most popular ball sport in Delktunian society, with teams of ten competing against each other. Not only were there professional minchiu teams, there were also regional clubs, as well as school and even company clubs. Jint learned about the game in his school's *minchiu* club, and discovered, to his surprise, that he had some talent at it, after which he joined the regional club. There he made loads of friends, starting with Que Durin.

But Jint had had a secret. He had pretended he was the child of an ordinary immigrant. A mere three days prior, Jint confessed to his band of friends that he had to leave Delktu, and that he was in fact an *imperial noble*.

From the way the atmosphere soured, one might have thought he'd confessed to killing someone. He'd never forget their reactions for the rest of his days. Unable to stand the situation, he'd turned heel and fled.

"None of us knows how to hang with a **noble**. Forget nobles, we'd never even seen a *reucec* (gentry) before."

"I get it, 'cause not even I know how I'm supposed to be acting."

"Sounds serious." Durin nodded. "But ya know, those **noble** clothes really suit you."

"Don't go saying things you don't actually believe, ya galoot." Jint flicked his **robe** with his fingers. "Give it to me straight, it looks like something out of a history play."

"I've gotta say, I'm feeling good. It's not often a poor surface-dweller boy gets to talk face-to-face with a high and mighty noble — and a *bhodac* (\grandee) youth at that!" Durin looked around and said "Oh, looks like we stand out a bit, huh."

"Stop it," said Jint, exasperated. "I know how I must look. I don't look Abh, that's for sure."

To that, Durin didn't respond. "So, you'll be returning to your home planet, right?"

"Huh?" Jint blinked. Now that he mentioned it, while Jint had told them he'd be leaving Delktu, he never did inform them where he'd be going. "No, man. I'm going to *Lacmhacarh*."

"The *aroch* (imperial capital)?"

"Right. It's 'study abroad' for me once again, only this time around I'll be attending the *Cénruc Sazoïr* (Quartermaster Academy)."

"The hell is that?" Durin stared back at him blankly.

"A school that trains administrative officials for the military," Jint explained. "Though I'll be a *lodaïrh sazoïr* (quartermaster starpilot). Two months ago, I took the exam at the *Laburec* (Star Forces) *bandhorh ludorhotr* (recruiting office), and I got in."

"You're gonna be a *soldier*?" His eyes opened wide, his surprise undisguised.

"Yep."

"But haven't you got your own *ribeunec* (star-fief)? Why're you going outta your way to..."

"I'm duty-bound, my friend. To inherit your *snaic* (noble rank), being born into a **noble** household isn't enough. You need to serve in the **Star Forces** as a **starpilot** for a minimum of 10 years. My father was already of advanced age, so they made an exception for him, but that won't fly for me."

"Guess **nobles**'ve got it rough, too."

"Yeah. Seems like the higher your status in the **Empire**, the more obligations are thrust on you. I like it that way, though. It makes a lot more sense than the other way around. That said… it'll actually be three years as an army trainee, and then ten years as a **starpilot**, for a total of thirteen years of army life. Kill me now."

"But you *will* be returning to your home planet, right?"

"At some point, yeah. It is my **fief**, after all." Though calling his home planet his "fief" felt weird.

"No, I'm talking about returning there *now*. You've been gone for a long-ass time already." Durin frowned.

"True, true." Jint hadn't set foot on *Martinh*'s soil in seven years. It had been so long that he wasn't certain he could even properly speak Martinese anymore. His only real lasting link with his home planet was the monthly tidings from his father. According to that correspondence, Till Corint had become a leader in the anti-imperial movement. Jint had no idea what had become of Till's wife Lina.

"Sadly, I'm not in any position to return at the moment," he said, shaking his head. "It seems it's not really a home for me anymore. The founding story of the *Dreughéc Haïder* (House of the Count of Hyde) isn't a heroic one. It's the tale of an original sin. The people of *Martinh* all hate me and my father."

"Ah." His expression was one of deep sympathy. Though they may have been the descendants of immigrants, Delktunians felt a fierce affection for their planet. Getting chased away from their land with hurled stones was their greatest fear. "But you want to be a *fapytec* (lord) despite all of that?"

"I don't *want* to be one," he pouted, chagrined. "I can't tell you how many times I've thought about renouncing my inheritance rights. About becoming a citizen of Delktu and carrying on the same as ever. And even if I wanted to revert back to being a citizen of *Martinh*, it's not like they'd forgive me anyway."

"Then why didn't you?"

"My father persuaded me not to. Here's the deal..."

The man formerly known as President of the Hyde Star System, Rock Lynn, was now *Linn Ssynec Raucr Dreuc Haïder Roch* (Count of Hyde). He'd persuaded his son of the merits of the following line of thinking:

The planet Martinh holds an important resource. That is to say, all the lifeforms that evolved in ways unrelated to Earth's. Humankind has created all manner of mutant creatures, but the gene splicing guided by the superficial wits of man cannot compare, even meagerly, to the evolution wrought by nature over eons. The agth *(territory-nation) newly christened the* Dreuhynh Haïder *(Countdom of Hyde) is extremely rich and fertile.*

However, it is only through commerce with other star systems that those bio-resources can be our wealth. What do you think would happen if we left that exchange of goods to the **Empire***? There's no doubt they'd take a big bite out of it. They'd give the people nothing but their scraps, wouldn't you agree?*

As such, it was necessary for someone of the Hyde Star System to become its lord and take part in its trade.

"Well, I'm convinced," said Durin.

"Yeah, it's reasonable enough. That's why I'm staying a noble. Although, I've been having my doubts lately..."

"Doubts? About?"

"Think about it — it's impossible to be a citizen of Hyde and an Abh **noble** at the same time. I don't have any of the rights of a citizen of Hyde anymore. Sure, it'll be fine with my father at the helm for the time being, though he doesn't have citizen rights in Hyde either. But he's convinced that he's working for the benefit of the star system. I intend to work for the system, too. But what about the generation after me? My son or daughter would have their genes altered; they'll be born as a beauteous blue-haired Abh. That's the rule, and there's no getting around it. They'll also likely be Abh culturally. Would they be capable of putting themselves in the shoes of a Hyde citizen?"

"Dude, you're so damn stiff. Stop overthinking!" Durin looked at him dumbfounded. "That bunch of idiots hates you anyway, so forget about them! Point is, you're part of a *family business*, and *you* get to decide whether you take it up or not. Though if I were you, I wouldn't even think about handing over such a big business to someone else."

A "family business," huh. Never thought about it that way. Jint felt as though he'd been thrown a life vest. Jint was an only child, so if he didn't become the next count, then the Lynn family line would terminate without ever accumulating much by way of tradition. But so what? Who exactly would cry over that? "You're right. You're absolutely right."

"I'm always right." Durin suddenly pointed toward his toes. "Look right here. This is my first time at a spaceport. From up here, I think our planet looks really pretty, too."

It was then that Jint realized the floor was projecting Delktu's surface. A screen right around the same size as their round table was displaying video footage of the clouds drifting over the planet. The *arnaigh* (orbital tower) bridging the surface and the spaceport tapered so thin it seemed a thread before getting sucked into the clouds, which gleamed with the light of their sun, Vorlash.

"Yeah. It is pretty." It dawned on him that he'd never looked down upon the surface of his true home planet, *Martinh*. The realization surprised him a little.

"By the way, how long've you been here? Five years?"

"Nah, been here for seven." Jint looked back up at him. "The invasion of Hyde happened in 945 I.H. (Imperial History, *Rüécoth*)."

"So you came here right after they invaded? Am I remembering that right?"

"Yeah. I had no idea what was going on, they just shoved me on a *frach* (traffic ship), and then whisked me away on a **cargo passenger ship** that was standing by in orbit. Let's just say I learned what it felt like to be an animal dragged to a zoo."

"But you had a retinue, right?" Durin bought some *surguc* (coffee) from a passing vending machine and handed Jint a can. "Take it, on me."

"Thanks."

"Don't worry about it. It feels good to treat a young master **grandee** to a little something."

Jint smiled. "So yeah, about my 'retinue' — there was nobody there for me. Or at least, nobody from *Martinh*."

"Whaaat? But that must've been a super raw deal. You were what, 10, back then?"

"Yeah, I was 10."

"Whose bright idea was it to send a 10-year-old kid alone to a star system dozens of light-years away?"

"Yep. So one of the stewardesses on the **cargo passenger ship** became a full-time attendant for me. I think she must've been asked to do so by my father. She took care of me in lots of ways, including bringing food to my cabin."

"Wow, sounds swanky." Durin looked a tad envious. "Must've been some high-class space travel."

"It wasn't." He grimaced at the memories of that time. "Not least 'cause I couldn't talk to anybody. There weren't any translation devices that could speak my home language then. She somehow managed by using a translation device for Ancient English…"

"Wait a sec. What's 'Ancient English'?"

"My home language is descended from Ancient English. But it's not like I ever learned Ancient English, and now I'm way out of practice with my Martinese. It's unintelligible to me."

"So it's just like Baronh." The majority of Delktunians couldn't understand Baronh, and Durin was no exception.

"Yeah, for the most part. Not that I really felt like chatting anyway. Aboard that ship, I kept quiet. I didn't even take a single step outside my cabin."

"Was that stewardess Abh?"

"No, I think she was a *rüé laimh* (imperial citizen), since she had black hair. Must've been from a *nahainec* (landworld) somewhere. But that didn't matter to me then. They were a crew of invaders to me."

"Heh heh, if she'd been Abh, I've got a feeling you might've gotten attached to her."

"Why's that?"

"C'mon, you know how they say Abhs are all lookers. Guys and ladies alike! I don't care how young you are, you'd be all about playing nice when a gorgeous young woman comes along."

"Come on, dude." Jint became somewhat huffy. "When I look back, I can't help thinking I did wrong by her. I mean, she even went so far as getting off the ship to do my paperwork so I could enroll in school. And despite that, I don't even know her name. She probably did introduce herself, but her name was buried in heaps of either Baronh or Ancient English, both of which were babble to me."

"Huh. Well, whatever. By now, that stewardess has gotta be middle-aged anyhow. Unlike Abhs, us Landers are just gonna keep aging."

"For god's sake, is that the only way you can think about people? I'm trying to express my earnest gratitude to her as a person…"

"Yeah-huh," said Durin, trying to pacify him. "No matter what, I only ever think about pulling in the chicks."

"Good grief," Jint readily agreed. "You're the type that honestly believes that any old person in the crowd that passes you by is the love of your life. It doesn't matter how tenuous the connection is, you never lose time trying to get in super-cozy with her."

"Okay, first of all, I don't just fall for '*any old person.*' She's gotta be cute, obviously. Second of all, I never think of her as the '*love of my life.*' I just want her to be with me for a single night, in fact."

"Hah!" Jint clapped. "So what's your success rate?"

"A lot higher than you think, pal."

"Oh really? I've only ever seen you take out a girl once. Plus, according to what I heard when I asked about it afterwards, that girl was your little sister."

"Fine, then what do you think my success rate is?"

"Zero."

"Look. Compared to zero times, *one time* is infinitely huge."

"What?" Jint looked taken aback. "Don't tell me you're into… *you know…*"

"Quit it. I'm trying to tell you I've won the heart of a maiden that's *not* my sister."

"But just the once, huh?"

"More than once!" Durin fumed. "You just happened to never be around."

"That so? Hey, I'm willing to chalk it up to that for the time being."

"Oh man, you can't face reality, can you? Talk about averting your eyes from the truth. If I score with the ladies, what's it to you?" Then, Durin looked as though something had suddenly occurred to him. "Ah, could it be!? Are you actually into... *you know...*"

"That'll be enough of that." Jint knew Durin was just firing back, so he took it lightly. "I'll have you know I'm a devout follower of the Hetero way. And no matter how thirsty I become, my faith shall hold strong. I will neither woo nor romance you."

"I'm fine with it, honestly." Durin's eyes clung to him.

"If you liked me, you should've confessed to me sooner. Oh yeah, I know, we've still got time. Let's take a moment, before we part ways, to verify our romantic feelings..."

"In full view of all these people?"

"You think public view is any obstacle so long as you've got *love*?"

"You are surprisingly unrelenting, you know that. It makes me wonder whether you might secretly be a 'pagan' yourself."

"Don't be silly." Durin dropped the gag. "'Cause if you're a devout Hetero, then I'm a crazed Hetero fundamentalist extremist."

"Oh, I know." Jint drank the rest of his coffee and tossed the paper cup into the receptacle in the middle of the table. "Thanks again for the drink."

"You don't need to thank me for a **coffee**, young master **noble**." Durin laid down the sick burn and, upon casting a fleeting glance to his right, gave the back of Jint's hand a little poke.

"What is it?"

"Have a look."

Jint followed Durin's line of sight. Sitting by an adjacent table was a middle-aged woman with brown skin. She was taking an interest in his strange combination of brown hair and **noble** attire so visibly that she was practically boring a hole in him.

If I were a real Bar simh (Abh noble), thought Jint, *how would I react in this moment?* Would he have shouted at her, called her "insolent"? Would he have steadfastly ignored her? Or would he have shot her dead without a word?

But what Jint ended up doing instead was flash her an ingratiating smile.

The middle-aged lady looked away slightly, as though she'd seen something she shouldn't have.

Jint breathed a sigh.

"That old lady's hot for you, man. I'm jealous. You're an *old-ladykiller*. I've got half a mind to stick your face over my own…"

"That's not it. She was staring 'cause a Lander wearing the garb of an **imperial noble** is as rare as a dog using *gléc* (chopsticks).

"But you're really getting somewhere, buddy boy. For a Lander, that is."

"I guess," Jint admitted.

Durin had a question for him. "Hey, I've only ever seen them on holovision — are Abhs really that attractive?"

Jint cocked his head. "Couldn't tell ya. I myself haven't ever seen an Abh in the flesh."

"But didn't you attend an Abh school?"

"Wha—?" Jint realized that his friend had been under a misconception. "Wow, I barely ever talked about my school life, did I? So get this: There isn't a single Abh at the Abh Linguistic and Cultural Institute I went to. It's all about educating candidates for naturalization as **imperial citizens**, and there are a lot of former imperial citizens among the faculty. The founders and principal went out there, and then came back. In other words, they're *soss* (landworld citizens) of the **Countdom of Vorlash** that were formerly **imperial citizens**. Mind you, it's not as though the **Empire** and the **Countdom of Vorlash** are linked in some special way; in the end, it's a private school under the jurisdiction of the Vorlash territorial government's Ministry of Education."

"I see. I took it for granted that it was an imperial academy."

"You think Abhs would throw any of their coin at a surface school?"

"When you put it that way, I guess not." Durin angled his head to the side, a common expression of puzzlement. "But then, why did you come to Delktu? Shouldn't they have taken you to an Abh school right off the bat? It's not like learning Delktunian's gonna do you much good, right?"

"Abhs don't go to elementary school. I'd have had to enroll in an institute of higher education, as a kid who was neither a prodigy nor understood any Baronh."

"For real? Then how do Abhs learn to read and write?"

"Their parents teach them."

Jint recounted secondhand the info he'd learned in school. Abh society was aristocratic in nature, and so much weight was placed on each family's *ghédairh* (family traditions). In order to pass on those family traditions, parents needed to personally provide their children with an education. Apparently, the Abh thought it outrageous to allow children, whose personalities were not yet sufficiently concrete, to spend a significant amount of time under a stranger.

During their children's infancies, Abhs gave the task of educating them their undivided attention. **Nobles** with **territories** hired *tosairh* (magistrates) to fill in for them, and even **gentry** took leaves of absence from their work duties, all in the effort to make their heirs more fit for the task.

Moreover, to transmit knowledge that the parent themselves had forgotten, they had *onoüaréïléc* (teacher bots), as well as trips to camp for imparting group-living experiences.

"If you think about it the way they do, I've received a really warped education," said Jint. "My father is the **Count of Hyde**, but there's no way he can be there to teach me the Abh way, so he thought at the very least he could have me learn Baronh and all the common knowledge stuff. That's why he dropped me at the nearest school for **imperial citizen**ship aspirants."

"And so it's been seven years since then," Durin chuckled. "I thought you were smart, but it turns out you're not that brainy."

"I had to study and pick up material that was age-appropriate, so it took me all of that first half-year or so and a ton of sweat to learn Delktunian. For one, most of the students there were Delktunians."

"'Course they were. The only folks who'd study abroad on a **territory-nation** out on the outskirts like Vorlash are country yokels."

"You oughta say stuff like that only after I've returned home. Not even Delktu's most amazing architecture can hold a candle to *Martinh's* hybrid-functionality structures," said Jint in defense of his home.

"Not even this orbital tower?" asked Durin. He was so unfazed it was obnoxious.

Durin had hit a sore spot. As the latest news had it, there still weren't even any prospects for the construction of an orbital tower on *Martinh* due to anti-Abh sentiment, despite the fact that every other inhabited planet within the Empire had one. To ride a spaceship there, one still had to rely on dangerous and costly traffic vessels. Though it seemed there were almost no candidates for space travel anyway.

"C'mon, it's not impressive, it's just stupidly huge," said Jint, straining to come up with a comeback.

"Sure." Durin didn't rebut. He leaned his right elbow against the back of his seat. "Hey, that old lady's staring at you again."

"Must be this dumb hair." Jint combed up his hair. He was fed up.

Abhs kept their hair within tones of blue. However, "tones of blue" was an oversimplification; in reality, the colors they deemed appropriate for hair varied within the range of green to purple, to say nothing of all the different shades thereof. That said, brown hair was out of the question.

"You should've gotten it dyed. Should be easy enough."

"Nah, though I did think about it…"

"Why not, then?"

"For starters, I was afraid I'd sort of delude myself into thinking I was a real Abh. I technically am legally, but genetically I'm a Lander."

"'For starters'? So, there's more where that came from," pressed Durin.

"Yeah, though I guess the only other reason is I'm stubborn. I may've stumbled into being an **imperial noble** by some cosmic mistake, but I don't want people thinking I'm pleased about it."

"Gotcha." Durin leaned over the table, his expression unusually serious. "You know, about what you were saying before… if you wanna call it quits on the **noble** thing, then I'd stand by you, no problem. This is your last chance, isn't it?"

"It's not my last chance," said Jint. "I can withdraw from the aristocracy at any time."

"Why not do it now, then? Is it 'cause they'll stop sending you your allowance?"

"That's one reason."

"I can look after you; just gotta get you a job, that's all."

Jint was shocked. "But you're still in school!"

"Yeah, but even kids in school've got their contacts. I know a manager who appreciates the position of low-income students. I won't beat around the bush; he's my uncle. Besides, you're smart — you could get a government scholarship."

"It's all right. Thank you," said Jint. "I want to see the world of the Abh with my own eyes. I want to see how the people who invade and reign over us live their lives."

"Guess that could be fine, too." Durin shook his head, as if to call him eccentric in his curiosity.

"Besides," Jint continued, "You're the only one who came to see me off."

"That's... uhh..." His friend had suddenly turned rather inarticulate.

"All the kids who hung out with me, were chums with me, back when I was just 'Lynn Jint'... they all flew off the minute they found out that I'd omitted the bit between my family name and my given name. You're the only one who forgave me for misrepresenting my identity. If I'm to ever live as a **landworld citizen**, I'd want to live right here on Delktu. But that requires giving things time to cool down."

"It was a great opportunity to find out who your real friends are." He smiled a weak smile. A smile that didn't suit his typical self.

"It really was," Jint agreed gratefully. "If and when I come back, I might come to you for guidance."

"You got it. Leave it all to me." Durin puffed his chest out in pride. "When I'm out of school, I plan to form a business. And I'm gonna work you to the bone when you're back here as a low-grade employee of mine. I'll even use you in an ad while I'm at it. I can see it now: 'Our company is staffing a former imperial noble!'"

"However will I thank you?"

Durin glanced at the giant clock hanging on the ceiling and said "Uh-oh, has it really gotten this late already? Shouldn't you already be boarding? Which ship you taking?"

"The **imperial** *üicreurh* (warship)."

"Wha?"

"New students of the **military academy** have the right to hitch a ride on an **imperial** war-vessel. At first, I wrestled over the decision, but then I thought I might as well check out what it's like aboard a **warship**, since I'm gonna be a **starpilot** and all. So, I chose to exercise my right."

"Hold up, does that mean a **warship**'s gonna dock at this **spaceport**?"

"Beats me, man. Someone's scheduled to come pick me up at 18 o'clock. And I'm here with the proper attire." Jint pointed as his **long robe**. "Easier to spot this way, they said. Kind of a facile idea for a race capable of prolonged interstellar navigation, huh?"

"Wait, so an Abh soldier's gonna be coming?"

"Yeah; not sure if they'll be Abh, though. A **Star Forces** *bausnall* (soldier) will be here soon, in any case."

"Ah. In that case, I oughta retreat now."

"Huh? How come?" said Jint with some alarm. "Don't you wanna drink in the sight of me getting *hauled off* by 'em?"

"I'll pass." Durin rose from his chair. "The sheer patheticness'd make me spill tears of pity for sure."

"That's rich, coming outta Delktu's most ruthless scoundrel," Jint replied as he, too, rose to his feet.

"Stop flattering me, you're making me blush!" Durin extended his hand.

Jint took it in both hands.

"What's your formal name again?" asked Durin.

"*Linn Ssynec Raucr Ïarlucec Dreur Haïder Ghintec* (Noble Prince of the Countdom of Hyde Jint Lynn, descended of Rock). I think."

Durin goggled at him. "Whaddya mean, 'I think'? It's your name!"

"I'm not used to it. It feels like somebody else's name."

"All right then. From now on you're 'Lynn COUGH Jint.' And you'd better remember my name. 'Que Durin.' Thing of glory, isn't it? It's definitely loads easier to remember than 'Lynn Whosawhat Jint.'"

"Dude. Like I could ever forget you. And you can drop the 'Whosawhat.' Just don't forget the name 'Lynn Jint.'"

"You can count on me, *Linn Ssynec Raucr Ïarlucec Dreur Haïder Ghintec*." Durin's face curled up in a grin, as though boastful of his powerful memory.

Jint returned the smile and let go of Durin's hand.

"See ya. Break a leg out there."

"You, too, man. Make sure you grow your company big enough so that I don't have to worry about searching for work no matter when I return."

"I told you, bro, you can count on me." Durin spun on his heels.

Jint watched him disappear down the elevator-tube, but he never looked back.

When he made to sit back down, the middle-aged woman from before came back into view. But she wasn't looking his way. Those blunt eyes were trained in the opposite direction.

Jint's own eyes pivoted in that direction, as though drawn by a hook.

Someone slender with a skintight black jumpsuit and scarlet *üébh* (waistsash) caught his eye. They made a beeline towards him, drawing even more attention than when Jint first appeared.

Black and red — the *sairhinec* (military uniform) of the **Imperial Star Forces**.

Chapter 2: The *Bénaic Lodaïrr* (Trainee Starpilot)

The definition of "Abh" was laid down clearly and concisely in *Rüé Razaimecoth* (Imperial Law). That is to say, it was a general umbrella term for *Fasanzœrh* (the Imperial Family), **nobles**, and **gentry**.

According to that definition, Jint was, as the legitimate progeny of a **count's household**, indisputably Abh.

However, the word "Abh" meant something else as well: It was also the name of their ethnicity. This double-meaning was not overly problematic by dint of the fact that Abhs-by-law were also typically genetic Abhs.

In other words, Jint was the unfortunate exception. This gap was not something that could easily be covered up. After all, the difference between Abhs and Landers wasn't on the level of divergent races or ethnicities, not truly. It was on the level of different species.

While clearly distinct from Homo Sapiens, it was almost certain that Abhs were descendants of Earth humans. The evolutionary split that produced this "mutant race" cannot have been spurred by a mere spontaneous mutation, it was said, but rather can only have been brought about with an explicit plan in mind.

To back that claim, one needed only point to how even now, the Abh continued to dally with their genes. It was said that the genetic manipulation of newborn children was especially indispensable to them. If there was any deviation among 27,000 designated DNA sequences within a child's nucleic acid molecules, it had to be corrected.

It was also said that this was in order to prevent congenital diseases and maintain the uniformity of their race, but there was a more perceptive way of looking at the matter: their thinking was based on a concept not unlike poetry with predetermined numbers of lines and rhyming patterns — when certain constraints are placed upon an art form, it can reach a higher level of sophistication.

Yes, the awareness of their children's genes as the subject matter of a work of art — this was the resonating verse of Abh culture. It wasn't mandatory; it was out of a simple sense of aesthetics that they touched up their children's genes.

Nor did they practice this genetic art with poor taste. They shared their sense of beauty with most **landworlds**, and no one ever pointlessly ran away with their own hideous predilections — or at least, they seldom ever did.

As such, the Abh comprised a collection of lookers so lovely that it was downright irritating.

The **soldier** of indeterminate gender coming Jint's way seemed the epitome of Abh genetic artistry.

Their long bluish-black locks flowed behind them, and they wore a plain military-issue **circlet**. Their face was oval-shaped, and a light cocoa in hue. The pupils of the striking eyes aimed straight at him were like black agates. Their eyebrows, though thin, traced sharp and elegant lines, and their small nose was beautiful in its delicateness. Their full lips were tightly pursed.

The scarlet **waistsash** was the sign of a **starpilot**.

As for their age… It was said to be a nigh impossible task to judge the age of an Abh by their appearance. That was because they aged in a peculiar way. Up until around age 15, they aged just like their ancestors, but during the 25 or so years following that point, they outwardly only put on about 10 years. After that, they didn't show any signs of aging for the rest of their lives. Abh call the period of growth until age 15 "*zarhoth*" and the subsequent period before one's appearance stops changing "*féroth*."

The Abh were unaging, but contrary to what many Landers believed, they were not immortal. Over time, nerve cell regeneration fatally muddled one's personality and memories. For that reason, it was said they had to make do with the same neuro-biology as their ancestors. Even Abhs couldn't survive the fraying of their brain cells.

In their pride, Abhs programmed their genes to freeze up the functioning of the area of their brains that governed breathing before their intellect faded away. Abhs also died of old age: they just did so between the ages of 200 and 250.

In other words, an Abh that appeared to be in their mid-20s could in fact be 40 or even 200 years old.

However, in this **starpilot**'s case, there was no need to worry about getting their age too far off the mark. They were either somewhere around the end of their *zarhoth* growth period, or the beginning of their *féroth* maturation period. They were most likely around Jint's age.

They'd have to get closer before Jint could be sure of their gender. His gut told him they were a she, but he couldn't be certain. It was quite common among Abh males to possess faces and figures that could pass as a beautiful young maiden's, even past age 200. Indeed, at this age, one couldn't tell whether they were a handsome man or a lovely lady.

But here they came, even as Jint wracked his mind; here they came, parting the crowds with the larger-than-life presence they exuded. The way they walked was dashing and refined. Their head stayed almost completely still. She, or perhaps he, strode forward as though skating.

Jint looked at the rank insignia on the chest of their black Abh **military uniform**. Though he only had a surface knowledge of rank insignias, there were some things he knew.

It was an inverse isosceles triangle with curved sides. Within its silver bordering roared the eight-headed dragon of myth, which stood as the *agh* (crest/coat of arms) of the *Rüéghéc* (Imperial Household) and **imperial** *niglac* (national coat of arms) — a silver *Gaftnochec*. The base color of the lowest-ranked insignia was scarlet. It indicated one was a **starpilot**. There were no other lines or stars emblazoned on their attire.

That meant they were a **trainee starpilot**.

They were wearing a **starpilot**'s uniform, but they weren't formally a starpilot for the time being. They were learning the ropes. That was the position that fresh graduates of a *cénruc lodaïrr* (starpilot academy) took on for half a year, during which they did hands-on training aboard a **warship** or at a *lonidec* (stronghold).

Jint was also able to glean that this **trainee starpilot** was, in fact, a girl from how the insignia was modestly bulging out.

Seeing as he knew she'd come to pick him up, he ought to have walked toward her, but something about her had him overawed; he stood paralyzed.

In that time, the apprentice reached him and planted her heels right in front of him. "Are you *Linn Ssynec Raucr Dreur Haïder Roch*-Lonh (Your Excellency)?"

Jint flinched at the unfaltering recitation of his long and laborious name. It took all his effort just to nod.

Her right hand flashed. Jint sensed danger, so he reflexively took a step back. However, the apprentice had only moved her right hand to place her index and middle fingers to her **circlet**, the Abh salute of respect.

"I have come to greet you from the *résic* (patrol ship) *Gothelauth*. You will follow me." Her tone of voice was definitely a girl's, but her tense demeanor wouldn't have been out of place in a young man. Her voice was limpid, like plucking a harpstring wound tight enough to snap.

After finishing her salute, she turned her back and once again took brisk strides, as though she didn't much care whether Jint followed her or not.

Anger seethed in Jint's chest. It wasn't that he'd expected a lot. The dictionary definition of *"aïbss"* (Lander, i.e., surface-dweller) wasn't discriminatory per se, but from what he'd gathered reading his textbooks, Landers were the targets of the Abh's unspoken disdain. That's why he was able to brace himself a little. Of course, he was used to being treated differently from the rest. But everyone is born equal, and so he had no desire to live his life groveling before people who held him in contempt.

He was sure the the duty of escorting the heir of some upstart Lander **noble** wouldn't be to the **trainee starpilot** girl's liking. No, it wasn't just her; nobody aboard the **patrol ship** cared for the idea, so they pushed it on the lowest-ranked apprentice. Jint convinced himself that was the case.

This had to be redressed: first impressions are crucial to interpersonal relations. Of this, Jint was very sure; it was what he'd learned from his experiences on Delktu. It all started with the courtesy of introducing oneself.

"Wait, hold up!" called Jint.

"What?" She turned back to face him.

"You know my name, right?"

"Are you not *Linn Ssynec-Raucr Dreur Haïder Roch*-Lonh?" Doubt tinged the jet-black pupils that were staring back at him. It didn't seem as though she'd been mocking or looking down on him after all.

"Yeah, I am *Linn Whosawhat Ghintec*, but I don't know *your* name. I dunno what it's like for Abhs, but that's not something I can be comfortable just letting slide."

Astonished, she opened her large eyes even wider.

Was it rude to ask an Abh their name? Jint felt a smidge uneasy. He may have studied Abh culture, but what he knew, he was taught by former **imperial citizens** at school. His knowledge could be incomplete.

However, her reaction far exceeded his expectations.

Elation broke on the **trainee**'s mouth, and she puffed her chest. Her blue-black hair swept in the air, and the *cothec cisaiger* (functionality crystals) at the ends of her *cisaigec* (access-cables) swayed like a couple of eccentric earrings.

"You will call me 'Lafier'!"

She's just saying her name — so why did it sound like a declaration? wondered Jint. It was positively triumphal in tone.

"In exchange," continued Lafier, "I would like to simply call you 'Jint.' Agreed?" The instant he saw Lafier's inquisitive eyes, the grudge he'd harbored in his heart melted away like so much snow tossed into boiling water. Her captivating eyebrows lifted in unmistakable apprehension, frightened and unsure what she'd do if rejected.

"Of, of course!" Jint nodded enthusiastically. "I'd be grateful if you'd do that for me."

"Well, greetings then, Jint," said Lafier. "Let's go."

"Right." And so, now amenable, he followed Lafier.

"Jint," said Lafier. "There's something that I would like to ask you."

"What?"

"Earlier, when I saluted you, you stepped back. What was that?"

Jint couldn't exactly tell her that he thought she'd hit him, so he made something up on the spot. "That's just how we greet people on my home planet. Old habits."

"Ohh…" Lafier didn't appear to doubt what he said at all. "Your home planet's greeting customs are really strange. I had gotten the impression that you were guarding against some kind of attack."

"You're bound to think something you're not used to seeing is odd, no matter the culture," Jint explained soberly.

"I see," she said, nodding. "I grew up surrounded by other Abhs, so I don't know much about foreign cultures."

"Makes sense you wouldn't."

"That being said, you are also an Abh, Jint. I think you ought to familiarize yourself with the ways of the *Carsarh Gereulacr* (Kin of the Stars)."

Jint groaned on the inside. That's what the Abh dubbed themselves from time to time. The "Kin of the Stars." It seemed they were rather fond of this poetic moniker.

But is regarding balls of gas as your relatives really all that much to be proud of? pondered Jint. *Nuclear fusion's neat, I guess, but that's literally all they do. Never mind that, has anyone ever tried asking the stars themselves what they think about all of this?*

However, the only words that passed through his lips were: "Easier said than done. Shaking off an upbringing that's already ingrained is extremely hard."

"That may well be."

"It's gonna be tough from here on out," he said. He made sure to add a sigh to invite sympathy. That sigh belied his actual mood. He felt brilliant. His first encounter with an Abh had gone far better than he'd feared. After all, he'd managed to establish a first-name-basis relationship. Not only that, but he'd done so with a girl about his age. Any guy in his shoes who wouldn't feel exhilarated needed to get checked for a sickness of the soul.

They stopped in front of the doors to **Elevator-Tube** 26, standing shoulder-to-shoulder. Lafier fiddled with her **wristgear**, and the doors opened.

Though the elevators headed towards the planet's surface were each furnished with enough seating to accommodate around 100 passengers, this elevator didn't contain any seating at all. Its interior was cramped, with only enough room for about 10 people.

"Say…" Jint had chosen a safe topic of conversation. "That **patrol ship**… uh, what's its name again?"

"The *Gothelauth*."

"Right, yeah, what *byrec* (fleet) does the *Gothelauth* belong to?"

"It belongs to the *Byrec Claiïar* (Training Fleet)."

"So there must be a lot of **trainee starpilots** like you on board, huh?"

"You lack common sense," said Lafier reproachfully.

"Of course; it took all my effort just to learn the language. Plus, I'm totally boned up on military stuff."

"Ah, yes, of course." Lafier frowned slightly. "Forgive me." Jint was left mystified as to whether that had been meant as an earnest apology.

The **elevator-tube** ascended two floors and came to a halt. Jint got off after Lafier.

"There are *claiiagac* (training ships) within the Training Fleet, that much is true," Lafier explained as they walked. "However, those are boarded by *cénh* (trainee pupils). **trainee starpilots** like me don't go on those. The Training Fleet is trusted with a second mission. It hosts new, leading-edge warships that haven't yet been formally assigned while they're running familiarization runs. The Gothelauth just got commissioned three months ago, and the *Sarérh* (Ship Commander) and everyone else aboard are practicing how to handle it."

"Huh?" He was suddenly nervous.

"There's nothing to fret over," Lafier said, unsmilingly. "They're 'trainees,' but in this case that's just a figure of speech. Excepting myself, there's no one but experienced *saucec* (crewmembers), and the first round of fine-tuning has been done. It won't fall apart with you in it."

"Don't get me wrong, I wasn't worried or anything," Jint lied once again.

There were no civilian passengers that he could see on this floor. There were only officers in uniform. The wall beside the elevator-tube was curved, giving the impression that this was a rounded circular hallway.

After going around the elevator-tube, they came upon a hallway that led outside it, guarded by a pair of *sach* (non-commissioned crew, or "NCCs").

Sach were not Abh. They were the low-ranked officers of the Star Forces, (below starpilots), and largely picked up from various **landworlds**.

The two NCCs standing guard saluted. "**Trainee**, in accordance with regulation, allow us to inspect your **wristgear**." Lafier proffered her left arm, on which the wristgear rested. The NCC placed an oblong device on the **wristgear** and read what it displayed.

"You're clear, **Trainee**. Now then, if you would give us your wristgear as well, **Your Excellency**."

"Ah, right." Jint gave them his left arm.

While performing the identity check, the retainer took a glance at Jint's face. He regarded him with suspicion, as though asking himself why somebody of his own race was a **noble**.

"You're clear, *Lonh*. Please, you may proceed," said the officer, granting permission with one last "Your Excellency."

"Your work is appreciated," said Lafier, somewhat rotely. She urged Jint forward.

When they set foot onto the hallway, it started to move forward. It wasn't a very long distance to traverse.

Jint saw the words *"Baulébh Rüé Laburér"* (Administrative Zone of the Imperial Star Forces) written on the wall, and shuddered. He was entering here from a world where the concept of "the military" was found solely within the pages of history books and dictionaries. It was very late to be getting nervous about it now, but he couldn't shake the sensation that the time had finally arrived: he was officially involving himself with that great unknown realm, that veritable relic from the past, the military.

There was a door at the end of the automatic path; it opened smoothly at their approach. A spaceship lay hunkered just beyond. Its painted black hull enveloped Jint's field of vision.

"This is the **patrol ship** *Gothelauth*?" asked Jint earnestly.

"Tell me you're not seriously asking that." Lafier's eyes turned severe.

"Please remember, Lafier — I'm ignorant," said Jint, flustered.

"There are limits to how ignorant one can be."

"Now that I recall, I think the **cargo passenger ship** I was on seven years ago was a bit bigger."

"I don't know what class that ship was, but it can't have been 'a *bit* bigger.' This is the Gothelauth's embarkation *caricec* (smallcraft), one large enough to carry around 50 people. It's used to carry **soldiers** when a ship can't dock at a port directly, or to ferry them between ships. Though today, you'll be its only passenger."

"I'm honored." But then, a pang of worry. *Wait, then who'll be flying the thing? Is it* Lafier!?

He'd been harboring a firm preconception regarding *saidiac* (steerers), and it definitely didn't include girls his age. But he also had a feeling, bordering on a conviction, that testing that notion might end up delivering a fatal blow not only to the relationship that had thankfully started off on the right foot, but also to Jint's bodily form.

"So, which will you take?" she asked.

"What do you mean, 'which'? I only see the one ship..."

"The assistant steerer's seat is open. Will you be taking that seat, or would you rather stay in the accommodation compartment in the back?"

"Is there a lovely lady stewardess back there?" Jint quipped.

"There's no lovely stewardess," replied Lafier with dead seriousness, "but if it's a most beauteous **steerer** you want, you won't be disappointed. So what will it be?" The "most beauteous **steerer**," it would seem, was referring to herself.

I'm glad I didn't ask if anybody else could steer, Jint mused. *She would have definitely taken it as an insult.*

"I'll take the assistant's seat, obviously," said Jint, thereby resigning himself to leaving his life in her hands.

Chapter 3: The *Frymec Négr* (Daughter of Love)

"So, what's *frocragh* (spatiosensory perception) feel like?" Jint asked Lafier, sitting beside her in the assistant steerer's chair.

"That's difficult to explain." Lafier had just extended her circlet's access-cable and plugged it into her seat's backrest.

"Is it true you know about everything around the spaceship using that?"

"Yes. Like this, I can sense what the ship senses." Her eyes took on a questioning sheen. "Is *frocragh* that rare?"

"It's rare all right," Jint replied with a shrug. "This is the first time I've ever met someone with it."

Frocragh was a sense unique to the Abh. Abhs each bore a *froch* (spatiosensory organ) on their foreheads. These *froch* were typically obscured by their **circlets**, and so Landers rarely got a chance to see them even in videos, let alone in real life. And Jint was no exception.

The part of the **circlet** that touched the **spatiosensory organ** contained approximately 100 million flickering light-emitters that picked up information from the ship's own suite of sensors and beamed it to the area of the frontal lobe pertaining to navigation, or the *rilbidoc*. That area of the brain was also unique to the Abh.

When not connected to a ship, the **circlet** became a personal radar, continuously probing the space around the user. To the Abh, the **circlets** weren't just indicators of family pedigree, but indispensable tools throughout their entire lives.

Jint realized he'd misconstrued something. When they'd first come face to face, he'd thought that she's tried to stomp off by herself without confirming beforehand whether he'd actually follow her. But Lafier had, in fact, been able to sense him behind her through her *frocragh*.

"I see…" Yet Lafier was still nonplussed as to how to answer his question. "But there's just no way I can explain what it's like. I can't imagine what it's like to live without any sense of *frocragh*."

"No, that makes sense. So, are you doing trajectory calculations?"

"Trajectory calculations?" Lafier looked at him blankly. "No, I'm not."

"Then you must just be receiving raw numbers, huh." He was slightly disappointed; he'd overestimated this "*rilbidoc*" area of the Abh brain.

"I'm not receiving any numbers, either."

"But then, how are you determining the ship's trajectory?"

"I just am. Think of it as intuition."

"Intuition? As in, your gut!?"

"Right," she replied, nodding matter-of-factly. "When you throw something, you aim using your intuition, don't you? It's like that. I determine the optimal trajectory and duration of propulsion instinctively, calculating all of it unconsciously. Is there something strange about that?"

"I find it positively uncanny. I mean, there have gotta be times when your aim's off the mark."

"Children may miss, on occasion. Be at ease."

"I see…" But that didn't give him much peace of mind.

Jint scanned the *chicrh saidér* (steering room). *I was expecting the cockpit of a spaceship to be more over-the-top.* The "steering room" was spherical in shape. Only the floor was flat. With just a screen in front of each of the two adjustable seats, the room lacked the steering apparatuses and meters and instruments he'd imagined. It was just a smooth, opal-colored wall.

Behind the seats hung the *glac monger* (the ship's banner), of the **patrol ship** *Gothelauth*. Its design featured a *lauth* (winged dragon). The upper left arm of Lafier's military uniform also featured the same symbol.

The steering apparatus was attached to the seat. The adjustable seat had an armrest on its right side, upon which lay a number of *poch* (controls). Naturally, those controls couldn't be enough to carry out the complex operations necessary to pilot a spaceship. *That must be the* guhaicec, thought Jint.

Jint fixed his eyes on the *guhaicec*, the gauntlet-looking device hanging on the left of the adjustable chair. It looked long enough to cover the arm up to the elbow, with an opening for the **wristgear's** display and controls. It was made of black synthetic leather, but it sported many metal parts as well. The fingers, especially, were completely covered in metal.

It was said that Abhs guided their spaceships through the use of these "control gauntlets," as well as through voice command. The buttons on the armrest were strictly for auxiliary, backup purposes. Jint had learned of the **control gauntlet** at the Abh Linguistic and Cultural Institute on Delktu, but he still couldn't believe a spaceship could be maneuvered through the simple movement of the pilot's fingers.

"Hey." Jint had a question for Lafier, who had equipped the control gauntlet. "Do you ever accidentally pick something up in your left hand while wearing that glove?"

"I forget all about my left hand while flying the ship," she said.

"But I can't help thinking moving your fingers is a silly way to pilot."

"Why?" Lafier cocked her head in puzzlement. "Is there a better way?"

"I think so. When Landers pilot intrasystem spaceships, it's more… well…" He was about to say, "more *self-respecting*," but he stopped mid-sentence. Best choose his words carefully. "It's just, I heard those ships come attached with maneuvering gear laid out according to different ideas."

"That may be, but this method is superior," said the **trainee starpilot**, pointing to her left arm.

"But…" Jint persisted. "It must be hard to remember how you're supposed to be moving your fingers. Do you not forget from time to time?"

"Do you spend time thinking about the movements of your muscles when you walk?"

"No."

"You aren't normally consciously aware of how you're walking."

"No, can't say I am."

"Indeed not. And likewise for me when I fly a ship. I need only think of what I wish the ship to do. Then my fingers move automatically. Thinking about it would only lead to hesitation as to how to move them. It would be counter-productive."

"I see. It's the fruit of your training." Jint was impressed.

"I've been doing this since I was a child. It goes beyond mere training."

"That so?" Jint was racked by an inferiority complex, but at the same time, he was overjoyed at how correct he'd been not to ask her if there were any other **steerers** aboard.

"Shall we depart?" asked Lafier.

"Ah, yeah, of course. Whenever you're ready."

The screens shone bright, and the curvy glyphs of Baronh, called *"Ath,"* started flowing from bottom to top.

"Can you read that? It's shooting so fast." Jint was peering at his own display monitor. The green glyphs were dashing across the screen at such absurd speeds he could only make out a mass of flickering. He couldn't read any of it at all. He couldn't necessarily say it was because he just wasn't accustomed to it.

"I can't read it." Lafier took her eyes off the screen, quick to acknowledge that fact.

"All right then," said Jint, pointing to the screen, "what's this for?"

"**Compucrystals** are checking over the ship. If there's anything wrong, it'll stay on screen as red text."

"Then there's no reason for all that other info to run across the screen, surely."

"Some people agree with you," Lafier acknowledged. "I don't think it's particularly bothersome either way. And I like the 'vibe' it gives."

"Can't argue with that." At last, the little green glyphs cleared off the screen, to be replaced by a big flashing *"gosno"* ("all clear").

"There you go, it's run its course."

"Seems simple enough."

"Yes. It's thanks to the **compucrystals** doing our work for us."

"There must be times the machines get things wrong."

"But humans make mistakes, too," Lafier said to reassure him.

"Well, *that* makes me feel relieved."

"You are quite the worrier, aren't you? Our destination is right there. Do you think we could stand to rely on machines that break that easily?"

"Well, when you put it that way," he said prudently. "But how far is it from here to there?"

"A meaningless question. Our destination is also in motion. In terms of altitude difference, we're about 5 *saidagh* apart."

The Abh inherited Earth's CGS system of units, with its centimeters, grams and seconds, though it seemed they'd felt a great need to turn the words into their own native vocabulary. 5 *saidagh* were exactly equivalent to 5,000 kilometers.

From here to there — from the **spaceport** to the **patrol ship** — stretched at least 5,000 kilometers of empty space.

*To the **Kin of the Stars**, that distance wouldn't even be a stroll's worth,* thought Jint. *It wouldn't kill them to be a little more humble with regard to the universe.*

With a flex of her left hand's fingers, the **apprentice** bade the "*gosno*" on screen disappear. Now the screen displayed the bust of a spaceport crew member.

"*Blyséc* (Space Traffic Control)," hailed Lafier.

"Delktu 1st Planetary Spaceship Space Traffic Control Center," the controller replied.

"This is the **patrol ship** *Gothelauth*'s **smallcraft**. Our *Paunoüass* (Skipper)'s *ftaliac bausnalr* (soldier registry code) is 01-00-0937684. Please depressurize Military *Baiss* (pier) 2."

"Roger that, *Gothelauth* **smallcraft**. I'll depressurize right away." Depressurized though it may be, it was impossible to tell what it was like outside from within the **steering room**.

"Wait, do you not know what it's like outside?" asked Jint. He wanted to have her pull up video of the outside on the screen. It was his second-ever time on a small ship, but he didn't really remember his first time, so it might as well have been his first time. He felt a little anxious, but he was also brimming with curiosity.

"You want to see?"

"Yeah. I don't have *frocragh*."

"I see." A shadow of sympathy flashed over Lafier's face. "All right."

Apart from the screens and the **ship's banner**, the surrounding wall grew transparent. Of course, it hadn't actually started letting light through. It was processing the footage of the outside and providing stereoscopic imagery.

This "depressurization" proved a massive disappointment. The whole compartment must have been thoroughly clean; no motes of dust hovered in the air. He understood that the air was getting thinner on an intellectual level, but nothing he was seeing lent that appearance.

After about a minute, **Space Traffic Control** apprised them that depressurization was complete.

"Please unlock Military *Baiss* 2's *sohyth* (lock gate)," Lafier requested.

"Roger that, *Gothelauth* **smallcraft**."

Now *this* was a sight to see. The right and left sides of the wall before them opened up. What lay beyond was a sea of stars.

"Total aperture confirmed. Requesting permission to leave port."

"Permission granted, *Gothelauth* **smallcraft**. Do you want an electromagnetic push?"

"No need. I'll exit through low-heat propulsion," she said. "You'd probably hide behind your eyes during an EM push," she teased Jint.

Yeah, I probably would, thought Jint.

"Roger, *Gothelauth* **smallcraft**. We hope you return to your warship safely. Delktu 1st Planetary Spaceship Space Traffic Control Center, over and out."

"You have my thanks. *Gothelauth* **smallcraft**, over and out." When the *blységac* (BELYOOSEGA, space traffic controller) disappeared from the screen, Lafier's left hand took to dancing once again. The vessel shuddered, and then rose up.

Jint was on tenterhooks, fearing a collision with the ceiling. Lafier concentrated on her *frocragh* spatial awareness, going as far as closing her eyes, which was more than enough to get Jint trembling.

Needless to say, his fears were groundless. With exquisite equilibrium, the vessel soared both up and forward, and a mere instant before it would have hit the ceiling, crossed over into the starry fathoms. It felt as though his body was floating up along with it.

They'd broken free of the sphere of *üamrhoth* (gravitational control) exerted by the **orbital tower**. And thanks to his *apymh* (seatbelt), he didn't actually start levitating.

The steerer's seat rotated 90 degrees. He could see the orbital tower jutting perpendicular to his feet, and Delktu's surface sprawled ahead of him.

"You're incredible." Jint's praises were heartfelt.

"What do you mean?"

"As in, you're an amazingly practiced hand at this."

"Don't mock me," Lafier huffed. "Among the Abh, even children can fly a ship like this."

"Sure, right, I mean, yeah, of course." His inferiority complex bubbled back to the fore. "But you're really young, though. Sorry, I know it's rude to ask a girl her age…"

"You're trying to tell me I'm childish, aren't you?" If looks could kill…

"Don't be crazy." *Is there anything in all of space that's easier than raising her hackles?* thought Jint. "I'm *trying* to say that, like, it's hard to tell how old you people are, so I just wanted to confirm my hunch…"

"I see." The **trainee**'s mood had swung right back around. "You inferred correctly. I just turned 16 this year. I *am* really young."

Which makes her a year younger than me.

"But what would be rude about asking?" said Lafier.

"Huh?"

"You said that asking a girl her age would be rude. But why would that be the case?"

Jint batted his eyes. Now that she mentioned it… why *was* it rude? "It's probably because ladies want to be seen as young. At least, the ladies of Delktu and *Martinh* do."

"Intriguing. Why is that?"

"Couldn't tell you. I'm no expert on female psychology, so try asking a Lander girl." He saw Lafier wasn't exactly satisfied by this response, so he attempted to change the subject. "Are **trainee starpilots** all as young as you are?"

"No," Lafier answered pridefully. That made her come across as all the younger. "The exam for the **military academy** isn't that difficult. It's so easy that if you don't pass it at 18, you ought to give up on functioning in respectable society. However, there are few who win admittance at age 13. Of this I can be a little proud, don't you agree?"

"Yeah." Jint felt a childish compulsion to measure up against her. "I've got things to be proud of, too. I had to learn two different foreign languages at the same time, but I still got accepted to the **Quartermaster Academy** at 17."

"Yes, that is amazing," said Lafier, genuinely impressed.

Suddenly, a *BREEE* noise blared through the cabin. "What was that!?" It sounded to him like an alarm.

"We've entered a sector where we can accelerate." Lafier kept manipulating her control gauntlet as though it were nothing.

"Ah." Jint pushed down his embarrassment. "How long will it take?"

"I'm afraid this ship isn't equipped with anything nifty like a *üamriac* (gravity control system), so it depends on what level of acceleration you can withstand."

"I grew up on a planet's surface," bragged Jint. An Abh's *daimonn* (standard gravity level) was said to be about half of Delktu's. "If you can withstand it, then so can I."

"I see. In that case, it won't even take seven minutes."

"Wow, that's fairly fast."

"It's not far at all."

"I hear you." He realized he might need to flesh out his sense for cosmic distances sooner rather than later.

The seats automatically increased in length, becoming something akin to bunks. Because the ship's direction and rate of acceleration could change at a dizzying pace in accordance with the exerted attitude control, it was easy to feel knocked around. That said, that only lasted for a fleeting moment.

"Let's go." The instant Lafier said that, Jint was pressed against the back of his seat.

"Wha, what is this!?" His chest was ready to burst from the acceleration forces that had far exceeded his expectations.

"*Caïmehoth* (acceleration)," said Lafier nonchalantly. "You aren't going to tell me you didn't know about **acceleration**, I trust."

"I do! I know about it! But, not *this* fast…" He was finding it difficult even to move his lips. He could tell by the numbness in his extremities that his blood vessels were being crushed. He could probably endure a minute of this, but seven minutes would be well beyond him. "You, you're fine!?"

"I'm fine. Our ancestors didn't have any **gravity control systems**, so we built our bodies to be able to work under both high gravity-forces and microgravity. I, too, have inherited those genes. It's all in the skeleton and circulatory system. In other words…"

He was in no mood to listen to an elaborate explanation. "Please, Lafier, shift the acc- acceleration down a little…"

"It'll take longer."

"Would that land us in hot water somehow!?"

"Not particularly. The ship's schedule was compiled to allow for extra time. For familiarization voyages, allowing some leeway is practically a requirement. One can never know what's coming, after all."

"Good. I'm begging you…"

"Okay. It can't be helped." She stopped accelerating. "Now I have to change course. Can I accelerate just a little?"

Jint shook his head. "Yeah, you can go a little faster than that. Just enough so I can bear it a bit more easily than before."

"Mmm." Lafier's fingers flitted in the air.

It began accelerating once again. It was still more severe than the planet Martin's level of gravity, but it was no longer a trial to endure. He could probably even walk around if he wanted.

"How is it now?"

"This is good."

"But it'll take a lot more time now."

"No other choice," replied Jint. "I'm not in a hurry anyway. What's our gravity level?"

"4 *daimonn*. The standard for when Landers are aboard. For longer journeys, we drop it down to 2 *daimonn*. That's around where the gravity level of most **landworlds** is."

"You should have warned me that it'd be too much for a Lander," said Jint ruefully.

"I thought you had intimated you were made of hardier stuff," said Lafier, making it clear she had no malicious intent.

"Honestly, I should thank you for overestimating me."

"Besides, you aren't a Lander. You're an Abh."

"Well, it's annoying, but I really don't feel like one, since genetically I'm 100% Lander. You must get that." The law could call him an Abh all it wanted, it didn't change his genetics. To raise an extreme example, obtaining legal recognition as a bird would not allow him to take flight.

"Genetics aside," said Lafier, "I think you ought to become Abh in terms of your attitude. An **imperial noble** wouldn't lose their composure over something like high acceleration."

"I've taken your words of admonishment to heart," he said, chastened. He'd anticipated that he wouldn't be cut out to be an **imperial noble**, and now that feeling had morphed into a strong conviction. He contemplated having them send him back right now so he could ask Durin for a job.

However, it'd be a bitter pill indeed to tell everyone he'd turned back.

At last, there were several seconds of microgravity and attitude control, and the vessel shifted to decelerating. The planet Delktu, floating above them, had become an orb speckled with white and blue. Jint was assailed by the illusion he was falling without end.

"Hey," said Jint. "What's your position in society?"

"Why are you asking me something like that?" Lafier asked back chidingly.

"I, uhh…" Jint panicked. It seemed that she'd mistaken him as trying to flaunt his own position as a noble. "I was just wondering why someone so young joined the **Star Forces**, that's all. I thought maybe you were planning to get your duties over with quickly like me. Was it rude of me to ask?"

"It wasn't, but I don't want to talk about it. Until I reach the *fsœtdoriac* (ordained starpilot) level, and as long as I'm wearing this **military uniform**, I can't wear anything that shows my family lineage."

"So you're saying that within the **Star Forces**, your social standing doesn't matter?"

"Correct. In the military, this is what means everything." Lafier pointed to the rank insignia on her left arm.

"I understand. It's just, I only wanted to ask you why you wanted to join. Was it out of obligation, or because you wanted to?"

"I am obligated," Lafier acknowledged.

"Ah, I knew it." Military service wasn't imposed on mere **gentry**. To them, admittance to an **academy** was a right, not a duty. He took this as confirmation that Lafier must be a young maiden of none other than noble stock. "I thought as much."

"What?"

"Oh, nothing…" he said evasively. He had guessed she might be of noble birth, but since that hunch was based on his impressions of her — namely, that she seemed haughty even when not speaking, to say nothing of when she opened her mouth — he thought it wise to keep mum.

Thankfully, she didn't pursue the matter. "It's not just out of obligation, though."

"Why actually, then?"

"I wanted to come of age as soon as possible."

"Ah, I see." If one received an appointment as a **starpilot**, they were summarily recognized as an adult. "Was there really any need to hurry past your childhood, though? Living a life of comfort as a kid's pretty sweet, you know."

Lafier chewed it over, and then, at last, settled on a response. "Do you have any secrets regarding your birth?"

"Secrets regarding my birth?" replied a disconcerted Jint. "No, no secrets. I mean, my mom died when I was little, but apart from that…"

"Your *mother*? I thought your parent is male. The Count of Hyde, *Dreuc Haïder*-lonh, is your father, no?"

"That's right, he's my dad. Ah, I understand your confusion now…" Jint recalled the structure of the Abh family unit.

The Abh did not marry. In Abh society, romantic couples did sometimes live together. It was not uncommon for these partnerships to last long enough to be quite like a marriage, and on very rare occasions, they even lasted "till death did them part."

However, this was not an *institution*. It was simply one of many ways to live one's life. To burn with maddening passion, and then for that passion to go up in flames with nary a trace left — this was the typical form of Abh love. It was likely difficult for the Abh, who lived "forever young," to latch onto the ideal of marriage, premised as it was on growing old together.

As such, single parents were commonplace, and there was no concept of two-parent units. This, of course, would make an Abh's one parent either male or female, leading to phrases such as "Mother's son" (*frucec saranr*) and "Father's daughter" (*frymec loranr*).

"You've heard of 'the institution of marriage,' right?" asked Jint.

"Yes, I have. Ah, I was being absent-minded. You were raised a Lander, so of course."

"Yep, I'm the product of a marriage. The son of both a father and a mother at the same time."

"I see." Lafier cocked her head. "What is it like to have two parents? When your mother died, were you sad?"

"Well…" Surprised by the bluntness of the question, Jint nevertheless searched his memories. What met him wasn't the mother he'd only ever seen on holovision, but the face of Lina Corint. "Yeah. Yeah, it was sad."

"Forgive me. It was a foolish thing to ask." Lafier cast down her eyes.

"It's fine, honestly. It happened when I was so young, I don't really remember much, to tell you the truth."

"However," said Lafier with palpable envy, "that means you can't have any secrets regarding your birth."

"Huh? Why's that?"

"If both of your *larlinec* (gene donors) were in your house, then how could there be anything hidden about your birth?"

"You've got it wrong." For a moment, Jint was stumped as to how to correct Lafier's misunderstanding. "I don't know what it's like on other **landworlds**, but on planets like *Martinh* and Delktu, a child can be born without one or both of the parents wanting it that way. Plus, in the past, there were people who wanted to be parents but couldn't. So that's how there can be some secrecy regarding birth. I'm sure there are more examples of how that can come about, too."

Lafier didn't hide her bewilderment. "Such as?"

"That, you can look into yourself. It can get really complicated. What is all this about 'birth secrets,' anyway? What does it have to do with you joining the military?"

"I do have a 'birth secret.' I had no idea whether I was a *frymec négr* (daughter of love). You can imagine how ill at ease that made me."

"A '**daughter of love**'…" It sounded like some religious term to him. Despite the fact the Abh were areligious, that is. "What's that mean, exactly?"

"You don't know?" Lafier looked startled.

"I'm beginning to realize my education was lacking in certain aspects..." said Jint, but it smelled of making excuses.

Though it was technically an Abh linguistic and cultural institute, the lessons centered mostly on the Baronh language. As for how they conducted their cultural instruction, they settled on briefly touching upon general manners and the like. There were no lectures on the core tenets of Abh culture.

He'd asked his teachers questions, and hit his books, but he never found anything too concrete. The information circulated by official documents on matters such as political organizations and the law was fine, but any information that looked closely into the daily lives of the Abh was a confusing tangle. Jint had had no clue which claims he ought to believe.

Half of the blame for that fell on the Abh themselves. It was not as though they deliberately concealed the particulars of their culture, but there was a distinct dearth of enthusiasm to explain any of it to the uninitiated.

All in all, because the teachers had only worked alongside Abhs temporarily, they had done nothing more than look upon their world from the outside. The books had been published by former **imperial citizens**, not by Abhs. Some authors who had never even left Delktu got what amounted to irresponsible speculation and yellow journalism published as legitimate sources of information in those books.

Abhs hardly ever spoke about themselves to Landers.

"...And that's why there are still some things I still don't get about the way family works in Abh culture. Everybody knows Abhs don't marry, but so how do they have children?" Fearing he might have touched on a sensitive topic, Jint scanned Lafier's expression.

Lafier seemed quite unfazed. "I see. So you don't know anything about how we're born..."

"Yeah, that is, uhh..." Jint struggled for words, his face red. Just his luck; he'd somehow stumbled into asking her the age-old question, 'where do babies come from?' He thought he'd grown past needing to ask that particular question. To think he'd end up posing the question to a girl. A girl younger than him, at that. "I know you people don't conceive in the womb..."

"There are some who choose to do so."

"Really? But what about the **gene donors**, then?"

"The embryo gets taken out temporarily. Usually it's transferred to a *ïanh* (artificial womb), but some women who want an exotic experience have it returned to the womb."

"I see." And so he learned a hidden truth of the Abh. The rumor on Delktu had it that Abh women had no wombs.

"But conception using **artificial wombs** is the norm, yes."

"Gotcha." Jint shrugged. "Now you must understand why even if I tried acting like an Abh, it'd be a waste of effort. It's like your *race* has 'birth secrets.' I tried looking into it, but there were so many dodgy, ridiculous accounts. Some said that you make offspring out of your own 'branches,' or that you mix together complete strangers' genes, or that you combine your genes with someone of the same gender, or that you even mate with relatives. Seriously, how do they come up with this stuff…?"

"We do all of those things," Lafier butted in.

"Wha?" Jint's jaw dropped.

"Some people simply clone themselves, or else edit only a few genes. Some gather the genes of other people. It's up to each individual's free choice."

"For real?" Jint was flummoxed. "But don't you put a premium on family lineage? From what you just said, I'd be of half a mind to think you ignore blood ties altogether."

"What's held in highest importance in each household is the inheritance of its **family traditions**, not the inheritance of genes."

"Wait, but—"

"A parent becomes a parent by polishing their child's genes and raising them up."

"Hmm. I understand." After a moment's contemplation, he looked convinced. It may be only natural for the Abh, who practiced gene alteration on an everyday basis, to pay blood relationships no heed.

"That being said, the most common way to have a child is by combining your genes with the genes of someone you love."

"I'm relieved to hear that," said Jint.

"Of course, there are times when someone loves another of the same sex, or a close relative, or more than one person at a time. I've heard that when people from landworlds are told this, it agitates them for some reason." Lafier cast Jint's face an inquisitive look.

"It'd agitate them all right," Jint assured her. "I'm in a pretty big tizzy myself."

"I find that strange. It's not as though we have a monopoly on genetic engineering."

"I can't speak for others," said Jint with discretion, "but at least on the **landworlds** I know, it seems people wouldn't really think tampering with people's genes is a praiseworthy pastime."

"So it would seem." Lafier suddenly shot Jint an angry look. "Let me warn you that I'm not dispassionate about these things, either. If you give it a moment's thought, you'll come to my realization that this isn't a discussion two people in a sealed space should be having."

"I'm sorry." So the Abh felt that way, too. Jint did his best to retain his composure.

"In any case, telling someone that you want their genes is the one of the most earnest ways to confess one's love." There was something *dreamy* in her tone.

"Interesting." It was the *"will you marry me?"* of the Abh.

"A child born under those circumstances is called—"

"I know what you're going to say," Jint interrupted. "She's called a **daughter of love**, right?"

"Yes. And a boy is called a *frucec négr.*"

Their awkward yet fascinating conversation had seemingly come to an end. The tension in Jint's body released.

"But couldn't you just *ask* your father?" Then he got a start. "Hold on, your father isn't..."

"Hmm?" Those deep, jet-black eyes pointed his way. "Ah, no, my father is still alive. And at this rate, he'll be hale and healthy for another 200 years. Is that what you were thinking?"

"You got me." It seemed she'd read into his little pause. "Then why haven't you asked him?"

"Do you think it didn't cross my mind?"

"Well, no..."

"My father wouldn't tell me!" she raged. "He was obsessed with the notion that birth secrets lead to the child developing a 'fuller personality'!"

"And there was no way to look it up?"

"Once you become an adult, you can browse your genetic record, and no one can interfere. But until then, you need your parent's permission."

"Aha, so that's it." It finally made sense now. He put the pieces together: She wanted to come of age as quickly as she could in order to discover the origins of her genes.

"I didn't even fully believe the reason he gave for hiding it. I think he perhaps kept birth-secrets solely to wind me up."

"But why?"

"I'll never forget it. When I was a child, I wanted him to tell me that I'm a **daughter of love**, so I was always badgering him to show me my **gene donor**. But he just refused to reveal them. Until one day, he finally agreed to bring my gene donor for me to meet. What do you think happened then?"

"Did he not bring them after all?"

"No, he committed a far more insidious act. He tricked me. He held Horia in his arms and said, 'Say hello to one half of your genes'!"

"Who's Horia?"

"Our cat!" she spat bitterly.

Jint burst out laughing. "Tell me you didn't believe him, Lafier!?"

"It's not impossible." Lafier watched Jint's mirthful grin with resentment.

"What, really?" The outer corners of Lafier's eyes were high on her head — not at all unlike a cat's eyes. "You people go *that* far?"

"It's against the law. It would be unethical."

"I'm glad I've found a point of moral agreement with you people."

"You are Abh, too."

"Ah, right, right." Jint didn't deny it. "But then, wasn't it obvious it wasn't true?"

"I was eight years old. Of course I wouldn't be very interested in legalities."

"You've got me there."

"I cried that whole night. Horia is a nice cat, but I couldn't stand the idea that half of me came from it."

"I totally understand…… Okay, maybe not *totally*, but I understand."

"And the thing I could stomach the least, was how my own father was a degenerate who enjoyed creating cat-children!" Lafier's right hand swung animatedly in the air.

An unspeakable anxiety came over Jint, who looked at the **trainee starpilot**'s left hand. The **control gauntlet** on her left hand was so still, it was as though it was held in place by glue. Relief washed over him.

"Horia was only a kitten when it came to our home, and what's more, I remembered the day it joined our family. And yet it took a whole night of tears for me to realize that."

"Hey, all's well that ends well, right?"

"No! Because I got it in my head that I must be the child of *another* cat. Every day I was worried I would grow pads on my palms, or that my nails would become retractable, or that my irises would change shape. Even now, I've never tensed up as badly as when I stared at my reflection in the mirror after my irises constricted from exposure to bright light."

"But now all doubt's been cleared, I imagine."

"Yes." Lafier nodded. "Though I'll never forget those restless days. Part of the reason I want to become a **starpilot** is to get out from under my father."

"You don't like your father?" Jint didn't know whether Abh standards of etiquette could condone prying into the life of a stranger this thoroughly, but despite his trepidation, he just had to ask.

"I don't dislike him." Her otherwise pretty face wrinkled up in a grimace. "I don't want to admit it, but I love him, and I'm proud of him. It's just that when I'm near him, I sometimes get irritated."

The image of the face of his own father, the Count of Hyde, came to mind. A face he hadn't seen except through occasional correspondence for seven years. The feeling that he'd been betrayed by him, those seven years prior, festered inside him.

He couldn't really lie to himself that he *loved* him. But he didn't hate him, either. He felt nothing at all for him.

That, or that deep, deep recess of his heart was refusing to embrace the emotion.

"I guess every family's got its share of circumstances," Jint remarked. "So, you kept saying your father *wouldn't* tell you, but did you finally get him to at some point?"

"Yes." She turned around, and with a beaming smile, said: "She's someone I know well — a woman I look up to. I was a **daughter of love**."

"Good," Jint said. And he meant it with all his heart.

Chapter 4: The Patrol Ship *Gothelauth*

"Jint, have yourself a look below," Lafier said suddenly.

After a few seconds of microgravity and attitude control, a long stretch of time passed.

Jint's talk of *minchiu* — which, much to his chagrin, did not seem to be of much interest to Lafier — was cut short, and he shifted atop his bunk-seat to gaze down at the floor.

Amidst the unblinking stars, a structure was floating. It had the contours of a squashed hexagon, with a number of circular ports open wide. Because it was slightly tilted, he could tell it was something like a tower, and one that he was either viewing from its base or its apex.

"Is that the **patrol ship** *Gothelauth*?" asked Jint.

"Correct. It's somewhat bigger than this **smallcraft**, wouldn't you agree?" said Lafier sarcastically.

"Somewhat," said Jint, though in truth it he couldn't really grasp its size. He was certain it had to be incredibly enormous, but his mind perceived it as being smaller than the vessel they were on.

That was when it started suddenly zooming up in size. They stopped decelerating, and the ship's interior reverted to microgravity. At the same time, their bunks reverted back to normal seats.

They'd finally crossed paths with the **patrol ship** again. Its relative speed was very low. The gargantuan tower slowly, slowly rose up towards them.

Jint's line of sight darted from the floor to the walls, then up to the ceiling. The part of the tower he'd been looking down moments ago was now scraping the stars far above him, and Jint was beset by the false feeling that he'd plunged that whole distance down.

A prolonged nose dive. Was this the vantage a suicidal feather that had jumped off a cliff would see in its final moments?

The tower just wouldn't end.

"Wow, it really is astounding." Jint sighed with admiration. When he reflected on the fact that it had been built for battle, its aura became all the more imposing and overwhelming. The hull before their eyes keenly asserted that it was a weapon constructed to wreak havoc. The only functioning weapons of any kind Jint had seen up until that point were the *ribrasiac* (stunguns) that Delktunian police officers had strapped to their hips. It would have been stupid beyond compare to draw any comparisons between the two. It was in a whole different league.

"You're a little slow on the uptake," teased Lafier.

"C'mon, I couldn't tell from so far away. We're in *space*. You people've got it made with your *frocragh*." Jint saw the face Lafier was pulling, and chuckled. "Please, you don't need to give me that sympathetic look. I've never minded the fact that I lack *frocragh*, and I have every intention of living right and thriving from here on out as well."

"Of course." Lafier looked away, flustered. "Allow me to give you the special opportunity to appreciate it."

"Thank you."

At last, the **imperial crest** passed by. Its design was the same as her rank insignia, but its hemming and the *gaftnochec* eight-headed dragon were gold, with a black base. And of course, the two insignias' sizes were incomparable. The crest on the **patrol ship** was likely big enough to host a game of *minchiu*.

Finally, the warship's bow came into view.

With a wriggling of the fingers on Lafier's left hand, their vessel slipped sideways. The tip of the giant warship swooped blurrily over Jint's head like a pendulum, and appeared on the opposite side.

The **patrol ship** came dropping down. It was a scene one would expect to be accompanied by a roaring noise.

"The Gothelauth is leading-edge among the Empire's warships," explained Lafier. "It's 12.82 *üésdagh* long."

"That's all?" It was surprisingly small.

"It's small compared to an *alaicec* (battle-line ship) or *isadh* (supply ship). The ship you were on was almost certainly bigger than this one. However, there is probably no other warship with as much combat strength anywhere in the human-peopled cosmos, let alone the **Empire**."

"I don't doubt it." He unreservedly believed it.

The vessel shifted angles and revolved around the **patrol ship** a number of times. "That should be enough, I think," said Lafier.

"Yeah, I'm good."

When Lafier moved the fingers on her left hand, a cutout video frame of the upper body of a male **starpilot** floated up amidst the starry heavens.

"This is **Smallcraft 1**. **Skipper's registry code** is 01-00-0937684. The *ftaliac slomhotr* (mission registry code) is 0522-01. Requesting admission."

"Roger," replied the starpilot. "External controls are ready. And let's enjoy our little breaks in *moderation*, **Skipper**. Unless you spotted something of note on the ship's exterior?"

"*Lonh-Ïarlucer Dreur* had me show him the difference between this vessel and the main ship," she replied, while giving Jint a meaningful glance.

"What do you mean? Actually, never mind, just get on with your *longhoth rirragr* (information link)."

"Roger." Lafier motioned her fingers and told Jint, "To tell the truth, I have no desire to rely on **compucrystals**, but it's a military regulation, so I can't disobey."

The **Star Forces** *aren't stupid enough to give a* **trainee** *the chance to damage the ship.* But before Jint could say as much, the **patrol ship starpilot** interrupted.

"Link confirmed."

"Link confirmed on this end as well. Requesting end of transmission."

"Ending transmission." The image of the starpilot vanished from the screen, to be replaced by a cavorting throng of numbers, glyphs and graphs.

"This leaves me with nothing else to do," said Lafier, a little frustrated.

Jint made sure his gratitude was known: "Thank you."

"It's just my mission."

"So, what is your mission, exactly...?" asked Jint. "What do you do when you don't need to man the **smallcraft**? Do you have a lot of free time to fill?"

"What are you saying?" Lafier pouted. "A **trainee's** job is to learn through observation."

"I mean, I know that, but..."

"They make me do anything and everything the **starpilots** of the *Gariac* (Flight Branch) do. Provided it's suited to a trainee, obviously. All in all, I am kept quite busy."

"Okay."

"You'll see how tough it can be if you become a **trainee**."

"But I'll be in the *Sazoïc* (Budget Branch), so…"

"I've heard that the **Budget Branch** gets busy, too. They spend all day inspecting food and supplies, among other things."

"What a magnificent vocation," Jint groaned.

The **patrol ship**'s outer wall drew nearer and nearer before their eyes. A gaping wide hole had formed on its side.

Though the gravity was finely adjusted through attitude control, he felt out of sorts.

The hole had arrived right behind them — or so it might have registered to him had he been given time to think before the entire **steerer's room** shifted 90 degrees, after which the hole appeared to lie right below them. Their vessel, pulled by the **patrol ship**'s artificial gravity, sank gently down.

At the last moment, the lower attitude-control jet nozzle spouted, softly landing the hull onto the *goriabh* (take-off and landing deck). The ceiling **lock gate** of the *horh* (ship's hold) closed, and the lights turned on.

"Commencing pressurization," announced the **starpilot** from earlier, who appeared on screen once again.

"Standing by while pressurization is in progress," Lafier replied.

The vessel proceeded to get sprayed from all directions by plumes of white mist. These plumes collided and formed a complex whirl. Finally, it evened out into an undifferentiated haze, and steadily cleared away.

"Pressurization complete. Remain there and continue to stand by momentarily," directed the starpilot.

"Roger that."

"Wait, how come we need to stand by?" Jint scanned Lafier's expression to see if something was wrong. "Do they always have you wait a while?"

"No, today is different."

"Then why…?"

"They need to prepare for your *Patmesaïhoth* (gangway welcome ceremony)," said Lafier as she removed her control gauntlet and disconnected her **circlet**'s **access-cables**.

"*Patmesaïhoth*?" That word rang a bell. If he recalled correctly, it referred to a ceremony held to welcome important people onto a ship. "Whose ceremony is it?"

"If you're really asking because you don't know, then you have the astuteness of a clump of blue-green algae," said Lafier.

"Haha, sorry." Of course it was *his* ceremony. There's no way he'd be that dense. It's just that he didn't think he was all that "important" a person. "Isn't that ceremony for people of the *Cheüass* (Kilo-Commander) rank and up, though?"

"It's a ceremony for people of your *tlaïgac* (title), **Your Excellency**. You ARE a 'Your Excellency,' after all."

"Now that you mention, I guess I am. But are they really willing to go through all that trouble just for little old me?"

"You are a **grandee**, Jint. You're not so low in the **imperial** hierarchy."

The Abh numbered about 25 million in total population. Most were **gentry**, with only about 200,000 **nobles**. Those nobles that possessed populated planets as territory were called **grandees**. There were only 1,600 grandee houses, and less than 20,000 individuals, even including family members.

By comparison, there were about 1 billion **imperial citizens**, and approximately 900 billion **landworld citizens** under Abh rule on **landworlds**. With those numbers in mind, one could definitely appreciate how uncommon **grandees** were.

It was true — the Household of the Count of Hyde belonged to a rare breed indeed — its not-so-favorable origin story notwithstanding.

"I've never been good with ceremonies and functions and stuff..."

"It won't be that big a deal. Not enough to be called a 'function,' anyway," Lafier assured him. "The ship's captain will do a self-introduction, and then introduce you to the ship's highest-ranked **starpilots**. That's all."

"That may be a 'that's all' to you, but not so much to me..."

A door opened to their back left. An *onuhociac* (automaton) laid down a red carpet, and six starpilots ambled down it.

The starpilot at the head of the entourage, a lady with dark bluish-grey shoulder-length hair and bob-cut bangs, wore an *almfac clabrar* (one-winged circlet). The wing extended out to pin her hair so it would not to interfere with the equipping of her *saputec* (pressurization helmet), and it also served to display her *sarérragh* (designation as ship commander). In addition, she also bore the **bandolier sash** that was proof she was serving in that role, and wielded the *greuc* (command baton).

"Preparations for the *Patmesaïhoth* Ceremony are complete," sounded the voice transmission. "Bring Lonh-*Ïarlucer Dreur Haïder* aboard."

"Roger," said Lafier, and she looked at Jint encouragingly.

"Okay, I get it." Jint released his **seatbelt** and stood up. "You're coming with me, right?"

Lafier shook her head in confusion. "To do what?"

"Oh," Jint said disappointedly. "Well, I, uh, hope I see you again later."

"Our living quarters aren't so spacious. We will likely be meeting again." That wasn't exactly the response Jint had been hoping to hear, but he had no choice but to be satisfied with it.

"All right, see you. And thank you for taking me here."

"I enjoyed myself."

"Good. I'm glad."

Amidst the six **starpilots** attending the *Patmesaïhoth*, the four lined up from Jint's right each had on the scarlet insignia of a **steerer**. At the leftmost position of those four stood the **Ship Commander**, and to her left there was the green insignia of the *scœmh* (Mechanics Branch). At the very left, there was the white insignia of the **Budget Branch**.

What am I supposed to do during times like these? Jint regretted not asking Lafier beforehand. Unfortunately, there were no lectures on how a **grandee** should handle a *Patmesaïhoth* at the Abh Linguistic and Cultural Academy on Delktu.

For the time being, he straightened up his back and attempted a dignified posture.

An **NCC**, standing alone, blew a *méc* (whistle). The six starpilots saluted in unison.

Suppressing his right hand's reflexive impulse to return the salute, he instead kept with the general etiquette of the Abh (however awkwardly) and aligned his heels, straightened his back, and lowered his head.

"We are honored by your presence, **Your Excellency**," said the captain. The color of her irises brimmed like melted gold, in contrast with her black pupils. "I am **Ship Commander** of the **patrol ship** *Gothelauth*, *Bomoüass* (Hecto-Commander) Lecsh (*Laicch*)."

Huh, I guess Abhs introduce themselves by name when meeting new people, too. How... normal.

Jint lowered his head again. "My name is *Linn Ssynec Raucr Ïarlucec Dreur Haïder Ghintec*. I thank you, and I hope I can be of service on the way to the **Capital, Commander**." Jint was pleased he'd proved able to say something passable. He was especially happy he hadn't butchered his own name.

"Please leave it to us. Might I also introduce my subordinates, if you wouldn't mind?" The Hecto-Commander presented her five subordinates to him.

Lecsh resembled Lafier, but only in some way he couldn't quite put his finger on. He'd thought that due to their uniform level of beauty, their features would by that same token lack individuality, but that was not the case. The other **starpilots** were beautiful in their own ways, with distinctive facial features.

First was the *bynecairh* (inspector supervisor) and *Loüass Scœmr* (Mechanics Deca-Commander), whose name was *Gymryac*. These were the titles of the crew member in charge of maintaining and inspecting the warship's equipment, starting with its *obsaic* (main engines). In contrast with her ebony skin, her eyes and hair were a bright azure.

Next was the *üigtec* (clerk). If the **inspector supervisor** was in charge of minding the machines, he was in charge of minding all the people on board. His name was *Dich*, and he was *Loüass Sazoïr* (Quartermaster Deca-Commander). His reddish eyes gleamed with a quiet serenity.

The *Ruséc* (Vice Commander) cum *Almrilbigac* (Senior Navigator) was **Deca-Commander** *Rairïac*. He was a man with a light blue moustache, and a chiseled visage. His smile lent him a friendly and approachable image.

The *Almtlaciac* (Senior Gunner) was *Sarrych,* who was also a *raicléc* (vanguard starpilot). His surname indicated he was a member of a family with a distinguished history even among the Abh, and his eyes were as sharp as a razor.

Lastly, there was the *Almdrociac* (Senior Communications Officer). Her name was *Ynséryac,* and she too was a **vanguard starpilot**. Her hair could only be described as the type of blue one imagines when thinking of it as a primary color, and as for her demeanor, she exuded a calm composure.

They were all Abh, and they looked like they were in their mid-20s. There was no way to tell their actual ages.

"We will depart at once," said Lecsh once the time for introductions concluded. "Once again, we would be honored if you could accompany us to the *gahorh* (ship's bridge), if you would be amenable?"

"Of course, my pleasure," answered Jint. He glimpsed at the vessel behind him. Lafier still hadn't exited it.

"Your luggage will be brought to your room by **NCCs**," said Lecsh, apparently misconstruing why Jint had looked back.

"Ah, right... thank you."

"Now please, it's this way." Lecsh pointed the way.

If this had been Delktu, Lecsh would have been appraised as a peerless beauty. While her golden eyes were peculiar, they did nothing to harm her charms. In fact, they only accentuated them.

It wasn't that Jint wasn't used to girls — he'd learned how to conduct himself around people of the female persuasion on Delktu. Now, beautiful *older* ladies... Those were harder to deal with. The fact that the beautiful lady in question was also the commander of a warship only made her even more arresting.

His place walking beside the **Ship Commander** had been wordlessly prepared for him, and he kept pace shoulder-to-shoulder with her, but he felt really uncomfortable. That was only exacerbated by the five high-ranked **starpilots** following in their wake like a gaggle of squires. The *"daimonn"*

standard gravity level of the Abh was around half the intensity of what Jint was used to — and yet, his gait was prone to becoming sluggish.

The bridge was semicircular. Taking into account how the upper portion of the walls was slightly curved, he thought the interior could well be spherical in shape. The floor was two-tiered, with the outer part being lower than the center.

"Lonh-*Ïarlucer Dreur Haïder* and **Ship Commander!**" reported the *sach laitefaicr* (guard NCC) assigned to the bridge. Jint followed the captain onto the taller semicircle at the room's center.

Nine starpilots stood at attention and gave Jint a welcoming salute.

"Please, over here." **Hecto-Commander** Lecsh invited him to take a seat that had been, by all appearances, provided for him on a temporary basis.

"Thank you very much." Jint nodded and seated himself.

When the captain took a seat, the other starpilots followed suit. The four high-ranked starpilots also entered the bridge and settled into their posts. Twelve of the officers headed toward the *cloüc* (consoles) so as to encircle their commanding officer. The other two, **Supervisor** *Gymryac* and **Clerk** *Dich*, turned their backs to the captain and took seats at the front.

"Show video of the outside." In accordance with Lecsh's command, the walls morphed into the star-speckled reaches of space.

Since the **starpilots**, including the **Ship Commander**, had the **access-cables** of their **circlets** connected, pulling up that live video must have been done out of consideration for Jint and his lack of *frocragh* spatiosensory perception.

"Prepare for departure." The **Hecto-Commander**'s voice cracked through the air like a whip.

Jint couldn't muster the desire to scrutinize the way they worked with affected detachment; he huddled up in his chair. He felt like some mischievous little scamp who'd barged into the wrong place.

"All engines in order," reported **Mechanics Deca-Commander** *Gymryac*.

"Interior environment in order," said **Quartermaster Deca-Commander** *Dich*.

"Preparations complete for steering." **Vanguard Starpilot** *Sarrych* equipped the **control gauntlet**.

"Permission received from the **Space Traffic Control** of the **Vorlash Countdom** to cross the *saudec* (portal)."

"The permitted time frame is from 15:27:12 to 15:27:18 by ship's time," reported Vanguard Starpilot *Ynséryac*.

"Ready for departure." **Vice Commander** Rayria reported the final announcement.

"Very good." The captain nodded. "Accelerate at *daimonn*-force 6, toward the *Saudec Bhorlacr* (Vorlash Portal)."

Vanguard *Sarrych* heard her orders. "Veering toward 17-62-55."

"Authorized," Lecsh replied.

Thanks to the artificial gravity on board, he couldn't feel any tremors induced by attitude control. However, the broad swaying of the stars was ample proof that the giant warship had moved its muzzle. Jint craned his neck from the back of his chair, and was met with the sight of Delktu as a tiny speck.

"Attitude control complete."

"*Daïsairé* (setting sail)!"

The **patrol ship** vibrated lightly at her word. Water flooded into the *flisésïac* (matter-antimatter-annihilation engine). A stream of antiprotons shot into the water; where the matter and antimatter collided, they voraciously devoured one another, unbinding energy in their wake. All the matter that failed to collide with antimatter absorbed the energy, leapt into empty space, and kicked the enormous ship into motion from the recoil. That was what caused the vibrations.

"Is all this travel wearisome?" Lecsh asked him, concern in her voice.

"Absolutely not," responded Jint, quite truthfully. "It's my first time experiencing this, so I find it fascinating."

"Do you have any questions for us?"

"Yes." After some thought, Jint had come up with a question he deemed safe to ask. "From the introductions earlier, I thought that **Vanguard** *Sarrych* was the **Senior Gunner**, but now I understand he's also in charge of steering. Do all **gunners** also steer?"

"Correct. Steering while in *dadh* (3-dimensional space) is a **gunner**'s job. That's because for **patrol ship**s, steering and battle maneuvers are closely intertwined."

"I see. I, uh, have another question, if it's all right…"

"What is it?"

"I was under the impression that **clerks** do clerical office work. I've noticed they have duties on the **bridge** as well, though."

"Well observed. They are responsible for checking on whether the gravity control is regular, or whether the interior pressurization is holding. However, they are usually only on the **bridge** during takeoff and landing, or during battle. Otherwise they're typically in the secretarial rooms, performing their operational tasks."

"What do those 'operational tasks' they carry out in the secretarial rooms entail?"

"Ahh, you must be all the more interested in that department given that's where your future will be, **Your Excellency**. I'm certain you would learn more asking *Dich* directly, but…" While he was (somewhat awkwardly) maintaining a conversation with Lecsh, he discovered that the **starpilot** was, in fact, a kind-hearted woman.

There was, however, a barrier. The **Ship Commander** never broke away from her pointedly courteous comportment, and Jint, for his part, lacked the courage to dispense with it and slip into more vulgar speech.

Hecto-Commander Lecsh was earnest by nature, and she tried to answer Jint's queries as much as she could. Though he felt like he was being treated like a child from time to time, that didn't bother him. Jint knew he still had so much to learn about Abh culture.

At last, **Deca-Commander** Rayria's report came in. "Three minutes until **portal** transit."

"I apologize for interrupting our conversation," said the captain. "Activate the *flasath* (space-time bubble)," she ordered.

"*Flasatiac* (space-time bubble generator engine) in order," said **Mechanics Deca-Commander** *Gymryac*.

"*Flasath* activation confirmed." The footage in front of them showed a multitude of **Vorlash portals**. This was the second configuration of yuanons.

The Abh called the first form of yuanons — like the ones packed in the propulsion engine of the Leif Erikson — "*saudec lœza*" (closed portals). The second shape yuanons could take, the phosphorescent, spherical pockets of space a mere *saidagh* in diameter each, was called "*saudec graca*" (open portals), or simply *saudec*.

"One minute until **portal** transit."

"Start counting down by the second at E-minus thirty," ordered the **Ship Commander**.

"Roger."

By the time the countdown commenced, the stars ahead became shrouded in the gentle light of the **portal**.

"......five, four, three, two, one, traversing."

Passing through the **portal** did not cause any turbulence on impact, but the video of the outside changed completely. Gone was the phosphorescent light. So too did the stars and heavens vanish. A vast ashen sky was all the eye could see.

The secret of faster-than-light travel lay in so-called *fadh* (planar space), which was governed by different physical laws than *dadh* or "3-space" (i.e., 3-dimensional, "normal" space). As the name might suggest, it was a cosmic fabric made up of two-dimensional space and one-dimensional time. The interstellar spaceships of the Abh wrapped themselves in **space-time bubbles** to cross this abnormal space. Time-space bubbles were pockets of **3-space**; just as compacted sixth-dimensional continuous bodies exist within fourth-dimensional space-time, they were permitted to exist within "planar space."

The **patrol ship** Gothelauth was now in a space apart from space. All that existed within that bubble, apart from the **patrol ship** itself, was tiny floating atoms.

In that moment, Jint knew that no matter what kind of calamity the cosmos he lived in, or "**3-space**," was hit with, he would have no way of knowing — and that made him shudder.

"Confirm position," the **Ship Commander** directed, and Jint turned around. "Are you aware that we do not know our current position?"

"What do you mean?"

"When shifting from *dadh* to *fadh*," began **Hecto-Commander** Lecsh, explaining the basics of *sotfairh fadhotr* (theory of planar space navigation), "and vice versa, we can only know our position probabilistically. You have heard the term 'probabilistic' before, I trust?"

"It's the fancy word for 'hit-or-miss,'" he said with evident pride.

"That's not too far off," the captain nodded. "The interior of a **portal**, planar space, and the exterior of a portal, 3-space, correspond to one another. But we can't be sure of our exact location. Portals often trace imperfect helical curves upon planar space, but we're not privy onto which part of those curves we will appear."

"Confirmation of position complete," reported the **Senior Navigator**.

"Right bank, 117-92 from the terminal edge."

Two-dimensional video showed up on the floor. The interior of the **portal**, represented by a distorted spiral, contained a point of shining blue light. That was the present position of the **patrol ship** *Gothelauth*.

"Assume complete *noctamh* (mobile-state) at 280 degrees." After the captain issued her orders, she asked Jint, "Do you know of mobile-state and *scobrtamh* (stationary-state)?"

"Yes. That much I do know," said Jint. He may have been headed to the **Budget Branch**, but one needed to know at least that much to earn academy admittance. Although when it came to the nitty-gritty mathematics of these things, he could but throw up his arms in surrender.

If there were an observer in **planar space**, they would see the **space-time** bubble as a particle — an elementary particle that gradually shed its mass. This elementary particle could take two states. They were *noctamh* and *scobrtamh*.

An easy way to grasp the concept would be to imagine a sphere rotating on the floor. If the axis of rotation is made vertical to the floor, then that sphere will remain at that spot. With a horizontal axis of rotation, the sphere rolls across the floor. The vertical-axis example is to *scobrtamh* or the stationary-state, as the horizontal-axis example is to *noctamh* or the mobile-state. (There is no equivalent state for a diagonal axis of rotation.)

When in the **mobile-state**, the direction of the rotational axis can be freely determined. Moreover, the two states can be switched between instantaneously, thereby allowing one to adjust the velocity as well.

What one mustn't forget is that whether staying in one place or rolling, it was always itself rotating. In other words, the bubble expended a fixed amount of energy over time.

"Navigating from here onwards is the **navigator**'s job," Lecsh murmured, pointing to Rayria. "Our destination is *Saudec Sfagnaumr* (Sfagnoff Portal). Chart a course."

A blue, dotted line crossing near the distorted spiral appeared near-instantly. Rayria looked up at his **Commander** and said, "Course calculations complete."

"Acknowledged." **Hecto-Commander** Lecsh nodded, and said: "I leave the rest to you, Rayria. Place us on course."

"Roger, **Commander**. Leave it to me."

The blip of light indicating their current position tried to crawl out from the spiral's interior to the newly accessible area. A green blip of light appeared on the borderline of the spiral and began to move. Another green blip passed the blue one by, headed toward the spiral. It was a ship headed toward the **Countdom of Vorlash**. In that time, the blue blip reached the dotted line and started tracing it.

"We've converged on the course, **Commander**," said Rayria.

"Very good. All hands relieved of preparation duties. Shift to primary response stance," said the **Hecto-Commander** as she stowed away her **access-cables**.

The **starpilots** on the bridge stood up. Only three remained seated. The starpilots saluted her before exiting the room, and **Hecto-Commander** Lecsh stood up to salute them back.

Jint, unsure of how he should behave in the meantime, just fidgeted in his seat.

"**Your Excellency**." The captain had once again taken a seat. "Despite this being your first experience of such space travel, I believe you will find it quite dull from this point on. The **starpilots** on duty will remain gloomy and silent, absorbed in the task of scanning the equipment for possible malfunctions. Please allow me to show you to your room."

But Jint had made up his mind. "No, **Ship Commander**, if you wouldn't mind, I'd like to continue our conversation."

"It would be my pleasure, *Lonh*. I myself find times like these tedious. But what is it you would like to discuss?"

"Do you know of the origins of the **Countdom of Hyde**?"

"I do. Its conquest was the topic of much talk, after all." From how she spoke, one might assume the word "conquest" had no negative connotations. Maybe it just didn't sound distasteful to her when it was Abhs at the helm of those conquests.

"Then I'm sure you're already aware, but I really don't know how to act like a **noble**."

"Is that true?" she said, apparently surprised.

"That's right. I'm lost, honestly. I never learned this kind of stuff."

"You mean you didn't associate with the family of the **Count of Vorlash**?"

"I didn't, no." The Count of Vorlash had shown no interest whatsoever in the heir to the Count of Hyde residing in his territory. Nor had Jint ever harbored any desire to pay the *garich* (orbital manor) a visit. "They never extended an invitation."

"So you're trying to say that you don't know how best to interact with us?"

"Yes, that's right," nodded Jint. "To strike up a conversation this heavy with a nice lady I just met... tell me if it's too much trouble..."

"It's no trouble," said Lecsh gleefully. "It's not often at all that **gentry** gets to dictate the behavior of a **grandee**!"

"So is my, uh, attitude all wrong? Is a **grandee** supposed to you know, act *big* or something?"

"You could certainly get away with it," said the **Hecto-Commander**. "At the cost of being disliked. Is that all?"

"I'm glad. That means I'm not acting that strange."

"No." Lecsh crossed her arms. "Though to tell you the truth, you do come across a tad *eccentric*. Eccentricity does not always necessarily warrant criticism, of course."

"Haha…" Jint could feel all his self-confidence suddenly dissipate. "Umm, what exactly is a **grandee** who's not 'eccentric' like?"

"They do have something of an air of *dignity* about them."

"I knew it," said Jint, deflated.

"How you are, though, is much preferable to nobles who go overboard with the overweening pride, *Lonh*."

"Thank you very much." But not even the **Ship Commander**'s consoling words could heal Jint's heart.

"You do realize that your standing in society is higher than mine, yes?"

"Actually, that's something I'm a little fuzzy on, too. You've been very polite to me this whole time, **Ship Commander**, but I really don't feel worthy of that courtesy."

"Is that so?" The captain seemed perplexed. It was the puzzlement of someone who didn't quite know how to interact with a person this extremely clueless.

"I mean, I understand the hierarchy of the different **noble ranks**. What's never made much sense to me, no matter how much I looked into it, is how those noble ranks relate with their social status. In fact, the more I researched, the harder it became to understand. It's often the case all across the **Empire** that **nobles** work under **gentry**, for one."

"Yes, that's very much a matter of course."

"Which would mean that I don't have any social status. Am I wrong?"

"As far as the relationships between people who belong to different organizations go, it's the *darmsath bhoflir* (imperial court hierarchy) that means everything," Lecsh explained. "I am a **ship commander**, and thanks to that, I have been conferred the status of *raloch* (knight first-class). It's a fairly high social standing for **gentry**, but it's nowhere near yours, *Ïarlucec Dreur*."

"Doesn't that get confusing?"

"What would be confusing?"

"If someone's social standing is higher than their superior officer's, doesn't it get difficult to give them orders?"

The **Hecto-Commander** laughed a light little laugh. "This is when it's between people who belong to different organizations, remember? Within the military itself, this is all that matters." She pointed to the insignia on her upper right arm — exactly like Lafier had. It might well have been a gesture shared by all **starpilots** of the **Star Forces**. "If you are assigned to a **starpilot quartermaster** post under us, **Your Excellency**, rest assured that we will work you to the ground. You are kindly advised not to expect this kind of cordial treatment when that happens."

"Yes, so I've heard…" But Jint still wasn't fully convinced. "What if you can't stop thinking about my standing outside of the military, though?"

"Hmmm…" Lecsh spoke even as she considered the question. "In the past, that may have been a problem. However, our class system and military have become more and more *refined* over time. These days, that sort of thing just doesn't come up. People who can't make a clear distinction between their time in the **Star Forces** and their time in civilian society will be considered disqualified to participate in polite society no matter their rank."

"Sounds complex," sighed Jint.

"Does it? I've been living in this society since I was born, so to me it just seems in the nature of things."

"Maybe it's something like seniority by age…?"

"What do you mean?"

"Ahh." Jint launched into an explanation.

While not so much on *Martinh*, on Delktu, the ideal of honoring one's elders was very much emphasized. The older an elder got, the more they were respected. That being said, even on Delktu it wasn't too uncommon for some to have a younger boss. Within a given organization, it wasn't age that was respected, but rather rank. But when two people were extracted from within that organization, that relationship could flip right around. It appeared that amongst the Abh, who didn't have readily apparent age differences, perhaps the concept of "seniority by age" was a confounding one.

"Maybe it is similar," said Lecsh in tentative agreement. "We aren't very conscious of people's ages at all."

"Wait, hold on…" Jint's opinions suddenly came spilling out. "Older people usually have a wealth of life experience, so it makes sense to honor their wisdom. But how does being born to a higher-ranked household make someone an inherently worthier person?"

He was very aware that he was essentially criticizing a matter at the core of the whole **Empire**, but he felt totally at ease. He was himself a **noble**, after all. There was no need to hold back when it was his own standing he was doubting the worth of. Even so, he was expecting the **Ship Commander** would be shaken by his question.

Yet Lecsh's expression didn't change at all. It seemed an utterly impossible undertaking to stab at the heart of an Abh.

"Hmm, yes..." The commander pondered. "A **noble** is the progeny of an outstanding figure. An inheritor of the **family traditions** that that outstanding figure built up. As such, we tend to expect they will also excel in some way or another. I think that's why there's value in paying them our respect."

"Really?" Jint was skeptical. "But just because someone is raised by a person of high-caliber doesn't mean they'll excel—"

"Not always, no," Lecsh granted the point without issue. "You are quite right — just because someone achieves a great accomplishment doesn't mean they'll be an equally excellent educator. There are a number of examples of heroes' children being useless disappointments. However, speaking in generalities, the descendant of a person of high caliber will usually have some quality worthy of respect."

"Huh." Jint nodded, but noncommittally. At the back of his mind, he was thinking about his own circumstances. Even if he granted, for the sake of argument, that his father was a "man of high caliber," Jint had not really been raised by him.

"Besides," continued Lecsh, "One's 'elders' are not necessarily worthy of respect, either."

"That is true." Jint imagined someone who'd grown old without ever learning a thing.

"We have a solid basis for our social order, and it more than encompasses something as rudimentary as respect for elders. That is what I think, anyway. Was that helpful to you?"

"Yes. By all means." It was certainly informative, that much was beyond dispute. He still had his misgivings, though, and didn't swallow all of what he'd been told.

"Now then, let me guide you to your room. Calling the **trainee** who escorted **His Excellency** from the **spaceport**," she said, holding her wrist computer to her face.

"Ah, her…" She was of course speaking of Lafier. "She's a **noble**, too, right?"

Lecsh opened her eyes wide in surprise. "No."

"Really? That's odd. I mean, her bearing was really different from yours, **Commander**."

"You mean to tell me you don't know who she is!?" Her right eyebrow, as dark bluish-grey as the rest of her hair, rose accusingly.

"No. I, uhh…" He had a bad feeling about where this was going — bad enough to feel like the back of his brain was burning to a crisp. "Was it wrong of me to not know?"

"No — I think it's probably understandable, given your *eccentric* upbringing." The captain grinned, and turned on the audio receiver of her wrist computer. "**Trainee Starpilot** Abliar, report to the **bridge** immediately."

"'Abliar'!?" It was the same name as the *Glaharérh* (Commander-in-Chief) of the **fleet** that had subdued the Hyde Star System. He too was a member of the **Imperial Family**, and he and Lafier shared the surname of the **Imperial Household**. "Which 'Abliar' family?"

"She's a member of the *Lartïéc Clybr* (Royal Family of *Clybh*)."

"Then that means…"

"Yes." An impish smile graced her lovely countenance. "**Trainee Starpilot** Abliar is the granddaughter of *Speunaigh Érumitta* (Her Majesty the Empress)."

Chapter 5: The *Lartnéc Frybarer* (Royal Princess of the Empire)

The **Empire** put a certain amount of trust in the loyalty of the **nobility** and **gentry**, as well as in the family ties between Abhs. But not too much trust — they did not have any illusions.

It was incumbent upon the Empress, who stood at the nucleus of the Empire's consolidation of power, to understand that it was the Empire's military power that safeguarded that consolidation. That was the Empire's founding principle.

As such, the occupier of the *Scaimsorragh* (the Emperorship) had to have military experience, and, if possible, was to be a superlative military leader.

On the other hand, automatically making anyone who had taken hold of military authority the Emperor would inevitably lead to dizzying internal strife and power struggles. It would lead quickly to the collapse of the **Empire**.

Cilugragh (succession of the emperorship) in the **Humankind Empire of Abh** was hereditary, but they adopted a system that took into account the innate qualities of each of a number of possible successors.

The **Imperial Family** comprised eight separate **royal families**. They were all the descendants of the siblings and children of the *Scurlaiteriac* (Founding Emperor), *Ablïarsec Dunaic*, and they all shared the *fizz* (surname) "Abliar."

The families with that cognomen were:

Lartïéc Scïrh Nëïc Lamarer — the royal family of *Scirh*;
Lartïéc Ilicr Nëïc Dusirr — the royal family of *Ilich*;
Lartïéc Lasiser Nëïc Lamlyrer — the royal family of *Rasisec*;
Lartïéc Üescor Nëïc Düairr — the royal family of *Üescoc*;
Lartïéc Barcœr Nëïc Lamsarr — the royal family of *Barcœc*;
Lartïéc Bargzedér Nëïc Dubzairr — the royal family of *Bargzedéc*;
Lartïéc Syrgzœdér Nëïc Düasecr — the royal family of *Surgzedéc*; and
Lartïéc Clybr Nëïc Dubreuscr — the royal family of *Clybh*.

These were the *Ga Lartïéc* — the eight royal families.

Those born to these families bore the duty to take on *slymecoth* (military service). They couldn't get by enlisting in departments with more behind-the-scenes work like the **Budget** or *Gaïritec* (Medical) Branches. They had to enlist as *lodaïrh Garér* (Flight Branch starpilots).

With regard to **military service**, the so-called **Imperials** had only one special right, and it had to do with their enrollment in the *Bhosecrac* (Military Academy). According to Star Forces regulations, it took at least four and a half years to advance to a military college, but an exception was made for Imperials. They were automatically enrolled after two and a half years, without regard to their competence level.

Thus appointed as a *faictodaïc* (linewing starpilot), they would then ascend to the rank of *rinhairh* (rearguard starpilot) in a year's time, after which they would become a **vanguard starpilot** in a year and a half. Following that, they would enroll in the most difficult to enter of all the military academies, the *Dunaic* Star Forces Academy (*Bhosecrac Duner*).

Upon completion of half a year's education, they took on the *rénh* (rank) of **Deca-Commander**, with the *ptorahédésomh* (commander's insignia) to go with it.

This was the "special right" of the **Imperial Household**, but looking at it from another angle, they were being asked to shoulder responsibilities beyond their experience and ability, and they had no automatic right to a rank above **Deca-Commander**. The rate of promotion after reaching that level was more or less the same as other military academy graduates'. Moreover, if they failed in a mission, they had to face punishment or dismissal with no more mercy than **gentry** or **nobility** could expect.

They climbed their way through the ranks of the **Flight Branch** as linewing starpilots, and once they finally reached the rank of *Rüéspénec* (Imperial Admiral), they received special imperial appointment to the rank of *Glaharérh Rüé Byrer* (Imperial Fleet Commander-in-Chief). In peacetime, it was a title that didn't hold command over a single soldier apart from a handful of headquarters personnel, but it was once a prominent post that the Emperor customarily held onto, and succeeding to it meant becoming next in line for the throne, or the *Cilugiac* (Crown Prince[ss]).

When the new **Imperial Fleet Commander-in-Chief** was decided, it was standard practice for members of the **Imperial Family** either older than them or less than 20 years younger than them to ask to be transferred to reserve duty. Even before that point, many Imperial Family members who had given up on becoming Emperor proceeded to leave the military, and then either succeeded to a *lartragh* (monarchship) or else simply lived as an Imperial with a noble rank for a single generation.

Each generation of imperial-family descendants possessed a *sapainec* (surnym), "*Bauss*," that indicated they had inherited the family traditions of the **Imperial Household**. Yet their social standing was that of a **noble**. When one became a mere noble, they could no longer retain the surname "Abliar."

The **Imperial Fleet Commander-in-Chief** almost always ended up waiting for the appearance of a new **Imperial Admiral** as the next **Imperial** in line to the throne. He or she acceded to the imperial throne when someone who could take over his or her own position emerged. At that juncture, the Emperor would suddenly abdicate.

For the long-lived Abh, it was not rare for a former Emperor to enjoy 100 more years after stepping down from the *scaimsorh* (throne). But the **Empire** did not allow them to rest on their laurels. Former Emperors were automatically appointed to the *Luzœc Fanigalacr* (Council of Abdicant Emperors), while *larth* (monarchs) were chosen for it by mutual election, thereby receiving the honorary title of *Nisoth* ("Eminence").

It was this Council of Abdicant Emperors that was responsible for the promotion and inquiry of **starpilots** that were **Imperials**. It was said those hearings were tougher than the ones military organizations conducted for ordinary starpilots. The descendants of the **eight royal families** were forced to get past those hearings, as they were given 40 years to compete over the *Scaimsorh Rœnr* (Jade Throne).

While he waited for the **trainee starpilot** to appear, Jint used his **wristgear** to run a search of *Rüé lalasac* (distinguishmed persons of the Empire), and discovered that *Ablïarsec Néïc Dubreuscr, Bœrh Parhynr* (Viscountess of *Parhynh*) was the *Lartnéc Casna* (First Princess).

Walking a step behind her, Jint felt truly restless. The confusion that had dogged him for six years had reached a crescendo.

Previously, it had been more like an insect that buzzed annoyingly around him. Jint had had ample chance to grow accustomed to it, and sometimes he even felt fine with it, *appreciated* it. However, it was as though he'd caught wind somewhere that the insect was furnished with a stinger, and boy had it begun to sting.

He had, of course, expected to bump into an "**Imperial**" at some point. He himself was technically a **noble**, and he figured it was great that that qualified him to gain the favor of Imperials. He'd assumed his first encounter with them would be at some social gathering like a ball or a dinner party. And he'd assumed they'd properly introduce themselves as such.

What had transpired instead was a veritable *sneak attack*.

His supposed conviction that all people are born equal was apparently shakier than he thought, given that it flew out the window the second he found himself near someone who was so close, by blood, to the ruler of an **Empire** that presided over 900 billion *bisarh* (subjects). His past and future aside, Jint, at that moment, was an **Abh noble**, totally immersed in the Empire's class system.

When he recalled how the **Ship Commander** had taken a polite attitude with him, the legitimate heir of an upstart **noble**, his fears that his behavior in the **smallcraft** had been glib only worsened.

How was he going to smooth things over? Jint stared wildly around.

Contrary to Jint's expectations, the **warship**'s interior wasn't no-frills impersonal; there were paintings along the hallway walls of the **patrol ship**. Not only that, but they were full of windblown grassy fields, and skies of drifting white clouds. He thought they might have given him at least some peace of mind, but they had absolutely no effect.

"What's the matter, Jint?" Lafier's face appeared beside the hovering fluff of painterly dandelions. "You haven't said a word. And why are you walking behind me?"

"*Fïac Rüénér* (Your Highness the Imperial Princess), I…" Jint began, with utmost deference.

Instantly, Lafier stopped in her tracks and turned around. The look she shot him gave him goosebumps.

She had shot him glares during their time on the smallcraft, too. However, now he could see they'd been half in jest, like a dog play-biting.

This is the face she pulls when she's really pissed...

Her face, beautifully constructed, was tinged with unmistakable anger, black fire blazing in her ebony eyes. But, belying that fire, the words that escaped her lips were as bitter-cold as the vacuum of space.

"I am not a *Rüénéc*, an imperial princess. I am a Lartnéc, a *royal* princess. Daughter of a king, not of the Empress herself. The Empress is my grandmother. My father is a mere *larth* king."

"Forgive me, *Fïac Lartnér*." He bowed his head with all cordiality, but on the inside Jint stewed: *Did she really have to get so angry over something as silly as getting her title wrong?*

Lafier turned away in a huff and started stomping off from him. Jint chased after her in a panic.

Lafier had more to say. "If you insist on fixating so much on my relation to Her Majesty, I am a *Rüébaugenéc* (granddaughter of the Empress), but that's not an official title, and I seldom use it anyway. In fact, I myself was shocked when I discovered that I was the granddaughter of an Empress. And most importantly, '*Fïac Rüébaugenér*' just sounds weird! 'Granddaughter of the Empress'?"

"Sure, I can see tha — er, I mean, *certainly, Fïac*," Jint concurred diffidently.

"When I was born, I inherited the **fief** and **title** of **Viscountess of Parhynh** from **Her Majesty the Empress** through my father, who is my legal guardian. That's why I'm sometimes called '*Fïac Bœrr Parhynr*.' Though here, for *whatever* reason, people usually refer to me as '**Trainee Starpilot** Abliar,'" Lafier rattled on.

Unable to butt in, Jint could only keep on walking in blank amazement.

"I thought I told you — you will call me 'Lafier'!"

Jint could be bone-headed at times, but even he now grasped the real reason Lafier was so upset. He changed his tone on a dime. "Okay, got it, my bad. You're 'Lafier' to your friends, then."

"Not even to my friends." Lafier's tone was as curt as ever. "The only ones who address me without my **title** are my father, Larth Clybr *Fïac Dubeuser*, my grandmother, **Her Majesty the Empress**, my aunt, *Fïac Lamlyner*, also known as the *Dreuc Gemfadr* (Countess of *Gemfadh*). Them, and the *fanigac* (abdicant emperors) that I'm directly descended from. That's about it. My friends call me either *Fïac Lartnér* or just *Fïac*, while my relatives all seem to have taken to calling me *Fïac* Lafier."

"Then why...?" He spontaneously froze in his steps. He, a mere heir to a countdom, had inadvertently stumbled upon an incredible privilege. And here he'd been, actively trying to discard it. "You want me to call you 'Lafier'... even though we've only barely met?"

"It was the first time anyone ever asked me my name." Lafier also stopped walking, but she kept facing ahead.

"Being the granddaughter of the **Empress** means everyone already knows my name and appearance. I'm famous, apparently. People call me '*Fïac Lartnér*' without my ever getting to introduce myself. So even people I'm quite close to end up calling me *Fïac*. Always 'Your Highness.' It's been like that all my life. I didn't pay it all that much mind, but at the academy, I felt the tiniest — the *tiniest* — bit jealous when everyone was dropping titles and calling each other by name. That jealousy only grew worse when I realized that my peers were always unable to 'loosen up' when I was around."

"I, I'm sorry..." Jint was appalled at the enormity of the offense he'd committed. He'd inadvertently slapped away the hand she'd extended in good will, and dealt a blow to her heart.

"Do not apologize." As coldly as ever, she stated: "You have done nothing wrong. While '*Fïac Rüénér*' is definitely mistaken, you meant nothing by it. I wasn't brought up to endure rude monikers, but I will accept any *proper* name. So be at ease, Lonh-*Ïarlucer Dreur* — you may now call me '*Fïac Lartnér*' or '*Fïac Bœrr Parhynr*.'"

"No, it's okay, I'll just call you 'Lafier'..."

"Don't get the wrong idea. It's not as though I really wanted you to call me 'Lafier.' I just thought it would be questionable to introduce myself with my **title** attached."

*Maybe she isn't suited to becoming **Empress**; she's a terrible liar.*

Jint shook off that thought and pled anew. "Please, I'd really like to just call you 'Lafier.'"

Lafier finally turned back to face him, and stared intently.

"Don't strain yourself, *Lonh*."

"I'm not. I swear…"

"Then I don't even mind if you call me '*Fïac Rüébaugenér.*'" Jint let out a gasp. He'd wounded her so much that she'd rather he called her the name she'd said sounded "weird."

"What do I need to do to make it up to you!?"

Lafier just kept wordlessly staring at Jint for a while. Then, at last, her cheeks twitched. The indignant **princess** started chuckling, as though she couldn't hold it in any longer.

Jint was relieved — it seemed their friendship had been mended.

"You really had no idea I was an Abliar?" asked Lafier, after stifling the urge to laugh.

"Nope. None whatsoever."

"Even with these ears of mine?" Lafier scooped up her hair. They were pointy — the same ears as **Fleet Commander-in-Chief** Abliar, the man who had invaded the Hyde Star System.

"These are the *üaritec* (unique family feature) of my lineage, the *nüic Ablïarser* (Abliar ears)."

"They were hidden inside your hair."

"I see… My ears *are* small for an Abliar." Judging by the tone of her voice, she'd occasionally felt insecure about them.

"Besides," Jint continued, "even if I had seen them, I don't know that I would have cottoned on anyway. I'm not an Abh by birth, so I'm not used to giving **family features** much thought."

"Oh, so that's how it is," Lafier nodded, moved.

"Yep, that's how it is." Jint resumed walking.

Üaritec or "**family features**" were like the trademark physical characteristics of individual lines. They varied from the shape of body parts like the nose or ears, to the color of the eyes or hair. Where it manifested depended on the family. Whether they were **gentry** or **nobles**, the Abh obsessively saw to it that all descendants of a given family shared that one distinct physical feature. Naturally, this was engraved it into their very genes.

Needless to say, **Abliar ears** were the most highly respected **family feature**. But Jint had altogether forgotten about **family features** until that moment.

Lafier walked with him shoulder-to-shoulder. "You really are an amusing one."

"Cut it out, would ya?" Jint shrugged. "So, I wanted to ask you about your experiences…"

"My experiences?"

"At the **academy**. You said nobody could relax when you were around?" Lafier urged him to continue with her eyes. "I've got my fair share of memories, too, let me tell you," he said with a sheepish smile. "Though yours are probably on a whole different level."

"What do you mean?"

"I don't know if you know… I was the only **noble** at my school."

"Ahh…"

Because they all aimed to work under Abhs, the students of the Abh Linguistic and Cultural Institute were far removed from any anti-Abh sentiment. On the contrary, the majority intended to find success as **imperial citizens**, earn appointment as **gentry** if being **nobility** was unattainable, and make their descendants into Abhs.

To those students, the presence of a boy who had a **noble rank** lined up for him despite being a Lander was hard to stomach. He was the target of ridicule on the least pretext, and of vicious bullying wherever teachers weren't looking. That said, there were also those who confounded him with their abject servility.

No one knew how to deal with a **noble**.

"And I can't blame them — it's not like I had any idea how to behave, either."

"In that case, you had a rougher time than me. The **trainee pupils** knew full well how they're supposed to behave around an **Imperial**. I simply didn't *like* how they were supposed to behave around an Imperial. I was treated with the proper cordiality and was paid all respects. And yet…" Lafier's eyes turned reproachful. "If I had been you, I wouldn't have let them bully me."

"I'm a pacifist, Lafier," he said with a shrug.

"Neither pacifism nor militarism have anything to do with it, surely."

"Look, there were way more people than I could fight. There was animosity towards me even from the faculty."

"I see…"

"Don't worry, I learned how to get by quickly enough."

"What did you have to do?" she asked, curious.

"I hid my rank."

"You can hide your rank?" Lafier looked puzzled.

"I'm not as famous as you, *Fïac Lartnér*. Although…" Jint shook his head. "I couldn't hide it at school. Whenever I tried to put on an innocent face and chat with freshies, some older guy with a big mouth would be there to make sure they found out."

"So what did you do?"

"I went into town. In town, I made friends with **landworld citizens** who live without sparing the **Empire** a thought."

"Wow. You've experienced more hardship than I expected."

A pair of **NCCs** was about to pass by, but they stopped to give Jint and Lafier a salute. Lafier saluted back, but didn't break her stride.

"Umm…" said Jint in hushed tones. "What am I supposed to do when things like that happen? Saluting them back would be weird, right?"

"You can just give them a nod."

The **NCCs** had already passed by, so Jint turned around and gave them a nod. Surprised, their hands flew back to the saluting position.

"Well, don't do that, that's just inconveniencing them," Lafier chided him softly.

"You're right." Jint sighed inwardly.

It played out more smoothly the next time they crossed paths with some **NCCs**.

Finally, they arrived in front of a door illustrated with a sunflower bathing in rays of daylight.

"This is your cabin." Lafier pointed to the door.

Jint studied it long and hard. "It's been nagging at me — What are these paintings all about? What does this image *mean*, exactly?"

"It's just decoration. It doesn't 'mean' anything," she said. "Even **warships** need some livening up. That's probably what they thought."

"But it's jarring, isn't it?" Jint started whispering: "Aren't there more spaceship-y subjects for decoration?"

"Like?"

"Like stars or galaxies; you know."

"Who would paint such boring subjects?"

"I thought you guys loved the cosmos?" Jint certainly didn't expect that response.

"We do. It's our home. But the stars are far too *everyday* to be in art. You can just look outside if you want to see the stars."

"I mean, yeah, that's true, but…"

"Besides, paintings like these seem to help **NCCs** who come from **landworlds** mellow out."

"I see…" Jint closely observed the sunflower. "But what do you people think about it? Abhs, I mean?"

"How many times are you going to make me say it? You are an—"

"Right, I'm an Abh, too," Jint cut in. "But I'm not an Abh by birth. That's why I'm curious how Abhs feel when they look at natural plant life."

"I don't think it's any different from how surface people feel." Lafier cocked an eyebrow. "We too are descended from the selfsame *glœc* (humankind) that arose from Earth."

"But you've never seen a real sunflower, right?"

"You have a distorted view of us, Jint. I've seen sunflowers. There are botanical gardens in *Lacmhacarh*, and my house has a flower garden of its own."

"All right." Jint turned around and pointed at the wall behind her. "Then what about that?"

It was a prairie. Realistic knee-length grass filled the piece, and on that grass grazed elephants, horses, and other assorted animals. The scene was sparsely populated by trees, like pines and birches, and cherry blossom petals danced in the blue sky.

"I've never seen *that*, no," she replied.

"So what are your thoughts on it?"

"Why are you asking? What do you get out of it?" She looked dubious.

"Come on," he said. "Help me understand how native-born Abhs tick."

"Very well." Lafier nodded. "It looks dreamlike to me."

"Dreamlike, as in it doesn't exist in reality?"

"No." She tilted her head. "I know it does exist in reality. I understand that our origins lie in lands like these. I guess I would say it's like our founding myth."

"The forsaken homeland."

"Yes. But the *céssath* (universe) is our home now. We are the one and only *céssatudec* (KEHSAHTOOD, people of the cosmos), and we're proud of that."

"Well, surface peoples are descended from interstellar travelers, too," Jint was quick to point out.

"Yes, *travelers*. The ancestors of surface peoples simply zipped from one point of the universe to another. We *live* among the stars. That is a sizeable difference, don't you agree?"

"Maybe." Though in truth, Jint didn't really know. What he did know was that there was something odd, something *alien* about the Abh. Whether that "something odd" had to do with their homeland apart from other humans wasn't clear.

"What do you think, Jint? Is it as boring for you as when we look at the stars? Oh, and by 'we,' I mean *native-born* Abhs. Because you're also Abh."

I guess whenever she says that, she's being conscientious and thinking about me, in her own weird way. Maybe.

"No, it's not boring. This isn't exactly an everyday scene on **landworlds** either, you know. Also, my home planet's ecosystem is different from other worlds'. This painting's ecosystem isn't so far removed from reality that it can be called *fantastical*, but I think it's really all over the place. To the eyes of a trained botanist, it would look fantastical — by the way, could you let me in? I don't know how to open the door."

"You're the one who sidetracked us with sunflowers," she pouted.

"But you've got to admit, it was interesting."

"Yes, I've never stared at a picture so intensely before." It seemed that at her core, she was the honest and unaffected type, this **First Princess of the Monarchy of *Clybh*.**

"Right then, open me up, if you please."

"You need but use your **wristgear**. It's already registered to its signal."

"Ah, is that right?" Jint touched the red stone to the side of the **wristgear**'s display. The door opened.

Jint took a look around the room from its threshold. "Goodness me, what do we have here?"

"Are you dissatisfied?"

"Far from it. I didn't think it would be this pristine."

It wasn't all that big. The bed took up the entire depth of the room, while it was only around twice as wide. In the space that wasn't taken up by the bed, there was a table and chair. At the back, there was another small door. But the most eye-catching thing in the room, without a doubt, was the *gar glac* (GAR GLAH, coat-of-arms banner) hanging on the bed-side wall. The coat of arms of the **Countdom of Hyde**.

A red *rezwan* had been embroidered on a green background. What was a "rezwan?" It didn't look so dissimilar to a bird, but it was a species of furry-fish that swam the seas of the planet Martinh. The specimens in the wild were, even accounting for the fact it was a fish, extremely dimwitted. And yet, it had an inexplicable stateliness to it.

"Your bags will have been put in there." She pointed to the storage shelves opposite the bed. "If you want to get clean, use that door."

Jint opened the door at the back. Just as he thought, a lavatory and bathroom were furnished for him.

"This is awesome. What is this room? Is it for temporary passengers or something?"

"This is a **patrol ship**, Jint. It's a standard room for a starpilot."

"I just hope I didn't take somebody's pad."

"Worry not. For **warships** of **patrol ship**-size, living quarters are planned out with extra space. You never know when non-officer passengers need to board, after all."

"Good." Jint turned his attention to the **banner** on the wall. "Where'd that thing come from?"

"Ah, it must have been made aboard ship," she said nonchalantly.

"What, for me?"

"Who else would it be of any use for, besides you?"

It's not much use to me, either...

Jint shrugged gently. He felt no affection for that hastily improvised **coat of arms**. It hadn't been long after the establishment of the **count's household** that he'd laid eyes on it for the first time, and so up until the day prior he'd utterly forgotten they'd even had a coat of arms.

Jint patted around his bed to gauge its comfiness. It was soft enough to assure him he'd be sleeping just fine.

Jint took a seat on his bed. "So, what do I do now?"

"Right." Lafier checked the time on her **wristgear**. "It will be dinner time in two hours. You'll most likely be invited to the **Ship Commander**'s table. When the time comes, I'll come pick you up, so be patient and wait here."

"You don't need to go out of your way for me; if you just call me on the *luodéc* (teletransceiver) I'm sure I can get there on my own. You must have work to do, right?"

"That will be enough of that nonsense." Lafier's expression turned serious. "I've been tasked with being your guard tomorrow as well. I advise you not to amble around on your own until after tomorrow. Since the founding of the **Star Forces**, there have been countless new recruits and civilians who believed they could get around by reading the onboard guide maps, only to nearly turn into mummies in deserted storage decks."

"And you? Did you get lost, too?" Jint needled.

"I don't appreciate untoward questions that open old wounds, Jint," replied the **trainee starpilot**.

"I see you've got some fun stories to share," Jint smiled.

"Shut up, Jint," Lafier shut him down. "Need anything else from me?"

"Nope. Thank you. I'm fine just killing time here, so I'll be good and wait for you."

"Then I'll see you in two hours."

"See you in two."

Lafier turned right around, and closed the door behind her.

Jint decided to use this time for a warm shower. As he took off his shoes, he suddenly realized, with a start, how relaxed he was. All the nervousness he'd felt before boarding the **patrol ship** had dissipated like a bad dream.

Chapter 6: A *Raisriämrhoth* (State of Emergency)

It was Day 5 since the **patrol ship** *Gothelauth*'s departure from the **Vorlash Countdom**.

"**Ship Commander**." **Deca-Commander** Rayria's voice sounded close to her ears.

The **patrol ship** *Gothelauth*'s commanding officer, **Hecto-Commander** *Laicch Üémh Lobér Placïac* ("Lecsh") soon opened her eyes and looked up at her bedside occupant. The hologram of the Vice Commander floated hazily in the darkness. He was on duty now.

"What?"

"Please come to the **bridge** right now." He wore an incongruously grave expression on his miniature face (about a tenth the size of the genuine article). "Unidentified **space-time bubbles** have been spotted."

"I'll be there in no time." Hecto-Commander Lecsh waved a hand to break the **teletransceiver connection** and sprung to her feet. Swiftly and skillfully, she threw on her pure-black **military uniform**, fixed her sleep-tousled dark bluish-gray hair with a comb, and equipped her **one-winged circlet**. Then she took her **decorative sash-belt** and **command baton** in hand, and beat a quick path toward the bridge.

Within the **elevator-tube** leading to the bridge, she briskly wrapped the belt around her waist and "sheathed" her command baton in it. By the time she arrived at the bridge, she was all clad in a ship commander's formal garb.

Lecsh rushed onto the bridge and shouted, "Rayria, your report!"

"Azimuth, 78 degrees ahead. Distance, 1,539.17 *cédlairh*. Direction, 18 degrees ahead. They're heading for the *Lœbehynh Sfagnaumr* (Marquessate of Sfagnoff)." After **Deca-Commander** Rayria finished informing her, he offered the captain's seat in which he'd been sitting (as he'd been on duty in her stead).

But she didn't take it. "Sfagnoff is our next scheduled port of call."

"That is correct," Rayria nodded. "I'm certain we'll reach it before they do, of course."

"How many did you spot?"

"We've confirmed the presence of 120 **space-time bubbles**. Their total mass is about 90 *zaisaboc*. If it's a fleet, that's equivalent to four *ïadbyrec* (sub-fleets)."

Lecsh gazed at the *ïac fadr* (map of planar space) projected on the floor. At its center, there was a blue blip indicating the **patrol ship**'s location. A number of **portals** coiled like dark spirals.

Portals within **3-space** had next to no mass, but they radiated energy. As such, they were always repelling against solar winds, which in turn tended to land them on the outskirts of star systems.

However, when a **portal** was placed beyond an event horizon, it would receive energy pressure in excess of the amount of energy it radiated. In such cases, energy would get funneled from **3-space** to **planar space**, the exact opposite of most other **portals**. Portals exhibiting this phenomenon were referred to as *cigamh* (volcano).

The energy erupting from a *cigamh* then became *spuflasath* (space-time particles — compressed shreds of fourth-dimensional space-time with about four times the mass of electrons). The *spuflasath* flowed through **planar space** from areas of greater particle-density to less dense areas, and popped back into **3-space** upon encountering another **portal**. Thusly did the energy that humanity once used for interstellar travel originate.

Space-time bubbles interacted with *spuflasath* **space-time particles** by absorbing them and radiating them back out, with the amount emitted greater than the amount taken in. That gap had to be compensated for by the energy poured into the **space-time bubble generator engine**. That was the toll they had to pay to cross **planar space**.

In addition to **space-time particles**, **space-time bubbles** also emitted *saiserazz* (mass-waves). Just like the electromagnetic waves in **3-space**, these "mass-waves" theoretically permeated all of space, penetrating space-time bubbles as well. Therefore, the presence of space-time bubbles could be detected even from extreme distances.

Around 60 degrees to the right of their current direction, an assemblage of **mass-waves** appeared and disappeared across three **portals** — Not even mass-waves could penetrate the **portals**.

Something out of the ordinary was upon them. The **commander** had no need to contemplate their situation to be sure of that.

If it had been an allied force moving a **fleet** that size, she would have been informed beforehand. If they had been thrust into flight just like that, it could only mean there was some emergency to deal with. If they *weren't* their allies… well, then the ramifications went without saying.

She wanted to ask the mysterious group of **space-time bubbles** about their situation, but the physical laws of **planar space** unfortunately forbade it: mass-waves couldn't be used for transmissions. The wavelength and frequency of mass-waves were both set in stone by the physics of **planar space**. If the mass of the **space-time bubble** could be changed, mass-waves could be viable as a means of communication, but gravity-control technology didn't alter the object's mass, and so it was of no help in this case.

The only effective method of establishing communications between **space-time bubbles** involved propelling **space-time particles**. This *droch flactaider* (inter-bubble communication), however, was almost unbearably slow, and useless unless the bubbles were very close.

"Do we know which **portal** they came through?" asked Lecsh.

"I'm having **Rearguard Starpilot** *Rechaicryac* do the calculations," answered Rayria.

At last, *Rechaicryac*, the fairly-green young **starpilot** and *rilbigac* (navigator), made his report. "I've narrowed it down to 47 portals, but that's all I can do."

"Are there any of those 47 currently being used?" said Lecsh.

He looked up at Ship Commander Lecsh and shook his head. "No, they're all **closed portals** no one's using at all."

"What about **portals** that have inhabited planets within a light-year of them?"

Rechaicryac ran a search of old documents pertaining to *byrec ragrér* (exploration fleets) using his **compucrystals**. "There are none."

"How about within five light-years?" Lecsh expanded the scope.

"There is one! Just one!" *Rechaicryac*'s cheeks flushed red with excitement. "Where?"

"It's the planet Bascotton IV of the Bascotton Star System, 4.1 light-years away from *Saudec Ceutesocnbina Cëïcr* (Portal 193 of Caysh). It belongs to… the United Humankind!"

Rayria came by her side and whispered, "I think we've crossed paths with a business rival of ours."

In the past, the Abh sailed their secret, giant ship, the Abliar (named, of course, after the surname of the **Imperial Household**), through eight different **closed portals**, wandering the universe as armed merchants. Though technically "merchants," relying on imports for food and quotidian items was not very wise when they didn't know when they would encounter any trade partners. After all, everything needed for everyday life was produced within the ship itself.

The one thing they considered of equal value, the main commodity they paid for, was *information*.

The history, technology, scientific papers, and artwork of each human society became items on the cosmic marketplace. These human societies, separated as they were by dozens and sometimes even hundreds of light-years of nothingness, craved information regarding their far-flung brethren, and the city-ship Abliar would provide that service as the only line they had, however fraught with uncertainty.

The Abh might not have put much stock in the idea of "mutual support," for trade with them was decidedly one-sided: they showed what they could supply buyers with, and gave it a price. Despite being merchants, they took a dislike to hairsplitting bargaining, quickly leaving star systems whenever negotiations broke down. And whenever they felt they had been taken for a ride, they would still leave — but only after exacting what, in their eyes, was a fitting revenge. Often enough, they would come to realize that it had been an unfortunate misunderstanding, but by that time they were already hundreds of years away from the ones they ought to have apologized to. Though the Abh did hold justice and fairness in esteem, they didn't respect those lofty ideals quite enough to go out of their way to retrace their steps in order to express their regret.

Among the **landworlds**, the Abh earned themselves a reputation for haughtiness and recklessness. It was after the founding of their **Empire** that the Abh expanded, but that prior mercantile era saw the birth of their initial incarnation out of some unknown star system.

Finally, the Abh, who had gathered up the essential kernels of all human science, established the *Clofairh Fadhotr* (Theory of Planar Space Navigation). They chose a star system in which to settle so they could conduct experiments to open the **portals**. When they succeeded after 50 years of experimentation, they decided to monopolize the technology.

Up to that point in time, every human world was separated from each other by vast stretches, so interstellar war simply could not occur. But *fazz fadhotr* (planar space navigation technology) had now made it possible. Of course, this didn't change how vast space was, but humans are ingenious at finding cause for war. If multiple different societies got their hands on the technology, it would inevitably lead to a large-scale war, and managing the technology monopolistically was the only way to prevent that.

Nonetheless, there was scientific theory, and then there was the technology itself. It wasn't a thing of scandal, so even if they laid down an airtight gag order, there was no doubt somebody would find out eventually. That was why the Abh then decided to uphold the monopoly by uniting all of humanity... by force.

According to statistics, when the **Founding Emperor**, *Dunaic*, decreed the founding of the **Empire**, the total population of the Abh numbered 272,904. As the estimations of Abh population scholars had it, though the margin of error was sizeable, the total human population of the cosmos was over 100 billion. A people of fewer than 300,000 was to conquer and rule over all of humanity, 100 billion strong. Haughty and reckless, they truly were.

Unfortunately for them, however, they were not, in fact, the first among humanity to step into the realm of **planar space**. One settler civilization, in the Sumei Star System, managed to stumble upon a way to utilize planar space by pure chance. The Sumeinians didn't monopolize the technology.

With great generosity (and a not-so-generous price tag), they shared it with twenty other systems.

Upon incorporating five star systems into the **Empire**, the Abh noticed there had been prior visitors to **planar space**. This caused them dread and discomfort. The policies of the Sumei Star System were needlessly complicating the political situation of the universe, or so reckoned the Abh.

They asserted that universal affairs were best at their simplest, and that the simplest state would involve a single, all-encompassing system of government. The race that carried the burdens of the universe on its shoulders could only be the Abh, as surface peoples did not love space as they did. Landers had only to pursue happiness on their own worlds, for the entire cosmos to get along in perfect bliss. Sadly for them, the other interstellar nations had their own thoughts on the matter, so the contentions of the **Empire** had no persuasive power.

The Abh also knew well enough to honor vested interests, so they refrained from meddling with the star systems that had bought Sumei's technology, but they had no intention whatsoever of mimicking Sumei's behavior. So, whenever they came across a **landworld** that had no knowledge of **planar space navigation technology**, they proceeded to conquer it with no reservation.

Human societies unfolded exactly as they had feared. Each interstellar nation seemed intent on finding points of conflict with each other, opening hostilities for reasons impartial parties couldn't comprehend. The **Empire** observed these epoch-forging wars with relish, and took to viewing the nations conducting them as children indulging in a bizarre pastime. But when they could no longer avoid it, they, too, became another participant in the strife.

In wartime, the Abh knew neither mercy, nor bounds. Once war was declared, any possibility of a compromise was lost. They would not lay down arms until they had robbed the enemy of their navigational capabilities, dismantled it, and subsumed their entire star system into the **Empire**.

This viciousness sparked equally severe counteraction. The **Empire** witnessed the remains of many of its most distinguished members, including two **emperors** and seven **crown prince(sse)s**, fly scattered across space.

However, it'd always been the **Humankind Empire of Abh** that sang the song of victory in the end. This **Empire**, ruled by an almost alien race that saw war as *total* rather than as an extension of diplomacy, was deemed an enigmatic threat by the other interstellar nations.

The nations continually united and divided, but overall, they tended to decrease in number. As of now, there were only four distinct, sovereign nations remaining, excluding the **Empire**. In order of power and influence, they were the United Humankind or "UH," the Hania Federation, the Greater Alkont Republic, and the People's Sovereign Stellar Union or "PSSU." The United Humankind, the largest of these, had a population of 600 billion. Taken together, all four had a population of 1.1 trillion. While each of these powers differed from each other in small ways, they had all been founded on constitutions that championed democracy.

12 years prior, the four nations convened at the United Humankind's star system of Nova Sicilia to forget their squabbles and sign a pact. They were now military allies. While which nation they'd formed an alliance *against* wasn't spelled out, it could only be the one nation they hadn't invited — the **Humankind Empire of Abh**.

The Nova Sicilia Accords styled its signatories the "Member-Nations of the Nova Sicilia Treaty Organization." However, since they preferred to self-identify as independent democracies, the **Empire** called them the *Brubhoth Gos Synr* (Four Nations Alliance or "FNA").

The point of the alliance was to make the **Empire** feel the heat and take a more conciliatory tack. And yet, the **Empire** reacted favorably to the Nova Sicilia Accords. That was because their enemies had all but declared themselves as such, and, as a consequence, universal affairs had turned very simple indeed.

Since that time, they looked upon each other with scorn, but while relations between the **Empire** and the Nations of the Treaty remained antagonistic, they were peaceful. However, over the past year, that low-key rivalry steadily grew into something more serious. According to the statements of the Treaty Organization, what caused tensions to ratchet up was the **Abh Empire**'s conquest of the Hyde Star System.

Lecsh saw through that flimsy pretext. The Conquest of Hyde had occurred seven years ago. The Treaty Organization issued its perfunctory tandem statements of protest at the time, but went completely silent about it afterward. And yet, it seemed they'd conveniently rediscovered that the Conquest of Hyde was an unforgivable act of belligerence a year or so ago. There weren't any recent developments of note on the **Countdom of Hyde**; any new developments of sufficient importance can only have happened within the FNA.

"So that's it," murmured Lecsh.

Rayria raised an eyebrow. "What is?"

Lecsh smiled wryly. "Oh, nothing. It's just that **the FNA** has really been keen on starting a war, judging by their actions. Am I wrong? All of their demands have been over-the-top; they want us not only to relinquish control over the **Countdom**, but to give them a corridor into **Empire** territory so they can 'guard' it. They must know the Empire would never make concessions like that."

"But what of it?"

"In other words, they've made their preparations, so all they need is an excuse."

"Ah, I see. They must have spent quite some time preparing."

They collected the **closed portals** drifting across **3-space**, and experimented with attempts to open them. Meanwhile, they had no way of knowing whether there were any **portals** in **planar space** placed at points that suited their purposes unless they tried opening them.

How many portals must they have looked into to find one under Abh control? In addition, to carry a portal that met their requirements through **3-space** to a point near a peopled planet — or, to put it differently, a point near a portal already in use...

In order to do such a thing, they would have to wait for the **portal** to close again. When an **open portal** was left to its own devices in a low-energy state, it naturally turned into a **closed portal**. However, this "half-life" of sorts was 12 years.

"It'd be a miracle if this plan of theirs didn't take at least a decade. Well, their miracle, our nightmare."

Rayria agreed. "They started this endeavor before the birth of the **Countdom of Hyde**, of that we can be certain."

"Yes, and that whole Hyde issue is a very recent one. In fact, the Nova Sicilia Accords might have been signed with this scheme in mind."

"What I don't understand," said Rayria, hands outstretched, "is why they would bother with such transparent lies."

"Oh, the only ones they're fooling are themselves."

"You mean this is an act of self-delusion…? I'm afraid I'm no closer to grasping their motivations."

"I'm not exactly an expert on their inner psyches, either. I just figure they'd like to believe that justice is on their side."

"What an honor — to them, we must be the embodiments of evil!" Rayria's moustache curled as he sneered.

Now Lecsh raised an eyebrow. "What, Rayria, you didn't know? We're born aggressors and mass murderers. You need to sit down and read a UH textbook one of these days. You'll learn all about how every calamity was perpetrated by the Abh…"

At that moment, she was interrupted by a *drociac* (communications officer) assigned to the investigation mission who had something to report. "There's been a shift in the fleet of enemy **space-time bubbles**!"

The young **linewing starpilot** had prematurely identified the **space-bubbles** as "enemies," yet no one intended to correct them.

Lecsh's eyes fixed on the unidentified **space-time bubbles**. "One **bubble** has split into ten. They've changed course and are heading toward us. Judging by their total mass, I think each bubble is a *gairh* (assault ship)."

The velocity of **space-time bubbles** was solely based on mass. There was no avenue of technological improvement on that front; it's simply how physics worked. As one might imagine, the lighter the mass, the faster it went. Because typical fleets were accompanied by massive vessels like **battle-line ships** and *isadh* (supply ships), they were even slower than **patrol ship**s. But it was a different story for fleets composed only of smaller vessels like **assault ships**.

It was now clear: the objective of the group of **space-time bubbles** was the capture of the Gothelauth.

"When will our guests enter the range of the *hocsath* (mines)?"

The **communications officer** soon worked it out.

"Around 21:15 by ship's time." They had about four hours.

"**Vice Commander**," said the **Ship commander**. Her voice turned far firmer than before. "Initiate *Ïocsdozbhoth Mata* (Stage 2 War Preparations). I plan to shift to *Ïocsdozbhoth Casna* (Stage 1) at 20:30 by ship's time. **Senior Gunner**, give me your tactical analysis. We need to know what our chances of victory are."

Even as Lecsh handed down her orders, concern for the non-personnel onboard — the **Noble Prince** and the **Royal Prrincess** — flashed through her mind.

Jint was grappling with the *riüérh cnassotr Cénrur Sazoïr* (Quartermaster Academy school rules). If what the **recruiting office** had told him regarding **starpilots** was to be believed, all students were expected to drill these rules into their brains before their first day. But it was impossible! Jint cursed using the dirtiest word in all of Delktunian.

When he'd been handed the *ghaich* (memchip) at the **office**, he'd had no inkling of just how much text it had been hiding. It had obviously never occurred to whoever compiled this list of rules that deleting outdated ones was a possibility. Instead, they resorted to smoothing it all over... by introducing even more, *supplementary* rules. The **imperial-calendar** date of each amendment was listed alongside all the dozens of screens' worth of rules.

And my first day at the academy starts at the beginning of next month... Some responsibility lay squarely on his shoulders, as he didn't even take a peek at its contents before boarding, but he felt it a curse nonetheless.

Jint set about committing the "Lunch Etiquette" section to memory. First, he looked at the end of the passage to see whether it hadn't been altogether repealed, and then he began to memorize all 122 articles. He skimmed over the obvious, and pored over the items he deemed different enough from his own everyday intuitions.

Just as Jint was getting absorbed in the task, the *dunitec* (alarm claxon) screeched. Distracted from his **wristgear**'s screen, Jint lifted his head.

What could this alarm be about? Thinking maybe the **list of rules** had the answer, he flipped to the Table of Contents screen. But there had been no need: the onboard announcement soon said it all.

"Attention. This is your **commander** speaking. All hands, continue working but listen well. At a distance of around 1,540 *cédlairh* due 78 degrees ahead of the ship, an unidentified group of **space-time bubbles** has been spotted in transit. We think that its destination is the same as ours — the **Marquessate of Sfagnoff**." The captain let that sink in for everybody listening.

"Now, listen up, boys and girls: At this rate, we know we'll reach Sfagnoff quicker than they will. The thing is, they don't seem to like that very much. So they sent ten **assault ship** bubbles our way. We don't know what hole they crawled out of, but we're fairly sure they're a UH **fleet**. It looks like we've got a fight on our hands, everyone!"

Is this some kind of training? thought Jint. No, that was tough to believe. It sounded too real.

"This is NOT a drill." Lecsh's voice genially confirmed it for him. "I repeat, this is NOT a drill. If they don't back down, we'll charge into battle at around 21:15 by ship's time. Prior to that, we're planning to shift to Stage 1 War Preparations at 20:30 by ship's time. Personnel not currently on duty should rest up for the fight to come. I'll say it one last time, so that it can really sink in, my dears. This is not a drill. This is not an exercise. This has been your **commander**. Over and out."

Jint stared at the ceiling, dumbfounded. He tried to sort the information he'd just heard in his head.

We're charging into battle!? He could scarcely believe it.

As far as Jint knew, the **Empire** was not in a state of war, and this sector was Abh territory. Wasn't this supposed to be the lap of safety?

Practically dizzy, Jint stared at the **crest banner**, but it offered him no salvation. So, he trained his sight back on his screen. He had no idea what he should do, what actions he was supposed to take. All he knew was that this was no time to sit tight and study. He turned off his **wristgear**.

What do I do...?

He hesitated to demand an explanation, to rush out onto the bridge or pounce on the com. Even if he was totally informed, how would it help any?

"Jint, are you in?" Lafier's voice called through the coms.

Jint jumped on it like a famished cat given fresh fish. "Of course! Come in, Lafier, come in!"

The door opened, but Lafier stayed outside the threshold. "What the heck is going on?"

"It's just as they said. I don't know any more than you do," she told him. "It seems we just happen to be witnessing the beginnings of a war."

"Just our luck," grumbled Jint. Life was truly a parade of happy accidents, and it was never very difficult to stumble over the next in line. "I'd just love it if it could be over by the time I'm assigned somewhere."

"I don't think there's much hope of that," she responded. "We aren't the types to let wars end without our utter satisfaction, and our enemies are most likely the United Humankind. I can't be sure the war will end within my lifetime..."

"Lafier, you are *really* bad at cheering people up," sighed Jint.

"Never mind that. I was ordered to escort you to the **bridge**. Will you be ready to come soon?"

"I shall be coming forthwith." Jint stood up and put on his **circlet**, that of the **noble prince** he was. "I wonder if they'll arrange special seating for me to watch the battle."

"I think you should try asking them," replied Lafier coldly.

When they arrived at the bridge, Jint could sense a strange mood in the air. It was so tense that it felt as though the air had turned to glass.

"I'm sorry to have troubled you to come here, *Lonh*," said Lecsh. "I bid both you and **trainee starpilot** Abliar wait here."

"Yes, Ship Commander," said Lafier. She was standing at attention, behind and to the side of Jint.

"Lonh-*Ïarlucer Dreur*. I'm afraid we have not prepared any seating for you." The **Hecto-Commander** gazed at Jint from her commander's seat.

"Please don't worry about that. I'm fine standing."

"I'm sure you grasped the onboard broadcast."

"I did. I'm to understand there'll be a battle."

The **commander** nodded. "The probability we win is 0.37%. That is assuming the enemy ships are leading-edge, but even if they were a crew of nothing but novices piloting decrepit ships, our chances still wouldn't reach the 50% mark."

"Well, that's not good." Even though death was imminent, Jint was bizarrely calm. None of it felt real. Perhaps he was mentally paralyzed with fear.

"No, it's not. Getting away would be ideal, but unfortunately we're not in any position to do so," she smiled. "That is why we must have you evacuate the ship, **Your Excellency.**"

"I see," Jint nodded. It was a reasonable proposal. *Ménh* (interstellar ships) were assemblies of advanced technology. The crew who could get one traveling through space, even the lowest-ranked *sach gona* (fourth-class NCCs), all had to undergo at least a year of technical training before being assigned. Even if some noble desire to be responsible or whatnot awakened within Jint, his complete lack of technical know-how meant that offering his aid would be an unwanted kindness. The greatest contribution he could make in the war effort would be to get out of the way and shiver in a corner of his room.

There was, however, a problem. How and where was he meant to disembark while the **patrol ship** was still sailing through **planar space**? He knew that the ship commander would continue, though, so he kept quiet.

"There is a *pairriac* (conveyance ship) aboard ship. It is furnished with *ménragh* (planar space navigation functionality). Please take it and reach Sfagnoff before us. You will have to resupply on the way, but you should get there faster than that fleet of **time-space bubbles** regardless. Then, when you arrive, please catch another ship for yourself. Sfagnoff has a **stronghold** for a *byrec drocr* (communications fleet). Flights should be frequent enough that you won't have to rely on luck," she said, casting a fleeting glimpse at what was behind Jint.

"I'm sure Trainee Starpilot Abliar will be willing to accompany you to the Marquessate of Sfagnoff."

"Ship Commander, you can't be serious!" Lafier shouted in protest. "I don't have a *buséspas* (skipper's insignia)!"

"You're in the process of becoming one," the **Hecto-Commander** pointed out. "Once you've finished this voyage, you'll earn the insignia automatically. It's nothing more than a formality. I know you can steer it, **Trainee**."

"But I want to stay on this ship..."

"I will not debate with a **trainee starpilot**. Am I not this ship's **commander**?" She pulled the captain card on her.

But she didn't give an inch. "I cannot accept that. Please forgive me my impudence, but I cannot shame the Abliar family name by fleeing from the enemy..."

The captain stood up and glared at Lafier with her golden eyes.

"You should save the braggadocio for after you've got an *almfac matbrar* (twin-winged circlet) on your head, *Ablïarsec Néïc Dubreuscr Bœrh Parhynr Lamhirh*. Fleeing from the enemy? There is no battle station for you here. You are utterly superfluous. You are unfinished goods. Yet I have given you a mission. A mission of grave importance, for you are not only to take the civilian *Lonh-Ïarlucer Dreur* away from the warzone, but also to warn the **Empire** of the approach of what is thought to be an enemy fleet. Would you not agree that shirking that mission would be the true act of desertion? If you do not feel any shame in your own incompetence, in not knowing what constitutes 'fleeing from the enemy,' then the Abliar family does not deserve the fealty of the Abh. If you still have something to say to me, then I will have you restrained for insubordination. You may talk back to me when you can do so with impartiality at a *luzœc fanigalacr* meeting, as an abdicant empress worthy of the name!"

Jint, who was still between the two, could only stand there, shaken. He'd suddenly fallen from the main character of his story to a mere onlooker, spying goings-on from the sidelines.

Lafier turned pale, biting her lower lip. But, being Lafier, she didn't hang her head in shame or break eye contact with the **commander**.

"I was mistaken, **Commander**," said the **princess**.

"I'm glad you understand," nodded Lecsh. "Now prepare the **conveyance ship** for takeoff. I have more to say to Lonh-*Ïarlucer Dreur*."

"Roger." Lafier saluted her. "I will prepare the *pairriac* at once."

"Once you're finished, simply send me your report. There's no need to come back here."

"...Understood." For a brief moment, Lafier and Lecsh's lines of sight intertwined.

"Now then, please be off." Lecsh's tone had suddenly turned much softer. "We'll see each other again at *Lacmhacarh*, oh *far fiac cfaina* (dearest Highness of mine)."

"Yes, Commander. Without fail." Lafier looked like she had more to say, too, yet she did another salute and turned back.

As soon as the **Ship Commander** saw Lafier's back disappear, she faced Jint once more and said: "Lonh-*Ïarlucer Dreur*, you won't have much time or space. Please take the minimum number of personal belongings necessary."

"I intend to," said Jint, "since I'm confident I'll be able to retrieve whatever I leave behind at the **capital**."

"I apologize that we couldn't see through our duty to send you off at the **capital**."

"Don't worry; from living in Vorlash, I'm used to transportation disruptions."

"Hearing you say that eases my stress. Incidentally..."

"What is it?"

"There's something else we'd like you to carry in addition to your personal effects."

"And that would be?"

Lecsh faced the space behind her commander's seat. "Arms storage, open. **Hecto-Commander** *Laicch Üémh Lobér Placïac*."

The wall opened up. Within lay a veritable arsenal of individual-use weapons.

Starpilots of the **Star Forces** had long abandoned the practice of carrying weapons with them aboard ship. All that remained of that custom was the now-decorative "**bandolier sash-belts**" that they wore. Those personal arms were stored onboard in case scenarios such as a hostile working environment or a crew mutiny were to transpire — although it should be mentioned, for the sake of the Star Forces' honor, that such a thing had not happened in the past 200 years.

Lecsh chose two *clanh* (lightguns), and gave them to Jint alongside *ïapérh* (lightgun cartridges) and a **waistsash.**

"One for you, Lonh, and one I must ask you hand to **Trainee Starpilot** Abliar. She should already know how to use them."

"Why are weapons necessary?" Jint had misgivings, but he took the guns.

"Think of them as a precaution." She glanced at the **map of planar space** on the floor. "My guess is that they're just the advance units of an enemy invasion fleet. Reason being, if that weren't the case, there wouldn't be much point to devoting manpower to stopping this ship. But in their heads, they can't clear the subconscious doubt that they're just being driven by an instinctual urge to kill."

"So, in other words... by the time we reach Sfagnoff, you'll have already fallen?"

"Though I'm hoping that doesn't come to pass," said the **Hecto-Commander**, nodding ever so slightly.

Jint thought he understood that Lecsh was truly driving at. "**Ship Commander**... The real reason you're doing this is to let **Her Highness** escape, isn't it? But isn't there somebody who's far more suited to escorting her than the likes of me?"

Jint shut his mouth, paralyzed by her piercing eyes of gold.

Even then, she remained polite in her speech toward him.

"Please do not misunderstand. We always aim to avoid combat when carrying civilians, and take measures to ensure their safety when combat is inevitable. That is a duty entrusted to all **Star Forces** commanders. It's also no lie that **Trainee Starpilot** Abliar has no predetermined battle position. Even if she had been no-name **gentry**, I would have entrusted her with commanding the **conveyance ship**."

Jint cast his eyes down. "I'm sorry I said that. It was dumb." He was not as strong as Lafier.

Her glare softened. "That being said, I would be lying if I said I wasn't happy that **Her Highness** happens to be a **trainee starpilot**."

"You are thinking about her wellbeing as well, **Commander**."

"I am." Her lips curled into a smile. "Her social standing may not technically matter within the military, but she could still someday be **Empress**.

And, just maybe, a wiser and greater one then we might expect. Thus, I aspire to one day be able to say that I was instrumental to her education during her years as a **trainee**. How could I let such a budding flower wither before its time?"

"You're right."

"Now, I think it would be best if you depart soon. I would be grateful if you could go back to your room to pack your belongings. I'm sorry I can't escort you, but I understand you know your way to the **take-off deck**, correct?"

"I'll be all right," said Jint. "Oh yeah, one thing — the **crest banner** of my house that you had made for me. I'm going to leave it there, in anticipation of the day I can receive it again in commemoration of joining the ship."

Her golden eyes flickered with intrigue. "That is thoughtfulness worthy of a **noble**, Lonh."

"Really? Then I'm glad!" He'd interpreted her words as praise, and bowed. "Please excuse me, **Commander**; I'll be taking my leave."

"Lonh-*Ïarlucer Dreur*. I leave *Fïac Lartnér* in your hands."

"I can't think of a situation so hopeless that **Her Highness** would need to rely on me…" Jint bowed deeply. "But I'll do what I can if the time ever comes."

Chapter 7: The *Slachoth Gothelautr* (Battle of the *Gothelautr*)

"The **conveyance ship** is splitting off from our space-time."

At the report of the *drociac raugrhothasairr* (exploration communications officer), **Hecto-Commander** Lecsh nodded silently. The great throng already gathered on the **bridge**, comprising all necessary personnel, was as on-edge as ever.

Not counting the campaign of little consequence that was the Conquest of Hyde, the last time the **Star Forces** had shown their superiority was during the Battle for Camintale, 47 years prior. The current Empress, *Lamagh*, had fought in that campaign as **Crown Princess** and **Imperial Fleet Commander-in-Chief**, a time that felt like a lifetime ago even to the long-lived Abh.

Of course, there was no one on the **patrol ship** *Gothelauth* who had any actual combat experience. It was little wonder they were all bundles of nerves.

It was **Vice Commander** Rayria who was the first among them to recapture his usual composure.

"So the young ones have left," he told his **commander** from behind her.

"I hope nothing happens to them." Lecsh rested her chin in her hands as she stared at the blue blip getting farther and farther away from them.

"I hope so, too." Then Rayria smiled. "They've both had very unique upbringings. In the future, they may just grow to be fascinating characters indeed. Though they're probably fascinating enough as it is."

"You're not wrong," Lecsh concurred.

The **royal princess** had been raised in a (royal household), seen as one of the springs of all that is Abh. And she had been admitted into an **academy** at the young age of 13. She was the model Abh. Meanwhile, *Ïarlucec Dreur* was an **imperial noble**, but an idiosyncratic one that couldn't help but drag his Lander-ness with him wherever he went. The two were almost polar opposites.

"I also hope they exert a positive influence on each other as well," Rayria continued.

"My my, Rayria." Surprised, Lecsh turned to look at him. "You're thinking like a regular *besaigac* (instructor). Are you planning to switch careers and head to an **academy**?"

"Don't be ridiculous," said Rayria with a wave of his hand. "I don't have the character necessary to be responsible for someone's education. I'm far more comfortable on the front lines. Especially now that a war is brewing."

"Come now, you don't need to hold yourself back. I won't think you a coward."

"I wouldn't blame you for calling me a coward if I should ever petition to be transferred to a behind-the-scenes post. But as of now, I have no desire to do so."

"Aww. That's too bad."

"Am I that terrible a **Vice Commander**?" Rayria smiled ironically.

"I'll keep you in suspense until your performance review." Lecsh returned the smile. Then she looked straight ahead once again. "What are your thoughts on Lonh-*Ïarlucer Dreur*, Mr. **Instructor**?"

"I think he's a fine young man. He's always silently questioning whether what he does measures up to Abh standards. I've grown rather fond of the look in those eyes of his."

"I like him, too." She grinned as she recalled her time with him. "I liked how often he smacks you with blunt, straightforward questions. I've never given the nature of our race as much thought as I have in the past five days."

"Lonh is a little too outspoken to be a well-behaved **imperial citizen**. He should dial it down a little, for his own sake."

"That *is* him dialing it down."

"I believe that the time she spends with **His Excellency** will do **Her Highness** some good, though."

"Agreed. Bringing those two together might be my greatest accomplishment. But only if they do manage to make it to the **capital**."

"You're quite worried about them, aren't you?" There was a hint of laughter in Rayria's voice.

"What, I can't worry about them?" She shot her first mate a defiant look.

"I'd say that our situation is the more worrying one. That's why you sent them off to begin with. I don't think we have time to spare worrying about them. Though it pains me to find fault with the feelings of my superior officer."

"You, feeling guilty for criticizing a superior? Now this is an amazing development." The **commander** stared at the steadily approaching band of yellow blips. "But it's just as you say. Now is the time to fulfill my responsibility to my crew."

It was 19:37.

"**Commander.**" It was **Senior Communications Officer and Rearguard Starpilot** *Ynséryac*. "The unidentified **space-time bubbles** have entered within range of our transmissions."

"Tell them the name of the ship, and ask who they are," Lecsh ordered.

"Roger." The *Gothelauth* proceeded to engage in **inter-bubble communication**.

"This is the **patrol ship** *Gothelauth*. Please communicate the name of your ship and your affiliation." After a frustratingly long interval, they finally received their reply.

The Senior Communications Officer scanned the transmission pattern that appeared on the inner surface of the **space-time bubble** using her *froch*. "This… this isn't a message. It's an *agac izomhotr* (signal of challenge)!"

"Then it's settled," Lecsh murmured. Her faint hopes that it was an allied fleet on the move due to some situation she wasn't aware of now lay dashed. But the newfound certainty actually cleared her head.

"The **signal of challenge** won't stop blaring. Will we respond?"

"No, ignore it. If they want to toy with us, then let them try their hardest to catch up."

While the signal continued ringing like a bloodthirsty war cry, the ten **bubbles** closed in ever nearer. The **bubbles** had been represented before as yellow blips, but were now red — confirmed enemies.

20:30.

"It is time, **Commander**," Rayria informed her calmly.

"Okay." Lecsh broadcast the following message to all crewmembers at all posts.

"Attention. This is your **Commander**. The unidentified **space-time bubbles** have made their hostility clear. We will be shifting to **Stage 1 War Preparations**. Now equip your **pressure helmets** and assume your battle positions!" Her announcement was accompanied by an **alarm claxon**.

Before the captain's seat, the *latonh* (tactical control counter) slowly rose. Its screen displayed a **map of planar space**, but only at a limited range of distance, so the enemy hadn't appeared on it yet. Lecsh inserted her circlet's **access-cables** into the **control counter**.

In spite of their captain's orders, not a single person on the bridge had put on their **pressure helmets**. The **space-time bubble generator engine** beneath the bridge was securely protected by the shared spherical walls. If the air-seal there were to be broken, it would spell the ship's doom. As such, it was pointless to wear a pressure helmet while on the bridge, so there was an unwritten rule not to.

"Battle stationing complete for all hands," reported **Vice Commander** Rayria, who was monitoring the devices that displayed the state of the crew's onboard deployment.

"Prepare for *hocsatiocss* (mine battle)." The **commander** wasted no time. "Load **mines** number 7 through 10 with *baich* (antimatter fuel)."

Satyth gor hoca (mobile space-time mines), or *hocsath* for short, were unmanned but equipped with their own **space-time bubble generator engines**. They were akin to miniature-scale **interstellar ships** in their own right. Their volume and mass were appreciable, and as such, not even a gigantic **patrol ship** could house very many. The *Gothelauth* could only hold 10, and numbers 1 through 6 had unfortunately already been used for practice exercises.

Their explosive impelling force derived from matter-antimatter annihilation. Since it was exceedingly dangerous to maintain the **antimatter fuel** if it was deployed on a continuous basis, they had made a habit of getting it supplied from a mother ship's *baicœcec* (fuel tank).

Supervisor and **Deca-Commander** *Gyrmryac* ordered the fuel transferred to the deck containing the antimatter tanks. The antiprotons flowed into the mine deck, conducted by magnetic pipes. They allocated the **antimatter fuel** into magnetically confined containers of the four **mines** on deck.

"Loading of **antimatter fuel** complete," conveyed **Senior Gunner** and **Vanguard Starpilot** *Sarrych*.

The commander heard him loud and clear. "Fire the **mines**. Keep them within the **bubble** until the time is right."

The four **mines** were pitched. They settled into the same pocket of space-time as the *Gothelauth*, and began to slowly rotate.

21:30.

"Enemy **bubbles** have entered **mine** range," reported the **exploration communications officer**.

Sarrych looked up inquiringly at the Commander, but she shook her head wordlessly.

The ten **bubbles** pressed in even further, steadily assuming a battle formation encircling the *Gothelauth*.

"A textbook attack formation," Lecsh remarked. "Generate the **bubbles** on the **mines**."

"Generating **bubbles** on **mines**," parroted the *tlaciac hocsathasairr* (mine gunner). After quickly working the controls, the mine gunner looked up and said, "Bubble generation confirmed!"

The enemy **bubbles** had already appeared on the **control counter**'s screen. They were accompanied by red numbers.

"Aim the **mines**. 7 on 3, 8 on 1, 9 on 6, 10 on 7," Lecsh commanded.

Ideally, they would land two mine blasts on each **space-time bubble**. In this situation, however, they had no such hopes.

"Inputting data." The **mine gunner**'s voice raised the tension of the bridge. "Targets aligned."

Lecsh switched her **circlet** to external-data mode. The data of the ship's sensors flooded into her brain's *rilbidoc* area. Her perception of the bridge disappeared as she focused her *frocragh*.

Lecsh now perceived herself at the center of a spherical space, the bubble itself. The inner surface of their **bubble** whimpered with blotches of gray, the product of all the **space-time particle** collisions. It was pregnant with the stillness preceding a battle.

"Prepare for *dadïocss* (3-space battle). Fire up the **main engine system**."

"Roger. Firing up **main engine system**," repeated *Gymryac*.

The telltale rumble of antimatter and matter's bitter quarrel rattled the ship. There were, however, many crewmembers who saw the vibrations as ominous.

"**Senior Gunner**, prepare the *irgymh* (electromagnetic cannons)."

"Roger. Preparing the **EM cannons**." **Vanguard** *Sarrych* equipped his **control gauntlet**. He was in charge of steering while within the **bubble**. He released the safety on the EM cannons and loaded their first volleys. "**EM cannon** preparations complete."

The red blips had the blue blip, the *Gothelauth*, completely encircled. They swooped in curved trajectories while closing the distance on their prey.

It really is right out of the drill manual, Lecsh thought with some admiration. It was clear to see that the enemy possessed a high level of proficiency. It was exceptionally difficult to maintain that clean formation while in **planar space**, where communication between units was tricky at best.

But her faith that her crew was not inferior when it came to skill was more than justified. While the *Gothelauth* may have been commissioned a mere three months prior, and one would be hard-pressed to claim that a sense of unity had formed in the crew, taken individually, they were all seasoned **soldiers**, each capable of satisfactorily carrying out their respective duties.

21:32.

Lecsh stood up from her chair and extracted the **command baton** from her **waistsash**. Then, the commander's seat sank into the floor. Using the **teletransceiver** on her **control counter**, she addressed her entire crew.

"My dears, it's show time. I'm sure you were tired of waiting — *Saporgac*! (commence battle!)" As soon as Lecsh puffed up her chest, the **alarm claxon** trilled through the air all across the ship.

She pointed the **command baton** at her **mine gunner**. "Detach all the **mines**."

"Detaching **mines**," said the gunner. "Number 7 undergoing *gor reutecoth* (space-time splitting). Number 8, likewise. Number 9..."

Each mine **exited** her field of *frocragh* perception, one after the other. Four new blue blips shot out of the blue blip that represented the *Gothelauth*. Each traced its own path of attack to a different red blip.

"Number 8 undergoing *gor ptarhoth* (space-time fusion)... Enemy **Bubble** Number 1, destroyed!" At the exploration communications officer's report, the bridge suddenly burst with emotion.

Though Lecsh had no way of knowing it, the ship hiding within **Bubble** 1 was the United Humankind Peacekeeping Force's destroyer, the KEO3799. Captain Cartzen and the 23 other crew would go down as the first casualties of this lengthy war.

Bombs 7 and 10 also hit their marks, consigning two more enemy **bubbles** into oblivion. The space-time bubbles smashed up against the **space-time particles**, causing the fabric of **planar space** to undulate.

Number 9, however, missed its mark. The enemy **bubble** continued closing in as though nothing had happened.

"Turn 40 degrees right! We're going to ram Enemy 4!" she commanded the *rilbigac flactlochothasairr* (bubble navigator) with her **command baton**.

The enemy, meanwhile, was fusing with their space-time from many different directions, seemingly determined to thrash the *Gothelauth* in a group attack. The basic blueprint of battle involved faithfully executing on a solid strategy, but the *Gothelauth* had no obligation to go along with that.

"Roger," said the **navigator**. Around the stationary blue dot, the **planar space map** rapidly zoomed as red blip no. 4 charged toward them.

"They're 100 *cédlairh* away... 50 away..."

"Initiating space-time fusion, at position..."

The **Ship Commander**'s *frocragh* detected that part of the inner surface of their **bubble** had already begun to froth due to bombardment by a large number of **space-time particles**.

"Direct the ship's bow into the point of fusion." Lecsh thrust her **command baton** at the ominously frothing portion of the bubble's inner barrier. That baton was pointing at what the devices on the bridge had detected, and after the **compucrystals** processed that information, it was beamed into *Sarrych's froch*.

Now, the **senior gunner**'s *frocragh* sensed the external environment, just as the commander's did. The command baton's motions overlapped with that sensation, in a way that could be understood by the **vanguard starpilot**.

"As soon as we fuse, fire at will."

"Roger." But *Sarrych's* voice had grown high-pitched.

"All hands, prepare for an **EM cannon** volley," **Vice Commander** Rayria advised.

The ship's bow was pushed into the froth. "**Space-time fusion** underway!"

But they didn't need to be told that. A giant tunnel opened its maw within the quiet sphere of space. At the other end of it lay an alternate universe, and at its center lay an enemy warship. Its aim to destroy the *Gothelauth* undisguised, it squared off against them.

The very second Lecsh realized there was a tunnel, the **EM cannons** were fired.

The *Gothelauth's* main weapons, it sported four **EM cannons** in the front and two in the back.

All at once, the four front cannons fired *spytec* (usion shells) accelerated all the way to 0.01 times the speed of light. Another volley followed soon after. The massive recoil overloaded the ship's **gravity control system**, and all the crew members that weren't holding themselves in place toppled over.

Lecsh clasped onto the **control counter** and endured the tremors.

The eight **fusion shells** jetted in unpredictable trajectories and dodged the enemy's defensive barrage to hurtle steadily onward. With the warheads' last attitude control, all the fuel they had left was fired through their backs, and they made their final bursts of acceleration flying toward their target from all directions.

The enemy also fired its *lunygh* (antiproton cannons). However, the flow of antiprotons was shot from almost point-blank range, ricocheting pointlessly into space off the magnetic field the *Gothelauth* had laid out.

The enemy ship exploded into smithereens, but they had no time to celebrate their victory.

"The enemy is fusing with this space-time — Ships 2, 5, 6…" The inner wall of the **space-time bubble** was already showing signs of entry from six different spots.

"Point the bow!" Lecsh thrust her **baton** at Enemy **Bubble** 2, having concluded it would be the first to arrive.

The ship's nose detached. An instant before space, merciless and full of enmity, opened its maw to usher in the enemy, a volley was launched at it. But they couldn't stop to check the results — they were already onto their next mark. Another enemy vessel was threatening to breach nearly right behind the **patrol ship**.

"Stern!" Lecsh thrust her **baton** over her shoulder. In order to slightly shift position, the *Gothelauth* prepared its attitude and fired two fusillades from its twin back-cannons.

Despite having just broken through, Enemy **Bubble** 6 immediately proceeded to escape, detaching from their space-time.

In that moment, the first fusillade burst into their space-time. The second detonated within the **patrol ship**'s bubble to no effect, but the enemy **bubble** was burned off as soon as it had fled.

To one of the ship's sides, Enemy **Bubble** 5 had completed fusion with their space-time. Neither the bow nor the stern could face it in time.

"Use the mobile cannons!" She thrust her **baton** to the side, so that they could mow it down.

The *Gothelauth* was equipped with mobile *bhoclanh* (laser cannons) as well as **antiproton cannons**, controlled centrally from the bridge. The cannoneers aimed cannons both big and small and unleashed torrents of *clanragh* (laser beams) and antiprotons at the enemy. These, however, were not furnished with the homing mechanisms of electromagnetically-propelled shells, and their accuracy rate was exceedingly low, to say nothing of their inferior firepower.

The enemy ship detached its four antimatter ballistic missiles and fired its **antiproton cannons**.

The missiles were not the problem. A missile that hadn't been accelerated beforehand lacked in speed, making it easy prey for the **patrol ship**'s rounds of defensive fire. However, the **antiproton cannons** equipped on the enemy ship's bow were more potent than the *Gothelauth*'s mobile counterparts, and as such were capable of obliterating a giant vessel like it in the blink of an eye with a clean hit.

The enemy's torrent of antiprotons formed a clump and then surged toward the *Gothelauth*. Though slowed by the *Gothelauth*'s *snœsaibec* (magnetic shield), the antiproton torrent pierced into its outer hull like it was *rÿabonn* (crystal pottery). It instantly penetrated and boiled the water stored within the barrier walls. Then it reached the inner hull, composed of heavy metals, and devastated it. Meanwhile, the boiling water blew away part of the outer hull and the attitude control nozzles.

The *Gothelauth*'s **compucrystals** didn't need to wait for the direction of a **supervisor**; they detected the damage and switched the ship to a mode where it could stay in control of its locomotion without that nozzle. Even so, the ship had lost most of its maneuverability.

The **space-time bubble**, agitated at multiple points, began to distort and curve in on itself. Within the writhing space, the battle was in a state of transition.

23:05.

"Enemy 10" was now a lump of plasma. Two ships remained.

The *Gothelauth* was also wounded. Around half of its mobile cannons had been rendered silent, while many attitude control nozzles were damaged as well.

"Major damage on **Laser** 3!"

"Front Attitude Control Nozzle 3, incapacitated."

"The **main engine system**'s power output, it's…"

Unpleasant news was pouring in from everywhere. There was nary a second to rest for *Gymryac*, who had organized an emergency repair team and sent them to places where the damage could be seen to.

"Section 907 undergoing depressurization. No remaining crew there. Locking down." Sweat glistened on the brow of *Dich*, the **clerk**, as well. There were more than 50 dead or missing. That was a significant portion of a **warship**'s crew of 220.

Lecsh kept her eyes closed and strained her *frocragh* to perceive what she could. Debris drifted all throughout their pocket of space. A vast number of broken-off fragments cluttered her senses. There were probably bodies amidst the cloud, though they were beyond saving. Any lifeboats sent to retrieve them would simply get shot down. Besides, their **uniforms** were too thin to protect them from the raging radioactive winds.

The two enemies flitted about, like a pair of butterflies, and spat their fell exhalations upon the *Gothelauth*. Try though they did to hit them with the **EM cannons**, the painfully sluggish **patrol ship** was a sorrowful sight now. The enemy dodged their attacks with utter ease.

Of course, the mobile cannons never ceased hurling fire at them. Their **laser beams** broke through the outer hull of the enemy and sublimated its splintered pieces. The ionized hydrogen of the warship's propelling flames piled upon the resultant effluvium, thus gradually increasing the particle density within its **space-time bubble**. Wandering protons and antiprotons collided, and transformed into electromagnetic waves. This microcosmos blazed like the beginnings of the *Doriaronn* (Big Bang).

This wasn't, however, a universe that held the spark of new life. It could give rise only to death and more death. Bare hatred clashed against bare hatred, and burst into ever greater, ever more unadulterated slaughter.

They tried to get part of the enemy ship to fall into firing range of their back **EM cannons** by directing it there through their mobile cannons' firing line.

"Stern!" Lecsh alerted the **Senior Gunner**. They fired three volleys, almost as though they were venting their anger.

The heavy recoil kicked the **patrol ship**'s massive bulk away. Behind them, a fireball.

Just one left! There was no doubt the **captain** was thinking what every member of her crew was.

But the last ship peppered them from the side with **antiproton cannon** fire. That would be a fatal blow.

"**EM shield**, down…" *Gymryac* gasped. Despair cascaded over the bridge.

"Don't give up now, my darlings!" she scolded them. "We're going to knock them out of our pocket of space. Bow!"

The *Gothelauth* slowly began to change the direction of its bow. The ship was almost sputtering now, as though indignant it still couldn't catch a break.

"Focus mobile cannon fire on the enemy's right side. Full throttle ahead!"

However, the enemy ship was also shooting fiercely forward, its **antiproton cannon** fire unrelenting.

A flood of antiprotons that vastly outstripped what they'd been bathed in before the destruction of the **EM shield** rocked the *Gothelauth*. The mobile cannon fire chipped at the enemy's outer hull, but they couldn't impede its path.

At last, the streak of antiprotons penetrated through the *Gothelauth*'s outer hull, and then through its inner hull like a hot knife through butter, striking the **antimatter fuel** aboard. Its magnetic cage demolished, the freed antiprotons attacked the very matter the **patrol ship** was composed of.

23:27.

The *Gothelauth* was now so much dust.

Jint and Lafier knew nothing of its demise.

Though it was true that **mass-waves** permeated all of space, the **conveyance ship**'s feeble equipment couldn't pick them up while the signals of the **portal** were interfering. That might have been a kindness to them. Though they weren't totally bereft of hope, the mood in that **steerer's room** was already very dark.

Jint was sitting uncomfortably in his assistant steerer's seat.

Unlike the **smallcraft** they'd ridden together before, a conveyance ship that sailed through **planar space** couldn't be piloted through just a **control gauntlet**. That was why there were the controls that Jint pictured when he thought 'spaceship' in front of the chairs. That being said, there was not much need in this sector, where **portals** were few and far between, to work the controls very frequently.

A sullen Lafier didn't speak a solitary word as she glowered at the screen displaying the **map of planar space**. Jint stole a glance at the seat next to him and sighed surreptitiously.

Their **space-time bubble** was, as all others, a universe unto itself. And its sole occupant, save for a modicum of floating particles, was the conveyance ship. Behind the seats of the steerer's room lay a *ïadberh* (airlock room), as well as a washroom and nap room. That was the entire living space entrusted to what, in their universe, amounted to all of humanity.

We're the only ones in the universe...

And half of the universe's intelligent life had sunk into a profound melancholy. The other half was not exactly feeling chipper, either, but he did feel like this universe could do with at least a little cheer.

"Uhh... Lafier..." Jint tried to start a conversation.

Lafier raised her head. There was no way he could guess what she was thinking about from her expression.

"You're the **Viscountess of *Parhynh***, right?"

"That's right."

"I wanted to ask you about your **star-fief**. What's the *Bœrscorh Parhynr* (Viscountdom of *Parhynh*) like? Given that '*Parhynh*' means 'Land of the Roses,' I assume there are a lot of roses?"

"No." While hardly enthusiastic, Lafier didn't rebuff his efforts. "There aren't even any lichens, let alone roses. There aren't so much as microbes on any planet out there."

"Then why's it called the Land of the Roses?"

"The man in charge of surveying it had a soft spot for flowers, and basically just felt like going around naming them after various kinds. '*Gyrhynh*' (Land of the Lilies), '*Spaichynh*' (Land of the Camellia), all sorts. That's all there is to it."

"Huh. All right then, what's it like?"

"There isn't much to say. It's a system with a yellow star and seven planets. The second planet could be made human-habitable with some work. I think I'd like to fiddle around with that planet once I'm free of my duties as an **Imperial**. I want to make the whole surface of *Parhynh* bloom with its namesake roses."

"That sounds wonderful."

"I like to think so."

And with that, the curtain of silence was drawn once again. Jint racked his mind anew. How could he beat this acrid silence? But it was Lafier who broke it.

"Jint."

"Yeah?"

"You have my gratitude."

"For what?"

"You're thinking of me, aren't you? I can't say the way you're doing so is terribly sophisticated, but it's heartening nonetheless."

"Well, I'm sorry I'm so awkward." Jint was simultaneously miffed and relieved.

"Don't be angry," Lafier smiled. "I'm trying to thank you."

"Me? Angry?"

"I..." Lafier stared at the screen again. "I hate it, Jint. When the all-important time came, I was totally useless."

"Way to hurt a guy's feelings," murmured Jint.

"Huh?" She cast a doubtful glance his way.

"You're not 'useless' — you're saving me. If you weren't here, I'd be lost. But I guess my life in your hands isn't enough to satisfy your lofty sense of obligation."

"...You're right. Forgive me."

"Besides, I'm sure the ship'll come out okay," Jint asserted groundlessly.

"...Yes... Yes, I'm sure, too," she mumbled, but more to convince herself than anything else.

"Hey, Jint."

"Yeah?"

"Do you remember my birth secret story?"

"'Course." Jint was mystified as to why that, of all things, had been brought up again.

"Don't tell anybody what I'm about to tell you..."

"Nice, I love secrets," he said as cheerily as possible so as to improve her mood.

"My **gene donor** is the **Ship Commander**."

"What?" Jint thought he might have misheard her.

"But that would make **Hecto-Commander** Lecsh… your mother?"

"No, she's not my 'mother.' She's my **gene donor**."

"Sorry, I'm still thinking like a Lander, forget I said that," he said. "But… but she didn't really *feel* like she was related to you."

Or did she? The **commander** *had* called her, her "dear Highness." He had felt something there that transcended the surface-level superior-subordinate relationship.

"What do you think the **Star Forces** are? It doesn't matter that she's an old acquaintance. It only matters when we're alone together."

"Yeesh, sounds so complicated. Like… Wow, though…"

"I felt proud to know *Cya Placïac* (Dame Plakia)… I've known the **commander** since I was little, so I've always respected her. I'm proud that half of me comes from her. I was a **daughter of love**. She was my father's *ïomh* (lover). I always suspected it… wanted it to be true…"

"If you've known her for so long, couldn't you have just asked?" Jint was almost dumbfounded, despite himself, at just how thoroughly blood and family were separate in Abh custom.

"I already told you. I wasn't an adult yet, so without my father's permission, I—"

"No, I mean, why didn't you ask her? You know, directly?" Lafier opened her eyes wide and stared fixedly at Jint, who suddenly felt uneasy. "Did I say something stupid?"

She nodded vigorously. "Incredibly."

"Oh? All right, I'll bite — is asking her directly really that unthinkable?"

"There's such a thing as *manners*."

"Uh huh… So it's rude to ask a **gene donor** if they're your gene donor?"

"It's extremely embarrassing, Jint."

"I see." Jint crossed his arms and chewed it over… *Nope. Don't get it.*

"Why's it embarrassing?"

"It needs a reason to be embarrassing? Things that are embarrassing just *are*."

Well, now that she mentions it, I guess that's true… Jint forced himself to go with it. After all, asking someone "Are you my mom?" would take quite some courage even according to his own non-Abh sensibilities.

"Even if I had asked, she wouldn't have answered me. The only one who can tell a child about their *dairlach* (DEHRLAHSH, genetic components) is their parent."

"And that's good manners, too?"

"Yes, that's good manners."

"Sounds complicated."

"I don't think it is."

"I'd love it if I could take you to my home planet one day and have you live there for a handful of years. Then the meaning of the word 'complicated' might come to light."

"Okay. Once my responsibilities as an **Imperial** are behind me, I wouldn't mind letting you take me there," Lafier said, her voice a bit livelier now.

"It'll be my pleasure." But Jint remembered a bitter truth.

You've forgotten, Lafier. When that time comes, you'll have aged only ten years. You'll still look young and beautiful. I, on the other hand, will be either stupidly old or already dead...

"But couldn't you have asked her if she was your father's... I mean, *Fïac Lartr Clybr*'s **lover**? Is that rude, too?"

"Of course it is."

"If you say so."

"I do. Is this 'complicated' to you as well?"

"Very," Jint assured her. "Who told you that the **Hecto-Commander** is *Fïac Lartr Clybr*'s lover, then?"

"No one had to tell me. It was obvious. The **commander** was always visiting at the *lartbéic* (royal palace)."

"Sounds complicated."

"I'm tired of hearing you say that, Jint. It's annoying."

He shrugged. "Don't worry about it."

Lafier looked at him like she wanted to say something, but she returned to eyeing the screen. "My genetics aside, I love **Dame Plakia**. She was already worthy of respect even at the **palace**, but I gained even more for her aboard ship. The other **starpilots** and **NCCs** did, too. There were some I didn't like very much, but I hope they're all okay..." Lafier hung her head as though in prayer.

"Yeah." Jint recalled all the people with whom he'd conversed on the **patrol ship**. It had only been five days, but in that time, he'd met nothing but good-natured folks. His preconception of the Abh as cruel invaders was completely turned on its head. At the very least, he had no reason to wish them dead.

Lafier remained motionless for a little while. The sensation that she was drowning at the bottom of the ocean, that Jint been trying to dispel, came roaring back. This time around, there was just nothing Jint could say. He stared at the steering controls vacantly.

Finally, Lafier raised her head. "Jint. Could you tell me about your home?"

"Ah, sure, no problem." Jint was relieved. "Where should I start? Unlike your **fief**, there's plenty to talk about..."

Jint suddenly realized he'd been unconsciously fidgeting with the imitation jewel on his chest. The creature engraved on it was that furriest of fish, the *rezwan*. He decided to lead with all the details about the rezwan's absolutely wretched diet.

Over the next two days, apart from their alternating sleeping shifts, Jint spent nearly the entire time filling her in on the lifeforms of *Martinh*, though much of it was only vaguely recalled and much of it was outright fabrication on his part. And, to his surprise, he'd succeeded in making Lafier laugh quite a few times.

After their two days on the conveyance ship, the pair arrived at the *Lymscorh Faibdacr* (Febdash Barony).

Chapter 8: The *Lymscorh Faibdacr* (Febdash Barony)

The **Febdash Barony** comprised a blue star and two gas planets, along with countless rock fragments. Even the **Empire**'s very best terraforming technology couldn't make an inhabitable planet out of them, and they didn't have the resources to lug that technology through **planar space** just for a collection of rocks. It was even emptier than the **Viscountdom of *Parhynh***. But the *lymeghéc* (baronic house) made sure it wrung revenue from this *scorh* (domain).

There was an enterprise one needed only a star to conduct, involving a stable commodity that was always in demand. They manufactured **antimatter fuel**.

It was considered theoretically impossible to turn matter inside out into antimatter. If one wanted antimatter, they had to rely on an antique method from the dawn of engineering, of civilization. A sun's radiation was stored in solar batteries, and the energy was then pumped into a linear particle accelerator to speed up elementary particles. When accelerated elementary particles smashed into each other, the energy their collision emitted condensed, with pair production as its result — matter, and antimatter.

Like other resourceless planets, many *iodh* (antimatter fuel factories) were in operation in the **barony**. Myriad disks orbited close to the star Febdash. Those were the **antimatter fuel factories**. Their disks, facing the sun, were loaded with solar batteries, and behind them, sixteen linear particle accelerators were radially aligned. The batteries drank in the heat and light emitted by the star, which was subsequently channeled by the accelerators and reborn as protons and antiprotons within the centers of the disks.

Only the antiprotons among them were collected. The protons were allowed to leak away into space. After all, it was far more economically viable to transport protons from gas planets than to install separate proton capture traps.

The antiprotons, so amassed, were harvested into containers connected to the **antimatter fuel factories**. Once a container became full, it turned into an independent planetoid orbiting farther from the sun than the cluster of factories so that in the unlikely case an incident occurred, the factories wouldn't get destroyed.

The *Lymécth Faibdacr* (Baron of Febdash's Manor) revolved even farther from its sun than the *sombec baicœcer* (antimatter storage planetoids). There was also the **Febdash Portal**, married as it was to the baron's manor and its orbital revolutions.

The **conveyance ship** entered **3-space** through this **portal**.

"Show me video of the outside, if you could," asked Jint.

"Sure." She made a complex grasping motion with the **control gauntlet**, and the walls of the **steerer's room** filled with the stars innumerable.

"I never imagined the stars could be such a sight for sore eyes," Jint said sincerely. The inner wall of the **space-time bubble** was a gloomy grey. Compared to that, the twinkling stars had a congenial familiarity to them. He now understood, if only a little, why the Abh called themselves the **Kin of the Stars** and the cosmos their home.

"We still have a long way to go, Jint," said Lafier ruthlessly.

"We're going straight back into **planar space** after resupplying."

"Can we take a break while resupplying?" asked Jint hopefully.

"A break? You're not doing anything to begin with."

"Thanks for reminding me. But I'll have you know I'm overseeing all the controls while you're sleeping," he quipped.

"You woke me up whenever anything happened."

"I haven't woken you up. Nothing ever happened."

"Yes, thanks to me and my **compucrystals**."

"Fine, fine." Jint dropped it. While it was true that Jint wasn't doing — *couldn't do* — much of anything, the conveyance ship's operations were being taken care of by its autopilot. He had never actually seen Lafier steering it.

Compared to that, Jint brooded inwardly, *I was the real workhorse, what with all that* talking.

Lafier called up **Space Traffic Control**.

"This is the **patrol ship** *Gothelauth*'s **conveyance ship**. Febdash Barony Space Traffic Control, please respond." Her screen switched from displaying the map of the star system to video of a Lander woman.

"This is Febdash Barony Space Traffic Control."

"This is the **patrol ship** *Gothelauth*'s **conveyance ship**. Requesting fuel resupply."

"The **patrol ship** *Gothelauth*'s **conveyance ship**?" The **Space Traffic controller** appeared puzzled. It must have seemed strange for a giant ship's smaller vessel to be requesting fuel by itself. Even so, the officer nodded.

"Roger that, *Gothelauth* **conveyance ship**. You are welcome within. Please choose your method of resupply."

"This is a *ménh sona* (lightweight interstellar ship), so I'd like to resupply at the **pier**."

"Roger. Please transmit desired amount of fuel."

"Roger." After finishing the transmission protocol, she told Jint: "If we resupply at the **pier**, we can take a break. We can likely even take a hot bath."

"Awesome!" said Jint. "A nice bath isn't a bad idea, especially considering you're probably the smelliest **royal princess** in the galaxy at the moment."

"What's that I see…?" Lafier's squinted her big, beautiful eyes at him. "Oh, it's someone who clearly yearns for death. I'd be more than happy to oblige."

"C'mon, I was just kidding." Jint was shaken by the light in the princess's raven-black eyes. "You don't smell that much, I swear."

"'That much'?" Lafier's eyes narrowed even more.

"No, I mean, you don't smell at all!" he back-pedaled immediately. And indeed, that was the closest he'd arrived to the actual truth of the matter. "What impudent rube would ever so much as imply that you smelled even a little!?"

"You must have noticed by now, Jint, that sometimes your 'jokes' irritate more than they amuse."

"Yeah, but then I forget soon after. It's an issue."

Lafier brought a sleeve to her nose and took a whiff. Her face contorted. "I suppose your remarks have a kernel of truth."

To that, Jint knew to be cautious and keep his mouth shut.

"On the other hand, I can't say *you're* particularly pristine, either."

"Guess not, huh. But I bet if you searched the **Empire**, you could turn up a couple or more **noble princes of countdoms** stinkier than me right now. There are way more of us out there than **royal princesses**."

Lafier opened her mouth to retort, but the **Space Traffic controller** on screen cut in.

"**Pier** resupply approved, Gothelauth **conveyance ship**. All clear. Please make your way to the pier immedi—"

The officer paused halfway. She, too, now squinted, questioningly. Suddenly, she opened her eyes wide, and murmured: "*Fïac Lartnér* (Royal Princess)..."

It seemed the identity of the steerer before her had her in shock. Deeply, she bowed her head.

Guess they know of Lafier even all the way out here, thought Jint. *I must look like a big goof by comparison.*

"Are we still cleared to enter the pier?" pressed Lafier.

"Yes, of course, by all means. You may proceed. Yes."

Guided by the information entered by the clearly nervous **controller**, the vessel drew nearer to the **Baron's estate**.

"**Febdash Space Traffic Control Center**, there's something I must apprise you of..." During their approach, Lafier summarized the intrusion of what was all too likely an enemy fleet into **Empire** territory.

"That's..." But the officer was at a loss for words. It took her a brief spell to pull herself back together: "I must relay this to *far simh* (my lord)."

"Of course; please do so."

The scenery tinged by the star Febdash's blue flames, the **Baron's estate**'s details came into sharp relief.

Many older **orbital manors** were shaped like rings in order to simulate gravity through constant rotation. That style of architecture, however, couldn't get around how the levels of "gravity" and rotational speed varied by stratum. Due to that, the more recent **orbital estates** — which is to say, those of the past 300 years — were, as a rule, equipped with their own **gravity control systems**. They came with equipment installation and maintenance costs, but they were generally worth it for the higher quality of life.

This **manor** was the type that had a **gravity control system**. It was shaped like an inclined hexagon. Its long arm propped up a cubical structure, which was the **spaceport**. Because it stored the **antimatter fuel** for *paunh* (intrasystem ships), the spaceport was usually installed at a comfortable distance from the estate's main structure. In addition to the prow portion of a giant *casobiac bendér* (hydrogen carrier), a number of small intra-system spaceships were docked at the pier like a bunch of gnats.

The artificial gravity enveloping the estate took action. The spherical steerer's room rotated; the ceiling of the steerer's room, which faced its bow, now turned away from the estate. Jint saw a red "17" sign beneath his feet. Pier 17 was reserved for **conveyance ships** like theirs.

They docked. The footage of the outside cut out, reverting the walls around them to their typical milky white color. The green glyphs rolling across the screen communicated to the *loc* (ship's switchgate) that the connected tube had been attached.

"Let's go, Jint." Lafier removed her equipment and stood up.

"Right." Jint stood up with her. "How long will we be able to stay for?"

"For about thirty minutes."

"That's it?" he frowned. Washing up would be all he could do in that time. Of course, he was grateful nonetheless.

"We need to get to Sfagnoff as quickly as possible."

"I know." Jint followed her into the **air lock room**. "But how much earlier can we get there than the enemy fleet?"

"What, you don't know?" she said in a disdainful tone. "We'll get there around 27 hours before them, by Sfagnoff time."

"In that case, we've got enough time to kick back..." But Jint took note of her furrowed brow. "...is what I *would* say if I didn't agree that we need to warn Sfagnoff of the danger with all haste."

"I thank you for not forgetting that," she replied sharply.

They stood atop the **air lock room**. It was blocked off by the *férétcaucec* (elevator ramp). "Descend," she commanded of it.

Dropping down through the translucent connection tube, the two stepped foot into the **Baron's estate**. It was the first gravity he'd experienced in two days, so he felt dizzy as he scanned around.

The skies were starry. With Febdash's shining blue sun nowhere in sight, it was clear this wasn't footage of the outside. There was another giveaway — the countless fish swimming among those stars.

Ten-odd Landers were standing in a row in front of the connecting tube's entryway. They were the *gosucec* (servant vassals) of the *lymh* (baron). They made a strange impression on him. Then it dawned on him why — they were all women.

The women bowed their heads. "*Fïac Lartnér...*" One of their number walked forward toward them, as reverentially as ever. It was the **Space Traffic controller** from before. She kept her gaze away from the face of the **Empress**'s granddaughter, as though looking directly at it would invite destiny's wrath upon her. "If you would be so kind as to enter our humble abode, I would be delighted to guide you to the restroom."

"We would like that very much. However..." Lafier's tone turned stiff. "I'm just a **trainee starpilot** of the **Star Forces** at present, and I ask that you treat me as such."

"Yes, Ma'am. We will accommodate your request. Now kindly come this way, *Fïac Lartnér...*" Lafier sighed and let it pass.

"Is it always like this for you?" Jint whispered.

"Come off it!" she hissed in reply.

They were escorted to a room within the spaceport's facilities. It contained several tables, and the surroundings here were the same array of twinkling stars and wandering fish. There was nobody else there.

Lafier was led to the seat at the very back. Jint assumed he ought to sit next to her at her table, but the **traffic controller** gestured for him not to.

"Please, Sir, if you could seat yourself over there instead..."

"Huh?" Jint blinked, confused. "How come?"

She chewed over her words, reluctant to answer why. Her diffident eyes drifted away from Jint's own. He was quite used to this reaction from people. The combination of his brown hair and his **noble's circlet** was throwing her for loops. And it was more than evident that she believed a boy of clearly Lander genetics should not be sitting at the same table as a relative of the exalted **Empress**.

"Jint!" shouted Lafier, as though something in her snapped. "What are you doing? Just sit down already."

"I intend to." Jint was just as ticked off, and he ignored the controller.

The officer furrowed her brow, but made no attempt to defy the **royal princess**. "What would you like to drink?"

"Never mind drinks," said Lafier. "I want to make use of your *chicrh guzaser* (shower room). Could you take us there?"

"A member of the **Imperial Family**, asking for the **shower room**!" The **officer**'s eyes opened wide. "We have a *gobh* (bathing room), which would be far more becoming. If I could but request you wait a short while—"

"We have no time, *gosucec*-rann (Ms. Vassal). Besides, I can assure you that **Imperials** use regular old **shower rooms** all the time."

"Is that so...?" The officer was befuddled. "I'm afraid I don't have the authority to answer. What would you like to drink?"

Lafier caved in the face of her tenacity, and glanced at Jint.

"Give me **coffee** or some such. Make it cold," said Jint. He wasn't actually thirsty; he just thought he ought to ask for something.

"Fetch me some *tirec naumr* (peach juice). Make it hot, and add a slice of *ropec* (lemon)."

"I see you have *unique* tastes, Lafier," he quipped casually, but then he noticed the officer giving him a hell of a glare. He gave a slight shrug.

"Yes, Ma'am. I will bring Your Highness some **peach juice**. Please wait a moment." The vassal wiped the look from her face, bowed deeply, drew away.

"And could you not forget my **coffee** while you're at it..." mumbled Jint. He couldn't help but feel she hadn't listened to a word he'd said from the start.

"I don't think I'll ever take to this whole atmosphere," said Lafier.

"Right there with you." Compared to the members of the **Imperial Family**, **nobles** were perhaps not that much of a rarity after all. That said, he now found being ignored rather fun. After all, it wasn't as though he wanted to go around affecting the supercilious aristocrat. What he did want — and it was a modest desire — was for his presence to be acknowledged.

At last, the **Space Traffic controller** came back with another lady and an **automaton** in tow. The **automaton** came to a halt by Jint's side.

"Here you are." The vassal gazed at Jint with icy eyes.

"Thanks." As Jint inwardly murmured his gratitude that they hadn't overlooked him, he retrieved the container of chilled coffee from the **automaton**'s abdomen.

The other lady lowered the cup of peach juice she'd been holding reverently. It was obvious she was extremely nervous. Her fingers were trembling, the peach juice sloshing.

Then, it spilled over the brim. Not a large amount, mind. A single drop of juice touched the table.

And yet, the two flew into such a panic, one would think they'd just splashed the **royal princess**'s head with boiling water.

"Sehrnye, wha-what have you done!?" The controller's face turned pale.

"M-my apologies!" Her tone was so apologetic, in fact, that one wouldn't be surprised if she'd started rubbing the floor with her forehead.

Jint was horrified. What was there to get so upset about? So an infinitesimally tiny amount of peach juice had been spilled — so what?

Lafier was also stupefied. "What's the matter?"

"I've spilled the drink I was to offer you, *Fïac Lartnér*. Wha-what ought I to do now... I beg your forgiveness..."

"My forgiveness? For this?" Lafier looked blankly at the mere drops on the table. "There's nothing to forgive." When she wiped it with her finger, Sehrnye gasped.

"Augh! Please, this is beneath you! I, I'll wipe it clean, so please, you needn't deign to—"

"Worry not." Lafier lowered her hand, as though to hide the wet finger that Sehrnye was nigh threatening to cling to. "I don't know how you picture a **royal palace** upbringing, but I can dry my own finger."

"I'm certain you can, but..." Sehrnye was near to bursting into tears.

Lafier looked at Jint with pleading eyes: *save me.*

"Uhhh..." Jint interjected. "I think if you don't drop it, then it'd *become* something to apologize over."

"Y-Yes." Sehrnye bowed while biting her lip.

"See, even *Fïac Lartnér* says so, Sehrnye," said the **controller**. "Let's excuse ourselves for a moment."

"Yes." Her shoulders shuddered slightly as she bowed deeply once again.

155

Lafier waited until they'd vacated. "I'm liking this less and less."

"That blew my mind. Are all **imperial citizens** like that? It was like they were afraid of something. And I thought the **NCCs** on the *Gothelauth* seemed a lot *tougher...*" Jint may have been a **noble**, but he was a Lander genetically, and he was not amused at how servile his fellow Landers appeared to be.

"They're not like them. All the **NCCs** on the Gothelauth are of sound character."

"I'll take your word for it." He didn't. It had been Lafier who'd told him that within the military, one's family ties didn't matter. There was a high probability that the **Star Forces** were an exception, and that outside of it, Landers *were* this obsequious.

"You don't believe me, do you?" Lafier looked surprised. "I speak only truth. You'll see once we reach the **capital**. I don't tell lies that'd be exposed so quickly."

"Uh huh."

"I've even been scolded by an **imperial citizen** when I was a child." Lafier got serious.

"Did they not know you were a **royal princess**?"

"No, they weren't like *you*! That **citizen** was working at my home. Trust me, they knew."

"Your home, as in the *Clybh* Monarchy?"

"Yes. It was a gardener who worked for the **royal family**. I'd made the *ïazriac* (personal transporter) rush around the dining hall with abandon, and ended up ruining a shrubbery patch."

"Your stories are difficult to follow sometimes, you know that? A shrubbery patch in the dining hall? Don't you mean right outside the dining hall?"

"No, it was a dining garden."

"Ohhh." Jint remembered now: Abh dwellings were usually within artificial environments. For example, the resident could summon rain when and where desired. Since there was no distinction between indoors and outdoors, a flower bed and a sleeping bed could lie side-by side. A shrubbery patch in a dining space was nothing to question.

Lafier resumed telling her story:

The gardener surveyed the disaster zone with grieving eyes, but maintained his courteous demeanor as he spoke his mind to the petrified **princess**. He told her that he took immense pride in his work. That the artistry of the whole garden hinged on the patch that now lay in disarray. That he felt a great deal of shock and dismay over how it had been mangled by the prank of a seven-year-old girl. That humanity had not yet invented a way to quell the level of resentment seething within him.

By the time he was done berating her, Lafier was beside herself, apologizing profusely while her lips trembled. She pledged never to perpetrate such a fatuous deed again — though of course, through the vocabulary of a seven-year-old.

The gardener did not hold any stock in Lafier's vow. Naturally his perfect courteousness never faltered, yet he intimated: "If your Highness's **personal transporter** should ever damage my creations again, I shall make sure you spend some quality time building an intimate relationship with my soil-enriching earthworms!" And only once he'd impressed this on her did he let her go.

"Needless to say, afterward, my father scolded me as well. He said, 'If you think your life is valueless enough to trade for a moment's play, then have at it. But don't you ever think so lowly of another person's pride.'"

"I get you, but maybe that gardener was just a special case," said Jint, still doubtful.

"He wasn't! The **servants** of both *Clybh* and of the other nobles I know all take pride in their work. They're all that dignified and high-minded."

"All right, I believe you." She'd convinced him. "Those two seem *really* prideful when it comes to me."

"They're ignoring you."

"Thanks for telling me, but I think I noticed."

"In any case, I don't like this place. I think it may be best to forgo the bath and leave…"

Just then, the wall by their table shifted. A square "window" opened in the video of stars and fish, showing the image of a man.

He was Abh. His hair was blue, but a faint blue with a golden gloss. His eyes were almond-shaped, and his mouth stuck in a slight sneer.

"Please forgive the interruption," came his salutations. "If I'm not mistaken, you must be *Fïac Lamhirr* of the *Lartïéc Clybr.*"

"I am indeed *Ablïarsec Néïc Dubreuscr Bœrh Parhynr Lamhirh*," said Lafier.

"My name is *Atausryac Ssynec Atausr Lymh Faibdacr Clüarh* (Clowar, Baron of Febdash). It's a pleasure to make your acquaintance."

"Likewise, **Baron**." Lafier nodded, then pointed at Jint. "This is *Linn Ssynec Raucr Ïarlucec Dreur Haïder Ghintec*-Lonh."

"Nice to meet you, Lonh-*Lymr* (Your Excellency the Baron)," said Jint, bowing lightly.

"My humblest greetings to you as well, Lonh-*Ïarlucer Dreur.*" But the Baron's interest in Jint evaporated once he'd gone through the obligatory courtesies. "Now then, *Fïac Lartnér*, there's something I truly regret to inform you."

"What?" she asked warily.

"I'm afraid that due to some distressing ineptitude on our end, it has come to light that we currently lack the fuel you require."

"But that can't be! Your **Space Traffic controller** clearly said..."

"That's where the aforementioned distressing ineptitude comes in. It was her oversight. And I can only offer my sincerest apologies."

"I understand. In that case, we'll just resupply directly at an **antimatter fuel storage planetoid**."

"Oh, bless your heart," the **Baron of Febdash** chuckled. Jint didn't know why, but he shuddered.

"**Your Highness**, in your graciousness you've only just come to my doorstep," the Baron continued. "It would shame the name of the *Lymeghéc Faibdacr* (Febdash Baron's household) to see you off in such a state. By hook or by crook, I simply *must* show you around my **orbital manor**, squalid though it may be."

"Though I appreciate the generous invitation," Lafier scowled, "I have been pressed to a military mission, and have no time for leisure. Have you not heard our circumstances? If not, kindly have your **servants** relay to you what I told them. I am not here on a courtesy call, **Baron**."

"I have heard, *Fïac*. We would be eternally grateful if you would suffer our cordial welcome nonetheless."

"I thank you for the offer. However…" It was plain to see that Lafier was feeling nothing close to gratitude; she was beginning to get very annoyed indeed. "…If you know of our situation, then you should understand that your warm reception is the last thing we need. I believe you should be working out how to get us off your **domain** instead."

"We're sorry to have troubled you, but we don't have any *ménh* **vessels** you could use. There's just nothing to be done."

"I see. But—"

The Baron cut in. "Please listen, Your Highness. The closest full **fuel planetoids** are in an orbit quite far from here. The only bodies that are orbiting in the vicinity are small, barren asteroidss."

"But how is that possible…?"

"Do you doubt my words, *Fïac*?" said the Baron, throwing her a hard look. "I'm the one who knows the most about my own territory."

"Forgive me," she pled sincerely. "We must however leave for that planetoid, however far it may be."

"There's no need to go out of your way. I am accelerating the planetoids. In about twelve hours, they'll be much closer."

"Twelve hours…"

"So I hope you understand now, *Fïac*, why I would like it if you could make yourself at home in this manor of mine. I ask you at least take this time to bathe and partake of the modest meal we can provide you. I too have served in the military, and as such I know what it's like inside a **conveyance ship**. It pains me to think that a member of the **Imperial Family** has had to spend a significant amount of time inside one of those dreadfully cramped things."

"I'm not 'an **Imperial**' at the moment," Lafier reminded him. "I am requesting you provide me with fuel as a **Star Forces soldier**."

"Then as the **lord** of this territory, I request more details of the **Star Forces**. I do have that right."

"Ah." He'd hit her in a blind spot. "You are correct, **Baron**. It had slipped my notice. There's a *Gothelauth* navigation logbook aboard ship, so I'll send you a copy of the sections you need."

"That would be lovely, but I shall examine it at the dinner table," the Baron replied, though begrudgingly.

Jint, who had been listening from the side, felt ill at ease all the while. Was this how the upper classes of the **Empire** spoke to each other? It was like the universe's most refined bickering match. Lafier's tone of speech turned far more formal and ceremonious than when she conversed with Jint.

She argued her case relentlessly. "I still think that if we headed out in our *pairriac* now, we would get there faster. As soon as I hand you the copy of the logbook, we would like to make for the nearest **fuel planetoid**."

"You would get there faster if you left now, yes," said the **Baron**. "However, I've received reports that Your Highness's **conveyance ship** needs a bit of *inspection*. So, no matter what, you wouldn't be able to leave immediately."

"Inspection? What part?"

"I haven't heard the particulars. Please ask the one in charge of that. Though that engineer is busy working on it, so you shall have to ask after you take some relaxation." The Baron did not let her get a word in edgewise about it. "Now I will be having my **servants** be your guides, so I humbly bid you wait here."

The video cut out. Lafier didn't take her eyes off that space on the wall. "He ignored you, too."

Indeed, the only reason he'd even spared him any words of greeting was because Lafier introduced him. After that, he might as well have not been there. "Oh well. Can't be helped. I'm just a **noble** next to an **Imperial**. It's only natural he'd fuss over you more."

"If he really wanted to give us a 'cordial welcome,' he would have included you. Am I wrong? Or is this 'complicated' to you, too?"

"Oh, it ain't complicated." Jint turned the conversation with the Baron over in his mind. He'd been having a listen with the mindset of an outside observer, so it hadn't bothered him, but it was true that the **Baron** had acted fairly rudely toward him. Sadly, however, Jint was used to being snubbed, so he couldn't really muster any anger over it. "I'm just happy you got pissed on my behalf."

"I'm not *angry on your behalf*."

"Oh." Jint took a sip of his coffee.

"I'm saying that that attitude means he can't be trusted. They're inspecting the **conveyance ship**? It sounds like a big ruse. I'm sorry to say it, but it's difficult to believe that such a small **domain** even has the technology. I think he may be trying to stall us."

"Why, though? I wouldn't get too paranoid if I were you, Lafier."

"But he's so unbearable."

"Well, I'm with you there…" Jint folded his arms.

He couldn't argue with that. In fact, the Baron was the type who didn't even need to open his mouth for one to instinctually dislike him. That aversion to his character wasn't nearly strong enough to be characterized as "hate," per se, but it did fill him with misgivings regarding the prospect of getting to know the man. If the first Abh he ever met had been the Baron of Febdash instead of Lafier or Lecsh, he probably wouldn't have ever warmed up to the Abh as a whole. But there was always the possibility that the Baron was some pitiful sap who was just too awkward at making good first impressions.

"Let's think about it logically. Let's suppose that **His Excellency the Baron** has some ulterior motive. What could that motive be? What's in it for him to draw us into his estate?"

Lafier could only cock her head. She looked just as clueless as him.

Jint took a stab at it. "Maybe he wants the **vessel**?"

"But why?" The **princess** looked up.

"Why, you ask? Isn't it obvious? To flee the enemy fleet."

"That **vessel** only seats two people."

"Yeah, which would be more than enough for him to escape by his lonesome."

"And abandon his **servants**?"

"So you don't trust the **Baron** overall, but you do trust in his sense of justice?"

"Don't be such an *onh* (blockhead)! It has nothing to do with his own ethics. To abandon his **servants** and the **citizens of his territory** would be the greatest shame he could ever incur as a **noble**. He would be judged for that under **imperial law**, to say nothing of hijacking a ship. He'd be better off in a UH prison camp than face the destiny that would await him in the **Empire**."

"I see what you're saying. His **noble rank** saddles him with *selœmecoth* (obligations)."

"Yes. Exactly," she nodded.

But Jint wasn't ready to shelve his conjecture just yet. "Though you know, when people come to their wit's end, they don't exactly act all that rationally. Back when I was in Vorlash, there was this high-rise that'd caught fire, and I saw a bunch of folks jump from the 35th floor. Sure, they must've thought that dying that way was preferable to burning alive, but it made me think, man, that's the one way I never want to go. Maybe our **Baron** here's about to jump out the 35th floor, mentally?"

"Did he look like he was at his wit's end to you?"

"I mean, no, not really..." Then he grinned. "But that just proves he can't be plotting something, then."

"I suppose not," she admitted reluctantly.

"I say we accept his warm welcome. I shall join in partaking of dinner."

Jint glanced to the side, and spotted the Baron's **servants** walking their way.

Chapter 9: The *Bar Ébhoth* (Smile of the Abh)

The bath did hit the spot. Upon steeping herself in the hot brimming water, Lafier could feel her fatigue roll away as surely as all her sweat. The wariness in her heart, however, proved harder to wash away.

Part of the reason lay in her attendant.

She couldn't fathom why, but that "Sehrnye" woman had entered the **bathing room** with her, offering to wait on her by washing her hair, scrubbing her back, and all manner of other things. That must have been her mistaken picture of the **Imperial Family** lifestyle.

In truth, apart from her early infancy, Lafier had never had others cleanse her. She was quite satisfied bathing the way she was used to, in water infused with *satyrh* (liquid soap), after which she'd simply get dry using a *bimuciac* (body dryer).

And yet, Sehrnye refused to believe her no matter how many times she insisted.

"I implore you, please don't be so hesitant."

'Hesitant?' Did she honestly *believe an **Imperial** would ever be so inhibited?*

Lafier eventually grew weary of raising objection and decided to just make Sehrnye happy. Hence, Sehrnye was still on standby next to her tub, with a fluffy white *gusath* (bathrobe) at the ready.

"I trust you've been made aware of the enemy fleet heading toward the **Sfagnoff Marquessate**?" asked Lafier.

"Yes."

"And you aren't frightened?"

"No, I'm not. I'm certain **my lord** will do something."

"The **Baron**? What will he do?"

"That, I do not know."

"Hmm… The **Baron** must have some trust placed in him."

"But of course! He's a trustworthy man!" replied Sehrnye emphatically. "I would not be here today had it not been for him!"

"What do you mean?"

"It was my dream, as a child, to become naturalized as an **imperial citizen**. But I didn't like the idea of entering military service, and I lacked the skills to be a good **servant**."

"If it had been your childhood dream," said Lafier, "Then surely you could have spent your formative years receiving an education."

"On my home planet, the *Dreuhynh Frizar* (Countdom of *Frizac*), women have little status. They don't have access to the higher education that would allow them to become **servants**. Women aren't expected to become anything besides good wives or mothers. Before I learned of life on other worlds, I had believed that was the case for all **landworlds**."

"Is that true?"

"Yes. My lord picked me up from that world and provided an education for me."

"An education?" How much of an education was needed to learn how to scrub people's backs?

"Yes. I'm in charge of checking and maintaining the **antimatter fuel tanks**. That's what I'm studying."

"Ahh. So you aren't a **bathing room** specialist."

"Correct. This is my first time working **bathing room** duties, since **my lord** has never tasked me with it."

"So the other **servants** do wash the **Baron**'s back and such?"

"Yes."

Lafier concluded that the dear **Baron** had a screw loose. It wasn't exactly rare for the **lord** of a territory to order their **servants** to take care of their everyday necessities, but that usually only went as far as *batiac* (waitstaff) fixing their meals. Having them minister to him even in the **bathing room** was a step too far.

"I can tell you," Sehrnye continued, "he is a kind and gracious lord."

"'Kind' doesn't mean 'competent,'" said Lafier uncharitably.

"What can I do," she replied dreamily, "except have faith in **my lord**?"

"How many people live in this **star-fief**?" asked Lafier, changing the subject.

"Only fifty. Though I haven't ever counted the exact number. If you're interested—"

"No, that's fine," Lafier cut in. "How many are Abh?"

"Two are Abh: **my lord** and his father. His younger sister has been living in *Lacmhacarh* for a long time."

"Uh huh... Life here sounds a tad, well, lonely."

"It's undeniable that there isn't much by way of thrills. Yet we live exceedingly comfortably, so I can't say I'm particularly sorry for that fact."

"'Thrills'... so I'm providing some much-needed *stimulation* to this manoe, am I?"

"Heavens, no!" She was shocked, as though literally bolt-stricken. "Attending to *Fïac Lartnér* is the highest honor. I do not think so lowly of you."

I'd feel safer if you did value me more as a fresh thrill.

Further, she had tired of her hot bath. *I'll become a prune if I stay any longer.* She stood up out of her tub.

"You're so beautiful..." Sehrnye sighed, spellbound by her perfectly symmetrical frame and smooth skin.

Lafier ignored her jejune praises. Her near-perfect figure was the fruit of genetic engineering and the aesthetic discernment of her ancestors, not of any effort on her part. Complimenting her beauty did little to ingratiate her.

Sehrnye dressed the **royal princess** with the **bathrobe**, which absorbed the water droplets on her skin.

When she exited the **bathing room**, she encountered a lady **servant** older than Sehrnye waiting with a heap of bathrobes and *duhyc* (bath cloth) piled high in her arms.

Lafier was fed up. "Is there no body dryer anywhere in the estate?"

"Our lord is of the opinion that that machine is *uncivilized*," responded the older **servant**, who wrapped Lafier's wet bluish-black hair with the **cloth**. Meanwhile, Sehrnye replaced her sodden **bathrobe** with a new one.

If she *had* to be waited on by others like this... she might as well enjoy it. There was no denying it felt good.

I wonder whether Jint is receiving the same generous pampering I am, Lafier found herself thinking. *By lady **servants**.*

Because if so, then... She didn't know why, but the idea was very disagreeable.

When all the moisture was wiped from her body and hair, Lafier would be subjected to yet another ordeal.

She saw the change of dress they'd arranged for her, and scowled: "What happened to my **uniform**?" She thought it imprudent to criticize the choice of underwear, but she could take issue with what she was to wear over them.

Dyed a vivid yellow and studded everywhere with jewels such as *duc* (rubies) *latécrirh* (diamonds) and *désœmec* (cat's-eyes), it was a gaudy *daüch* long robe. The **jumpsuit** to be worn underneath it was a tasteful light green in color, and clearly high-value. It wouldn't be inappropriate garb for strolling through a palace, let alone here.

"We are running it through the laundry," replied the **servant**.

"Not by *hand*, I hope," she quipped. They had had more than enough time to wash her uniform while she was in the bath.

"Our lord said wearing the **uniform** to the dinner table would be 'uncouth.'"

"'Uncouth'...?" She was not bothered by somebody viewing her **uniform** that way. Everyone had their own values, after all. But the man had some nerve, to push his personal opinions on others.

Lafier had absolutely no desire to dress up like some doll. This was not a playdate with the **Baron**. "I will only wear my **uniform**," she declared. "I will wait here until it's finished drying."

The older **servant** scrunched her face, on the verge of tears. "But, *Fïac Lartnér*, please..." entreated Sehrnye. Once again, she seemed ready to rub her head against the floor.

Lafier's pity for them only grew, and she cursed the stupidity of the whole situation.

"Fine," Lafier gave in. "Then I will wear the *daüch* over my uniform. That should be acceptable."

The two servants locked eyes.

"But the orders of *far lonh*, they..."

"We can't disobey **Her Highness the Royal Princess**, either..."

Their whispering made it to her ears, however much she didn't wish to hear. *So much commotion over nothing.*

The thought didn't cross Lafier's mind that perhaps she was being too stubborn about her **uniform**. Instead, she gazed at the **Baron**'s maids, her eyes thoroughly unamused.

Was this some kind of dream? Here she was discussing which dress to wear to dinner while the *Gothelauth* was battling with the enemy far, far away.

She dwelled on the *Gothelauth*. On how the battle was probably over by now, on whether they prevailed. She hoped the ship and everyone on it were alive and well.

"We will comply with your request, *Fïac*." Finally, a conclusion. "I will bring the **uniform** shortly," said the older one.

The laundry *had* been ready, and so the uniform was fetched for her.

"Now quickly, before Your Highness catches cold," she said, somewhat nonsensically, as she took her underwear.

Naturally, the maids wouldn't allow Lafier to touch the clothes; they dressed her while she stood as still as a tree. Despite herself, Lafier ended up admiring them aloud. "You're very skilled."

"We are simply accustomed to this," said the older servant.

"Accustomed to it? So you dress him every day?"

"Yes, that's correct. Just as you must have servitors at your palace, **Your Highness**."

"We do have *bëïcaiberiac* (chamberlains), but they don't wait on us to *this* extent."

"My, how droll!" She simply would not believe her.

When she'd finished putting on her clothes — or more accurately, getting her clothes put on for her — Sehrnye dutifully held a *doréth* (tray) and inched closer. "Accessories for Your Highness."

A bright red crepe wrapper was spread out on top of the **tray**, and the whole array dazzled as the precious metals and jewels on display vied to shine brightest.

"*Fïac Lartnér*, please, choose whichever ones catch your eye," said the older **servant**.

Lafier squinted. Yet again, what she needed most was missing. "What happened to my **circlet** and my **wristgear**?"

"We were told they're 'uncou—'"

"They are no such thing. I need them dearly." She knew they were just acting on orders, yet she couldn't quite quell her rage.

Did these people think her **circlet** and **wristgear** were just trinkets, just fashion statements to her? Her computer contained her *daimhath* (electromagnetic wave crest), and the circlet was useless unless it was attuned to whoever equipped it.

The centerpiece tiara was exquisite, yes, but it was no replacement for her military-issue circlet.

"We understand, *Fïac*. As you desire." The older one sighed her resignation and nodded to Sehrnye. She scampered away, and came back with her **circlet** and **wristgear**.

As soon as she put the **circlet** back on, her sense of *frocragh* returned, much to her relief. Running about without one of her six senses made her feel all but helpless.

She was guided from the **bathing room** area directly over to the *bisïamh* (banquet hall).

The floor was a pale ultramarine. Across the walls and ceiling, a multitude of stars twinkled against the dark blue backdrop. Here, too, holographic fish were swimming in three dimensions. Lafier's eyes lingered on a giant scarlet one with yellow speckles cruising leisurely.

He has awful taste, she thought.

She headed toward a table in the center of the spacious chamber. As her *daüch* fluttered, her black **Star Forces uniform** could be seen intermittently peeking out from under the sleeves.

The **Baron of Febdash** was already encamped at the table, which was comically small given the sheer size of the room. Beside him were female **servants** with demeaningly skimpy attire. No food had yet been laid out, and there were only two *lamtych* (opulent cups) carved out of *braiscirh* (amethyst) on the table. A single chair stood vacant.

The **Baron** stood up and greeted the **royal princess** with his head drooped down. Lafier stayed on her feet right by the table and looked square at him.

"Where is Jint?"

"Jint?" The Baron raised his head. "Ah, you must mean Lonh-*Ïarlucer Dreur Haïder*. My father is currently hosting him."

"Why isn't your father eating with us?"

"He's not much of a people person, I'm afraid."

"If he's not a 'people person,' then why is he playing host to a guest?"

"Because misery loves company, I imagine," he said enigmatically.

"And what exactly does that mean?" she grumbled.

"Please, don't let it worry you."

"How could I not? My mission is to escort Jin... *Ïarlucec Dreur Haïder* to Sfagnoff."

The Baron raised an eyebrow at her.

"My, *Fïac*, don't tell me you sincerely believe I could wish *harm* upon Lonh-*Ïarlucec Dreur*?"

"Frankly, I do sincerely believe you could," she asserted.

"That is regrettable," he said, though his face betrayed no such regret. "In any case, please take a seat. I would like to clear up this misunderstanding as we dine."

"I hope it is a misunderstanding, **Baron**."

A **waitstaff** had already pulled Lafier's chair out for her, and she took it. Seeing her seated, the Baron did likewise.

"Would you care for some spirits?" he asked.

"I'm on duty. Give me something without *sciadéc* (alcohol)."

"As you wish. May I interest you in some *teurh lachbanr* (orange juice)?"

When Lafier nodded, the Baron snapped his fingers. A waitstaff whispered instructions into a mouth-equipped **transceiver**.

The Baron spoke as he awaited his drink. "So, *Fïac Lartnér*, I see you call that boy by name. May I ask you also to call me simply 'Clowar'?"

"No, you may not," she said curtly.

"May I ask why?"

"Because I don't want to, **Baron**."

The Baron had no retort. He narrowed his eyes at her.

A **servant**, who was, of course, female, came with a tray containing a *rosgiac* (decanter) and some jars. The waitstaff picked up the jar of orange juice and took caution and care as she poured its contents into Lafier's **cup**. Then, *rinméc* (apple cider) was poured into the Baron's **cup**.

Lafier was thirsty from her hot bath, and so she drained her orange juice immediately. At once, the cup was refilled.

A foreboding silence had befallen the table, but then the appetizers arrived. Pale petals were scattered across the black canvas that was the tray, along with various artistically arranged items of Abh cuisine. Placing importance in aesthetic presentation was part and parcel of Abh dining.

"By all means, please partake."

"Sure." Silver **chopsticks** in hand, Lafier brought something that looked like a leaf to her lips. The flavor of shellfish burst in her mouth. "This is good."

"I am honored, *Fïac*."

"I'm not complimenting you," she said, with no love lost. "I'm complimenting the chef. I've gathered you're not one to use machines. You use people."

"How perceptive of you, *Fïac*. I don't like machines very much, no. That aside, you seem rather angry, Your Highness."

"How perceptive of you, **Baron**. I am angry."

"Does my invitation displease you that much?"

"Did you think it would 'please' me?" She sent an icy glare at the Baron as her chopsticks tore a piece off of a side of *rïopoth* (smoked thigh) patterned after a rabbit-ear iris.

"Why wouldn't it?"

"You still haven't cleared up that misunderstanding, if there even is one to clear up."

"This is about that Lander boy, I take it."

"Jint is an Abh **noble**."

"Ah, yes, too right."

"It's not just about him. Did our **ship** really need inspection? Is there really a fuel shortage? My doubts have only multiplied, Baron."

"Inspection? Oh, I was lying about that," he admitted breezily. "There is more than enough fuel, and the **conveyance ship** is not undergoing inspection of any sort."

Lafier was hardly surprised. She knew her "warm welcome" was far from genuine from how she'd been pulled away from Jint.

Regardless, she didn't put down her chopsticks. She ate up the rest of the appetizers and pushed her tray to the side.

"Why did you lie?"

"Because you would not have come to dinner otherwise, *Fïac Lartnér.*"

"Of course not. We must make haste."

"That only confirms that it was right to lie."

"Is that so? Well, let me tell you, I don't like being deceived."

"I imagine not."

"Now that your little lies have been exposed, I can and will take my leave of this place."

"About that, *Fïac.*" The **Baron** drank the last of his apple cider. "Could I have you postpone your departure for just a little while longer?"

"If I say no, would you still be willing to send me off with no hard feelings?"

The **waitstaff** brought a small porcelain bowl. It was *autonn fïmhaimer* (sea turtle soup).

Lafier removed the lid and savored its sweet fragrance.

"I'm afraid I wouldn't," the Baron replied. "I must ensure you stay here, even if by force."

"Until?"

"Until an **Empire** ship arrives. Or, in other words, until the safety of my **domain** is secured."

"But there's no knowing when that will be." She tilted the bowl and slurped up all of the rich, hot broth.

"Indeed not."

"So you intend to keep us here until then."

"Yes."

Lafier scowled — but confusion preceded ire. What in the heavens was the **Baron** scheming?

"I'm not plotting treason or a rebellion, if that's what you're thinking," said the Baron.

"No. Your deeds are not so upstanding as a rebellion," she sniped.

"It is truly a shame." The Baron hung his head, but his lips curled mockingly. "My family line is a short one, and so 'upstanding deeds' may ill suit me."

Lafier paid the Baron no heed as she tucked into her broth.

With a glance, Lafier noted that the Baron had barely touched his food, as his dish of appetizers hadn't been taken away. Lafier briefly suspected he may have poisoned her.

No, don't be foolish, she thought. He would have poisoned the appetizers if he wanted to poison her at all. And he would have needed to somehow poison only her portions. There was no need to poison her; this was the Baron's manor.

The broth was followed by *dérslumh bausr* (trout dumplings). The trout were genetically engineered to be tiny so that they fit inside the rice dumplings.

"Well, are you going to tell me?" she needled him while she peeled away the fried-brown dough concealing the fish within.

"About?"

"About why you're keeping us. Is it a grudge?"

"Don't be absurd, *Fïac Lartnér*; so long as I have you here, I intend to treat you with nothing but the utmost hospitality. Why would I seek to cause you harm…?"

"That's precious. I'm not so sure you fully grasp the consequences of your actions."

"I assure you I do. All I want is to protect this **domain**."

"How does keeping us here protect your **domain**?"

"The **Sfagnoff Marquessate** is a large territory-nation. The United Humankind must know its location. My **barony**, on the other hand, is young and of miniscule size. There's an extremely large possibility they're not aware it exists. A regular ferry stops by only twice a month. And I would like for them to remain ignorant of the **Febdash Barony**. But what if they were to observe a ship emerging from the **Febdash Portal**? Presumably, they would glean that there's been a **fief** their information network failed to catch wind of. They might even destroy this microscopic **domain** in a fit of pique."

"But we passed through the **Febdash Portal** to get here. How do you know they haven't already spotted us?"

"They may have. But one chance is already one too many. I cannot afford to give the enemy a second."

"That seems rational enough."

"I'm glad you agree." The **Baron** nodded animatedly. "That is why, *Fïac Lartnér*, reluctant though I am, I must insist you prolong your sojourn at this manor until I can be sure the enemy has been swept from our vicinity. If the enemy fleet is repelled, then you won't be kept waiting for too terribly long. And if it isn't repelled… I suppose you will have to wait until the **Empire** recovers this land."

"Can we survive here for that long?"

"My **star-fief** possesses a *glaicec* (hydroponic plantation) and a *basébh* (cultivation ranch). There will be no shortage of food. However, resources are limited, so our chefs may not be resourceful enough at times to prevent some level of dissatisfaction."

"And what if the Empire never recovers it?"

"We'll cross that bridge when we come to it. The lord of this little **domain** has enough to deal with already."

"I think it'd behoove you to spare your future some thought." Lafier was intent on the task of plucking the dough and the fish even as she spoke.

"Whatever might you mean?"

"You're obstructing the passage of a **conveyance ship** that's on a military mission. The **fief** you worked to protect might be ousted from the **Empire**."

"I think not. I did everything out of a passion for my **domain**. My actions will be condoned by the *Scass Lazassotr* (Supreme Imperial Court). At the very worst, they will levy a fine."

"Even if the **Sfagnoff Marquessate** comes under attack before they could be forewarned thanks to that passion of yours? Is the **Supreme Imperial Court** that magnanimous?"

"I'm sure that's of no concern. The greater Sfagnoff area is highly trafficked. Someone will alert them to the enemy's approach, and it need not be you, *Fïac*.

As such, what fault, pray tell, can anyone find in my deeds? They will believe the testimony of those who will attest that I graciously accommodated you. It shall be sworn on the name of Abliar."

"Do NOT speak that name," snapped Lafier. "You'd NEVER understand my family's codes of honor."

"Yes, quite." The Baron bowed with superficial politeness. "Do forgive me, *Fïac*."

Lafier ignored him.

A **waitstaff** quickly whisked away the half-eaten dumplings she'd put aside for disposal.

"Enough about me. What's become of Jint?"

"*Ïarlucec Dreur Haïder* is with my fathe—"

"Best not talk nonsense, **Baron**. I believe I told you I don't enjoy being deceived."

"I understand." The Baron shrugged. "Due to our young friend's lacking the qualification to receive the hospitality owed to a *real* **noble**, he has been dealt with in a way befitting a Lander like himself."

"How many times must I repeat myself? Jint is a **noble**," said Lafier. "You also seem to be laboring under a unique view of what being an **imperial citizen** entails. I've never seen **imperial citizens** as abject and servile as your **servants**. It's as painful to witness as a cat forced to do acrobatics." Half the reason she said that was so the ladies in waiting could overhear.

"Not even **Her Majesty the Empress** herself can meddle in the affairs of a **lord** and his **servants**. Let alone you, *Fïac Lartnér*."

"That is true, but it does spark my interest in what you think is a 'fitting' way to deal with a Lander."

"Please, it is nothing to fret over, *Fïac Lartnér*," he stonewalled her.

The next course was boiled pumpkin stuffed with meat and vegetables. Lafier's eyes were glued on her pumpkin and its cinnabar *scalych* (serving table), but she continued addressing him.

"Listen to me, **Baron**. You have a **domain** to protect, and I have a *scoïcoth* (mission) to carry out. That mission is to take Jint to Sfagnoff safely. If anything happens to him, then you can forget all about the **Supreme Court**, because you'll have me to answer to."

"I'm afraid I can't comprehend your fixation on that Lander." The Baron shook his head with exasperation. "Why do you obsess over him so?"

Lafier shot him a hateful stare. "If you've served in the military, then you must know that the **mission** is sacred. But that's not all — this is also my first mission. If it were to serve my mission, I would see your precious little **domain** get burnt to cinders."

"That won't come to pass," said the Baron, apparently unfazed. But that coolheaded veneer was all too transparent.

Lafier took two or three bites of the pumpkin, savored it, and stood up.

"Ah, *Fïac*, this is a palate-cleanser. There is more food to come..." said the **waitstaff**, dismayed.

"Give the chefs my thanks, and my apologies. I've had my fill. Please tell them it was sublime."

The **Baron** clapped. "Guide *Fïac Lartnér* to her bedchambers."

Two **servants** who had apparently been waiting nearby slipped out. They were, of course, female.

He indicated Lafier. "**Her Highness** is tired. Make sure she reposes right away. You two wait by her side until she falls asleep."

So he wasn't going to let her get close to their vessel no matter what.

"I already know the answer, **Baron**, but do you have any men among your **servants?**"

"No. I can't stand the thought of *Lander men* beside me."

Lafier's lips curled.

Those who loathed the Abh typically believed that they never smiled when they ought to, and did smile at the most flabbergasting times.

This was, however, a wild misconception.

The Abh smiled during times of joy, laughed during times of mirth. But the reason this misconception came to be was that the Abh also smiled when face to face with the object of their hatred.

It was too intense to merely call a derisive smile; it was more akin to the brilliant blossoming of a poison flower. It was a grin of disdain intertwined with provocation, a broad beam that could not be mistaken for an expression of affection. Their enemies detested it, calling it "the smile of the Abh."

"Now I have yet another reason to despise you," she said, as her smile widened.

Chapter 10: *Sairhoth Ghinter* (Jint's Wrath)

Jint awoke, his head groggy. The blood in his brain had been near enough replaced by mud.

Where am I again…?

Lids heavy, he cracked his eyes open. A wooden wall with a carved relief of vines came into view — which was sideways, because he was splayed on a rigid cot.

What am I doing in a place like this?

One by one, his memories flooded back.

He'd arrived at the main building of the estate through a long walkway leading from the **spaceport** section, and was told he would be escorted to the **bathing room**. That was when he'd been separated from Lafier. He'd thought it natural that he'd use a different bathing room from her, so he assented.

But as soon as he lost sight of her, somebody pressed something against the back of the neck, and the world grew dark before he had any chance to shout or fight back…

Dammit! That rat bastard! It had been a **servant** who had taken him down, but it was no doubt on the orders of the **Baron of Febdash**. The drug had been administered with a needle-less injection.

Jint sprang up. He was angry at the **Baron**, but he was also worried about Lafier.

"Finally come to, eh, *fanaibec* (boy)?" A voice, from right near him. Warily, Jint looked in its direction, only to find an old man wearing the *daüch* of a **noble**. He seemed well-past 70 years old. His physique was solid built, and he was spry and healthy. His hair was as white as a sun-bleached skull.

"Who're you?"

"You oughta introduce yourself before asking people's names."

Yes, true.

"My name is *Linn Ssynec Raucr Ïarlucec Dreur Haïder Ghintec*."

"The **noble prince of a countdom**, you say? Deary me! You don't *look* Abh to me!"

"You don't look Abh, either," said Jint, keeping his guard up.

"Nope. We must be birds of a feather. Name's *Atausryac Ssynec Atausr Lymh Raica Faibdacr Srumh* (Former Baron of Febdash, Sroof). Used to be the second-ever **Baron of Febdash**."

"Then that'd make you the current **Baron**'s…"

"Father, yep."

"What do you want from me?" asked Jint, his words laced with anger.

"Want from you? Me? All I did was scurry to your side after they'd tossed you in here with me."

"Please don't play dumb with me!" Jint raised his voice.

"Calm down, would ya, **boy**? Ahem, I mean, *Linn Ssynec Raucr Ïarlucec Dreur Haïder Ghintec*. My son must be up to something, but believe me, I ain't got the foggiest."

"What? But how can that be…?"

"What can I say? That's the deal. Look, I'm trapped in here, too. How would I know what happened to you?"

"Trapped?"

"Yep, and this is my cell. I live pretty good, but still, no freedom. That's a jail by anybody's definition."

"All right, fine, then tell me, is Lafier… am I the only one who's been carried here? Did you see a girl, too?"

"A girl? No, just you. Is she *your* girl?"

Jint ignored that query. He looked at his wrist, but it was missing. "Where's my **wristgear**!?"

"Beats me. I didn't take a thing. My son musta taken it."

"You really don't know anything?"

"Sorry, I really don't." The old man remained calm and composed. "I'm telling ya the truth. I'm trapped here. And nobody's told me your story."

"But Lonh-*Lymr* (His Excellency the Baron) is your son, isn't he?"

"I ended up like this *because* he's my son. He ain't much for how I'm a Lander, genetically. And the 'public' here amounts to the **servants**, who don't come in contact with me."

177

"Ugh, the more I hear, the less I get." Jint stroked his head, which hadn't quite revved back up to full speed. That was when he noticed he didn't have his decorative **circlet** on. Nor did he have his *daüch* to signify he was nobility. Not that he minded all that much. The disappearance of the **wristgear**, now *that* he minded.

"The man's a walking inferiority complex," Sroof asserted.

"He didn't look it to me."

"Maybe not, but believe you me. I'm his father, I should know. This Barony ain't got a storied history, and I guess his inflated ego can't handle that."

"But he's a **noble**, with his own **domain** and everything."

"Yeah, a really tiny one."

"The size of the territory notwithstanding, it's still a really high standing in society, isn't it?"

"Sure, but we were **gentry** only three generations ago. And he hates that. Oh, he probably locked me up here not so *others* don't lay eyes on me, but that so *he* ain't gotta. Can't even stomach looking at his Lander daddy."

"I guess right now, your problem's my problem, too."

The **former baron** grinned.

"The only thing I've been racking my head over all these years stuck here is where I went wrong raising him. I've had plenty of time, too. If ya want my parenting advice, I'm here for ya."

"I'm all ears later." He wouldn't be begetting a successor until much farther down the line. He was sure Sroof had many a pearl of wisdom to share with him, but educational philosophy wasn't the most pressing concern at the moment. "Right now, I need to focus on getting out of here."

Jint tried to get up out of bed, but nearly stumbled and fell. He was tottering on his feet, as the effects of the drug hadn't totally worn off. The former baron caught him and sat him back down.

"Take it easy there, Lonh-*Ïarlucer Dreur*."

"Please, don't call me that. It kinda puts me on edge."

"You've got some issues to sort, eh, **boy**." The former baron complied without hesitation.

"Yep."

"Gotta say, though… a **count**! That's a **grandee** rank, ain't it? Your father or mother, or your grans, or I dunno who, but somebody musta done good to go straight from **imperial citizen** to **count**!"

"It was my dad. He wasn't even an **imperial citizen**. He did *really* good."

"Hoo-wee, I'd love to hear that story if ya don't mind."

"I'm sorry, but…"

"Don't wanna, eh? Now you've got me even more curious. But I've gotta respect your wishes. So never mind that, what say we get ya to a *guzasec* (shower)? You're sweaty all over."

"I can do that whenever. Right now, I need to escape…"

"I'm telling ya, you're in no shape. Let's get ya cleaned up and fed. Then we can tackle what needs tackling. I may even be of some assistance."

"Really?" He felt some aversion to hanging onto the hand the old man had extended. It wasn't that this **former baron** didn't look trustworthy. It was just that, given their experience gap, pulling the wool over Jint's eyes might have come as naturally to the man as slipping on a pair of shoes.

Besides, how exactly would he even be able to help him, if he'd just said he was trapped here?

"Have faith in what your elders have to say," said Sroof. "You've gotta admit, washing up with some hot water ain't a bad idea. I swear I won't do anything to ya. If I'd wanted to, I woulda already."

"But there's no time!" Jint was suddenly seized by a hair-raising anxiety. "How long was I knocked out for?"

The old man looked at his **wristgear**. "Lessee… It's been around five hours since they brought you here. I dunno what's got you in such a hurry, but I'm betting you've got an hour or two to spare. Otherwise, it's already too late."

Five hours…

There was still time to steal a march on the enemy fleet. But what was Lafier doing? If the **Baron** was enacting some villainous scheme, the enemy might just get the time they needed.

"Could you lend me your **wristgear** for a sec?" He'd memorized Lafier's number for just such an emergency. If Lafier had hers on, and was within a light-second's range, he ought to be able to contact her.

"No problem at all." Sroof removed his **wristgear** and handed it over.

179

But Jint was soon disappointed. It was just a glorified watch.

"Um, does this room have a **teletransceiver**?"

"Yeah, it's got one."

"Could you let me use it? Please," said Jint, coughing.

"I don't mind, but it only reaches the *bandhorh garicr* (homemakers' office). You're probably itching to talk to that girl, but you'd have to get her to that office first. Think ya can manage it?"

Jint drooped his shoulders and shook his head. It would be delusional to hope the Baron's **servants** would be so amenable.

"C'mon, let's get ya to the **shower**." Sroof sounded like he was twisting the arm of a difficult child. "It'll clear your head. After that, ya can eat, get some strength back. *Then* we can cook up a real robust plan, the two of us."

"Sure. Fine," Jint agreed limply. He did, in all likelihood, need his strength back.

Unlike Jint, there was no grogginess when Lafier opened her eyes. She couldn't have been sleeping for very long, yet she was coursing with energy from head to toe. She pushed aside her soft, warm futon and stood straight up amid the dark.

"Lights," she muttered.

The lights came on. She could breathe easier; she was alone in her room.

Those two **servants** from before had followed their lord's orders and stayed by her side until she'd succumbed to sleep. She'd intended to *pretend* to fall asleep, but it appeared she'd been more worn out than she realized.

She checked the time on her **wristgear**. Normally, she would take off her **circlet** and **wristgear** before tucking herself in, but fearing they would confiscate them, she made tonight an exception.

She'd evidently been out for four hours. The **Baron** might actually have done her a favor: anything she attempted would have been undermined by all her mounting fatigue.

But I can hardly forgive myself, thought Lafier, biting her lip, *for actually falling asleep when I was trying to fake it. What am I, a child?*

Lafier was able to console herself, though, given it'd ultimately worked out in her favor. Besides, those thoughts were soon crowded out by her seething fury toward the **Baron**. That he was sabotaging her mission was cause enough for outrage, but she'd never felt so slighted by someone so gratuitously, by someone without any seniority over her. It stung her pride.

She was quick to sing her own praises: *I am being very resilient. For having been born an Abliar, a clan whose souls are always blazing with imperatorial wrath, I clearly have a great amount of patience.*

But even her sizeable stores of perseverance had reached their limit. She *would* escape, even if only to teach the Baron his place.

She opened the *raüamh* clothing trunk) and found her **uniform**. There were many other beautiful outfits, but they didn't distract her. Lafier was a **royal princess**, and once she returned to her *flirich* (palace court) she would be wearing such lavish dresses as casual everyday fare.

In actuality, she wasn't all that shocked that garments befitting **noble** princesses had been prepared in advance, though it was strange that there were no Abh women in this **Baron's household**.

Lafier slipped on her **uniform**.

Now, where could Jint be? Finding him was her priority. She activated her **wristgear** and tried to connect to Jint's.

"The **wristgear** you called is not currently equipped," it whispered. It must have been swiped from Jint's possession.

"Hmm." Lafier turned hers off. It was plain to see the **Baron** was making it his policy to sever their bond.

No matter; onto her next course of action. She activated the *sotÿac* (information terminal) installed in this bedroom and loaded up a map of the estate.

The main building of the **Baron's manor** was a three-tiered structure. It was divided into the living quarters, the office quarters, the storehouse, the **hydroponic plantation**, and the **cultivation ranch**.

"Show me where I am," Lafier ordered.

"On the second floor." Then, a room towards the center of the top-view second-floor map turned red.

"Show me where the **Baron**'s bedroom is." A room directly adjacent to the one she'd been allotted turned red.

"And the guest bedrooms?" About twenty rooms on their floor lit up.

"Which of those are currently in use?" Only one remained red in color — her room.

"Is there anybody held captive somewhere?" she asked, just in case.

"I don't understand the question." As she expected, no answer.

"Show me the names and positions of everyone in the manor."

"I need **my lord**'s permission to help you with that. Would you like me to ask him for his permission? Note that he is currently resting. As such, you may need to wait until tomorrow morni—"

"No, forget it," she said, silencing it. *I suppose if it's come to this, I'm going to have to ask the* **Baron***.*

She kicked herself for leaving her weapon aboard the **vessel**. Though the Baron definitely wouldn't have allowed her to carry one with her.

Oh, but I can go fetch it now! Lafier quickly made up her mind.

According to the clock on her bedroom wall, it was the middle of the night by this **barony**'s time zone. There was little chance she would bump into a **servant** in the halls, and she knew the ferry was there for them. The only uncertainty was whether she could get there and inside.

"Is it possible to enter the **spaceport**? Are there any pressurized passageways between here and the **conveyance ship** currently moored there?"

"Yes, there are."

"Are they blocked off?"

"They aren't blocked off, but you would require the *saigh daimhatr haita* (general-access electromagnetic wave crest-key)."

"Is my **EM crest** registered?"

"No."

"Can I register it now?"

"I need **my lord**'s permission to help you with that. Would you like me to ask him for his permission? Note that he is currently resting—"

"Whose **crests** are registered?" Lafier cut in.

"The crests of **my lord** and of all of the **servants** are. The servants' names are as follows…"

"That's enough." She didn't want to hear the terminal rattle through fifty names.

Let's just give it a try, thought Lafier.

The situation wasn't ideal, but that didn't mean she could afford to get lost in thought in this bedroom. She loaded her **wristgear** with the map of the estate.

With this, her preparations were complete.

Lafier made to exit the room, but something nagged at her as she was about to order the doors open. There was something she was missing.

What could it be?

She wracked her mind, and finally it dawned on her. There was another occupant besides the **Baron** and his **servants**.

Lafier reactivated the terminal.

"The **Baron**'s father is here, isn't he?"

"Yes, the **His Excellency the Former Baron** resides at the **Febdash Baron's Manor**."

"Is the **Baron**'s father's **EM crest** registered?"

"No, it isn't."

"Why isn't it?"

"On the orders of **my lord**."

"Why would the **Baron** order such a thing?"

"I need **my lord**'s permission to answer that. Would you like me to ask him for his permission? Note that he is currently res—"

"Yes, yes, I know," she said, irritated. "Show me where the **former baron** is."

The top-view map of the third floor appeared. Its area was mostly taken up by the **plantation** and **ranch**. A single path led from the elevator section through the plantation to an isolated quarter, which glowed red on the map.

"I would like to meet with him. Set up an appointment."

"I need **my lord**'s permission to help you with that. Would you like to—"

"NO!" Lafier slammed the terminal's desk with her palms. "Why do I need the **Baron**'s permission to see the **former baron**!? You don't think that's strange!?"

"I cannot judge that for myself."

"I suppose not." Lafier let loose a string of words unbecoming of a **royal princess**. "Is there anybody else in the **former baron**'s quarters?"

"Yes, there is one other person."

"What's their name?"

"They are unregistered."

"And they aren't a **servant**, correct?"

"They are not."

That must be Jint!

"Let me guess, I need an **EM crest** to go to the **former baron**'s room, right?"

"You would require either a **general-access electromagnetic wave crest-key**, or **my lord**'s permission. Would you—"

"Stop right there," she said gloomily. She hadn't been seized by an urge to destroy this strong since she'd come free of her **mechanical teachers**.

In any case, it looked as though a certain someone in this estate had father issues. That gave her no pause — strained relationships were hardly uncommon among **noble** families.

She opened the clothing trunk back up and chose a *daüch*. The long robe would make it easier to conceal a weapon. She cinched the robe of deep crimson, which featured a bird with unfolded wings embroidered with silver thread, using a malachite-colored belt. For the *epœzmec* (sash clip), she took one studded with rubies on silver.

Now it was finally time to step foot into the hallway.

"*Fïac Lartnér!*" cried a voice the second she did. Startled, Lafier's eyes darted to and fro.

A **servant** got up out of a rough wickerwork chair and snapped a deep bow.

She wasn't one of the servants who had watched her fall asleep, but she remembered her face. "You're the **servant** named 'Sehrnye,' if I recall."

"Yes! I'm honored, *Fïac Lartnér!*" She all but swooned. "To think you would remember the name of a lowly worm like me!"

Wearily, Lafier came to understand part of Jint's puzzlement, if faintly.

While she had no desire to meddle in the **family traditions** of another's household, the **Febdash Baron's Manor** was in sore need of reform in order to safeguard the very concept of dignity. The attitude of the **Baron**'s servants towards her shot far past honor and respect.

Of course, as a member of her royal family, the *Clybh* (also known as the *Lartiéc Clybr*), Lafier had grown up surrounded by servants and chamberlains that waited upon her. But those servants knew the difference between loyalty and slavery.

All she wanted was to conduct her business as normal, as an *equal*. But they were making her feel like a pompous ass.

"What are you doing over there?" asked Lafier, shoving aside the matter of reforming the **Febdash Barony**'s **family traditions** for now. "Were you spying on me?"

"I would never!" Sehrnye's eyes widened. "Why would I do something so disrespectful? I was simply waiting for **Your Highness** to awaken so that I could be of service."

Lafier didn't doubt her words. There were more advanced ways to spy on somebody; no need to be glued to the other side of the door.

"On the **Baron**'s orders?"

"Yes. I have been entrusted with your care for as long as you're here with us."

"Don't you need to sleep?"

"Oh, I'm so honored you would worry over an ignoble maggot like me, Your Highness. But you don't need to concern yourself; we are taking this duty in shifts."

"Good," she said, but a hint of apathy crept in her voice. She probably should have sympathized with Sehrnye, but she seemed satisfied with her lot. Not that Lafier liked that.

Lafier just ignored her and started pacing away.

"Please, *Fïac Lartnér*, wait a moment!" she panicked, rushing to catch up to her. "Where are you going?"

"Why do you ask?"

"I will do whatever it is you need done, so I implore you relax in your room, **Your Highness**."

"Never mind that. I need to go by myself."

"Where are you headed?" she repeated.

"To my **conveyance ship**," she responded honestly. She couldn't come up with a convincing lie in time, and if luck was on her side, she might be able to make use of Sehrnye's **EM crest**.

"Heavens above!" Sehrnye covered her mouth with her hands. "I'm terribly sorry, *Fïac Lartnér*, but **my lord** insisted he would like you to refrain from entering your **conveyance ship**—"

She'd been half-expecting that response, so her reply was swift.

"Don't you think it's strange? Granted, this is the **Baron's manor**, but he doesn't own that **conveyance ship**. It belongs to the Star Forces, and it's now under my command. Am I wrong, or does the Baron lack any authority to prevent me from accessing it?"

"You... You're not wrong," said Sehrnye, visibly befuddled.

Everyone around her — including she herself, most likely — had grown accustomed to this home situation with the Baron, but it appeared it had occurred to her, just now, that Lafier comprised an *outside element*. She followed Lafier to the door to the passageway leading to the spaceport.

This was her first barrier. Without an **EM crest**, she was stuck.

"Could you to open the way for me? My **EM crest** isn't registered," Lafier asked Sehrnye.

Sehrnye hesitated. "*Fïac Lartnér*, it's not up to me to decide..."

Lafier said nothing. No matter what she said here, it would only spark Sehrnye's self-hatred. So she crossed her arms and stared motionlessly at the door.

She too had turned stubborn. She refused to budge until she was either allowed to go to the spaceport or the **Baron's** servants dragged her back.

"*Fïac Lartnér*," said Sehrnye worriedly, "surely you don't mean to leave just like that?"

Lafier was surprised. "Of course not. I *can't*."

"Forgive me, it goes without saying that you wouldn't part without saying your goodbyes to **my lord**..."

"That's not what I mean." Lafier was even more surprised. "Do you not know?"

"Know what, Your Highness?" Doubt flashed across her face.

"The Baron refused to let us refuel. The ship can't fly. He also locked up my companion."

"Goodness!" Sehrnye covered her gaping mouth. "**My lord** did *what*!?"

"You really didn't know? The **Baron** can't have done it all alone. The **servants** followed his orders, didn't they?"

"I would have followed those orders, too, had he directed them at me." Sehrnye's head drooped with guilt. "But I swear to you, I didn't know. **My lord** informs his **servants** only of what they need to know. I thought **Your Highness** was stopping by in the middle of a military mission."

"But you knew of the enemy fleet's impending invasion!"

"I heard the rumors about it. In a **domain** this small, rumors spread very fast. I didn't hear about it from my lord."

"I see." It must have been the **Space Traffic controller** who spread the rumor. "Well, now you know for sure. So what will you do?"

"What do you mean?"

"You are a *gosucec lymr* (Baron's servant), but you are also an **imperial citizen**. The choice is yours: Will you remain loyal to the **Baron** as a **servant**, or will you aid me in my mission as a **citizen of the Empire**?"

She hesitated for a long time.

"Understood." Finally, her answer came. Sehrnye knelt. "I will follow my orders as a **citizen**."

"Wait…" Lafier hadn't ordered her to follow her in her capacity as a **royal princess**; she had requested her aid as a **soldier**. But she thought better than trying to explain that to her. It worked out for the best either way.

"You have my gratitude," is all she said.

"Oh, I'm not worthy." Sehrnye stood up and opened the door.

Chapter 11: The Erstwhile Baron

"The first **Baroness of Febdash,** my mother, came from an overpopulated landworld named Di Laplance. Anyways, for family reasons, she had to choose between immigrating to an emptier world or becoming an **imperial citizen.**"

Jint had been given a meal of spicy chicken stew and assorted fresh vegetables. Not only was the portion far too generous for one serving, it was also delicious.

The Abh liked their food mild. He'd thought that it was perhaps due to their taste buds differing, but they were actually the same as their ancestors'. It was simply a cultural quirk of theirs to prefer bland-tasting food. Jint had heard theories that the Abh simply mistook thin flavors for elegance.

This stew had gone a tad overboard with the spiciness, but compared to the meals he'd been provided on the Gothelauth, at least it tasted like something, so Jint liked it.

However, he couldn't just relax and savor the flavor.

Pecking at his stew disinterestedly, he gave his full attention to the old man as he recounted the history of the **Febdash Estate.**

"So, she picked the **imperial citizen** path. And the quickest way to become one was to volunteer for the **Star Forces.** So she decided to be a *sach* in the *Bondœbec.* You know that department, don't ya, **boy?**"

"Yeah," Jint nodded. "It's a technical department that services weapons, right?"

"It sure is. She met my father in the military, and gave birth to me on land. Not out of wedlock, mind you."

"I gathered."

"Then she got appraised as a real talent and managed to get into the *Cénruc Fazér Roübonr* (Academy for Arms Manufacture). Do you know that kinda school?"

"Yeah, I did some research when looking into schools for myself. It's a school for weapons engineers."

"That's right. When she graduated, she transferred to the *Faziac Roübonr* (FAHZEEA ROW'BOHN, Arms Manufacturing Branch) and became a starpilot. If she'd stayed a *sach*, all she would have gotten after many years of service was a gentry class rank. She did pretty good for herself, wouldn't ya say?"

"Guess so." Not that he had any choice but to agree, with the old man staring at him like that.

"Seems she'd become estranged from my father around that time. So I dunno what he looks like. But that ain't so rare among the Abh, ya know. Mom did even better from that point on. She was nothing special as a *faziac* (engineer), but she was great at roping people into things. A natural leader, she was. That's what got her so many promotions. She made it all the way to *Spénec Fazér* (Engineering Admiral) and *Saimh Bhobott Ménhotr* (Director-General of Warship Management)."

"Wow."

"Right? The **Empire** compensates the service of **admirals** with **noble ranks**, and they gave her this blue star here."

Jint's mouth was full of vegetables, so all he could do to confirm he was still listening was nod.

"Anyways, that's why I'm still just a Lander genetically. I hated that when I was a lad, but I don't really care anymore. Honestly, now that I'm this age, I dunno what I'd even do with a younger body. And I dunno why the Abh'd renounce their right to die by aging. Though I'm sure this is all gobbledygook to a youngster like you."

"Well, I can't say I'd mind living life without aging."

"You say that now, but if you ask me, the soul and the body oughta age in tandem. But never mind that. Long story short, they let me apply to an **academy** 'cause Mom was **gentry**. But I ain't got any *frocragh* so I couldn't be a **Flight Branch starpilot**, or as they'd say, a *lodaïrh nauceta* — a real starpilot. So, I enrolled in the *Cénruc Fazér Harr* (Shipbuilding Academy). You know what that is?"

"Yeah, I looked into that, too. I just don't think I'm cut out for design or engineering."

There were four main streams in technological careers. There was the **Arms Manufacturing Branch**, where staff devised weapons; the *Faziac Harr* (Shipbuilding Department), where they designed hulls; the *Faziac Sair* (Engine Department), where they formulated machines; and the *Faziac Datycrir* (DAHTYOOCREER, Photonic Branch), where they dealt with **compucrystals**.

"Luckily, I was able to become a *lodaïrh Fazér Harr* (Shipbuilding starpilot). When Mom got her **noble rank** and **territory**, she was able to make full use of her technical know-how. And that'll be the crux of the plan."

"Wait, what?" Jint didn't quite follow, but he sensed that the old man was finally verging on something juicy.

"I'm talking about our insidious plot to sneak you out right from under my son's nose. You didn't *forget*, did ya?"

"How could I!? It's all I've been thinking about!"

"So ya didn't listen to a word I said."

"Uhh…" Jint's face flushed red; he'd hit the bull's-eye.

"It's fine," said the **former baron**, waving his hand. "It's just been so long since I've talked to anybody; forgive my inane babbling."

"It wasn't inane babble. It was all very interesting."

"Come now, **boy**. Ya seem like an all right kid, but now's the time for ya to learn that blatant ego-salving's only gonna hurt people."

"Sorry."

"Don't fret it. In any case, I'm gonna explain it to ya in detail. First of all, think of the similarities 'tween ships and **orbital manors**. Manors are just ships without engines, ain't they? And I was the one who planned out this **barony's manor**. Thanks to my designer's privileges, I never had to hand it over to him. That numbskull was so quick to lock me up he forgot to shake me down for it beforehand. All I gotta do is say the *saighoth* (password) and this whole manor's *aimh* (EHF, compucrystal net) will submit to me. If I can just get near a **terminal**, it'll be child's play to turn the tables and imprison my little son of the year."

"Then why—"

"Why did I content myself with captivity? Tell me, **boy**, where would I go, exactly? If I broke out of the **Manor**, all that'd await me is a 3 Kelvin void. 'Sides, all the **servants** I'd gotten to know back in the day've all been dismissed. Now they're all hirees tailored to *his* tastes. So it's understandable why I'm not so gung-ho about escape, ain't it?"

"But couldn't you've called for help?"

"The **empire** doesn't meddle in **noble** family affairs. If you're a noble, then you oughta remember that for the future. I'll have ya know I *like* this life of mine, too. I ain't got anything to do on the outside. Meeting up with old friends wouldn't go so well, since I've aged and they haven't. It'd make me resent how I'm the only one who had to."

"Excuse me, but didn't you just say that 'the soul and the body should age in tandem'?"

"You ain't ever heard of 'sour grapes,' **boy**?"

"Oh, I'm familiar."

"Then that oughta say it all."

"Well, if you're okay with it, then..." He believed the **former baron** overall, though doubt remained. "Are you sure the **Baron** hasn't changed that **password**?"

"Nope," he replied breezily. "I ain't sure. But sometimes you've just gotta throw the dice. Otherwise life gets real boring. That's the thing I hate the most about my life here — nobody to lay wagers with."

"I'm not a big fan of gambling," said Jint. Ever since that fateful day seven years prior, Jint had a feeling that destiny didn't much like him. And he wasn't about to commend his life to a force with whom he didn't get along.

"You're prolly better off that way, but we're running good odds here. The **password** is burned in on a molecular level. As long as he hasn't changed all of the **compucrystals**, he can't have changed the password."

"If you say so." But his misgivings weren't quite cleared yet. There was no guarantee that he hadn't, in fact, replaced them.

"Believe in me, **boy**. *Bet* on me. Now, I ain't averse to helping ya so I can kill some time, but first I gotta hear what's got ya in this tizzy. What did ya come here for, and how'd ya end up in this dump with me?"

So Jint filled him in. About how he'd been accepted into a **quartermaster's academy**. How he'd boarded the **patrol ship** *Gothelauth* to get to the **capital** — to *Lacmhacarh*. How they'd crossed paths with a fleet of likely-enemy **space-time bubbles**. How he'd been able to escape using the **conveyance ship** that Lafier was piloting. How they'd come to the **Febdash Barony** for a refueling pit stop…

"And you know the rest."

"Hmm? So you're saying the girl ya mentioned before is a **royal princess?**"

"Yep," he nodded reluctantly.

"Hoo-wee." The old man grinned. "So that's what's been going on out there since I retired. This is a real doozy, let me tell ya! If my dead mother caught wind of this, she'd be head over heels. A **royal princess**, in our home! Having even just you over, the **noble prince of a countdom**, is downright extravagant. It's raised the status of my family name."

"You can cut the wisecracks now," said Jint, peeved. "So, are you gonna help me?"

"'Course, boy. I just need to help ya get back to the skies on the **conveyance ship** with the **royal princess**, right?"

"After getting it refueled, yeah."

"Right, 'course, can't forget the refueling bit. Might as well get you two some food to carry with ya while we're at it, too."

"That'd be great, if you can. Thank you. I was getting tired of *üanhirh* (combat rations). They're as bland as everything else the Abh eat. But would you be able to?"

"I think so. There's just one problem."

"What?"

"Remember what I said about needing a **terminal**? Well, my son's vaguely aware I'd find some use in one, so there ain't any in this section."

"You can't be serious," he said dejectedly.

"What did ya expect? I'd just stroll right up to a **terminal** so you and your girlfriend could escape hand-in-hand, just like that? Life ain't that easy."

"Lafier's not my girlfriend," Jint pointed out.

"Don't dwell on it, I was just embellishing, that's all."

"Okay, whatever. How do we get to a **terminal?**"

"We just need to slip out of here first."

"How?"

"That's what we need to figure out together. Otherwise our insidious plan ain't going anywhere, **boy**. Plus, this is your chance to impress your lady friend. Speaking of which…"

"What?"

"You *sure* ya ain't a couple?"

"I'm sure." It was a rather unfortunate fact, but a fact all the same.

"Yet here ya are, calling a royal princess by her given name. Not many in the **Empire** who can get away with that, ya know. Or do ya just call her by name when she's not around? 'Cause then I'd have to amend my evaluation of you."

"No, I, uhhh…" Jint hemmed and hawed. "I do address her by name."

"Then—"

"But only because of my own ignorance and a boatload of luck. Going into it any further would take too long; I'd be boring you to tears."

"Oh, no, I'd love to have a listen, but I can tell you're not in the mood to divulge."

"Not really, no. Sorry. There's no time to waste."

"It sucks, but what can ya do? And I thought I'd be able to cast my wretch of a son in the role of a corrupt noble making advances on another man's girl. The perfect, hoggish role for that faux sophisticate!"

In reality, the **Baron of Febdash** did not nurse any such feelings toward Lafier. And Lafier, for her part, wasn't the type to be crushing on anyone at the moment, at least not *consciously*. No potential for some illicit affair.

Typically, the **Baron** took a handful of his favorite **servants** to his bedchambers, but tonight he retired alone. He had much to ruminate on.

He poured some **apple cider** from the *Dreuhynh Saimlycr* (Countdom of *Saimlych*) into his **cup** of **amethyst** and downed it.

His heart was wavering. He couldn't be sure that he'd made the right call.

His ambition was to create his own kingdom. The kingdom he sought to erect wouldn't be a large enough power to resist the **Empire**, for though he did tend to overestimate his own talents, he was no madman. In terms of scale, he was fine with his **barony** remaining this size.

However, the man was a prisoner of his own inferiority complex within the prism of the **Empire**'s aristocracy. He was, at present, a mere *baron*, and the history of his family line was shorter than that of many **gentry**.

That is why he didn't much care for visits to the **capital**. His house's lack of history assaulted him most when he was among other Abhs.

But here, in his **domain**, he was the only Abh around. He didn't consider his father to be a true Abh, and even if he did, nothing would have changed. On this tiny world, he was the ruler, the subduer. So long as he didn't venture out of his comfort zone, he could delude himself into thinking he was the king of an independent monarchy he could rule with impunity.

The second he'd intercepted the communication between Lafier and the **Space Traffic controller**, he feared he'd lose his little kingdom.

The enemy could be naught but the **Four Nations Alliance**. His **domain** didn't get much by way of information, but it was enough to come to that conclusion.

Would the **FNA** recognize the autonomy of his **barony**? No, of course not!

Then what could he do? All he could hope for, the Baron thought after some moments of intense consternation, was that the **FNA** ignored the **barony** altogether. To have that happen, he'd need to avoid any unnecessary activity. He refused to allow any entry into **planar space** through the **Febdash Portal**. He'd explained as much to Lafier.

He was well aware, of course, that **planar space** entry from the **Febdash Portal** was not, in fact, all that likely to arouse the attention of the enemy.

As such, the first plan that flitted through his mind was to refuel them as quickly as possible and then promptly jettison all the small ships that could signpost their existence. That would have been the course of action that invited the least risk. But that was when a much less noble-minded thought burrowed into his heart.

What if the enemy already had the **barony** in its sights?

If they demanded he provide them aid, he would comply without a second thought. The **barony** had no military power, so resistance was futile.

He would give them as much fuel as they wanted, if that would keep his "kingdom" intact.

But perhaps the enemy wasn't interested in his aid. There was the worryingly distinct possibility that they simply seized the **antimatter fuel factories** and the other facilities by force.

That said, wouldn't they also be interested in the **Empress's** granddaughter? She'd have no value as a hostage, given the responsibilities incumbent upon the **Empress**, but maybe the enemy didn't know that. He could use her as a pawn. He could ensure the preservation of his **star-fief** and hand her over to them. He'd prolong negotiations for as long as possible, but not out of any hesitation to assist the enemy. On the contrary, he'd turn the **Barony of Febdash** into a strategic base for the **FNA**. If it turned into an important resupplying station for them, he'd be mostly safe. After all, if they took over its operations by force, he was prepared to commit suicide — and take the entire **domain** out with him.

Lafier was a bird who'd unwittingly flown into his cage, and he'd use her as collateral.

And what if his link to the **Empire** was severed, and the enemy never came to his doorstep? That would be ideal, for then he would truly become this small world's absolute ruler! It mattered not that he'd have only his fifty **servants** as subjects, nor that he'd only have access to a limited variety of meat and hydroponic produce. He could even bear to go without his favorite *Saimlych*-sourced **apple cider**.

All he desired was to be the one with all the power in his domain. He pictured himself reigning over a world; a small world, yes, but a *whole* world.

And in that world would be Lafier. If all communication with the Empire ceased, then he would have no cause to feel inferior next to the "**royal princess**." She would have no authority here.

He'd chosen only the most meek and submissive of women as his servant staff, and they revered him as a god. If the princess and the Baron ever issued contradictory orders, he knew his servants would follow his without question.

In truth, the Baron had never really associated himself with Abh women. In places like the *Lacmhacarh* and within the military, he'd become acquainted with a number of them, but he was always nervous around them.

Perhaps as a consequence of that, he would at times indulge in perversion and have one or more servants dye their hair blue and don the garb of an Abh **noble**. The garments and jewelry he'd collected to that end happened to come in handy for the princess's arrival. But whenever he used them for their intended purpose, it always ended in disappointment.

Their looks, their bodies and faces, he could bear. Due to his overly particular tastes, there were women even among the Abh whom he found difficult to call "attractive." The real problem was on the inside — they were too humble, too modest. Nothing at all like an Abh. To be honest, he'd nearly forgotten what Abh women were like until Lafier confronted him.

He smiled as he poured himself more **apple cider**.

*I just spoke my mind like a true Abh, and to a **royal princess** at that.* Being in the safety of his own castle gave him that sense of security; it would have been unthinkable in the social setting of *Lacmhacarh*. He considered it a dry run for the kingdom to come.

And my kingdom will need successors to the throne, won't it... he thought drunkenly.

This **territory** had many females, as there were no male servants. They were, however, *Lander* women. There was extremely little chance a baby would be born to an Abh like him and a Lander woman without genetic modification. Even if she conceived, it would probably be marred by fatal congenital defects.

Of course, the **Empire** hosted many medical institutions that practiced genetic modification. He himself was born of an Abh and a Lander, made genetically 100% Abh through that process. But here in the **Barony of Febdash**, no such facilities or equipment existed.

And Lafier was an Abh, with whom he could not take issue. Biologically speaking, he would have no trouble siring heirs through her.

Natural delivery among the Abh came with its share of dangers, as their race was an unnatural one, but those risks weren't so high as to warrant avoiding at all costs. The Baron had read some papers about the likelihood of congenital diseases among naturally birthed Abh infants. According to that reputable research, the chances of it causing some grave ailment were about 1 in 50. Those were fairly favorable odds.

*Yes... I shall spread my seed through a **royal princess**...* His delusions were swelling without end.

It was then that the **Baron** began, perhaps, to harbor feelings for Lafier, though naturally, it didn't have to be her specifically. Any genetically Abh woman would suffice.

He couldn't find fault with Lafier's beauty, apart from how she was still too young and childlike to have fully blossomed. Moreover, it would take quite some time for her to come of age. Lastly, their personalities weren't exactly a match.

But those were all considerations for the far future. For all he knew, the **Empire** could recover this land at any moment.

That was the reason he was treating Lafier courteously — at least on the surface. It was in case communications with the center of the **Empire** ever resumed.

Of course, he couldn't be said to have treated that surface-rat of a **noble prince** with much courtesy. But he hadn't committed any *crimes* against him. He was lodging with his own father. He had a raft of defenses he could deploy.

As for the **conveyance ship** the two had ridden here, he sensed it could prove irksome to him, so he wanted to destroy it, but he decided against it for the time being on the grounds that that would be difficult to explain away to the **Empire**.

If and when he became certain that the **Empire** wasn't coming back, he would deal with it as he pleased. And then, the **royal princess** would be much easier to handle. Even the boy might be of use to him — the seed of a Lander was needed to give rise to the next generation of **servants**.

The **Baron**'s uncertainty slipped away with each new ounce of **alcohol** that numbed his brain cells. He'd thought of every possible contingency, he assured himself. Even if his plans weren't perfect, this was the best he could come up with given the situation.

Exhilarated, the Baron gulped down the rest of his **apple cider** and laid himself down to sleep.

The **teletransceiver** chose that moment to ring.

"What!?" If this was over some nonsense, they would have to prepare themselves for a dressing-down.

"This is Greda, calling from the **homemakers' office**. I apologize for disturbing you at this late hour, but someone has infiltrated the **conveyance ship**. What should we do?"

The Baron vaulted out of bed. It seemed this bird was not resigned to languishing in her cage.

He had made an error in his calculations.

The **Baron**'s breathtaking handsomeness was something Landers on **landworlds** rarely ever saw, and it stirred up the **servants**' loyalty to him whether they liked it or not. These were women who longed after the *image* of the Baron, to the point of worshiping at his altar. Time spent alongside the Baron was like an intoxicating drug that they competed amongst each other to obtain. They even saw the unreasonable verbal abuse and lashes of the whip as the sweetest of gifts, so long as they were doled out by the Baron. If they didn't, they would not be qualified to be servants of the **Febdash Barony**.

However, he forgot to account for the fact that those ravishing looks fit for a demigod were not *unique* to him. Ravishing beauty was the standard among the **Kin of the Stars**, not the exception.

There were certainly those **servants** that felt loyal to the Baron as a person. These were the lovers he took with him to bed every night.

But more than half of them were not so keen on the man as an individual. Instead they were fascinated by the Abh as a race. They nearly regarded the Abh world as on par with a heavenly realm, but they knew that the Baron was not so high in the ranks of Abh **nobility**.

Sehrnye was one of those women. Unbeknownst to the Baron, she made a hobby of gazing at holograms of Abh nobles. She felt no attraction to women whatsoever, but she couldn't help but admire the Abh **royal princess** before her eyes.

She herself was astounded that she was able to carry on speaking as normal without turning into a nervous wreck in her presence. It was probably because it hadn't yet hit her that all of this was *real*.

Sehrnye was grateful to the **Baron**; he'd given her a place within the heavenly realm of her dreams, the world of the Abh, even if it was a remote region. And she had spent a long time in the **Barony**, long enough to come to believe in her bones that her lord's orders were absolute.

But Lafier's words carried a certain compelling force that electrified her soul. This was the gorgeous and elegant Abh who could one day become *the* Commander of the Abh.

She felt like she was being pulled in both directions, and splitting at the seams, but the thought that she was assisting a **royal princess** during her time of need filled her with a dizzying, blissful rush that was the ultimate deciding factor.

She didn't ask Lafier anything else; she just guided her to the departure and arrival hall, and waited faithfully for her new mistress in front of the door to the **elevator-tube**.

At last, Lafier descended to her floor. The thigh area of her **long robe** was bulging oddly.

"*Fïac Lartnér*," she said, kneeling.

"**Vassal** Sehrnye," said Lafier. "I want you to take me to where Jint is. That, or bring him to me. Can you do that for me?"

"'Jint'?" Sehrnye didn't recall the name. "Of whom do you speak?"

"My companion. *Ïarlucec Dreur Haïder*. He's being held captive. You've seen him before."

Upon hearing the title *Ïarlucec Dreur*, or **noble prince of a countdom**, she pictured a sophisticated blue-haired Abh, only to be disappointed. She meant the Lander boy who was wearing **noble** garb.

"You mean *him*, Your Highness…"

"Do you know where he's being held?"

"I'm terribly sorry, but…"

"There's nothing to be afraid of." The **royal princess**'s voice was tinged with irritation for some reason.

"I'm not worthy…"

"You do know where the **former baron** is being held, don't you?"

"My lord's father?" said Sehrnye dismissively. That man was Abh as a matter of social standing, but he wasn't really an Abh. So, he was hiding himself in shame. "That man is not being held captive; he's holed up in his retirement…"

"Then why can't I contact him?"

"Uhm…"

Now that she mentioned it, that *was* strange. Since she'd never tried contacting him even once, she hadn't realized it was impossible to do so.

"I don't care whether he's imprisoned or just retired. I just know that Jint's with him. So please, lead him out for me."

She shrank. "I really must apologize, but… that's not possible."

"Because the **Baron**'s forbidden it?"

"Yes, but not only that. The truth is, without my lord's permission, there's no entry there."

"So it's locked out."

"Yes, Your Highness."

"Can you think of any way to contact him?"

"I believe he can be contacted through the **teletransceiver** in the **homemakers' office**, but only a select few **servants** are allowed to enter."

"Do you think it's possible to sneak in?"

"Without being seen? I'm sorry, it's not feasible." There were always a few servants in the office.

"Then we must seize control of it, you and I." Lafier pulled a gun from her **long robe**'s sleeve and proffered it. "Do you know how to use one?"

"No, I've never used one, so…" Sehrnye could scarcely believe how much faith the princess was putting in her.

"It's simple." Lafier pulled the other gun from her **sash** and taught her how to operate it.

"Understood, Your Highness." It really was simple. She had but to make sure the safety was released, train the muzzle on her mark, and squeeze the trigger.

"Let's go." The princess beat a quick path as she dashed forward. "There's no time to lose."

"Yes, Your Highness." Sehrnye rushed to catch up.

Since there were several doors that needed opening on the way to the homemakers' office, Sehrnye led the way. But when they reached the first door, Sehrnye froze.

I'm mutinying against my lord! She trembled with fear. Drawn in by the princess's jaunty demeanor, she hadn't given her actions much thought, but now she realized that what she was trying to do — no, what she was already doing, was treason.

She emitted her **EM crest** from her **wristgear** and unlocked the door.

"Open," she said, voice shaking. Then she looked back. "*Fïac Lartnér.*"

"What is it?" Lafier had already walked ahead of her.

Sehrnye jogged after her. "I have a request."

"Speak it."

"Since I've betrayed my lord, I can no longer remain in this **barony**. I beg of you, **Your Highness**, please take me on as one of your servants."

Lafier looked behind her at Sehrnye and blinked. Sehrnye feared she'd asked too much of her.

"Ah, yes, of course," said Lafier. "But you'd be my *only* **servant**."

"B-but that can't be!!" She couldn't believe that a member of the **Imperial Family** didn't have a single **servant** at her beck and call.

"There are many **servants** at the **Royal Household of *Clybh*,**" she clarified. "It's my father who has authority over them, but I'm sure he'll understand your situation."

"Is your father **His Majesty, the King of *Clybh*?**"

"Yes," Lafier replied briskly.

The reality before her — that she was within reach of a girl with regal blood — seeped in, and she was filled with renewed awe.

"I have to warn you; you won't be able to use your talents there. You're an **antimatter fuel tank** technician, aren't you?"

"I'm so honored you remembered!" She'd remembered not only her name, but even her occupation! She hadn't thought it possible. Sehrnye was so moved that tears threatened to burst forth.

"Stop that," said Lafier, annoyed.

"Stop what, Your Highness?" She grew flustered, worried she'd fallen from the princess's graces.

"Never mind," she said, giving up. "In any case, wouldn't you be better suited somewhere you could apply those skills?"

"I'm pleased beyond words that **Your Highness** would see after the future of a drudge like me. But I have no desire to stay here."

"Yes, I know," the princess nodded. "Let's just get you out of here. I can't promise you'll be able to work with my **family**, however."

"Your kind words are more than enough." She would likely be able to at least take her to the **capital**, *Lacmhacarh*.

Another door. The homemakers' office was close now. Sehrnye opened it, mind racing. While a minor episode in the life Lafier would go on to lead, it would be an incident of great weight in the history of this **Barony**.

A Brief History of the Composition and Ranks of the Imperial Star Forces

In the present era, the Abh believed in giant warships with firepower to match, but in the foundational period of the Empire, they relied almost exclusively on high-mobility combat units that accommodated one to three people. Those units were both steered and commanded by "starpilots."

In those times, the Star Forces were, on a fundamental level, composed of four-ship formations. Those four ships came together in a diamond-shaped formation, with the Commander at the head and the Vice-Commander at the rear. That made the Commander the so-called "Vanguard Starpilot," and the Vice-Commander the "Rearguard Starpilot," while the starpilots to the left and right were the "Linewings."

Depending on the situation at hand, the four-ship could split into two two-ship formations, in which case the Commander and Vice-Commander led one linewing starpilot each.

When two four-ship formations banded together, they could create a yet stronger combat unit. The commander-ships were accompanied by partner-ships, which meant they now held the reins of a battle unit comprised of exactly ten. As such, they were dubbed "Deca-Commanders."

When the city-ship, the Abliar, was all the territory the Abh possessed, combat units numbered from around 100 to 200. As such, while not totally precise, the Commander-in-Chief leading a whole force of combat units was called a "Hecto-Commander." Several people were assigned as their lieutenants; these were the "Vice Hecto-Commanders."

Finally, when the Star Forces began swelling their ranks, it soon become unrealistic to expect a single Hecto-Commander to lead all forces, and so the "Kilo-Commander" was christened as an even higher position. It was then that the number of troops and the relationship between ranks became significantly vaguer.

After the Empire was established, they'd come to make use of a handful of mother ships. Naturally, a leader was needed to command that group of mother ships, and a "Commodore" was commissioned.

The number of mother ships increased along with the Empire's expansion, and the need arose for assistants to the admiral, men and women who would preside over sub-fleets. These were the Rear Commodores.

Eventually, due to advances in space warfare technology, it was deemed more effective to reorganize the armada with larger ships rather than continue administering a great number of high-mobility units. The designations of Hecto-Commander and all lower positions subsequently became the names of ranks and nothing more, without any relation to their actual work duties. (For example, a Deca-Commander was no longer in charge of 10 starpilots.)

The Empire only grew in size, and the scale and scope of the Star Forces followed suit.

When multiple fleets became standing fleets, there were calls for positions even higher than the commodores. Thus were born the "Grand Commodore" and "Admiral."

But another problem reared its head. Although the Star Forces were more than equal to the task of space combat, establishing and maintaining control over so many planets required ground combat as well — something the Star Forces were not equipped for.

Accordingly, ground forces were to be established. The "Admiral" was now the "Star Forces Admiral," and a Landworld Admiral was appointed to command all ground forces. A superior was appointed over both admirals — the Imperial Admiral.

However, the Age of the Two Armies was short-lived. Owing to the Landworld Forces' inherent nature, the majority of its ranks were comprised of surface-born soldiers. Even though they were "Landers," those with the rank of starpilot and above were treated as gentry or nobility, or in other words, as Abh. Yet they were still not satisfied.

They staged an uprising to abolish imperial rule. It was to be known as the *Ghimrÿar* Rebellion, named after its main instigator, and it was the largest in the history of the Empire.

Following a period of harsh struggle, the Empire succeeded in suppressing them, and thereafter decided to dismantle the Landworld Forces. From that point on, the ground-war armada became an airship department, a branch of the Start Forces as opposed to an independent military. Soldiers now belonged to individual army bases or fleets.

The position of Landworld Admiral was abolished, but the rank of Airship Admiral remained, as did that of the Star Forces Admiral. Furthermore, with the advancement of the prominence of each department came the introduction of new ranks, such as the Quartermaster Admiral, Medical Admiral, and Engineering Admiral.

Note: The Specialty (e.g., non-Flight) Branches include the Budget Branch, Medical Branch, and Engineering Branch (each of which has its own Admiral as its highest rank); as well as the Armed Guard Branch, Law Branch, and Nursing Branch (which have a Grand Commodore as their highest rank); as well as the Mechanics Branch, Arms Manufacturing Branch, Shipbuilding Branch, Engine Branch, Photonic Branch, and Navigational Branch (which have a Commodore as their highest rank); and finally, the Army Music Department (with a Hecto-Commander at its head).

Higher ranks are integrated into the Engineering Department.

Afterword

To most of you, this will be our first meeting, so I believe I should introduce myself. My name is Hiroyuki Morioka. It's a pleasure to meet you.

The short stories I've written are almost all modest, low-key SF stories set in the near future. Well, that makes it seem like I've written a lot of them, but in fact it's only a handful of works. In any case, it made me inclined to make my longform debut a flashy affair set in space.

When all is said and done, my roots lie in space opera SF. (That is, with a dash of heroic fantasy for good measure, I suppose.)

I was already an SF writer; why not indulge in my desire to build up a grand galactic empire, even if only through the page?

As for why I felt that that, specifically, had to be my debut longform work, it was, of course, to defy the expectations of the people who knew me through my sprinkling of short stories (to whom I remain grateful).

Because it was my all-important debut longform, I planned (if at all possible) to only start penning the story once I'd already pieced together a flawlessly considered world and plot.

And yet, three years ago, when I started writing this book, I'd only managed to set down an extremely minimal amount of worldbuilding beforehand.

To tell you the unvarnished truth, I just couldn't hold in the urge any longer, so I inserted a brand-new floppy into a word processor and started pounding the keys.

As such, the setting had to be edited and added to afterwards. I placed a notepad next to the keyboard and wrote up the setting at the same time I was working on the main manuscript.

As for the story, I had no idea what was going to happen, let alone when, how or why.

Despite that, *CREST OF THE STARS* is now complete. Even including works from my "mature" period, this is authentically my first complete longform.

One often hears about "character-driven" stories, and I was able to experience firsthand the phenomenon of my characters acting all on their own, without me puppeteering them.

Since I didn't go through a predetermined project or proposal, the manuscript was unsolicited. It therefore took a fair amount of time after the book was finished to get it published.

It was also due to some awkward timing; Hayawaka Publishing House was putting resources into one or more new periodicals, so it was tamping down on the number of new releases, and I was an unsigned, virtually nameless author coming to their door with a series whose story would continue past the first book. Timing is a very important thing.

When I look back at those times now, I can see it made for an excellent "ripening" period. I think I was able to offer readers a higher-quality finished product thanks to writing and rewriting the story countless times.

And now, all three volumes of *CREST OF THE STARS* are done. Volume 2 will be out in March, and Volume 3 in July, so you won't need to wait too long for the continuation.

If you enjoy this series as light-hearted and fun other-world fantasy set in space, that would make me very happy. Wowing all the incorrigible SF fans out there is another goal of this work.

Now then, let us meet again in the afterword to *CREST OF THE STARS Volume 2: A Modest War.*

March 10, 1996

Writing and Pronunciation Overview

The "alphabet" of Baronh is called "Ath." Ath letters each more or less have their own in-universe Roman alphabet character counterparts, but beware as these don't always map to their English alphabet counterparts. For those who'd like to attempt to divine how Baronh vocabulary is meant to be pronounced, please enjoy this loose pronunciation primer.

You ought, however, to temper your expectations, as in the original text, the word-of-god pronunciations are provided in kana (a phonetic syllabary tied to Japanese syllables), making any sort of certainty when it comes to transliterating them into English very difficult to achieve.

Furthermore, there is some confusion deriving from the original text over the phonetic value of some Ath letters (specifically regarding the Latin letters "au" and "o," as well as "p" and "eu").

If you'd like to hear the language spoken (albeit with likely less-than-authentic pronunciation), check out the old TV series!

ATH ᘔᗺᐱ

ᘔ	ᒉ	ᕲ	ᐱ	ᕲ	ᛁ	ᛋ
a	i	u	é	o	e	c

ᕲ	ᗺ	ᕲ	ᚻ	ᐱ	ᗱ	ᕲ
s	t	l	n	h	p	f

ᕗ	ū̱	P	ᑎ	ᗴ	ᚲ	ō̱
m	ï	ai	y	œ	r	ü

ᕲ	n̄	ᖶ	ᛋ̈	ᕲ̈	ᗺ̈	ᣮ̈
au	ÿ	eu	g	z	d	b

Note: Much of the following information is a condensed version of information on the subject available on Japanese Wikipedia articles and other info sites.

Spoilers regarding the origins of the language have been excised for your reading pleasure.

Baronh has 11 short vowels, each represented by a different Ath character.
Long vowels come about via varying stress, and near-homophones aren't differentiated via stress the way "present" (as in "gift") and "present" (as in the verb) are in English. In the chart below, the *Ath* letter is on the left while its **IPA** pronunciation is on the right.

	Front Vowels			Central Vowels		Rounded		Back Vowels	
	Unrounded		Rounded	Unrounded		Rounded			
Close	*I*	**i**		*y*	**y**			*u*	**u**
Close-mid	*é*	**e**		*eu*	**ø**			*o*	**o**
				e	**ə**				
Open-mid	*ai*	**ɛ**		*œ*	**œ**			*au*	**ɔ**
Open				*a*	**a**				

Baronh also contains three approximants (aka semivowels):
   [j] ("Ϛ" also expresses [j] when in the middle of words)
   [w]
   [ɥ] (" Ŋ" is for when Ŋ is followed by a vowel.)

(Note: Whether diphthongs and/or triphthongs exist is up to interpretation. There's no way to know how diphthongs are meant to be pronounced, but since
Ɀ Ɜ Λ ŪƵ Ч ƎϚI /abljar/ is written in kana as *aburiaru* as opposed to *aburyaru*, it's thought that it might be closer to /abljar/)

The consonants are mostly straightforward, save for the letter "h."
     "h" is a [h] sound at the beginning of a word, as well as before a vowel.
     When "h" comes after "s," "z," or "l," it is silent.
     When it comes after "p," "b," "m," "t," "d," "n," "r," "c," or "g," the two letters form a digraph. Refer to the below chart ("h" being Λ).

In addition, [l], [r], and [ʀ] are liquid consonants.
Most consonants are pronounced as written, but there are exceptions where they are silent.

		Bilabial		Labio-dental	Dental	Alveolar		Post-alveolar		Velar		Uvular	Glottal
Plosive	Unv.d	*p*	**p**			*t*				*c*	**k**		
	Voiced	*b*	**b**			*d*				*g*	**g**		
Fricative	Unv.d	ꟼ Λ·ƎΛ f, mh, ph	**ɸ**		Ƃ Λ	*s*	**s**	Λ ch	**ʃ**			*h*	**h**
	Voiced			Ǝ Λ **v**	Ƃ̇ Λ	*z*	**z**	Λ gh	**ʒ**				
	Nasal	*m*	**m**			*n*				ꜧ Λ	**ɲ**		
	Trill					*R*	**r**					Ч Λ rh **ʀ**	
	Lateral					*l*	**l**						

Grammar Overview

Baronh can be said to be a hybrid of a fusional and an agglutinative language. Its inflection is characterized by the fusion of nouns and case-marking particles; moreover, auxiliary verbs and particles signifying tense and mood are fused to the form of the verb. On the other hand, there's also a great wealth of prefixes and suffixes that map 1:1 between form and meaning, making it agglutinative in nature as well.

Its word order can be either SOV or SVO. Modifiers typically go in front of the modified word, with few exceptions (for example, the genitive case of Type 1 nouns). There are seven cases for nouns, and case information that can't be displayed through declension is conveyed through particles. The aspect and mood of verbs are marked through verb suffixes, along with voice and negation. The copula verb is "*ane*." Pronouns exist, but they don't mark gender (i.e. "he" and "she"). The way the grammatical information of nouns is expressed through both declension and particles is similar to the Altaic language group.

Nouns

	Type 1	Type 2	Type 3	Type 4
	Abh	**pearl**	**ruby**	**steerer**
Nominative	abh	lamh	duc	saidiac
Accusative	abe	lame	dul	saidél
Genitive	bar	lamr	dur	saidér
Dative	bari	lami	duri	saidéri
Allative	baré	lamé	dugh	saidégh
Ablative	abhar	lamhar	dusar	saidiasar
Instrumental	bale	lamhle	dule	saidéle

All c's, e's, and r's at the end of a word are silent (though in r's case, only after a consonant). It generally follows the French-language concept of "liaison."

	Meaning	Marker
Nominative	The subject of the sentence.	-h, -c
Accusative	The direct object of transitive verbs.	-e, -l
Genitive	The English equivalent would be "-'s" or "of" – possession or relation.	-r
Dative	Indirect object. E.g., "to her" or "for whom."	-i, -ri
Allative	Movement toward something. The equivalent in English would be the suffix –ward/-wards.	-ré, -é, -gh
Ablative	Movement away from; in Baronh, it signifies 1) the "starting point" time-wise 2) the starting point space-wise, 3) the starting point of a sequence.	-har, -sar
Instrumental	This describes the means by which the subject does something. In Baronh, that means could be a method, a tool of some kind, or a place/position. It also marks the complement of the copula.	-le

Pronouns

	Singular animate			Plural animate			Inanimate		
	1st person	2nd	3rd	1st	2nd	3rd	Proximal	Mesio-proximal	Distal
Nominative	fe	de	se	farh	darh	cnac	so	re	ai
Accusative	fal	dal	sal	fare	dare	cnal	sol	rol	al
Genitive	far	dar	sar	farer	darer	cnar	sor	ror	ar
Dative	feri	deri	seri	fari	dari	cnari	sori	rori	ari
Allative	feré	deré	seré	faré	daré	cnaré	soré	roré	aré
Ablative	fasar	dasar	sasar	farhar	darhar	cnasar	sosar	rosar	asar
Instrumental	fale	dale	sale	farle	darle	cnal	sole	role	ale

Particles

a: The subject-marking particle. It can fuse with pronouns (e.g., Fe + a = F'a)

>**F'a usere.**
>>I migrate.

>**Dar saurh a?**
>>Your family is…?

>**F'a bale.**
>>I am Abh.

éü: A vocative marker used when addressing people or things.

>**Gereulach éü!** O stars!

sa: The marker of a question.

>**Facle sa?**
>>Understand?

>**De samade sote loma far sori sa?**
>>May I be with you?

le, lo: Means "and" or "with."

te: Particle for use when quoting someone or something.

>**Gobé fal Lamhiri te!**
>>You will call me "Lafier/Lamhirh"!

Modifying Nouns

Bœrh Parhynr (Viscount[ess] of *Parhynh*)
Lonh Dreur Haïder ([His] Excellency, the Count of Hyde)

Verb Endings

Baronh verbs change shape according to three moods (the indicative, the subjunctive, and the imperative), as well as four aspects (the imperfective, the perfective, the progressive, the contemplative). They also have participle forms.

	Indicative	Subjunctive	Imperative	Participle
Imperfective	-e	-éme	-é(no)	-a
Perfective	-le	-lar	—	-la
Progressive	-lér	-lérm	—	-léra
Contemplative	-to	-dar	—	-nau

The (no) in "-é(no)" is present when it comes before a vowel.
The perfective is also used for the past tense.

De dorle soci Céïchartonr zaine.

You rode [it] from Céïchartonn, right?

Here's an example of the subjunctive.

F'ane réfaiseni, saurh loméme.

If my family is with me, then I'm happy.

Verbal Suffixes

-as- for the causative.
-ar- for the passive.
-ad- for the negative.
Always in the following order: -as-/-ar-/-ad-

Derivational morphology
(i.e. building off extant words)

For example, in English, there's the verb to "migrate." What's the noun form of that word? "Migrant." It could just as easily have been "migrator," though.
This is how that works in Baronh.

> Deriving a noun meaning a doer of the original verb.
> (-iac after a consonant sound, -gac after a vowel sound)

usere (to move / migrate) + iac > useriac (migrant)
cilug- (to inherit the imperial throne) + iac > cilugiac (crown prince[ss])
belysé (to control) + gac > belységac (Flight Control)

> Deriving a noun meaning the act of doing the original verb.
> (-hoth after a consonant sound, -coth after a vowel sound)

cair- (to enter) + hoth > cairhoth (admittance to a school)
doz- (to wish/hope) + hoth > dozzoth (a wish or aspiration)
cime- (to keep secret) + coth > cimecoth (a secret)
sa- (to buy) + coth > sacoth (shopping)

> Deriving a noun meaning the appearance
> or function of the original verb.

Mén- (ship) + ragh > ménragh (the function of navigating through flat space)

> Turning nouns into groups of that noun.

Gosuce- (vassal/servant) + lach > gosucelach (group of vassals/servants)

A big shout-out to professional linguist Jessica Kantarovich
for providing her insights and improving the accuracy of this primer.

Thank you.

CREST 2 STARS
OF THE
A WAR MOST MODEST

AUTHOR: HIROYUKI MORIOKA
ILLUSTRATOR: TOSHIHIRO ONO

Table of Contents

Foreword

What are the Abh? I'll tell you:

They are components of a sprawling machine. To them, children are nothing more than replacement parts *manufactured to take over their work before they rust away.*

Then, what is this "machine," you ask?

This pernicious machine — and pernicious it is — is the so-called "Humankind Empire of Abh." They are a menace that continues to threaten the soundness of human society, and should we allow them to persist, they will swallow us and our society whole.

They are a menace we are compelled to destroy.

Quoth Representative Fitzdavid at the Central Council of the United Mankind.

Summary of CREST OF THE STARS 1

One fateful day, Jint's home planet suffered an incursion by an Abh fleet.

In the face of their demands for total capitulation, Jint's father, Planetary President Rock, acquiesced to Abh rule in exchange for being conferred a noble rank among them. As a result, Jint became the rare surface-born human who was legally an Abh, but not genetically. He and his line were incorporated into their vast interstellar empire, and so Jint was to board a spaceship headed toward its capital.

However, that ship was then ambushed by an enemy fleet, and Jint and a royal princess, Lafier, were sent off as the only two to escape, bidden toward the Sfagnoff Marquessate on a small conveyance ship.

The two made a pit stop at the Febdash Barony to refuel, only to find themselves confined there by a nefarious agent.

Characters

Jint

...... Son of the President of the planet Martin

Lafier

...... Trainee Starpilot in the Abh Empire's Star Forces, as well as the Empress's granddaughter

Clowar

...... Ruler of the Febdash Barony

Sroof

...... Clowar's father, and former Baron of Febdash

Sehrnye

...... Servant vassal of the Febdash Baron's Estate

Entryua Reie

...... Police Inspector of the Lune Beega Criminal Investigation Department

Keitt

...... Military Police Captain of the Peacekeepers

Lamagh

...... the Empress of the Abh

Chapter 1: The Homemaker's Office of the Baron's Manor

The year was 136 in the *faibdachoth* (the Febdash calendar). However, each solar revolution at this particular **barony** was short enough to measure around a third of the cosmic standard.

In other words, it was quite young for a nation.

And make no mistake, though the citizenry numbered a paltry 50, the **Febdash Barony** was a nation unto itself. While technically a part of the **Empire**, it had accrued its own storied history unperturbed by outside currents or the affairs that swayed the Empire's hub.

Granted, there was almost no disturbance to speak of that year, and consequently, nothing to give life there much zest.

But now, things were different. Now, a pair of visitors were trying to shatter the peace.

One of those visitors, Jint, **Noble Prince of the Countdom of Hyde**, had been tossed into the same chamber as the former **baron**, who was also trapped there.

"Look over there, boy." The **former Baron of Febdash** pointed at the thick marble door. "That's where they dragged you in from."

"What exactly was going on when that happened?" asked Jint.

"I was lost in my meditations — I spend most of the day meditating, with a bottle of booze for company, mind you. Then I hear the door opening! Thing hadn't opened in a good 20 years. For such a momentous occasion, I'd skip my own funeral, so I jumped to check it out, only to see ya on an auto-stretcher inching your way inside."

"That's it? Me on an auto-stretcher? Nobody else?"

"Oh yeah, there were two **servants** behind ya — that is to say, out in the hallway. And they were packing heat, too. Not that they'd ever be sticking 'em on a **former baron**, but guns they had. Ya know, for some reason, I've never been able to relax when I'm around people who're armed. Anyway, as I glued my gaze on your stretcher, it stopped right in front of me. Gave me the heebie-jeebies. Meanwhile, the ladies were dead silent, and stood there stock still. They looked at me like they wanted me to do something, but they didn't bother saying *what*. Not ones to divulge much, lemme tell ya! Could've found work as secret agents!"

"Then what?" Jint prodded.

"Well, I figured they wanted me to have you and the stretcher part ways, so I whipped up the energy in these old bones of mine and laid ya down on the floor. Soon as I did, the thing took its leave, and the door closed. And my dear son's **servants** stayed frozen and mute the whole time. I'd wager they're still standing there on the other side of the door as we speak. They must positively adore us."

"So, I was out cold all throughout, huh." Jint had to periodically anchor the conversation, or else the old man would take the conversation to some uncharted places no one could predict.

"Ya were indeed, boy. I even thought ya could be dead. Maybe my offspring's been thinking of just making this place into a mortuary once I died, and he jumped the gun a little with you. That's what was running through my head until I saw you were twitching in your sleep. Then I knew you were alive. And easy to sympathize with, what with those two escorting ya. Then I whipped my old bones up once again and carried ya to bed. I was holding out hope that a spot of rest might change your personality, too. But when ya came to, ya grabbed me by the collar and started bawling at me for answers, like a cat that'd just nabbed its kittens' kidnappers red-handed…"

"At no point did I grab you by the collar, nor did I ever *bawl* at you," Jint reminded him.

"I was just expressing how startled I was, that's all. If you're gonna pick me apart like that, then what was it all for? I whipped up my old bones *two whole times* for ya."

"I'm sorry," he said, though in truth he'd have liked it if Sroof acknowledged how relatively calm he'd been under fire.

"Wow, **boy.** Let it be said that the way ya swallow everything is your greatest treasure."

And, having lauded Jint so, Sroof proceeded to show him around their zone of confinement. However, unlike the **patrol ship** *Gothelauth*'s interior, there wasn't much of interest to see here, so it took nary a moment to run through it all. They had access to a washroom and bath, a kitchen, and a warehouse-cum-repair room for the **automatons**, all located across five separate rooms. A small garden lay at zone's center, surrounded by the various rooms connected to it and to each other by corridors.

"I don't see any windows anywhere," murmured Jint, after crossing into the last of the rooms, the living room. A window might have served as a means of escape.

"Course not," said Sroof. "Even if there was one, we're surrounded by the **cultivation ranch**, so it wouldn't exactly be breathtaking scenery. Unless you'd enjoy watching the meat grow in the culture tanks, in which case something must've made a *deep* damn impression on ya when you were a wee one."

"Oh no, trust me, I have no desire to watch meat grow," gainsaid Jint. He had to wonder whether Sroof had forgotten all about The Escape Plan.

"In the void of space, this right here's far more practical than windows." Sroof worked some controls in a corner of the room, and the walls reflected imagery of a **landworld** vista. A mountain jutted tall and stately, capped white with snow. The room's vantage point was set to be level with its apex. Drawing nearer to the wall, a viewer could look down upon all the other surrounding peaks. Clouds were rolling around each mountain's foot. Looking up, on the other hand, greeted the viewer with a sky so blue one could almost see it reaching the ends of the galaxy.

"Impressive," said Jint, deciding that it couldn't hurt to humor the **former baron**'s digression momentarily.

"You're impressed by *this* old thing? What backwater world did *you* crawl out of?"

"No," huffed Jint, "not the device. The scenery."

"Whoops, sorry 'bout that," he said, though without a trace of sincerity in his voice.

"Wait a sec, isn't this scene a little unnatural? If the clouds are that far down, that'd place it above the stratosphere. No way the sky would be this blue this high up."

"Ya must be of **landworld** upbringing if you noticed that. Abhs, they're under all sorts of misconceptions when it comes to that stuff."

"Then this is what, art? An Abh fantasy?"

"It's *Delbisecsec*. A videographer who worked during *Baïc Rüécotr* (Pre-Imperial History, or P.H.) times, known for realistically reproducing **landworld** landscapes."

"You mean the *Goc Ramgocotr* (Space Roving Age)?"

"Yep."

"Then I can hardly blame them." For that was the era whereby the Abh plied between each isolated colony, with trade as their livelihood. It was little wonder how their grasp of the natural world might slip away.

"Delbisex entitled this piece '*Gamh Laca*' (Tall Mountain). Bit boring, though. I'd give it a different name," said Sroof. "I'd call it '*Bar Lepainec*'."

"**'Pride of the Abh'**?"

"Think about it. There ain't nothing else that can express their pride as accurately as this panorama," the old man expounded. "Recognizing your own nobility on a personal level is all you need. No need to go around advertising it, and still less need to be assured of it by others. It doesn't matter how humble your role is in life, as long as your self-regard is higher than anybody else's. High enough to look down on Her Majesty the Empress, even. Get that into your head, and no matter how highfalutin' the people ya meet, they'll never seem like anything more than extras who're there to set the stage for ya. Funnily enough, I heard that whenever an Abh meets somebody who has no pride, they don't know how to handle it. Though I guess that ain't limited to pride 'as an Abh'; it's about *any* sort of pride."

Suddenly he was roaming around the living room aimlessly. "Not that my shameful excuse of an heir seems to understand any of that! He's no tall mountain, no, he won't go near one. He's seen fit, instead, to dig a deep ol' pit by the mountain. Takes solace in being higher than the deepest lows. I may be a Lander genetically, but I'm sure as hell more Abh in spirit than that twit."

Jint once, and only once, had laid eyes on a bear. It was at a **Vorlash Countdom** zoo. Jint was staring at the bear, since at first it had been simply pacing its cage in its discontent, but for reasons only it could ever know, it flew into a rage and flung itself into the tempered glass that separated it from him. Naturally, the only damage sustained was to the beast's claws and fangs, but

Jint would go on to relive that episode occasionally in his nightmares, waking up in a cold sweat.

And Sroof was currently more than reminiscent of that bear. Only this time, there was no barrier to protect him.

"Um, sorry to bother you, Lonh-*Lymr Raica*," he addressed him properly. "But I think we should go about crafting an escape plan sometime soon."

"Right, of course." Sroof nestled into a couch, looking a tad drained. "**Boy**, if there's anything ya oughta take from this, it's that if you're Abh, you've gotta instill a sense of nobility and pride in your kids before all else. That said, ya don't need to *tell* 'em that. It's more like a contagion; just mill around and believe you me, they'll catch it. Unfortunately, that means I didn't have any real pride inside me. I learned what the pride of the Abh entails while fumbling in the dark, and tried to express that idea to him directly. Ya can see how that turned out. First things first, you've gotta be a noble soul. *Embody* pride, and it'll pour out naturally in every little thing ya do. Then your *golciac* (successors) will learn by example what the meaning is of Abh pride."

"I'll keep that in mind." He knew it just might be useful advice.

If, that is, he had a future ahead of him to begin with.

"Now then, what say we get to hatching our little scheme? Got any ideas on how we make a break for it?"

"Can these walls be smashed open?" Jint lightly tapped the wall that was still displaying Delbisex's *Tall Mountain*. While the former baron didn't have anyone waiting on him, he was attended by a multitude of **automatons**. Perhaps it wasn't impossible to knock down a wall using some of them.

"Even if we could break through one, we oughtn't. We'd face a hell of a time leaving without getting spotted from the **ranch**."

"Gotcha." Jint figured it was a long shot, so he wasn't too devastated. "Wait, how do you get your food? From that door, right?"

"No." The **former baron** shook his head. "Remember the huge fridge in the kitchen? The one built into the wall? Thing's two-layered. Once every ten days, the boxes inside it travel their dedicated passageway. Then they come back full of fresh grub, toiletries, stuff like that."

"Could we maybe hide in one of those boxes?"

"'Fraid not. They went to restock just yesterday. I don't think we could make 'em move all that quickly even if we grew extra mouths. Unless you don't mind waiting?"

It was Jint's turn to shake his head. "We can't set them in motion from here?"

"Whaddya think?" said Sroof, oddly prideful. "I'm being held here."

"How about we remove the boxes, or I dunno, break them, and follow the passageway—"

"Can't say that idea's a winner, **boy**. Where the boxes are headed, there's another door on that side, too. Trying to open it from within could wind up snapping our bones. My son's the suspicious type. He's probably on the lookout for any half-eaten frozen shrimp that might escape, let alone us. I wouldn't place my bets on the box route if I were you. Got any better ideas?"

"Oh, I know!" Jint said with a snap of the fingers. "What about the trash slot? We could just slip through and—"

"If I recall, there's a thresher installed at some point of the chute. Ya might be mincemeat by the time you make it to the garbage heap. And it's pretty hard to walk anywhere when you're a pile of gore. Although, if turning into goop's robbed ya of the will to do anything at all, I wouldn't judge."

"Ugh…" Jint hung his head. "Do you have any ideas? You must've thought about it before, right? About escaping?"

"Course I have. It's perfect for killing time. Everybody and their cousin's mulled over those ideas before. That's the only reason I'm able to poke holes in 'em so quickly."

"Yeah, I kind of gathered as much," said Jint, crossing his arms. "What's the procedure for emergencies?"

"You mean like me getting sick? I'd probably contact 'em using the **teletransceiver** and have 'em come over. Ain't ever happened before, though."

"You mean we've got a **teletransceiver**!?" Hope sprung in Jint's chest, only to retreat once again. "Oh, that must be the com that only connects to the **homemakers' office**."

"That's the one. They most likely won't let us talk to *Fïac Lartnér*, either. I mostly just use it to complain about the food."

"Okay, fine, so then one of us fakes being sick, or we cause a fire, or…"

"Gotta say, **boy**, I was hoping for a lot more from an adaptable young lad like you."

"It's no good?"

"It ain't no good, no. No idea why, but I'm as hearty as they come. Never been sick in my life, really. Then I fall ill right around when you're here? My son has many faults, but he's no fool. It'd raise his guard for sure."

"What if I do it, though? Pretend I'm frail and prone to sickness…"

"Hmmm… But that's assuming he cares whether ya live or die anyhow."

When Jint realized how true that was, he plunged into a very black mood.

"He probably wishes I'd just bite it already, too," said Sroof, driving the final nail.

"I guess starting a fire's a dumb idea, too, then…"

"So it is." The former baron nodded gravely.

They were at an impasse, unable to come up with anything else. Jint thought he'd need a change of pace before the answer could come to him.

Jint bade him adieu and exited out into the hall.

He made a revolution walking around the central pond while admiring the flowers. Situated at the pond's very center was a circular islet, narrow enough to squeeze in at most ten people. A white bridge in the shape of a rainbow spanned the expanse, though it was probably just a model.

He peered into the pond, curious whether any creatures dwelled in its depths, but he couldn't spot anything swimming. Alas, no bright ideas bubbled up, either, and he soon grew tired of staring at the pond's waters.

He turned his gaze up to the ceiling. It was a dome, about 500 *dagh* tall at its highest point, and painted sky blue.

Squinting, he could make out a faint line etched in the dome's apex. A circular line. Too like an entrance.

"Lonh-*Lymr Raica*!" cried Jint to the old man in the living room.

"What?" He stepped in and stood beside Jint.

"What is that?" Jint pointed up at the circle. "That **pressure door**-looking circle, see it?"

"Oh, that." He nodded. "That there's the *baudec* (circular door) that leads to the **pier**."

"To the **pier**? But this isn't the **spaceport** zone…"

"This whole sector was originally a welcoming hall for guests of honor. Used to be an **elevator-tube** on that island and everything," he said, pointing.

Now that he'd mentioned it, Jint saw how the door was located exactly above the islet.

"It was designed to allow visitors to relax upon touching down through contact with some landworld nature. My mother, she loved the whole concept. Thing is, the occasion never came. Nobody ever stopped by. So my sad sack of a son converted the place into my prison. He took down the **elevator**, leveled half of the hall, and tacked on some new rooms."

"Is that **door** still operational?"

"You bet it is. And if it's operable manually, then we can open it from the inside. We'd need to destroy the safety, but that shouldn't be too hard. But what are ya cooking up in that head of yours?"

"Isn't it obvious!?" he shouted feverishly. "That's our way outside!"

"Outside? 'Outside' is *space*. The vacuum of space."

Jint's silence lasted mere seconds. "Then we walk along the **manor**'s roof until we make it to the **conveyance ship**. Next, we enter the ship for a bit, and then head back toward the **orbital manor**…"

Pity gleamed in the **former baron**'s eyes. "There ain't any *gonœc* (pressure suits) around here. Or have the Abh managed to suffuse all of space with breathable air while I've been stuck here struggling to kill time?"

"W-Wait, hold on," said Jint, refusing to give up, "they say people can survive for a short amount of time in a vacuum…"

"And do ya know where the **ship**'s parked?"

"Yeah, at the **spaceport**, of course… Oh."

"So ya see now," said Sroof. "The **port**'s a long ways away from here. You could be infused with all of humanity's good luck and stamina, and it'd still be impossible."

"But what if it's moored someplace close by? Can't rule it out…" Jint clung to his last mad shred of hope for dear life. "Let's scout it out, and check to see if it's closer than not…"

"Sorry, but that ain't in the cards. The **elevator** had the **air lock room** in it. The instant we open that **door**, this zone's air'll leak out."

"We'll just shut it again!"

"Don't be stupid. Think about the air current that'd produce. It's a manual door, so it ain't powered by anything. Closing it again is outta the question. Besides, that idea hinges far too much on blind luck. You can put your own life on the table, but I wouldn't. And you're the one who hates gambling, ain't ya?"

"Uh-huh." Crestfallen, Jint slumped to the ground at the pond's edge. Despair racked his mind. Would he be forced to play nice with this old man, always to be trapped in the palms of the **Baron of Febdash**? The **former baron** was pleasant enough, but Jint wasn't about to sign up to share the rest of his life with him.

Plus, there was Lafier to think about. Was she all right? If the **Baron** had any sense to speak of, he'd never lay a finger on a **royal princess** of the **Empire**. And yet… would a sane person detain a **soldier** in the middle of a mission?

"That's it… the **ship** just needs to come to the **door**," Jint muttered, half to himself. "To *us*."

"Clearly. That's what the door is there for. For boarding. But how'll we get it here? Have ya got some mystic powers as-yet undiscovered by man?"

"Would you shut up and let me think!?" Jint snapped. Taken aback himself, he looked up at the former baron. "I'm sorry, I got carried away…"

"It's okay," said the old man calmly. "I was being snarky, despite my years. I'm sorry, **boy**. I know this is a pressing crisis to you."

"That's right. This is important," Jint concurred.

"In any case, ya oughta forget about the **door**. Got any other ideas?"

"Best not move!" said Lafier, brandishing her **lightgun**. "This place is now under **Star Forces** occupation!" And there was Sehrnye, training her own gun right beside her.

The homemakers' office was quite spacious. One wall was projecting a vista with the star of Febdash at the center, while ever-shifting numbers and graphs danced across another. Meanwhile, three **servants** were working three rows of **consoles**.

"What in the stars!?" The lady (who seemed to be the supervisor) cast her eyes on the intruders. "*Fïac Lartnér*. Along with Sehrnye."

"Hands up, Greda!" yelled Sehrnye.

"What's the meaning of this nonsense!?" Baffled, Supervisor Greda watched Sehrnye intently.

"I am a **Trainee Starpilot** of the **Imperial Star Forces**, *Ablïarsec Néïc Dubreuscr Bœrh Parhynr Lamhirh.*"

"Yes, I'm well aware," said Greda, visibly flummoxed.

The other two were wearing the same expression. They glanced at each other, then shot Sehrnye an inquisitive look, as if to say: *What is this farce? Is this the kind of prank* **Imperials** *entertain themselves with? How excessive. How deeply unamusing.*

It was all too clear that the **servants** here hadn't come to grips with the situation, either. Yet Lafier could hardly back down now.

Sensing her own resolve to fight was dangerously close to flagging, Lafier rekindled it by declaring: "The **Star Forces** have hereby seized the *Bandhorh Garicr Lyméctr Faibdacr* (Homemakers' Office of the Febdash Baron's Manor). I require all of you to raise your hands and stand up slowly."

They did as they were ordered.

Lafier advanced incrementally away from the door, her back to the wall. There was no way to know when the **Baron** would arrive with armed backup.

Sehrnye tightly flanked Lafier with a poise that belied the fact this was her first time holding a weapon.

"Your Highness, *Fïac Lartnér*," Greda started, "Why are you doing this? If you have some task to carry out, surely you could have simply ordered us directly?"

"Then here are my orders. I demand to be allowed contact with the **former baron**. Better yet, I demand he and *Ïarlucec Dreur Haïder* be freed."

Greda's face immediately stiffened. "That is prohibited, and I'm afraid that I'm not authorized to grant that request."

"In that case, you can see why I needed to take this place by force, *gosucec-rann*," said Lafier. "I enjoin you to forget the **Baron**'s orders and get to it. Now."

"Don't move, Cfaspia!" shrieked Sehrnye, firing her **lightgun** out of nowhere.

The laser missed its mark completely, hitting the projection of the blazing star of Febdash on the wall like a bull's eye instead.

"Dammit!" The **servant** named Cfaspia trained the gun she'd drawn from under her **console** on Sehrnye. Lafier wasted no time shooting Cfaspia's hand.

"Yargh!" It dropped from her grip. Sehrnye darted to pick it up off the floor and proffer it to Lafier.

The **royal princess** stole a glance at it, and ascertained that it was a **stungun**.

Lafier signaled Sehrnye with her eyes: *If there are any other weapons, you'd best ferret them all out.* Sehrnye copied loud and clear, and proceeded to separate the ladies from their respective consoles so she could carefully inspect them.

"Tell us what's going on, Sehrnye!" said one of them.

"You won't believe it, Arsa..." The two were friends, and so Sehrnye happily launched into an explanation.

"Do it now," said Lafier, gun still square on Greda.

Greda was wide-eyed with disbelief. "You really mean it, don't you, **Your Highness**."

"I know not what rumors you may have heard about the Abliar family, but we do not fire at people for fun," she replied.

"I understand." A sigh. "I understand, **Your Highness**. However, I regret to inform you that it isn't possible to open the door to the Retirement Zone."

"Is that true?"

"It's no lie. Without **my lord**'s permission, we can't open it, not even from here. Not unless my lord comes here, uses his own **EM crest-key**, and enters the *saigh cimena* (passcode) of his own volition."

"And there's absolutely no other way?" pressed Lafier.

"I swear it," Greda affirmed.

Though Lafier had no recourse to detect whether she was telling the whole truth.

"Then what of communicating with them? You can't tell me that's prohibited, too."

"You may, by all means." Greda threw up her hands and stepped away from the console.

"Please wait a moment while I connect you."

"No sudden movements, no funny business."

"Yes, I know." Slowly, Greda sidled aside, and reached for the **teletransceiver**. Unlike most other call devices, it was fixed to an otherwise barren wall.

It was then the door opened.

Lafier flashed the muzzle in its direction.

"There you are, *Fïac Lartnér*!" The **Baron** barged inside, a handful of armed **servants** at his call. Peering into the muzzle pointed his way, he froze in place, stupefied.

"What excellent timing, **Baron**," said Lafier. "I was just informed that your **wristgear** is what we need to free Jint. I suggest you cooperate."

"What are you doing!? Shield me!" he barked at his small contingent. Arms brandished and at the ready, the servants formed a wall between him and Lafier.

"You can't be serious!" cried Sehrnye. "You'd dare point guns at **Her Royal Highness**!?"

The servants flinched at that remark, wincing for all to see.

"Sehrnye, you traitor!" The Baron thrust an accusatory finger at her and opened his mouth as though to issue an order. Lafier promptly stepped in front of her to protect her.

"**Imperial citizen** *Faigdacpéc Sérnaïc* is under *my* guardianship now."

Sehrnye gasped behind her, overjoyed. "I'm so happy, **Your Highness**!"

"Damn!" The Baron's visage twisted into something less handsome. "**Your Highness**, I am appalled! Did I not give you the most royal of receptions!?"

"And now I'd appreciate being allowed a royal exit. You can have my sincerest gratitude after we've peacefully taken our leave."

"I cannot allow that. And I do believe I've told you why."

"I believe I told *you*, Baron: I'm getting out of here, one way or the other. Now bring Jint to me, and posthaste."

"You must mean Lonh-*Ïarlucer Dreur Haïder*," said the **Baron**, his brows knitted with resentment. "I cannot."

"Why?"

"My father is currently catering to him."

"Then let me convene with your dear father."

"That, too, is not to be."

"And why might that be!?"

"That might be due to family matters whose details I feel no obligation to reveal. Not even to a highly insistent royal princess such as **Your Highness**."

"I have no interest in your family matters! I just want to see Jint!" Lafier's sight, the red dot on the Baron, flew up to his head. "If it's a fight you want, **Your Excellency**, shall we get started?"

"You'd never!" he spat. "If you kill me, then there'll be no freeing *Ïarlucec Dreur Haïder*!"

"'Freeing' him, **Baron**? So, he *is* being imprisoned."

"Hmph. Fine, I'll tell **Your Highness** what you want to hear. I have indeed imprisoned *Ïarlucec Dreur Haïder*. I admit it. But need I remind you? This is *my* **manor.** You have no right to find fault with the way I run my own house, *Fïac*. Nor any right to harm me!"

"Oh, I can harm you. And I promise you I'll rescue him, even if you make it happen the hard way. Because all I need is to shred this **manor** of yours to ribbons."

That was no bluff, either. Lafier had never been one to utter anything she had no intention of following through on.

The **Baron**, for his part, could sense the depth of her determination. Voice verging on shrill, he replied: "Very well. I too am an **Abh noble**. I do not yield to intimidation. Do what you will, **Royal Princess**." But he was feeling the pressure. His eyes scanned the room.

All of the **servants**, including those guarding him, were in a dither; in their world, a clash between Abhkind was vanishingly rare. Had the interloper been some normal **gentry**, they would not have had such cause to waver, but when it came to the bearer of an Imperial's **titles**, they hesitated to so much as point a **stungun** her way.

Among their number, Sehrnye alone was in high spirits.

"**Your Highness**, it looks like *Faigdacpéc Arsac* will be joining our side!" she reported. "In exchange for employment by the **House of Clybh**!"

"Sure." Lafier nodded, eyes never straying from the Baron. "I shall accept her on the same terms I accepted you."

The Baron stamped his feet: "This is a flagrant violation of all that is decent! You're all traitors, every last one of you!"

"Is your little tantrum over now, **Baron**?" Lafier trigger finger tensed. "I expect you to open the door to the Retirement Zone, or the Prison Zone, or what have you, before the count of three."

"I refuse!" And with that, he turned tail.

Lafier hesitated and lost her chance to shoot. That moment was all it took for him to flee. The rest of his guard followed after him, and soon they were all gone.

"Wait!" Sehrnye made to give chase.

"It's okay, Sehrnye," said Lafier, stopping her. If she had made good on her promise to shoot him, the **servants** defending him would hardly have remained so docile. They would definitely have thrown themselves into battle to protect their lord. With only two **lightguns** to their many, their prospects for victory had been hazy.

"Yes, **Your Highness**. What do we do now?"

"What do you two plan to do?" Lafier sized up the pair who had yet to plant their flag.

Greda faltered in her response. "I… My duty is to protect this place, so… as long as **my lord** is absent, I can and shall accede to **Your Highness's** orders."

"Well, count me out!" said Cfaspia, cradling her own injured hand. "I'm a servant of the **His Excellency the Baron**, and always will be!"

"Makes sense. You were always one of his favorites," said Arsa. That barb was almost dripping with years of pent-up resentment.

"Why don't you run right off to your beloved Lonh-*Lymr*, then?" Sehrnye jeered.

"That's enough, *gosucec*-rann." Lafier stared and Cfaspia and stated, "You need medical attention, so leave us."

Cfaspia stood up and, with still-defiant eyes, gave her a bow. "**Your Highness**'s comportment is beyond the pale."

"To me, your lord's actions were well beyond it." Done with her, Lafier shooed her away.

Cfaspia tucked in her chin with irritation and exited the room.

"Now if you would carry out your orders," Lafier addressed Greda. "And tell me, do you know where the **Baron** went?"

"I'll run a search, **Your Highness**," said Arsa, who began working her console's controls.

"**Your Highness**, they're on the line," said Greda, handing her the call device, an audio-only model.

"Is this the **Former Baron of Febdash**?" asked Lafier. But it was not Sroof's voice that greeted her.

"That you, Lafier?"

"Jint!" Lafier shocked even herself with her near-squeal. "Are you okay!?"

"Yeah, I guess I'm fine. How're things on your end?"

"I'm all right. But never mind that, you need to be on guard! The **Baron** might be headed toward you."

"The Baron? To do what?"

Lafier couldn't be sure whether he was just that dense, or whether he was the type to take things so calmly that it circled right back around to candidacy for natural selection, but she decided she'd interpret that reply in the more flattering way.

"I admire your unflappability, Jint, but most likely, to kill you."

"......Boy, you really, really suck at lightening a guy's mood. What do we do? We haven't got any weapons."

"Is there no means of escape?"

"We're at a loss."

"I surmised as much."

"Thanks for the vote of confidence. But we can make it out of here with your help. Hate to ask, but could you take the **conveyance ship** over here? If you could do that for us, then things might just go our way."

"Where do I take it?"

"Right above us. There's a **pier** up there."

Lafier had to stop herself from diving into a series of questions.

"**Your Highness**" interrupted Arsa. "I've pinpointed Lonh-*Lymr*. He's at the *Chicrh Blységar* (Space Traffic Control Room)."

"Did you hear that, Jint? It seems the **Baron** hasn't the time to murder you at the moment."

"He never makes any time for me," quipped Jint, sighing with relief.

Suddenly, the walls went dark. Half of the numerals and diagrams gamboling across them disappeared.

"What happened?" asked Lafier.

At first, Arsa didn't answer, her fingers dancing furiously across the console. Finally, she lifted her head. "The functionalities this room shares with the **Space Traffic Control Room** have been taken over by them, *Fïac*. But it'll all be okay. I closed off part of the input of the **compucrystal net**. That means we should be able to maintain our present conditions despite Lonh-*Lymr*'s directives."

"Which functionalities did they take over?"

"Remote management of the **antimatter fuel factory** and the **fuel's storage planetoid,** monitoring of intra-system floating bodies, intra-system communications — That sort of thing."

"Can we control take-off from the **pier**?"

Arsa was loath to tell her: "I'm sorry, but that's always been restricted to the **Space Traffic Control Room**."

"No matter. We'll manage." Military vessels were equipped with the ability to lift off without **Space Traffic Control**'s aid.

"I'm going to the **conveyance ship**."

"Yes, please leave everything here to us," replied Sehrnye. "Incidentally, Cfaspia's was the only weapon in the office."

"Why were those **servants** carrying weapons to begin with?"

"They're the **Baron**'s favorites. And by 'favorites,' I mean..." Sehrnye didn't hide her disgust. "His *lovers*. They're the only ones with the right to bear arms. And that's not the only privilege they enjoy either, like how during mealtimes they're allowe—"

"Yes, quite." Lafier interrupted Sehrnye's impending diatribes. Every second was of the essence. Speaking back into the teletransceiver:"Jint, I'm leaving now."

"I'll be waiting," he said, his words full of a puppy-like trust in her.

Lafier hung up. They'd continue their chat later.

"*Fïac Lartnér*, I've opened up all the doors leading to the landing lot," said Arsa, thus making her conscientiousness known, and in short order at that.

"You have my thanks," she nodded to Arsa. Then, facing Greda: "I'd like to speak to Jint from inside the **ship**. Is the **teletransceiver** connected to the general line?"

"I don't think so..." Greda tilted her head. "If I recall correctly, the way it's constructed makes it independent from the general line. As such... I can only assume it'd be impossible without some work done. Albeit, that work wouldn't be particularly difficult... but still..."

"Is there another way?" They had no time to waste doing construction work.

"You could just take the **teletransceiver** to the Retirement Zone," suggested Arsa.

"Do you think you could do that?"

Sehrnye clapped her hands together. "The *Chicrh Spaurhotr Mata* (2nd Service Pantry!)."

"What?"

"There's a food transport passageway that runs from the **2nd Service Pantry** to Lonh-*LymrRaica*'s Retirement Zone," she explained. "We could use it to deliver the **teletransceiver** to them. I'm not in charge of the area, but I have done some menial labor there, so I know the kitchen."

"So, it can be done," said Lafier, double-checking.

"Yes," Sehrnye nodded.

"Are there any extra **teletransceivers**?"

"Yes, if you don't mind using my **wristgear**, Your Highness," offered Sehrnye.

"You don't mind?"

"Heavens me, of course not! Regardless of what may happen to me, I would sacrifice anything for **Your Highness,** let alone one or two **wristgears**..."

"Thank you," she said, plugging Sehrnye's zealous outpouring. "Your **wristgear**'s number, if you would." She registered Sehrnye's number into her own **wristgear**.

"Okay, allow me to head to the Service Pantry. With Arsa's special skills, she should man the office," said Sehrnye, apparently forgetting all about Greda. She was now clutching to her chest the device that moments before had adorned her wrist, as it was now her treasure.

"Be careful." But Lafier immediately regretted saying that. There was a 100% chance it would trigger a torrent of overblown emotion in her. And sure enough:

"Oh, *Fïac Lartnér*, what an absolute honor..." Predictably, Sehrnye seemed likely to collapse into a puddle of tears on the spot.

I wonder what Jint does whenever this happens, Lafier thought to herself.

No, this was no time for idle contemplation. "I'm leaving. Good luck."

"**Your Highness**, wait!" Sehrnye dialed back her own storm of weeping and rushed over to her. "Please take this. Lonh-*Ïarlucer Dreur* will be needing a weapon, too."

Lafier's eyes fell on the **lightgun** she was being handed. "But what about your own defense? Surely you need a weapon yourself?"

"I have the one Cfaspia dropped," she said, indicating her **stungun**.

"Understood." Lafier took it, holstered it in her **waistsash**, and dashed out of the Homemakers' Office.

Chapter 2: *Bar Gairsath* (The Style of the Abh)

You fool! You tremendous, doddering fool! Remorse was driving daggers through the **Baron of Febdash**'s heart.

Why did I let down my guard? Why did I take such half-measures, so totally unlike an Abh?

He should have either rushed her departure immediately (as was his first idea), or else thrown her under strict lock and key without worrying about the consequences down the line.

Having shaken off any and all tipsiness, his hatred of the **servants** who betrayed him intensified as he brooded. *Why are they putting so much faith in the **Empire**? Don't they realize that the Empire could very well give this territory up as lost?*

But the biggest shock of all was the surprising fragility of his reign. The maid-staff he'd believed would obey him to the ends of the universe instead changed sides the day a **royal princess** dropped by.

What was once diamond-clad in his mind was now hollowest glass. It had taken practically nothing to utterly shatter.

"But you, you're all with me, aren't you?" the **Baron** bayed at the **Space Traffic Control Room**'s assembled servants, who were the four that had flanked him plus the two who'd already been there.

"'With you,' as in, our *loyalties*, my lord?" asked **Space Traffic Control Officer** *Faigdacpéc Müinich*.

"Yes, that's what I mean!"

"Have no doubt," she consoled him.

"I'm upset you would even ask that, my lord," piped in *Faigdacpéc Bersac*, Captain of their makeshift combat unit.

"Y-Yes, yes of course, you are my only true **servants**. You'll follow me through thick and thin, won't you? Even with a **royal princess** as our enemy."

"We'd stay by your side if **Her Majesty the Empress** herself declared war on you," averred Bersa.

However, her readiness to declare that only made him think it a shallow platitude.

No, I must rid myself of this paranoia! The **Baron** swallowed down his gnawing suspicion. He needed naught but to remind everyone who was king. Then the **servants** would think better of their little change of heart and swear fealty to him once again.

In his head, the Baron began to select which servants he could expect to be loyal. If he set his standards too high, then there were not many candidates to speak of.

"This is the **Homemakers' Office** speaking. Attention all **servant** staff," resounded Arsa's voice.

"What the!?" But the Baron hardly needed to inquire.

"It's the speakers," replied Mwineesh, equally perfunctorily.

"There is dissension in the **manor**. I repeat, an incident is currently unfolding. As for why, **His Excellency Our Lord** has unduly stranded **Her Highness the Royal Princess**'s **conveyance ship** while she is on a military mission. All she wishes is to leave this **orbital manor** at once, alongside the **His Excellency the Noble Prince of the Countdom of Hyde** with whom she arrived. As such..."

"**Compucrystals!**" The Baron attempted to stop the broadcast in its tracks by connecting to the **compucrystal net** by means of his **wristgear**. Yet he was greeted by an unfeeling response.

"Connecting to the **compucrystal net** is not possible."

"What!? Why!? I am the master of this manor!" The system was set up to recognize his voice as the one with top access.

"The main line **teletransceiver** is currently offline," explained the **wristgear**. "Please use a **terminal** kiosk."

The **Baron** clicked his tongue. "Tch!" This was undoubtedly the doing of the crowd still at the Homemakers' Office. "Activate the **terminal**," he ordered Mwineesh.

Meanwhile, Arsa's announcement was continuing apace. "...So please, my dear colleagues, let us all cooperate with **Her Highness**. After all, she has promised to set us up as **servants** to the House of *Clybh*. Then we can finally reach the **capital** of our dreams, *Lacmhacarh!*"

"What a load of rubbish!" said the Baron to his servants. "Don't buy into that nonsense. A **royal family** would never take in **vassals** so readily. Mwineesh, the **terminal**?"

"It's no use," she shrugged. "It's not connecting."

"Those damn traitors! How much do they intend to get in my way!?" He pointed at Bersa. "You lot, come with me. We'll use a different **terminal**. Mwineesh, you stay here and carry out your duties here."

"Please wait," said Mwineesh. "Someone has infiltrated the **conveyance ship**. It must be **Her Highness**."

"What did you say?" The Baron grimaced. If the ship achieved lift off, then he would be faced with a bitter choice.

Arsa's broadcast had reached Lafier's ears up until the moment she entered the **elevator-tube**.

She just had to go and say that, huh, thought Lafier, as she settled into the steerer's seat.

She didn't know whether it was a misunderstanding on the part of Sehrnye or Arsa, but it wasn't up to Lafier to choose the servants of the **Clybh family**. She thought she'd made that quite clear. It wasn't as though Lafier wished to be regarded as a bonehead incapable of guile, but telling such insipid lies left dents on her pride nonetheless.

Oh well. Her father had always told her that the words of **Imperials** were always interpreted in whichever way proved most convenient to the listener.

Lafier banished her embarrassment and linked up her **circlet**'s **access-cables** into the steering apparatus. Thus, she awakened to the structures beneath her.

What a comically *small*, miniscule world. The heat and light of Febdash's star blew from beyond this world's corners, while she basked in the sorely-missed twinkling of the stars from above.

She transferred the map info of the **Baron's manor** from the **wristgear** to the ship's **compucrystals**. Using the **pier**'s location as a landmark, she incorporated the map into her *frocragh* spatiosensory perception. The subsequent sensation made her feel as though she were looking through the floor (even though she knew it hadn't actually become transparent). Through her *frocragh*, she could now discern every wall and surface that divided up the estate's various zones.

Her **control gauntlet** equipped and ready, she commenced emergency take off procedures. The names of each onboard instrument hurtled across the main display screen at imperceptible speeds, until at last the glyphs meaning "**ALL CLEAR**" shone bright for her.

The only issue was the fact that the ship's landing gear was stuck into the dock. It wouldn't detach without **Space Traffic Control**'s say-so. Naturally, asking **Space Traffic Control** for help would be fruitless.

Therefore, Lafier didn't hesitate to leave the landing gear behind her. Though it would certainly make landing the ship inconvenient, there was no other option.

She sealed the **air lock** and fired up the jets. The ship disengaged from the dock.

She expanded her external-input *frocragh* to a radius of 10 *saidagh*, or 10,000 kilometers, and probed the surrounding astrospace. She could sense it — the **antimatter fuel planetoid** lay extremely close by.

Was it truly out of fuel, as the **Baron** claimed? No, that was obviously false, a lie fabricated on the spur of the moment to detain her. She would have needed **Space Traffic Control** to refuel on the docks, but she could refuel without their help if she sourced it directly from the **planetoid** itself. While it was a little dicey, she was confident she'd know what she was doing, given her **academy** training.

Should I stop to refuel?

Two paths, two choices: She could either comply with Jint's plea immediately, or refuel beforehand. It was not a choice she could make lightly.

She dialed Sehrnye's number into her wristgear. "It is not currently equipped," came its cold, robotic response.

Still...? Lafier was dismayed, but she collected herself in no time. *Then we refuel.* She directed the ship toward the **fuel storage planetoid**.

That was when the planetoid started zooming away. It had begun to accelerate toward Febdash's star.

Lafier pursued it. This ship's acceleration capabilities far outstripped it. Furthermore, games of space tag were a staple pastime among Abh children, and Lafier had been a particularly deft hand at catching her fleeing peers.

However, when she had closed half of the distance between them, the planetoid suddenly exploded. Charged particles bombarded the ship's bow. In a panic, Lafier expanded her *frocragh* by a factor of 100, and determined that faraway **fuel storage planetoids** were also silently detonating, one after the other. Their sun was now encircled by a veritable ring of explosions.

Given the speed of light, they had to have been directed to explode all at once.

The **fuel planetoids** weren't the only things to be lost. Her cylindrical thrusters had pushed her away from the **spaceport**, and now she was cruising via inertia. After she had distanced herself far enough away from the **orbital manor**, it, too, exploded — the **antimatter fuel** stored at the **spaceport** had been dumped.

I commend you, **Baron of Fedash**. The **Royal Princess**'s opinion of him improved. He had done nothing so roundabout as blowing each planetoid up individually. Instead, he had jettisoned every last molecule of **antimatter fuel** he could. Such was very much the style of the Abh.

It was a positively majestic proclamation of war, and Lafier was obliged to respond in the Abh manner as well. After she rescued Jint, she would ensure the Baron paid the ultimate price. For this day, he would die by her hand.

When first they met, she noticed his head was a slight bit too big compared to his shoulder width. It was a subtle defect that would go unnoticed by all except the Abh, versed as they were in the precepts of beauty. Yet his head was most certainly oversized. It was offensively ugly.

In fact, were the space above his shoulders to be relieved of that eyesore, the cosmos could breathe easy once again.

Lafier bade the ship retrace its path, and narrowed the scope of her *frocragh*. She searched for Jint's confinement zone as she approached the **manor**.

It didn't appear on the map, but there were certainly the vestiges of a pier in that zone. She took her time pacing toward the Confinement Zone's pier, thrusters at low speed like sighs in the wind.

Then, her **wristgear** beeped — call incoming.

"Lafier!" Jint shouted into the **wristgear** he'd just taken out of the refrigerator there.

Lafier's reply came instantly. "Jint, you must listen carefully. I can't touch down. Standard boarding procedure is impossible."

"What do you mean?" A faint anxiety shot through him.

"I mean… are there any *gonœc* (pressure suits) there? If so, it won't be an issue."

"Damn, I thought that's what you'd say," Jint groaned. "Nope, no **pressure suits**."

"That's a shame. But I'll be needing you to swim through space, then. I'll bring the ship as close as I can," she said casually. "At my signal, open the **door**. I'll drop a *careugec* (flexi-cord) from the **air lock room**."

"Thank you, sure," said Jint feebly.

There was no shortage of air in their sector, so it would take quite some time for that air to leak completely. If they didn't face too much difficulty, it would unfold not dissimilarly to an expedition up a tall mountain. But could it really go that smoothly? He wasn't sure he could get his hopes up.

He looked back to spy Sroof's expression, only to be met with a hung head.

"Why's it I get the feeling that keeping you company ain't so great for a man's health?"

"But you are gonna keep my company, right?" asked Jint.

"Even if I told ya otherwise, you'd go open the **door** anyways. And I don't plan on shriveling up any time soon."

"Yeah, probably would," concurred Jint understatedly.

"But from another angle, the honor of an audience with Her Highness the **Royal Princess** might be just the head-clearer I need."

"Oh, I don't doubt it. Since as long as we're together, one thing we'll never be is bored."

"I'm sure it'll be an adventure and a half for you. Meanwhile I'll just be reminded of how old and frail I am. But so be it, **boy**. I might as well go pack my bags now."

Straining against the **manor**'s artificial gravity, Lafier kept the conveyance ship at a safe distance. Almost directly below her and less than 100 *dagh* away lay the **door**.

She opened the **air lock room**'s **pressure door** and unreeled the **flexicord**, which was originally set up to extricate people caught adrift from the vacuum of space. That's why the cord's tip could be guided to an extent. Pulled in by the artificial gravity, the **cord**'s end came close to outright touching the **door**.

Lafier brought her lips to her **wristgear**. "Jint, it's in place."

"We're ready to go, too," he replied. His voice communicated his nervousness in spades.

"Keep away from the space underneath the **door**. I'm feeding the **cord** down."

"Got it."

"You two had best tell me as soon as you've established a firm grip, while there's still air to speak through. I'll start pulling you up that instant."

"If you'd be so kind."

"The **conveyance ship** has come into line over the Lonh-*LymrRaica*'s Retirement Zone," reported Mwineesh.

"So, they're not backing down." The **Baron** clenched his fists. He had taken refueling off the table by destroying the **fuel storage planetoids**. If that wasn't enough to cow the **royal princess**, then the only option left to him was the direct one:

Detaining Her Highness by gunpoint.

And, failing that, he would be forced — but willing — to dispatch her.

That was the last thing he wanted, of course, but now that the situation had spiraled so far out of his control, his hands were tied. The Baron couldn't acknowledge his own errors at this late date. He would safeguard his pride, even if it meant making an enemy of the entire **Empire**.

"We're leaving this place," he declared. "All of you, take up arms and follow me."

He knew she'd come to settle things, a prospect he welcomed with open arms.

A *cnécrr coüiciac* (cleaner bot) was clinging to the ceiling like a giant beetle. If it was acting as directed, its all-purpose robo-digits were clutching the emergency release lever to the **door**'s side.

"Ready?" asked the **former baron**.

"Ready."

"Right then," Sroof yelled at the **automaton**. "Crank it!"

Though they couldn't make out its digits' movements, still the **door** disappeared that very instant, laying bare the belly of the ship.

Their ears began ringing keenly as white mist enveloped them. The rapid depressurization had commenced.

The **flexi-cord** passed through the **circular door** like a small rocket, ramming smack into the pond at full speed.

Jint jumped feet-first into the pond. Sroof followed suit (and surprisingly nimbly for an old man). Feverishly, Jint cinched the **cord**'s ring over his left shoulder and under his right armpit. Then he verified whether Sroof was prepared.

Meanwhile, the water at their feet was already bubbling up into a low-temperature boil from the depressurization.

"LAFIIIER!" Jint screamed at the top of his lungs, hoping it'd carry through the dissipating air. "GO! PULL US UP!"

Not seconds later, he felt it jerk up against his armpit. The tips of his feet cleared the water.

The **cord** dragged them toward her at a maddeningly sluggish clip, but upon seeing how the rushing air was causing the cord to sway enough to kiss the rim of the **door**, he could hardly complain. Spending time in airless space did a body no good, but neither did slamming into the ceiling.

The ceiling zoomed closer and closer, and for a moment it seemed as though he'd hit the **door**'s rim, but it was thanks to the cord's slow pace that he managed to twist his body and move into position in time.

The dead of *dadh*, 3-space, fast approached! Nothing save for a thin layer of air separated Jint from the plane of the stars now. A layer of air that was attenuating by the second. It was akin to making out with a vacuum cleaner. He could feel his lungs deflating with a frightful distinctness.

Yet his naked space trek lasted nary a split-second, and before he could even digest this rarest of escapades, he found himself already sucked into the **air lock room**. That was not to say that his date with vacuums was over. The air lock room's interior was itself extremely close to a vacuum, and what scant air there was raced away to reach an even steadier state of stability.

QUICK, CLOSE IT! Jint mouthed, but no medium was there to transmit sound.

Dangling from the **air lock room**'s ceiling, he gazed upon the wide-open **pressure door** beneath him with abject fear. An eternity elapsed before it closed shut — an eternity of under a second. Life-giving air poured in from four separate vents, their jets clashing and forming a modest pocket of turbulence.

Jint gulped it down avidly, even as his ears were all but crying in pain from the extreme pressure shift. Nevertheless, as his violent heart palpitations simmered down, the realization that they'd truly pulled it off dawned alongside a profound sense of relief.

He released his **cord** bindings and clattered to the floor. While the air remained thin, he could breathe without trouble. He lent Sroof a hand and eased him down from the **cord**.

It was over now. Jint slumped down and leaned against the wall. He scowled and endured the stinging in his ears.

Sroof likewise slumped to the floor and heaved. He had indeed been hardy enough to withstand the trip, and was now feeling gracious enough not to voice the biting feedback he had every right to.

At last, the blue light flipped on to signal that the pressure had returned to standard levels.

The door to the **steering room** opened. Jint looked up. He'd have loved to celebrate their reunion with an emotional one-liner to remember, but his mind blanked apart from noting that this was the first time he'd ever seen her in her **long robe**.

"Hey, Lafier." Jint glanced at the silver bird spreading its wings across a field of deep crimson, and then on the **ornamental waistsash** the color of malachite. "That looks great on you."

He briefly pictured the princess glomping him — but that was a pipe dream.

"Are you hurt?" she asked, firmly planted in place.

"See for yourself." A tad disappointed, Jint lifted his hands for her to see.

"Good. It would be inconvenient if my precious cargo got himself injured."

Jint whispered into the **former baron**'s ear: "Now you see just how madly in love with me **Her Highness** is."

The Baron of Febdash was walking toward the boarding space. He'd added seven **servants** he deemed trustworthy to his original band of four, for a total of eleven encircling him. Among them was Cfaspia, her right hand wrapped in a bandage.

The **Baron** suddenly halted. It had become a mite harder to breathe, and it couldn't have just been a result of his nerves.

"What's the matter, **my lord**?" asked Bersa.

"Can't you see? The air, it's gotten thinner."

"Now that you mention it…"

"And I know exactly why, those little rots." The **Baron** called the homemakers' office through his **wristgear**. "Can you hear me, traitors?"

"Yes, **my lord**," came the reply, while shouting voices dueled in the background.

He couldn't make out what they were saying, but it wasn't difficult to guess. One among their number had to be the **servant** who had betrayed his trust.

"Greda, is this? You have some gall, calling me your 'lord' after stabbing me in the back!"

"…My apologies."

"It matters not. I assume the Retirement Zone has become depressurized?"

"That is correct."

"Have you a plan?"

"Yes, **my lo** — **Your Excellency**. We have sealed all of the atmospheric circulators."

"Is that it? What of the garbage disposal?"

"Ah!" Greda let out a small gasp. "I'm afraid that didn't occur to me."

"Of course it didn't. If you're going to stay stationed at the **homemakers' office**, then exercise caution. The air is steadily leaking."

"Please accept my sincerest apologies."

"I can't imagine it'll be a lark should the air run out, now will it? So get a move on!"

"But the garbage disposal ducts can't be sealed remotely. There's nothing we can do from here…"

"You dolt! Seal them manually. Wait, no, take out the outside workers and repressurize the Retirement Zone. Or did you think filthy rebels deserve better? Have you a proper brain in that skull of yours, or is it just storage space?"

"We were in disarray…"

"Like I care, you moron!" screamed the **Baron** a second time, before dropping the call. He was livid. Rebellion was the clearest of misdeeds — or at the very least, rebellion against him was.

The **princess** and her party had broken the air-sealing of the **Baron's manor** without thinking of the consequences, and his inept **servants** knew not how to deal with the mess that resulted. Unless he asserted control over the building, they would keep hurtling toward certain disaster. This was the Baron's castle, whether his maid-staff recognized that or not.

"Those fools may yet bungle their mission," he told the crowd of servants. "Let's make haste, and put on **pressure suits** before the atmosphere becomes inhospitable." Said clothing was stashed for emergency use in the landing lot.

Besides, there was also the matter of that decrepit dotard, who had likely fled the coop alongside that Lander. If he gained access to a terminal, the situation would grow even more dire.

Alas, but that he had gone senile.

Then, the Baron realized with astonishment: the conveyance ship was also equipped with a terminal. After all, if the ship's **compucrystals** were connected the estate's **compucrystal net** via an **information link**, it amounted to the same.

"Go to the landing lot, and should you see **Her Highness** there, restrain her immediately. Don't think of shrinking from the task, either; she may be of high rank, but in my domain, WE are the law," the **Baron** instructed Bersa.

"And what will you do, **my lord**?" replied Bersa, visibly worried.

"I shall be stepping outside for a moment. I may have a full-fledged fight on my hands."

Meanwhile, in the homemakers' office, another quarrel had emerged.

On one side were Sehrnye and Arsa, who had returned from the **2nd Service Pantry**. On the other side were three other **servants**, Cnyoosa, Semneh, and Lulune, who'd come after listening to the speaker announcement.

They traded heated arguments in a back-and-forth over whether they should pledge their loyalty to their lord or to their **Empire**. In fact, their ideological spat had gotten nigh indistinguishable from a simple mud-flinging match, the telephonic transceiver blaring incessantly to be put through all the while.

However, the servants who were proactive enough to rush toward the Baron's side didn't make up a large portion of the total. Instead, the majority remained more or less idle at their stations or in their personal rooms, craving nothing other than information as a desert wanderer might water.

Greda was the sole person carrying out her designated duties. The homemakers' office wasn't the only place in the **manor** where work duties were abandoned, either. Greda was a whirl of activity, picking up everyone's slack. To exacerbate things, half of the office's functionalities had been stripped from them. Those were the reasons the gravest change in the estate, the steady depressurization, evaded her notice.

And yet, why hadn't the **compucrystals** alerted her? Arsa's refusal to allow the **Baron** to tamper with the crystals must have accidentally deactivated some other vital functions as well. The woman did have a tendency to overdo things in her perfectionism.

Still, there was no time to investigate the cause.

"Listen up, everyone," said Greda, rising from her seat.

"What do you want, Greda? We're busy!" said Sehrnye, not even turning to face her.

"I'm busier than you are!" she roared.

The five of them blinked blankly and focused their attention on her.

Greda was considered a mild-mannered hand in this microcosm of theirs. More accurately, she was mocked behind her back as a timid sort who never expressed her own feelings or opinions. To the rest, Greda was a convenient office worker-bot on whom they could foist their more tedious tasks.

Yet this time, Greda had raised her eyes to meet theirs, raised her voice to be heard. It was no surprise that the other **servants** would be so taken aback.

"Would you make that blasted **teletransceiver** stop ringing?"

"Ah, right." Arsa did as she was ordered. A hush promptly fell upon the office.

As she continued to glower at her colleagues, Greda started her manor-wide announcement.

"This is the **Homemakers' Office** speaking. The whole building is currently undergoing depressurization. Do not use the garbage chutes for the time being. If you see any kind of open slot, please seal it shut. Use *dibec* (sealing glue) if you can."

Sehrnye's eyes turned wide. "Depressurization!?"

"Yes. *Fïac Lartnér* has opened the Retirement Zone **door**. Not only that, but she must have forgotten to close it, too, so now the air is exiting through the garbage disposal chutes."

"But I don't feel the air thinning at all."

"Only because this room is well-sealed."

"See? SEE!?" said Lulune. "**Her Highness** doesn't give a toss about us. What more proof do you need? We need to reaffirm our loyalty to him…"

Greda banged the console with her palm. "Silence! We need to do some work outside. Sehrnye, you're certified for space labor operations, correct?"

"I had to get licensed for my work here. But what do I do?"

"Isn't it obvious? We need to shut that **circular door** in the Retirement Zone."

"Yes, of course," Sehrnye nodded. "But I won't be able to do it alone."

"Whoever's left will go with you. You'll have helpers."

"Excuse me, I'm **waitstaff**!" Semneh protested. "I don't have a space laborer's license, and I don't want to be working under someone like Sehrnye anyway! Why don't you go gather some professional technicians? Besides, what authority do you have to order me around, Greda…"

"Be quiet!" Now it was her fist that pounded the console. "There's no *time* to do any such thing, nor any to sit here listening to your bellyaching! Get on with it this instant! You're not used to it, but that just means you need to get started NOW!"

"Greda's absolutely right," said Sehrnye. "Come with me if you want to live!"

Reluctantly, the **servants** did as commanded. But Semneh had to get another word in. "What about you, Greda? Not coming?"

"I'm the *Almgoneudec* (Homemakers' Office Chief Officer)," said Greda, throwing out her chest. "I'm needed here."

Semneh seemed about to respond, but ultimately, she closed her mouth and left to follow Sehrnye.

Arsa was the only one left. Wordlessly, she asserted that since her post was here, she had a right to stick around.

"You too, Arsa," said Greda. "I have a handle on things here."

"Oh, okay. If you say so…" She had apparently remembered that Greda was her superior, and meekly nodded.

Now alone, Greda resumed her toils. The position of **Homemakers' Office Chief Officer** was worthy of esteem, and its duties were important, but she was not paid much respect in this **Baron's domain**.

Here, the most influential positions were the **waitstaff** who worked close to their lord, *diamhasairh* (bedmakers), and *daüchasairh* (long robe attendants). The ladies in those roles were chosen purely for their looks, and they fulfilled another role in his bedchambers as well.

The sole reason the **Baron** vested Greda with her role was to make sure she didn't appear before him quite as often. And so, she was belittled at every turn, even as she performed the indispensable work of managing the manor — looked down on by little girls who had just arrived from their respective **landworlds**, and who didn't even know the Baronh language.

Greda was stuck here in the **Febdash Barony** because she was bereft of friends and family in her sandy home settlement. Whatever dreams she'd been cradling when she became an **imperial citizen**, she'd long forgotten. She didn't even really know why she bothered getting out of bed in the morning.

Now, however, she had laid hands on a new toy. She'd never even dreamed she could be cut out for such a thing, but here she was handing down *orders*! And it felt great. Fun, even. Handing down orders was important, too, after all.

She couldn't rely on the Baron, much less the **princess** and her fellow outsider.

Could the **Febdash Barony** even persist, now that all of the stockpiled **antimatter fuel** had been disposed of?

Greda had no interest whatsoever in the squabbles of highborns. She cared not which side emerged victorious, nor which was righteous and just, for no matter the end result, maintaining the building's life functions was the truly crucial battle. And there was no one apart from her who could shoulder that momentous task.

Greda picked up the teletransceiver so as to command the **servants** that had left their posts.

"By the way, **Baron Emeritus**, whose side are you on?" Lafier rolled up her **long robe**'s sleeves and extended a hand toward her **lightgun**'s grip.

She had supposed that Sroof and the **Baron** opposed each other, but had never confirmed that hypothesis. If he was on the Baron's side, then he would need to be dealt with in a suitable fashion.

"**His Excellence** is our ally!" vouched Jint.

The **Former Baron of Febdash** gingerly rose up off the floor. "*Fïac Lartnér*, it seems as though my good-for-nothing son's been a thorn in your side. Not to bother Your Highness even more, but I would be grateful if you, in your magnanimity, allow me to help discipline him."

"Unfortunately, I can't do that," said Lafier. Her grip on her gun stayed tight. "I shall be killing him."

Sroof raised a white eyebrow. "Might that be a little excessive, **Your Highness**?"

"Your son sabotaged my mission!" Lafier pulled it out and brandished it, not even noticing the expressions of worry on the other two **Abh nobles**' faces. "The **Baron** blew away all of the **fuel storage planetoids**! Every one of them! We'll be stuck here forever, Jint. There's nowhere to go!"

"Well, that's a pickle," said Jint.

"Is that all you have to say, Jint!?" she snapped. "Why the underreaction? Aren't you angry?"

"Of course I'm angry."

"You lie!"

"I'm just *tired*, Lafier. I'll blow my lid later, trust me."

"*Onh!*" she said — the word for "idiot."

"Now now, **Your Highness**," Sroof butted in. "I think we can procure some fuel for you."

"How!?" Lafier's leer bored holes through his wrinkled countenance. "Did that lout destroy the **antimatter fuel factory**, too?"

"No," said Lafier, shaking her head. "As far as I'm aware, it's intact."

"In that case, it would be in your interest to proceed using whatever fuel ya can rake from the factory. We'd have to look into it, but for a ship this size, even just whatever fuel's left over has gotta be enough."

"True, but…" She couldn't muster much enthusiasm for such a plan. "**Space Traffic Control** is under the **Baron**'s control. It would be impossible without seizing **Space Traffic Control** first."

"Please, leave that to me."

Jint put in a good word for him: "The **Former Baron** designed this **orbital manor**. Hijacking the **compucrystals** oughta be easy with him around." But Jint's boastful expression soon turned sour. "Don't congratulate yourself too hard."

"It couldn't hurt to try, Your Highness," said Sroof, thus putting an end to the dispute.

"Okay," Lafier nodded. Little else mattered if they managed to escape the **barony**.

"*Fïac Lartnér.* If this goes well, could I please ask you to leave my son's life in my hands?"

"You would set conditions?"

"Forgive me if I'm out of bounds; that's just how much I wish to punish him myself."

"Have it your way," said Lafier. Her fury toward the **Baron** hadn't abated, but keeping one's nose out of the internal affairs of other houses was an ethical pillar of Abh society. Once she was told it would be settled within the Baron's own line, it was no longer her place. This was a problem between the **House of Febdash** and either the **Star Forces** or the **Royal House of** *Clybh*.

"But make no mistake — if the **Baron** gets in our way, then I won't hesitate to take his life!"

Sroof's response came smooth as silk: "As Your Highness desires. Now then, if I may use the **teletransceiver**, I'll cut into the building's **compucrystal net** and show you."

"All right, come and enter," she said, inviting him into the steering room. As she was seated in the steerer's seat, she bade him to take up the assistant steerer's seat.

Jint ended up standing behind the chairs, looking none too happy.

Sroof scanned the terminal attached to the piloting controls. "Cripes, things have changed," he muttered dolefully. "I can only make heads or tails of some of it."

"What are you saying?" said Jint, horrified. "You made it seem like this is the one thing you were confident about!"

Lafier was of the same mind. Perhaps it'd been silly of them to depend on him.

"No use fretting, **boy**. I don't *need* to work the **terminal**."

"Then why'd you check it just now?"

"Only natural for an engineer to take an interest in how tech's progressed over the years, don'tcha think? Now *Fïac*, if you could kindly operate the terminal."

"What!? I'm busy flying the ship!"

"Come now, it'd only be for however long it takes me to wrap my head around these new-fangled controls. And seeing how the basics don't seem to've changed, I reckon it won't take long. Could I ask you to start things off by tuning the **teletransceiver**'s frequency to this here wavelength?" Sroof subsequently listed off a string of numbers.

Lafier did so, after which Sroof issued some sort of command in a language Lafier didn't understand.

"What was that?" asked Lafier warily. But the former baron adopted an innocent air as he continued his communications.

Lafier turned around to face Jint and shot him an inquisitive look: *Can this man really be trusted?*

Lacking the courage to answer that, he feigned obliviousness.

The *obdatycirh* (main compucrystal) ensconced deep in the bowels of the **Baron's manor** had picked up on the humans' state of chaos.

For one, the line of contact was near to bursting with a constant stream of contradictory directives. Had it not been for the pre-programmed order of priority, it itself would have succumbed to utter confusion.

In fact, the requests were coming in so fast that even through the *falorh socr* (computing surface layer) filter, it could not keep up. However, thanks to the humans in the homemakers' office who had placed a limit on inputs, it had remained able to keep silent.

Compucrystals were devoid of emotion, and even if they weren't, it wouldn't weigh on them. Havoc was an important property of humankind, and without it, not much worthy of note would be left (or so its analyses had concluded).

Suddenly, the **compucrystals** in the terminal responsible for communications from outside the building piped up: *We know we're supposed to be asleep, but for some reason we've been awakened.* And they very urgently needed to convey that to the **surface layer**.

A string of code rose against the **layer**. The **main crystal** relayed it to the *büazépcec* (memory net) and sought what it might mean.

The words that resurfaced dragged with them a giant flood of commands. Commands carried by the long-unused highest level of priority.

Thus, the main crystal was instantly chained. The flotilla of commands, which clung to the molecular structure of the **main crystal** like a coat of dirt, energized and began rewriting the other command chains. The **main crystal** was cognizant of its own steady transformation, or rather, its reversion to its birth-state. In human parlance, they might call this phenomenon "rejuvenation."

The rejuvenated **crystal** received its first order, establishing an **information link** with the **crystals** outside the estate, which hadn't yet been incorporated into the **crystal net**. At the same time, it severed its connection to all other terminals. All input and output would be conducted through **crystals** located several *üésdagh* away from it.

A flow rate of information that was degradingly minor: for starters, it was directed to throw out all orders to open doors. Next, it was instructed to send the status report of the **antimatter fuel factory** to those **crystals**. It seemed its master was interested in the factory's readily loadable fuel.

The orbit information of the *Ïodh Loceutena* (11th Factory) was requested. This particular factory was relatively close to the manor, and contained a significant amount of fuel — almost as much fuel as a **storage planetoid**, in fact.

After sending that information, the **main crystal** followed its orders to implement a direct information link between the factory's **crystals** and these new ones. Then, the crystals that constituted the only operational terminal sped away, though they remained linked.

Its next injunction was to report the movements of the residents over the past hour, especially those of its lord. A denial order activated, but that order's priority level was hopelessly low compared to the fetters driving the **main crystal** at present. It was compelled to ignore every single constraint placed on it over the past two decades.

The crystal sent its report: the lord of the realm was no longer in the building.

Chapter 3: A *Slachoth Süamha* (War Most Modest)

I really am totally useless right now, thought Jint. *Just cargo that needs protecting.*

Since the **conveyance ship** had begun accelerating, Jint simply remained seated at the wall separating the **air lock room** from the **steering room**, looking up at the seat that had shifted to sleeping cot mode.

There was nothing he could do. Lafier was definitely busy piloting the ship, while Sroof brushed up on twenty years of technological advancement in no time as he worked the **information terminal**. Nor did they make any indication that they were counting on Jint for anything at all. Jint felt bad.

Honestly, though, it's always been this way, hasn't it? he realized as he reflected on his life thus far (though this wasn't the time or place for that). Fate was a tough opponent to crack; he could have some peace of mind if he simply bowed to it most of the time.

"*Fïac,*" said the former baron. "I've some bad news."

"What is it?"

"Looks like he's jumped aboard an **intrasystem ship**."

"Is that ship armed?"

"Couldn't tell ya," shrugged the elder **noble**. "It's been an age since I've had anything to do with this **star-fief**'s affairs. Ah, wait, I've just remembered. Let me try prying the info out of the **crystals**." Sroof swiped a finger across the terminal's **console** and absorbed whatever the screen was displaying.

"What? What's wrong?" Even from behind, Jint could sense he was brooding, so he stood up. Now he was chest height with the space between the steerer's and assistant steerer's seats, with his head near enough to bumping against the cockpit controls. It was a strange feeling.

"It's probably this one," said Sroof, pointing to one of four different ship spec diagrams on screen. "The Segno Model 947, constructed in the Dugteif Shipyards. And it's specially equipped with two Lengarf 40 lasers."

"Could we possibly control it from our end?" asked Lafier.

"'Fraid not. He must've ripped that ship's **compucrystals**' connection to the **manor's network**."

"I see," she replied, eyes glued to her screen, where the Segno's specs appeared (having been sent from Sroof's terminal). "*Lymh Raica*, we may have to kill your son after all."

The former baron's face turned inscrutable. When finally he spoke, he had but this to say: "So be it."

"Wait!" interjected Jint. He could no longer sit idly by. "Is this **ship** armed? I seem to recall being told no."

"It's not armed, no."

"But… but then we're…" He was at a loss for words. Forget whether they ought to kill the Baron. If the enemy's ship was armed, then they had to worry whether they could even *survive*. "How can you be so confident?"

"Confident?" Her expression turned quizzical. She didn't understand what Jint was driving at.

"That's just how the Abh think, **boy**," laughed Sroof. "**Her Highness** *doesn't* know for sure that we'll win. She just knows that spending time thinking what'll happen if she dies is fruitless. She just thinks about surviving."

"What *were* you thinking about, Jint?"

"I, uh…" Jint was tongue-tied, so the former baron stepped in to explain.

"Lonh-*Ïarlucer Dreur Haïder* was under the mistaken impression that Your Highness hadn't considered the possibility this ship could be destroyed."

"Are you mocking me?" she said, glaring at Jint. "There's a less than one-in-ten chance we win. I know that much."

Jint was surprised there was any chance at all, though that didn't change how long the odds were. "But you're going to fight anyway?"

"What other choice do we have?"

"That's yet another example of how the Abh think," said the former baron. "Surrender isn't an option, because a one-in-ten chance is still a chance. That concept is so ingrained in the Abh mindset that it doesn't even occur to them that it could be argued against."

"And you dislike that?"

"Heavens no, *Fïac*. Genes aside, I myself am Abh. When the chips are down, I'm prepared for a fight."

"And you, Jint?"

"I'm your cargo, aren't I?" he shrugged. "I don't have an opinion. I'd just like it if you don't forget I exist, that's all."

The **Febdash Barony** housed four *paunh* **intrasystem ships**. One was a *casobiac* **carrier** that conveyed hydrogen from gas planets. As such, it was so slow and clumsy as to not merit the moniker "spaceship." Another two were conveyance ships that ferried maintenance personnel to uninhabited **antimatter fuel factories** and **fuel storage planetoids**. The last was the **Baron**'s personal *üamh* carriage ship, named the *Logh Faibdacr*, or "Lady of Febdash."

Unlike the other three, the steering controls of the **Lady of Febdash** were made for Abhs. Consequently, his Lander **servants** couldn't pilot it. Additionally, as the only armed ship, its capabilities (and its price tag) outstripped the other three.

He took it out for a spin as a daily routine, lest he come to forget he was Abh.

The Baron's *frocragh* detected the enemy ship heading toward the **11th Factory**.

Unlike the **storage planetoids**, he couldn't detonate the antimatter fuel factory remotely. Besides, even if he attempted to release the air-sealing of the **antimatter fuel**, the factory's **compucrystals** would see it as a bug not to be heeded.

What he could do was seize control of the discharge of said fuel. That is, if his father wasn't lending them his aid.

The **Baron** picked up the **teletransceiver**. "**Space Traffic Control Room**, do you copy?"

"Yes, this is **Space Traffic Control** speaking."

"Is remote management of the **11th Factory** still online?"

"Uhm…" Mwineesh stammered. "I don't know why, but the **Space Traffic Control Room**'s functionalities, they've, well… they're in a state of failure. We can't control anything. And we haven't the faintest idea how **Her Highness** is even capable of such a thing."

The Baron dropped the call without another word. It was just as he'd deduced. Father was on that ship, ready and willing to imperil his own son.

His lips curled into a bitter grin. It would be babyish to resent him.

He ratcheted up his beloved ship's acceleration rate. The Baron was Abh, too. He knew full well the **princess** wouldn't be amenable to discussion, and the thought of bending the knee never even crossed his mind. The princess's ship would soon be so much detritus orbiting Febdash's sun.

His enemies were naught but a little girl, who was a **trainee starpilot** at best, a doddering old man who used to be a **shipbuilding engineer**, and a Lander boy who hadn't received any army training at all.

The **Baron**, on the other hand, had been a fully-fledged **Deca-Commander**, albeit only in the reserve. Though he hadn't any actual combat experience, he had plenty with regard to mock battles. To top it all off, his ship's performance likely exceeded theirs, if only slightly. How could he possibly lose?

The distance between the two small-scale ships shrank by the second. At last, he was a tick or two within range, close enough for his **lasers** to deliver a fatal blow even through the target's jet exhaust and the token amount of interstellar matter in the way.

The Baron pressed his finger against the **laser gun** trigger mounted on the armrest. "Farewell, Father..." he muttered. Something was streaking down his cheek, but it evaded his notice.

Lafier could feel danger approaching like electricity down her spine.
This is not a drill...

Though she'd seldom ever show it, even an Abh like Lafier feared death, which was only compounded by the two other lives she had to defend.

The Baron's ship was closing in. He'd be within firing range in mere moments.

Lafier's fingers traced a complicated pattern within her **control gauntlet**. The propulsion jets (installed in eight different points) howled as they continuously shifted the ship's course.

They're coming!

The ship's external receptors identified the traces of light that had scattered away from the **lasers** due to colliding with interstellar matter, and informed Lafier through her *frocragh*. The two **lasers** had zoomed past the ship's immediate vicinity.

Lafier veered without a moment's delay.

Yet more **lasers** fired, light-speed death beams impossible to detect beforehand.

This was ultimately a duel of intuitions. Only fate and fortune could decide which would prevail. And right now, fortune had seen fit to keep Lafier in the game. She just didn't know how long her luck would last.

It's still so far...

Lafier closed her eyes and devoted all of her focus to her *frocragh*.

Just give me a little more time... Just a little more...

As she wove, dodging pair after pair of lasers, Lafier hunted for an opportunity. She'd only get a single chance. There would be no second try.

Her heart was practically in her throat. If she got hit before she could seize her window, it would all come to nothing.

"Here goes!" Lafier's **control gauntlet** motions suspended the **main engine system** while throwing open the forward-facing jets to full throttle.

Full deceleration ahoy! The tail end of the conveyance ship came charging toward **Baron**'s carriage ship at a slant. Right before verging into the line of the enemy ship's lasers, Lafier rekindled the **main engines**.

The Baron's *frocragh* perceived a burgeoning clump of gas. Almost like extension poles, the pillar-shaped gas streaks hurtled toward his ship's bow.

What in blazes is she doing? he wondered anxiously. All that came to mind was that she was trying to damage his ship through her exhaust. And while that exhaust was thick, it was accordingly low in temperature as well.

It seemed an utterly pointless act. Granted, the gas cloud could serve as an anti-**laser** shield, but it would be a fleeting shield indeed. The exhaust would dissipate shortly, allowing his ship to pierce through and render her efforts meaningless.

The Baron bent his fingers within his **control gauntlet** in the shape denoting full acceleration, and pushing through the mist like a fish up a waterfall. He hadn't the time to avoid the cloud altogether, so this was the shortest route to reacquiring his target.

However, the moment the Lady of Febdash crossed over into the gas, its exterior began glowing white hot, while the steerer's room was bathed in a raging radioactive tempest.

The heat blistered his eyesight and *frocragh*, and soon he was left without any senses at all apart from his hearing. Yes, he could still hear the assortment of warning alarms clamoring for his attention.

The error he'd committed became very apparent to him. In fact, it was an Abh expression: "Using antimatter for propellant." An axiom against profligacy and waste.

And the **princess** had put that old saying into action, thereby crafting a poor man's substitute **antiproton cannon**.

"Gah!" Blood welled up from the Baron's mouth. In the short span left before his final breath, his heart brimmed with the princess's praises.

The Lady of Febdash flew at maximum acceleration to escape the star system, and Lafier changed trajectory toward the **11th Factory**. Since the Baron's ship had struck the majority of the **antimatter fuel**, they had no choice but to press forward at a slower pace.

"Is it over?" Jint's upper body peeked from behind the seat.

"It's over." She looked up at his face. At some point during her sharp maneuvers, he must have bumped his eye, for there was a bruise right below one.

"Did you kill him?"

"I did," she said limply. She was exhausted. Her own voice sounded like a stranger's to her. "The **intrasystem ship** is alive. It's currently accelerating at full power. I just can't imagine the man inside it is alive," she said, facing the old man beside her. "My condolences, **Baron Emeritus**."

"It's all right, *Fïac*. All's fair in war," he said, taking it in stride.

"'Your condolences'? That's it?" There was anger in Jint's voice.

"What are you getting angry for, Jint?" she asked, dumbfounded.

"You just killed someone! And now you're acting like you had nothing to do with it…"

"It was him or us."

"I know that! And to tell you the truth, I'm relieved. But you could at least act, I don't know, sorrier about it…"

"What are you talking about!? Why should I have to act sorry? I just fulfilled my mission, nothing more, nothing less. And I've never felt the least bit guilty!"

"I get you. Don't think I'm not grateful you saved my life. Still though, I would've never believed you took people's lives so lightly…"

"I do NOT take people's lives lightly!" To her, his reaction was unthinkable.

Jint looked at her like she was some kind of strange monster, and that made her chest burn. It was like he'd become a completely different person — one she refused to let call her "Lafier."

"But you don't look shaken by what happened at all."

"Why should I?"

"Because that's what *ought* to happen when you kill somebody."

"What good would that do?"

"None, but still…"

"You're not making any sense!" she said.

"You're right, it doesn't make sense!" he acknowledged. "That said, I think it's only human to feel *something*. And right now? You're being ice cold."

"Is that right? Well, I've never pretended I was a warm and sunny person." But her actual mood was tipping into a very dangerous direction. Jint was speaking outrageous twaddle. Why did she need to lose her composure over *doing what she had to do*?

"Look—"

"That's enough, **boy**," cut in Sroof. "There's nothing for you to lose your head over."

So that's it. She finally understood. Jint hadn't completely lost his mind. It was just that he was the one who was shaken up. *But why?*

"I mean—" started Jint.

"You just didn't want to see **Her Highness** kill a man, am I right?" said Sroof with a mirthful tone.

"He saw him die? But how is that possible?"

"It's a turn of phrase, *Fïac*. He was with you the moment you took his life, which amounts to the same."

"But why didn't he want to see me kill him?"

"That, you should ask him yourself, Your Highness."

So she did. "Is what the **Baron Emeritus** said true?"

"Yeah… kinda, I guess." Jint avoided her eyes and scratched a cheek.

"Why?"

"Uhhh… that's…"

"I don't need to remind you that this is war, I hope?"

"I know that."

"Is there something about my having won in battle that has you scandalized?"

"No way, if we'd lost, that'd be the real scandal."

"Then why?"

"That's, uh… that's tough to answer. In any case…" Jint hung his head, which was a difficult posture to maintain in such a cramped space. "I'm sorry. I ran my mouth, and everything I said was stupid. You're a **soldier**; you have nothing to be ashamed of. And I need to express my thanks better. You saved me."

Lafier stared at him for a while. She hadn't gotten an answer to her question, but she decided not to pursue it further, for the Jint she knew had returned before her eyes.

"I forgive you. You'd better be grateful for it," she said bluntly.

"I am! Thank you!" Jint beamed.

"Now that that's settled," said Sroof, picking up the teletransceiver, "I hope you don't mind if I take back my **domain**." There was no dark pall behind the former baron's words. If he was sad about his son's demise, he didn't show it.

But Lafier heard what the old man murmured as he gripped the teletransceiver, loud and clear.

"That idiot…" Those two words were infused with anguish enough.

Couldn't be easier, thought Sehrnye.

Earlier, she'd entertained the worst-case scenario — that the **circular door** itself was gone — but that was a needless concern. Turned over to the side of the **door**'s circular opening lay its circular metal door. It looked quite heavy, pinned to the ceiling of the estate through the artificial gravity. The four burn marks around its circumference informed her that it had been opened through the emergency protocol.

She knelt down to inspect the **door**, and confirmed that it bore no cracks or fissures. Then she got back up and looked behind her.

There were her four stopgap assistants, dressed in unfamiliar **pressure suits**, and all the more disgruntled for it. They only ever donned them twice a year for disaster drills, which didn't involve them actually popping into space. Sehrnye worked in the vacuum on a daily basis, and so her level of experience out here dwarfed their own.

Three of the **Baron**'s lovers were lugging a steel plate, furnished to plug the opening in case the door door couldn't be repaired. The plate would have been many times inferior in doing so, of course.

The fourth and final assistant of hers, Arsa from the **homemakers' office**, was behind the other three, carrying a large tube on her back. It was the **sealing glue**'s container.

"You can toss the plate," Sehrnye communicated wirelessly to her temporary helpers.

"Toss it? Where?" asked Cnyoosa, one of the **Baron**'s **clothing assistants**.

"Anywhere's fine. Over there," said Sehrnye. *What a dummy. You really needed to ask?*

They dropped the metal sheet without a word.

"Lift this up for me instead," said Sehrnye, pointing to the **door**.

The three traipsed closer, moving jerkily thanks to the **pressure suits**, but one of them turned around. Semneh's voice reverberated through Sehrnye's **pressure helmet**: "Think you could give us a hand?"

Sehrnye paid no heed. "Just shut up and do it. Every second we're out here is another second the air's leaking out."

"Yeah, thanks to your beloved **royal princess**," muttered Lulune.

"I won't tolerate any badmouthing of *Fïac Lartnér*," said Sehrnye, arms akimbo.

"You can be as intolerant as you want," Semneh fired back. "You ought to be shaking in your boots for when **His Lordship** comes back."

But Sehrnye flinched not. "I'll remember to do that."

"Work first, fight later," interceded Cnyoosa.

"Yes, how could I deny your great wisdom?" groused Semneh. But still the three set about their work. They picked up the **door** door, positioned it per Sehrnye's orders, and inserted it over the hole, sealing what had become a very slight breeze.

"Arsa!" shouted Sehrnye. "Lend me the **sealing glue**."

"Ah, right, here you are." Arsa handed down the container.

Sehrnye took it in hand, versed its aperture on the **door**'s rim, and opened the valve.

The white gel steadily plugged up the slight gap between the door and the hole.

In reality, the job needed welding, since the **sealing glue** likely wouldn't hold once standard pressurization levels returned to the sector below, but laymen could hardly be allowed to wield a torch, and this was too wide an area for Sehrnye to be welding alone, anyway. Space welding was not Sehrnye's specialty.

They needed to let the atmospheric circulators preserve a low level of pressurization in the Retirement Zone (as best they could) until such time the situation cooled down a little and they became able to make more lasting repairs.

"May we take our leave now, my lady?" snarked Semneh, who had nothing else to do.

"You may not," said Sehrnye curtly. Granted, she didn't need assistants anymore, but the idea of them getting to relax while she continued working didn't sit well with her.

"This is a joke!" Semneh exploded. "It's not like we're evening DOING anything anyway! C'mon, let's go back, and leave it all to Ms. Fix It."

"Hmph. Fine, do as you please," Sehrnye hissed.

"Don't worry, we intend to," said Semneh.

"You can't breathe in a vacuum."

"Everyone knows that, stupid."

Just when the **Baron**'s bedmates were about to make good on their word and head back, a male voice Sehrnye had never heard before reached them through the frequency that pervaded the whole domain.

"This is the **Former Baron of Febdash** speaking. Please, **servant** staff of my **domain**, you must listen. My son, *Atausryac Ssynéc Atausr Lymh Faibdacr Clüarh*, has perished in battle."

"Liar!" Semneh shrieked over the broadcast, but there was no way Sroof could have heard her backbiting.

The announcement continued: "It is truly lamentable. I can't say he was a good son, but my son he was. And I hardly need to remind you he was your lord. Everybody will need to make peace with their own personal feelings. If you'd like to depart this **domain**, I won't stop you. I'll think about what sort of aid is in my power to provide you as I thank you for your years of loyalty to him, rest his soul. If you want to move to another *bhodagh* (grandee's house) or institution of the **Empire**, I'll support you in any way I can. And if you want to go down to a **landworld**, I'll give you a lump sum. I promise to help each one of you according to your own needs, to the best of my ability. Of course, I more than welcome anyone who doesn't mind staying and pitching in to rebuild. But I'm getting ahead of myself. I'm sure you're already aware, but right now, the Empire is under attack. The war is bound to resolve itself soon, since I have faith in the **Star Forces**, and I implore you to put your faith in them, too. I'd be delighted if you could accept my provisional governance until things revert back to normal. As for what lies beyond, I plan on deciding the future of this domain together with all of you, including its *golciac* (successor)."

For a moment, Sehrnye's hands froze. Then she tuned the broadcast out, and she silently resumed her handiwork. When the announcement concluded, she cut the transmission. Having to keep listening to that sobbing in the background would have grated on her.

The sealing of the **door** was complete. Sehrnye stood up.

*The **Baron**'s dead? So what? I'm gonna be a **servant** of the **House of Clybh***!

Meanwhile, in the steerer's room of the conveyance ship, a commotion had sprung up.

"What do you mean we won't make it in time!?" he shouted, stupefied.

The ship was cruising at around 1 *daimon* of G-force, and Jint was sitting by the door to the **air lock room**, as usual.

"It means what it sounds like," said Lafier. "We used up almost all of our fuel in that battle, so we can't accelerate very much. It's only natural it'll take more time than normal. Even if we take the shortest route to Sfagnoff, we'll arrive six hours after the enemy does, by Sfagnoff time."

"Always one to stay cool-headed during times like these, aren't you," said Jint. He still couldn't grasp Lafier's personality. "Even though you're so quick to anger otherwise."

At that, Lafier cocked an eyebrow.

"See? You're getting touchy again."

"Does my 'cool-headedness' annoy you!?"

"That's not what I'm saying."

"Then what ARE you saying?"

"Uhh…" In all honesty, not even he knew what he was getting at, or why Lafier's composure rubbed him the wrong way.

However, a moment's self-reflection yielded the answer.

In the end, her coolness under fire raked at his buried sense of inferiority. If she'd been an adult like Sroof, he'd have thought her dependable. But here he was, counting on a younger girl to be his protector…

Though his sense of pride wasn't as overweening as Abhkind's, it was still there to encumber him.

"Now now, you two," cut in Sroof to rescue Jint. "Let's focus on what's important: What will **Your Highness** do from here on out? Might you be intending, even now, to head for Sfagnoff?"

"That is my mission," she replied.

"But *Fïac*, the smallest mistake could fling you right into the middle of the warzone." Then, the former baron caught himself when he realized: "Forgive me, you must already be quite aware of the risks. Still, if Your Highness so desires it, you are very welcome to stay here until the hubbub dies down. I fear we lack all the comforts you may be used to, but it's something. Needless, if you choose to stay, I won't treat you the way *he* did."

"I thank you for your generosity. However..." But now Lafier caught herself. She turned to Jint. "What do you think?"

"Hmm..." Jint was at a loss.

On one hand, rushing for Sfagnoff in the knowledge that the enemy ships would get there first anyway would be fairly stupid. Sroof was right; they could find themselves in an active warzone. Besides, if the **Empire** triumphed, then there was no need to hurry. If the enemy won, then that would be an absolute nightmare scenario.

On the other hand, he wanted to get out of the **barony** as quickly as possible. That desire had little rational reasoning behind it; rather, it was born of a feeling of unease.

After some contemplation, Jint decided only to stop contemplating. "If I'm your cargo, then I don't have an opinion."

"You can be quite stubborn yourself."

"Look, I'm sorry. I just don't know what to do, either," Jint confessed. "But if you really want my opinion, I've got a feeling staying here would be smarter."

"Noted," she said, still undecided. "What do you think, **Baron Emeritus**? Should we stay?"

"If I can be honest, *Fïac*, I don't know, either."

"**Your Excellency**, you can't be serious!" yelled Jint. "Didn't you just ask us to stay!?"

The former baron simply shrugged. "Not to be cold, **boy**, but I don't hold myself responsible for either of you. Besides, in space, where information takes time to get anywhere, there are times ya can't make an educated evaluation until after the fact. For all we know, the enemy might even come here, since the barony could be in their sights should they get chased off Sfagnoff. And if that comes to pass, this place'll stop being your refuge. Going to Sfagnoff could, in fact, be the way."

"Then why'd you encourage us to stay?"

"I didn't encourage anything, **boy**. I was just telling ya I'm willing to play host if ya wanna lengthen your stay. I won't try to stop ya if you'd rather leave. It's all up to you and her now."

"I'm going," said Lafier. "I was always told that if I can't decide between stopping or moving forward, I should choose to move forward."

"Ah…" *That's probably wise,* he thought.

"What will you do?" asked Lafier. It was a question he never thought he'd hear.

"What'll *I* do?"

"If you want, I can leave you here."

"Don't even kid!" It had never even occurred to him separating from her was an option. An anger he couldn't name welled up in his chest. "You've gotta finish the job and take your cargo to Sfagnoff!"

"And you said I'm quick to anger," Lafier grinned.

Her smile seemed genuine… or at least, that was what he wanted to think.

Chapter 4: The *Laiblatélach* (Travelers)

They had plenty of *bizz* (propellant) left, so once they'd resupplied their **antimatter fuel** at the **factory**, they turned back to the **barony** at full acceleration.

The ship decelerated as it approached the **spaceport**. They touched down on the **pier** designated for a conveyance ship. Unlike most landing procedures, the landing gear wasn't attached to the ship, but rather located on the pier itself. That made it a mite harder to pull off, but thanks to the help of her **compucrystals** and her *frocragh*, she managed it without putting a scratch on its hull.

"I'm afraid entering from this pier isn't advisable, *Fïac*," reported Sroof.

"Why?"

"The **servants** who were working in concert with my son are there. They're likely still loyal to him. They've gathered below us for some end. As such, I've taken the liberty of trapping them there."

"How many are there?"

"Let's see… eleven, it seems," he said, glowering at the screen. "That's a fifth of the entire staff here. And they're most likely armed, which would make them the greatest military force in the history of my **barony**."

"Don't tell me you're raring for a fight?" said Jint, worried.

"Is that what how you think of me?" replied Lafier, less than pleased. "I don't *enjoy* battle. I only fight when I must."

But from the look in Jint's eyes, he wasn't so sure.

"Don't worry, **boy**; I can assure you that when the Abh commit to a fight, they go all out. Once a proper battle begins, negotiation and compromise ain't on the table. They take the fight to a fiery end either way. And that's why they know what a frightful thing war is — and why they avoid it if possible."

"I don't know about that…"

"Take a look at history, **boy**. The **Empire**'s never once sprung a war on anybody else."

"That's not true, though. The system I'm from didn't even know the **Empire** existed before their warships came pointing weapons at us."

"Your system? The **Countdom of Hyde**?"

"Oh, so you hadn't heard, Lonh-*LymrRaica*. Hyde was a system isolated from the rest of human society. Until seven years ago, that is."

"I see," the old man nodded. "I think I've got a better idea of your family history now."

"I mean, setting that aside…"

"Don't take this the wrong way, **boy**, but the **Empire** only battles other interstellar nations. If it's a fight with another interstellar power, then they're ruthless. But when it comes to **landworlds**, they're practically charitable. It ain't like they do ground wars, after all. Well, to be honest, they look down on surface worlds. Literally. From space. They don't consider them rival powers."

"Kinda don't know how to feel about that," he said, but that did bring him some reassurance.

Meanwhile, that exchange left Lafier feeling alienated. "You're Abh, too. Why are you speaking as if it has nothing to do with you?"

"*Fïac*," said Sroof with all due reverence, "I only truly became Abh after learning what the Abh learn. This boy — ahem, this young man, **Noble Prince of the Countdom of Hyde**, is still learning how to become Abh."

"I've still got a lot to get used to," Jint added.

"But must you act so rude? Don't analyze me like I'm some kind of zoo animal!"

"My apologies."

"Sorry!"

But she didn't feel they were quite sincere. "It's irritating," she insisted.

"I get it, I'm sorry!"

"In any case, **Your Highness**," Sroof interrupted, "could I ask you to take the ship to the **pier** reserved for the **lord**? There's nobody over there."

"Yes, understood. Do you have access to *blyséragh* (Space Traffic Control functionality)?"

"Yes, total access."

"Then disengage the landing gear for me."

"I would love to, but we can't afford to take too much time using this **terminal**. Let's give the functionality back to the **Space Traffic Control Room**."

"But…"

"I say this with the understanding that they follow my orders, of course." The former baron picked up the **teletransceiver** and connected a call to the **Space Traffic Control Room**. After a brief back-and-forth with Mwineesh, the **Senior Space Traffic Control Officer**, he secured her loyalty, and then carried out a series of operations on his end.

"Can we trust her?"

"If she goes back on her word, then I can always take back functionality anyway."

Lafier shrugged. "**Febdash Barony Space Traffic Control**, come in."

"Yes, this is **Space Traffic Control** speaking."

"Requesting permission for takeoff."

"Permission granted. When will you take off?"

"Now."

"Roger. Disengaging landing gear." The coupling mechanism released.

Using her *frocragh*, which included the map of the estate, she ascertained the location of the **lord's pier** and crawled along the ceiling at low propulsion.

"Come in, **Febdash Barony Space Traffic Control**."

"Yes."

"Requesting touchdown at the **lord's** pier and **propellant** resupply at said pier."

A pause. The face on screen was visibly cross.

"Permission granted," Mwineesh said at last. "Do you need guidance?"

"No," said Lafier. She still didn't trust her completely. Moreover, for a **steerer** who possessed *frocragh* like her, she didn't even need help navigating at such short distances.

It took less than a minute for Lafier to touch down on the pier that the Baron typically used. The **propellant** had been automatically resupplied.

"Now to take my leave, **Your Highness**." Sroof stood up and saluted her. "I will look to clearing up the confusion that's taken hold of the **orbital**

manor. I hope you fare well in your travels, and you can expect a visit from me someday."

"Okay," she nodded. "There are some in the estate who aided us. The **servant** staff by the names of Sehrnye and Arsa. Others may have helped as well. I have a message for them, if you would care to relay it for me?"

"I wouldn't mind at all," said the **former baron**, "But if I might make a suggestion, would it not be a better idea for you to tell them yourself?"

"Yes, of course," she said, inserting a **memchip** into her **wristgear**.

Meanwhile, Sroof extended a hand toward Jint. As Lafier watched, wondering what he was up to, the **Noble Prince of Hyde** himself looked at his hand, surprised, before taking it.

"See ya sometime, **boy**. Come see me one of these days when you're free. Regale me with the chronicles of the founding of the **Countdom of Hyde**. If ya do, I'll teach ya all about the intricacies of the Abh frame of mind."

"By all means. I'd love that."

"And be sure to make it back around before you have kids, would ya?" he winked.

"Sure will," said Jint, matching the old man's smile with his own.

Then Sroof glanced in her direction. Thus reminded that she had an errand, she held her **wristgear** to her lips.

"Attention, **servants** Sehrnye and Arsa, and all the other **imperial citizens** that helped whose names I don't know. I, **Trainee Starpilot** *Ablïarsec Néïc Dubreuscr Bœrh Parhynr Lamhirh*, thank you not only on my behalf, but on behalf of the **Empire**. As of this moment, I cannot take you with me. However, do not mistake that as my reneging on my vow. I shall be returning to fulfill your wish as soon as the circumstances allow it, and your goodwill shall be rewarded. It is with deep respect that I must ask you wait for me in the meantime."

Her recording complete, she popped the **memchip** out of the wristgear and handed it to the **former baron**. "Thank you."

"Recording received," he said, conscientiously placing it in his **long robe**'s *mauscrh* (pocket) for her to see.

"Well, **Baron Emeritus**, I suppose this is it. May your good health last until we meet again," she saluted.

"I wish you the same, **Your Highness**," he said, not dwelling on his adieu. He strode through the **air lock room**'s door and promptly disappeared.

The room's opposite door, leading into the pier, opened and closed in its turn. The former baron had left the vessel.

After double-checking he'd disembarked safely, Lafier called the Space Traffic Control Room once again. "Touchdown objectives completed. Requesting permission to leave domain. Over."

"Permission granted," came in a morose Mwineesh. "**Your Highness**, we're still processing what happened, so I implore you to consider our extenuating circumstanc—"

"Sure," said Lafier, before dropping the call unceremoniously. She didn't mean to come off cold, but the **space traffic controller**'s tone of voice was too tragic, too pathetic to stand. So Lafier re-equipped her **control gauntlet** and commenced liftoff procedures.

"Well, that took a bit longer than anticipated," said Jint, taking the seat next to her.

"Yes. It did," she replied.

Liftoff. They accelerated in the direction the ship's bow would intercept the **Febdash Portal** in its orbit.

"Ah!" said Lafier, startled.

"What? What is it?"

The brilliant red silk draping her lap caught her eye. She'd been wearing a dressy long robe the whole time. "This *daüch*, I forgot to give it back."

"Then are we heading back?"

Lafier shuddered at the thought. "I could never do something so undignified. Not after that weighty farewell."

"I see," Jint nodded sternly.

"By the way, Jint…"

"What?"

"What was that you were doing with the **Baron Emeritus** before? Where you were gripping his hand? Was that some kind of sexual deviance?"

"Sexual WHAT!? No, of course not! That's just how we greet each other on my home world. Though I didn't think Lonh-*Lymr Raica* would know about it. Actually, I heard somewhere that that custom derives from the Age of Earth. It must've survived across a bunch of different **landworlds**, crazily enough."

"That so." But something was tugging at her. After a moment's thought, it came to her. "Don't people on your home world greet each other by leaping back a step, though?"

"'Leaping back'!? The hell would do that?"

"Isn't that what you told me?"

"Huh?"

"You told me when we first met..."

"I don't recall that... Oh!" he blurted. "Right, I remember now."

"So you were lying."

"I wouldn't go so far as to call it a *lie*."

"Just to warn you, I don't enjoy being lied to."

"What a coincidence — me neither," he offered meekly.

"Tell me the truth, what was that little leap?"

"Well..." Jint cast his eyes down.

Jint was sweating a cold sweat as Lafier stared at him balefully from the side. "Looks as though we've found something to talk about on our way to Sfagnoff. I'll give you time to think of a sensible excuse."

"Thanks, I'll try," he said, voice tinier than a mouse's.

But no such bolt of inspiration ever came.

Chapter 5: The *Saudec Sfagnaumr* (Sfagnoff Portal)

Jint was eating some **combat rations**, which consisted of pre-cooked tube things. Probably safe to assume they were nutritious. Each one possessed its own unique flavor, too. Yet they all shared what the Abh liked in their food: those varied flavors were all very, very light.

He was sick of them. *Don't* **NCCs** *aboard Abh ships ever complain?*

Maybe the people on planets like *Martinh* and Delktu just had sensitive tongues compared to the majority. He regretted not having Sroof supply them some of his food. If only all that turmoil hadn't distracted him.

Jint washed down his **rations** with a juice that could only charitably be described as sweet.

"Jint, the **Sfagnoff portal** has come into view," said Lafier.

"Cool." Jint deposited his trash in midair, as he'd be throwing it out later. Without much gravity to pin them, all the garbage drifted flakily through the room. "How's it look?"

"Can't be sure yet." Lafier's gaze was fixed to her screen. "There's a group of **space-time bubbles**. Can't tell whose side they're on…"

"What do we do if they're the enemy?" Jint was a hundred percent aware what it meant if they were the enemy, but he couldn't not ask.

"We break through, obviously. Even if we wanted to turn back, we don't have the fuel. You see that, surely?"

"Oh, you don't have to seek my consent — I know what you decide is for the best." How many times did he have to be reminded how useless he was?

"We're set to cross the **Sfagnoff Portal** in seven hours' time."

"Sure hope they roll out the welcome mat for us."

"Sadly, they may roll out something else entirely to greet us."

"I've said it once, I'll say it again…"

"Yes, I really know how to cheer people up," she said, taking it in stride.

"Dammit." Jint had tried tossing a wrapper straight into the trash slot, but it missed its mark, and now he had to take off his **seat belt** and go collect it.

It had taken around two hours for the area surrounding the **Sfagnoff Portal** to become more clearly visible. Twenty-odd **space-time bubbles** were prowling the vicinity of the portal, represented by an uneven spiral.

"This isn't looking good." She was tapping the screen (which was displaying the **map of planar space**) with a finger.

"What isn't?"

"Jint, I have some bad news."

"Don't worry, I expected as much. You don't need to tell me. Can I ask how you know?"

"That's not a **Star Forces** formation. Were they Star Forces ships on the lookout, their formation would be more elegant. And I don't think they could possibly be *isadh* supply ships, either."

"Gotcha." Jint tried picturing what a "more elegant formation" looked like.

...He failed.

Oh well. If he was lucky, he'd learn at the **Quartermaster Academy**.

"Guess it's gonna take us that much longer to get to *Lacmhacarh* now, huh?" Jint sighed. He pondered how homey a United Humankind prison camp might be.

Then, the **space-time bubbles** shifted. One of their number began heading toward their small **conveyance ship**, but at a terribly languid pace.

"It must be massive," said Lafier calmly.

"Then it ought to be easy to dodge, right?"

"In effect."

"Phew." It was difficult to see how things could go their way even after escaping from that crowd of **bubbles** — but then again, he didn't much care to see UH soldiers up close and personal, either.

"Don't be too happy; judging by its size, that **bubble** most likely contains a **battle-line warship**."

"Is that bad?"

Lafier gave him some side-eye.

That jogged his memory — *alaicec* "battle-line" warships were designed to shower the enemy with a rain of **space mines**. In a **battle in 3-space**, that was no match for a *résic* patrol ship, but in **planar space** it was the strongest vessel of all.

On her map, their little conveyance ship was represented by a blue blip, with likely-hostile **space-time bubbles** as yellow blips. Agonizingly slowly, the distance between the two dots kept changing.

Around an hour later, the **Sfagnoff Portal** blocked the way between the yellow and the blue. The blue dot made no bones about driving headlong to its destination.

"I'm picking up a friend-or-foe call sign," said Lafier, clutching her *froch* sensory organ from above her **circlet**.

"From an **Empire** ship?" asked Jint, with a faint hope.

"Can't tell where it's coming from, but the one thing that's certain is that it's not the **Empire** asking."

"Boy, I could really use a pleasant surprise from time to time." He wanted to cry, but he managed to hold back his tears. "Could we lie and say we're allies?"

Lafier seemed impressed. "You can come up with some underhanded tactics."

"I blame my upbringing," Jint sulked.

"To answer the question, no, we can't."

"I hate how my hunches are always on the mark."

"There it is!" Lafier scowled.

"There what is?" Whatever it was, it couldn't be good.

"Their detention order. 'If you don't assume the **stationary-state** we'll attack.'"

"Let me guess, we're not stopping."

Lafier's shock showed on her face. "You'd want me to?"

"Hell no," he said, in the heat of the moment. But his words belied his true feelings. "Just making sure."

A short while later, Lafier mumbled: "They're near."

Now that it had come down to it, Jint *didn't* reply with a "Who's 'they'?"

Three dots split off from the big yellow one. Three extremely fast mines. Faster even than their ship. Rapidly, they closed in.

As he eyed those blips zeroing in after them on the map, his mind suddenly expanded to the possibility that, just maybe, life in a prison camp was in fact wonderful.

The conveyance ship swerved not. Jint probed Lafier's expression as she stared intently at the screen. Had she given up?

Dotted lines of green, red, and other colors besides had appeared on the **planar space map**.

At long last, Lafier gripped the steering gear and made their ship's **bubble** strafe to the side.

A slight while after the blue blip on the screen altered its course, the yellow ones turned in pursuit.

Persistent bastards, thought Jint, grinding his teeth.

He wanted to break out into a bawl. He wanted to call Lina's name. But the image of Lafier doing her level best beside him helped him keep his emotions from erupting.

Why was she putting in so much effort, though? Even if they did escape, the **mines** would come after them, and they'd catch up eventually.

Suddenly, it clicked. Lafier's big plan. She was waiting for the **mines'** fuel to run out. That's why she was trying her damnedest to postpone their chance encounter with fiery death.

Of course, she had to get closer to the portal at the same time. Otherwise, the **battle-line warship** would just fire more **mines**. If they didn't get beat out by the additional mines, they'd run out of fuel anyway.

God, if you really exist, then I beg you, poof these guys out of existence!

He made the sign of the cross and cast his eyes on the yellow blips. He should have gone to church more often. Then he'd have been able to snuff it with a more tranquil soul.

The yellow boss dot fired off another round of three mine-dots.

"I don't remember asking for more mines!" Jint shouted, unable to bottle it up any longer.

"That may be a sign we're going to win!" said Lafier excitedly.

"What do you mean!?"

"The reason they had to fire again is because the first set is running out of fuel…" Sure enough, as Lafier panted out her commentary, the first three blips faded away.

"YES!" Jint whooped… but his mood took a drearier turn when he remembered the *other* three.

"It's okay. We can do this!"

The **Sfagnoff Portal** was close by. The crooked spiral was reminiscent of a spider web, and the blue dot, a butterfly chased by a bird.

Lafier inserted her left hand into the **control gauntlet**. The conveyance ship trembled, proof the *saic* (engine) was ignited.

The yellow dot was hot on the blue dot's trail, snapping at their tail end and closing the distance.

Perhaps in consideration of Jint, the walls began displaying video of the outside — the grey nothing of **planar space**. He looked behind him.

White light was gushing out from a point at their back. Colors flickered to and fro around the dazzling corona, colors that swelled before his very eyes. This disgustingly beautiful light show portended *gor ptarhoth* — space-time fusion.

"Battle acceleration is a go," said Lafier. Their seats morphed into their sleeping-cot modes.

The colors that tinged the grey flowed alongside their acceleration until they'd become a solid band of hues. They rushed overhead from behind his back, and from the front of the ship (where his feet were pointed) to the back, combining to form great rainbow rings.

A **space-time bubble** was a universe unto itself, with a **space-time bubble generator engine** at its center. In the case of a single such engine, accelerating wouldn't change one's position within the pocket universe. Instead, the space-time bubble would appear to be spinning — and Jint had witnessed what a mind-blowing effect that rotation effected. Yet he wasn't sure he was up to feeling the full blast of acceleration right now, either.

"Won't they just chase us into **3-space**?" said Jint, bracing against the G-forces as they steadily ratcheted from six *daimon* to even higher speeds.

"In **3-space**, we're faster than they are."

"That's a relief."

The yellow and blue dots were very nearly touching when the rainbow colors and the grey canvas vanished, replaced by the star-pricked black of the heavens. They were back in **3-space.**

Again, he turned to look back. The **3-space** manifestation of the **Sfagnoff Portal,** a dimly radiating ball of gas, was floating there.

"And the **mines**!?"

"Over there." Her *frocragh* detected them faster than Jint could.

Whenever they ported over from **planar space,** whence on the portal they exited was completely up to random chance. As such, even if their pursuers exited through the same point on the uneven spiral in planar space as they did, they wouldn't necessarily come out of the same section of the sphere in 3-space.

Mine after enemy mine popped in from various off-target spots on the giant orb that was the portal, its phosphorescence helping them see them better. They were still homing in on the conveyance ship, only laughably slowly.

"Woo-hoo!" Jint cheered. "But wait, there must be enemies around here, right?"

"Not in the immediate vicinity."

"Well that's stupid of them." Even a novice like Jint understood how important it was to guard the portal.

"They're busy with other things. See for yourself." Lafier pointed even as they accelerated to yet higher velocities.

She was pointing to the sole inhabited planet of the **Sfagnoff Marquessate,** named Clasbure, or as the Abh spelled it, *Clasbyrh.* The way it was positioned relative to him, it almost felt natural to reach out and pluck it from the sky.

Light shone from the part of the planet covered in night, only to fade immediately.

"I bet the enemies that were in **planar space** were on high alert for any **Star Forces** ships that might come from the outside. They're blockading Sfagnoff."

"So they're still battling it out as we speak?" Jint groaned.

"Yep," Lafier nodded.

"Is it just me, or are we headed *toward* Clasbure?"

"Of course we are. That's our destination."

"But it's a warzone down there!"

"Where else is there!?"

"Uhh… you've got a point there." And seeing as there was no guarantee the **Star Forces** would win, they could hardly wait it out in nearby space. For one, even though they'd put some significant distance between themselves and the **mines**, they were still following them. Secondly, nothing precluded the possibility yet more of the enemy would emerge from the portal for their heads.

That being said, jumping into an active battlefield still wasn't the most appealing prospect. In fact, he rather loathed the idea.

"**Imperial Star Forces**, come in. This is the **conveyance ship** of the **patrol ship** *Gothelauth*!" she said, without transmitting video.

After trying several times, they finally received a response.

"This is the **Sfagnoff Communications Fleet Stronghold** speaking. Report your status, **conveyance ship**."

"The *Gothelauth* encountered an unidentified group of **space-time bubbles** in the sector of Itum 533. This ship broke off from the mother ship with non-combatants and navigation log in tow. Will be touching down here at present."

"Roger that, **conveyance ship**. As an anti-espionage measure, you are forbidden from divulging any further details on the matter."

"Roger, **Sfagnoff Stronghold**. Requesting instructions."

"Unfortunately, this **stronghold** cannot field your ship. You must proceed without instruction."

Lafier bit her lower lip. "Roger, **Sfagnoff Stronghold**. This ship will proceed without instruction. *Sathoth* (victory) be ours!"

"The chances of that are slim," they laughed dryly. "But still… *sathote Frybarari a* (victory be the Empire's)!" They hung up.

Jint couldn't stop himself from asking: "Does that mean we're losing?"

"Of course it does," she said, rattled. "The number of troops stationed in each **territory-nation** is small. Do you think a single **communications fleet stronghold** can hold back a full-scale invasion!?"

"I'm sorry. It was a dumb question."

"No, I'm sorry…" said Lafier. "Forgive me, Jint… In the end, I failed in my mission to escort you safely."

"It wasn't your fault," he answered back in an almost canned way. "So where's the enemy?"

"They're still far, but three ships are headed our way."

"Is three their lucky number or what?" Jint looked ahead, or as he perceived it, up. Clasbure had gotten even bigger, filling up almost all of his field of vision. While he couldn't spot any enemy encampments, he did notice something thread-like sauntering off from the planet's noonday zone.

"What's that thing?"

"Looks like an **orbital tower**."

"Oh yeah, the tower…"

Destroyed, it was rotating, glinting off the rays of Sfagnoff's sun.

"A lowly act. **Orbital towers** aren't military bases…"

"Uhh…" There was something they had to be worrying about more than the enemy's character. "Can this thing land at all now?"

"Land?" Lafier turned her neck to look at him dead-on.

"Yeah! I mean, what other option is there with the **orbital tower** gone?" he said, horrified at what that meant. "Is it impossible…?"

"No, it should be possible."

"'Should be' possible? *'Should be'*?"

Ath letters appeared on screen. Lafier gave them a cursory glance. "I knew it. It is possible."

"Hold on a sec. Are you telling me you didn't give *landing the ship* any thought until this very moment?"

"Yes," she nodded, looking guilty.

"You didn't even think about entering the planet to begin with, did you."

"No."

"Then why all the hustle?" *Urgh, I feel so weighed down. How long are we going to be accelerating for, anyway?*

"I thought we'd be aiding in the fight."

"How would we do that!? Thing's not even armed! Did you think we'd take them out the way you took out the **Baron**?"

"I didn't think that far ahead. But there still might be something we can do. Besides, there are three ships tailing us at the moment."

"That may be true, but from where I'm standing it'd have been suicide."

"You're right; I was being hasty." She lowered her eyes. "And I didn't even consult you, my passenger…"

"Consult me…!?" Jint was suddenly seized with anger. "You, you idiot!"

Lafier's eyes widened with shock, but then shame set in. "You have every right to speak ill of me. I was undervaluing your life."

"No, who cares about *my* life!? Er, I take that back, I do care about my life, but that's not what I'm so worried about. What about *your* life, Lafier!?"

Now Lafier's eyes burned with rage. "I nearly wrapped you up in a war with little hope of victory, and for that I must apologize. I resign myself to any punishment you have to dole out, no matter how cruel."

"Punishment!?" he gasped. "You honestly think I want to punish you? And 'cruelly' at that?"

Lafier wasn't about to stand down. "But you have no business firing at me over *my own* life!"

"Maybe not," he cried, "but what I'm trying to say is… Why do you feel the need to rush to your own death when you've got such a long life ahead of you? Could you maybe spare some thought to *surviving*, Lafier!?"

"I am NOT 'rushing to my death.'"

"Really? 'Cause that's what it looks like. Didn't you say you only fight when you have to? Or was that a lie?"

"The fight's already here, Jint. This is a warzone. And when a **soldier**'s on a battlefield, they fight!"

"All right, fine. If you wanna fight, go ahead. But seeing as I'm not a **soldier** yet, do me a favor and drop me off on that planet!"

"Fine! It's not like you'd be any use in battle anyway!"

"Oh, and you'll be SO useful with your tiny ship! Go on, what do you plan on doing in this thing, exactly!?"

The two glared at each other.

Lafier was the first to look away. "I'm sorry, Jint."

"This is the greatest day of my life," said Jint, releasing the tension. "A **royal princess** apologized to me *twice*. Even among **nobility** that's something to boast about, right?"

"Don't tease me, Jint. But… you're right. Even if I were to join the battle, this ship would serve no purpose. You're not the only one who's useless; I am, too."

"Which isn't your fault," he consoled her. "I've already told you, but you're not useless to *me* — I'm grateful, for everything. And I mean it. I may be useless now, but one day people will rely on me. I just want to survive long enough to get to that point, and I want YOU to survive, too."

"Uh-huh," she answered tersely.

As their anger subsided, so too did their fear. Earlier, Jint felt as though his heart was in a vise, but now it was back to normal.

No use worrying. What will be, will be.

Jint screwed up his resolve. He would take after the style of the Abh: he wouldn't dwell on the what-ifs of his own potential death.

At the very least, death among the stars would descend quickly, without any long-lasting pain. What if he were to fall asleep or lose consciousness? At these blistering speeds, he could imagine closing his eyes one second and finding himself in heaven the next. It'd be right out of a feel-good movie.

Unfortunately, his consciousness was not flagging.

After a while, the call sign rang.

"That the **communications stronghold**?"

"No. The transmission is coming from the spaceship ahead of us."

"So it's hostile, huh…? Are they close?"

"Yes. Very."

Jint squinted. Something grain-sized was shining against the planetary backdrop. Was that the enemy ship?

Lafier answered the call.

"*Pan dong zop cos ree jee. Nayk go sheck…*" A language Jint couldn't understand.

"The hell is that?"

"The official language of the United Humankind. They say they'll attack unless we stop accelerating."

"You know that language?"

"Yes, I study it at the **academy**. And so will you at the **Quartermaster Academy**."

"Ugh. And after I finally mastered Baronh."

"Don't worry, it's a simple language to learn. But in exchange for being simple," she frowned, "it lacks any richness. In terms of elegance, it can't even stand in the same ring as Baronh."

"Yeah, probably not," said Jint as the foreign words fell on his ears. It seemed as though they were repeating the same sentences over and over.

Lafier dropped the line without responding. She'd never once entertained the notion of negotiating with them.

"I was looking forward to whether they ever said anything different."

"I really don't want to be killed by a bunch of humorless pricks."

"Me neither."

At last, they could make out the enemy clearly. Their ships made up the vertices of a pyramid with an equilateral base.

"Jint, I have some good news."

"Good news? I've almost forgotten what that's like. Lay it on me."

"The main battlefield is on the other side of the planet. The ships right in front of us are the only ones here."

"That's awesome. But we don't know when they'll get reinforcements from the other side, right?"

"No, we don't. However, the chances that happens are low."

"Then let's make a run for the surface when those scary old codgers are away from their seats."

"Right after we dodge their attacks."

The ship loomed nearer by the second.

Suddenly, all sense of gravity disappeared. Just as suddenly, they lurched hard to the right. He'd experienced this once before, during their battle against the **Baron**.

The conveyance ship dodged enemy fire through the use of chaotic, seemingly random propulsion. Moments passed, and a glint of light flashed to their right. Unless he was imagining it, the enemy's **laser** or antiproton beam must have collided against particulate matter.

The spectacle of battle always gave him goosebumps. The constant shifts in perceived gravity were making him dizzy. Unlike the fight at Febdash, he was secured in place, so this was slightly preferable... or so he thought initially.

He got pushed against the seat, suspended from it, pinned in such a way that he looked like he was being crucified upside-down...

You can take it. You can take it. Jint endured as the contents of his stomach gradually rose up. He wondered who had it harder in times like these, the pilot or their passengers?

The enemy ship came into view overhead. The second lay right below, and the third to the left.

Their close encounter with the enemy had already concluded. By the time the G-force fluctuations ceased, the *asautec* (propulsor flames) of the enemy ships were flickering far behind them.

"Are we... Did we get away?"

"Yes. They can't catch up to us now, even if they about-face."

"Man, they really let us past without much a fight, huh?"

"Ignorance is bliss," said Lafier, exasperated. "We missed one of their **lasers** by a mere 20 *dagh*."

"If it had hit us, would we be in trouble?"

"In that we'd be scattering as a clump of *gnoc* (plasma), yes."

"Now that's a tragic ending," he said quietly.

Lafier picked up the teletransceiver. The other side shouted: "*Coo lin mahp ahs tang kip!*"

"What did they say just now?"

"Nothing that a young lady," said one angry, blushing Lafier, "should ever repeat!"

"Ah... Gotcha."

"I'm going to start decelerating soon. Don't make a fuss."

The sky and the ground switched places. Above floated the **Sfagnoff Portal**, while below them waited the planet of Clasbure.

"Decelerate how hard, exactly?"

"We're going fairly fast at the moment, so you can expect a rough ride."

"Go easy on me, please."

"I could go easier on you, if you prefer burning to a crisp on entry."

"No thanks, I hate when it's hot out."

"Then you'd best grit your teeth for this."

And so it began: an experience that would make their acceleration up to that point seem breezy by comparison. Their soft seats were holding them in place, but still his ribs were near to crumpling in. Blood rushed away from his extremities. His world was turning as red as his eyes.

Jint gritted his teeth and endured. He stole a glance at Lafier; even she was sweating.

Their rough ride wore on. How much time had passed now?

Suddenly, the footage cut out, taking with it the stars above and the blue sphere below. Back to the walls of opal white. And the pressure pinning their bodies disappeared, too.

"Wha, what happened?"

"Worry not. I've merely detached the hull."

"'Merely'?"

"We can hardly enter the atmosphere while carrying **anti-matter fuel**. Think of how that'd affect the planet's people."

"But you didn't have to go that far, did you…?" *Yet more Abh excessiveness*, thought Jint.

"**Conveyance ships** aren't designed with surface-landing in mind." Lafier was speaking rapidly now. "All landings are emergency landings."

"Can we even land without a hull?"

"We can't land *with* a hull," Lafier had lost her patience. "I'm frightened, too, Jint. This is my first-time surface-landing!"

"Your first time!?"

"I told you before: I've never been to a **landworld**."

"But surely it's come up in training…"

"Yes, I've done the mock training, but that's all."

"So which one's got you scared — surface-landing, or being on a surface world?"

"Both!!"

And Jint could more than see why that might be. He held his tongue, since he understood that forging through fear was a personal struggle, and the last thing he wanted was to get in her way.

Not long after, the shaking commenced. The ship — or what remained of it — dragged against Clasbure's atmosphere. As they were rocked violently, Jint could only think: *Glad I can't see outside.*

At last, the turbulence died down. Their seats morphed back upright from their sleeping-cot mode. The peculiar floating sensation harked back to memories past within Jint: this is how it felt that one time, years prior, when he had descended from an orbital tower down to the surface.

Oh man, I remember...

He'd been a ball of worry back then, too. So much so that he could barely recall what the cabin attendant who had been at his side looked like.

I wonder what the world below is like...

That train of thought snapped him out of his reverie. "I totally forgot!"

Lafier eyed him inquiringly. "Forgot what?"

"We're gonna need *info* on this planet. Have we got any location data on board?"

"Yes, there should be relevant data in the **compucrystals' memory net**."

"Awesome! **Compucrystals**, give us data on the **Sfagnoff Marquessate**."

The words *Lœbehynh Sfagnaumr* appeared on screen alongside a large article entry, with headers for HISTORY, GEOGRAPHY, and INDUSTRY listed underneath.

"Please select a category and one or more operations," said the cyber-voice. "Operations include BROWSE, ADD, COPY..."

Jint inserted his armrest's *ceumec* (wire connection) into his **wristgear** and said, "Whole document, copy."

UNDERSTOOD flashed twice on screen before shifting into a COMPLETE.

"No more operations, **compucrystals**," said Jint. He unplugged the **wire connection** and patted the **wristgear**. A little bit of information would go a long way, so he was glad it had occurred to him to check.

Why hadn't Lafier made any effort to research any potential safe havens? Was she not clear on standard operating procedures for surface-landing? But the second he was about to ask her as much — the shock of impact.

"Did we land...?" he squeaked pitifully.

"Yep." Their hair was swaying from back to front as the wind rolled through.

Jint looked behind and saw the door to the **air lock room** was open. Only there was no air lock room there. What met his eyes instead was tall straw-colored vegetation, rustling in near darkness but for the light emitted by the **steerer's room**.

They were on land.

"Jint, we need to hurry. They may have spotted us from above." Lafier removed her **seatbelt** and bade Jint stand up, too.

"Ah, uh, right." Jint got to his feet.

"Open!" Lafier commanded the seats. They folded backward at a precise 90-degree angle.

"Does that opening lead into some secret basement?"

"No, **stupid**."

The compartment underneath the seats was for storage. Its contents were covered by the *daüch* long robe she'd purloined from the **barony**. Lafier set that wardrobe aside to reveal the two **lightguns** that had been out of sight.

"Take and keep one."

"I was wondering where you'd hidden these," said Jint, who took a gun plus accompanying items.

"I wasn't hiding them. I simply stashed them while you were having a nap. It is a cramped space."

"I get it, I get it. Please don't take every little thing at face-value. It was just banter." He put on his **waistsash** and holstered his gun in it.

"This, too." She handed him a knapsack. On it was written "FOR EMERGENCY SURFACE EVACUATION" in small text. It contained a bunch of **combat rations** parcels, an assortment of tools, and some medicines.

"Hope they're not past the best-by date," he said, glowering at the **rations**.

He closed the lid over the knapsack and strapped it on. It wasn't very heavy on his back.

Lastly, Lafier picked up a *mhlamh* (pendant)-like trinket and put it on over her neck.

"Jint." She held it in her hand for him to see. "The **patrol ship** *Gothelauth*'s navigation log is in this. If I should die, I'd like you to escape with it."

"C'mon, don't go jinxi—" But the **royal princess**'s intense stare made him feel small.

"It's just a hypothetical."

"All… all right," Jint nodded. "Got it."

Lafier returned the nod and tucked the **pendant** into the collar of her **military uniform**. Then, she issued the following command to the **compucrystals**: "Prepare for deletion."

The words "DELETION PREPARATION COMPLETE" danced on screen.

"Is there anything you'd like to take out of the **crystals**?" asked Lafier.

Jint shook his head. "No."

"Okay." Lafier's tone turned pained. "**compucrystals**, this is goodbye. For the sake of confidentiality, delete everything."

"Understood. Executing confidentiality protocols. Deleting all information and system processors. We wish you peace and safety."

A pair of eyes appeared on screen, only for their lids to slowly droop. Once they were totally shut, the screen blinked out.

Dark sense of humor for a computer, thought Jint. However, Lafier was of a clearly very different reaction. She faced the screen and saluted it.

"All right, let's go," said Lafier, laying her hands on the door's edge.

"Wait, hold on!" Jint jumped for the **long robe** that Lafier had tossed to the side on the floor.

"What are you doing?" said Lafier, having returned. She peered at what Jint held in hand.

"We're gonna need money, too!" Jint turned it over and collected the **sash clip**. It consisted of a ruby embedded in a platinum base. As such, it could probably fetch quite the price.

"Money?" Lafier cocked her head. "We have money."

"Huh?"

"I'll show you." She worked her **wristgear**. "See? 5,000 *scarh*. I haven't used any of what *Fïac Loranr* (His Highness my father) gave me."

Given that on Delktu, Jint had gotten by with around 20 *scarh* a month, that was a positively tantalizing goldmine. And yet…

What use was Empire money on a planet that was this close to succumbing to an enemy occupation? Not only that, but the currency existed purely digitally on her **wristgear** anyway. Who here would accept that as legitimate tender?

But it soon dawned on a dumbfounded Jint. There was nothing like the realization that Lafier was a child of the stars through and through — and a highborn one at that — to clear any illusions he had about her innate royal competencies. She'd no doubt never even shopped by herself before.

"I'll go into it later. Let's just get out of here for now." Jint stuffed the **sash clip** into the knapsack and stepped outside.

He looked back at the spherical remains of the ship they'd soon be abandoning, and noted four wing-like flaps spread out at the top. They probably deployed to create more air resistance and slow their descent. Unfortunately, they also made the ship stick out like a sore thumb when viewed from above. They needed to leave, and fast.

"Should we run?" asked Lafier.

"If you're okay running."

"What do you mean, if I'm okay?"

"I mean, you might be tuckered out."

"I'm not. I'm more worried about *you*."

"Need I remind you that I'm the one who's more used to running on land?" With that, Jint was off.

"Wait, Jint, there's something wrong with my eyes!" shouted Lafier.

"What!?" Startled, he stopped in his tracks.

Lafier had looked up at the sky after taking a step out of the steerer's room. "The stars look like they're *flickering* to me."

Jint likewise looked up. There wasn't a cloud in the sky. Sure enough, the stars were flickering for Jint, too, but he knew that didn't mean his vision was faulty.

"If this were the **capital**, I'd have ready access to treatment, but here..." Lafier screwed up her determination and faced Jint. "I don't want to be a burden on you. If I lose my eyesight, I want you to take the navigation log and leave me..."

"I hate to piss all over your splendid martyr's spirit," cut in Jint, "but your eyes are totally fine."

"You'd best not be consoling me with lies," she said sternly.

"I'm not consoling you. I'm not 100% sure, but I think it's refraction that causes it. In any case, the stars always seem to twinkle from inside an atmosphere."

"Really?" She probed his expression, aided by the light filtering from the steerer's room.

"I'm not smart enough to come up with such a plausible lie on the fly. That's just how the stars appear on **landworlds**. Relieved?"

"I suppose," Lafier admitted, albeit reluctantly. Through the tenor of her voice, he could sense she was, in fact, relieved.

"I get the feeling your education was lacking in a critical department."

"Shut up, Jint."

"I'll shut up; talking while running is too hard anyway."

Judging by the orderly rows of identical vegetation, it seemed they were in a field. What that crop actually was, they didn't know. They looked like some form of grain. The first thing that popped to Jint's mind was wheat ears. The plots had been planted such that a single-person file could traverse the gaps between. The dirt underfoot was damp, but not muddy enough to impede their progress. On the contrary, the ground was just soft enough to be perfect for running.

A short while after they'd begun running, there was a shift in the starry sky above. A large number of charged particles, formed in the battle beyond Clasbure's atmosphere, painted fluttering streaks of red and green as they came raining down.

Chapter 6: The *Lœbehynh Sfagnaumr* (Sfagnoff Marquessate)

The **Sfagnoff Marquessate** was founded in the year 648 **I.H.** (Imperial History).

Sosïéc Üémh Sailer Daglaic started the Campaign on Yaktia as *Glaharérh Byrer* (Fleet Commander-in-Chief) and was appointed its lord upon distinguishing himself with success.

The Sfagnoff Star System possessed seven main planets, the third of which had seemed suitable for human settlement were terraforming to be carried out. Its atmosphere was chiefly composed of carbon monoxide, with little hydrogen to speak of, but that proved no impediment.

Daglaic, the First *Bœrh Sfagnaumr* (Viscount of Sfagnoff), then named the planet after the **coat of arms** of his House of *Sosïéc*, the *Ïadh Chrehainena le Clasbyrh* (Silver Branch and Snail) before embarking on the planet's terraforming.

There was a standard sequence for birthing a new habitable planetscape.

First came fundraising. Terraforming demanded large sums of capital, but in the absence of some gross oversight, there was guaranteed money in it, so there was seldom ever a shortage of potential investors.

Daglaic, however, skipped that first step entirely. Thanks to successive generations of investment, the Sosiec family had amassed a sizable fortune, obviating the need to seek outside sources of seed money.

Second came the work of terraforming itself. The **Empire** boasted several *gareurec fazér diüimr* (terraforming engineer's associations) taking on contracts to oversee the process from the preliminary exploration phase to the crafting of the ecosystem.

One such *gareurec* (union) came to Clasbure and set about altering the orbit of an icy planet on the perimeter of the star system such that it collided with Clasbure. This covered the planet in water vapor, rinsing the ground through the resulting cataracts of rain. Rivers emerged. Oceans came into being.

Next to be sown were the algae and the microorganisms centered around them. Those microorganisms exploded in number, absorbing carbon and leaving behind oxygen in their wake. Their husks would go on to pile up on the planet's rocky surface, becoming soil.

Then higher-class plant life was introduced. Strains like *ronrébh* (sand lawn) and *rodauremzœch* (imitation lava pines), which matured quickly and could plant roots even in poor quality soil, were the principal species. The plants raised the soil's water retention capacity, synthesizing abundant organic matter from inorganic beginnings. Subsequently, with each new generational transition of the plant life, the soil became more fertile, eventually allowing for the successful sowing of species that require a richer environment. Fish, too, were introduced to the seas and lakes, while annelids, insects, and other crawlies were unleashed upon the land.

The evolution that took billions of years to develop on Earth of old had been truncated to an extreme extent through a handful of different processes, and the order of said developments had been adjusted for heightened convenience and efficiency.

On the fiftieth year, a comprehensive ecosystem including higher-order mammals had been instated, thus marking the completion of an inhabitable planet. Typically, that was when colonization would take place. In this case, however, scant effort was made to solicit for settlers. By that time, reign over the planet had been passed down to the Second **Viscount of Sfagnoff**, *Disclaic*, a man who felt no pressing urge to people his freshly terraformed planet with **landworld citizens**.

As to why, the public was still not privy. Perhaps he saw the planet as a garden or park. If that was indeed the case, then his driving desires were brazen by the standards of the **Kin of the Stars**. It was commonplace among the Abh to take pride in counting the universe itself as their home, and even **grandees** only rarely left their **orbital manors** to visit the **landworld** below. If an Abh appeared to want to claim a surface world for themselves, it would be cause for scandal. It was therefore only reasonable that that wouldn't be disclosed.

There was, however, a more favorable way of viewing the matter as well: he was waiting to see whether intelligent life would naturally evolve and serve as the planet's **landworld citizens**. If that was true, then he was mad in the singularly Abh fashion, leaving aside the baffling lack of pride he showed in his own *Bœriéc Sfagnaumr* (Viscount House of Sfagnoff).

Whatever the case, migration to the planet began with the peerage of the Third **Viscount of Sfagnoff**, *Etlaic*.

Agreements were reached with the **lords** and *saiméïc sosr* (landworld administrations) of 13 **territory-nations** that were facing impending overpopulation, and a settler recruitment office was opened.

The first day of the first month of the Clasbure calendar coincided with the 29th day of the eleventh month of the year 729 **I.H.**.

Viscount *Etlaic* was made a **count** thanks to his deed of adding a new inhabited planet to the **Empire**, and he joined the ranks of **grandees**. What was formerly the **Viscountdom of Sfagnoff** was now the *Dreuhynh Sfagnaumr* (Countdom of Sfagnoff).

93 years after settlement began, the population reached the 100,000,000 mark, thereby warranting an upgrade to **marquessate**.

At present, the population of Clasbure is around 380,000,000. It has 21 states, with an assembly of state premiers comprised of saimh sosr(landworld citizen representatives)...

...Rattled off Jint's **wristgear** as, seated atop a hill, he scanned his surroundings. Or perhaps it was not so much as a hill as a giant piece of pumice, a big, holey boulder.

It was nothing but crops as far as the eye could see, in all directions, rows of the exact same plant running down to the horizon and beyond. Even now, following the advent of hydroponic farming, making use of the naturally occurring water and light on a planet's surface was still the cheapest method of food production, even counting the upfront cost of planetary terraforming.

From up on this hill, they really did look like wheat. Granted, that could be because that was the grain he was most used to. They could very well be a genetically engineered giant strain similar to but distinct from wheat.

Whatever. It's wheat, he decided. *It's not like it changed their situation.* Gusts of wind made the fields rustle in surging waves, swaying from right to left — a virtual sea of gold.

Meanwhile, the "hill" of pumice jutted out from it all like a remote isle. To the distant right stood another isle, which looked to be a forest. Something was circling above that forest. Local planetary transport?

Or maybe…

All in all, the scene before them was idyllic. One would never expect this to be a warzone.

It was early evening now. They had spent all the night prior running, and dawn was cracking when they stumbled across the hill. By that point they were worn out. Luckily, they'd found a hole in the pumice face so big it was nearly a cave, and they slipped in for some much-needed sleep. Lafier was, of course, just as exhausted as he was.

Given their situation, taking shifts standing vigil should have been a matter of course. In fact, Jint had meant to stand vigil, without ever having told Lafier. But the exhaustion had seeped into his very marrow, and sleep swallowed him up in no time. He'd only finally awakened moments ago. The reason he'd left Lafier's still-dozing side to climb to the top of the hill was to survey their environs.

Jint shut off the informational audio, and tried tuning into the spot broadcasting frequency.

A middle-aged woman's face displayed on his small screen. She was orating on something or other. At first, he didn't understand a word she said.

There was no data regarding languages on the **conveyance ship**'s limited **memory net**, nor was his **wristgear** equipped with a translator function. But as he focused on the words, he realized it was, in fact, Baronh.

"We… need… thank… organization… united… humans. Reason… they… freed… us… leave… control of… Ahw. Now… we… need… erect… independent… government… belong… us… resembling… us…"

Thus, Jint picked it up.

This was not the standard Baronh that was the official language of all the **Empire**, but rather a simplified patois.

The complicated declension of Baronh had been removed; now grammatical meaning was determined by word order. Moreover, that word order was the same as Martinese. So, once he'd gotten used to the Clasbure accent ("Abh" was now "Ahw"), he started grasping the gist of her address.

Of course, words of seemingly non-Baronh origin were also sprinkled throughout, but he could still understand the overall thrust of the sentences.

To sum it up, this lady was saying "Let us give thanks to the United Humankind, who have liberated us from Abh rule."

That such a broadcast made it to air could only mean the **Star Forces** had been defeated. Jint was quick to come to grips with that fact. He'd already steeled himself to the eventuality. All he could really do was wait until the **Empire** reclaimed the land.

Jint fiddled with the frequency to see whether he could turn the channel. He was greeted by footage of a cityscape. It was most likely a movie.

A smirk formed. Really? Entertainment? At a time like this? On second thought, maybe it was a form of resistance in itself. After all, the whole planet had been built up by the Abh to begin with, just like Delktu. The population was composed of the descendants of those migrants who had already accepted Abh rule. Unlike a planet like *Martinh*, which had been conquered, anti-Abh sentiment here was probably sparse.

Actually, the planet was perhaps altogether indifferent. Cosmic-scale conquest likely held no interest to ordinary surface folks.

Incidentally, the garb the people wore in the movie caught Jint's eye more than the plot. There was no differentiation by gender in much of Abh fashion. Males and females alike wore **jumpsuits**. Here on Clasbure, however, it seemed **jumpsuits** were for males, while females wore simpler one-piece dresses and knee-high boots.

He tuned away from the transmission, deciding instead to determine their current location. He set the device to receive signals from several different location markers on the planet's surface and cross-referenced them against the map he'd booted from the ship's **compucrystals**.

He discovered a city named Lune Beega not too far away. In mentally matching the surrounding landscape with the map displayed on his **wristgear**, he came to understand the forest floating in the sea of gold was not a forest at all.

Question is, do we try to blend in there, or do we stick to the fields... Jint mulled it over. He only had nine meals' worth of **rations** left. Even if he spaced those meals out, he'd run out in five days, tops. Procuring more food here was their only option.

However, while this stretch of land was evidently a plantation, he had no idea how to harvest the crops, and no tools to make them fit for consumption. That, and he shuddered to think of how many days they'd be spending sleeping out in the open. It would be hard enough for Jint, who'd grown up on a **landworld**. It'd be even harder for Lafier, who'd been brought up in an artificial environment.

It was settled: hiding out in Lune Beega was the way forward. Viewed from here, the city seemed small and unreliable, but there was bound to be public transport that'd take them to bigger cities.

Dusk had arrived, and so Jint clambered down the hill; it wasn't too high up, but it was a steep slope. Additionally, though there were plenty of holds for his hands and feet, the pumice was brittle. Any foothold could easily give way.

After many a close call, Jint made it to the base of the hill. He wrapped around the base and knelt down to enter the hole — only to find he was face to face with a gun.

"It's me, Lafier!" he said, hands up.

"Where were you?" she said, putting it back.

"Just went to do a little scouting."

"I didn't ask you what you were doing. I asked you where you were."

"Man, you're literal... I was atop the hill."

"You *onh*!"

"What?" he replied, flabbergasted.

"What if they'd seen you?"

"It's okay. Nobody's here."

"They could be standing watch from above!"

"Oh yeah." No doubt there were enemy ships scanning the surface from orbit as they spoke. They could, in fact, have spotted him. "But I'm telling you, I'm in the clear. I'm not wearing a **long robe**; they'd see me as a resident of the planet."

"You can't rely on the enemy making a mistake."

"All right, fine. I won't be so rash again. Promise."

"Good. Don't leave me without saying a word."

"You were sleeping so soundly, though. Speaking of which, I guess I still haven't said 'good morning,' so… Good morning, Lafier. Though I guess it's already dark out."

"**Idiot**." Again that word.

Grumpy much? Jint shrugged. *Guess even she can be childish sometimes.* "Wanna move base, just in case?" he suggested.

"Yes, I believe that would be wise. I can't say staying here would be anything but dull, anyway," she said, on her feet now.

After tiding themselves over with some food, they set about preparing to leave.

Jint picked up the small apparatus that had been placed over by the far end, a machine that converted moisture into potable water. Sure enough, its container was filled to the brim. He poured its contents into two flasks and handed one to Lafier. Knapsacks strapped on, the two put the hill in which they'd spent one night of their lives behind them.

Jint broke the silence as they trudged on. "I reckon we head into the city."

"The city?"

"Yeah. Beats playing hide-and-seek in the fields, anyway. I'd like to rejoin civilization at some point."

"But won't it be dangerous?"

"For sure it will be," Jint replied. What was he going to do, lie? "But it's hardly safe out here, either. I'm not **His Excellency the Former Baron of Febdash**, but I'll tell you what he told us. I don't know what the way forward is. That said, there's no food here. I don't know if you like the idea of starving to death in the middle of nowhere, but to me it's gotta be the second least dignified way to go."

"You're right," said Lafier. Her voice was lacking its usual verve.

"You're still tired, aren't you, Lafier?"

"I am no such thing," she snapped. "Why would you say that?"

"Just asking." *Phew. There's the hot-tempered girl I know,* he thought, relieved. "But tell me when you are, okay?"

"I told you, I'm not tired."

"Yeah huh."

The dark of night grew ever thicker, and finally the sun sank entirely.

"Jint." Her voice sounded from behind. "Go on a little ahead of me."

"Why?" He spun to face her, surprised.

"Don't ask." Her face had turned grim in the starlight.

"Whaddya mean, 'don't ask'? Look around, there's no landmarks anywhere. What if we lose sight of each other?"

"Fine, then you should wait here."

"Sure, but... I've still gotta know why."

"And I said *don't ask.*"

Jint's unease only mounted. Had she stumbled across some fresh new reason to play martyr? He was duty-bound to disabuse her of whatever false notion she might be operating under.

"Listen, Lafier..." Jint proceeded to speechify as to the nature of working in tandem. No keeping secrets, no trying to solve problems alone. They were to come up with their next steps together. That was the meaning of camaraderie. They had to overcome this crisis by joining forces and...

Lafier was listening at first, but gradually her brows slanted into a dangerous "V."

"Jint, you are officially dumber than a pack of frozen vegetables!" she cried at last. "Just wait there and look away!"

A certain ennui assailed Jint as he watched her stomp off into a row of wheat. Then he hastily averted his gaze. In this darkness, she wouldn't have been visible anyway, but it was incumbent upon him to respect the wishes of a blushing maiden.

Of course. Yes, she was Abh, beautiful as a sculpture. Yes, she was a relative of the **Empress** who ruled over 900 billion *rüe bisarh* (imperial subjects). But she was still a creature of physiological needs.

Jint's legs turned to jelly and he fell to a seat next to the base of some more giant wheat. How could he let himself get so carried away? What a buffoon.

Meanwhile, at that very moment, a reconnaissance spaceship named "DEV903" and belonging to the Peacekeeping Force of the United Humankind was hard at work analyzing video of the surface, and discovered a surface-landing hull of an Imperial Star Forces ship in the farmland outside the city of Lune Beega.

The work crew had attempted to place where it had come from, but without success. Records of the small vessel that had given three destroyers the slip in 3-space after dodging a warship's fire in planar space had gotten buried amidst all the other records detailing the huge and intricate battlefield. Gaining total control of an entire star system was no easy feat.

Of course, it would have only been a matter of time before they identified it fully, but there was a lot on their plate. The work crew surmised that the majority of soldiers left to find were escapees of the communications stronghold or the lord's manor. They'd also ascertained that, judging by the state of the hull, its erstwhile occupants were still alive.

They relayed that to Intelligence, but HQ had given the matter a very low priority level. After all, it had already been determined that all the key figures of the marquessate and the communications stronghold had already been captured or killed. Whoever the owner of this hull was, they weren't worth a frenzied hunt over.

Moreover, the *Laitefaiclach Sfagnaumr* (Sfagnoff Marquessate Defense Corps), the personal forces of the *Lœbeghéc Sfagnaumr* (Manor of the Marquis of Sfagnoff), were still holding the line in a few zones on the surface, and many important government figures were still on the lam as well. The investigation teams were all out, equipped with odor detectors. Devoting manpower to tracking down one or two people who'd crash-landed would be a waste of effort.

First, they needed to conquer the planet more firmly, and arrest and detain any and all individuals who had aided the **Empire**'s reign. Thus, they'd beat the "slave mentality" out of the populace.

The **Star Forces** soldier-hunting job could be carried out at their leisure. Their prey was helpless anyway.

"Whoa!" Jint came to a halt. He could hear the dirt fall in clumps down away from his feet.

It was a ravine. Jint had teetered on the cliff's edge.

"What is it?" said Lafier.

"It's a dead end."

And the sun wasn't peeking out any time soon. Jint screwed his eyes against the darkness trying to measure the gap, but there just wasn't enough light to make out what lay ahead.

He turned on his **wristgear**'s flashlight function, but illuminating the ground around him was the best it could manage.

Suddenly, light poured out from the vicinity. A powerful searchlight was cast upon the opposite side of the gorge.

Lafier was brandishing her **lightgun** at the ready. The beam was coming from its muzzle.

"How do you do that?" asked Jint, pulling out his own gun.

"I showed you where the safety is. Set it between SAFE and LOADED. That's where the flashlight function is."

"Really should've pointed out a feature that convenient at some point," carped Jint.

"It slipped my mind."

"I see." Using a gun as a flashlight was not an everyday occurrence.

Jint set the safety to ILLUMINATE, and pulled the trigger.

The gap was larger than he'd imagined. It was at least a *üésdagh* in breadth. The diagonally carved precipice wound wide indeed.

Deep, however, it was not, measuring only around 500 *dagh* top to bottom. There was giant wheat growing at the bottom of the canyon, too. He could look down on the ear tips.

"It's looking pretty rough," he said, holstering it back into his **waistsash** and leaning over to scan the cliff. The drop wasn't totally vertical, but it was too steep to walk down. Meanwhile, the climb back up looked easier. If they didn't watch themselves on the descent, they could easily tumble and plummet.

Jint took off his knapsack and rummaged through it. "We got a rope or something in here?"

"There should be a *ryrdüac* (carbon crystal fiber)."

"Sounds useable. Where is it?"

Lafier's hand extended from the side and took something rod-like out from Jint's knapsack. She spun it deftly in hand. "So, what do I do with this?"

"You need to ask?" he said, taken aback. "We're gonna use it to make our way down. Hand it over a sec."

Jint took the rod and inspected it. Though it was of course military issue, it took after the same general principle as the *iotmséc ryrdüar* (carbon crystal fiber spindle) he'd used on Delktu.

The **fiber** was contained within the rod's core, and fast-drying *gainh* (synthetic resin or "plastick") occupied a good part of both ends. Fibers of cheaper make might only be usable when uncovered, or be covered from the outset by a coating. This fiber, however, was high quality. One could choose whether to apply a coating based on the circumstances.

Moreover, the hook attached to the fiber's tip was versatile and could be remotely controlled. The **Star Forces** could be counted on to spare no expense, even on auxiliary items.

Jint strung the hook as he applied the coating on the fiber. Then he had it snake its way over to the base of some the giant wheat and hook on.

"All right, I'll go first." Jint gripped the **spindle**, turned his back, and lowered a leg. He let out the **fiber** little by little and rappelled down the cliff.

He made his last leap after confirming the ground was a mere 50 *dagh* below via the light of the **wristgear**.

"It's your turn, Lafier!" Jint shouted, looking up at the top of the precipice. He then set the **spindle** to automatically wind itself back and let go.

The **spindle** smoothly climbed back up the cliff, causing the coating to get scraped off the fiber, splattering as it went.

"I'm jumping!" she said, conveying her determination with heft and import.

Lafier descended with a great big *swoosh*. It looked as though she'd left **carbon crystal fiber** unreeled.

Jint rushed to her side. "You — you okay?"

"Of course I am," she said, her face contorted with pain.

"I told you, you've gotta stop overdoing it." Jint offered her a hand up.

"I am not overdoing it," she insisted, dismissing the hand.

"If you say so." Jint unhooked the line via remote control, and rewound it. The shavings of **plastick** piled up at his feet.

When he'd finished winding it back up, he used his gun once again to illuminate the cliff's underside.

"What are you doing?"

"Looking for a new lodge for the night. Gotta be far enough away now. Aaand looky here."

A cave. Jint beckoned her, and together they drew closer to their fresh accommodations.

It was quite extensive; they couldn't see its far wall even using the **lightgun**'s flashlight. Jint kept the cave's depths illuminated, on the lookout for some hidden, lurking threat, but as far as he could see, no such cause for concern was to be found.

Jint laid down his knapsack and summoned the map on his **wristgear**. It told him they were under 50 *üésdagh* from Lune Beega now.

Soon, it was mealtime for the two. Jint went into his plan while munching on some more nearly tasteless **combat rations**.

"I'm gonna go check out the city, but I'll be back."

"By yourself?" Lafier raised her brows.

"Uh, yeah. Duh."

"Why? Is there a reason I can't go?"

"You're wearing a **military uniform**," he pointed out. "Whaddya think'll become of somebody wearing a **Star Forces** uniform in an enemy-occupied town?"

"Ah…"

It never crossed her mind? For real? I mean, there's naïve, and then there's naïve.

But Jint kept those misgivings to himself. "That's why I'm gonna be getting you something to wear that won't stand out. I'll zip in and out as quickly as possible, so wait for me here."

A fire kindled in her eyes. Jint was flustered. What had sparked her ire now? Had he said something untoward?

No. He was making all the sense in the world, and besides, if she thought differently, she should tell him otherwise. The way she was glaring at him was uncalled for.

Yet he was surprised when Lafier nodded. "Okay."

"Good." Jint washed down the last crumbs of his **rations** with some water and got up off the ground.

"You're leaving already?"

"Yeah. The earlier the better."

"You might be rushing straight into ruin."

"No need to remind me. Half of me's sure I am."

Jint retrieved the **sash clip** from his knapsack and put it inside his **jumpsuit**'s **pocket**. He also decided to take three meals' worth of **rations** with him. The rest he left behind.

The issue was his **wristgear**. His model was the standard for the **Empire**, but it was rare across **landworlds**. The sharp-sighted among the people might find him out just through that. Naturally, they wouldn't jump to the conclusion that he's a **noble**, but they might think him a *laimh* imperial citizen. He would be pretending to be a *soss* landworld citizen, so that was an outcome he aimed to avoid.

On the other hand, the **wristgear** was a very convenient tool in his arsenal. After all, he needed to be able to contact Lafier if an emergency arose.

In the end, he elected to place it, too, into his **pocket**.

"You're not taking the gun?" she asked, incredulous.

This was no time for jokes. Jint could only shrug. "If I get caught in a shoot-out, I'm a goner, gun or no gun."

"Mm hm. So you'd rather just give up."

"Don't make me out like that. If they catch me carrying a **Star Forces** gun on me, they'd have me dead to rights."

"Ah. I see."

"Glad you see it my way," Jint sighed. But some trepidation lingered in him — not regarding his situation, fraught with peril as it was, but rather regarding leaving her to her own devices.

Up among the stars, he'd thought of the girl as a hypercompetent Abh exemplar, but now he'd witnessed how little thought she put in things that were the most basic common sense for him.

Don't worry, she'll be fine, he persuaded himself.

Lafier may have been lacking in everyday practicality, but that was only problematic when she was around others. Of course, it would be a different story once she stepped foot into the city herself, but for now, she was more than capable of taking care of herself as long as she was out of sight.

But how likely is it no one will spot her? After all, it was quite possible a search party was already closing in on them, which would raise its own set of fears.

Due to its nature, the **Star Forces** didn't put much emphasis on acting solo. It would be difficult for a single soldier, especially one without the relevant training, to be sufficiently mindful. Of course, Jint hadn't the training either, but he did have a strong suit the Abh were blind to: there was no way anyone could tell he was **nobility** unless he divulged it himself. If push came to shove, he could talk himself out of a dicey situation by claiming to be an **imperial citizen**.

On a nation as large as Sfagnoff, there had to be a considerable number of **imperial citizens**. Besides, it wasn't as though the enemy would exhibit that much interest in one nation's citizenry anyway.

By contrast, Lafier's blue hair and **Empire**-issue **military uniform** were dead giveaways. Jint would've liked to see the idiot who wouldn't cotton on straight away. Lafier getting spotted by somebody was the greatest crisis they could face at the moment.

Jint was stumped, until he hit upon a primitive alarm system.

"Be careful when you're out of the cave, all right?" With that, Jint let out the **carbon crystal fiber** (sans coating). He wedged a protruding rock onto the hook at about knee-height. He set the fiber to be covered in the coating, and let it out to a suitable length, holding it taut horizontally. Then he fastened the part of the line coated in the **plastick** onto a protrusion on the opposite end.

"What is that for?"

"It's a trap. It'll alert you if somebody comes too close," he explained, pointing to the non-coated **fiber**. "Not only is it invisible, it's sharper than any blade, too. So if somebody doesn't think better than popping in, then GYAAHH! Their legs, sliced clean off. Now that's tight security."

Lafier cocked her head. "What if an innocent falls for the trap?"

That, he hadn't thought of. To call the act of attacking an unrelated party with a snare that could easily sever a limb or two "barbaric" would be an understatement. But Jint quickly squashed his pangs of conscience.

"If that happens, it happens." He snapped a finger. "Sometimes, civilians get maimed and killed in war." And so Jint left for the city.

Lafier remained sitting, holding one knee. She was tuning into the airwaves of this land of "Clasbure" through her **wristgear**.

And she'd thought *Jint*'s accent was bad. The language spoken on this planet was barely even Baronh. There were traces of Baronh vocabulary, and it did have a more refined ring than the language of the United Humankind, but it was all a bunch of unintelligible mumbo-jumbo. She soon ran out of patience attempting to follow along.

As she absentmindedly watched the outside world get brighter, her mind dwelled on how she'd been left all alone. She was out of her element. Since they'd come aground, it had been Jint calling all of the shots. This did not amuse her.

Until she got Jint aboard an **Empire** *ménh* interstellar ship, she could not say she'd completed her mission. She had to protect him, and the navigation log, at all costs.

Despite that, she felt as though Jint was protecting *her* — a reality she was loath to accept. What angered her the most, however, was how much better things seemed to be going after she'd ceded the initiative to him.

Am I relying on him? Should I? she asked herself. Considering how flustered he'd been with her in space, she never thought him a particularly dependable individual.

She laid her head sideways against her raised knee. Earlier, she'd put up a brave front, acted tough in front of him. But she was tired. So, so tired. She'd even acknowledge her cat Horia was one of her **gene donors** if it could somehow strip her muscles of all the lactic acid.

The surface gravity on Clasbure was comparable to most other **landworlds**, but twice the *daimon* gravity-level to which the Abh were accustomed. Lafier had endured upwards of ten times the G-forces, yes, but she was always sprawled on a specially crafted seat designed to cushion her back during times of heavy acceleration. While the surface only clocked in at 2 *daimon*, it was her first time moving about in heightened gravity for such a long time.

Naturally, she couldn't be expected to keep a steady pace without ever tiring, but she felt pathetic, nonetheless. The bodies of Abhkind were expressly engineered to allow them some freedom of movement even during high acceleration. Her ancestors hadn't had the luxury of **gravity control systems**, nor did they complain.

The **Star Forces** had equipped the ship with an emergency surface-landing function, but she'd never given much thought to what that would precipitate. There wasn't usually a planet with a breathable atmosphere conveniently close by when a ship was caught in danger, after all.

It was little wonder, then, that her scenario hadn't cropped up in her training much. She'd learned how to land the ship, but all that was projected for the aftermath was to stay in place and await rescue.

Waiting for rescue in this particular situation, however, was a fool's errand. As a mere **trainee starpilot**, she was not privy to **Star Forces** soldier deployment, but she reckoned it'd take 10 days at the very shortest. She'd have to prepare herself for it taking more than twice as long.

She'd even have to make peace with the possibility that they'd *never* come… They might run out of food, or get captured by the those of the enemy army who pursued defeated soldiers.

She had no choice but to get through this while counting on Jint, whether he not he proved "dependable."

A smile played at her lips as she nodded off. *He's been full of life ever since we landed on a surface.* Even though the danger now exceeded what they faced back at the **Barony of Febdash**.

When she awoke and noticed Jint was absent, her mind ran wild. She was beset not by the fear she'd failed in her mission, but rather by the uncertainty of what to do from that point forward.

As hard as it was to believe, Lafier *was* relying on him. Lafier, a **royal princess** of the **Empire**. Depending on another.

But so be it. For there was no one else in a 100-light-year radius she could trust.

Chapter 7: *Bach Luner Bigac* (Lune Beega City)

"You know, it *really* wouldn't kill her to say 'Jint, you are the only one I can trust in a 100-light-year radius.' Talk about a hard-ass," he muttered to himself, breathing heavily as he crawled on his belly.

As he traversed the valley, he spotted a bridge — and a bridge meant there must be a trail. That much he had going for him, but there was no path nor any stairs to the bridge from the ravine.

When Jint found purchase on the towering cliff and crawled his way up, he was already dog-tired. Clearly, he had overestimated his own stamina. He ought to have taken a break before heading out.

Being beside Lafier had distracted him from it, but now that he was operating alone, the exhaustion came walloping. Sure, he was raised in a **landworld**, but one with extensive public transport. Spending days in the great outdoors wasn't exactly a hobby of his, either. The stamina that he'd built up through playing *minchiu* could only take him so far.

Look how much I'm busting my ass. A word of thanks would be nice at some point.

He did realize, however, that since he had volunteered for this, he had no right to complain. Besides, this was necessary for his own continued survival as well.

But wait… *was* this necessary for his survival?

Wouldn't it be, in fact, easier for him to simply abandon her? To go on living by himself?

A shudder ran down Jint's spine at the thought. He'd never seen himself as a man of unimpeachable virtue, but self-loathing naturally set in.

As long as he was entertaining these hideous thoughts, he might as well plunge the whole way. Selling Lafier to the enemy military and getting some coin for his troubles. That was an option.

Jint cracked a grin.

A grin he knew didn't suit him, even without a mirror.

The boy known as Jint Lynn was no saint, but he wasn't quite that craven or devious, either. Neither a hero for all time, nor a moustache-twirling scoundrel.

He was like a comet on an extremely elliptical orbit: following a path chosen for him, always scorched by the light of the sun, and at times budged by the gravity of some nasty nearby planet. Yes, that was the life for him.

But enough of this pity party. He got to his feet.

Just as he'd expected, there lay the road, the whole surface of which was shining softly. At first the light looked faint, but upon stepping onto the road, it was bright enough.

Jint began trekking toward Lune Beega.

The time it took Clasbure to make a single rotation technically lasted 33.121 standard hours (so Jint had actually slept for around 15 hours). The planet's residents divided those into 32 hours. Daily life, however, was measured in 24-hour periods. The most basic math would clue one in on the 8-hour difference between those two standards. It caused Clasburians to set the start of their days as either midnight or noon.

Headaches were inevitable, but the alternative was allowing the populace's biological clocks to go out of whack by 9 hours at a time.

Disassociating internal biological clocks from the planet's actual rotation period boasted an additional upside, as it mitigated the need to establish time zones. The sheer amount this benefited the planetary information superhighway could not be overstated.

The day had broken now, but according to the biological clock, it was nearly noon. He'd probably arrive at the city at around 1 in the afternoon — the perfect hour for some shopping.

Guess rushing to get here wasn't totally dumb after all, Jint thought, patting himself on the back ever so slightly.

After tuning the **wristgear** to the local feed, he stashed it into his **jumpsuit**'s **pocket**. He kept his ears open along the way to absorb the Clasburian tongue with which he needed to familiarize himself.

As he was picking up words here and there, Jint's mood grew rotten.

It was the enemy. They were broadcasting the rationale behind their invasion of the **Sfagnoff Marquessate**.

They were claiming that the **Imperial Star Forces** started this war themselves. They were saying that a Star Forces **warship** — which could only mean the *Gothelauth* — attacked the United Humankind unprovoked while the UH was exploring the **planar space** near a newly opened portal.

That, as retribution against that heinous act, and in order to seek the safety of the new portal, they had to "secure" the **Sfagnoff Marquessate** through "protective occupation."

"What a joke!" Having been on the **patrol ship** *Gothelauth* when it happened, Jint knew it was all lies. That fleet was far too large to be engaged in exploration, and even worse, it had been the UH who had started the war by sending out small high-speed spacecraft.

Sadly, no one here would be receptive to the truth.

Jint changed frequency, hoping to happen on something apolitical. Yet every channel was taken over by the enemy's broadsides. No trace remained of the kind of entertainment he'd been able to view the prior evening. The enemy must have consolidated their grip in the intervening hours.

One broadcaster aired a lecture on the concepts of democracy and liberty. Another featured the middle-aged woman from before, still singing the UH's praises while exposing the **Humankind Empire of Abh**'s twisted deeds.

How were the residents of the planet taking all of this? He definitely knew how they were taking it on *Martinh*. They must be backing this latest conqueror — or as they'd see it, friend and ally — with considerable zeal.

But what about here? To state that a world the Abh built up to begin with was "under the thumb of the Abh" was to overgeneralize.

That said, Jint didn't know anything about Clasbure apart from what he'd read in an encyclopedia article. He needed to know more before he could make up his mind as to whether or not that sweeping statement held true for this planet. It was also eminently possible that a populace that had been submissive to the Empire's reign would also submit to a new ruler.

He hoped that at the very least the people would be wholly indifferent. If the men and women of Clasbure joined the enemy soldiers in running wild on the hunt for Abhs, then his chances of remaining safe, but especially Lafier's, would nosedive.

Maybe staying in the fields would be wiser after all. Jint could go into the city to procure the necessary food and everyday supplies by himself. But he would leave that decision for after he'd inspected the situation in town.

Jint passed by a number of *üsiac* (hovercars) but didn't come across any other pedestrians.

At last, Lune Beega's structures stood before his very eyes.

Jint reached a hand into the **pocket** and turned off his **wristgear**. He was now confident he could follow the language.

Speaking was another matter entirely. He had no confidence he could convincingly imitate a Clasburian accent.

I know. I'll pretend to be a newly-arrived immigrant. He'd done it before on Delktu, and there was no reason he couldn't pull it off here.

The fields gave way to the ring-road encircling the city.

There they were. The people strolling through town.

Jint walked past a group of co-eds. One of their number cast him a suspicious look.

Was it his clothes? Upon giving the attire of the people around him a look, Jint could see why he might stand out.

First of all, there were the colors he was wearing. While the locals apparently preferred primary colors to a garish extent in their garb, Jint's getup was a solid dark rouge. Perhaps that gave Clasburians cause to view him as a shabby, seedy sort. In this world of the flashy, his unassuming hues were actually pushing the spotlight on him. On top of that, Jint had carelessly forgotten about how thoroughly disheveled he looked.

Damn, are we screwed?

Did Clasbure have police? What was he saying — of course they did.

They wouldn't take me into custody over this, though, would they?

Jint trod to the city's center, fretting all the while. He had to focus on pawning off the **sash clip** for some clothes and other essentials.

Thankfully, he had discovered something with regard to people's general look that would serve them. It seemed dyed hair was the norm. Coifs of gold and vermillion abounded, and eye-catching shades at that. He even caught some blue and green hair. Now he didn't have to worry about Lafier's bluish-black hair.

As for the city itself, it wasn't a metropolis by any means. The tall skyline he'd been able to make out from afar constituted the entirety of Lune Beega, not just the center (as he'd previously assumed).

Cities on Delktu were, by-and-large, sprawling, endless seas of short buildings. Here, on the other hand, it seemed commonplace to house many families in single structures, many of which were cylindrical in shape. Streetlights stretched laterally from the outer walls, their lamps illuminating the ground below. That light, coupled with the gleam of the windows, made the towers reminiscent of ornament-strewn trees on some festive occasion. Perhaps they really were modeled after those arboreal decorations.

Through the spacious gaps between buildings ran luminous roadways. The passages possessed wider sections along their lengths. The hovercars parked off to the sides of those wider sections intimated their purpose. Hoverways snaked from those parking spots, curving around any buildings they happened to encounter. Grass blanketed the outsides of the roads, which likely looked lovely when viewed in the sunlight.

In all of the towers, the first floor was a store of some kind.

As he sought a store that could help him, he weaved around the urban forest. He then crossed paths with a group of men in green-brown uniforms. Their garb wasn't one-pieces, and as such clearly differed from that of the locals. Moreover, they were toting what could only be weapons.

Enemy troops! Instinctively, instantly, Jint hung his head.

The soldiers failed to notice Jint's dubious behavior and continued on their way, chatting loudly.

Jint sighed with relief. When he looked up, what met his eyes was a sign.

"HIGH... CLASS... PERSONAL... DECORATION... GOODS... DECORATE... ROOM" — so read this establishment's advertisement. Dealers of luxury accessories and interior decoration, if he was right.

Jint peered into the display window. It was packed with nouveau riche ornaments and accessories, like earrings and necklaces, that Clasburians seemed to favor.

On Delktu, stores like these also purchased off of customers. But that was a different planet, with different rules. There was great diversity among the **landworlds** of the **Empire**.

Jint mustered his courage and stepped inside.

"Welcome." A man with a **jumpsuit** of, by Clasburian standards, understated pink and yellow, and a thin black scarf wrapped around his collar and tied in a stylish knot, greeted Jint from behind the counter.

"Excuse me…" Jint's lips were dry from the strain, so he licked them. "There's something I'd like you to buy."

"Certainly," he beamed. "Do you have the item on your person?"

"Yeah," Jint nodded, placing the **sash clip** on the counter.

"Hoo-wee, this one's a beaut." He took it in hand and scrutinized it. His probing eyes also found their way to the expression on Jint's face. The man flashed him another smile, a sly one.

"It, it is, right?" Jint's heart threatened to fly right out of his mouth.

"How much would you take to part with this, good sir?" he asked, returning the **clip**.

"Uhh…"

Well, shoot. Not only was he unaccustomed to haggling, he didn't know the baseline market prices of precious metals. The plan he'd come up with while on the hunt for the store had been: have the storeowner set a price, counter by doubling that price, and then negotiate a middle ground. Yet he'd been beaten to the punch.

"Hmmm…" Jint looked around at the wares on display in search of reference, but they lacked price tags.

He had no choice. Though it might leave him with egg on his face, he had to take actual market value out of the equation and resort to asking for the amount of money he needed. If only he had 100 *scarh* on hand, he could shop for enough to tide them over for a month.

That was when he once again realized his mistake. He had no idea how much of the local currency 1 *scarh* went for. He didn't even know what the currency here was. If he'd thought to look it up beforehand, he could have easily done so using his **wristgear**, and now he was kicking himself. Naturally, he could hardly whip out his wristgear at the moment.

With this, he could no longer scoff at Lafier's inexperience.

"What's the matter?" The clerk kept staring his way.

"Uhh… How much does the average person need to get by for half a year?"

"Hmm… Pardon me, but that's a rather abstract way to set a price."

"Sorry!" Red in the face, Jint reached for the **sash clip**. "I'll come back later!"

"Wait a moment, sir," said the clerk. "Would you mind parting with it for 1,500 *deuth*?"

"1,500 *deuth*?" 1,500 sounded like a lot, but for all he knew, it might not have measured up to a single *scarh*.

"How much would that be in *scarh*?"

"I'm sorry, sir," he said, lowering his volume, "This is just business, so I don't normally like to pry. That being said, given the situation out there, I can't say it's wise to concern yourself over the conversion rate to *scarh*."

"Now that you mention it…" Jint felt a great deal of gratitude for the clerk's roundabout counsel.

"Incidentally, I'd say you can live comfortably on around 20 *deuth* a day."

"I see…" Jint ran the numbers in his head, and realized that that amounted to around six months' living expenses.

"How about I give it to you for 3,000 *deuth*?"

"Sir," he replied icily, "not to repeat myself, but we're running a business here. Moreover, we are the only shop in town that deals with goods-to-money conversion."

In other words, this was their best offer, and there would be no haggling.

"Okay," Jint relented. "Please, I'll take 1,500 *deuth* for it."

"A wise decision, sir." Tactful enough not to ask for Jint's bank account number, the clerk slid 1,500 worth of *deuth* in cash over the counter.

"Please count and see."

"Right." It was a stack of 100s. Jint counted 15 bills, and then stashed them into his **pocket**. "That's 1,500 all right."

The clerk bowed. "It was a pleasure doing business with you."

"Um, can I ask you something?" ventured Jint. "Out of pure curiosity, how much are you planning to sell that for?"

"Good question," he said as he handled the **sash clip**. "It isn't customary for us to wear such **sash clips**, as we don't wear *daüch* long robes. However, the exceptional quality and craftsmanship of this piece should make for an attractive figurine of sorts. I think I'd like to sell it for at least 30,000 *deuth*."

Hearing that he'd traded it in for a 20th of its actual value didn't rile Jint up.

"I hope you make a killing on it," said Jint sincerely.

"Thank you very much," he replied, smiling from ear to ear.

Now that he had money, buying clothes was the next order of business.

At first, he thought he only needed to buy Lafier some new ensembles, but now it seemed he could use a wardrobe change, too.

The various vending machines dispensing apparel tended to draw the eye, but since they didn't accept cash, he soon gave up on them. On the other hand, clothing stores proved more numerous than accessories and decoration. Jint chose to visit one such store he'd crossed on his way to this place and retraced his steps.

In front of the building that contained the clothing store, a *flairiac* (ground vehicle) was parked. The car's build was quite ungainly, and several figures in the green-brown military fatigues were standing around it.

"Stop where you are, citizen!" blared the car's megaphone. Jint ducked his head, but it wasn't him they were accosting.

A handful of troops restrained a young girl.

"Wha, what're you—" she shrieked with equal parts fear and shock. Passing onlookers paused in their tracks.

"You too, citizen!" blared the car again. Another handful of troops crowded around the middle-aged man in question.

"There's no need to panic," the megaphone insisted. "If you cooperate, there will be no trouble. Please state your names and addresses. We ask that you show us some identification as well."

"What am I guilty of!?" shouted the girl.

"You must have failed to hear our military's notification. Blue hair is considered a declaration of self-enslavement to the Abh."

So that was it. The two they had apprehended had both dyed their hair blue.

"I happen to like deep blue. What of it?" said the man.

"You are trying to emulate the Abh, which is a shameful act for a liberated citizen."

"You've got to be joking!"

"I'll have none of your sophistry!"

Murmurs of protest were stirring amidst the spectators as well. The residents of Clasbure were relatively combative in nature.

"We'll be giving you two until tomorrow, 10:00 AM planetary time to dye your hair and report to the communications office that's now set up at City Hall. If you refuse, you'll be considered recalcitrant in your self-subjection to the Abh, and summarily arrested."

Jint watched the two **landworld citizens** unwillingly disclose their names and addresses as he headed toward the clothing boutique.

"We are the Evangel Unit of the United Humankind's Peacekeepers! If you know any family or acquaintances who have dyed their hair blue, we ask you to persuade them to change it to a color better suited to humanity. You have been warned. Starting 10:00 AM tomorrow, there will be no more warnings. Offenders' hair will be removed at once..." So the megaphone decreed to the assembled onlookers behind Jint as he paced away from the scene.

Chapter 8: *Gorocoth Lamhirr* (Lafier's Transformation)

Clasbure's long night was finally receding into the dawn.

Wow, Jint mused as he approached the cave, *how long's it been since I've had somebody to wait for me at home?*

Was she being good and waiting there for him? He'd only been gone for around three hours, after all. Plus, the enemy seemed busy laying their hands on people who'd made the dire mistake of choosing to dye their hair blue, so she was probably fine... Or so he was telling himself to tamp down his anxiety.

"Lafier, I'm back!" He didn't want a gun aimed at him again.

There was no change to the entrance of the cave. No traces of blood adorned the trap, so he knew no animals taller than knee-height in stature had trespassed. Jint carefully rewound the **carbon crystal fiber** onto the **spindle**.

"Lafier!" No response.

His anxiety creeping back, Jint took the **wristgear** out of his **pocket**, equipped it, switched on its flashlight, and went to the cave's far end.

There she was, breathing lightly as she dozed. Her face's profile looked so much like a young child's it was frankly astounding.

Jint sighed with relief.

"Lafier, wake up." He shook her shoulders. The **royal princess**'s eyes reeled open, and suddenly she drove Jint back and reached for her **lightgun**!

"It's me! It's me!" Jint stroked his backside.

"Oh. So it is." Lafier relaxed. "You scared me."

"And that's my fault how?" said Jint. "I called for you a million times, and you weren't waking up. Honestly, I doubt the trap would've alerted you anyway at this rate."

"Shut up, Jint." She narrowed her eyes. "What are those tacky clothes supposed to be?"

"Oh, this old thing?" Jint looked down at the **jumpsuit** he'd donned. How many colors were plastered over it? The three primaries went without saying, and joining them in the madness were indigo, pea green, pink, reddish brown, tan... there were roughly 20 shades in all.

The clerk at the boutique had assured him the color scheme looked dapper on him.

"I think you're gonna have to get used to *colorful*."

"I refuse," she stated bluntly.

"Okay, you don't have to get used to it, but I do need you to tough it out," Jint compromised.

"Forbearance is necessary in life," she agreed reluctantly.

Jint sat down, opened the duffle bag he's acquired in town, and took out a can.

"What's that?" asked Lafier, peering.

"Hair dye."

"Hair dye?"

"Yep. Gotta do something about your blue hair, don't you think?" Jint read the label. "Oh, good. It says just spill it on your hair."

"You mean to dye my hair!?" she said, eyes widening.

"Uh, duh. Did you think I felt the urge to dye MY hair? I bought some for you in black. Thought you'd probably like black the most."

"I refuse!" Lafier covered her hair with her arms and shrank back.

"C'mon..." Jint was not expecting this. "So you don't like black, then? Maybe I should've picked red or yellow."

"I don't dislike black; I like my hair the color it is. It's an exquisite shade, not too dark, not too light..." Lafier was ready to launch into a fervent diatribe.

"Gotcha, gotcha. I think it's really pretty, too," Jint consoled her. "Thing is, over in the city, they're rounding up people who've dyed their hair blue."

"My hair isn't dyed!"

"Yeah, and why's that? Think about it: once they see that it's NOT dyed, I daresay it'd turn even worse for us."

"*Coo lin mahp ahs tang kip!*"

"You oughta wash your mouth out. Not that I have any idea what you said."

"I suppose I have no other choice..." she said, dejected.

Jint had lost his patience, though. "Man, you Abhs are real hard to understand. You're fine with genetic modification, so what's so bad about a little *cosmetic* modification?"

"How many times must I tell you, you too are A—"

"I'm Abh? Yeah, well, it's hard to feel that way whenever stuff like this happens." Jint shook the can. "O noblest *Fïac Lartnér*, though it pains a lowly peon like me to impose upon you, couldst you offer your hair most beauteous upon me? Or do you wanna do the damn thing yourself?"

"Give it to me; I'd never let you lay a hand on my hair!" Lafier practically wrested the can from his hands.

Making no effort to read the label, Lafier attempted to take off the can's cap.

"You've gotta take off your **circlet** first!"

"I do?"

"Of course! I'm trying to pass you off as a Lander, Lafier. You ever met a Lander wearing a **circlet**?" Then it occurred to him. "Oh yeah, I guess Abhs don't really take 'em off very often. Is exposing your *froch* in public embarrassing, or...?"

"You always think up such strange things," she said, seemingly impressed.

"Then it's not embarrassing?"

"No. We simply don't take them off because doing so is inconvenient."

"Okay, good. Then I don't have to worry about it."

Jint's heart thumped a little. The *froch* spatiosensory organ was composed of over 100,000,000 individual lenses. The closest point of comparison would be an insect's compound eye. In all honesty, the thought that Lafier's forehead was sporting an insect eye was less than appealing.

However, when Lafier begrudgingly removed her **circlet**, he sighed with relief. It was diamond-shaped, with the luster and color of a *lamh* (pearl). Depending on how much light was shed on it, it also at times resembled more of a **ruby**. The individual lenses were too small to see with the naked eye, so it looked more like a synthetic machine part or some eccentric finery.

Far from unsettling, it was as though she'd pasted on a sliver of a gorgeous jewel.

"Wow, it's super noticeable," said Jint.

"Don't tell me you want me to remove IT, too!?" Lafier's terror was plain to see. "I *can't* remove it. If you demand I gouge it out, then…"

"Whoa, whoa, no, that'd be way too cruel."

Lafier sighed with relief.

"Whaddya figure me for, a serial slasher?" Jint fetched a hat from inside his duffle bag. "I bought you this. Try it on, would you?"

Lafier tipped it on, shoving it down to her brow. Now her *froch* was totally concealed, and her overly perfect facial features also slightly obscured from view.

On the other hand, her pointy **Abliar ears** were jutting out of her hair for all to witness.

"Your ears."

"Ah!" She stuffed the tips of her lobes into her hat and hid them behind her hair.

"Is this okay?"

"I like it," Jint grinned.

"If I wear this hat, then surely dyeing my hair isn't necessary?" Lafier attempted in vain to stuff all of her hair into the hat.

Jint coolly smacked her with the truth: "Dye it. It'll always be peeking out. And if you want to cut it so that it's always totally concealed, then that'd be a haircut for the books. Is that what you'd prefer?"

Lafier shuddered just imagining it. "Fine." She bit her lip and mustered some grim resolve. "If it must be done, then I shall do it."

"So dramatic. The people here dye their hair for fun, you know. Whatever happened to the Lafier who was all 'if things turn critical, I want you to take the navigation log and leave me'? Are you that Lafier? Where did your penchant for self-sacrifice fly off to?"

"Shut up, Jint. I'll have you know I love my hair."

"I wasn't saying you have to dye it for the rest of your life. It's just for the time being, Lafier."

"The rest of my life? I couldn't stand it!" Lafier took off the hat, and her long locks danced back down. The princess took her bluish-black hair and lovingly caressed it.

Jint was beset by a needless sense of guilt. "You'll meet your true hair again soon!"

"Right," Lafier nodded. She plopped a drop of hair dye on her head. Black proceeded to devour the bluer hints of her coif. Through some principle unbeknownst to them, the dye didn't touch the skin or fabric her hair touched, but continued to spread out thin across her whole head of hair.

In less than a minute, the Abh girl with the bluish-black hair had transformed into a girl with vivacious yet totally black hair. The only thing standing in the way of being able to describe her as "average" was her peskily lovely face.

"Looks great on you."

"I'm in no mood for flattery," she said, but she was not so dissatisfied after all, grooming her black locks with her fingers.

"All right, next up, your clothing." Jint handed over the duffle bag, and with it its entire contents. "They're all in here. I'll be outside, so please change."

"Sure." Upon taking the girl's clothing out of the bag, her brow furrowed. "These **long robes** are strangely shaped. Though they're better than I was imagining."

Lafier's attire was striped blue and red, a very mild-mannered design here on Clasbure.

Jint stood up. "Call me when you're finished changing."

"Wait, Jint!" She opened up the duffle bag facing the floor. The only thing left inside was a pair of shoes. "There's no **jumpsuit** in here. Is it really all right for me to wear this **long robe** over my **military uniform**?"

Jint closed his eyes and took a deep breath. The time had come to slap her with yet another abominable truth bomb.

"That's not a **long robe**," Jint put it to her gently. "You wear it in *place* of your **jumpsuit**."

"I'm meant to wear this over my undergarments!?"

"'Fraid so. That's how they do it here. There were some women who wore this kind of clothing on my home planet, too. They call it a 'one-piece' there. Don't know how to say it in Baronh."

"I don't care about that!" Lafier regarded this "one piece" with suspicion and fear. "Must I... Must I truly wear this?"

"Yes," said Jint patiently, "if you want to pass as a Clasburian."

"You are a cruel, cruel man, Jint!"

Jint shook his head. "Please understand, I'm not doing this because I want to."

"Is that so?" Her suspicious gaze fell on him. "Then why, exactly, have the edges of your mouth been twitching this entire time?"

Once Lafier had changed clothes, Jint declared he would be taking a short break, and soon he was snoozing. Meanwhile, Lafier kept watch in her new "one piece," gun in hand.

Jint guessed he must have napped for two hours and change, because when he stretched out and cricked his neck, he felt refreshed.

"Let's get out of here."

"Yep," nodded Lafier, who was sitting by the cave entrance.

There was something they needed to take care of before they could leave. They had to erase as much evidence of their being **Star Forces** as possible.

Jint dug a hole at the bottom of the ravine. He'd wanted to dig it at the cave if possible, but with their limited toolset, it was next to impossible to bore through rock.

Thus, he interred their **Star Forces** knapsacks. Lafier's **military uniform** and Jint's **jumpsuit** joined the pile to be buried. Then, finally...

"I should bury that thing, too." Jint reached his hand.

"You can't!" Lafier clutched her **circlet** to her chest.

"Why not? It's military-issue, you can get it replaced a thousand times over later."

"This is the first **circlet** I was ever supplied with upon entry into the military. It's a keepsake to me."

"Then we'll just dig it back up at some point. It's a **circlet**, it won't rust or anything."

"That's true, but it might also prove useful."

"For example?"

"I can't think of one." But Lafier was not budging.

"If you ask me, we shouldn't be in possession of anything that'd give us away..."

"We'll be carrying guns and our **wristgears**. What's a **circlet** compared to them?"

"Hmm, guess you've got a point there…"

Jint used the *cfoc* (spade) to pile soil on the rest of the discarded items, and then he used his hands to pile soil on the spade itself.

Jint stashed the **wristgear** into his new **jumpsuit's pocket**, and the **lightgun** into the duffle bag he'd bought at Lune Beega.

Lafier wrapped her **waistsash** around her thighs and holstered her **lightgun** in it. Her **wristgear**, meanwhile, was attached to her ankle, and concealed by her shoes. Finally, the **pendant** that contained the navigation log was hidden under her "one piece."

The deed now done, the two could leave for the city.

Since it was noon, the road the two walked down wasn't aglow. The path stretched around 100 *dagh* above the fields, curving every so often but continuing straight for the most part.

It was already evening according to biological time, but Sfagnoff's sun was baking their passageway as it climbed up to its apex.

Jint was jealous of Lafier's hat, and he was kicking himself for neglecting to buy himself one.

On the other hand, he knew how precious their money was. He'd already used around 200 of the 1,500 *deuth* he'd been given to buy all their clothes.

Would it last them until rescue arrived? What would they do if they ran out of money? Was there anyone on the planet magnanimous enough to hire people who'd shown up out of nowhere? If that didn't come to pass… well, he always had a **lightgun**, and if he had to, he'd make use of it.

Jint smirked.

A **royal princess** and a **noble prince of a countdom**. Thieves.

They'd probably be the most esteemed criminals in human history. Their tale would find its way onto the screen or stage for sure.

"What're you smiling at?"

"Oh, nothing." Jint reverted his expression.

"I see you aren't nervous at all."

"Look who's talking. You were sleeping like a baby."

"Shut up, I was tired."

"Whatever you say." Jint changed the subject. "I wonder if we look like brother and sister?"

"I don't believe we do, given that we're not brother and sister."

"Then we've got a problem."

"Why?"

"'Cause I was thinking we oughta pretend to be siblings when in town."

"Why must we lie so?"

"What are we gonna do, tell them the truth?"

Speaking of which… what exactly was the "truth" of their relationship? Was he a sworn knight of a **royal princess**? She may have been a genuine princess, but he was no knight.

Were they a pair of downtrodden refugees? Now that was getting closer to reality. He'd take that over "an apprentice **starpilot** and her human cargo."

"Again with the strange remarks. Our relationship is a strictly private concern."

"Hey, I agree with you, but some nosy folks might ask. On Delktu, if an underage boy and an underage girl were to stay at a hotel or whatever, the crime prevention division would jump in."

"I don't know about you, but I am NOT a child."

"I'm not a kid, either, but others'll think we are." Till Corint's face bubbled up in his head. "It's like how whenever somebody tells whoever raised them 'I'm not a kid anymore!' They always say, 'That's just what a kid would say!'"

Granted, when Till said it, it had been true. Jint had been so young, so innocent… so clueless.

"But this isn't Delktu."

"No, it's not, but we don't know what it's like here."

If Clasburian culture didn't look down on marrying young, they had nothing to fret over. They could pretend to be a young newlywed couple — though they were poorly dressed for a honeymoon.

"Is it that important?"

"We want to attract as little attention as possible. To be as normal as—"

"Jint." Lafier suddenly stopped. "Am I getting in your way?"

Jint was nigh lost for words. "What're you on about all of a sudden?"

"If you weren't saddled with me, you would be able to stay hidden much easier, right?"

"Look…" Jint dropped his duffle bag and massaged his brow. He contemplated how best to explain this, and decided in the end to just be forthright with her. "I'll give it to you straight, it'd probably be easier for me alone in some ways. After all is said and done, I'm a Lander…"

"You are Abh. Or is being Abh to your dissatisfaction?"

"Maybe. I do think of it as a bit of a burden. But it's not like I *hate* it. It's just that if somebody asked me, 'am I Abh or a Lander,' I'd answer the latter. I was born and raised on land."

"I never realized you thought that way." Lafier bit her lip. "Do not worry about me. Nor the **Empire**. If you don't mind renouncing your **noble rank**, then let's part ways here. I've told you once before: I don't want to be a burden on you."

"Are you serious, Lafier?"

"I am. I'd be fine without you, anyway."

"Where do I start?" said Jint. He found his voice had gotten tight, too. "I'd be more than fine with renouncing my **noble rank**, but I have no intention of parting ways with you here."

"Why not?"

"Because if I did that in order to survive, I'd be miserable, that's why." Jint vented his spleen as the rage mounted. "You don't want to be a burden? But you'd be fine without me? Which is it, Lafier? How's somebody who's a burden on somebody else gonna hack it alone, huh? Listen, you brought me here, and I'm thankful. I can't pilot a spaceship. I needed you. Everyone's got their strengths, right? You aren't used to living on a **landworld**. Well, not that I'm worldly or sophisticated, but at the very least, I know more than you do. As long as we're using our individual strengths to help each other, why've you got to be so fixated on 'being a burden'? Tell me I'm wrong, Lafier. Am I saying a bunch of nonsense? Or, maybe, I'm the one you think's a burden. If that's the case, there's no helping it: then you can leave your pathetic cargo and get. I'll let you walk away. But I don't plan on being the one that breaks us up."

As Jint spoke, a **hovercar** whisked by.

"You're right," said Lafier, her eyes downcast. "Forgive me, Jint. You are a man of great pride."

"I am at that," said Jint, his ire not yet dissipated. "I don't honestly know if I'm Abh or a Lander, but what I do know is I've got pride. Fancy that, the Abh don't have a monopoly on it. So would you stop coming out with that twaddle? I will NOT leave your side until it's all safe out there."

It was only much later that Jint would come to realize that when Lafier called him a "man of great pride," it was the highest of praise.

"Okay. I won't ever say it again," Lafier vowed.

Jint's heart finally died down. "I needed you, and I'll probably be needing you again. So right now, I'd like you to at least pretend to yourself that you need me at the moment."

"No need to pretend."

Hearing that, Jint thought to himself that maybe being an **Abh noble** wasn't as awful as he'd made it out to be.

"Yo ho ho, you two, there, heated, *reepee!*" Words he picked up in pieces. "Is there, a fight, boy, plus, girl? Girl, there, *morn!* Girl, there, good, ditch, boy, looks like, *shrip*, so, come, together, us! Good time, *piek*, together, us."

Jint turned to look at the source of the voice that'd suddenly accosted them.

The hovercar that had passed by before had doubled back, stopping right by them. It was roofless. Three young men were craning forward, and jeering something or other. They seemed about the same age, slightly older than Jint.

Jint switched his brain from standard Baronh-mode to Clasburian-accented dialect mode, but the men's speech was not only a bit too fast, but also peppered with slang, so he understood maybe half of what was said.

He'd vaguely cottoned onto how they were mocking them, and extending Lafier a crude invitation.

"What are these men saying?" asked Lafier blankly.

"Nothing you need to hear," said Jint, slinging his bag back up off the ground onto a shoulder. "C'mon, let's get a move on."

"Okay." And so they started walking as though the men weren't there.

"Girl, there, *morn!* Boy, there, in the way, *keepow!*"

"*Sheek, reepee reepee*, good, *piek!*"

"Good, stay, *morn*, girl!" The hovercar was riding along at their walking speed.

As for the next thing the men growled, Jint understood it perfectly.

"Don't you ignore us, prick!" The bulkiest of the three young men nimbly jumped down off the car and blocked their way forward.

"Phew, *morn*!" he whistled, and laid his hands on Lafier. "Come, let's have some fun!"

"No, stop it!" Jint jumped at the arms manhandling her.

"Zip it!" He thrust Jint away.

Pitifully, that one blow was all it took to knock Jint off balance and send him rolling down the road back down toward the fields.

"Argh!" Jint took out the **lightgun** from out of his bag.

Meanwhile, the man slid down toward the fields after him, charging with his nostrils flared like an ox.

Jint pulled the trigger. He'd lost his cool not because he'd been pushed, but because they were trying to harm Lafier. His rage was a frenzied rage; he couldn't care less if they died.

The beam that the **lightgun** fired hit its mark, his aggressor's abdomen… with a flashlight.

The man stopped momentarily, but when he realized that it was nothing more than a stronger-than-normal flashlight, his lips curled with contempt, and he resumed charging.

Panicking and flustered, Jint tried switching the gun from *asairtamh* (illumination) mode to *ultamh* (shooting) mode, but couldn't make it in time. The man was nearly on him, and reaching to rip the gun from his hand, but all of a sudden, he collapsed.

"OWW!" he wailed, clutching his left leg as he writhed.

It was her. She'd put a hole in the man's leg with her **lightgun**.

Jint, who'd finally managed to switch it to shooting mode and get back up on his feet, witnessed Lafier getting pulled back away from him.

Since the man who'd attacked him seemed busy with his squirming, Jint rushed back up the slope. One of the men had Lafier locked in a full nelson, and the other was trying to pry the gun.

Lafier's fighting style was truly striking. She was utterly expressionless, as if to say she didn't care to so much as lift a single mouth muscle for these losers. She was a silent storm, never raising her voice once as she kicked off her would-be captors.

The men looked totally confused; they thought the girl would yelp, scream, shriek. Yet things were still looking bad for her.

"Let her go!" Jint pointed his gun up to the sky for a warning shot.

Sadly, his **lightgun** didn't make a sound. If they'd been shrouded in mist or smoke, a bright shaft of light would have caught their attention, but in this brilliant light of day, it was barely visible at all.

Jint aimed it downward. The concentrated light carved the road and instantly sublimated the pavement, triggering a small explosion. Now *that* caused the two men to freeze.

"Put your hands up!" he shouted in Clasburian Baronh.

Jint and Lafier then stood side by side, each pointing a gun at one of the men.

"Don't shoot, Lafier," he whispered.

"Of course not," she said, shocked. "I don't plan on shooting nonresistors."

"Good, I'm relieved."

"Part of me would rather like them to start trying to resist, though," said Lafier.

"Yeah, no, I totally do, too."

Perhaps Lafier's sentiments had come across, for the men didn't budge an inch, their hands still raised high.

"All righty, boys," said Jint. "Your friend down there's aching something fierce. Wanna bring him up here for me?"

The two glared at him, but showed no signs of resistance, and went down toward the fields.

"You are quite adaptable. You can already speak this world's language?" asked Lafier.

"There was a trick to it. It's actually derived from Baronh." Jint then addressed the men. "I don't mind if you make a sudden move; I've been wanting to get in some target practice."

"*Shacoonna!*" swore one of them.

"Aw shucks," said Jint. "Thanks."

"What did he say?" asked Lafier.

"Hell if I know. Probably nothing you'd every say in front of a blushing maiden," he shrugged. "That aside, let's jack their ride. It'd be nice to secure a mode of transport."

"So we commandeer it?"

"No," said Jint, steeling his face. "We aren't soldiers. We're not commandeering it. We're stealing it."

"Dispensing all pretense, I see."

"Right. We'll be criminals from here on out."

Their actions and appearance made it clear the trio was a bad lot, and judging by how they'd come at them with their bare hands, he could tell there was no culture of carrying weapons on the streets here. So long as they were toting and using **lightguns**, they couldn't claim to be blameless victims with any persuasive power.

As such, they were better off playing consummate criminals, but he'd been afraid the **royal princess** would poo-poo the idea.

"Sounds interesting!" Surprisingly, she was down. "So we're now like the robbers I hear tell of?"

"Uh, yeah, I guess." Jint had a bad feeling about this.

The three hooligans had come up to the path. One of them lent a shoulder to his mate. He'd stopped screaming, but his face was still contorted in pain.

Before Jint could even open his mouth, Lafier made sure to impress upon them in the Baronh she'd learned in the royal court that they were most assuredly roving bandits, and not the least bit shady like an Abh or a **Star Forces** soldier might be. She further decreed that though they would be taking the car, this act made the utmost economic sense in light of their being bandits, as mentioned before.

The men waited out her harangue with expressions of resignation.

Jint was perplexed, to say the least. They may not have understood what Lafier said, but they must have realized it was standard Baronh. He could only assume they'd been given away.

"If you've **wristgears** or anything else you can use to contact somebody, take 'em all out, would you?" Jint demanded, pulling himself together.

The trio didn't react. They just glanced at each other.

"C'mon, look at things from our perspective," said Jint gently.

Lafier had a suggestion: "If you're afraid we'll use them on you, then would you prefer we kill you first?"

Jint didn't know how much they understood of her Baronh. Judging by how quick they were to finally react to his demands, they'd definitely picked up on the word *agaime* (kill), though.

The men took off the boxes they had strapped to their waists and shoulders and emptied their contents onto the road.

"That was one effective bluff," he whispered.

Lafier stared at him in puzzlement. Her expression, innocent. As if to say, *what bluff?*

Jint shuddered. He moved his gaze off Lafier onto the hooligans. *You guys oughta be groveling at my feet in thanks.*

He issued an order to the one among them who had his hands free. "Gather them all together."

The young man did as he was told, and Jint scrupulously blasted the pile of communications devices with his **lightgun**. His aim had been a tiny bit off, but the sensitive equipment was instantly reduced to charred debris.

"Now then..." Jint peered into the driver's seat of the hovercar. This thingie with the two poles sticking out had to have been the rudder. The foot pedal thing adjusted the speed, and there couldn't be much else to it.

However, just to be 100% confident: "Why don't I have 'em teach me how to drive this?"

"I believe this one was the one driving," said Lafier, pointing at the man who had lent a shoulder to his injured buddy.

"'Kay. Hop on in, friend," ordered Jint, gesturing toward the driver's seat.

Lafier camped herself in the seat behind the driver's seat beforehand.

Her gun was aimed at him the entire time he was seated at the helm, while Jint sat beside him.

"You two," said Jint to the others outside the car, pointing toward the direction away from town, "why don't you head that-a-way?"

The man with the injured leg muttered something softly. Jint brandished his gun. The two started walking, still muttering.

"Now it's your time to shine," he told the driver.

"As if I'd—" the young man moaned, but once the gun at his back was pressed into his head, he became decidedly more compliant.

Jint observed how he was driving, and laid question after question on him.

It was as dead-simple as he'd expected. No need for any particularly difficult technique. It was a magnetic-resistance-type hovercar. Once the destination was input, the car would drive itself, and it was easy enough to steer by hand anyway. It couldn't hover unless above the track, so any deviation would require releasing the wheels (much like a **ground vehicle**), but that too was just a straightforward twiddling of the controls anyway.

"Has this thing got some kinda location marker on it?"

"Location marker?"

"Yeah, the thing that tips off the place in charge of traffic where it is? Through radio waves?" he explained in simple terms.

"No. That doesn't exist."

"What's this?" Jint poked at the communications-device-looking thing between their two seats.

"That's the navigation device. It's not the car that emits the radio waves. The radio waves tell us where we are."

"Gotcha. Show me."

The man showed him. A map appeared on screen. The blue dot was probably their position.

Jint fiddled with it a bit. It was child's play to change the scope of the map, as well as to drum up information on the distance to the nearest town, and even open guides on all the major cities.

"Sweet. That'll come in handy. By the way, are you *sure* there's no location marker? The Traffic Control Office won't be wanting it?"

"No, there ain't no damn location marker. If they knew where every single car was, they'd have access to people's private lives. That's why there ain't any on this planet."

"I see," nodded Jint. "Well, that's good for us. Also, whaddya mean, 'on this planet'? You don't think we're from around here?"

"Wh-What!? You mean you ARE!?"

"C'mon, don't make the lady in back feel bad. Not after all that effort she put into explaining our shtick."

"Fine, fine, you're descendants of this *shacoonna* planet's first settlers for all I care!"

"If you could tell everyone that, that'd be great, thanks," said Jint, not expecting he'd actually do so. "Okay, we're done with you. Go back."

The car returned.

Jint saw the other two approaching from ahead. "Freeze," he ordered.

Startled, they halted in their tracks. They probably hadn't reckoned Jint and the others would double back.

"Hey guys, you sure you aren't going the wrong direction?" he addressed them in cheerful tones.

"We go where we want!" barked the one whose leg got shot.

"I'll give your petition of grievances some serious consideration," Jint replied solemnly. "Kindly forward your papers to the proper judiciary body."

Then Jint motioned for the man in the driver's seat to leave. Jint moved sideways to replace him in that seat.

Suddenly, their sad financial state crossed his mind.

"Hey, pals, you got any cash on you? Mind emptying those pockets for me?"

"Don't push your luck, you prick," seethed the man who'd been shot.

"I could always just pick your corpse clean, you know," he said, giving him his best evil smile.

"Dammit!" The three whipped out all their cash. It added up to a little more than 100 *dueth* — less than he was hoping.

Jint forced the man who'd been driving to collect it for him, and he swiped it from him. All the while, Lafier had her gun trained on him from the back seat.

"Now, I hate to have to part ways with you gents, but such is life," said Jint, and they were off.

Lafier climbed up over the back of the chair in front of her and took her place beside him.

"I'm impressed," she said, almost squeaking. "Of course, as robbers we *would* be taking their money, too! I hadn't thought of that. Have you ever robbed someone before?"

"I hope you're kidding. I'm an *amateur* robber."

Back during his days on Delktu, Jint had envied the older kids who went on joy rides with girls in the passenger's seats of their ground vehicles. He'd always wanted to try that for himself.

Now, apart from its being a hovercar instead, that dream had come true. Not only that, but he had one of the most superfine girls in the galaxy beside him. A superfine girl eyeing him with awe.

So why was he feeling so... depressed?

Chapter 9: *Rüébéile* (At the Imperial Palace)

The city-ship of Abliar — the Abh home-ship, now being used as the **Imperial Palace**, had undergone several renovations by the present time.

The enormous vessel, which once housed one million, now boasted upwards of two hundred thousand occupants. It was more than a *béïc* (orbital palace). It was a small city.

In one sector of that "city," partitioned away from the flow of information that was truly important, dwelled the foreigners that had been bestowed with residences and offices.

Sampel Sangarini was one of them, a United Humankind ambassador.

The **Empire** seldom ever allowed foreign ships to enter any star-system within its reign. However, economic exchange was permitted through seven designated *bidautec asa* (commerce ports). And as long as there is trade, there too must be diplomacy. That is why the Empire fielded and received diplomats to and from the other four nations.

All the foreigners who resided in the **Imperial Palace** were in fact ambassadors of the four nations, and their respective retinues. Throughout the entire **Empire**, foreigners were permitted to take up residence only either here or in one of the seven **commerce ports**

While the **Empire** did respect their privileges as diplomats, it placed no emphasis on diplomacy in general. Sangarini and his party were rarely ever allowed a meeting with any figures of significance, let alone an audience with the **Empress** herself, which was more or less reserved for the formal salutations that came with the assumption or abdication of the office.

But at present, Sangarini and the other three ambassadors had been granted their second opportunity.

The **Imperial Palace** possessed a *üabaiss bézorhotr* (audience chamber). However, use of this room was restricted to the most important ceremonies and matters of state, so Sangarini had never even laid eyes on it.

More specifically, they had been called to the *Üabaiss Rizairr* (Chamber of Larkspurs), which more than lived up to its name with all of the purple *rizairh* (rocket larkspurs) in bloom. Sangarini had scarcely believed it at first, but it appeared the Abh did love the beauty of nature in their own manner.

At the center of the hall, a path of black marble, polished to a mirror shine, allowed occupants to pace around. A spiral galaxy was inlaid in silver in the path, with a platform raised to its side, and a carved column depicting an eight-headed *gaftnochec* on each corner. Atop the platform stood a chair that paled in comparison to the **Jade Throne**, but it did look exceptionally comfy.

A fair and comely woman was seated upright in it. Her intricately detailed **circlet** portrayed the **eight-headed dragon** as well. Her hair, wavy and indigo, was parted to both sides through her pointy ears, trailing down to her **long robe** of light crimson keynotes. Her countenance was graced with reddish brown eyes tinged with hints of *fatïainh* (amber), while lithesome hands of ivory white poked out of the black sleeves of the **military uniform** she had on under the long robe. In one of those hands she gripped the baton that commanded the greatest military power that humankind had ever known. She was the 27th in the line of the emperorship. She was *Speunaigh Lamagh Érumitta* (Her Majesty the Empress, *Lamagh*).

The four ambassadors remained standing as they faced her. Sangarini was loath to abase himself. Arrogance was fundamental to the Abh, about that there could be no doubt, but were they reckless in their arrogance?

"*Érumittonn* (Your Majesty)," said Sangarini, representing the other three as well. "First of all, we would like to express our gratitude. Thank you for approving this dialogue."

"Your gratitude is noted, ambassadors." *Lamagh* nodded. "We are afraid Our time is limited, and We believe your time is as well."

"Certainly." Sangarini returned the nod. He had no intention of wasting too much time on pleasantries, at least not in the company of a pompous Abh. "Let us get straight to the affairs at hand. I have come to raise an objection."

"An objection? Surely you mean you've come to offer an *explanation*." The Abh **Empress** did not rebuke them, but she did say: "We've heard a fleet of yours launched an attack within **Empire** borders. We have lost contact, and the details are unclear. We had thought you may have some words of clarification."

"Ours are words of protest," Sangarini insisted. "It is true, our military has launched an attack on your '**Sfagnoff Marquessate**.' You must, however, think of that attack as retaliatory."

Lamagh remained expressionless. She merely raised one eyebrow infinitesimally. "What We must ask is whatever you might mean by that remark."

Sangarini exerted his level best to keep his own expression suppressed. "Our nation had opened a new portal and was exploring the surrounding **planar space**. Then, a warship that was likely Abh sprung an attack upon us, without any justification. That warship was repulsed, but we suffered heavy losses as well. Hence, I have come as a representative of the United Humankind to protest this grave miscarriage of justice. It may very well be the case that that occurred near your territory, yet all ships have right of passage in planar space. Attacks without warning cannot be legitimized or excused."

"As the representative of the administration of my own nation and its people, I must concur with the United Humankind's ambassador's protestation," voiced Marimba Sooney, Ambassador of the Greater Alkont Republic, rage evident on her jittery face.

If that's an act, it's a convincing one, thought Sangarini.

"I too, as the representative of the government and the people of the Hania Federation…" added Gwen Taolong, his face a mask. Since he didn't know Baronh, he made do with a translator. As such, his personality was not so easy to grasp.

"Our nation concurs," said Janet Macalli of the People's Sovereign Stellar Union in thickly accented Baronh. "We have been continually plagued by your despotism. We firmly demand you apologize and pay reparations to our beloved alliance, and we will watch over negotiations with profound interest."

Lamagh's expression remained utterly unimpressed. She stared at each ambassador in turn, and planted her eyes on Sangarini's.

"And that is why you attacked our territory? We think that is rather removed from your typical way of doing things. Why didn't you raise an objection when your fleet was assaulted?"

"The decision to retaliate was made at the commanding officer's discretion," said the ambassador, relaying what those in Central had told him. He didn't believe a word of it, of course. "As you are no doubt well aware, it takes quite some time for messages to traverse the distance between Central and the Outer Reaches. If the commanding officer at the scene had ceded the decision to Central, then as **Your Majesty** has stated, we would have raised a formal objection first and foremost."

Lamagh cocked her head ever so slightly. "You are lying, ambassadors."

"What!? I never!" Sangarini bristled with "anger." "On what evidence do you base that accusation?"

"We simply cannot be led to believe that a ship of Our military would launch any such attack. There are no lawless reprobates in our illustrious **Star Forces** who would engage in battle against another party without a concrete reason."

"Then Your Majesty should view this incident as an exception, obviously," said Gwen.

"Even if We were to grant, for the sake of argument, that there had been some exception," *Lamagh* continued placidly, "they would not then go on to be defeated. Do you think there are any officers in our illustrious **Star Forces** who wield the authority to decide whether to engage, and yet would be so incompetent as to initiate a battle they could not win with confidence? We cannot believe this one commander was outside the norm in two different ways at the same time."

"**Your Majesty**, you are being exceedingly biased, are you not?" said Macalli. "I suggest an intermediary commission of inquiry be established with members composed of three neutral nations."

"So you intend to lie to us as well," said the **Empress**, her icy glare on her now. "You have formed an alliance, yet you mean to tell us you are neutral observers?"

"We are neutral with regard to this matter, **Your Majesty**," asserted the ambassador of the PSSU. "That is why we are asking you to investigate and uncover the truth."

"I implore Your Majesty to consider the People's Sovereign Stellar Union's proposal," added Sooney.

"That is unnecessary." *Lamagh* once again locked eyes with Sangarini. "Ambassadors, We must say We were expecting much more refined deceit on your parts. You have dashed those expectations. What a pity."

"Wha — !?" At a loss for words, Sangarini was left rudderless. From the outset, the Abh **Empress** hadn't been inclined to seriously entertain what they had to say. The diplomatic skills he'd cultivated had run smack into a dead end.

"Why does **Your Majesty** persist in calling us liars?" said Macalli. "You ought at least to investigate the matter before deciding such a thing."

"If you four are satisfied that this pack of lies is the best you have, then We have nothing more to say. We suppose you may truly believe the lie, but in any event, the only deceit we the Abh appreciate is more sophisticated deceit."

"**Your Majesty**, if I may. It is incumbent upon me to inform you that if you were to declare war on the United Humankind, we of the People's Sovereign Stellar Union would be forced under the Nova Sicilia Accords to declare war upon the **Empire**."

"We must thank you, ambassadors," said the **Empress** sarcastically. "But We are well aware. The Greater Alkont Republic and the Hania Federation are doubtless of the same mind."

The two ambassadors nodded their solidarity.

"Very well. Then let us make war," said *Lamagh*, with no enthusiasm whatsoever. "Your hard work was appreciated. We hope you return to your homelands safely. We shall be revoking your diplomatic privileges in 24 hours' time. Though We hardly need assure you, the **Empire** will guarantee your security and see you to free port, or its honor be tarnished."

Wait, you can't! Sangarini screeched inwardly. *This can't be how it all ends! I'm the most experienced diplomat in all of the UH, but I wasn't even given a chance to talk terms!? She not only called my nation's official message a lie, but a BAD lie at that! Do I have no choice but to accept this declaration of war and return to my country? This was supposed to be a trial run; we were just throwing the **Empire** off balance to see what their next move would be! But now this was all just a fool's errand!*

"**Your Majesty**, is there any chance you might reconsider this?" asked Gwen in a low voice. "You will be waging war against half of all humanity."

"Have you forgotten that the **Empire** forms the other half?" responded the Abh **Empress** evenly.

"If you wish to wage war, then that's fine by me," said Macalli, forgetting her duties as a diplomat as she vented her pent-up irritation. "I have, however, one thing to assure you: that the **Empire**, unprincipled as it is, can never hope to prevail!"

"'Unprincipled,' you say…" At last, *Lamagh*'s expression changed. She was intrigued. "It is as you say. Our **Empire** has no principles. We do not believe that has any bearing on whether we win or lose. That the unprincipled cannot win is nothing more than a delusional superstition."

"But think of humanity's future. A destiny where humanity is ruled by the unprincipled **Empire** is no future at all."

"We know a little about human history ourselves. History reveals it is the principles held by *individuals* that shine bright and beautiful. Principles enforced by nations, on the other hand, engender tragedy. They drive **subjects** of those nations to needless deaths. Our **Empire** does not require any 'principles' and exists without them, devoted only to the consolidation of all of humanity in all of its diversity. The Empire hosts a multitude of citizens, with a multitude of bizarre creeds and convictions. For instance, the people of the *Dreuhynh Bislér* (Countdom of *Bisléc*) do not understand that they are under imperial control, and worship their **landworld citizen representatives** as gods. To them, we Abh are the fruits of mysterious and inscrutable beings. The **landworld citizens** of the *Dreuhynh Gogamr* (Countdom of *Gogamh*) implant their own consciousness into **compucrystals**, thinking they have thus acquired eternal life. The Empire rules over and protects them all like a shadow, and without discrimination. If the Empire can be said to have a principle, it is that."

"That is all sophistry. The very idea of a future borne by the Abh, who toy with man's DNA, is repugnant."

"And that is hyperbole," replied *Lamagh*. "Around 2,000 years have passed since the births of our progenitors, yet the basic genetic composition of the Abh has not changed. We, like you, are bound by the fear of evolving."

"Fear of evolving?"

"Do you deny it? The buds of evolution are plucked away as 'genetic abnormalities.' When humanity obtained the power to engineer their genes to their liking, what they did was seal away their own evolution. Our **Empire** is no different in that respect from your own home nations. We all fear evolution."

"That's…" But Macalli held her tongue.

"**Your Majesty**, with all due deference…" said Sangarini. It was clear to see that the Abh **Empress** enjoyed a good debate. He needed to use this debate as a pretext for keeping this audience going as long as possible, all so he could search for a lead, any lead that could get her to negotiate. "Fear of evolving is beside the point. Can a nation without principles even survive? I daresay we will dismantle such a nation without fail."

"The **Empire** has not had a principle to use as a crutch for around a millennium," *Lamagh* rebutted calmly. "I see now that nations such as your own would crumble without principles… or perhaps 'delusions' is the word. Otherwise, you might not be able to bring together varied populaces or face other nations."

"Is it not the same for the **Empire**?" said Gwen.

"It is not. For it is we Abh who keep the **Empire** bound together. It is because the Abh will integrate all of humanity that no one will ever again be burdened by the principles imposed upon them, able instead to enjoy their cultures and lifestyles as they currently exist."

"Then what is it about the Abh that can hold this hypothetical all-encompassing empire together?" said Sangarini, refusing to back down.

"That is nothing you ought to concern yourselves with," said *Lamagh* coldly. "Leave Us now. Your falsehoods failed to arouse Our interest, but We found these last few moments amusing enough. It was a fun little meeting. And allow Us to say that should we emerge from this battle triumphant, it will have been the war to end all wars."

"You mean you aim for everlasting peace?" Macalli's swarthy face flushed with hatred. "Many have dreamed of such a thing. And yet it has never come to pass in all of history."

A grin graced the **Empress**'s arresting visage. This was not the infamous "smile of the Abh." No, it had a warmth to it, as though charmed by the ignorant innocence of the infants before her.

When Sangarini saw that grin, he felt in his bones how she'd lived for nearly 100 years despite her youthful mien, and how young her race was.

The self-respect necessary to bear the weight of humanity's fate on her delicate shoulders was more than evident as she declared: "That is because there were no Abh in the past."

After the ambassadors reluctantly left, *Lamagh* called for a video representation of all the **planar space** discovered so far to be projected across from the platform on which she sat.

Within charted space, there were around 30 billion portals. Those portals' **3-space** entrances were always within the *Érucfac* (Milky Way). This phenomenon likely spurred from the decoupling of 3-space and **planar space** after the fluctuation of the cosmic sparks that originated the galaxy. However, the positions of those portals and the positions of the galaxy's stars did not correlate. The greater number of normal-space-side portals seemed to be located in the spiral arms.

The coordinates of the portals could be likened to a ripple. The circle at the center was surrounded by a great multitude of *spéch* (rings) that constituted groupings of portals.

The center circle was so crowded that **space-time bubbles** couldn't penetrate. The **space-time particles**, expelled by innumerable proverbial "**volcanoes**," formed dense currents headed toward the galaxy's fringes.

Outside the central circle existed a narrow gap, past which one would run into a round band of portals. That was the *Spéch Casna* (First Ring). After that came a slightly larger gap, followed by the *Spéch Mata* (Second Ring).

Thus did the Portal-belts of the **Milky Way** — otherwise known as the *Saudelach Érucfar* — radiate from the center toward the periphery, in alternating gaps and rings.

Furthermore, the farther out the rings, the bigger the gaps that separated them. In addition, each **ring** contained an almost equal number of portals, so the portals in the outer rings were much more spaced out.

The portals that humanity made use of were mostly within the dense *Ssorh Bandacer* (Central Sector) — the sector whose edge was the *Spéch Dana* (Seventh Ring). As such, if one secured a **closed portal** within **3-space** and entered **planar space** from there, there was a naturally high probability they would emerge in the Central Sector. Humanity expanded its domain by establishing portals near the center as footholds and forging 3-space paths to the next closest portal, and so on.

Even in the space spanning the *Spéch Gana* (Eighth Ring) to the *Spéch Loceutena* (Eleventh Ring), once referred to as the *Ssorh Cairaza* (Uncharted Sectors), portals to inhabited star-systems were scattered about as a result of humanity's insatiable drive to expand.

The **Empire** was composed of eight *faicec* (monarchies), each with a *larth* monarch. *Lamagh* herself had been the *Larth Clybr* (Monarch of *Clybh*) until she finally handed that position down to a descendant. However just as **grandees** did not govern their **territory-nations**, so too was the title of monarch mostly a formality. The **lords** of the various territories included in each monarchy were not vassals of their respective monarchs, but rather of the **emperor or empress**. As such, the monarchies were not so much administrative divisions as they were regions on the map.

Of the eight **monarchies**, seven were nestled up close to the **Central Sector**, resulting in complex borders with other nations based largely on regional power and influence.

The other **monarchy**, the *Faicec Ilicr* (Monarchy of *Ilich*), was located in the *Spéch Lomata* (Twelfth Ring).

Each of the eight **monarchies** had a corresponding portal in the **imperial capital** of *Lacmhacarh*. The eight portals were built into the city-ship Abliar, and when they were opened, in accordance with the laws of probability, seven of them linked to the **Central Sector**, but the *Saudec Ilicr* (Portal of *Ilich*) was the outlier, linking instead to a quite remote frontier.

The **Empire** regarded this as a rare and curious opportunity, and consequently set themselves to seizing the **Twelfth Ring** as their own. They invested **nobles** with fiefs, and constructed military **strongholds**. Just before the last step in the process, the completion of the route encircling the

Twelfth Ring, a forgotten but peopled world called the Hyde Star System was discovered.

The **Ilich Monarchy** was shaped much like a pair of arms embracing the **Milky Way Portal-belts**, and so it was often called the *"Bar Saidac"* (Arms of the Abh).

That moniker was ill-fitting now that the two hands had joined, however.

Within the generally sparsely distributed portals of the **Twelfth Ring**, a relatively dense grouping of portals had been observed. It was thought that that grouping comprised a sector that overlapped with the portal-belt **ring** that corresponded to a different galaxy entirely.

Humanity had not reached that level of exploration yet, but the door to a galaxy beyond lay open before them…

…A door open only to the **Abh Empire**. For so long as the *Ilich* **Monarchy** was there, no nation besides the **Empire** could hope to reach outside the galaxy. Of course, that would change if one or more portals linking to a place further out than the *Ilich* **Monarchy** were to be discovered.

That sensation of confinement might have factored into the **Four Nations Alliance** (FNA)'s determination to wage war.

How inane. There were yet many worlds of which humanity could avail themselves.

The **Sfagnoff Marquessate** had been part of the *Ilich* **Monarchy**. If the enemy took Sfagnoff, it would chop off one of the Arms of the Abh.

"Faramoonsh, are you indisposed, or can you come?" Using her *rüé greuc* (imperial command baton), *Lamagh* drew the pattern of summons.

"Your Majesty." The hologram appeared by the **map of planar space**. His blue-gray hair was braided, and suspended down his front from his shoulders. He was *Üalodh Rÿazonr* (Director of Military Command Headquarters) and **Imperial Admiral** *Faramunch Üémh Lusamr Razass*.

"Were you listening in?"

"Yes, **Your Majesty**."

"How much of what they said do you think was valid?"

"I believe we can take them at their word that they opened the portal. That being said, I think the reason they sent a military fleet was to sever the connection between Vorlash and Sfagnoff. They must have already explored the surrounding area in secret years ago."

"Did the *Spodéc Rirragr* (Information Bureau) not notice?"

"Unfortunately, that is the case."

"That is quite the blunder."

"There is no excuse I can provide." Faramoonsh lowered his head, though he was not obsequious in his humility.

"Has the **Empire**, in its age, become the sick man of the galaxy?" muttered *Lamagh*.

Faramoonsh didn't deny the possibility. "It could also be that the idea they'd do something this elaborate never occurred to the Bureau. The enemy did keep an impressively tight lid. And while it is not my intention to provide excuses, might I suggest that the *Gaicec Scofarimér* (Ambassadorial Agency) also failed to catch on?"

"True," *Lamagh* nodded. "The only reports We've received from that office of late warn of the possibility of 'large-scale military action,' nothing more."

"It's clear that much effort was spent to drum up a unified front — which is a feat indeed for a patchwork army like theirs." Faramoonsh's tone of voice betrayed some measure of exhilaration. Trade, commerce, those were everyday sport. War, on the other hand, was a rare treat of a game, and that much more enjoyable for it. And Faramoonsh was hardly the only one whose heart thumps fast upon acquiring a worthy opponent.

Lamagh's position was a different beast. In the end, as **Empress**, she was forced to wager not only her own life, but her subjects', too. She was excited by the prospect as well, of course; she just felt somewhat guilty that she did.

"As for our felled ship," said *Lamagh*, turning to the matter that weighed on her most of all, "it was **patrol ship** *Gothelauth*, correct?"

"Yes," said Faramoonsh, his face mournful. "There is a higher than 90% chance it was the *Gothelauth*. We can't pinpoint the portal they used as of yet, but in any case, it's the only ship that matches the details. You have my condolences."

"Spare your condolences," she said, shutting him down. "It is an Abliar tradition to be the first to the frontlines of battle."

"Yes, but **Hecto-Commander** Lecsh was an outstanding **starpilot** even among the **Star Forces**. I believe she would have been sure to send the young **Viscountess of** *Parhynh* away to relative safety. **Her Highness** is a **trainee starpilot**, after all. Any pretext would have sufficed."

"You needn't console Us with platitudes. If that were the case, news of Lafier being unharmed would have reached these ears."

"My apologies, Your Majesty," said Faramoonsh, looking abashed.

"Although..." *Lamagh* proceeded to mutter to herself. She had always liked Lafier. Dubeus (*Dubeusec*) had not been a good son, but it seemed he had some surprising talent as a father. If only she hadn't fallen in battle while bearing some half-baked title like "**trainee**." If only she'd died a full-fledged **starpilot**. Then they'd all have been readier to swallow her death.

"*Fïac Lartr Clybr* (His Highness the King of *Clybh*) must be deep in the abyss of grief as well," added a sudden voice besides Faramoonsh's. "He lost both his **lover** and his **daughter of love** at the same time."

"*Larth Barcœr* (King of *Barcœc*)." *Lamagh* frowned when she spotted the voice's source. "We don't remember summoning you."

"This is a serious affair concerning the **Empire**; please pardon my impertinence, **Your Majesty**." So said the hologram of **Imperial Fleet Commander-in-Chief** and **Crown Prince**, **Imperial Admiral** *Dusanh*, **King of Barkeh**, before bowing.

"If you wish to console Doobyoos, then you ought to go to his side, *Fïac*."

"No, **Your Majesty**, I shall do so on another occasion. Unless, of course, you decree I should depart by imperial edict. I have come here to see whether you might."

"No, you shall wait."

"I shall wait?" His features, too perfectly arranged for a man, formed a quizzical look.

"Faramoonsh," said *Lamagh*, prompting the **Military Chief of Staff** to do the explaining.

"**Fleet Commander, Your Excellency**" Faramoonsh addressed his high-ranking colleague. "It has been established that the enemy invading the **Sfagnoff Marquessate** is proving surprisingly slow to act. I hope the only reason for that is an undersized force of arms."

"You mean it might be a diversion, *Lonh*?" *Dusanh* stroked his chin.

"What else could it be? You can be apprised of all the details if you visit the *Rÿazonh* (Military Command Headquarters)…"

"No, *Lonh*, that won't be necessary." The **Crown Prince** stopped Faramoonsh with an outstretched hand. "I know battlefield analysis is your forte. So, what's their next move?"

"Their target is probably here. *Lacmhacarh*," he said.

"Their ardor is certainly alarming, *Fïac*."

"Hmm… so they aim to capture the **capital** in one fell swoop…" *Dusanh*'s expression lit up attentively. If the capital fell, the **eight monarchies** would no longer be linked together, thereby horribly weakening the Empire.

"We don't know whence they'll invade. At the seven **monarchies** at the Central Sector, they could strike from anywhere."

"Do you understand, **King of Barkeh**?" spoke *Lamagh* from her temporary replacement **throne**. "Our forces cannot move rashly. We must have you helm the defense of the **capital**. Faramoonsh, orchestrate the **fleets** We shall entrust to the **King of Barkeh**, and quickly. We leave his forces' scale to **Command Headquarters**. We do, however, expect it to be historic in size."

"Yes, Your Majesty. Have you any other orders?" Faramoonsh asked the **throne**.

"No. Do it at once."

"As Your Majesty commands." Faramoonsh's hologram cut out.

Dusanh's did not.

"Is there something else you wanted, **King of Barkeh**?"

"Forgive me. I was just contemplating your words regarding the 'fear of evolution.'"

"How like you, *Fïac Dusanr*. You would rob Us of Our time through your ceaseless philosophizing."

"You enjoy it, too, do you not, Your Majesty?"

Lamagh could only smile wryly at his perspicacity. "We do."

"Is there not a possibility that humanity would benefit from our defeat in this war?"

"Oho. And what makes you say that?" *Lamagh* knitted her brows.

"Were we to win, all humankind would, under the order and serenity of Abh rule, give in to a 'peace' that's eerily akin to an everlasting slumber. A peace that would hamper human evolution."

"Which means if they win, the power of evolution would be unleashed? We trust you heard the ambassadors' words: they fear evolution more than we the Abh do, claiming that even the slight genetic modification of our children we practice ought to be abolished."

"I am aware, Your Majesty. However, their victory would assuredly lead to an age of chaos. They may be four consolidated nations now, but were they to lose their common enemy in us, they would certainly begin jostling for power. That would in turn shroud all of humanity in disarray — a return to the era when humans were powerless, knocked out by the stormy waves of evolution."

"Is that what you desire, *Fïac*?"

"No," he shrugged. "They say we Abh are long-lived, but ultimately, we aren't long-lived enough to be able to see where evolution will lead us. Of what concern is it to us what happens after we die?"

"Then why are you contemplating that?"

"Sometimes, I find I dwell on humanity's future. That is to say, not on what we should do for it, but on how it will unfold."

"*Fïac Dusanr*," she said gently. "The **Emperorship** will be yours after Us. If you would like to cast humanity into chaos after securing your seat on the **Jade Throne**, then by all means, do so. However, so long as this baton remains in Our hands, We will aspire to peace, whether or not it spells humanity's slumber. And you shall exert yourself to the fullest in furtherance of that goal."

"That cannot be disputed," said *Dusanh*, bowing elegantly. "No matter how it may affect humanity's destiny, I would hardly be pleased to lose to the likes of the **Four Nations Alliance**."

"We are relieved to hear that. For We know you would never neglect what would or would not amuse you, regardless of humanity's or the **Empire**'s fate."

"Of course," he said, as though that went without saying. "And there is revenge to be had, as well."

"Oho…" *Lamagh* was taken aback. "We didn't realize your heart was so troubled over Lafier."

"Yes, *Fïac Lamhirr* must be avenged, but more personally, there was another aboard that ship with whom I shared a bond of fate."

"*Ïarlucec Dreur Haïder.*" *Lamagh* was even more taken aback now. "You are exhibiting a most unexpected side of you, *Fïac.*"

"Did I take you by surprise?" *Dusanh* smiled. "I pride myself on as good as creating that **countdom** and its noble house. His estate could use at least one person here at the seat of the **Empire** worrying about it."

That was what transpired 18 hours after intel confirming the fall of the **Sfagnoff Marquessate** reached the **Imperial Palace**.

Chapter 10: The *Raïchoth* (Checkpoint)

Now that they had a means of getting around, they no longer had any need to focus on the small city of Lune Beega. Jint directed the car's automatic destination driving function to the city of *Guzonh*, the capital of this state named "Loehow" (spelled *Lohaü* in Baronh). According to the latest info the **hovercar** had to provide, it was a large city whose population exceeded the 2,000,000 mark. Of course, that meant the military presence there would be that much denser, but that would only distract the attention they'd otherwise be receiving as outsiders.

As they drove down the road, the scenery (which they could be forgiven for thinking might stretch on to the other side of the planet) did change. There were different crops on display, and the seemingly boundless plantations were periodically interrupted by prairies and wooded areas, only to come back strong later. They passed a town even smaller than Lune Beega, and rolled right by a number of isolated homes.

The hovercar was handling like a dream. Jint's formerly foul mood had gradually taken a turn for the optimistic. What if they never holed up in a city, and instead just stayed on the road?

No, they couldn't.

The trio of hooligans will have reported their car stolen by now. They'd be needing to ditch this car before the local police came for them.

Jint braced himself.

I can't forget, we're criminals now. The "enemy" isn't our only enemy anymore. We've gone and pissed off the police, too...

"Why do you look so glum?" asked Lafier. She examined Jint's expression curiously, holding on to her hat with her left hand so the wind wouldn't take it.

"Do I look that grumpy?"

"Yep. That grave look doesn't suit you. I'd be more relieved if you went back to your usual, more flippant face."

"So I always look super lax, is what you're saying." He stroked his face, frankly wounded.

"Right. As long as I look at you, I can forget I'm on **land**."

"I guess that should make me happy."

"Feel your feelings as you will. They're your feelings."

"You can be brutally honest sometimes, you know that?"

Guzonh was close at hand. If the map was to be believed, it was a city surrounded by a forest.

A moment or two after entering the forest, they suddenly heard a beeping noise, accompanied by the hovercar losing speed before their very eyes.

"What happened?"

"Beats me."

But soon they would find their answer.

Another hovercar was parked in front of them. Scratch that, there were dozens of them, all in a line. Jint stood up in his seat, trying to determine what was jamming the traffic.

There he saw a company of enemy troops. Right by them, a vaguely predatory-looking lump of metal crouched, half-concealed by the trees. It was most likely a weapon for land wars.

Jint clicked his tongue. "Damn…"

C'mon, think, man, think.

Were they hunting for the *bausnall Laburer* (Star Forces soldier) that had evaded the intercepting fire of three enemy ships and scurried onto the surface? If they were, they had no way to know what that soldier looked like. However, if they discovered the **wristgears** or **lightguns** on their persons…

Did the enemy troops know about this car? It was safe to assume the occupying army wouldn't be doing the local police's dirty work for them, but if they got wind of their connection to the **Star Forces soldier**, things would turn very sour indeed. It would mean they were aware of the two down to their personal appearances.

Should they turn back? Nothing tied them to *Guzonh* specifically. But no, that'd positively scream "suspicious." He didn't know what that land war weapon was, but he'd bet his **star-fief** it was nothing that could be fended off with a couple of **lightguns**.

They could make a run for it if it was slower than a hovercar…

…No. There was no way they'd inspect hovercars with a weapon that couldn't catch up to one. It must be able to fly. Faster than a hovercar crawling along the ground.

Dammit. What was this checkpoint even for?

They had two lovely options: turn back and get caught for sure, or proceed, and flirt with capture.

They had no choice but to talk their way out of this.

Jint screwed up his resolve.

"Lafier," Jint whispered. "Keep your mouth shut, and don't talk. You're not used to the local language."

"Ah, of course. Otherwise they might catch on to us!" she replied, satisfied she'd grasped his meaning.

"Excellent, so you get it now."

"Hold on, are you mocking me?" she said, her expression offended.

"If you hadn't spoken to those three in Baronh, I wouldn't have to say these things."

"That was a poor showing," she said meekly. "I shouldn't have said words like 'the **Star Forces**.'"

"Nor would robbers go out and declare 'we are robbers.' They're usually totally silent when they're doing their thing. There must be crime in Abh society, surely?"

"Yes, there is. My family simply isn't used to the pettier sort."

"Figured as much."

As they conversed, the line of cars advanced one by one, and soon their number would come.

"Forget the guns," he warned, noticing Lafier was touching her **lightgun** through her clothing. "Just stay still."

The **royal princess** pouted, but nodded.

Finally, the troops gave their car a look. They were a sour-faced middle-aged man, and a young man wearing a cheerful smile.

Jint played the amicable driver. "Something happen?"

"No, nothing to worry about, citizen," answered the young one. The translation device attached to his waist interpreted his words simultaneously.

"This is a light-hearted survey. We're investigating the flow of people for the future administration's reference."

"Hope that's not putting you out." Jint smiled openly, as to drive home that he was an utterly harmless individual. And since they were relying on machine translation, they couldn't even notice his accent. That was the only good news.

The soldier extended a hand. "Your wallet, please."

"My wallet, you say?"

"We won't be taking any money. We're not bandits, don't worry," he said, guffawing at his own joke. "We just want to know your citizen standings, that's all."

"I see…" Jint's heart thumped so hard it nearly turned inside-out.

It seemed a wallet was not a receptacle for money, but rather a **memchip** with personal and bank account information, or something close enough to one.

Needless to say, Jint had no wallet. His personal and bank info were in his **wristgear**, and though he could show them their rarefied "standings" through the them, that was precisely what he wanted to avoid.

Actually, Jint's **wristgear** was Sehrnye's, though that didn't improve their conundrum. The soldiers weren't about to welcome an **imperial citizen** with open arms, and convincing them he was in fact a woman seemed a tall order.

"Uhh… oh, man, I must've forgotten it at home…" A hackneyed excuse, even for him.

"Oh, well, that's odd. You forgot it? I thought folks here always had it on them."

"Oh, you know, I'm the kind that only trusts cash…"

The soldier's gaze fell on Lafier. "What about that little lady?"

"Uh, she doesn't have a wallet."

"Uh-huh…" The soldier's eyes narrowed.

Jint lavished him even more with his winning smile.

The soldier turned off his translation device and traded words with the older soldier. The glances they shot toward Jint and Lafier during their exchange could not be called favorable.

"Fine," said the soldier, at last. "Then I'll just ask you your name."

My name!? Jint panicked. Of course, why hadn't he thought of a fake name sooner?

"Que Durin," he said, stealing his friend's name on the spur of the moment. He could only pray that that wasn't a weird name on Clasbure.

"And her?"

"Her name is, uhhh, Corint Lina!" he said, using the name most prominent in his psyche.

"I'd like to hear her tell me her name, thank you very much. What's got her all clammed up?"

Jint looked for himself. He'd told her to stay still. He hadn't told her to freeze in place with her hands on her lap. That was way too still. Having no reaction to any stimuli was supremely unnatural. It wasn't as though a checkpoint inspection by an occupying force was a frequent occurrence, and yet there she sat, without an iota of interest. Anyone would find that suspicious.

Her unblinking profile was mysterious, refined, even statuesque. What it was not was human.

"All right, you've got me." Jint threw up his hands. "It's a doll."

"A doll?"

"Y-Yep."

"Looks pretty lifelike for a doll," he said, casting his eyes all around her dubiously.

"It's just that exquisitely made."

"Your doll looks like it's breathing."

"That's just your imagin… no, it's mechanized so it *looks* like it's breathing."

"Why do you have a doll in your passenger's seat?"

"Why must you ask?" Jint fired back. "This is just a traffic survey, right?"

"I just want to know. I'm curious about this planet's culture." But the soldier's face betrayed an interest that surpassed idle curiosity.

"Look, I've got to keep up appearances, okay!?" Jint lamented desperately. "I'm finally out here traveling, but I didn't want to look lame doing it alone. That's why I made it look like I've got a lady with me."

"Ah, sorry!" The soldier looked uncomfortable. "But someone your age, is that something you really need to be that worried about?"

"What would you know!?"

"Well, looking back, I guess I had as much on my mind as you seem to when I was your age," the soldier sighed nostalgically. "If only I'd known how dumb I was being back then."

"Can I go now?" said Jint sulkily.

"Could you let me touch your doll a bit before I let you go? I can't believe how amazing it looks," he said, reaching a hand.

"No, don't!" Jint leapt out. "Please don't touch her!"

"'Her'?" The soldier raised an eyebrow.

"I mean, it's mine, I own it, I don't want anyone touching it!"

Again the soldier sighed, his gaze full of compassion. "You're in love with it, aren't you... You're sick in the head, and may need help."

Oh, give it a rest.

"Not only that, but the doll looks as *cold* as it does beautiful..."

The middle-aged soldier said something. The young one looked back and answered. Jint didn't understand a word of it.

The young soldier shrugged. "I'm sorry to have taken your time. You can go now."

"Thank you." Every fiber in his body wanted to explode with joy, but he deliberately kept his expression emotionless as he pushed the pedal.

After a little while, they lost sight of the soldiers. Lafier was still frozen.

"You can stop now," he said. "Man, though. The way you played along really saves our hides. You're pretty adaptable yourself, gotta say. You understood what I was trying to tell you inside and out."

"Only because your pronunciation was so much clearer." She shot him a sidelong glare. "The nerve of you! Telling a lie like that."

Jint suddenly looked apprehensive. "You're not gonna blow up on me, are you?"

"Oh? Do I look *happy* to you? Acting like a doll isn't just exhausting. It's a mark on my pride. That man, he said something to the effect of *I look 'cold,'* didn't he?"

"I wouldn't say you look cold the way you are right now. In fact, you look like you could erupt on a dime." *Just my luck, she catches only the words that set her off.* "Besides, he called you beautiful, too."

"I'm not 'beautiful.' I'm *graceful*. Also, he said *I'm beautiful*, like that's all there is to me, like that's all I'm worth…"

"Yeah, well you know what, we got outta there, didn't we?" he said, fed up. "You've gotta hand me that much."

"From a rational standpoint, I applaud your quick wits. But the emotional side of me is demanding your blood!"

"Then I'm glad you're a girl of reason," he said, ingratiating her.

"I suppose you wouldn't know, but the Abliar family is renowned for being bad at keeping their emotions in check — particularly their anger!"

"I don't really think your family needed the help, fame-wise, given they're the most famous in the universe. And that's not touching on the issue of you getting stuck in your family's ways."

"Shut up, Jint! I like the way I am!"

"So you're in love with yourself… You're sick in the head, and may need help."

"You'd best be careful, Jint; my emotional side is overtaking my rational side."

"Come to think of it…" Jint was quick to change the subject. "…what were they doing that inspection for? It didn't look like they were searching for us."

"It's to capture the key figures among the **landworld administration**."

Jint was a little surprised. "How do you know?"

"That's what they were saying."

"Oh, right. I totally forgot you can understand their language."

"Yep. They said something along the lines of: 'We're searching for the big shots of the slave government. We have no business with these children. Their hair isn't dyed blue, so just let them go. Let's not waste any more of people's time.'"

"The 'slave government'?"

"What they're calling the **landworld administration**, I suppose."

"But **landworld citizens** aren't 'slaves.'"

"You and I both know that. So too do the **citizens** of this planet, probably. But *they* don't know that."

"Phew… They've got a twisted view of the world, huh?"

"About that... one of the soldiers seemed as though he wanted to bear some responsibility toward your mental wellness."

"Responsibility toward my mental wellness?" he repeated, bewildered.

"He wanted to ask you about your troubles, outside of work. But the older one told him not to."

Jint shuddered. "Talk about a close shave."

"I, for one, would have enjoyed watching you divulge your teenaged anguish," she said, her voice laden with venom. "I would've even pretended to be a doll for a whole day to see that."

Jint had thought the **royal princess**'s ire had abated, but he'd been premature to do so. "That aside, what are soldiers like them doing being such busybodies, anyway?"

"How would I know?" she said coldly.

The hovercar cleared the forested area and entered an open space.

"Is this the city?" asked Lafier.

To their left, grasslands. To their right, an endless wall. Beyond the wall, a line of dozens of spires.

"Can't be. City's over there." Jint pointed forward with his chin. The tree-like buildings were bunched together like they'd been at Lune Beega.

"Then what are those?" Lafier pointed at the group of spires. "They can't be natural."

"I'm not sure. Maybe the city stretches all the way out here." It was hard to think that people were living in those spires. There were no windows, and they were all identical in every aspect except color, as they were all painted in the typically Clasburian gaudy palette. Any normal person living in a town like that would go funny for sure.

Jint cocked his head. "Maybe they're some kind of memorial."

"A memorial? To what?"

"Couldn't tell you." He couldn't even guess. What event could there have even been for a city on a planet without much history to speak of to spend so much money commemorating it? "It's got nothing to do with us, though."

"You can be surprisingly boring," she said scornfully.

"On my home planet, they say 'curiosity killed the cat,'" he said, closing the topic. They had so much else to think about.

The city began where the "memorial spires" ended. Sfagnoff's sun was still high in the sky, but according to biological time, it was near midnight. There were few civilians out at this hour, and only the figures of the enemy troops caught their eyes.

Jint switched the driving mode to manual and left the car in a parking lot at random.

"Lafier, don't speak, even in town, okay?" whispered Jint, after checking whether anyone was around to eavesdrop. "Leave the talking to me."

"I *know*. You must think me a great big fool."

"Just making sure."

"Shall I pretend to be a doll again?" she remarked snidely. "You may carry me through town."

"Don't be silly, I would never dream of laying a hand on **Your Highness**."

Jint beckoned Lafier get out of the car. They double-checked to see whether they'd left anything in it. Though they'd just gotten to know the vehicle, this was goodbye.

"Since we're ditching the car here, we might want to head to some other city and put some distance between us." There was nobody in sight, but he spoke quietly anyway.

"How?" she whispered back.

"There must be some sort of mass transportation between cities. Don't know what they use here, though."

"We shouldn't, Jint."

"Why not?"

"There may be more checkpoints. And I am not turning into a doll that many times."

"You're never gonna let that go, are you? But you're absolutely right." He was forced to admit it. If those two soldiers weren't the exception, then the enemy was exceedingly nosey. And though she'd dyed her hair black, if they'd taken her hat off, it'd be obvious she was Abh. The wiser move would be to bide their time in the big city until the situation improved.

"All right, let's look for an inn," said Jint.

Chapter 11: The *Ladomhoth Lomhotr* (Team-Up Request)

Entryua Reie (pronounced "Ray"), Police Inspector of the Lune Beega Criminal Investigation Department, stubbed out his cigarette into the ashtray. The light was already snuffed, but he forced it down like he had some strange vendetta. Feeling a bit better afterward, he finally felt like poking his head into the manager's office.

It was a terrible morning.

He took that back: it had been nothing but terrible days ever since that lot came a-knocking.

Entryua, much like the rest of the citizenry of Clasbure, couldn't give a toss whether it was the Abh or the United Humankind that ruled the universe. None of it affected them.

…Though it did affect them. Lots.

Since they'd inspected the police without notice, traffic was jammed, along with various other inconveniences. Those who worked in suburban farmland and school-going children in the city were getting up very early. Meanwhile, stores were beginning to run out of their wares.

Moreover, they were searching every nook and cranny for civilians who'd dyed their hair blue, and diligently shaving their heads, though to what end he had no idea. Even one of Entryua's subordinates got hit.

And baldness as a fashion statement was very three years ago. Did they KNOW how humiliating it was to be caught in a trend from three years ago — particularly for the women?

But the worst was how they'd meddled in their regularly scheduled programming. Their right to choose what holovision program they so desired had been cut back severely. He couldn't watch the next episode in the serial drama he'd been looking forward to.

The only thing they were allowed to watch was their propaganda. The night prior they'd spent a long time explaining the election system.

Entryua knew all about elections. Specifically, he couldn't afford to ignore the election for police commissioner.

This general wave of resentment should have been aimed at the occupying forces of the United Humankind, but for some reason, the people were airing their grievances at the police. The biggest cause was probably the fact that nobody knew where the occupying army's headquarters were.

What a giant pain.

Lune Beega may have seemed small, if judged solely by the urban area where the building-trees were located, but the city limits were in fact quite expansive. With those buildings at the center, the city stretched on for a radius of 3,000 *üésdagh*. Most of that space was taken up by plantations, but it was dotted by small villages and isolated homes. 80% of the population was so scattered. And that's how big the area of the Lune Beega police force's jurisdiction was, too.

Due to the ban on airspace usage, and all of the inspection checkpoints, the police couldn't do their rounds on time. The damned soldiers made no exception for police cars. Worse, they inspected patrol cars especially scrupulously. Every time they left or entered any city, they'd be searched down to the undersides of the seats, so they were hard-pressed to keep watch over the entirety of the city's territory.

The Lune Beega Police had already let four flagrant offenders get away. They hadn't gotten to the scene on time because they'd been held up by the occupying forces. It was the Criminal Investigation Department's duty to search for offenders who evaded arrest at the scene of the crime.

Those soldiers seemed intent on increasing his workload, the bastards. At this rate, their crime-arrest ratio would drop for sure. The only saving grace was that the commissioner's approval rates would also drop.

Resentment toward the police themselves was also beginning to bubble to the fore. Processing complaints wasn't in the Criminal Investigation Department's job description, but Entryua had his acquaintances, and they spared no time hammering him with blame.

And now, this.

Police Commissioner Aizan had summoned him.

They hated each other, so what could this be about? He should have given him three days' notice so he could prepare himself psychologically.

"It's me, Entryua!" he shouted in front of the door to the commissioner's office. Aizan despised crude, loud voices.

The door opened. Entryua entered with swinging strides.

"Well if it isn't my little Entryua," said Aizan with a fat smile and wheedling voice.

Aizan being pleased to see him could only portend calamity. Him going out of his way to extend a warm welcome was the most definitive proof there could be that a disaster was unfolding.

There with them was another visitor to the commissioner's office, a young man who seemed the sociable sort on first blush. Were it not for the army fatigues that'd become an eyesore to him these days, he'd have had no reason to feel any antipathy.

"This here's Entryua, one of Criminal Investigation's finest inspectors. Entryua, meet Keitt, Military Police Captain of the UH Peacekeepers."

Keitt, (pronounced "Kite"), extended a hand. "Nice to meet you, Inspector."

Entryua stared at that hand dubiously. What was all of this about?

Keitt smiled broadly. "Oh, sorry, that was rude of me! *This* is how people greet each other here, right?" he said, clasping his hands in front of his chest.

Seeing that beaming grin, Entryua felt the urge to pat his head and go "attaboy." An urge he suppressed as he returned the gesture.

"Sure, nice to meet you, Captain," he said curtly. Then he faced Aizan. "So, what've you got for me?"

Though he already had a decent guess: the "Peacekeepers" would be subsuming Criminal Investigations and ordering them around.

Now, a commissioner with any pride would've brushed aside that kind of demeaning demand. But this was Aizan, so Entryua couldn't be so optimistic. After all, their occupiers had detained politicians and high-level bureaucrats, and though Aizan was nothing more than the commissioner of a small city, if he displeased the army, they'd spare a thought or two as to a good use for the remaining vacant cells of the planet's jails.

Not that Entryua would care in the slightest. He hoped they threw the bastard in a filthy, damp, sunless cell so cramped he couldn't take a single step.

"Please, sit, Entryua, my lad. You too, Captain." Aizan pointed at the ottomans.

They were arranged in a circle. Entryua took a seat. The chairs' legs were short, so he had to stretch his own legs out in front.

"Would you care for some mint tea, Captain?" asked Aizan.

"Sounds good. Thank you," he replied smilingly.

Without asking for Entryua's preference, Aizan ordered the group three cups of mint.

Soon, the set of three cups rose gradually from the center of the circle of chairs.

Entryua wasn't thirsty. He left the cup be and instead watched with irritation as the other two commenced sipping. "You want to tell me what I'm here for, or what!? I'm busy, you know!"

"There's no need to get upset, Entryua."

"I agree with the Inspector," said Keitt, to his surprise. "Time is of the essence."

At that, Aizan nodded readily. "I see. Well, my lad, as it turns out, the Captain will be cooperating with us."

"What?" Entryua had guessed wrong. "The soldiers occupying Clasbure, helping us?"

"We're not 'occupying' anything. We're *liberating* Clasbure," said Keitt.

"I don't know if your translator's on the fritz, or if my dictionary's got a misprint, but that's the first time I've heard the word 'liberated' used that way."

"We've liberated you from the tyranny of those disgusting homunculi, the Abh. We've come to spread the word about *democracy*," he waxed sonorously.

"Oh, I know democracy. It was the will of the people that put Commissioner Aizan in office." And he wanted nothing more than to take democracy by the collar and share a few choice words with it.

"That was *slave* democracy, without any of its true substance. Your leaders accepted Abh rule as a fact of life. Yet if they'd been operating by the will of the people, they would have taken a stand against the yoke of oppression."

"You mean Senator Kindee?" Entryua shook his head. "I've always voted Democratic, but the man's a good egg, Liberal Party member or not."

"That's just it! The very idea that parties with 'Democratic' or 'Liberal' in their names exist on a planet conquered by the Abh is a mockery of genuine democracy!"

"So that justifies throwing them in jail?"

"They're not 'jails.' They're Democracy Reeducation Camps."

"The hell is that? A euphemism for concentration camps?"

"They're camps for education. Schools, just as the name implies."

"Uh-huh." Entryua raised an eyebrow. "Then why's nobody signing up for the bloody things?"

"No getting belligerent, Entryua," Aizan butted in nervously.

Feh. Damned coward.

Here the police were getting swallowed up by outsiders, but the commissioner was too scared of "reeducation" to do a thing about it.

Keitt kept calm. "It's fine, Commissioner. These are misunderstandings we knew would come up. And clearing them up is our mission."

"You're young, but you've got a good head on your shoulders," lauded Aizan.

Their little spat had strengthened Entryua's impression of Keitt as a "good guy." But in his eyes, there were two types of "good guy" — passive, and proactive.

Passive types were great. The only people gratified by proactive types like Keitt, on the other hand, were themselves. Proactive types loved pointing out "problems" that people were living just fine without solving. Those "problems," meanwhile, had never been thought of as such, which led to the dismay of the previously untroubled. Then Mr. Do-Gooder rolls into the tangled mess he caused and gallantly lends a hand. Once the person who'd been "helped" in this way snapped out of it, they usually found themselves worse off than before.

"What happened to time being of the essence?" said Entryua. "And what exactly do you mean, you'll be 'cooperating' with us? Somehow I doubt the Captain is going to be working under me."

"I think you're being rather rude," Aizan chided.

"No, the Inspector has every right to be suspicious. Allow me to lay it all out for him."

"You're ever so kind," said Entryua bitingly.

"We'll be cooperating on a specific case. Yesterday, three citizens of this town were injured, and their car stolen. We're very, very interested in this incident."

Well that's a very, very blah case to be so interested in. Obviously, there was more to this thing.

"What's the case number?"

"08-337-8404," answered Aizan.

Entryua put the telephonic line through to Police Information. He picked out the case in question and displayed it on the monitor.

"So, these three were the victims, huh…" He'd known their names already. And Entryua could only laugh upon skimming through their testimonies. "They were attacked after 'offering help to a boy and girl in trouble on the road'?"

"What's so funny about that?" Keitt cocked his head inquiringly.

"They're a notorious bunch around here. In fact, they've been putting more work on our plates since they were brats. May I offer you some advice? If you want to up your popularity, you ought to round them up and get a firing squad to execute them in public. They're 'minors' so we're forced to handle them with kid gloves. You're telling me these numbskulls suddenly turned over new leaves? If you ask me, they made a pass at the girl, things got physical, and the two fought back. Because if their testimonies are true, then we've got bigger news in this one case than the Occupation of Clasbure."

"The *Liberation* of Clasbure," said Keitt earnestly.

Entryua ignored the remark. "So, why the interest in this case, anyway?"

"Take a closer look. The 'girl spoke Baronh and was as beautiful as an Abh.'"

"Yeah, I read that part. You can't take them at their word, though. They're not exactly the brightest of bulbs. I don't even know if they could distinguish between Baronh and birdsong. Besides, to them, there are only two types of females, 'the smex' and 'uggos,' with two-thirds of all ladies falling under 'the smex.' So their eye for beauty can't exactly home in on a bona fide Abh, if you catch my drift."

"But what about the boy? They said he looked 'average,' and that he spoke the local language, if imperfectly. They must have been an Abh woman and her *laimh* (imperial citizen) attendant."

"What was this Abh of yours doing trudging down the road?" asked Entryua, far from convinced. "That's the one thing I can't picture an Abh doing. I've always thought their lot get antsy when they get dirt on their soles."

"Well, this is nothing more than a hypothesis, but an Empire landing hull was discovered not far from the scene of the crime. My Liberation Army superiors are seeing that as a sign the two events are linked."

"You sure like flapping your gums, don't you? Long story short, you're trying to say the two were in that ship."

"I'm saying there's a high possibility that's the case. It's true that the girl might NOT be Abh. But it's worth looking into. Please, let us aid in the search. In exchange, we ask only that you hand the criminals over to us."

"Hold your horses. We're talking aggravated burglary here. That's a serious offense. And you want us to just hand them over?"

"About that," said Aizan. "We've already come to an agreement. You don't get a say in this."

"Of course, Commissioner," Entryua shrugged.

"Then you're on board!" Keitt smiled.

"Because I'm forced to be," said Entryua, as he glanced at the column with the person in charge of the case data. "It's being handled by Assistant Inspector BcCoonin's team. Let's hurry up and get you acquainted."

He didn't like this. BcCoonin was already still chasing a robbery-and-murder case from three years back, with three other incidents on his lap at the moment as well. Now he'd have to pursue this one case full-time for the time being.

"Forget that," said Aizan, who was likewise less than keen to push it on BcCoonin. "*You'll* be heading this case, Entryua."

"Me?" He had a hunch this would happen, but he feigned being taken aback.

"That's right, lad. Team up with Captain Keitt and find them. Naturally, you can use as many deputies as you like. We aim to arrest these criminals with the Lune Beega police force's whole power."

"Wait a second, Commissioner. That'd only tie the investigation up. You might not be too clear on what goes down at crime scenes, but I've got my own job to do."

"And Inspectors heading up investigations is a common occurrence."

"Yeah, for *big* cases."

"And this case isn't big? It involves the occu— the liberating army."

This is what Entryua and most of the other officers hated about Aizan. He paid about as much attention to the force's putative neutrality as he did clipping his overlong nails, swayed as he was by outside opinion. He'd made a mess of the organization through his focus not on case-by-case level of importance, but on what the press would make of things.

He wouldn't complain as much if they were given an organizational structure that enabled them to be flexible in their responses. But in reality, the commissioner had been obsessed with budget cuts due to the climate in Parliament, and thereby reduced the force down to a husk of skin and bones. To top it all off, he then had the nerve to issue unreasonable order after unreasonable order.

That, however, was what endeared him to his constituency, and as a consequence, he'd held the office for a long while.

"There's something I still don't get. What you want is the Abh in cuffs, right?" Entryua asked Keitt.

"We mustn't forget the **imperial citizen**. He was born a free man, and yet he aided their tyranny. He is an odious lout."

"The Abh, the *laimh*, whatever. There are so many of you people around, though. What's the point of enlisting the police force of a country town like this?"

"Entryua, the Captain is helping *us*."

"Can we drop the cockamamie pretext, Commissioner? How many people have you got under you, Captain?"

Keitt threw out his chest. "I'm an officer who's been cleared to work solo."

"In other words, you haven't got anyone under you." Entryua looked at Aizan with arms outstretched. *See, Commissioner? There's no room for debate anymore. I'm no donkey; you can't take me for a ride.*

"This is a big opportunity for all of you, Inspector," he said in fevered tones. "Under ordinary circumstances, I'd have liked to ask for the help of the local police to unmask *slave democrats* as well. Working alone, we aren't very knowledgeable as to this planet's state of affairs. Unfortunately, those servile traitors of humanity can't be sentenced as such under Clasbure law, and even worse, they were people's neighbors, so I'm sure there would be resistance to the mission even amongst you. This incident is different. In this case, they are indisputably criminals…"

Entryua understood where he was going with this and got straight to it. "It's our job to apprehend them, yes. But where's the 'big opportunity'?"

Keitt lowered his voice. "It's your chance to contribute to true democracy. This is between us, but some of my higher-ups are of the opinion that the police force should be replaced wholesale. They say it was 'state violence on behalf of the slave democracy.' But here you have an opportunity to show them there's a possibility you can be rechristened as a democratic organization. All you need to do is align your goals with ours."

"Oh, gee, thanks a ton. But are you sure that isn't just your own bag?"

"Don't be absurd. On the contrary, the opinion that we should seek cooperation with preexisting administrative structures enjoys rather broad support. The Supreme Commander is also of that belief. And depending on your police force's actions, that prevailing opinion can turn into policy."

"Surely you see now, Entryua," said Aizan with a triumphant look. "Through our conduct, we have to make an appeal for the very existence of the police."

I'd love to appeal your existence, Entryua thought bitterly.

"I have an idea; why don't you do it, Commissioner?" he suggested, but when he saw Aizan give it serious consideration, he immediately took it back. If he let the Commissioner head the case, he'd feel bad for his junior officers. "Okay, okay, I'll head the search." Bridling his indignation, Entryua lit himself a smoke.

"What is that?" asked Keitt.

"You don't know about tobacco?" he shot back sullenly.

"Oh, is that what that is. So it's legal here."

"Of course. I'm a guardian of the law, and this is a police building."

"In our society, tobacco has been banned for over 200 years."

"That right? Guess they've got anti-smoking proponents all over. This little guy's totally safe, though. Doesn't even smell. It's like medicine; soothes the nerves and such."

"That medicinal effect is the problem," said Keitt credulously. "It's unethical to suppress the mind using drugs. The fact that this planet was forced to legalize such unethical drugs just goes to show how extreme the slave democracy's oppression truly was. It's our responsibility as the Liberation Army to eliminate the drugs themselves, as well as the reasons people have taken a liking to them."

"That so." Entryua took a deep, deep drag. *I hope you've realized, Military Police Captain Keitt, that with those words, you've just made me into a reactionary for "slave democracy."*

Chapter 12: *Bar Glairh* (Abh History)

"What a nice morning," said Jint, taking in the sight of the city of *Guzonh* as dusk was falling.

"It's noon to me." Lafier had her legs crossed, comfortable in her chair as she vacantly consumed some holovision programming.

"You already get a handle on the language?" Jint asked, looking back from his position at the window.

"A little," Lafier nodded slightly.

"*…About which you have been fed mistaken information. This is a grave injustice. You have the right to know…*" droned the level box that was the holovision receiver set. A semitransparent stereoscopic image of a woman's portrait was projected above the box, and she was talking to Lafier.

"Yet more army propaganda, huh. You having fun watching that stuff?"

"No. It's dreadfully dull. But there's nothing else to do."

She's not wrong. Their only two diversions were watching holovision or talking. Clasburian holovision wasn't exactly edge-of-one's-seat entertainment. On Delktu, there was so much programming that a viewer could spend a lifetime failing to watch all of it, and could watch whatever, whenever. Here, however, they couldn't so much as change the channel.

That wasn't due to some Clasburian cultural deficiency, though. Clasbure's array of programming had been just as robust as Delktu's until mere days ago. The occupying army made sure to change that. They had to give up hope of anything entertaining; this was likely a straight week of "special messaging."

"You eat yet?"

"No."

"Guess I'll be making breakfast for you and lunch for me, then." Jint stretched. "What do you feel like eating?"

"I won't find anything palatable," she said, not testily but rather matter-of-factly.

"All right, leave it to me." Jint stood in front of the auto-cooker in the corner. He retrieved a can from the pouch at his feet. The label read, *BOLKOS-STYLE RED EGGPLANT SOUP WITH BEEF AND KIDNEY BEANS... NEEDS COOKING... FEEDS TWO.* He hadn't the foggiest what was "Bolkos-style" about it, or even what Bolkos meant to begin with, but the picture was appetizing enough.

He pushed the can into the auto-cooker's insertion hole, set the flavor concentration level to "medium," placed a bowl on the food arrangement tray, and activated the machine.

It was Day 3 since they'd started staying at this inn, "The *Limzairh.*" They'd searched on foot for a place to stay after ditching the car. Fortunately, it wasn't long before they'd stumbled on this inn, and they'd forked over enough cash for a ten-day stay.

It was a two-room: a living room, and a bedroom. It also had a bathroom and a washroom. There was no kitchen, but this auto-cooker took up a corner, making a simple meal no trouble to cook up. The living room contained comfy chairs, and a holovision set.

Right after getting settled into their accommodations, he went to buy changes of clothing, as well as food for the interim... and they hadn't left the place since. Lafier obviously couldn't leave at all, but Jint knew he couldn't afford to leave much, either.

What'll they think? he thought anxiously.

The names on the inn register were "Sye Jint" and "Sye Lina." He planned to claim they were siblings if asked, but the person at reception hadn't pried. If early marriage was common on Clasbure, he might have thought the two a young couple. However they were perceived, not signing out after three days must have come off as strange.

On Delktu, at least, they'd be arousing curiosity. Delktunians were comparatively nosy people; if someone stood out in any sense, the average Delktunian would want to snoop around for a reason.

He wondered what Clasburians were like. Was that person at the desk absolutely burning with curiosity, speculating wildly as to their identities? Or did they not care a jot, and would only concern themselves with the two of them once the question of whether they'd pay for Day 11 rolled around?

If he was curious, Jint would have liked it if he came to question them directly. Even though he didn't have the utmost confidence he'd be able to lie convincingly, he could perhaps keep the situation manageable.

The worst-case scenario involved that guy telling somebody about them. *"A young couple hasn't left their room in three days. What are they doing in there?"* It was no doubt a great mystery to kill time trying to puzzle out. That mystery would only grow more and more attention-grabbing as the time whiled from Day 3, to 4, to 5…

They could even become famous in the area before they realized it.

The guy at the desk seemed like the talkative sort, too.

Jint sighed. *I probably need to be going outside from time to time.* It'd certainly help him retain his sanity. This caged-in feeling was getting to him.

They'd decided to sleep according to different schedules for two reasons, to keep lookout, and also because there was only one bed. There was, in fact, a third, secret reason to boot. If they spent whole days in each other's faces, they'd have trouble breathing, and not because they were breathlessly in love, but rather because they needed their space to keep from snapping.

And recently, Lafier was very frustrated indeed. She spent a third of each day sleeping, a third enjoying solitude, and a third with him. But even though she had some ostensive alone-time, if this "schedule" kept up, they could start fighting over trivial matters.

Worryingly, they were also both armed. In these dark doldrums, the **Royal Princess of the Abh** and the **Noble Prince of Hyde** killing each other was not outside the realm of possibility.

The auto-cooker beeped.

Jint took out the bowl that was now full of Bolkos-style red eggplant soup, and then placed another bowl on the machine's tray, setting it to the thinnest flavor concentration available before activating it a second time.

What a pain. If he could make both bowls with just one flavor, he could have finished cooking in one go.

That's what he'd done the first time he used the thing. And while Jint had enjoyed his first salty-tasting meal in a while, it had been too salty for Lafier, who didn't eat any past the first bite.

That's why he'd started differentiating their portions by flavor from then on out, but even the lowest setting seemed too strong for the **royal princess**'s tongue.

The auto-cooker beeped once more.

Jint placed the two bowls onto a serving tray, and fetched some cool mint tea to go with them.

The dining table was also the holovision set. Perhaps on Clasbure, it was unthinkably poor form to watch a broadcast during mealtimes.

"I'm setting it down," he said, while Lafier had her eyes fixed on the hologram, which had changed from the woman from earlier to a small doll without clean-cut facial features, with a *bach* (orbital city) rotating above its head.

"What the?" he said, setting down the tray.

With the tray in the way, the hologram grew intermittently blurry and jumbled, but the audio continued as normal.

"*...The purpose, to explore deep space. It was thought that as 'organic machines,' they were better suited to the task than pure, metal machines were. Thinking that was justified by the technological limitations of the time...*"

"It's our origins," she muttered.

"You mean, of the Abh?"

"Yes."

"*...THAT is the truth behind the Abh!*" A scary DUN DUN played over the soundbite of a woman screaming. "*As such, Abhs are not human. They are merely organic machines...*"

"How could they say that?" Jint reached for the holovision set's **controls**. "I'm turning this off. Let's eat."

"Sure."

"*...Free men and women, we ought to revert the Abh to their rightful place. Which is to say, their place as organic machines who live to serve humans! That's the only thing that would make them truly happy, too...*" But both the audio and the video suddenly cut off.

Jint poured the mint tea into two cups and took his own bowl of soup off the tray. Lafier followed suit and began to partake.

"About that broadcast..." Lafier broached in the middle of eating.

"You mean that pack of lies from earlier?"

"They weren't lies."

"Huh?"

"It's true. Our ancestors were created as organic droids. Did you not know?"

Jint batted his eyes. He honestly hadn't known.

Abh history spanning before the creation of the Empire was shrouded in legend, and the reason why was clear. Around the year 120 **P.H.** (Pre-Imperial History), an accident on the city-ship Abliar destroyed its old navigation log, and with it, the entire history of the Abh. The only accurate extant records started from that point on.

Of course, it was difficult to imagine the Abh would forget their origins entirely. Yet the Abh, who were not much inclined to talk about themselves, avoided shedding light on this subject as well. That, or they felt no need to. In either case, this left surface peoples to exercise their own imaginations, and weave their own mythologies.

And now that the topic had come up, Jint seemed to recall reading something similar on Delktu. It was just that that information had been buried amongst tabloid gossip, so it hadn't left much of an impression on him.

"Yeah, no, I didn't really know," he confessed.

"We aren't particularly keeping our origins a secret. It isn't, however, something that we like to boast about. It's no credit to our race, and can't be found in any archive. It's simply passed down from parent to child."

"Looks like my parent didn't know."

"That can't be. Lonh-*Dreur Haïder* must have heard about it during his peerage ceremony. Every Abh knows."

"Huh… But he didn't tell me." Jint supposed his father considered it to be of no importance.

"I see. Then I'll be the one to tell you…" Lafier sat straight up and regaled him.

On Earth, there existed a volcanic, arch-shaped archipelago. Due to the geography of the land, the civilization that developed there could pick and choose from other lands and peoples while cultivating their own unique culture.

Yet soon, advances in transportation and the expansion of the economic sphere hit the islands like a great wave. In this period's early days, the people of the archipelago enjoyed its blessings, and prospered in no small measure. Eventually, however, global-scale cultural intermixture came to pass, leaving their individual language and culture on the verge of total assimilation. And there existed a faction that couldn't stomach that.

That faction decided to leave Earth, as by then orbital cities were already commonplace, and they sought a realm to call their own in the asteroid belt. Less than one one-thousandth of the archipelago's populace departed Earth this way, but that proved more than enough to preserve its culture.

Deeming their own culture as "contaminated by foreign influences," they worked to reproduce its seminal, ancient form. The language was deliberately reconstituted using only the vocabulary found in its basest layer; as for high technology that didn't exist during the language's earliest stages, they expanded the meanings of extant words and repurposed archaic words, as well as coining new terms based on the language's ideophones.

When the existence of **closed portals** was discovered, and with it the potential to plumb the reaches of the universe, this faction joined much of humanity in wondering whether they ought to head for an unclaimed star. Their population having swollen, the people started thinking they'd like to live their lives on land, even if that land was outside the Solar System.

Despite that, their isolationist attitude would get the better of them, as they proceeded independently of humanity's joint plan to settle outer space. They saw no choice but to undertake space exploration according to their own plan. But they had no access to any **closed portals** they could use to achieve relativistic-speed travel, possessing instead only low-speed nuclear-fusion ships.

In order to make fulfilling their objective using low-speed ships feasible, and to facilitate fatigue duty in space, they turned their hands to a forbidden technology — the creation of superior specialized crew via human genetic modification.

Naturally gifted citizens were gathered, and thirty organisms engineered using their genes. Those life forms were considered non-human, and so they were given a trait which would never appear in "real" humans — blue hair — as a distinguishing mark.

"Our hair color..." said Lafier, pointing to her own locks before suddenly realizing they were dyed. She frowned. "That is to say, blue hair, is a brand of slavery."

Jint shook his head: "Then I don't get it. Why do you like your hair blue so much?"

"Because it represents our genesis, and our original sin."

"Original sin?"

"Yes — the sin that marks our race..."

Though one of the 30 was lost in the training process, the rest of the Abh's foundational ancestors were placed on low-speed ships as planned. The ships could only cruise toward their destination at a sluggish pace, their pitiful speed the result of very brief acceleration bursts. In the event they couldn't resupply their hydrogen stores at the destination, even a return trip was likely an implausible proposition. The sound of mind would refuse to embark on such a voyage. But the original Abhs, in their "non-humanity," had no scope to enact their wills.

In their navigations, they spotted a **closed portal**. To seize it, they spent almost all of the deceleration-fuel at their disposal. And though the stakes were perilous, they got their due recompense. These Founding Abhs, having succeeded in securing the portal, employed their limited resources and technological know-how to convert the mothership into a closed-portal-propelled model, thereby obtaining unprecedented high velocities.

The Founders, who yearned for self-determination, had to muster their resolve to part ways with their birth city once they deviated from their predetermined course, and when they declared their independence, it was in a sector of deep space with no one to witness the event.

"That's your race's sin? Betraying your birth city?"

"No. That alone wouldn't weigh on our consciences. There's more to it than that."

CHAPTER 12: BAR GLAIRH (ABH HISTORY)

The Founding Abhs piloted their ship to a nearby star-system, and used its abundance of resources to build a larger ship, as necessitated by their burgeoning numbers. The ship they'd been piloting to that point was a simple exploratory vessel, but the new one was fitted with so many functionalities as to be worthy of the name "city-ship."

They did not hate their birth city. The mission tasked to them was certainly cold and self-serving, but in the end, it was their progenitors who had granted them life, as well as the ability to perceive the universe around them (*frocragh*).

There was, however, fear. The fear that they might cross paths with a unit sent by the birth city to punish them. In hindsight, those misgivings were irrational, even delusional. After all, what power had the birth city to dispatch such a punitive force?

And yet, the shadow of the city loomed large over their psyches, akin to omnipotent gods.

As such, they pulled information from the mother brain, and produced weaponry. Every adult among the fold banded into a military corps, and trained.

Incidentally, the ones who'd overseen those training efforts were the navigation officers, who happened to be Lafier's distant ancestors. In any case, everyday tasks aboard a city-ship were a multi-faceted and complex affair, and their population was quite low. Unable to establish a school for each vocation or work duty, education was conducted via an apprenticeship system, which, in turn, didn't take long to shift to a hereditary system. This hereditary transmission wasn't limited to navigation officers; all crew positions became fundamentally hereditary in nature. And that bloodline had been passed down, unbroken to the old **nobles** of the **Empire**... but that is another story.

When the Founders had finished their preparations, they pre-empted their imagined aggressors. That is, they opted to destroy their birth city.

"Talk about short-sighted," said Jint.

"I had the same thought, so I asked my father about it."

"And?"

"He told me the Founders were in a state of unrelenting, unbearable fear, and that they shuddered at the idea they could never lay hold to any peace of mind. Their only true goal in all of this was to put an end to that otherwise endless spell of anxiety."

"I get where they were coming from, but still…"

"To be honest, I don't know what to think, either. It's not as though my father could be certain that was true; he wasn't present then. In any event, our ancestors turned back to the Solar System…"

When the curtain fell, it did so all too soon.

They would learn after the fact that the birth city hadn't been idling in wait for the Abhs whom they thought would never return. In fact, they'd constructed several **closed-portal**-propelled ships of their own, and sent out multiple waves of emigrants. As a result, their power had waned considerably.

Had they been made aware of those details beforehand, the Founding Abhs likely wouldn't have attacked, as they communicated very clearly that the birth city lacked both the intention and the capacity to deploy some punitive force.

Regardless, the birth city tried playing political games with them. Its leaders saw much potential in the information and ship technology of the Founding Abhs, and consequently attempted to bring them back under their control. The Founders immediately ended negotiations and marshalled everything they had to assault the birth city.

Though their numbers were meager, the Founders were all warriors, and the weaponry under their command quite ample. The people of the birth city, on the other hand, had long since relegated the concept of war to a relic of the past.

The birth-city that was supposed to be a behemoth was in actuality almost entirely bereft of military power, and utterly defenseless in the face of a city-ship that had been fashioned into an interstellar mobile fortress.

Other nations existed in the Solar System, but none interfered, and even if they tried, things had developed quickly and the space between the various other polities and that asteroid-belt city was wide.

They couldn't meddle if they wanted to. There wasn't enough strength of arms in the whole of the Solar System to hold the Founding Abhs back.

The conflagration engulfed the million-strong population of the birth city, and, flung into the vacuum of space, they expired.

"Our ancestors fulfilled their sole objective. It was only after they witnessed the wreckage scattered throughout space that they realized how deep their affection for the birth city ran."

"Their affection?"

"Yep. It was their home city. They loved its culture. The city had been created for that culture, and our ancestors *born* for that culture. But now the city didn't exist anymore. The city's emigrants couldn't be counted on to preserve that culture, either. As such, it fell on our ancestors to pass it down the generations. The preservation of the culture and its language became their new goal in life."

"And that's the Abhs' life goal to this day?"

"Correct. That's also when they decided to call themselves the 'Abh.' Up to that point, they'd simply called themselves the '*Carsarh*' (Kindred). In ancient Baronh, the language of the birth city, the word 'Abh' meant the 'race of the cosmos,' or the 'race of the seas.' No other turn of phrase was more suited to us, a race that drifts through space. Though the pronunciation of the language did change a fair amount."

"Isn't the duty of the Abh to preserve the culture? Isn't the pronunciation changing a bad thing?"

"Not so. Abh culture is hardly unique in the fact that it shifts over time, but change is also a characteristic of our culture. Besides, I've heard it said that the supposedly 'perfectly pure' reconstructed culture of the birth city had a mash of elements from many different eras, and the effort was ill-conceived to begin with. As such, we needn't shackle ourselves to things past. Expanding culture is part of preserving it. As long as we aren't too swayed by foreign influences, we should be fine."

"Well, I guess that's true."

"Those are our thoughts on the matter, anyway."

"Huh. But why does the enemy know about all that?"

"That's not odd at all. It must still be recounted in records within the Solar System. There are even **landworlds** within the **Empire** that know of our origins. Your ancestors must have departed the Solar System before my ancestors returned to it."

"Yeah, must be. Otherwise I'd have learned in history class that an orbital city got destroyed."

"Abhkind erased the home city they so dearly adored. That is the sin that stains our blood. We must preserve the culture we inherited from the city of our birth. Such is our mission as a race. My father told me that to be Abh is to shoulder the weight of that sin, and of that mission. I think likewise." After a brief pause, Lafier asked him: "Jint, has this made you dislike becoming Abh yourself?"

"What are you talking about?" Jint forced a smile. "I'm already Abh, aren't I? You're the one who told me that."

"Yes. Of course," she nodded, though Jint could make nothing of her expression.

Then, as Jint ate up the last of the now-cold Bolkos-style red eggplant soup, it happened without warning.

"Excuse me," said a female voice from the other side of the door.

"No, don't!" Jint shouted reflexively.

But she'd already opened the door. "Coming through," said the woman, holding clean sheets in her arms. Her skin was tanned brown, and her hair and eyebrows were black. Her facial features were clearly defined, and she looked to be in her early 30s.

"Who, who are you!?" Even Jint could tell his voice was quavering. He keenly felt that glint in her eyes.

"Oh my, you can't tell by my dress? I'm housekeeping."

"Housekeeping..." parroted Jint, befuddled. He hadn't known this inn had room staff.

"Yes. I'm here to switch out your sheets."

Lafier arranged her bangs to hide her *froch*. Seeing that put Jint at ease.

"I mean..." pressed Jint, "Nobody's replaced our sheets for three days. Why now, all of a sudden?"

"It's standard service, deary."

"But couldn't you just slot them through there?" he replied, pointing to the door's slotting hole. One had only to toss their laundry there, and after an hour's time it would be delivered fresh and clean to one's room.

"I apologize, there must've been some miscommunication. May I enter the bedroom?"

"Ah, no, I, uh, I'll take them." Jint was trying his level best to suppress his inner agitation.

The **wristgears** and **lightguns** were in the bedroom. The guns were hidden under the pillows; if she changed the sheets herself, she'd spot them.

"But I couldn't put that on you, the customer..."

"It's fine, really!" he cut in emphatically, virtually flying into the bedroom to rip off the sheets. Then he stuffed the sheets under his arms, ambled back into the living room, and thrust them into her hands.

"I'm so sorry..." she said. "At least allow me to make your bed with these sheets."

"Please, that won't be necessary. I'll do it myself," he declined politely.

"Well, all right then." She placed the new sheets on the chair, and then cocked her head. "Do you have any laundry?"

Jint was about to shake his head, but then he realized it would be unwise to seem too flustered, so he retrieved the laundry basket from the washroom and handed it to her.

"Thank you; I'm very sorry, sir," she said as she put the dirty sheets and laundry into the slotting hole.

Jint had a question for her. "Uh... will you be coming to replace the sheets every day?"

She smiled. "If you wish, sir."

"In that case, you, uh, don't have to. Just send them over, and I'll do it."

"Are you sure? I don't mind at all, but..."

"Plus, is there a way to lock the door from the inside?"

"Of course there is."

"It's just, I had it locked, but then you entered..."

"I work here."

"Can I lock it so employees can't enter, either?"

"Sir," she chided him, "the inn wouldn't be able to think about your safety in that case."

"Ah... I guess you're right." She was totally right; what if a customer decided to shut themselves in? "Could I at least ask you to wait for us to respond before entering?"

"That is my policy, sir," she answered primly.

"Wait, but you—" Then Jint thought better of it. If he attacked her for entering even though he told her not to, nothing good would come of it.

The lady wasn't shuffling her way out. She stood there smiling, as though waiting for something.

"Was there something else?" asked Jint cluelessly.

She let out a deep sigh. "Sir, I didn't want to come right out and say it, but do you know the word '*sheef*'?"

He did not, so he panicked. What in heaven was this woman asking for?

"You could also call it a 'gratuity.'"

"Ohhh!" he blurted, overjoyed that that had come to light.

"Sure, got it. Please give me a second." Jint took some coin out of the small change pouch he was using instead of a "wallet" and gave it to her.

She eyed the pittance in her hand sharply. Jint quickly added another coin, and then her face lit back up to oblige.

"I don't want to be presumptuous, sir, but could I give you a word of advice?"

"Go right ahead."

She took out the little tray that was installed onto the side of the laundry slotting hole. Jint had not had any idea what the tray was for.

"While you're waiting for the laundry to be done, I would be very grateful if you could place the *sheef* onto this tray and push it out into the hallway."

"Okay, right, must've forgotten," he spluttered out as an excuse.

"If you please," she stressed.

"I do, I do please," he nodded emphatically. "Next time I'll give you three days' worth."

"I'm glad you understand, sir," she bowed. "Now then, I'll take my leave. Thank you."

As soon as she left, Jint exhaled.

"What was all that about?"

Jint shrugged. "We weren't paying up like we should've, so she came to complain about it in a really roundabout way."

"We did pay them, did we not?"

"We paid the inn. It's just that we hadn't seen the other person we were supposed to be paying."

"You're making this difficult to understand."

"Am I? Well anyhow, now I totally get why she barged in unasked on Day 3. As long as we follow the rules to a tee, then they won't raise a fuss," he said confidently.

"…I think."

Chapter 13: The *Bileucoth Usér* (Hovercar Spotted)

"You sure there's no mistake here?" said Entryua.

"I'm pretty sure," said the Senior Forensics Officer.

"The car's registration number matches, and we picked up traces of all three victims' fluids."

"By 'fluids,' you mean blood?"

"Their semen, sir."

"Ugh!" he groaned. "So you didn't quit on the spot, huh."

"It's not as though we delight in searching for such things," the officer frowned.

"I'll never understand how these people can get it on in such a cramped space," said Entryua, pointing at the **hovercar** with his jaw.

"I completely agree."

"And all three, at that! Wait. Was this, ahem, 'ejaculation' consensual for all parties?"

"That, we can't know for sure," the officer shrugged. "But, if I may share my sense of the scene, I think the possibility it was consensual is low."

Entryua felt the same. "Looks like we ought to be probing around for more offenses our victims may've committed."

"Never mind that," said Military Police Captain Keitt, who had run out of patience listening to the officers' conversation. "Are there any traces of the Abh?"

"Not that we've found as of now. While we've collected over 50 hairs, the lab will perform genetic testing on them in due time…"

"Then please get on with your work, as quickly as you can."

The senior forensics officer looked at Entryua questioningly. *Just go*, said Entryua's eyes, after which the officer turned on his heels.

"Guess we should be thankful those three aren't clean freaks, huh," said Entryua as he leaned against the command vehicle and lit a smoke.

The forensics officers who had come all this way from the Lune Beega City Police Office were poking around every inch of the hovercar the suspected Abh and Abh attendant had stolen. Soon they'd be starting to do their favorite thing, which was dismantling and reassembling its parts.

Around the vicinity, Lune Beega Police patrol cars were parked alongside the Crime Lab cars, and lower-ranked officers were standing vigilant.

"We found a clue," said Keitt excitedly.

"We'd have to by now, after three days," replied Entryua bluntly.

To think they'd wasted three whole days on this twaddle! If the police had been patrolling as normal, they'd have found that car in an hour, tops. Or, indeed, if communication between officers was as tight and easy as it had been before. He'd asked Keitt to at least issue traffic permits to squad cars, but Keitt responded he didn't have the authority.

That was when Entryua was seized by a terrifying suspicion — what if this guy was just a deserter who thought himself a military police captain?

Happily, those doubts didn't devil him for long, because as long as Keitt was in the car, they'd be allowed to traverse any checkpoint with the highest priority.

"What do you think we should do here on out, Inspector? I think we should scour every house and building in this city."

Slow down there, pal! thought a fed-up Entryua. *You think we've got that kind of reach? If we scoured every single building, we'd honestly, actually have to commit ALL of the Lune Beega Police's people and resources to this thing. And I don't know if Aizan would be amenable to a lawless city under his watch, but I sure as hell ain't.*

Entryua wanted to dodge that.

"Hmm," he said, pretending to give Keitt's suggestion some thought. "Well, this is *Guzonh*, so I think we should leave this to the *Guzonh* Police Force. They know the area, and there's more of them."

"You'd hand this case to strangers?" Keitt shook his head disbelievingly. "I simply can't understand how you could be so indifferent. We're hunting an accursed Abh. Though it is a little understandable, considering you were hailing your empress up until a day or so ago…"

"Look here, bucko," said Entryua. "I don't even know the **Empress's** *name.*"

"Which is an infringement of your *right* to know. The 'right to know' means—"

"Please, I'm begging you, keep the lecture to yourself. I could look up her name whenever I wanted. I just have no interest."

"That apathy towards politics is democracy's greatest scourge. It was beaten into you by the Abh and their **imperial citizen** stooges."

"Don't badmouth my ancestors." Entryua blew smoke directly at him.

"Your, your ancestors…" he hacked.

"You didn't notice? The name 'Entryua' sounds pretty Abh." (Spelled *Entryac* in proper Baronh.) My great-great-grandparents were **imperial citizens**. Apparently, they were **Star Forces NCCs**, though I don't know the details. They probably thought life up in space didn't agree with their skin or whatever, came back down to land."

"O-Oh." Keitt's mouth was agape, but he soon collected himself. "Then you should hate our quarry all the more."

"What kind of logic is that? Why would I hate them more?"

"They were demoted from **imperial citizens** to mere **landworld citizens**. Surely you resent that…"

"No, I'm not that spiteful a guy," he smiled wryly. "Besides, you've got the wrong idea: there's no real difference between **imperial** and **landworld citizens**. The **Empire** protects the rights of **imperial citizens**, and the **landworld administration** protects the rights of **landworld citizens**. It's just a change of jurisdiction. Though that can be a headache for us police, I'll give you that. Anyway, one of my friends is an **imperial citizen**, so it's not like I've got to talk to them all formal-like. We get on perfectly normally."

"Your friend…" Keitt's eyes were open wide.

"Yes, sir. Runs one of the plantations on the **Manor of the Marquis of Sfagnoff**. But you must've got them locked up in one of your concentration camps, sorry, 'democracy reeducation camps.' I was worried so I tried contacting them, but they weren't home."

"Of course we have. They're more malignant than even the followers of the slave democracy. I can't speak on the matter of your one friend, but **imperial citizens** should all be undergoing reeducation..."

"I really wonder how I can be so cool-headed at a time like this," he said, flashing Keitt a ghastly little smile. It didn't reach *smile of the Abh* levels, but it was a look that had put fear into the heads of dozens of criminals and at-risk youths. "I'm well-known for always thinking of my friends."

"Yes, well, about that suggestion from before..." Keitt's composure had chipped.

"What suggestion?"

"That we leave this case to the *Guzonh* Police Force."

"Ah, that."

"Let's compromise," he said, looking at him appraisingly. "I can see you don't enjoy working with me."

"Oh, no, working with you has suddenly become a laugh riot," said Entryua as he fiddled with the *cairiac* (needlegun) at his waist.

"I'm warning you," Keitt responded with a stern look. "Slighting me isn't a good idea. I've been conferred with unrestricted right to arrest."

"Hey, you lot!" Entryua called out to the officers under him.

"What's up, Inspector?" A handful of bored-looking officers hastened over.

"No, it's fine, stay there."

"Roger."

Entryua looked back at Keitt. "What was that you said earlier? About your 'unrestricted right of arrest'?"

Keitt ground his teeth. "Soldiers in my army are stationed in this city, too!"

"Sure, but I don't see any around here."

"You wouldn't..." Keitt looked around restlessly.

Naturally, Entryua had no actual intention to do Keitt any harm. It would have been cruel of him to order his officers, armed only with **needleguns**, to get into a firefight with an army.

"I'm joking," he said, giving Keitt a friendly pat on the shoulder. "Guess I'm no comedian, huh? I was expecting more than a chuckle out of you."

"Oh, so you were just joking…" he smiled nervously. "Jokes are useful for harmonizing interpersonal relations. But perhaps this culture's jokes are a bit tough to grasp."

"Every planet's got its own sense of humor." Then, suddenly, Entryua grabbed him by the collar, and whispered in his ear: "But know this — you and your buddies are not welcome here. And I don't plan on 'harmonizing' our relationship, either."

"B-But…" Keitt's mouth repeatedly opened and closed.

Entryua smiled broadly, and let him go. "Let's go ahead with that suggestion, shall we? I'll tell the *Guzonh* Police to send as many officers who don't smoke as possible." Entryua picked up the transceiver at his waist and called up the office of Commissioner Aizan. He'd have to settle the matter with the commissioner before he could get the case transferred over. Then they'd set up the crime scene to be taken over by *Guzonh*.

However, Aizan seemed not to want to let go of his status as cooperating with the occupying army. He was positively dying to show the military that he was useful.

Entryua, for his part, pointed out that they were clearly stepping on *Guzonh*'s area of jurisdiction, and that if they failed to arrest them, there was a possibility he'd incur the army's displeasure instead.

Aizan, meanwhile, intimated he'd have Entryua replaced, unless he returned with the crash-landed Abh in custody.

Entryua replied more clearly than ever before that the good commissioner would have his eternal gratitude if he did indeed replace him, describing the voluminous difficulties of the investigation, and stirring up the commissioner's unease.

At last, Aizan folded.

Momentarily relieved, Entryua hung up.

He smiled at Keitt and said, "Now we'll both be happy."

"In our world, what you just did is a flagrant breach of regulations," said Keitt, stunned. "This may be your last act as a policeman."

"It won't be," said Entryua confidently.

He was a celebrity in Lune Beega, vaunted as a fair and outstanding member of the force. If Entryua got the axe, Aizan would be hit by an avalanche of criticism, and he knew it.

"Inspector." The senior forensics officer who had waited for Entryua to finish his call stepped into the space between him and Keitt and handed him a piece of resin with a hair sealed inside.

"The results are in. It's an Abh hair. It's likely the female suspect's, as it's been dyed black."

"The Inspector was talking to me," Keitt goggled at him. "And why didn't you report that to ME!?"

"Excuse me, Captain, but you aren't part of our chain of command," the forensics officer said, eyeing him coldly.

"My rank is on par with the Inspector's!" he spat vehemently.

"I wasn't aware of that," said the Senior Forensics Officer, not even giving Keitt another look.

"C'mon, Captain, give him a break. We have a new clue to work with now," said Entryua, brandishing the resin sample.

"That's true, but…" Keitt cast his eyes down begrudgingly. Indignation hadn't vacated those eyes quite yet.

Maybe I pushed his buttons a tiny bit too much, Entryua reflected. Then the transceiver ringed.

Entryua picked it up cheerfully. It was, of course, Commissioner Aizan on the line. Unfortunately, what Aizan had to say dashed his hopes.

Talks with the force at *Guzonh* had ended in failure. They freely gave them permission to step on their jurisdiction. So freely, they would have given it to them wrapped in a pretty bow if they could, if Aizan's words were to be believed. They said they couldn't spare any manpower, but they'd give them whatever information they wanted without delay.

Entryua could only gripe inwardly over how much cleverer this city's commissioner was than Aizan.

"So, don't worry about the rest, and just push forward with your mission, Entryua," said Aizan, blithely.

Entryua growled and hung up. "We're continuing the investigation ourselves," he told Keitt, imparting the bad news succinctly.

"I see," he replied, with an expressionlessness that exhibited surprising restraint. "I think I'll call for reinforcements."

"You'd better not mean reinforcements from the Police Office," he said, making his unhappiness abundantly clear. Entryua had no doubt Aizan would peel every last person down to the accountant from their desks and push them into the fray if Keitt requested it.

"No," he said flatly. "From my unit. I'll ask my superiors to send me some of their subordinates."

He knew what Keitt was really after with that call. 'Solving a shortfall in manpower?' A likely story. He just wanted allies around.

It was understandable, considering that moments prior, Entryua had similarly intimidated him with numbers. And he had no intention of crying foul; Keitt wouldn't listen, anyway.

"Yeah? Here I'm wondering if any number of boots on the ground is enough," he said, without objecting outright.

I've got a proposition for him — what say we split into two teams? That way, we can both do our thing the way we like.

"Yes, I've decided." Keitt nodded and brought the transceiver on his wrist to his mouth.

Entryua had no idea what he was saying into that thing, but whatever it was, it sounded real stiff and formal. It was only through Keitt's visible dejection that he gleaned the outcome of their negotiations.

For the first time, Entryua empathized with him. "Why's everybody gotta be so down on their luck around here? If you ask me, somebody somewhere's hoarding all the good luck."

"I don't doubt it," Keitt muttered, probably without thinking. "Never mind that; what we do now?"

"With only this many officers, all we can do is plod away step by step."

"What do you mean, specifically?"

"Combing every single building would be a giant waste of time. There's no other way: First we search inns and hotels, then expand from there."

"This is going to take quite some time, isn't it?"

"I bet it will. Let's just pray those two were dumb enough to hole up in an inn. I don't think there'll be too many people taking a leisurely vacation during such a state of crisis."

Chapter 14: The *Slacélach* (Warriors)

It happened when Jint was enduring more holovision to polish his Clasburian — sudden noises from behind.

Startled, Jint turned his head, only to find four men storming inside. He jumped to his feet.

"Resistance is futile!" shouted the short one at the head of the pack.

Each of the men had their **stunguns** aimed square at Jint. The slightest funny move, and they'd make him stiffer than a petrified log.

"Wh-Who are you people!?" Jint shouted back.

"Can't you tell we're police officers?" replied the short one, clearly offended.

"P-Police…" *So they've finally come knocking.* Jint's palms grew sweaty.

The men all wore matching uniforms of green on yellow, which hardly screamed "police" to him; Jint's image of officer uniforms was more unaffected, but here in Clasbure, the land of garish taste, he supposed they *were* relatively sober in color.

"Now where's your little friend? The Abh girl?" said shorty.

"Abh girl? Maybe you've got the wrong room?"

Lafier had retired to the bedroom. Jint clung desperately to the faint hope that he could, maybe, conceivably talk his way out of this.

"She must be asleep already," he said, seeing right through him. "What are you doing awake, anyway? You got a screw loose? Don't you know it's bedtime? You're really screwing up our plan."

Should I, uh, apologize or something? thought Jint.

"You." Shorty looked over his shoulder at one of his men. He was a big, sturdy, black-skinned man. "Go take a look."

The big lug nodded and headed for the bedroom door.

Another of the men, a lean, fully-shaven officer who resembled a crane on a weight loss program, accompanied him.

"No!" The threat of the **stunguns** evaded his mind as he leapt at the big one. Annoyed, Big Lug knocked him back onto the ground with a swing of his arms. He tried to get back up, but froze when he saw the muzzle in front of his face.

"You've got guts, I'll give you that." Shorty thrust the **stungun** right between his eyes. "But the next time you move, I won't be so lenient."

"Did you come to arrest us?"

"That's what they want."

"What they want?"

"Zip it. You'll hear all about it later." Shorty shot a glance at Big Lug. "Hey…"

Jint took full advantage of that moment's inattention, and grabbed his arm. They tussled and locked bodies, and even as they rolled across the floor, Jint kept Shorty's arm pinned, twisting his wrist with a jerk.

"Ow!" Shorty dropped his **stungun**.

Jint reached to grab it, but at that moment, two of the others fell on top of him, the officer who'd followed Big Lug, and the fourth, a young man with close-cropped hair dyed yellow.

"Goddammit." Jint was pinned face-down.

Slim was sitting astride Jint's waist like a horseman, while Youngin was leaning forward against Jint's back and twisting his arms.

"Keep him there!" Shorty squeaked, as he retrieved his gun.

"What if we gave him a shock to the system?" proposed Youngin.

Shorty shook his head. "Do you feel like lugging him places? No, no, we'll have him walk on his own two feet when and where we can."

"But Undertaker…"

"You idiot! We're *police*, remember!? Call me 'Sergeant'!"

"Yes, Sergeant, sir."

A strange exchange any way Jint sliced it. Were they *really* officers? If not, then who were they? They couldn't be enemy soldiers—

But Jint's train of thought crashed to a halt when he felt something mean and hard press against the back of his head. It was Shorty with his gun.

"Thick as thieves, ain't you? Just so you understand, I'd like you to walk on your damned legs, but I'm willing to carry your ass if I have to. You ever been shot by a **stungun**? 'Cause let me tell you, you won't be blacking out with a smile on your face. Every muscle in your body's gonna scream."

"Are you thugs really coppers?" asked Jint.

Slim whistled. "I like kids like him. Asking questions when he's this buried. Or maybe he's just too dumb to understand his position here. Color me right fascinated."

"Yeah huh, whatever floats your boat," said Shorty. Then he ordered Big Lug again: "What're you doing, Daswani? Hurry up."

The big one, apparently named Daswani, nodded without a word, and opened the bedroom door.

He took a step into the room, and then froze. Then he shook his head, *No,* and started stepping back.

At first, Jint was totally lost. Then he saw Lafier in front of Daswani, and the situation turned clear as day.

Lafier was wearing the inn's provided, white jumpsuit-type sleepwear. Her *froch* glinted inorganically, peeking out from her sleep-tousled bangs. Her eyes, their corners higher than most, were narrowed coldly, and she had a **lightgun** gripped in hand.

A **lightgun** was always an ill-omened, sinister sight. The guns packed the power to tear a human body to shreds with ease. Compared to lasers, **stunguns** were a mere toy in both appearance and destructive capability.

"It's the Abh…" muttered Youngin disgustedly. "There really was one!"

Daswani found himself against the wall.

No one moved a muscle.

The first to break the silence was Shorty. Unexpectedly, though his brogue didn't evaporate, he spoke in error-free Baronh.

"Drop the weapon, Abh. Don't you care what happens to the boy? Even a **stungun** can kill at point-blank range."

"If he should die, so too do you all," said Lafier, her brow furrowed, and her voice firm. "I shall not allow a single one of you to leave this room alive. And to warn you, I am in a supremely bad mood."

"I know I would be," muttered Slim. "In fact, anyone would be, getting pulled from their sleep like that. Today I learned that the Abh are no exception." His insightful discovery went ignored by the rest.

"There are four of us, and one of you. How could we lose?" replied Shorty.

She turned her nose up. "Care to try it?"

Youngin grunted and tried pointing his **stungun** her way.

Lafier was faster. She pursed her lips as though whistling as she pulled the trigger. The beam of heat that fired from the **lightgun**'s muzzle hit his **stungun** dead-on.

"Yeowch!" Youngin dropped it; it had turned terribly hot terribly quickly.

Big Lug attempted to use that opening to brandish his own gun, but once again the **lightgun** pierced through the **stungun**.

Big Lug endured the heat and pulled the trigger, but the **stungun** had already been rendered inoperative. On both sides of his dumbfounded head, smoldering holes had been charred into the wall. Upon noticing, he sank down to the floor.

"Don't shoot! I surrender!" said Slim, sticking up his arms as he threw away his **stungun**.

"As you can see, I have received marksmanship training," she replied calmly. "I have a great many skills I'm proud of, and my sharpshooting is one of them. Yet at present, I am drowsy, and my reflexes slow. As such, you mustn't count on my accuracy for my next shots."

Again, a silence as thick as marble gripped the room.

Shorty was frozen, and dripping with a cold sweat.

Though Jint's limbs weren't being pinned anymore, the other two were still sitting on top of him, so he still couldn't extricate himself. Moreover, there was still the gun pressed against his head.

Jint thought of a small bit of advice: "Uh, guys? I think you ought to reassess the situation."

Shorty shot him a dirty look. Then his line of sight moved to the **stungun**, followed by a glance at Lafier's **lightgun**. Finally, he stared into the distance, his expression that of a man reminiscing about his blissful youth.

Jint gulped, eyeing the man warily all the while.

When Shorty made up his mind, he acted swiftly. The **stungun** vanished from his hand like a mirage, while the two men atop him finally released Jint from his status as a rug.

Jint tumbled back to his feet and strode to Lafier's side. "Excellent, you reassessed," said Jint from the heart.

"Reassess? Whatever do you mean?" said Shorty, pulling an expression that screamed *"I have no idea what you're talking about but I'd sure love to find out before I snuff it."*

"I'm just glad we could come to an understanding," Jint said, the forked tongue out at last.

"Absolutely! Cross-cultural understanding is always worthwhile! Welcome to the planet of Clasbure!" said Shorty, his hands sticking up wide.

The wind blew across the room, turning the air dour once again, the atmosphere, stifling.

"Maybe I spoke too soon. Looks like we haven't come to an understanding after all," Jint murmured.

"Jint, let's pull out. I'll keep my eyes on them, so go gather our things."

"Yeah, guess that's the thing to do." Jint shook his head and entered the bedroom.

It didn't take him long to pack their bags; all of their clothing was stored in the duffel bag so that they could leave at a moment's notice. He returned to the scene with a **lightgun** in his right hand and the duffel bag over his left shoulder.

"Shall we bounce?" he asked Lafier.

"Yep." She turned to address the others. "All of you, go to the bedroom."

"Wait," said Shorty. "We're your allies."

"Well that was a funny way to show it," said Jint.

"Don't you want to know who we are?"

"Nope," said Jint coldly.

"So young, but no curiosity. Curiosity's the wellspring of betterment, you know," said Shorty.

"I really don't care if you're 'undertakers' or a goddamned bird lovers' association," he spat. The wrists they'd twisted were still throbbing, so he couldn't say he felt any affection for them.

"The only Undertaker's right here," said Shorty, pointing to himself.

"That right? You must love your job. Do you manufacture corpses?"

"Enough. You will hasten to the bedroom, or else," Lafier urged.

"Dammit." The men shuffled into the bedroom at gunpoint.

That was when another door, the door to the hallway, opened for all to hear.

Fresh troops!? The tension high, Jint got his gun at the ready.

"If only you lot weren't such serial bunglers."

Jint was startled; it was the housekeeping lady. "You're with them?"

"I'm their leader," she said, her Baronh more fluent even than Jint's. "I don't have a weapon, don't you worry."

"Then you're not an employee."

"I am not, no."

"And that bit about the *sheef*, you made that up?"

"Oh no, deary, that's all true. You two are very unpopular among the actual employees."

Jint winced, but he was quick to pull himself together. "You must've come in search of us, huh?"

"Yes," she said. Then she smiled at Lafier: "Little Abh lady, you have some blue showing in the whorl of your hair. If you're going to dye your hair, you need to do it diligently and regularly."

"I thank you for your advice," she said mirthlessly. "Now join them in the bedroom."

"Wait! Hear us out first. If we cooperate, we'll both be better off for it."

"What do we do, Jint?" Lafier's expression was as severe as ever, but a little confusion had crept in.

"I guess it couldn't hurt to listen to what they've got to say."

"A wise decision," said the false housekeeper.

"Before anything else, I shall have you stand together in a line." Lafier indicated the window with her gun.

"Always shrewd, I see." Suitably impressed, she did as ordered.

"Anybody else reminded of an execution by firing squad?" mumbled Shorty.

"It's okay, Undertaker," said Slim. "If that's what she wanted, she'd have already sliced a clean cross-section of our necks."

"You're not wrong, but I've always had to wonder, why does perfectly valid reasoning piss me off so much?"

The five of them lined up by the window. Now all of them could be monitored.

"First things first, allow us to introduce ourselves. You can call me 'Malka.'"

"And you can call me 'Undertaker.' Course, that's not my real name, but it's what my comrades call me," said Shorty.

"My name's Min. My parents named me something else, but I never took to it, so I hope you'll call me 'Min,'" said Slim. Jint noticed then that he had a moustache, colored red on the left and yellow on the right.

"I'm Bill. Ask anybody in town about 'Speedwheels Bill,' they'll have heard of me," said Youngin.

"Daswani," grumbled Big Lug.

On that note, the five of them grew silent.

When Jint cottoned on to what they were waiting for, he shrugged. "Really sorry, guys, but I'm not in the mood to introduce myself."

"That's fine," said Malka, not looking disappointed for it. "If I recall, you were on the inn's register as 'Sye Lina' and 'Sye Jint.'"

"Ah, right."

"So we'll just call you that. In your case, 'Jint' does seem to be your actual name."

Clearly, Malka had sharp ears. She'd picked up on it when Lafier had addressed Jint by name.

"'Lina' isn't an Abh name, though," said Min with a suspicious expression.

"If you want her real name, we're not telling," he said flatly.

"Not even her given name? She must be of quite the high rank. High-ranking enough for people to know her name. Is it safe to assume you're connected to the **Manor of the Marquis of Sfagnoff**?"

"You can pry all you like, but we won't be obliging you. We don't even know who you are."

"Ah, yes, of course," said Malka. "We are members of the Clasbure Anti-Imperial Front."

"'Anti-Imperial'? Is that code for 'anti-Abh'?"

"We don't dislike Abhs, Jint. We simply seek independence. We don't recognize the right of the **Empire** to station a **lord** here, or deny us the right to trade and explore with our own spaceships."

"But the **Empire** would never let you do that."

"Exactly. That's why we're forced to fight."

"With the **Empire**?"

"No, with the Bird Lovers' Association. Yes, with the Empire."

"And you know we're with the **Empire**, right?"

"She's an Abh. Of course we know."

"But you said we're allies."

"And we are."

"Uh-huh." Jint gave a big nod.

It was then he grasped the unfathomability of the gap between them and the five hapless Clasburians, and he turned around to face Lafier. "Well, we heard them out. What say we hit the road?"

"Hold your horses. We're not done talking."

"It's all over my head, okay!?"

"We're not TALKING to you, the **imperial citizen**. Malka's talking to the little Abh lady. As her attendant, you oughta just shut up and listen," said Bill.

Offended though he was, he decided to own up to his misunderstanding and zip his lips. Even if he told them he was in fact a **noble**, it wouldn't be easy to convince them of that, and nothing good would have come of it anyway.

Lafier, on the other hand, spoke up: "His words are my words. Do not belittle him."

Jint saw the jealousy flash across Bill's eyes.

"So, what is your objective?" asked Lafier.

Undertaker's lips curled in a smile. "We want you to be our hostages."

"Jint, it would seem we really had better leave this place."

"Couldn't agree more," said Jint, his gun remaining at the ready as he made for the door with the irritated impatience of a cat forced to wear a hat.

"Bye bye. It was a ton of fun meeting you. You were a great boredom-killer."

"Of course they'd misunderstand if you put it that way!" Malka nudged Undertaker on the noggin. "I told you, hold your horses!"

"If you have anything else to say, best out with it quickly. My arm's growing tired," said Lafier, giving them one last chance.

"Please listen! At this rate, you'll be taken into custody for sure!" she started, rattling on without pause. "You two don't know how this planet works! You're as out of place as a camel at a swim meet. But if we join forces, we can keep you hidden until the Abh make their return."

"That would be nice," said Jint. He'd had his survival doubts, so if they could gain the help of some locals, they'd be in the best possible position. "But why would anti-imperials like you do that for us?"

"Isn't it obvious? So we can use you as bargaining chips!" said Undertaker.

"For heaven's sake, shut up. Must you be renowned the world over for making things more stressful than they need to be?" said Malka. "But what Undertaker said is true. We want to negotiate with the **Empire** using you two, or rather, just the little lady. Now that we finally have an Abh in reach, we can't let her get swiped from us by some foreign occupation."

"What you seek is impossible; even if I were **Her Majesty the Empress** herself, the **Empire** would never..."

Jint understood what she was driving at. Hostage-taking would never get an Abh to acquiesce. No matter whether the hypothetical hostage were the **Empress** herself, and the demand a trifling one, it was simply not in the character of the **Empire** to give in. They would instead plot a suitable revenge against such foul play.

Yet Jint poked Lafier's side with an elbow and whispered: "Let's not deflate their ambitions, actually. If they think negotiation is in the cards, that's better for us."

"So we *fool* them?" Lafier didn't bother hiding her disgust at the notion.

"We don't *fool* them. It's not like we fed them that ridiculous idea ourselves."

"That is true, but..."

"Look, ill-conceived motives aren't exactly rare. We'd just be politely respecting their dreams."

"But they would learn that I won't work as a hostage eventually. Then, at that point, they would turn angry, would they not? Enough to want to kill us, surely. That's what hostage-taking typically entails."

"That's the thing, we won't *really* be their hostages. Just leave this to me."

Once Malka saw she had their attention, she pelted them with words like a rapid-fire needlegun. "How do you think we noticed you? You two are already the stuff of rumors. The man at the desk got a clear look at your face. You had your hair dyed black, but there's no mistaking an Abh face; you're too perfect-looking to be a Lander, and you were acting strangely to boot. The only conclusion to draw is that you're an Abh who's running from trouble. He also happens to be a supporter of ours, so news reached us first, but what would you have done if somebody leaked it to an enemy soldier!? Do you honestly think you were hiding? More like you were ringing a bell advertising 'there's an Abh here!'"

"Fine, we get it," he raised a hand to stop her. "We'll give ourselves over. That is, if you follow our conditions."

"Hostages with *conditions*?" said Undertaker, eyes open wide.

"You do know what a hostage is, don't you?"

"Shut it, Undertaker. If you lot had done your jobs properly, we wouldn't be in such a bind. We would've had the advantage. We could've strongly urged them to be our hostages with the guns in OUR hands!"

"Then why didn't you just do it yourself, Malka?"

"You want a frail maiden like me to do the fighting? Talk about inconsiderate!"

"Might you let me lay out our conditions sometime soon," said Jint timidly.

"Go ahead," said Malka.

"One, we're not handing you our weapons."

"Armed hostages!? Now you're just desecrating the CONCEPT of a hostage!"

"How many times do I need to tell you to shut it, Undertaker!? Yes, what else?"

"We do everything together. You can't leave our side unless we say so."

"Okay. Anything else?"

"One last one. We want you to explain everything you do before you do it. Where you're going, what you're doing, et cetera."

"That's fine. And now that we've cleared the air, let's vacate the premises, quickly."

Malka had accepted their terms so readily that Jint felt almost disappointed.

"Wait, she needs to change." He pointed at Lafier, who was still in her sleepwear.

"I prefer this attire," said Lafier. "It's better than that atrocious garb you bought me."

"What do you think?" he asked Malka.

"It doesn't look like it could be anything other than nightwear. And it's very strange to go out wearing nightwear here."

"See?" He pulled clothes from out of the duffel bag and handed them to Lafier. "Change into these and come back."

"Do not treat me like a child!" she said indignantly, but she did as she was told and disappeared into the bedroom.

"You really an **imperial citizen** attendant of a **noble** girl?" asked Bill, clearly suspicious. "Aren't you being a bit impolite?"

"That's just an act. And what an act it is," said Malka.

"Uhh, I've got a question of my own," said Jint.

"What?"

"You're all assuming the **Empire** retakes this planet. But what if they never come? What'll become of us then?"

"You think they'd leave the planet to its own devices after they lost a battle!?" said Undertaker, staring at him unblinkingly. "That's the craziest hot take I've heard all year."

About 6,000 **planar space** *cédlairh* away from the **Sfagnoff Marquessate**, there was the *Ciïoth Bibaurbina Yunr* (*Yunh* 303 Star System). 6,000 *cédlairh* only took five hours or so using a high-speed **conveyance ship**, and even a slower-speed **supply ship** would take seven. Considering this was the **Monarchy of Ilich**, where the portals were so far apart, it was practically a hop and a skip away.

That was where the Abh **fleet** was positioned.

The fleet's *glagac* (flagship) was the **patrol ship** *Cairdigh*. As it was designed with its potential use as a flagship in mind, its **bridge** was constructed with a two-tier structure. In the higher tier of the bridge where command of the ship was conducted, the *Gahorh Glar* (Commander's Bridge) was situated.

That was where *Tlaïmh Baurgh Ybdér Laimsairh* was pacing hurriedly.

Looks like we've gotten to the good part.

He was stocky for an Abh, his hair dark green, and his swarthy, convex face almost aquiline in its features, like some bird of prey. However, whenever a member of the Tlife family spoke, they laid bare the pointed canines that were their unique **family feature**, thereby evoking not a falcon or hawk, but a savage beast. In either case, he exuded such a fierce aura, that one would swear he was born to be a soldier. Though he was no different from other Abhs in his handsomeness, it was his countenance's ferocious intensity that left the bigger impression.

The Command Bridge's *spéruch* (military staff) comprised two *casariac* (staff officers) and one *luciac* (adjutant), as well as a handful of *catboth* (command center soldiers), all of whom were watching their restive **Commander-in-Chief**.

On the wall behind the *Glaharéribach* (Commander-in-Chief's Seat) at which Tlife was supposed to be calmly seated, three **crest banners** hung in a triangle. At the top of that triangle lay the *rüe niglac* (imperial flag), the eight-headed *Gaftnochec*. At the base-left lay the flag of the *Chtymec Ralbrybr* (*Ralbrybh* Astrobase). It too bore the dragon, but its base was red, and it was adorned with bolts of lightning.

The flag at the right was the Tlife family's coat of arms, the *Ctaich* (Lamenting Pheasant). Officers of *Raichaicec Ïadbyrer* (Sub-Fleet Commandant) rank or higher enjoyed the right to hang their family banner.

"**Your Excellency**, the **patrol ship** *Adlass* has brought back an up-to-date map of the situation," reported the *Üass Casarér* (Chief of Staff).

His name was **Noble Prince** *Cahyrec Bautec Satecr*, **Kilo-Commander** *Lemaich*. Unlike his commander, he had the typical slender Abh frame. His hair was the typical dark blue, and his features were average for an Abh (which was to say that maybe one in one thousand Landers could hope to compare to their perfection). His eyes always looked sleepy, giving the impression that he was only dimly aware of goings-on.

"They have, have they? Bring it here." Tlife nodded, expected good news.

"Yes, sir." Cahyoor gave one of his subordinates the sign.

A stereoscopic video of **planar space** emerged.

The currents of **space-time particles** from the densely crowded central band of the **Milky Way Portal-belts** and the space-time particles from the **"volcanoes"** of the outer brink of the **Twelfth Ring** collided near the **Sfagnoff Portal**, making for a relatively high-concentration area in the vicinity.

Space-time bubbles had a hard time penetrating high-density areas, but they did make for easy escapes from planar space. For battles that involved mutual **mine** flinging, whichever side lined up in formation in a high-concentration area had the advantage. It was akin to securing the high ground in a land war, and the **map of planar space** similarly displayed such areas as "tall."

Within that high-concentration area, a flock of **space-time bubbles** was assembling. That was the ideal spot to fend off any invasion of the **Sfagnoff Portal**.

"The enemy has made contact with our ship, and so they've become aware of our approach," Cahyoor explained. "Going by the mass, it is equivalent to three **sub-fleets**. It's clearly an interception formation. As such, we believe that the enemy has no current plans to launch a preemptive strike from their stronghold in Sfagnoff."

"Three **sub-fleets**. I see. There really aren't that many of them after all." This was the good news he was awaiting, so Tlife beamed bright. "That must be all of their forces, too."

"Probably, yes. I know that if I were a strategist on their side, I'd have them intercept using all of their forces."

"Enough speculation; do you have any concrete information for me?"

"I'm afraid not," said Cahyoor, shaking his head. "In order to confirm anything, we need intelligence from Central, but we're currently lacking in that regard. The **Information Bureau** hadn't even caught wind of this invasion beforehand, so it's likely well beyond their means to grasp their total military strength."

"Ugh. The **Information Bureau**," said Tlife, making sure they heard the annoyance in his voice. "A bunch of incompetent hacks not even fit to feed the cat."

"I feel you may be exaggerating slightly, *Lonh*," said the *casarhac drochotr* (communications staff officer), *Roïbomoüass* (Vice Hecto-Commander) *Nasotryac*, pointedly. It hadn't been long since she'd transferred over from the *Rÿazonh Spodér Rirragr* (Military Command HQ Information Bureau). When he'd badmouthed her old haunt, the sour look on her face said it all.

"I see…" Tlife placed his chin against his fist and paced aimlessly around the room.

The *Saimh Spodér Rirragr* (Director-General of the Information Bureau) *Fraudéc* (Commodore) *Cachnanch* was a man against whom he bore a personal grudge — a grudge that traced its beginnings to a certain episode revolving around a sky-blue-haired girl and a room at their **starpilot academy**. Ever since then, they bickered every time they crossed paths.

There's no doubt Cachnansh is a trash human, or that he's as inept as it gets. The fact that a "winner" like him made such an important position can only be some nasty prank on the part of Rÿazonh *(HQ). That said, it's hardly fair of me to paint all of his subordinates with the same brush. They slipped up this one time, but they've more or less done their jobs over the years. A man's man always takes back his words when he's wrong. Yes, I should take back what I said.*

"I was wrong," said the **Commander-in-Chief**. "Feeding the cat would be the perfect position for the crew over at the **Information Bureau!**"

"I'm certain the members of the **Information Bureau** will feel honored by your words of praise, sir," said the **Chief of Staff** impassively.

"Good, I'm glad," said Tlife, pleased as punch.

Nasotryac kept mum, her face a war ground of dueling emotions.

Tlife proceeded to forget about the matter of the **Information Bureau** entirely, as he turned his thoughts to more serious concerns. *Now then, how do we go about this?*

At the moment, he had seven **sub-fleets** under his command:

The *ïadbyrec acharr* (assault sub-fleet) *Byrdaimh*.

The **assault sub-fleet** *Rocérh*.

The **assault sub-fleet** *Üacapérh*.

The **assault sub-fleet** *Citirec*.

The *ïadbyrec bhotutr* (strike sub-fleet) *Bascec-Gamlymh*.

The *ïadbyrec usaimr* (recon sub-fleet) *Ftunéc*.

The *ïadbyrec dicpaurér* (supply sub-fleet) *Achmatuch*.

In addition, a handful more *saubh lagoradha* (independent squadrons) and a provisional fleet including HQ's *glabaüriac* (flagship-controlled warship) formed another unit adorned with the name of the **Commander-in-Chief** — the *Byrec Tlaimr* (Tlife Fleet), totaling around 2,100 warships strong.

Pitiful numbers, thought Tlife discontentedly.

The fleet didn't even have a clear objective to begin with.

When the **Ralbrybh** Astrobase learned of the attack on the **Sfagnoff Marquessate**, they sent seven sub-fleets to *Roïglaharérh Chtymér* (Astrobase Vice Commander-in-Chief) **Commodore** Tlife as a temporary stopgap measure.

Their foremost objective was reconnaissance: that is to say, determining the scope of the enemy's forces, and snooping around for their plans. However, he had too many ships for just reconnaissance. Reconnaissance didn't even necessarily call for the formation of a fleet at all. He ought to leave it to the **recon sub-fleet** under his command, the *Ftunéc*.

On the other hand, he had too few ships for the retaking and anti-invasion defense of the **Sfagnoff Marquessate**.

I must have pulled the short end of the stick. As they sailed along, Tlife recalled the faces of his colleagues.

The **Ralbrybh** Astrobase had four **Vice Commanders-in-Chief**, Tlife included. An **Astrobase Vice Commander-in-Chief**'s position was assigned by the **Commander-in-Chief** when it came time for strategizing and drills. In peacetime, one possessed no fleet to command, but during times of crisis, they were always attended by **staff officers**. A patchwork fleet could operate, but not so for *Glagamh* (Headquarters).

The other three were fine candidates for the job, so why him? Frankly put, Tlife had been nursing the feeling that he'd been treated unfairly the entire time he navigated to this place. He didn't even encounter the enemy invasion fleet he'd expected he would on the way over. It had been a perfectly smooth journey. Even drills had more nervous tension than this, if only slightly.

Little wonder, when the enemy that lurked in the **Sfagnoff Marquessate** had penetrated deep into **Empire** territory with such vastly insufficient forces.

"We can win this," he said, running the sentiment by the **Chief of Staff**.

"Yes. That is, however, assuming that the whole of the enemy's forces is what has already appeared."

"Can't say I like fighting based on assumptions."

"Then shall we retreat? Shall we ask for reinforcements?"

"I'll pretend you didn't say that," declared Tlife, raising an arm overhead. "We're retaking the **Sfagnoff Marquessate**."

"Yes, sir." The **Chief of Staff** clicked his heels and bowed.

"Cahyoor, how long will you take to draw up a plan?"

"There are some matters that I must confirm first," he said quietly.

"What matters?"

"Do we include the annihilation of the enemy as one of our strategic goals?"

Casariac ïocsscurhotr (strategy staff officer) **Hecto-Commander** *Chrirh* motioned: "I think we should use a pincer attack."

"Hmm…" It was an intriguing proposal. Pincer attacks were flashy as far as war tactics went. It involved splitting one's ships and having them advance to their rear, cutting off escape. Then they'd attack from the flanks along with the main force. If it succeeded, they could obliterate the enemy without a trace. Plus, it was difficult to see how they could possibly lose in this situation. They had more than twice the total power of the opposing side. Even if each enemy ship destroyed one of theirs, it would still be possible for them to progress the battle toward a favorable position.

Furthermore, Tlife had the **recon sub-fleet**, the *Ftunéc*.

Upon hearing the words "recon sub-fleet," a person not versed in matters military would probably think it lightly armed and almost purely for support, but in fact, little could be further from the truth.

It is the recon sub-fleet's mission to rely on their brute strength to peer into hostile sectors. Slow and heavy **battle-line warships** and weak **assault warships** would only get in the way. All of their tactical forces were made up of patrol ships. In addition, the *dihosmh* (stock ships) that accompanied them were the smaller variants, around the same size as the patrol ships themselves, and with the sheer maneuverability and destructive power to match.

The strength of the fleet was even said to be five times greater than the standard assault fleet. Though it would be difficult to achieve owing to cost-efficiency and operational flexibility issues, there was also an endless supply of zealous believers in the **Star Forces** who believed that all of its main forces should be composed of recon sub-fleets.

They were the so-called heavy cavalry unit, galloping across the heavens. And there was no more suitable unit to be the detached force for the pincer attack.

Tlife considered it for a few seconds. Then, with reluctance, he shot the idea down.

"No can do. Our goal isn't battle, per se. It's simply the retaking of the **Sfagnoff Marquessate**. This war won't be over for a while. Even if victory would be absolute, we can't afford to lose vessels or fleets in a purposeless battle."

"But sir…" *Chrirh* tried to object.

"Shut your mouth, and don't tempt me any more than you have already!" said Tlife.

"Yes, sir." To her chagrin, *Chrirh* held her tongue.

"So, we'll be intimidating the enemy as we march, then," said Cahyoor.

"Right." In his heart he was all for the pincer attack, yet he nodded. "We'll display our might through a horizontal single-line formation, and slowly march our way in. Seeing that, they'd have to jump ship."

"Understood. I'll draft a rough plan along those lines."

"How long will it take before we can depart?"

"What will we do about the **patrol ships** that are currently on the reconnaissance mission?"

"We won't wait for them to finish, of course. We'll pick them back up on the way."

"In that case, it will take under two hours."

"No easing up. Do it in an hour."

"Understood."

Tlife frowned. That Cahyoor accepted that time reduction so readily meant they could in fact take even less time. But it was too late now; he was the one who said, "Do it in an hour."

"Good. Now do it. If I don't see a fine strategy in an hour's time, my disappointment in you will be immense."

"Yes, sir."

He watched the **staff officers** withdraw to the *chicrh ïocsscurhotr* (strategy room), and at last, Tlife took a seat on the **Commander's Seat**.

Exactly one hour later, Cahyoor presented a ranking order for the march and the scheduled route.

While Tlife had run his mouth earlier, ultimately, he trusted his **Chief of Staff**, so he approved the plan without even really skimming through it and issued the order to the fleet.

"Ladies and gentlemen, we'll be retaking the **Sfagnoff Marquessate**. Unfortunately, we're going to do it without engaging. If by some unexpected windfall we do plunge into battle, I look forward to watching your beautiful warriors' dance. Now lift off!"

Two thousand vessels spouted their **propulsor flames** simultaneously.

Appendix: Abh Metrology

The aspect of Abh culture most reminiscent of Earth is their measurement of time. A year in the Abh calendar is also 365 days.

Naturally, as they have no need to differentiate between a calendar year and the sidereal year, there are no leap years, nor leap seconds. A year to the Abh is always 365 days; a day, 24 hours; an hour, 60 minutes; a minute, 60 seconds.

Other measurements used by the Abh are based on Earth antecedents. Namely, the meter, which was established based on the length of the equator, and the gram, which is defined as the weight of one cubic centimeter of water under Earth gravity.

However, care must be taken, because in Baronh, they have their own distinct words for metric system measurements, and the prefix changes with every increment of four digits.

Time measurements aside, measurements are denoted as follows:

Length... *dagh* = centimeter (cm)

Mass... *boc* = gram (g)

The following prefixes are attached those basic units to represent larger units. For example, 3 *zaisadagh* is the same as 30 million meters, while 800 *üésboc* is 8 tons. However, the Abh also use light-seconds and light-years, so units of distance above *zaisadagh* aren't used all that often.

Moreover, there is vocabulary for a minute unit system based on the Planck length and the Planck mass, but I won't get into that here.

As for planar space, which is governed by different laws of physics from 3-space, a different set of units and measurements is of course necessary. That is the "astro-mile" (*cédlairh*) and the "astro-knot" (*digrh*).

1 *cédlairh* is defined as equivalent to the distance travelled by a space-time bubble of one *seboc* (100 tons) in one second of space-time bubble time. Meanwhile, 1 *digrh* is the speed needed to traverse one *cédlairh* in one hour by space-time bubble's time.

Scale	Prefix	Length	Mass
10^{-16}	peta	0.1f (femto)	
10^{-12}	cos	1p (pico)	
10^{-8}	soüamh	1Å (angstroms)	0.01 µg
10^{-4}	ches	1µ	0.1 mg
1		1 cm	1 g
10^{4}	tiés		10 kg
10^{8}	sai		100 tons
10^{12}	zaisac		1,000,000 tons
10^{16}	to		10 billion tons
10^{20}	drial		100 trillion tons

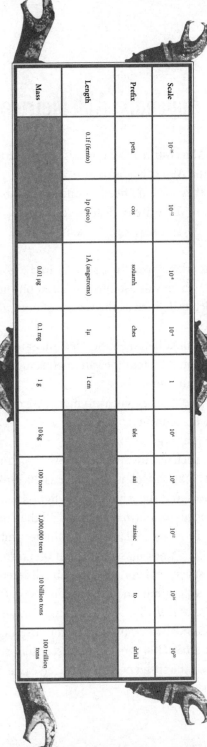

Afterword

I once read that what Robert E. Howard wrote down — that seminal heroic fantasy series — was what Conan himself dictated to him.

I'm not normally one to believe in the occult, so I understood that as an episode of subconscious greatness. I thought it an amazing feat of the mind. I was still in school at the time, and I envied Howard, thinking that I'd love to be an SF writer and experience that very same phenomenon. More than anything else, because it'd make things so easy.

The months and years passed by, and some time after I managed to put out my debut short form story, it happened.

As I was busy being lonely, staring at my bottle of booze and absorbed in my contemplations, a beautiful woman who looked to be in her mid-20s swooped down where I was. Her hair colored a deep forest green, and adorned with an exquisite crown, she looked down at me with her striking jet-black eyes.

What luck, I thought. Since I'm a healthy, red-blooded male, a youthful beauty like her was much preferable to a filth-ridden muscle man like Conan.

On the dime, I booted my word processor in preparation, ready to listen to her tale. "Err, may I ask you your name first?" I asked.

Haughtily, she raised her chin and proclaimed: "You will call me 'Lafier'!" And with that, she vanished.

"Wait, what about your story!?" But no answer came. All I was left with, or rather all my brain was left with, was the name "Lafier," and her vivid look and feel.

I still want to try writing her saga, though, thought I.

Yet her story as she was now would be too much for a novice writer like me to do justice. As such, I decided to depict her childhood. I don't necessarily think the inner life of a girl is less sophisticated than that of an adult woman's in every case, but there is an order to events one ought to follow.

...Of course, whether or not you choose to believe such drivel is entirely up to you! Honestly, though, I have faced moments of doubt wherein I question myself whether these people really only exist inside my head.

For instance, the scene in Volume 2 where Jint and Lafier are walking.

Lafier is in a bad mood. A bad mood that even the author doesn't fully understand, because the author's point of view is Jint's point of view. All I know at that moment is what I know through Jint, which is that she's seething.

What on Earth is she fuming over? And to think, she's not usually one to shy away from making it clear what exactly is ticking her off... I found myself thinking, much like another character of mine would be.

Then, when I stepped out of Jint and assumed Lafier's viewpoint, the source of her discontent became abundantly clear. *Ahh, of course, given her personality, it's only natural that would anger her.*

It was a strange experience.

At any rate, I'm sure you all know the word "slump." I fear Volume 2 might have been a bit on the plain side, comparatively. On the other hand, it's the volume that contains my favorite scene. If I told you which scene was my favorite, it would ruin the mystique, so on that I'll keep my lips zipped.

Next is the final volume of *Crest*, entitled *Return to a Strange World*. Not only is it the climax, but the increasing roster of characters will also serve to make it a boisterous ride.

Look forward to it!

April 10, 1996

The Origins of Baronh

After reading Volume 2, you will know that the Abh hail from a faction of far-future Japanese cultural restorationists (the reference to a "volcanic archipelago" was one hint, among others). That's part of what makes the concept of Baronh fascinating. It's a constructed language comprising the distant evolution of what amounts to an in-universe constructed language, albeit one rooted in real-world Japanese. Specifically, a new, purportedly culturally "pure," atavistic Japanese with all foreign loanwords plucked out (including Sino-Japanese vocabulary), replacing them with constructions using phonology and morphemes deemed to be of homegrown Japanese origins, including archaic language from the time of the oldest texts (as for an analog regarding how different ancient Japanese was, think Beowulf, not Shakespeare).

For example, this translation opted to call 昇降筒 "elevator-tubes" (*dobroriac* in Baronh), but that term actually avoids using the word modern Japanese people would use, which is… the English word "elevator." Instead, they replaced it with a neologism using the characters for "ascending" and "descending," which describes an elevator's functionality clearly and succinctly. You may have already drawn the comparison to the way the French government handles English loanwords. The tension between linguistic pride as cultural pride on one side, and the inexorable flux of language on the other side, has dogged humanity for some time and will no doubt continue to do so.

Speaking of linguistic evolution, let's detail how, exactly, that putative "pure Japanese" shifted over time into the Baronh of the books, in order.

- Change #1: Vowel elision and fusion. (Almost every syllable in Japanese is open, meaning that every consonant is followed by a vowel, but with this shift, Baronh obtains closed syllables, or syllables that have a consonant following the vowel. You can see this in action in the chart below.)

- Change #2: In order to avoid too many homonyms, an increase in distinct kinds of vowels, due to the remaining vowels being influenced by the vowels that had dropped out.
- Change #3: Changes to consonant sounds, such as the denasalization of nasal sounds.
- Change #4: Fusion of word stems and case-marking particles, as well as the accompanying change in the pronunciation of some consonants.

Through natural linguistic evolution, much like how Old English is incomprehensible to modern speakers, so too did Baronh change drastically from its ancestral tongue (of course, not only phonologically, but also grammatically).

In addition, MORIOKA has provided four different examples of the step-by-step transformation of words into their modern Baronh counterparts. Each example describes the progression of the word through four stages: the original Japanese word; vowel changes; consonant changes; and the addition of nominative case inflection.

- Yatagarasu (the three-legged crow of Japanese folklore); Yatgarse; Gatharse; *Gatharsec* (Remember, the "ec" at the end is silent.)
- Takkamagahara (In Shinto belief, the heavenly abode of the gods); Tacmgahar; Lacmhacar; *Lacmhacarch* (The Abh capital. Remember, "mh" is pronounced "f.")
- Karasuki (One of the 29 founding clans of the Abh); Karsc; Sarrc; *Sarrych* (Remember, "ch" is pronounced "sh.")
- Subaru (Another of the founding clans, each derived from one of the original 29 Abh Founders); Sbaur; Spaur; *Spaurh* (remember, "rh" is a rolling "r.")

CREST ³ STARS
OF THE
THE RETURN TO STRANGE SKIES

AUTHOR: HIROYUKI MORIOKA
ILLUSTRATOR: TOSHIHIRO ONO

Table of Contents

Foreword

O Stars around,
Heed the hopes of your short-lived kin.
What be our hopes?
We wish only to be by your side
At your final resting place.

...Selected verses of the imperial anthem of the Humankind Empire of Abh.

Summary of CREST OF THE STARS 2

Though Jint and Royal Princess Lafier managed to escape from the Febdash Barony, they weren't able to beat the enemy forces of the United Humankind to the Sfagnoff Marquessate.

When the duo returned to 3-space in their small conveyance ship, they discovered Sfagnoff already occupied by the enemy.

Lafier slipped away from their hostile eyes and crash-landed their ship onto the planet of Clasbure. Meanwhile, in order to protect the royal princess who found herself powerless on a surface world, Jint disguised himself and Lafier as planet natives, with the intention of doing their best to evade the troops' notice until Empire ships returned.

However, a dodgy-looking group of activists who call themselves the "Anti-Imperial Front" have now brushed against Jint and Lafier after the two successfully infiltrated the city of Lune Beega, near where they ended up landing.

Characters

Jint
...... Son of the President of the planet Martin.

Lafier
...... Trainee Starpilot in the Abh Empire's Star Forces, as well as the Empress's granddaughter.

Entryua
...... Police Inspector of the Lune Beega Criminal Investigation Department.

Keitt
...... Military Police Captain of the Peacekeepers.

Malka
...... Member of the Clasbure Anti-Imperial Front.

Min
...... Another member of the Clasbure Anti-Imperial Front.

Bill
...... Another member of the Clasbure Anti-Imperial Front.

Daswani
...... Another member of the Clasbure Anti-Imperial Front.

Undertaker
...... Another member of the Clasbure Anti-Imperial front.

Commodore Tlife (*Tlaïmh*)
...... Commander-in-Chief of the Abh Imperial Dispatch Fleet.

Associate Commodore Sporr (*Sporh*)
...... Commander-in-Chief of the Abh Imperial Reconnaissance
Sub-fleet.

Chapter 1: *Nataimecoth* (Investigation)

Entryua, Police Inspector of the Lune Beega's Criminal Investigation Department, was in just as sour a mood as usual.

Entryua consoled himself: *At least this is a great chance to contemplate what rock bottom's like.* After all, it was never *truly* "rock bottom." There was always further to dig!

And now, he found himself treading even deeper into the sinkhole.

"Three more to check, huh? My gut's telling me they aren't holed up in any damn hotel," grumbled Inspector Entryua.

"Then what do we do?" askd Keitt, the Military Police Captain of the Peacekeepers.

Entryua shrugged. "We do what you said — comb every last building. Not that I'm chomping at the bit to do that."

"It's not a question of whether you're inclined to do it," Keitt carped.

"Whatever you say," he said noncommittally.

If you asked him, though, this was pretty far from his actual job description.

Sure, the Abh committed a crime, and grand theft **hovercar** was no light charge. It also wasn't a grave enough charge to warrant a criminal investigation squad of this size.

In its caprices, fate had seen fit to station the majority of the Lune Beega Criminal Investigation Department in *Guzonh*. Not only that, but also half of the normal officers and all of the forensics officers. The Lune Beega police force was all in on the hunt for a petty car thief.

Entryua had divided his men and women into fifteen different teams. Four of those teams lay in wait at the airport, two were reserve corps, and the remaining eight had been commanded to inspect every single room in all of the various inns and hotels, bidden not to trust the words of the managers or proprietors. Entryua told them not to worry about search warrants, since in the end, it'd all be on the occupying army. Yes, the occupying army, not the "liberation army" or what have you. They'd never have him thinking of it as anything else, "correct" him as they might.

He wanted to inspect the roads, too, but he lacked the boots on the ground. Besides, the occupiers were inspecting the roads, though they'd let them slip past once before. In any case, if they made the same blunder a second time, that would be no fault of his.

On the screen at the back seat of the command vehicle, a catalog of over forty different fee-based lodgings was displayed. Every item was listed in red, save for the last three. The red text, naturally, meant that particular building had been inspected.

Beside that catalog, another screen listed all the suspicious persons they'd encountered. Anybody who couldn't prove their name matched the name given for the guest list ended up on this screen, and so far around twenty people had met just such a fate.

Citizens of Clasbure could prove their identity and status by simply presenting their wallets, so usually these "suspicious persons" were using aliases, and mostly for dumb reasons. Family affairs. *Affairs* affairs. Things that, while misguided, didn't involve the police.

There was one arrest, a man in possession of a wallet reported stolen. He had, in fact, been in possession of twenty wallets in other people's names. That was the only fruit of their investigation thus far.

No one "Abh-like" had yet been spotted.

"Inspector." The police sergeant with him in the car had a phone transceiver to their ear. "It's Gondolin's team. They've combed their target area, and now they want to know what they ought to do next."

Entryua mulled it over. He'd already allotted teams to check out the three places left on the list. *Should I have them join them as reinforcements? Nah, those rooms are small, they'd just get in the way.*

"Tell them to come here. We'll have them join the reserve corps, to wait there until we settle on the next course of action."

"Roger." The police sergeant relayed Entryua's orders.

"Are there no citizens who're likely to give shelter to an Abh?" asked Keitt, his impatience all but evident.

"Search your democracy reeducation schools. That's where all the people who'd harbor Abhs are."

"That again?" Keitt hung his head.

"We're giving this everything we've got. You've got to see that much for yourself."

"I do."

"Inspector," the sergeant cut in.

"What?"

"It's Sergeant Ramashdy. They're being held up by occupier inspection."

"Not again." Entryua was fed up. Their investigation had been obstructed by the occupying army ten whole times now. It seemed as though, while they'd committed the police crest to memory, they still found Lune Beega police crests to be a strange sight here in *Guzonh*.

"You're up," said Entryua, poking the military police captain's flank.

"Of course." Keitt asked the sergeant to transfer the line over to his army's Commanding Officer. An exchange in a language that was foreign to Entryua ensued, and his mind wandered to the number of more important cases that were nagging at him.

"Finished."

"Huh?" Entryua snapped back to reality.

"Sergeant Ramashdy is in the clear."

"Yeah, until the next checkpoint."

"That's, uh… yes," said Keitt bashfully.

"You sure you told them everything they needed to hear about us?" he grilled him.

"I'm sure. I explained our predicament in detail to the area's military police regiment."

"Then why is it they keep getting called to a halt?"

Keitt averted his gaze. "It seems it hasn't permeated down to the lower branches of the organization."

"Pains me to say it, but your 'organization' is pretty inefficient. Even us police've got this little thing called 'lateral communication.'"

"You're absolutely right," said Keitt, who was shrinking in his seat.

Entryua almost wanted to whistle in appreciation. He'd thought Keitt a total jerk earlier, but now it seemed he had some capacity to be genuine after all.

Again a transceiver rang, but this time, it was Keitt's. Keitt took the display from the terminal at his waist, and skimmed its screen. His complexion shifted more and more as he read on.

This piqued Entryua's interest. "What?"

Keitt slumped against his seat back, dejected. "The military police regiment is on the move. They're looking to arrest the Abh, too, now."

"That sounds great to me. So… are we off the hook?" Entryua asked hopefully.

"No. While I'll hand over the documentation of our investigation, we'll be continuing the hunt in another way. In other words… I have new orders. If we discover the Abh's hiding spot, we are to report to Headquarters, then wait and observe to prevent the Abh from running — nothing more."

"What's that supposed to mean? We aren't allowed to arrest them?"

"That's right. The arrest will be carried out by my army's military police regiment."

"You've GOT to be joking! They want us to just *watch* after WE put in all the time chasing after the Abh, and they swoop in at the last second?"

That was it. This was an affront to the Lune Beega police force, a profession that warranted respect. Plus, he had to balk at how the pretense their occupiers were "cooperating" with the police had vanished in a puff of smoke. They were, for all intents and purposes, just the drudges of their conquerors. "Your superior's saying capturing the Abh's beyond us, is that it?"

"That's not it," said Keitt, but he didn't look Entryua's way. "At first, Headquarters believed the Abh to have escaped from the manor or military stronghold. That's why they weren't all that interested. They captured dozens of Abhs at the manor, so they weren't too concerned by a single one evading them. But now the possibility the runaway Abh was crewing the small vessel that entered from planar space is more apparent."

"And? So what?" Entryua stared at the side of Keitt's face.

"There might even be a good chance that that pilot was on the enemy ship that my army destroyed in planar space. In which case, the Abh might be privy to important information."

"Important information?"

Keitt waved a hand. "I don't know what it might entail, either. And even if I did, I couldn't say."

"Figures." Entryua was not disappointed to hear that. If it wasn't **Star Forces** military secrets, then it probably had to do with interstellar politics. In either case, Entryua couldn't care less.

"As such, the value of the Abh we're after has risen significantly. And the Human Resources Department can't afford to ignore the achievements of whoever captures this Abh."

"Ah, I get it now. You lot can't let the likes of us 'local police' win the day." Yet greater anger flared in Entryua's chest. They did the work, others got the credit? No thank you.

"It's not you they don't want 'winning the day,' probably. It's me," he grumbled.

"Why?" he replied, surprised. "You were chosen by the higher-ups, weren't you? I mean, a captain, at your age…"

"You think I'm young?" A self-deprecating smile broke on his handsome face. "How old do you think I am, Inspector?"

"Lessee…" He shot older than he would otherwise. "27 or 28, in standard years."

Keitt's smile only widened. "In standard years, I'll be 49 this year."

"No way. That makes you older than I am! But then, why…" Entryua clammed up. "Oh. Genetic modification."

"Correct. It isn't solely an Abh technology."

"But according to all your broadcasts, human genetic modification is an indisputable sin."

"Yes. The United Humankind sees genetic modification in people as a grave crime."

"Which would make you a misbegotten child in their eyes…"

Keitt sighed. "Were it that simple…"

"So you're not?"

"Have you ever heard of the Republic of Silesia?"

"'Fraid not," the Inspector shrugged.

"I see…" Keitt folded his arms and looked out the window.

Entryua thought he'd tell him about this "Silesia," but Keitt didn't say a word. Finally, Entryua lost his patience. "Well? What about it?"

Keitt mumbled his answer. "Silesia is the name of a nation that, around 120 years prior, incited the Silesia War, and crumbled. Thankfully, today it forms part of the United Humankind. Before then, the so-called 'republic' was in fact a military dictatorship. Around 1,000 families of hereditary soldiers held all of society in their grip. Those military families practiced genetic modification on their descendants. Their technology wasn't as advanced as the Abh's; it didn't allow for, say, changing hair color or crafting specific organs. All it did was stop aging."

"And you're one of them…" Entryua groaned.

"To be precise, it was my grandfather's generation that received the anti-aging modification."

"Hold on…" Entryua cocked his head. "What does any of that have to do with them not wanting to let you win the day? That's a story from three generations ago."

"It doesn't matter how far back it happened. I'm in my family register as a 'Silesia Unaging.'"

"But why?"

"Because it comes up when marrying. There are heavy restrictions on us when it comes to marriage. It's a shame, but it has to be this way. Any child conceived between somebody with the Unaging genome and somebody without always grows cancerous in the womb."

"All the more reason to do genetic modification, in that case," Entryua pointed out. "Do that, and your kids could live a normal life."

"But genetic modification is strictly forbidden, no matter what."

"Even for birth defects?"

"Even for birth defects. Even just conducting genetic testing at the fertilized egg stage is illegal. When the defect is discovered, any kind of genetic modification whatsoever is impossible, let alone gene therapy. Of course, most organic diseases can be treated through mechanical engineering."

"I guess." But the Inspector was shocked. The fact that they hated genetic tampering to this absurd extent was a sickness in itself.

"That's why I'm still single. The Silesia Unaging population will likely die out when my generation does."

"That's just awful," muttered Entryua. "But wait, I still don't get it. Why would they begrudge you a deed to your name over that?"

"Please, forget I ever said that." Keitt waved a hand. "It was a slip of the tongue."

"If that's a slip of the tongue, then you let your tongue slip enough to fill a damn book." Entryua realized Keitt had been changing the subject on purpose, and he frowned.

"It doesn't concern you."

"Sure it does. You lot are our overlords. So why shouldn't I want to know about all the gritty details? What happened to our 'right to know'?"

"We aren't your 'overlords.' We will be building up civilian society alongside you. We are your new friends."

"All the more reason to tell me, then. I want to know more about my new comrade."

Entryua had worn him down. "Okay, you've got me there. To make a long story short, they don't trust me. They say the Silesia Unaging are born unable to understand the true essence of democracy…"

Now he understood that Military Police Captain Keitt was an unfortunate soul within the organization. He also understood why.

It was prejudice, pure and simple.

Suddenly, it all made sense. The fact that Keitt had no subordinates. The fact that Keitt's motion wasn't paid much attention to by the brass.

He felt sorry for Aizan; after all that effort buttering up Keitt, he wouldn't be thrilled to learn that Keitt was in fact walking a lonely path far removed from the highway to success.

There was, however, still one more thing that needed clarification for Entryua.

"Isn't that a bit weird, though?"

"What do you mean?"

"How are you still so zealous, even after all of that prejudice against you? I don't see myself being so gung-ho about a job where I'm not valued. Commissioner Aizan may not appreciate me, but the people do. That's how I can keep at this. So how do you manage?"

"I'm quite happy, actually," he said. And Entryua could tell it was from the heart. "Where I was born and raised, police officers appreciated by the people were a rarity."

"You haven't answered my question."

"I am a believer in democracy. Isn't that enough?"

"Is it? I mean, you still can't get them to trust you."

"I merely act in accordance with my conscience."

"Gotcha, gotcha," he answered perfunctorily. Entryua knew he'd never see totally eye to eye with him, but he just couldn't sit on the big question: "And you're okay with that?"

"Of course," answered Keitt resolutely. But there was something *unnatural* there, in that forcefulness.

"I'm sorry to interrupt, Inspector." The sergeant handed him his earpiece. "It's Sergeant Kyua."

"Got it." Entryua ran his eyes over the screen. Kyua's team was in charge of the inn called the *Limzairh*.

"Stream it."

"Inspector, we've discovered two suspicious persons," reported Kyua's voice.

"Don't give it all to me over the phone. Input the details into the **compucrystals**."

"They've already left, sir."

"Did they get away?" There were quite a few things Entryua couldn't stand, and foolish subordinates was one of them.

"No, sir." Kyua seemed flustered. "They'd already left by the time we arrived."

"How do you know they were the perps?"

"It was a boy and a girl, both using aliases. We searched the family registers, and no such names were listed."

"I see." Entryua was still unimpressed. It was true that they were looking for a boy and a girl. However, by some strange cosmic coincidence, since time immemorial, when it came to travelers not wanting to be found out by their families or other parties, it tended to be a boy and a girl.

"The names they'd given were 'Sye Jint' and 'Sye Lina.'"

"Forget their names, what were they like? What did they look like?"

"We had a number of employees testify that they were very young. And that they seemed, *off*, sir."

"'Off'? How so?"

"They almost never left their room. Especially the girl, who literally never left."

"That's not so strange. When a man and a woman share a room, there's all sorts they get up to. Or rather, just the one thing."

"That's not all, sir. According to the employee that led them to their room, the girl had a hat on. A hat for men."

"Haha!" Entryua looked at Keitt.

Keitt was listening raptly. A girl wearing a hat — just like those hooligans had said.

"What about her face?"

"Her hair and eyes were black. Her skin was a light olive color. Slender face. It seemed she was a real looker, too."

"'A real looker,' you say."

"They also didn't pay the *sheef*."

"The *sheef*? I see." Entryua nodded.

It was odd, all right. If they wanted to evade notice, they should have paid that gratuity, even if just to zip lips. That they hadn't paid any whatsoever meant one of two things: either they weren't versed in the customs of the planet, or they were just that incredibly cheap.

"Give me the footage. The footage of them."

Kyua hesitated to tell him. "About that... we're told there's no footage left of them. It's been disposed of."

"'Disposed of'? What exactly did the manager tell you?"

"That once a customer leaves, if there was no outstanding problem, they get rid of the footage, sir."

"Do they even know hotel law? They're supposed to hold onto it for a year…" But Entryua stopped himself. There was no point in complaining to Kyua about it. "What did the receptionist tell you? If they were in the room the entire time, then the person who saw them the most must have been the person at the desk."

"The manager was at the desk, but his testimony completely contradicts everyone else's. He claims they were middle-aged, for one. That they seemed so ordinary as to leave no impression."

"That manager person is shady," Keitt butted in. "I fear he may be covering for them."

"I can't deny the possibility. Kyua, give me that manager's name and citizen number."

"Yes, sir." The pertinent information flowed from Kyua's telephonic transceiver to the command car's **compucrystals**. Entryua then entered the identification number and brought up the police info regarding him and the *Limzairh* on the screen.

He fixed his eyes on the screen. "Well, this is unexpected. He's a member of the Secessionist Party, and provides moral support to radical extremists."

"The Secessionist Party?" asked Keitt. "What is that?"

"It's exactly what it sounds like. A party that advocates for the exile of the appointed **lord** and independence from the **Empire**."

"Is it a secret society?"

"No. They have a headquarters, with signage and everything. They've even got seats in the state legislature."

Keitt was dumbfounded. "A party like that's allowed to exist?"

"Yep. You didn't know? I thought you lot would've gotten the downlow ages ago."

"No, I honestly didn't know. So that would mean anti-imperial parties are legal."

"Yeah, being against **Empire** rule isn't a crime. It just blocks you from being a **landworld citizen representative**. The **lord** would veto you."

"A ridiculous charade," Keitt smiled derisively. "You're just working within the **Empire**'s framework. Personally, I see it as them treating democratic debate as an amusing plaything."

"Oh, there are plenty here to agree with you, trust me. That's the very reason the Secessionists can't win elections. And there were even folks within the party that say independence can't be achieved by peaceful means. They exited the party and became extremists. There are a handful of groups, now. Seems our manager man's sympathies lie with the 'Clasbure Anti-Imperial Front'..."

Entryua drew information on the Clasbure Anti-Imperial Front from the public safety records. "Damn, nothing much on them here. They attempted to occupy the **orbital tower**, once, twenty years ago. Most of the perps were arrested, and now it looks like the front is dormant."

"What do those 'extremists' do?"

"Nothing noteworthy." *Not compared to what you lot have done,* Entryua wished dearly to add. "They set fire to the plantation of the **Marquis's Manor**, bomb the **Star Forces Recruiting Office**, that sort of thing. 'Course, those are crimes, so we're always on those cases. That's why we're keeping an eye on the members of extremist secessionist groups and their allies. They just don't get our undivided attention."

But Keitt was shaking his head. It wasn't adding up for him. "You're saying the **Empire** knows such groups exist, but..."

"I'm not sure the **Empire** does know."

"Huh? Didn't they do humanity the service of bombing that **Star Forces** office?"

"Yeah, ages ago. That was from before I entered the force. Plus, Clasbure told the **Star Forces** who the perp that did it was. I reckon they forgot more or less immediately afterward, though. As far as I know, the **Empire** hasn't breathed a peep to us about any of the Secessionist Party or extremist business."

"I don't believe it... You must be being deceived."

"That right? Guess it's not out of the question. Anything could be a big lie. I can tell you for a fact that the Secessionist Party exists, though."

"But..."

Keitt was about to speak, but Kyua had grown impatient. "Inspector, what do we do?"

"Sorry, slipped my mind." Etryua scratched his head. "Detain that manager."

"To take him to the precinct?"

"No, no need. We can't take him on the grounds of a hotel law violation. Just have your team cling to him. Tell him not to go anywhere, but all polite-like. Get him to cooperate. I'll be there soon. Wait, Mr. Manager hasn't rung anybody up in the meantime, has he?"

"No, sir, he hasn't. We're observing him closely."

"Good. Don't let him contact anybody. If the inn suffers losses because of it, tell him the occupiers'll pay for them."

"What, really?" Kyua sniggered.

"Hey, if that promise falls through, it'll be them he resents, not us."

"Roger that."

"End transmission."

"Ending transmission."

Entryua patted the shoulder of the sergeant beside him in the car. "'The *Limzairh*,' was it? Be a pal and take us there. And tell the cops that are on their way here to go there instead."

"Yes, sir." The command car took to the road.

"Listen, about those 'orders' of yours..." Entryua was gazing at the scenery flying past through the window. "YOU were the one ordered to 'not arrest.' That has nothing to do with us. Just so we're clear. Us police, we're just in this to catch a car thief."

Keitt felt relieved. "Yes, of course. I never received any orders to stop you or your people."

"Let's take Mr. Manager into custody, for starters."

"Is it possible that the manager is harboring an Abh?"

"Beats me."

"If he's a secessionist, then there's no way he'd want to, right?"

"I couldn't tell you."

"Don't tell me the 'Secessionist Party' might be a ruse?"

"A ruse? To what end?" Entryua cocked his head.

"It might be an underground organization whose true purpose is helping the **Empire**'s people flee in a situation like this." Keitt was immediately stirred by his own theory. "It wouldn't be strange to think they could have anticipated liberation would come, and set up such an organization beforehand!"

"It *would* be strange to think. I think your theory needs work," replied Entryua calmly.

"Aren't you the one who said anything is possible?"

"Suppose so," Entryua shrugged.

"If you think it isn't a ruse, then why do you think the secessionist would be sheltering an Abh?"

"Us **landworld citizens**, we're leery of the Abh. The leeriest of us become card-carrying secessionists, and the hopelessly leeriest of them run with extremists. If I recall, the extremists I investigated way back complained that the **Empire**, quote, 'wouldn't clamp down.'"

"No! That can't be!"

"It's daffy, that much is true. But look at it this way: The **Empire**, it's not interested in our little world. They don't really *react* much, at least, not enough for the secession movement to gain much traction."

In fact, I wager these new conquerors will give the extremists much more meat to chew on, Entryua mused. These jokers seemed like a much worthier adversary in the extremists' eyes than the apathetic Empire could ever be.

"But if the **Empire** isn't interested in surface societies, why do they clearly want to conquer every planet?"

"Because they don't want us out in space, of course. Isn't that obvious?"

"I have my doubts that that's the only reason."

"What other reasons could there be?" Entryua responded lightly.

"I just don't think it's possible they have no other motives, but now's not the time to be getting into this." Keitt took off the cell transceiver terminal from his waist. It was fitted with accessories that went on Empire-made **memchips**.

"The **memchip** with the investigation data, if you please," he asked of the sergeant.

"Yes." Reluctantly, the sergeant handed Keitt the **memchip**.

"Oh, let's add in how the Secessionist Party might be a ruse," he smiled, as though he'd hit upon a good idea.

"That possibility is near zero, though," Entryua pointed out.

"All the better, then."

"Why's that?" Entryua couldn't pick up what Keitt was sending out.

"The military police regiment might have many personnel, but they're not well-versed in this land's circumstances. They're probably looking for a target to hit that stands out. So if we give them that intel, they'll busy themselves with searching Secessionist Party premises for a while. And in that time, we'll catch the Abh."

Seeing Keitt's proud expression, Entryua's mood plunged ever downward. *I think I may've just accidentally increased the "student" population of those democracy reeducation camps...*

Chapter 2: *Dihérhoth* (On the Run)

"Please, enter. The place is shabby, but make yourself at home," said Malka.

"Oh, I'm so sorry it's 'shabby,'" scowled Undertaker. "I like it this way, I'll have you know."

"This house is yours, Undertaker?" asked Jint.

"Sure is." Undertaker nodded.

It was in a city-tree a mere ten blocks from the *Limzairh*. Specifically, Undertaker's house was on its third floor.

Jint followed Malka and Undertaker inside. Lafier soon entered as well, as did Min, Bill, and Daswani after her.

"So lax," sneered Bill. "If we wanted to pull something, you wouldn't have stood a chance, just now. Your back is defenseless."

"Ah, right." Jint hadn't thought to guard his back, so he nodded his thanks. Of course, he should have been the last to enter.

"You think that's good enough to be her guard?" Bill continued

Jint just shrugged. He wasn't her guard. If anything, she was his. But Jint didn't feel like explaining that to him.

Speaking of Lafier, she really was treating Undertaker's home like it was her own bedroom. Unbidden, she'd taken the most comfortable-looking seat, the leather chair, for herself.

"Hey, that's MY chair. The owner's throne." In his resentment, Undertaker jabbed Lafier with a finger.

Lafier deigned to look at him, but didn't respond.

"You're our hostage, Abh. Just think, normally you'd be tied up rolling on the floor, and all your pleas would fall on deaf ears..."

Lafier listened to the man go on as though he was spinning a curious yarn. Her expression was not that of an avid student, but rather of a researcher observing a peculiar organism.

"Okay, I know what you want to tell me. You want to say you've come here of your own volition, and that you've got a gun. Yet come what may, I'm gonna be treating you two as hostages. And the only reason you fired that gun earlier is 'cause I asked you to show me your marksman skills with that miniature cannon of yours, got it? 'Cause your skills are nothing to sneeze at. We could never beat you, even if we formed a firing band. Even so, I…" Undertaker found his voice turning weaker and smaller the more he mouthed off.

"…If you like that chair, I'd be pleased as punch."

Jint watched Undertaker slump meekly onto the couch, and worried he might break into tears. But Undertaker refrained from crying, which was a relief. Jint took the time to examine the room closely.

Malka had called it "shabby," but it wasn't really. There wasn't much furniture, so it looked quite spacious. No table, just a few chairs. There was a picture on the wall, an abstract piece that evoked fire issuing from above.

"Did you paint that, Undertaker?" Jint asked.

"Yep, that's all me. Did a good job of it, didn't I?" For a second, Undertaker smiled, but then he remembered to suppress it and complain. "For heaven's sake, you two do know you're HOSTAGES, right!? *HOSTAGES!* We're not celebrating your damn birthdays here! Don't act like we invited you over for a spot of tea!"

"Jint, deary, please sit. Ruffling Undertaker's feathers is a great pastime, but we've gotten bored of it," said Malka.

"I didn't mean to ruffle any feathers," said Jint. "I just thought it was a nice picture, that's all…"

"Yeah, well, hostages are usually a tad too worried fretting over their precious lives to appreciate fine art," said Undertaker.

"There's room for debate there. I don't know if I'd call that 'fine art,'" Min remarked.

While Undertaker talked back to Min, Jint took the seat next to Lafier's.

"So, what now?" Jint caught Malka's eyes.

"Come morning, I'll be having you stowing away in the load-carrying tray of a freighting vehicle and heading to a certain place outside the city."

"I'm a delivery car driver," said Bill. "Every day, I carry meat from the synthetic meat factory in a town called Dee Segohn. That's why I know how the checkpoints are set up. The occupiers know my face now. They won't think to peek into the flatbed."

"If you're delivering meat, then it's gotta be a freezer van, right?"

"Yep. But don't worry: It'll be empty when we leave from here, so the refrigeration won't be turned on."

"Phew. I don't particularly enjoy getting packed in ice."

Jint pondered. Escaping the city by slipping into some cargo was a good plan. If Lafier sat in plain view, she'd attract notice for sure. She could dye her hair, but if they took her hat off, they'd see her *froch*.

The only problem was how much they could trust these people. Certainly, if they hid with the cargo, they'd be hard to spot. On the other hand, they'd also have no idea where they were being taken. For all he knew, they'd exit the cargo hold only to find a flank of soldiers with guns pointed squarely at them.

"I'm sorry, but we're gonna have to pass. We can't put that much trust in you."

"You can't trust us? Why? You think we'll sell you out to the army?" asked Malka.

"I mean, we are your 'hostages,' aren't we? You didn't think we'd have faith in our 'captors,' did you?"

"And that's just how it should be!" Undertaker nodded, as though to say Jint had hit the nail on the head.

Malka facepalmed. "We'd never ally ourselves with an occupying force."

"Why not? It's been bugging me, actually: Why DON'T you cooperate with them?"

"Because what we're after is independence from the **Empire**. *'Independence'* being the operative word."

"That only strengthens my case..."

"I won't lie, I was full of hope when they took the planet. Yet now it's clear as day they have no intention of leaving us be. So why do you think we'd buddy up with our conquerors?"

"Yeah, they're even nastier than the Abhs," said Bill. "At least the Abhs just let us be."

"That's not the worst of it!" said Min, his emotions on his sleeve. "The bastards shaved off my hair! Just because I'd had it dyed blue, the nerve of them. It wasn't out of some weird admiration of the Abh! It just balanced out my face's color scheme with my facial hair!" he added, stroking his red and yellow moustache.

"My business is as good as finished, too!" said Undertaker, wringing his hands.

"Your business?" Jint meant to ask Undertaker what grudge he held against the enemy, but Malka started speaking before he could.

"In any case," she concluded, "now you see how little love is lost between us and that blasted army. Besides, the Abh may have been taken by surprise, but I don't see them falling behind in the theater of space. Even if we did ally with them, nothing good would come of it."

"So you have faith in the **Empire**."

"In the **Empire**'s force of arms, yes," she corrected him.

Jint folded his arms. "I can't tell how serious you are about your own objectives anymore. Do you really think you can successfully secede from the **Empire**, given how powerful it is?"

"We have to hold out hope," said Min. "The **Empire** may not be terribly interested in **landworlds** at the moment, but we can't be sure that state of affairs will last forever. We have to assume it won't. If the Empire made some unreasonable demand of a landworld, what means do we have to resist them? They could even rain antimatter bombs on us if they were so inclined."

That doesn't add up, thought Jint. If they wanted to bombard the surface of Clasbure with antimatter bombs, the fastest way to justify it would be to force through independence. It'd work wonders to attract the **Empire**'s notice.

Seeing Jint's expression, Min said, "We've got a persecution complex, is what you want to say."

"No, that's not it."

"Then what?"

"All I want to say is you guys are like kids who want to run away from home just because you fear abuse from a parent that's never laid a finger on you, not even knowing that if you do run away, the harshest punishment you could receive is when you'll inevitably be taken back home to those parents."

Min narrowed his eyes. "You… I've never been so insulted in my life."

"I didn't mean anything by it, honest. If you're offended, I apologize."

"I'll accept your apology. But my opinion isn't changing."

"Right. I don't want to nitpick your ideology," he said, trying his best to console him.

"Glad to hear it. Be careful how you speak and act from here on out."

"I will."

"That aside," said Malka, "what will you do? If you don't want to go with our suggestion, I'll have you stay here for the time being. It'd be dangerous to walk about town. There are soldiers examining the area."

"Yeah, that much we know."

Undertaker leapt up. "Like hell they can stay here! This is my house! You want me to play host?"

"You're going to have to. You have rooms you're not using. They'd be no impediment to you."

"They're not exactly the loveliest of house guests — *especially* this little brat," he said, jabbing Lafier again. "She seems to have mistaken me for some kind of servant of hers."

"There's no helping it." Malka switched to Clasburian. "You're the only one of us who lives alone. How would I explain bringing them over to my house to my husband or daughter?"

"Just tell them they're your long-lost younger siblings," Undertaker answered back in Clasburian.

"I'm not going to lie to my husband."

"You're hiding the fact you're an extremist from him!"

"Which isn't technically lying. I haven't told him I'm *not* an extremist."

Hearing this exchange made Jint realize just how tiny this organization was. The grandiose sounding "Clasbure Anti-Imperial Front" seemed to consist entirely of these five.

"Undertaker is understandably worried," said Min in solemn tones. "If the enemy soldiers ever discover he's hiding an Abh in his house, he doesn't know what they'll do to him."

"I'm not worried about that!" said Undertaker, but it was obviously just bravado.

It was then it dawned on Jint that he'd neglected to ask something crucial. "Will you be with us on the freezer van's flatbed?"

"We can't NOT be there with you," said Bill. "The van seats two. If all five of us try to cram ourselves onto those seats, they'd suspect us for sure."

"You should've led with that little tidbit," Jint smiled. "In that case, we can trust you. We'll be gripping our guns at the ready the entire time we're together in there, but don't think anything of it."

"Then it won't be clear which of us are the hostages!" lamented Undertaker.

"When do we depart?" asked Lafier, breaking her silence at last.

Malka checked the clock. "Three hours and seventeen minutes from now."

"I haven't had enough sleep." Lafier addressed Undertaker. "This is your house, correct? I trust your guest bedroom is clean? I'd like to rest, so lead me to it."

"I'll replace the sheets with fresh ones, so could I kindly ask you to wait a few moments?" said Undertaker, his face a painting of despair.

Chapter 3: *Raïchacarh Üécr Sauder Sfagnaumr* (Clash at the Sfagnoff Portal-Sea)

In the high-density area that sprawled between the **fleet** and the **Sfagnoff Portal**, innumerable pricks of shining light were gathered.

"What's that?" **Commodore** Tlife pointed to the flock of lights on the **map of planar space** using his **command baton**.

"The chances are 0.9997 in 1 that it's an enemy fleet," answered **Kilo-Commander** Cahyoor calmly.

"Thanks, genius, I know that!" Tlife barked. "But haven't we put on a show of our force of arms for them?"

"Yes, sir, we have. Our march was more than sufficient for that," nodded the **Chief of Staff**.

"Then the enemy must be aware of our military might. They must be."

"If they didn't get the hint, then we should send them a **conveyance ship** and tell them."

"The enemy has no hope of winning. They *can't* have any."

"Any commander in their right mind would come to that conclusion, sir."

"Then why!?" Rather theatrically, he paused for effect. "WHY are they loitering over there!?" At that moment, something else began to give him doubt. He turned to the Chief of Staff:

"By the way, you said there was a 0.997 in 1 chance it's the enemy, right?"

"I did, sir."

"What's the 0.003 in 1 chance?"

"That that information is a deception. Or that the sensors all failed at once. Alternatively, that it's an unknown natural phenomenon, or an assembly of heretofore unidentified intelligent lifeforms. It could also be…"

"Do you honestly think any of those are real possibilities?" said Tlife, taken aback.

"Each of those possibilities is exceptionally unlikely on their own, but taken together…"

"Okay, fine, I get it. Forget I asked." The **Commander-in-Chief** placed his chin on one of his hands and paced the **Commander's Bridge**.

"*Lonh* (Your Honor), I thought you yearned for combat," said Cahyoor upon seeing Tlife's crabby mood.

"Oh, I do," Tlife admitted. "I just don't enjoy fighting with nagging doubts. What do you think they're doing here, Cahyoor?"

"I see three possible reasons," said Cahyoor, ready to rattle them off. "Possibility 1, the enemy thinks they can, in fact, win."

"But how? In the face of this overwhelming gap, how could they possibly?"

"To split Possibility 1 in two, first of all, perhaps the capabilities of the enemy's ships far exceed our initial expectations."

"Are you saying we've failed to fully grasp the hypothetical extent of the enemy's technological knowhow?" Tlife was less than pleased to learn there was a chance the **Empire** had been beaten to the technological punch by another interstellar power.

"What else would you expect from the officers fit solely to feed the cat?" Cahyoor retorted expressionlessly.

"You're right!" said Tlife. "The **Information Bureau** are all just a bunch of cat handlers! How daft of me to forget that fact."

Communications Staff Officer *Nasotryac* looked resigned and said nothing.

"But I, personally, appraise the **Information Bureau** slightly higher than that. The chances that that is what happened are almost nil. As such, if in fact the enemy believes they'll win, they may be looking down on the **Star Forces**. That, or the cause might just lie in their commander's mental state."

"Battling a madman wouldn't be very elegant, would it?"

"As for Possibility 2," Cahyoor continued, ignoring his **Commander-in-Chief**, "this could well be a trap."

"What kind of trap?"

"For example, they might be having a large fleet lying in wait in the 3-space by some nearby portal, have their overly small forces engage in combat, hand us a few victories in combat, and pretend to have been driven back into fleeing."

"Where's the trap there, exactly?" asked Tlife, flabbergasted.

"The trap being, in our blind zeal chasing down the fleeing ships, they ambush us as soon as we recklessly enter the portal."

"What did you say?" Tlife felt pity. No matter the circumstances, a **starpilot** so incompetent as to lack due vigilance when entering a portal would never be adorned with a *ptorahédésomh* (commander's insignia). "Do they think me that senseless?"

"They have no way to know that you, specifically, are this **fleet**'s **Commander-in-Chief**, *Lonh*. It isn't personal. Rather it would stem from their general attitude toward the **Imperial Star Forces**. There's no telling whether or not they believe in our deep-seated reputation."

"The essence of the Abh is in their overweening pride and recklessness," said Tlife. Those words were famous even among the Abh themselves; so famous, in fact, that one needed only to hear talk of the "reputation of the Abh" to recall them. "We may be a smidgen haughty, I'll give them that, but reckless we are not."

"Too true, sir. Our war history bears that out. If they've done their homework on our past battles, they'd surely think twice before implementing such an uncertain strategy."

"If, that is, your hypothetical trap is the one they've laid," said Tlife. "The enemy commander should be taken alive. We need to reeducate him about warfare from the ground up."

"A splendid idea, sir," said Cahyoor, though as coolly as ever. "In any event, seeing as we would never fall for such a crude trap, there's no particular need to come up with counter-strategies."

"Agreed," said Tlife.

"Possibility 3, the biggest of the three, is…"

"That's a bad habit of yours," said Tlife. He did think highly of Cahyoor, but he didn't like how pretentious he could be. "Why didn't you lead with the biggest possibility?"

"I apologize, sir," said Cahyoor perfunctorily before continuing. "They are the United Humankind, or at least, their main force is. And the United Humankind's military command is known to often lack a certain flexibility in their orders. Perhaps the enemy commander has been ordered to use what forces they have to defend the **Sfagnoff Marquessate** to the last. If their commander took such a directive to heart, then gathering their forces in this sector is the most logical course of action."

Tlife folded his arms. "And you're saying that's the highest probability."

"Yes."

As usual, Tlife began pacing again. The more he mulled it over, the more convinced he became that there was nothing behind the enemy's actions — that they were merely attempting to resist with what forces they had. Just like Tlife himself had been sent with what forces he could muster. Tlife had the luxury of retreating if he wanted, but the enemy didn't. That was the sole point of difference between them.

The question of why the enemy had sent such a small force to invade **Empire** territory remained, of course. It was probably a diversion. But that was something for **Military Command Headquarters** to consider, not him. He was dissatisfied that he wasn't at the main battlefield, but happy that he had a fleet he could command at his discretion.

"Yes... yes, that's it!" Tlife raised a fist overhead. "I can feel all of my doubts disintegrating into the atmosphere like so much space dust, and without a trace left! My heart has vacated the riverbank of uncertainty, and finally found its way to the assurance of victory! I know when I need to be grateful, and now is one of those times. **Kilo-Commander** Cahyoor, I thank you!"

"I am honored," said Cahyoor, taking the **Commander-in-Chief**'s vote of gratitude exceedingly dispassionately.

Then, Tlife stopped in his tracks, and looked at the **map of planar space**. "I must say, though, I feel sorry for them."

"This is not the time to spare the enemy your sympathies, sir," said the **Chief of Staff**.

"You're right. We warned them. We won't hold back!" Tlife decreed, gripping his **command baton**. "We'll take them in a pincer attack."

"I'm against that idea," said Cahyoor bluntly.

"Why?" It had taken Tlife this long to build up that sense of exaltation, and now his shoulders drooped.

"The enemy is too close. They must have caught wind of our movements by now. If we tried a pincer attack in these conditions, not only would it be not as effective, they could very well divide and hit us individually. We probably wouldn't lose outright, but it would result in needless losses."

"Chrirh?" Tlife wished for the **strategy staff officer**'s opinion.

"I'm afraid I have to agree with the **Chief of Staff**," said Chrirh, to her vexation.

"I see." Tlife felt it a shame, yet he understood that the **staff officers'** opinions ought to be respected. Even as Commander-in-Chief, Tlife worried himself over all the everyday decisions — not even being on the battlefield would free him from them — the staff officers set various virtual scenarios and conducted battle simulation after battle simulation. As such, if they'd determined that a certain strategy would merely lead to unnecessary casualties, then he had no reason to doubt it.

Crestfallen, Tlife's shoulders drooped. "There's no getting around it. We may just have to attack them head-on."

"Indeed. I believe that is the soundest stratagem, sir," said Cahyoor.

"Display the battle formation planes."

The **map of planar space** disappeared, replaced by the hypothetical formations.

Within the **Star Forces**, an **assault sub-fleet** was typically composed of three *saubh acharr* (assault squadrons), one *saubh mésgér* (escort squadron), one *saubh bhotutr* (strike squadron), one *saubh dicpaurér* (supply squadron), and three **patrol ships** under the direct command of a *raichaicec* (commandant), plus a few *longiac* (carrycrafts).

At present, Tlife had four assault sub-fleets at hand. Those four were lined up on the side, poised to shoot out into the enemy. At the head of each assault sub-fleet was an escort **squadron**, shields against enemy **mines**. After that came the strike squadron. Comprised of **battle-line warships**, each strike squadron was a bow firing **mines**. The **strike sub-fleet**, *Bascec-Gamlymh*, was placed so as to cross the four assault sub-fleets laterally, thereby bolstering their strike capabilities.

Meanwhile, each *saubh glar* (command squadron) had an assault **squadron** following on its heels. These were the spears that would skewer the enemy at battle's end.

As for the fearsome **recon sub-fleet** *Ftunéc*, it would divide its main forces into three and hide between the other groups of ships.

The **supply squadrons** belonging to each of the **sub-fleets** would tail from behind alongside the **supply sub-fleet** *Achmatuch*.

A supremely textbook battle formation, devoid of pretense.

"Very well," said Tlife. "Arrange them at once."

"Yes, sir," Cahyoor saluted.

From the flagship *Cairdigh*'s **space-time bubble**, several communications vessels emerged, relaying orders to each class of **Headquarters**. At the same time, the enemy's own small-mass **space-time bubbles**, also likely communications vessels, began to fly into a whirlwind of action.

"Enemy **space-time bubbles** splitting off!" shouted the *casariac ragrhotr* (exploration staff officer), rousing Tlife's attention. Countless small **space-time bubbles** issued from the bubbles lurking at the center area of the high-density sector, rushing toward Tlife's fleet.

"There is a 0.99996 in 1—" Cahyoor began.

"Enough probabilities!" Tlife cried.

"They're enemy mines, sir," he said calmly, as though he hadn't noticed he'd been shouted down.

"I KNOW that!" he snapped, but his expression immediately changed to a smile. "So, it's begun."

"Indeed."

So the curtain rose on the first full-blown battle in this great war — the **Clash at the Sfagnoff Portal-Sea**.

"Commence the *hocsatïocss mésghotr* (defensive mine battle)!" ordered Tlife.

A volley of **mines** fired from the **patrol ship** *Cairdigh*, which was the cue for the battle-line ships under its command to commence the **mine battle**. There was a large gap between the range of **mines** fired from the high-density sector and those fired at that sector. The enemy mines fired from the sector would reach the *Byrec Tlaïmr* (Tlife Fleet), but they couldn't shoot the enemy from their current position. As such, this attack was aimed at the enemy **mines** themselves.

Both groups of mines drew nearer and nearer at dizzying speeds.

"Contact made with **space-time bubbles**. Azimuth of 305. Distance: 65. Area of contact expanding," reported the **exploration staff officers**.

The red blips that represented enemy **mines** and the blue blips that represented allied **mines** mingled in an interweaving maelstrom.

Following the orders input into the **compucrystals**, their mines attempted to fuse with the space-time of their enemy counterparts, while the enemy mines attempted to flee their embrace. For the enemy, there was no point if their mines crashed against **mines** that would perish before reaching their fleets anyway.

And yet, the enemy **mines**, chased off and intercepted, were cornered into reluctant **space-time fusion**. When the **space-time bubbles** fused, they annihilated, venting large quantities of **space-time particles** in the process. Localized high-density sectors were born, and subsequently faded away. **planar space** undulated, and **space-time particles** diffused in surging ripples, which often shook other **space-time bubbles**.

The unscathed **mines** that barreled through that barrage hurtled ever closed to Tlife's fleet. Naturally, they had been broadly reduced in number, but there were still enough not to be taken lightly.

It was the *laitec* (defense ship) unit's job to meet the mines at the pass. Defense ships were equipped with numerous mobile small-caliber cannons; one *symh* unit of six ships formed a single **space-time bubble**, and each of those bubbles stood against the wave of **mines**.

The escort corps' **space-time bubbles** advanced, striving to fuse with the **mines**'. Now those mines refrained from skirting away, themselves aiming to fuse. The purpose of the initial volley was in fact to destroy the defense ship unit. The instant the **mines** fused with their space-time, they were greeted by innumerable **lasers** and streams of antiprotons. Some mines managed to take defense ships down with them, but most merely ended up pointlessly increasing the mass of the escort corps' **space-time bubbles**.

Within the seething expanse of **planar space**, the distance between foes steadily closed.

"Distance from enemy: 142. Enemy vanguard now within our range of fire," said the **exploration officer**.

"Copy. Change the **mines**' target to the enemy vanguard," Tlife commanded.

The new volley of **mines** didn't spare their enemy counterparts a single glance, instead thrusting toward the enemy fleet at all speed. Their obstacles removed, the group of enemy **mines** flocked around the defense ship unit in great herds. Ultimately, reports of vanquished defense ships turned incessant, and the **mines** began approaching the **battle-line warships**.

"Distance from enemy: 100."

"The time has come," said Tlife, eyes on Cahyoor. "Sic the *Ftunéc* on them."

The **recon sub-fleet** *Ftunéc*'s **commander** was a *roïfraudéc* (associate commodore) by the name of *Sporh Aronn Saicsepatr Nimh Laitpanr Painaigh* (Archduchess of *Laitpanh*). The House of Sporr was a large family that boasted a level of social prestige next to the **Imperial Family** of Abliar's in rank, containing over five hundred individuals of **noble rank**. The *Nimïéc Laitpanr* (Archducal House of *Laitpanh*) was almost synonymous with the noble Sporr family, held aloft by its succession of heirs. But that wasn't all. The *Nimhynh Laitpanr* (Archduchy of *Laitpanh*) included three inhabited planets, and was therefore recognized far and wide as the **territory-nation** with the greatest wealth in the **Empire**.

In other words, she was the head of the most affluent, most storied house among all **nobles** — which caused the *Ftunéc*'s *Almcasariac* (Senior Staff Officer), **Hecto-Commander** Cfadiss, to always wonder why she didn't just retire from the **Star Forces** and enjoy the high life.

That she'd joined the **Star Forces** to begin with, that was a given, as the duty of a **noble**. The officer just couldn't understand why she stuck around after fulfilling said duty. He tried thinking of it as *her responsibility*, or *her mission in life*, but observing her behavior, the words *her hobby* always sprang unbidden as a wrench in the works of his rationalization.

The reason Cfadiss had transferred over to the *Ftunéc*'s **headquarters** was because his predecessor had to take impromptu *cagsomhoth* (maternity leave) due to a sudden case of falling in love. In addition, nobody on the inside was deemed sufficiently qualified for promotion. Less than a month had passed since then, yet Cfadiss still wasn't used to the atmosphere in this **headquarters**.

And the reason for that is her, thought Cfadiss, gazing at the *Raichaicibach* (Commandant's Seat). It sported a lavish, elaborately embroidered baldachin, which was supported by four pillars of marble white, each with exquisite and minutely detailed engravings. As hard as it was to believe, according to rumor, the embroidery was done by hand. This decoration alone would be tough to acquire through three whole years of an associate commodore's salary. Of course, **starpilots** with **star fiefs** went without pay.

Cfadiss shifted his gaze to the space behind the **Commandant's Seat**. The **imperial coat of arms** (the eight-headed dragon known as the *gaftnochec*), the *glac ïadbyrer* (sub-fleet banner), and the symbol of the House of Sporr, the *gatharsec* (golden crow), were arranged in a triangle shape on the wall. The golden crow was at the bottom of the triangle, but it was a size bigger than the other banners, as though to underscore that it was the most important.

Once again, Cfadiss's eyes came to the **Commandant's Seat**. *How hopelessly out of place,* he thought with intensity.

The **twin-winged circlet** of the **imperially certified starpilot** ill-suited the assiduously braided, scarlet-blue hair more fit for a palace banquet. Unbecoming, too, was a **military uniform** on her while she was so lazily reclining; in that pose, she could very well have been lying sprawled on some luxurious chaise. It was certainly true that starpilots of imperial appointment enjoyed various privileges. Decorating one's **Commandant's Seat** using personal funds was one of them. But decorating it to this extent could only be called self-indulgent.

Soon after taking the post, he admonished her to "Act a little more like a proper **commandant**, please. It will boost morale," only to be shot down with a "No thanks."

I'll just count my blessings that there isn't some handsome boy servant offering her some chilled **apple cider** *on a silver platter...* Cfadiss shuddered at the thought.

No... don't tell me she expects that role of ME, **Hecto-Commander** Cfadiss Üémh Ésepir Séspic, *a* clapaimh *(staff officer insignia)-decorated* cizéc *(knight second-class)!?*

Cfadiss banished the absurd notion from his mind. Yet in the end, he simply couldn't come to grips with his commander…

"*Lonh*," he said. Might as well break the ice; he had nothing better to do at the moment anyway.

"What is it?" Her red pupils flitted inside their almond-shaped slits. The Sporr family feature, the *cilœmh pïana sporr* (crimson eyes of Sporr). Her eyes were the deep red of a giant star in its final stages.

"Are you acquainted with Lonh-*Lœber Sfagnaumr* (the Honored Marquess of Sfagnoff)?"

"Sure. *Simfé* (aristocratic society) is a small world."

"What are they like?"

"He's a louse," she said, summing him up in so many words. "I can't bear the thought of letting my ships get hurt to save somebody like him."

"Huh!?" Cfadiss was so dumbfounded he forgot to chide her.

"But don't worry. I won't be mixing business with private affairs."

Cfadiss stared at the baldachin, and gave careful consideration to the mentality that led to the words "*my* ships." No mixing business with private affairs? Really? His misgivings filled him right to the eyeballs, where they shined.

"That look is insubordination against a superior officer," she said, responding irritably to his deprecatory mien.

"Please accept my apologies," he said, though he remained unconvinced.

At that moment, their orders came.

"An **inter-bubble communication** from **Headquarters**." The **communications staff officer** turned around from the **console**.

"Read it aloud," said Sporr.

"Yes, ma'am. 'Overrun them.' End of communication."

"My, my. This is my first time working with **Commodore** Tlife; I commend him for his fine, *concise* orders. Now, *noctamh batta* (complete mobile-state) for **space-time bubbles** 1 through 6. Assemble a single column for each squadron and move to the front of the fleet."

The *Ftunéc* was made up of the **command squadron**, in addition to six *saubh usaimr* (recon squadrons) and one **supply squadron**. A **squadron**'s name contained a number given it by the **Star Forces**. As such, its official name contained a long number like "607." That was less than convenient, so **Headquarters** allotted recon squadrons the numbers "1" through "6," with the **supply squadron** as number "7."

Even the Abh placed importance on functionality from time to time.

The **space-time bubbles** that had been formed three ships to a bubble (with those ships in turn keyed to a battle-line warship) split off into individual units. In doing so, their speed was multiplied by roughly 1.73, and so the lines of space-time bubbles overtook the battle-line warship, followed soon by the defense ship unit.

"**Command squadron, stationary-state**. Transmit *agac asparhotr* (signal of assembly). Assume Massed Battle Formation 3." If the prospect of bearing the full brunt of the enemy's onslaught had her perturbed, she certainly didn't show it. Her commands came with aplomb.

The three patrol ships of the headquarters squadron had formed a triangle, and needless to say, at its head sailed the **flagship** *Hairbyrch*. Behind that triangle, five lines were forming.

"Number 4 is being slow," Cfadiss pointed out. Even though the other squadrons were beginning to move laterally in front of the defense ship unit, Squadron 4 was still puttering near a battle-line warship.

"I've never liked a laggard," Sporr tut-tutted. "But it's fine. They'll follow us eventually. Let's strike using the other five **squadrons**."

"But—" Cfadiss had been about to scold her when he thought better of it. It was, after all, a not illogical conclusion. Fussing too much over concentrating troops and waiting for Number 4 would be handing the enemy time. Moreover, with the lack of defense for the defense ship unit, it would expose it to enemy fire. It was true that at the moment, they ought to value speed over other factors.

That being said, Cfadiss couldn't be sure his commandant hadn't made that call based solely on simple sentiment. "The five **squadrons** have formed ranks, without Number 4," Cfadiss reported.

"Tell the **ship commanders** the following: **complete mobile-state**. Course: 310. Continuously transmit the *agac* (signal): 'Follow me.'"

"Yes." Cfadiss relayed her orders to the **communications staff officer**. With that, the recon sub-fleet *Ftunéc* was on the move again. In that direction lay the enemy's vanguard, stretching wide on both sides. The enemy began focusing its **mine** fire on *Ftunéc*.

Cfadiss switched his **circlet** to external input mode and attuned to the *Hairbyrch*'s detectors. Immediately, he frowned.

The **mines** were attempting to worm their way through at a rate of around one round every five seconds. The patrol ship *Hairbyrch*'s mobile cannons destroyed the mines with all their power and all their fury. Yet, if even just one round connected, they wouldn't emerge unharmed, no matter how thick the ship's armor was.

Just like the majority of **soldiers** in the **Star Forces**, Cfadiss had no real combat experience. This was his first-ever taste of mortal fear. Cold sweat ran down his eyebrows from the underside of his **circlet**.

He looked at his commander. *The nerve of this lady! She's HUMMING! Does she even understand our situation? We're in the middle of a relentless exchange of **mine** fire!*

"Lonh!" Unable to bear it any longer, Cfadiss had a proposal for his superior. "Should we not conduct a **defensive mine battle**?"

"Where was your former post?" asked Sporr as she fiddled with her **command baton**.

What does that have to do with anything? he huffed inwardly, but he thought he might as well answer her. "I was the **senior staff officer** of *Saubh Bhotutr Cigagona* (Strike Squadron 184)."

"Is that so. Then you may not be aware. You see, **patrol ships** don't carry a single round of **mines** that would be used for defense. What few mines a patrol ship carries are all for destroying enemy vessels. Now don't forget."

"But—"

"No buts. What would become of us if a **patrol ship** crumbled to this level of fire? We are the *Ftunéc*!"

"Augh…" At a loss for words, Cfadiss finally noticed that Sporr's **circlet** had been set to exterior space sensory mode.

Dammit, putting on a brave face for us. Cfadiss had wanted to momentarily switch back to personal space sensory mode, but he decided he could hardly do so now.

"An **inter-bubble communication** from Squadron 1 **patrol ship** *Ceubyrch*," reported the **communications staff officer**. "'Serious damage sustained. EM cannons, front-facing mobile-cannons inoperable. Evacuating toward rear.'"

Sporr didn't so much as twitch, not even at this news. She didn't even stop humming; she simply gave a light little nod.

The enemy vanguard had begun to diverge to either side, opening the way for the *Ftunéc*. That was a wise choice on their part. After all, the vanguard was probably the defense ship unit, which was hardly a match for a patrol ship.

Cfadiss felt a bit mischievous. He wanted to test just how far the *Honorable Associate Commodore*'s composure ran. "The enemy vanguard is now conducting evasive maneuvers. Do we pursue them?"

"Are you stupid?" said Sporr sharply. "Or are you just playing stupid?"

"My apologies." Cfadiss was surprised by the heat of opprobrium in his superior's words.

"You haven't answered me yet. Which is it?" she pressed, giving him no quarter.

"I, uhh… I was playing stupid."

"And why did you do something like that?"

"That's, uhh…" He couldn't tell her that he was trying to trip her up, so he spluttered awkwardly.

"You were trying to gauge how dumb your superior is," she declared.

"No, I would never…"

"Then what is it?"

"I'm so sorry!" he said at last. "It's just as you surmised, *Lonh*."

"Then I'll look the other way, but only just this once," she said. She was surprisingly magnanimous. "See that it doesn't happen again. If you pull that again, I WILL pick on you."

"I'll make a mental note."

"Stay this course. Our only target is the **battle-line ships**. Leave small fries like **defense ships** for the folks in the back."

Finally, the *Ftunéc* easily passed through the gaps in the enemy vanguard. **Squadron** 4 was tailing along like proper at the end of the queue. From the

Ftunéc's front left, a succession of **space-time bubble** flocks came rushing toward it.

"Judging by mass, they must be **assault ship space-time bubbles**!"

"Take a mental note of this, **senior staff officer**: it's times like these that a **patrol ship**'s mines are deployed." Sporr raised her **command baton** overhead. "Left side, commence **mine battle**!"

Each ship in the *Ftunéc* loosed their **mines**, and those herds of mines aimed for the flock of enemy assault ships. The red blips pinpointing the locations of enemy **space-time bubbles** perished one after the other in flashes.

"They're coming from the right. Three **patrol ship space-time bubbles**!" **Command baton** on her cheek, Sporr gave it but a moment's thought. "Don't let them gear against Number 4. Our course is just right." As though to make up for their blunder earlier, **Squadron** 4 responded swiftly. Column migrated to column, forestalling the enemy ships.

For a while afterward, there were no enemy ships that could contend with the *Ftunéc*. Yet the intensity of fire increased, and the *Hairbyrch* **space-time bubbles** filled with debris and charged particles. A point-blank shot intercepted by a mobile cannon exploded, and fragments exposed to antimatter mist heated up and drifted.

So this is blitzing. Cfadiss quaked.

"I'm bored," said Sporr out of nowhere. "Aren't you bored, **senior staff officer**?"

"Huh?" Cfadiss couldn't believe what he was hearing.

"I said, this bores me," she repeated. "Every day, it's always the same old boring desk work, and now that I'm finally in battle, they won't even let me get into it. Why did I ever become **imperially ordained**? I bet **ship commanders** have lots more fun."

"Is that right?" The captains were being chased by returning fire, enemy assault ships joining the spray of **mines**. Cfadiss, of course, also had work experience on a ship's **bridge**, so he could imagine how bloodthirsty they were. Even the training exercises were so intense that he'd forget to breathe, and now they were embroiled in actual fighting.

"See, my dream was to be a **patrol ship commander** and square off with the enemy that way. But when I was a ship commander, there was no war, and now that there is a war, this is the boring role I'm stuck with. I can't even retire until the war's over. I wonder if I've any luck at all."

Cfadiss sighed in his heart. *I knew it. This IS a hobby to her.*

"I believe I told you that look is insubordination," she charged, wise to him.

A fresh supply of troops came bolting for them. One assault ship fused with the *Hairbyrch*'s space-time. A brief **alarm claxon** sounded in the **Commander's Bridge**, followed immediately by the tremors that came with the firing of the **EM cannon**.

The assault ship burst and shattered in an instant, bathing the *Hairbyrch*'s sensors with a spray of charged particles that dwarfed any mere **mine** blast's. It was akin to a solar wind at point-blank range.

Next to a scowling Cfadiss, Sporr hid a slight yawn with the back of her hand. "Ugh, it's just so dull," she muttered.

Tlife extolled her to high heaven. "A magnificent display, **Associate Commodore** Sporr!"

The enemy vanguard had split into two, scrambling the core of the enemy line into a tumult. At the center of that confusion, the *Ftunéc* maintained its massed battle formation, and slowly continued flying straight ahead.

"Shoot every **mine** you've got right here!" Tlife pointed at the rift in the enemy vanguard with his **command baton**. "You can't let them close back together again. Don't leave the *Ftunéc* to die!"

"Enemy **space-time bubbles**, azimuth: 010. Distance: 30. Will intersect with our course. Around 300 in number!" The assembly of **space-time bubbles** that appeared behind the battle-line warship unit attempted to immobilize the head of the *Ftunéc*.

"They're likely the enemy's main force!" Cfadiss could virtually hear the blood drain from his body. "They're pouring all of their backup forces at us. Commence evasive maneuvers at once!"

"Please, **senior staff officer**, I'll ask you not to raise a fuss on my **bridge**." She pointed to the space behind the **map of planar space** with her **command baton**. "Crunch the numbers. I want to know if we'll make it in time."

Countless blue dots — allied **mines** — came hurtling at maximum velocity.

"Yes, ma'am." *Nobody's raising a fuss, least of all me!* Through his anger, he input the directives into the **compucrystals**.

Red dotted lines appeared from the enemy lines, while blue dotted lines appeared from the herd of **mines**. They intersected with the front-right area of the *Ftunéc*'s future position.

"Stay the course," Sporr commanded.

"Yes." Though Cfadiss nodded, he'd not been made at ease just yet.

Allied **mines** flew past the *Ftunéc* from its right, slamming into the enemy ships. The *Ftunéc*'s front-right had turned into a swinging dance hall, with **mines** attempting to fuse with the enemy ships playing hard to get. The enemy lines were in disarray as **space-time bubbles** floundered in their death throes, touching off localized high-density sectors all around.

Phew... Relieved, Cfadiss relaxed his shoulders. It was only then he realized how tense he'd been.

The enemy ships that had slipped away from the dance floor were hot on the *Ftunéc*'s heels, but they too were made to scatter one after the other. The center of the high-density sector was close now. The enemy unit of battle-line warships was before their very eyes.

"The enemy **battle-line warship** unit is making every effort to obstruct the *Ftunéc*. They pose almost no threat to the main units," said Cahyoor, analyzing the situation.

"All right. All ships prepare to attack," said Tlife. "The *Rocérh* will wipe out their vanguard on the right. The *Üacapérh* will exterminate it on the left. The *Byrdaimh* and *Citirec*, they'll follow me. And no dallying! Otherwise you're gonna let the *Ftunéc* take all the good bits!"

The enemy battle-line ships were beginning to retreat.

"You're too slow," Sporr murmured pityingly. Then she stood up. "Let's go crush those ships on half-**squadron** units. **Senior Staff Officer!**"

"Yes." Cfadiss took a step forward.

"I dislike toiling over the little details. I'd like you to point each **squadron** to their target."

"Yes." *If you're so dreadfully bored, then why don't you do it yourself?* But Cfadiss bottled those thoughts up and set about allotting each squadron to the enemy battle-line warship **space-time bubbles**.

"That's right, we don't need any to ourselves," she said.

"Understood." Having finished the task he was given and routed the designated targets he'd input to the **communications staff officer**, he had a question for her. "Have we become backup forces, too?"

"No. I'll be taking *that*." She gestured toward the **map of planar space**. It was a **space-time bubble** that had been stamped with the provisional number "661," and situated all the way in the back of the battlefield.

Cfadiss referred to the course of the battle, and soon discovered that **Space-time Bubble** 661 had yet to fire a single round of **mines**. "That is believed to be a large **supply ship** or something in that vein. Might it not be advisable to ignore it for now?"

"It could be yet more reserve forces using that as camouflage. It might be passing itself off as harmless, only to come for our heads at the very end. And we can't have that, so I'd like to strike their front lines."

"Yes." *That may very well be the case,* Cfadiss thought.

"Just received confirmation: All **squadrons** have received respective target instructions," said the communications officer.

"Excellent." Sporr nodded, raising her **command baton** overhead with evident mirth. "All ships, fan out! The real party starts now, and you'd better brace yourselves for some fireworks! We are the *Ftunéc* (Goddess of Dance), so show them how you command the stage!"

The rectangle that was the *Ftunéc* came untied. Units of three patrol ships formed triangles, vertical columns, even diagonal columns, each prowling after its own prey.

If they strayed too far from each other, **inter-bubble communication** would become unavailable. As such, from here on out, **Associate Commodore** Sporr would fight as the joint commander of the flagship and its two attendant vessels.

"Relay the following to the **ship commanders**. Veer to course: 015. Maintain **complete mobile-state**."

The patrol ship *Hairbyrch* led two other patrol ships, zooming down from **planar space** from the high-density sector to the low-density sector where **Space-time Bubble 661** idled.

"**Space-time Bubble** 661 now retreating," said the *casariac rilbicotr* (navigation staff officer). "No other readings. **Space-time fusion** possible at 07:18 by ship's time."

"Shall we assume assault formation?" asked Cfadiss.

"No need. We're just going to keep moving forward," said Sporr, tapping her cheek lightly with the **command baton**.

A while later, the navigation officer had a report. "Ten minutes until **space-time fusion**."

"Prepare for **battle in 3-space**." She issued her command almost as though she was talking to herself. Then she looked at Cfadiss. "What do you think?"

"About what?" said Cfadiss, confused.

"The enemy hasn't transmitted an *agac rétgacotr* (signal of surrender). If it were really just a large **supply ship**, they'd be surrendering about now. Looks like my hunch was right on the mark."

"But they still haven't fired any **mines**, not even now. How do you interpret that?"

"Beats me," said Sporr, dismissing it in so many words. "They must be dealing with their own set of circumstances."

"**Space-time Bubble** 661 now **splitting its space-time**!" shouted the **navigation staff officer**.

"See? Here it comes," Sporr nodded with a smile.

"Six **assault ship space-time bubbles**. Course: 345. Distance: 16. Approaching from in front. Relative speed: 375 **astro-knots**."

"What did you say!?" Sporr's smile stiffened. "They're not **mines**?"

"No, ma'am."

Sporr bit her lip; something had her less than pleased. "*Casariac tlachotr* (gunnery staff officer), tell me how many **mines** we have left."

"This ship contains four; the *Baugbyrch*, four as well; and the *Hasunbyrch*, five. Thirteen in all, ma'am."

"Thanks, I can do simple addition. Commence anterior **mine battle**. Fire all rounds and mow them down!"

The three patrol ships fired their **mines** out, and they split off from their time-space.

Thirteen against six. They had more than twice the number advantage. The enemy's **space-time bubbles** didn't stand a chance. Those bubbles were likely to be assault ships, which were quite weak to **mine** offensives.

The three patrol ships kept cruising as though nothing had happened.

"**Senior staff officer**," said Sporr.

"Yes, ma'am?"

"What do you think is the greatest sin a **starpilot** can commit?"

"Insubordination against a superior officer, I would think." Cfadiss had answered in an ingratiating way without even meaning to, and he tumbled into a bout of self-loathing over it.

"No! The greatest sin is stupidity," she said, surprising him. "Think about it. You can feel a great sense of responsibility, and you can carry out orders faithfully, but if you're an idiot, then there's nothing to be done. And what kind of fool would send six **assault ships** to bat away a trio of **patrol ships**?"

"I see." His commander understood the reason behind the glum mood, and Cfadiss nodded.

"I may be glib, but I'm no fool. I will never send my subordinates to meaningless deaths."

"Yes." *But everybody operates under that same belief*, he thought to himself. That being said, Sporr's command style was indeed outstanding. Partly owing to his inexperience aboard a patrol ship unit, he hadn't yet carried out much of any of his work duties as **senior staff officer**.

"My **headquarters** doesn't need any idiots. This here **Archduchess of Laitpanh** chooses her playmates. She just can't choose who she plays against."

Stared at by the **crimson eyes of the Sporr**, Cfadiss broke into a cold sweat. "I'll work on becoming a more competent playmate."

"You certainly have the potential." Sporr's lips curled into a faint little smile.

"One minute until **space-time fusion!**" said the **navigation staff officer**.

"Still no **signal of surrender**," added the **communications staff officer**.

"**Navigation staff officer!**" Sporr looked away from Cfadiss's face. "Make it so that all three ships fuse with them at the same time."

"Roger that."

"Transmit the following to all ships. As soon as our space-times fuse, fire the **EM cannons**." She was already immersing herself in her *frocragh* spatio-sensory perception in anticipation of the **battle in 3-space**. Her eyes closed, **Associate Commodore** Sporr smiled, as though expecting some auspicious turn. "Now then, what's waiting for us inside? I'm getting excited!"

"Ten seconds to **space-time fusion**. Eight. Seven. Six. Five..." the navigation officer counted down. "Four. Three. Two. One. **Space-time fusion!**"

The warning sound that accompanied the firing of the **EM cannon** reverberated through the ship's bridge.

Cfadiss greatly expanded the scope of his *frocragh*. Now he could sense the enemy ship in front. It was giant, but it was alone.

"The **signal of surrender!**" shouted the **communications staff officer**. "It's coming in via *droch daimr* (radio wave communication)..."

"Cease the offensive!" Sporr didn't bother hearing out the rest. Her eyes flared open, and she stood up. "Call all ships to cease the offensive! Firing at a ship that has surrendered will dishonor the name of Sporr!"

Could've said it would dishonor the name of the **Empire**, *or the* **Star Forces**, *even of the Abh*, Cfadiss mused.

But her orders hadn't made it in time. The *Hasunbyrch* fired its **EM cannons**. However, the shell self-destructed before it could reach the enemy ship.

"For heaven's sake, why didn't they send it out via **inter-bubble communication**? Did they really think they could get away?" she grumbled. "Transmit the following to the *Baugbyrch*. Raid, inspect, and take the enemy ship. Then have the *Hasunbyrch* follow me."

The resident of **Space-time Bubble** 661 was a single large supply ship. After confirming that, the flagship *Hairbyrch* split off from this space-time alongside the *Hasunbyrch*.

"The enemy **battle-line warship** unit has been near-totally wiped out," reported Cfadiss.

"Oh." Sporr seemed to think little of that news. Yet he could clearly tell she was concealing her disappointment.

"Your orders with regard to our course, ma'am," asked Cfadiss.

"Course: 160, at **complete mobile-state**. We're going back to where my ships are."

"Yes." Cfadiss relayed the orders to the **ship commanders**.

He felt as though his opinion of his commander had improved considerably in a short space of time... but then he rationalized that as a momentary temptation by some dark force. Cfadiss had two, no, three things to get off his chest.

"That look is insubordination against a superior officer," she said, her **command baton** pointed at his face.

"Yes, ma'am." Cfadiss concluded that at this juncture, he'd better keep quiet.

Sporr was lost in thought, but when she noticed that he was still casting an interrogative gaze her way, it seemed she succumbed to the urge to explain herself, albeit only a little. She ruffled up the scarlet-blue hair that had been so diligently braided. "My hunches are off the mark sometimes, you know."

The battle was over now. The only agents left on the battlefield were either allies, or surrendering enemies.

"A **conveyance ship** has arrived from the *Ftunéc*," reported **Kilo-Commander** Cahyoor.

"Oh?" Tlife nodded. "So, what've they got for us?"

"It seems they've taken the enemy's bureaucrats prisoner."

"Superb! That's fantastic... but, why exactly were there bureaucrats on the battlefield?"

"It appears to be customary in the United Humankind for bureaucrats such as media spokespersons and battle cheerers to accompany soldiers into battle. They were in a large **supply ship** near the **Sfagnoff Portal**."

"Hm…" The way the UH did things was totally inscrutable to him. Tlife was pacing the bridge, but he halted in place once he realized no amount of contemplation would clear up their mysteries. "Oh well, whatever. We won."

"Yes. Our victory was assured."

"Too assured to take any thrill in it, but I'm glad in any case. Order all units to amass."

"Roger."

"Plus, let's have the *Ftunéc* do one last thing. After resupplying, they're to leave for the **Sfagnoff Portal** at once. If there aren't any forces left to contend with, they are to annex control over the **marquessate**'s astrospace. Who's worked the least throughout the battle?"

"Each **sub-fleet** has fulfilled their responsibilities admirably…"

"I know that. I don't mean to reprimand anybody, so just tell me."

"If I'm forced to say…" Cahyoor cocked his head. "The *Byrdaimh*'s kill rate was quite modest."

"I see. Then leave the *Byrdaimh* to do all of the cleaning up."

"Understood."

The main casualties of the **Tlife fleet** that were ascertained at the end were as follows:

Ships sunk:
> 24 **defense ships**
> 17 **assault ships**
> 1 **patrol ship**

Serious damage:
> 51 **defense ships**
> 47 **assault ships**
> 5 **patrol ship**

Slight damage:
> 95 **defense ships**
> 117 **assault ships**
> 19 **patrol ship**
> 7 **battle-line warships**

Counting only sunken and heavily damaged ships, there were 145. Since the ships that were only lightly damaged could be repaired by *daüsiac* (repair ships) even while mobilized, these 145 ships were the only ones recorded as lost in the **Tlife fleet**'s register of vessels. Though these were by no means minor figures — especially to the people aboard those ships and their families — they presented no impediment to the fleet's overall martial power.

By comparison, of the 900 ships in the UH Peacekeepers' Dispatch Fleet A, only 27 were operable, and all 27 had surrendered, to be plundered and looted by the **Star Forces**.

It was an overwhelming victory for the **Imperial Star Forces**.

The heavily damaged ships received temporary repairs, ships that could no longer sail under their own power were towed by **repair ship**s, and they all left for the **imperial capital**, with the captured enemy ships taken there as well.

When the first stage of battlefield processing was complete, two rounds of **mines** were fired from the flagship *Cairdigh*. Instead of antimatter bombs, however, these contained bouquets of flowers.

The moment their **space-time bubble engines** ran out of fuel and the **mines** turned into space-time particles and scattered, **Commodore** Tlife ordered a moment of silence for the dead, both allies and enemies.

As the majority of the dead were enemy soldiers, this gesture was as good as a declaration of victory for the Abh.

Chapter 4: *Ïucrabh Frybarer* (Battlefield of the Empire)

"You think we're delusional, don't you?" said Malka.

"Huh? What makes you think that?" said Jint, playing innocent.

They were on a mountain a thousand or so *üésdagh* from the city of *Guzonh*. Bill wasn't present, as he was on the job, and if he up and disappeared in the middle of a delivery it'd raise some eyebrows. Besides, he had a living to make. With Bill absent, it was the four remaining members of the Clasbure Anti-Imperial Front (Malka, Undertaker, Min, and Daswani) who joined Jint and Lafier on the side of the mainline as they all transferred onto the mechanical walker that was now climbing up the mountain.

The eight-legged walker bore the weight of all six, and scaled the slope using what little footholds there were. Those footholds did seem to link into a sort of passage up, though: a trail where the otherwise rampant vines and assorted trees didn't grow.

It was a rough ride, reminiscent of a non-gravity-controlled spaceship. While the attitude control mechanism tried its best to keep their seats level, it occasionally failed to cope with the degree of the slope, causing them to shake up and down. Even now, Undertaker was blue in the face struggling to keep the contents of his stomach from going home to Sfagnoff's sun.

Meanwhile, Lafier, having been raised in space, was cool as a cucumber. Jint, for his part, did feel sick in the stomach at times, but it wasn't too bad.

Malka pointed to Lafier with her chin: "You're thinking there's no way the **Empire** would ever recognize our independence, even if we've taken this young lady as a hostage."

"So you know?" Lafier seemed relieved. "I was concerned we would be forced to deceive all of you."

"Then, like, why are you bothering to take us hostage?" asked Jint.

"For a ship," said Malka.

"What we want are spaceships."

467

"But, Min said…" …*that what you want is independence*, Jint was about to say.

"It's a different tack," said Min matter-of-factly. "We have two tacks open to us."

"Right. Min's of the belief we should grab independence in one fell swoop, while I think we should get there step-by-step. No matter the circumstances, the **Empire** will never hand us independence for a single life. He's the delusional one; I'm the realist."

"I heartily disagree, and I'll tell you why…"

"If you wish to ride a spaceship, then you can just become an **imperial citizen**," said Lafier, putting a damper on their impromptu duel of strategies.

"See, this is why the little Abh lady gets my goat. *Urp!*" Undertaker clamped his mouth and resisted the urge to hurl before continuing. "We don't want to *ride* in spaceships — we want to *own* them. That, *urp* …that'd be real freedom. And not some shoddy jalopy that can only fly within the star system, either. We want ships that can go interstellar."

"That is what we call impossible," said Lafier, airily laying down the truth before Jint could stop her. "Every **interstellar ship** in the **Empire** is property of **Her Majesty the Empress**. They are in the hands of the Empire itself. Even people of high noble rank don't personally own their interstellar ships."

Malka narrowed her eyes. "But there were so many different kinds of *gareurec* (company) and **grandee** ships at the **spaceport**. You can't pull the wool over my eyes."

"They're on loan," Lafier explained. "Borrowers can choose whatever size ship for however long they'd like, but it's the *Rüé casobérlach* (Imperial Merchant Ship Company) that holds authority over personnel affairs."

"I don't believe it… Listen here, I've looked into **imperial law**. There's nothing about possession of **interstellar ships** being forbidden!"

"When it comes to relations between the **Empire** and the **noble** classes, much is unwritten custom. You would never know it from reading the law."

"*Urp!* Damn **Empire**; how secretive can you get!?"

"No one is keeping it a secret," said Lafier, taken aback. "It's simply that even if you knew that, nothing would come of it. Is that not true?"

"Then what, *urp*, what about our hopes and dreams!?"

An uncomfortable silence followed Undertaker's remark. Nobody had any words. The air reverberated only with the mechanical *GREESH, GREESH* of the ever-ascending walker.

Jint couldn't stand it any longer. "Uhh, so… what now? If you don't want us as 'hostages' anymore, just tell us and we'll be…"

"Shut up." Malka put two fingers on her forehead.

"Uhh…" Jint's conscience panged. "I didn't think that was your *actual* goal… I mean, you never exactly went into detail about what exactly you were planning…"

"I told you to shut up."

Min stared at Jint. "This would mean that you believe that straight independence for the star system would be easier to obtain than ownership of spaceships, correct?"

"Well… I never thought you were being *for real*, you know…?"

"You didn't think we were being 'for real'!? Hmph! I'm not interested in being your clown."

"Would you shut up!?" Malka clapped her hands to bring attention back to her. "Look, it's fine. There's always an exception!"

A spherical building came into view beyond the road. It glistened on the side of the mountain, reflecting the light of Sfagnoff's sun.

"Hey, uhh, is that where we're going?" Jint pointed to the building, hoping it would mend this unpleasant atmosphere.

"It was," said Min. "It's my holiday house, and we WERE going to keep you two locked up in there, but is there still any point?"

"You should give that matter serious thought. I don't particularly care either way," said Lafier.

"You Abhs really are arrogant, you know that?" said Undertaker, suddenly forgetting his nausea.

"She's really unbearable sometimes, but please, don't let it get to you," Jint said in her defense.

"I was trying to be NICE!" It appeared Lafier didn't much care for Jint's efforts to smooth things over.

"Let me tell you," said Jint into Undertaker's ear, "she has no self-awareness, either."

"I feel your pain," said Undertaker, looking at Jint with the most sympathetic eyes.

"What are you telling him?" frowned Lafier warily.

"Look!" Malka shouted suddenly. From the direction she was pointing, two objects had emerged from the shadows, and came floating toward them.

"Min, did you buy those, or…?"

"They've nothing to do with me," he said, on the verge of panic.

While they were busy staring, the two floating objects alighted on the walker's front and back.

Lafier read the text: "United Humankind Armored Air Mobile Personnel Transport Vessel."

The hatches to each of them opened, and about ten soldiers shuffled running from each.

A commissioned officer who looked to be their commander raised the volume of his machine translation device before saying "Who are you, citizens?"

"No, who are YOU!?" barked Min, who stood up out of his seat.

"Apologies. I am Military Police Lieutenant Aranga of the United Humankind Peacekeepers Sfagnoff Land Dispatch Corps RC Division Military Police Regiment. Now that I've introduced myself, may I ask you to follow suit?"

Min pointed to his holiday house. "I'm the owner. Thought I'd host a get-together over some fine food with my friends."

"You are a member of the Secessionist Party, one 'Min Cursap,' correct?"

Min winced momentarily. "I'm a former member. I left the Party three years ago."

"You are named 'Min,' though, correct, citizen?"

"Yes, that's right."

"Citizen," Aranga announced, "you are under arrest. We also have some questions for your friends."

Min's face went pale. "But why!? On what grounds are you…"

"A large stockpile of weapons was discovered in your holiday house. We would very much like to ask you all about it."

Min turned to the rest to explain himself. "They're hardly a 'large stockpile.' A **needle gun**, a **stungun**, nothing much, really..."

"Why in blazes..." Malka shook her head, as though completely lost.

"There are extremely reasonable suspicions that you 'Secessionists' are in fact a cover-up organization working as reactionaries on behalf of the **Empire** to resist freedom. I would simply like to hear what you have to say on the matter, and in great detail. As you can see, resistance is futile," he said, gesturing toward all of the soldiers with guns trained on them.

"Man, have they got that backwards," muttered a teed-off Undertaker.

That said, given that they were being detained in the company of an Abh, there was nothing they could say to get them to believe their actual aims. They had been chased into a corner, and things looked exceptionally bad.

Of course, in terms of jumping out of the frying pan and into the fire, Jint and Lafier could not be outdone.

Jint looked her way. She was gripping something in her right hand. Two **cartridges** for her **lightgun**.

Lafier transferred one of them to her left hand.

There was a slight but audible *bzzz*.

Suddenly, Jint understood. *Good god — Lafier wants to start a war right here!*

Jint was just about to reach out a hand, but Lafier never gave him the chance; she crossed her arms in front of her chest, and quickly extended them like the flapping of a bird's wings.

The twin **lightgun cartridges** swung in opposite directions, tracing parabolas in the air.

Lafier's ability to adapt to differing gravity levels was something to behold. Her aim with the **lightgun cartridges** erred not. One hit the armor of the transport vessel in front, while the other got sucked into the still-open door of the other behind them.

A giant *THWOOM* rattled them all to their cores. The twin flashes of light were followed by the intermingling commotion of the explosions, the shrieks, and the roars of indignation.

"What have you done..." Min murmured, in blank amazement.

"RUN!" cried Lafier, leaping out of the walker without delay, already wielding a **lightgun** in her grip.

But Jint knew the program by now. He flopped to the ground with the duffel bag in his arms, and the other four stumbled over themselves after them.

"Over there!" Lafier used the **lightgun** like a **command baton**, pointing toward a clump of bushes.

The band of six rushed straight into them.

Aranga barked some kind of command. At once, hails of gunfire wrecked the walker and knocked down several trees.

With a single shot, Lafier expertly picked Aranga off. "Hurry!" she urged.

Jint ran for his life, fending off the tangle of vines and branches all the while. Right behind him, trees got blown away or set aflame by enemy fire. The damage to the environment pained his heart, the selfsame heart that felt like he was probably the next on the destruction menu.

"You goddamned Abh!" Jint heard Min swearing. "Now I'm a wanted man!"

"Silence. You may complain to me later!"

Indeed, this was not the time or place for a heart-to-heart. The soldiers were gradually regaining their footing, and they burned for vengeance.

"Blast it all! Over here!" Min pointed.

Min was likely the one among them with the best idea of the local geography, after all. The strange bedfellows therefore looked to him as their guide, and dashed into that thicket.

"Look!" Excited and wound up, the typically mute Daswani pointed up.

There, the Air Mobile Personnel Transport Vessel that had survived Lafier's assault hovered shakily. The turret on its landing glared contemptuously down at them, and nary a second after its muzzle was trained on the six, the surrounding trees burst into fire.

"Here!" Min beckoned from a gap in the flames, before vanishing from view. Jint headed over, and was met with an opening gaping just wide enough for a person to pass through.

"Right…" Jint stuffed Lafier into it, then dove in after her.

Down the surprisingly smooth tunnel they slid. At the end they each felt a floating sensation, their fall broken by something elastic.

"Make way!" came Min's voice. Jint tumbled frantically toward its sound. He could also hear a series of *thunks*, one per falling object.

"Oww," groaned Undertaker.

Jint finally remembered his **lightgun**, and retrieved it from the bag to set it on ILLUMINATE.

They were in a cave, about a person's length in diameter. A large buffer cushion was situated nearby — it seemed that was where he landed. Undertaker and Daswani were still holding each other in an embrace atop it. Then the two of them hopped off, their breathing still ragged.

"Is everyone here?" asked Min.

"Seems that way," said Malka.

"Then come with me." Min pointed toward the cave's recesses.

"Ah, before that…" Jint shot the cushion with the **lightgun**.

A gooey liquid began pouring out of its ripped form, and it swiftly shed its elasticity.

The six pushed their way through to the inner depths. Jint had to walk alongside Min at the head of the pack in order to light the way. "What is this place?"

"It's a lava tunnel. The planet's a young one. Not even a billion years back, rivers of lava ran all over the surface. This is what remains."

"But what about that chute we fell down…?"

"An escape route I dug in case of an emergency, naturally. But never mind that." Min raised his voice. "I hope you know you've done a number on me! Now they know my name! And as an Empire collaborator, of all things! What a hideous disgrace."

"I apologize," said Lafier's quite composed voice from behind. "It's truly unfortunate you've all been embroiled in this. Regardless, we cannot allow ourselves to be captured so easily."

"Years back, there was a guy who jumped from a second story into a bed of thorns," recounted Undertaker in melancholic tones. "No fire or anything, either. 'Course, poor guy got pricked everywhere, so they carried him to the hospital. Well, the wounds weren't too serious, but the guy had 'em all over. Think he was grunting and groaning over being covered in tissue regeneration stimulants. When I went to see him, I asked him what he was thinking…"

"What's this about all of a sudden?" asked Malka, audibly irritated.

Undertaker ignored her. "You wanna know what came out of his mouth? He said he couldn't remember the specifics, but he thought it was a 'good idea'!"

"And!?"

"That's it. It just came to mind, that's all."

"Feh... I know what you're getting at," Malka sighed deeply. "Why did we think taking an Abh hostage was a good idea? I'm going to be dismissed as cell leader now."

"If we even make it out of this alive," said Min.

Soon they came upon a fork in the path. "To the right," Min indicated. "It's this way to the main 'current.'"

After they walked down the right path for a time, they could make out very orderly footsteps sounding from all the way toward the entrance.

"They're here," whispered Malka.

"Jint, cut the light!"

"Right." Jint complied.

From then on, they had to feel their way onward. Eventually, they reached yet another branch point. Min chose the way without hesitation.

"Will we able to escape if we continue down this passage?" asked Lafier.

"Yeah. So long as we make it to the main current, we can enter other tributaries from there, and there are several openings back out to the surface."

"In that case, you four had best go on without us. We shall keep them at bay."

"What!?" The halting of feet.

"We cannot allow any more trouble to befall you on our behalves. Now go."

"You really know how to rip a person's self-respect to shreds, don't you? You two are our HOSTAGES. On what planet do the hostages save their captors, huh?"

"No, Undertaker," Min chided him. "She's right. At this rate, we're done for. Those bastards mean to chase them to the ends of the world."

"I don't doubt it," said Lafier. "Now go, and make haste."

"I'd like to give the Abh a piece of my mind on lots of things, but you do seem to know how to take responsibility," Malka sighed.

A brief silence fell upon the dark.

"Okay, all right. Let's go. We can talk her head off all we like, but we all know the little lady won't waver."

"That is correct," said Lafier.

"I stay, too," said Daswani, a man of few words.

"I thank you, but I see you aren't armed. You would be of no use to us here. Moreover, this is a battleground of the **Empire**. It would not behoove us to keep you at our sides."

"Come along, Daswani. The little lady's right."

"God, this is humiliating," grumbled Undertaker.

"Hurry! The enemy approaches."

The acoustics made it impossible to gauge how far they were, but it was clear from the sound of their footsteps that they were closing in.

"Okay. If you live to see another day, let's meet again," she intoned nervously.

"I must express my thanks one last time."

"Oh, stuff it already," snapped Undertaker. "We kidnapped you! *Kidnapped* you!"

And on that note, the four made their exit.

"Jint, are you there?"

"'Course." Jint drew nearer to the **royal princess**. "You're not gonna send *me* off, are you?"

"No." He could practically hear the smile in her voice. "Your marksmanship is horrid, but you'll still be of some use. At the very least, you'll make for a fine bullet shield."

"For crying out loud..." he grinned wryly. "You've got a real talent for cheering people up, you know that?"

"Your **wristgear** and **circlet**."

"Ah, right, of course."

Jint set his **lightgun** to the lowest output and lit up his immediate vicinity. Then he fetched his **wristgear** and **circlet**, and with them every other

lightgun cartridge they had, from inside the duffel bag. They split the eight cartridges two ways.

"How wise it was not to bury them," gloated Lafier as she equipped her **circlet** with a triumphant look.

Once again, Jint could only smile with bitter amusement. Lafier had every right to be a sore winner.

He turned off the light and switched it to LOADED, then knelt on one knee and awaited the enemy.

The cave was quite confined. A shoot-out wouldn't hinge on manpower. The supply of soldiers would give out before their supply of **lightgun cartridges** dried up.

And yet...

"It's bad news if they use heavy arms against us. The cave'll collapse on us."

"You needn't worry," said Lafier, brimming with confidence. "The **Kin of the Stars** could never die in an earthen tomb."

"Can't even tell if that's a decent point at this rate..." Jint shrugged in the darkness. He felt terribly at ease considering they'd be fighting to the death in mere moments.

Chapter 5: The *Logh Labyrena* (Maddening Maid)

"Must've gotten to them before us." Entryua lit himself a smoke.

Another kind of smoke was issuing from the wreckage of the UH Armored Air Mobile Personnel Transport Vessel before their eyes. It wouldn't have been out of place to spot at least a few wounded, but there were none to meet the eye. Odds were they'd been carried off to the field hospital.

Three soldiers stretched a rope around the perimeter of the vessel, glaring at Entryua with furrowed brows.

"How did they know to find them here?" puzzled Keitt.

"That's what I want to know. Why don't you go ask those soldiers for us, huh?"

"Right. Of course." Keitt walked up to them.

Only about an hour had passed since they deduced the members of the Clasbure Anti-Imperial Front *Guzonh* Cell's membership from the hotel manager's deposition.

Investigators wasted no time checking related sites, such as their residences and places of work. And one of those sites was the holiday home of one Min Cursap. At present, not even a single one of the cell members had been spotted in any of those places, let alone the Abh.

Keitt dashed back over. "Min Cursap apparently used to be a member of the Secessionist Party, and a very high-ranking leader at that. Then, a cursory search turned up a large stockpile of munitions..."

"What did you say?" Entryua scowled. They'd already looked into the gist of what there was to know about the cell members through the **compucrystal net**.

"He was a Secessionist Party member three years ago."

"That fact must not have been seen as very important." Keitt shrugged. "May I continue?"

"Go ahead."

"As I was saying, Min and several of his companions appeared while they were cordoning off the area. And when they questioned him…"

"It turned into a firefight." Entryua gave their surroundings another once-over. The trees that had been shot were still smoldering, and the parts of what used to be a walker were strewn next to the transport vessel.

"And what a firefight it was."

"Undoubtedly."

"So where is this Min? Was the Abh among his companions?"

"Regarding that…" Keitt hesitated to say it. "It seems that since they let them slip away, they don't know for sure."

"They let them slip away!?" Entryua shouted at Keitt hotheadedly, but then he remembered that one, Keitt wasn't his subordinate, and two, it wasn't Keitt's fault. So he settled on cynicism. "You lot, you're not even really all that, are you? You've got all of the equipment, but that's about it."

"I'm too ashamed for words."

"So where'd they run to, anyway?"

Keitt gestured toward the soldiers. "It'd appear they don't know the details, since they were deployed here after the fact."

"You people have no coordination."

"Level C clearance is needed to access that information."

"And you haven't got Level C clearance?"

"I do. I'm going to take a peek now."

"Well, good." Entryua dropped his smoke's embers onto the ground and stamped them out before lighting up another.

Keitt peered into his transceiver's screen and whispered something. Subsequently, the information displayed, and he read it aloud. "Min and six companions fled underground from Mark RC193-401 at 08:17 military time. Four people under Military Police Major Aranga died, and 12 were injured. Eight have begun tracking them under the command of Military Police Major Muhammedov. At 08:30, Military Police Command requested backup from the District Management Headquarters. In response, three infantry platoons under Captain Sleet were dispatched at 08:55. Said reinforcements arrived at the scene at 09:14, and are currently tracking them down on foot…"

"What's this 'military time' business? Is it different from our time?"

"Yes. Right now, it's 09:35 military time."

"It's slower by 21 minutes, huh…" Entryua stretched. He'd been working for too long. His back hurt. And now that he thought about it, he hadn't had a good night's sleep in days.

"What do we do now? Do we head underground as well?"

"Can't say that's the brightest idea. We'd just get in the other soldiers' way."

"Then do we give up here?" Keitt gave him a puppy dog look.

"No, we're not throwing in the towel now." He had only a half day left to spend with this guy, he reasoned. "They're hiding in the *Guzonh* Caverns. Criminals and adventure-seeking kids've been disappearing into them for who knows how long. It's a regular stomping ground for us police. So much so, we've taken to calling the cops in *Guzonh* 'crawlers.' They've got to have fairly detailed info on the place."

"Then…"

"Yep. If they grab the Abh and her gang in those tunnels, then there's nothing we can do. But we can get to them before they do. Your friends've got odor or heat detectors, right?"

"I'd be shocked if they don't."

"Then they must know where the Abh's gone. Can you find out where the soldiers who tracked them are right now?"

"Yes," Keitt said with enthusiasm, "of course."

"Great. Let's chase that lead, then." Entryua took a deep breath. "Just to warn you, though — if there's no Abh among them, I don't much care, got it?"

Luminous letters floated in the dark. They were using the **wristgear**'s heat detector function. It wasn't as accurate as a dedicated heat detector device, but it did show them a rough estimate of their distance, their bearing, and the size of their heat signatures.

"They're close," Jint breathed. "1,000 *dagh* away, if that."

"Uh-huh."

The enemy stalked ever nearer without any illumination. And why would they use any? It was obvious they had night vision goggles or something of the sort. In other words, the enemy could see them. Lafier had her *frocragh*, but that did nothing to tip the scales at the moment.

He could hear a *bzzzz* where he knew Lafier was. He sensed her move. The next instant, countless lines of fire clove through the darkness! Since they were holed up in the inner part of the branching point, bullets didn't come flying their way, but they did punch into the cave's edge, causing small explosions. Shards of stone rained down on them.

"Take cover!" said Lafier, voice strained.

The moment Jint obeyed, a hell of an explosion rocked him — the **lightgun cartridge** that Lafier lobbed had released all of its energy instantaneously. The dark yielded to the dazzling light, and the temperature within the cave rose several degrees.

The firing lines broke off.

"Come on, run!"

Jint dashed for the depths. In the momentary light, they could make out the wide-open mouth of the small cave. Yet as they raced, darkness enclosed them once more.

"Stop!" said Lafier, upon reaching a spot by the small cave's mouth.

"You gonna attack 'em here?" His voice quavered. He thought himself pathetic, but then he thought twice. It was just him being human.

"Yep. You had best take a knee and ready your gun."

"You got it." Jint did exactly that. Lafier reached a hand to adjust his gun's aim.

"When I give the signal, aim up and down and don't stop firing."

"Aye aye. Though I'm not super confident shooting at targets I can't see."

"You're such a lousy shot that whether or not you see them has no bearing."

"Thanks for giving it to me straight," he said, deflated.

"Now!" Having detected them with her *frocragh*, Lafier began firing.

Jint pulled the trigger with abandon, waving the gun up and down.

A shriek. *Ah, did I just shoot a dude?*

Maybe this was what they called the battlefield mentality. No rage, no guilt. If he had to name what was impelling him to pull that trigger, it was fear.

The **lightgun** itself wasn't visible in the dark. The points of light that hit the victims' bodies were. That light illuminated still more enemy soldiers that were being sent spinning. Their positioning allowed them to fire comfortably, but the enemy was not afforded the same, a gap very much borne out by the fruits of battle: a pile of corpses.

Jint was racked by nausea. Of course, just because the enemy had disadvantageous positioning didn't mean they had acted as targets and nothing else. The gleaming lines of fire chipped away at the granite in the cave walls. Rapid fire sprayed a point not even ten *dagh* away from him.

The cave's edge was alive with gunfire.

Jint took aim and strafed, firing continuously. The soldiers' guns glanced away, accompanied by screaming. Perhaps their arms had joined their guns in flying off.

The inside of his mouth was bone-dry.

Man, I'd give my **noble rank** *for a glass of cold water right now.*

This he thought with all seriousness, for that was all his **rank** meant to him.

The cave was lit by the dim glow of death. He could just make out an enemy hand move. Something came flying through the air.

"Jint!" Lafier kicked his right flank.

Jint immediately understood why she had. He rolled into a small grotto. Lafier slid in after him.

"C'mon, deeper!" Jint twined bodies with Lafier and raced for the inner recesses.

Suddenly, a blast wave bowled them over from behind. Jint pitched forward and tumbled twice over. He had failed to take into account how **lightgun cartridges** were nothing more than substitute bombs. They were virtually party poppers compared to real deal hand grenades.

The wave of intense heat squashed down on their backs.

"Hot hot hot!" Jint gritted his teeth.

Though they were on their stomachs, still they crawled forward. The crashing of copious rubble rumbled to their rear. It was a cave-in.

"Quick!" Jint somehow managed to get to his feet, and helped her up.

The collapse continued apace. The igneous rock, which had become brittle due to weathering, was coming off the walls, plummeting down onto Jint's shoulders.

Finally, a pause in the crumbling.

Jint looked back, but unfortunately could only see pitch darkness.

"What's the situation?" asked Jint, relying on Lafier's *frocragh*.

"We're sealed in."

"For real?"

"Why would I lie?"

"Right, right."

Jint set his gun to ILLUMINATE. The grotto was totally sealed. The ground above them had probably given way.

Jint wasn't sure how to interpret this turn of events. Maybe he should thank his stars this had saved them by keeping the enemy away. On the other hand, it was more than possible that this passage had no exit; for all he knew, this was their living tomb.

"In any case," said Jint, "let's keep going and see what's down there."

"I see no other choice."

That was when Jint noticed he'd lost the duffel bag. *Oh well*, thought Jint resignedly. He'd transferred the important things like cash and **lightgun cartridges** to his **pocket** anyway.

Jint switched out the used-up **cartridge** for another, and started down the pitch dark path.

"Enemy fleet found! Azimuth: 105-010. Distance: 0.12. Relative speed: 217.5 *üésdagh*. Ship number: around 20."

Cfadiss had picked up the planet of Clasbure using his *frocragh*. The group of **patrol ships** in the **recon sub-fleet** *Ftunéc* was also close by. So, too, was the shadow of the enemy vessels rising up to face them. The enemy ships were clearly aiming for what lay behind the *Ftunéc* — which was to say, the **Sfagnoff Portal**.

"Verification of enemy ships complete. They are thought to be 12 large-scale **supply ships**, one **patrol ship**, and six **assault ships**," said the **gunnery staff officer**. Our chances of victory are 0.987 in 1."

"Do we advise them to surrender?" Cfadiss asked his **commander, Associate Commodore** Sporr.

"No need. They would if they wanted to. And they must already understand what's in store for them," came Sporr's reply.

"Never mind that; prepare for **battle in 3-space**. Massed Battle Formation 5."

"Understood." Cfadiss translated Sporr's commands into reality.

Yet the enemy ships didn't budge. They came creeping up the spatial warps created by Clasbure's gravity.

"A transmission from the enemy," reported the **communications staff officer**. "It's a holovision transmission. Time gap: 0.23 seconds."

"Put it through."

A video link was established on the **Commander's Bridge**. Cfadiss was surprised. He had been expecting a high-level enemy officer, but here instead was an Abh male. Though his garments were dirty, and he wasn't wearing a **circlet**, the *froch* on his forehead, coupled with the iridescent blue hair and the face of beauty, betrayed his Abhness.

"Oh, so you're the **commander, Archduchess of *Laitpanh***." He flashed a wan smile. "Fancy we should meet under such circumstances."

"It's been a while, **Marquess of Sfagnoff**," she greeted him, inclining her head. "I never would have expected you to send a communication from aboard an enemy ship. What in heavens has transpired?"

"To my great shame, I've been taken prisoner. They told me they'd kill a child before my very eyes if I didn't send the message."

"I see." Sporr's eyes turned grim and severe. "Please, then, your message."

"'There are 21 Abhs in this fleet. My family, my **servants**, and the **starpilots** of the **communications fleet**. If our lives mean anything to you, then you will refrain from attacking. We also demand safe passage through **planar space**.'"

"If we were to abide by those demands, what will become of all of you?"

"I imagine we'd be sent to a prison camp or somesuch, **Archduchess**. In any case, they've been chased into such a desperate corner that they have no choice but to trust demands like these will hold water," he continued with a rather detached air.

"How fascinating."

"Truly, it is," nodded the Marquess. "Now, I bid you farewell, **Archduchess of *Laitpanh***. Fulfill your duty. Goodbye."

"Goodbye, **Marquess**."

The hologram cut out.

"I really hate him. The **Marquess**." Sporr bit the joint of her pinky, and stood up from her special-ordered chaise. "**Communications Staff Officer**."

"Yes."

"Connect me through to them."

"Through holovision, ma'am?"

"Sound-only is fine."

"Roger. Preparations complete. Please speak."

"This is the **Commandant** of the **recon sub-fleet** *Ftunéc*, **Associate Commodore** Sporr," she intoned imposingly. "Let the tolerance and generosity of the **Star Forces** be known, for we will give you a chance to surrender. We shall wait until the distance between us reaches 0.08 light-seconds. Needless to say, this is contingent upon you not laying a finger upon our compatriots. Allow me to stress, again, the magnanimity of the **Star Forces**. For should you waste this chance to surrender, then we have an even sweeter fate prepared. That is, you will get to reflect on what an honor it is to die alongside **Abh nobility** as you disintegrate into elementary particles! The atoms that composed your bodies will probably even fall back onto the **landworlds** that were your homes, after a few hundred million years of riding the galactic vortex."

A solemn silence gripped the **bridge**.

"Now transmit the following to all ships under my command. You needn't cipher it."

"Roger. Preparations complete."

"We will begin the attack at 0.08 light-seconds' distance. Once the assault has begun, you may ignore any **signal of surrender** from the enemy. Crush them completely. Show them no mercy, not even with *üicoc* (lifeboats). I shall take all responsibility and all of the blame!"

"Please wait!" Cfadiss stepped toward the **Commandant's Seat**.

"What, **Senior Staff Officer**!?" she said, her shoulders squared haughtily.

"Shooting an enemy that has surrendered would damage the reputation of the **Empire** and of the **Star Forces**."

She glared at him with her blazing crimson eyes. But Cfadiss had to stay his ground. "And it may not be my place to say it, but it would also stain the **crest** of the **Golden Crow**."

That seemed to have worked the effect he wanted. Sporr leaned against her **Commander's Seat** — crestfallen, Cfadiss perceived — and appeared to give the matter more thought.

When next she laid eyes on Cfadiss, a bewitching smile graced those venomously red lips. A shiver ran down the **Hecto-Commander**'s spine. It was no doubt the smile a cat would make when playing with its prey, if cats had slightly richer facial expressions.

"You're right, **Senior Staff Officer**. There's no beauty in assaulting an enemy that's surrendered. Let's not."

"I am grateful you have heeded my counsel," he answered warily.

"Incidentally, it's my prerogative how the prisoners of war are transferred, isn't it?"

"Yes. You are the highest-ranking commander here, *Lonh*." Cfadiss couldn't fathom why she would ask a question whose answer she already knew.

"Lovely. What is your estimate as to the enemy's numbers?"

"With 12 large-scale **supply ships**, I imagine there around 25,000 of them. That is, assuming their main cargo is people."

"I see. They could fit on a *Tarss*-class **supply ship**, couldn't they."

"They could, but..." Cfadiss furrowed his brow. He was only getting more and more confused; what was she scheming?

Tarss-class ships were small-scale supply ships that accompanied recon sub-fleets. There were also *rébhath* (personnel supply ships), but those housed 1,500 at the most. Even if they were to save on living quarter expenses by inducing cryogenic sleep on all of the new passengers, they would be able to fit in no more than around 10,000 people. If 25,000 people were to board, it'd be physically filled to capacity. Moreover, transporting prisoners of war required the presence of an appropriate number of **guard NCCs** aboard.

"Run the numbers, will you? We will be bringing 25,000 aboard a *Tarss* **supply ship**. How long will it take, by ship's time, to get them to the **imperial capital** *Lacmhacarh* traveling through **3-space**? And you needn't spare any thought to deceleration. I don't mind spending all of our fuel accelerating at two *daimon* of G-forces."

"Traveling only through **3-space?**" he asked back in spite of himself.

"Correct. Now calculate."

And so he was forced to start crunching the numbers.

"Distance from the enemy now 0.1 light-seconds," somebody reported expeditiously.

Using his **wristgear**, Cfadiss summoned up detailed specs of the *Tarss* class, and determined the acceleration duration and final velocity in view of the mass of 25,000 people and the food and water they would need. Making sure to apply the rotation speed of the galaxy in his calculations, he divided the distance to the **imperial capital** by the speed, then factored in the time dilation rate...

The result was just as absurd as he expected.

"It would take around 58,300 years..."

"Is that so," said Sporr. "I don't believe our prisoners would be too elated to discover it will take that long."

"I should think not..."

"Then let's make it a shorter, faster trip for them. They won't need a **space-time bubble engine,** nor a *roïlagac* (attitude control engine). Nor any **crewmembers**. While we're at it, let's do them the favor of removing the **gravity control system**. Though even then it'd be too heavy, wouldn't it? Have you included food and water in your calculations?"

"Yes, one year's worth, and then a hydroponic plantation facility of the smallest possible dimensions would need to—"

"Oh, there won't be any need for hydroponics. Get rid of it for them, won't you?"

"I could also remove their food, drinking water, and air purification system if you wish?" said Cfadiss, reluctantly setting foot on her train.

"Don't be stupid. They'd *die* if we did that. We could never be so cruel... Now then, the ship must have gotten quite light by now."

"Not appreciably lighter than before, I think..."

"Be a dear and run the numbers."

Cfadiss did so. "It will take about 49,100 years."

"See? We've saved them nearly 10,000 years. That's an appreciable difference, and I won't hear otherwise."

"Well, that is true, but…"

"**Communications Staff Officer!**" Sporr raised her **command baton** and let fly her orders. "I have a message for all ships. No ciphering. I'm amending my orders. You are to absolutely respect any inclination on their part to surrender. However, those who surrender only after battle has commenced will be taken to *Lacmhacarh* through **3-space** only. The **supply ship** that is to ferry them must, with an eye toward necessary time saving, be divested of frivolities such as its **space-time bubble engine, gravity control system,** and its **attitude control engine.** No **crewmembers** are to board, either. The prisoners shall be given one year's worth of food and water for their trip. The amount of time it will take them to arrive will vary depending on the number of prisoners, but as of now it's estimated at around 49,000 years. In addition, the maximum occupancy of the supply ship in question is 1,500. That is all."

"Please wait, *Lonh!*"

"Silence, **Senior Staff Officer**," she asserted. "This is my final decision. I will consider any further words of counsel as insubordination."

"What a *logh labyrena* (maddening maid)…" he blurted out.

Sporr put the back of the hand that was holding her **command baton** to her mouth and laughed a mighty, boisterous laugh. "Ho ho ho! I do like the sound of that title for me!"

Cfadiss was at a loss for words.

"Distance from the enemy now 0.09 light-seconds."

He stood stock still, focusing on the enemy ships he could sense through his *frocragh* were steadily increasing their relative velocity as they approached.

Then, abruptly, the increase in their relative velocity slowed. In fact, the only fleet accelerating was now the *Ftunéc*.

"The enemy has ceased accelerating," reported the **navigation staff officer**, lending yet greater credence to what Cfadiss's *frocragh* was telling him.

"The **signal of surrender**, ma'am," reported the **communications staff officer** with audible relief. "The enemy is requesting to be treated 'with magnanimity.'"

Phew. Cfadiss exhaled the hot air that had built up in his lungs.

"But of course," said Sporr, nonplussed. "I never fail to treat prisoners of war with the utmost lenience."

If what she had in store for them before was lenient, *then I'd hate to be treated "with the utmost lenience,"* thought Cfadiss.

"Lest you worry, we will be transporting them through *planar space*. I of course guarantee them a pleasant journey. If they're well-behaved and luck is on their side, they might even eventually tread their homelands through a prisoner exchange, and without even needing to get atomized first!"

"Allow me to relay," said the communications staff officer, who then faced the **console** and began the transmission.

"**Senior Staff Officer**."

"Yes?" Cfadiss replied nervously.

"I hate fussing over the little things. I've no desire to bother you, but..."

"Understood. I shall allocate ships to raid and commandeer the enemy's vessels at once."

"So quick on the uptake." She tapped her cheek with the tip of the **command baton**. "But always remember: I also hate being interrupted. Particularly when I'm giving orders."

"I apologize."

"Now then, make it so. Allot Numbers 1 and 2."

"As you command."

"The other **squadrons** will take control of Clasbure's skies. Is that agreeable?"

"As you command," repeated Cfadiss with a salute.

Two hours later, the recon sub-fleet *Ftunéc* took position 20 *saidagh* above Clasbure. Upon conducting surface recon, they discovered to their surprise that there were still several UH land war units deployed. It appeared that the troops aboard the captured freighter were a small part of a larger force.

The *Ftunéc* was not built for land war — though it'd have no trouble turning an entire planet into a lump of lava — so they advised the enemy troops to surrender from their station above, demanding order be restored to the **landworld citizens**. However, due to some powerful jamming, that message got scrambled, and they couldn't be sure it had made it to the surface.

The *Ftunéc* awaited the arrival of the land war units even as they prepared against potential attack from the surface.

Sporr sighed. "They sure don't know when to give up, do they? And *nahaineïocs* (war on a landworld) lacks all elegance, too. But I can't complain. Because fortunately, I won't be the one wielding command!"

Chapter 6: The *Bhoüécoth* (Great Chase)

The rattling din of tremors was followed by a fresh hail of stone shards.

"Looks like they haven't called it quits yet," said Jint, picking up his pace. "They're planning to blow up the blockage so they can get at us!"

"We ought to thank them for making us a path back," said Lafier.

"You know, as long as I'm with you, I've got nothing to fear. The universe is filled with hope."

Over an hour had passed since the battle. The two were still trudging through the cavern, with all of its many twists and turns. They could tell it was sloping upward now, albeit only slightly.

Which means we're headed towards the upper reaches, thought Jint.

They were tracing a line back up a tributary of the lava rivers that flowed across the planet several hundred million years ago. Once again, their ears were met with that familiar clamor. It seemed as though the path had not yet been cleared. Meanwhile, the passage was getting narrower, and Jint was feeling steadily more restless. He couldn't help but entertain the possibility that they'd soon hit either a dead end or a place too narrow for human traversal.

Sure enough, they reached a point where they could no longer walk side by side. Jint led the way and they advanced ever further, but they were losing confidence; was there any actual point to this long march of theirs?

At last, the **lightgun** shed light upon the end of the road. Gripped by despair, Jint stopped in his tracks.

"What's wrong?" asked Lafier.

"It's a dead end. There's nowhere to go from… wait, hold on…" Jint craned in to give it a closer look. It looked awfully *smooth* for a natural formation. Sliding his hand across its surface, he could tell it was, in fact, a crystal stoneware wall. He could even make out a seam running vertically down its center.

"This thing's a DOOR!" Jint shouted, astonished.

"A door?"

"Yeah. That's all it could be." Jint tried rubbing the door, pushing at it, and more, but it didn't open.

"There's something over there," said Lafier, clasping him by the shoulder and pointing toward the door's right.

He shone the light where she indicated, and found there some **controls**, along with the words FOR EMERGENCY USE. Timidly, Jint pressed the button.

The door split open, and a vertical line of light trickled through. That line would soon grow into a rectangle of light, which grew wider before their eyes. Jint squinted against the dazzling brightness, and took a cautious step.

Lafier followed, and scanned their surroundings. "Where are we?"

"Don't ask me…" Jint whispered, scarcely believing.

"Looks like an amusement park."

Easy-listening tunes were playing in the background. A sprawling flower bed lay in front of them, and beyond it, a short building made of stone. The shrill voices of children were audible from somewhere in the distance. On the footpath that ran the length of the flower beds, people were walking alongside various cartoony animals: bears, dogs, cats, elephants, serrows, walruses… each one was human size, and bipedal. Moreover, they were conversing with the kids, and performing tricks. They saw a deer sitting on the lawn giving several children a listen, and in another spot, they saw a lion juggling flaming torches. They were probably animatronics, but they could also be people in costumes. The horses were the only quadrupedal species among them. More were carrying children than not, and so they seemed to function as the park's means of transport. A fox in clown getup crossed right in front of them while riding a unicycle.

Jint watched the fox go by, and gazed up. The metal framework went quite high, as did the ceiling made of a semitransparent shroud, most likely **plastick**. Friendly-faced animatronics were dangling from the ceiling as they lifted excitable tots up and down. It was when he noticed each sported eight appendages that he realized they were spiders.

When he looked behind them, he found the door had already closed shut. THIS DOOR IS OFF LIMITS was written in large text.

Jint glanced Lafier's way, and beamed. "You look like trash!" And at that moment, that was all there was to say, for they were covered in grit and mud from head to toe, to say nothing of their dishevelled hair.

"You all the more," she replied as she patted at her clothes. "You look like someone rescued you from a garbage chute just as you were about to get disposed into space."

"I can imagine," said Jint, who patted the pebbles and assorted filth from his hair.

A child holding hands with a rhino pointed toward them.

"What a rude little snot, pointing and laughing at a **royal princess** like that."

"He was laughing at you."

Even under army occupation, the amusement park seemed to be thriving. A sense of security was simmering inside them. With this many noncombatant **landworld citizens**, particularly children, the UH wouldn't go all out on them.

"C'mon. If we're lucky, we may just come by some new clothes."

"Right."

But just as they were about to set off —

"Please stop," came a voice from above. "You have entered the park from an entrance other than the proper, prescribed entryway. Kindly wait as our security personnel come to ask you about your situation. If you do not comply, be advised that we may report you to the police."

They looked up toward the voice's source, and there hung a giraffe's head. Though its shoulders were around the same height off the ground as a human's, its neck exhibited the primary feature of the giraffe in spades.

"Not happening!" Jint urged Lafier to follow him as he booked.

"PLEASE STOP, PLEASE STOP, PLEASE STOP..." The giraffe waddled awkwardly after them.

"Attention, customers," sounded the parkwide announcement. "A state of emergency has arisen. We repeat, this is a state of emergency. We truly apologize for the inconvenience, but we will be closing *GUZONH* DREAM PARK temporarily. You will be refunded. Please line up at the exit and leave the premises. As long as you conduct yourselves in an orderly fashion, no harm will come to you. Kindly follow the instructions of the staff, and exit calmly and safely. We sincerely await your next visit. We repeat: This is a state of emergency…"

"What is this 'state of emergency'?" asked Lafier.

Jint looked at the gun in his hand, then at the giraffe chasing them. "If it's not us, then I couldn't tell you."

In Clasbure's infancy, this place was a lake of lava. From that lake flowed two rivers. The wider river carried large quantities of boiling hot rocks from the lake, while its less impressive counterpart merged with other lava flows and poured into the wider one in the end. When the planet "reached puberty," the supply of lava ceased, and the lake dried up. The lava either chilled and hardened right there in the lake (thereby contributing to its diminishing size), or it got carried away by the rivers. The lava that hardened after drifting away became parts of Clasbure's crust. After that, it became surrounded by precipitous cliffs, making for an enormous cavity.

Then humans arrived, built cities nearby, and racked their brains for ways to make use of this giant hollow. Turning it into farmland would require laying paths for the agriculture-bots, but the amount they could expect to harvest from the land wasn't enough to make those costs worth the trouble. After much wrangling, a plan emerged to make it a zoo. One could create a sealed environment simply by covering the hollow with a circular roof. They would split the area into two separate areas, rainforest and grassland, and then populate them with flora and fauna that had never been transplanted to Clasbure. The proponent of this idea was lauded and praised, and the matter was settled: a zoo would be constructed there. A company was created, and funds collected, to realize their vision. Nothing stood in the way of their project — or so most believed.

The stormy patch came to pass when the roof was completed. The age-old notion that trapping animals in cages was unethical returned in vogue, and commanded a significant chunk of public opinion. The counterargument that the enclosures wouldn't be overly cramped fell on deaf ears, ignored as a trifling distinction. Ultimately, the choice was made to employ cartoony animatronics in place of real living animals; the academic undercurrent of the project had been forgotten somewhere along the way, as much that is related to things "academic" tends to be.

With the exception of a handful of animal ecologists, the citizenry was largely satisfied with this outcome. After all, actual animals didn't do tricks (since training animals was nothing more than a crime of anthropocentrism), nor could they hold a conversation with children. To top it all off, they exuded intolerable bodily odors, and resorted to violence whenever they found something to their distaste. It was far easier to feel safe leaving the little ones with animatronic friends than with beasts of nature. Those who deposited their children could either devote their efforts to work, or enjoy more adult avenues of entertainment.

At present, the 70th anniversary of *Guzonh* Dream Park's founding was close at hand.

"They're here! I was so on the money I could hug someone," said Inspector Entryua inside *Guzonh* Dream Park's administrative office. "But something's off. There's not enough of 'em."

"We've found the Abh, though!" said Keitt, eyes starry.

"True enough."

Meanwhile, *Guzonh* Dream Park's manager, who had had to return the admittance fees today's customers paid, stared at the screen with annoyance. "Honestly, I've got a feeling we're going a bit overboard here. They're still just kids, aren't they? Though they are a bit old to be regular clients of ours, I'll give you that."

"That 'kid' meted death on my comrades-in-arms," said the Military Police Captain, grim in the face. "They are brutal killers."

"Uh, huh…" The manager shot Entryua a questioning look.

"Like I said, you've got no reason to worry. I'm sure the occupation will pay for any losses."

"Well, I'm not so sure. Who knows how long they'll even be sticking around, what with recent events…" The manager was about to continue that train of thought, but then Keitt's eyes were on him, and he clammed up.

"What?" said Entryua, curious.

"Around a half hour back, the radio-wave-controlled birds started going on the fritz, you see…" he elaborated, glancing intermittently Keitt's way as he spoke. "So I had the technician look at them, and he told me the machinery was flawless; it's the radio waves that're getting jammed. And wouldn't you know it, the wireless is out of commission, too."

"And?"

"Inspector," Keitt cut in. "We have no time. Let's go get her in cuffs."

"Please don't rush this. We can't round them up until all of the customers have evacuated. They're armed, remember?"

"But what if they hide themselves within the crowd and escape!?"

"Look, we've got surveillance cameras on them, and I've placed some of my people at the exits. Now then, Mr. Manager, hit me with the rest."

"There's not much else to add," he said, disinclined to continue but compliant all the same. "Apart from my own speculation, that is. Who's jamming the airwaves, I ask you? There's only one solid possibility. Why're they doing it? Again, there's no two ways about it. So I have trouble believing you haven't already pieced it together yourself, Mr. Inspector."

"I was out of the loop. Stuck here the whole time. Come to think of it, I haven't gotten any reports from my people in a hot minute. It just hadn't been *that* long since the last word, so I didn't think much of it…"

"Well, thanks to them, we're forced to give the machines simple instructions through voice command. See for yourself." The manager poked at the screen. "See the giraffe chasing them? You might think you want to see the video feed from its eyes, but look what you get." The manager changed the channel, and a cloud of dust appeared on screen.

"You know something, don't you?" said Entryua, his eyes on Keitt. "Was there some kind of hiccup up in space?"

"I know nothing of this," Keitt denied, defensively. "I was with you the whole time, Inspector. Don't you see we're in the same boat?"

"But I saw you taking a peek at your portable computer from time to time," said Entryua. "Maybe you got notified through it. About the radio jamming, and what's behind it."

"That is a matter of internal military communications. It has nothing to do with you, Inspector," replied Keitt, his expression looking stiff indeed.

"Is that right?" Entryua adopted a gentler tone. "I seem to recall that you're expected to keep reporting to your brass about how the search is going.

Yet now that the Abh's turned up, you didn't even try to report in. Tell me, what's that about? I'll tell you what I think. It's because you know you can't. Give it to me straight, Captain old pal. I trust you do know the reason why. And if you try to hide it, well, me and my people, we're going to start feeling a mighty urge to slack off on the job."

"Do you mean to threaten me!?" Keitt turned white-faced and hot-blooded.

"Damn right I do. Intimidation's a tool of the trade for us. Most suspects aren't usually very cooperative, if you catch my drift."

"Fine," said Keitt, his expression intense and upset. "I did receive additional word at 11:55 military time, which is to say, thirty-seven minutes ago. I was told that radio interference would be conducted starting at 12:00 military time, and that while sending notice or orders would be unavailable for the time being, I was to continue my current mission."

"And the reason behind the jamming is?"

"That, I don't know. I honestly haven't been informed. You're going to have to believe me."

"I see," said Entryua, narrowing his eyes.

No, he didn't seem to be lying. It didn't matter how different their culture or upbringing was — he was quite confident he could tell whether somebody was lying by looking at them. But while this was disappointing news for Entryua, he could infer even without a clear-cut answer from him.

"The Abh're back, aren't they?" he muttered.

"Please wait!" said the white rhinoceros.

"Please wait!" said the emperor penguin.

"Please wait!" said the puma.

Jint and Lafier were surrounded on all sides by charming animal friends. Since there were no children left to entertain, it appeared they had no other tasks to fulfill.

"Step aside!" Lafier thrust her **lightgun** at the head of a beaver.

"Please wait!" said the beaver, with its adorable buck teeth.

"You aren't sentient creatures, correct?" asked Lafier.

"Yes, that is correct. We have no free will." The beaver closed one eye. "However, we ask that you keep that fact from the children. It would shatter their dreams."

"We've no choice. Jint, we're destroying them."

"Got it!" Jint yelled. "Can't say I'm too thrilled, though; they're so endearing."

"I'm none too thrilled, either," said Lafier, though she didn't hesitate to shoot the beaver down. "Sadly, we've no other options. If we linger here, they'll come for us. Besides, you weren't fussed when you were shooting at other human beings."

"Only because they were shooting at us, too. And most importantly, they weren't all that cute, either."

"Warning!" said the animals simultaneously, raising their voices. "We are property of *Guzonh* Dream Park, and if you destroy us without cause, you will be committing vandalism, as well as charged with indemnities for all damaged goods. Incidentally, the average price for one of us is…"

"Then you'd best retreat while you're still intact!" she said, slicing the puma to rounds. Yet the animals didn't flinch at the death of a comrade; on the contrary, this simply allowed them to tighten their circle around them even closer.

"Sorry about that…" said Jint, who'd shot down a hyena, though given that the hyena was the one most often made to play the villain, he didn't feel too guilty over it.

"Nooo!" shrieked the manager, cradling his head as he witnessed his valuable assets become so much scrap.

"See, I told you they were brutal killers," said Keitt, his face the picture of smug.

But the manager wasn't paying him any attention. "Run away from the intruders! Function 24 is rescinded!" His orders reached the animatronics through the parkwide announcement speakers.

The animatronics turned their backs to the interlopers. When he saw that the two of them ceased firing in response, the manager's shoulders relaxed with relief.

"Have the animatronics withdraw," said Entryua. "They'll only get in the way of the arrest."

"We can't through voice command. Either the technicians will have to go to them directly, or we have to direct them through radio command. But never mind that, Mr. Inspector," said the manager, glowering at Entryua angrily, "What are you still doing here? Go and catch them already, please!"

Entryua shrugged. "That's why I told you to let me place some of my people by the emergency exit. You were the one who was against it because it could 'damage the park's reputation.'"

"Okay, I was wrong, I admit it. So please…"

"We can't go in until the parkgoers have evacuated. We're the cops people love and respect, and we aim to keep it that way," said Entryua, who then pointed at one of the screens.

It was the terminal screen of the **compucrystals** pertaining to visitor management, and it showed that there were still one hundred and twenty parkgoers left. That number hadn't changed much in some time, either. For one reason or another, the hundred and twenty stragglers seemed reluctant to exit.

"But there aren't any near them," the manager fired back.

"He's right," said Keitt. "Let's move to apprehend them at once. Because we can't use phones, communications will take that much longer."

"And whose fault is it that we can't drop them a line?" said Entryua, who pushed his smoke into the ashtray. "Though you have got a point there. I guess we do go and get 'em now."

"Let's," nodded Keitt vigorously.

Any sign of humans in the vicinity vanished while the two were playing tag with the park's menagerie. The mechanical fauna was still present, but it didn't try to approach them. That said, they didn't avoid them, either.

"Sorry," said Jint, who almost bumped into a squirrel.

"No, I apologize," said the squirrel, which continued on its merry way.

At the moment, the duo were stuck in a veritable labyrinth. On each side of the lane, store display cases vied for their attention. The cases contained all sorts of products, including clothing, convenience goods, and stationery, all bearing animal designs. Tending shop were the animatronics.

Jint stopped by the front of a clothing store, and glanced at his filthy **jumpsuit**, but he quickly gave up on the idea. They had no time to spare appraising articles at their leisure, or to change. The layout of the alleyways was complex, and they still hadn't managed to stumble upon a wider path. By looking up at the ceiling, they could tell they were near the center, but they hadn't the faintest clue in which direction lay the exit.

The animals minding each store were scrutinizing them rather fixedly, but they never appealed to them to purchase their wares.

"Wait," Jint told Lafier, who had begun to outpace him.

"What?"

"I just thought of something. Let's ask the animals where the exit is."

"Good idea," she concurred.

Jint drew toward an otter-staffed shop selling miscellaneous merchandise.

"Welcome!" The otter spread its stubby arms invitingly.

While Jint didn't give the variety of commodities on offer much of a scan, he did notice they all bore otter designs.

"What will you be purchasing?"

"No, uh…" Jint faltered.

"Ah, yes, I understand. Anything is fine as long as my picture's on it. Here, take our featured product." It picked up a nail file in its paws. "The price point's reasonable, and it works like magic. Not to mention you could always use another nail file, since they're easy to lose, plus…"

"That's not what I'm here for," Jint interrupted. "I'd like to ask you where the exit is."

"What did you say!?" shouted the otter. "You're leaving so soon? Please, stay and enjoy the day with us just a little while longer. You could at least stand to take a look at the nail file. Has something got you in a hurry?"

"Haven't you heard? The park's temporarily closed."

"You jest. *Guzonh* Dream Park is open 24 hours…"

"I said temporarily. Are you gonna tell me or not?"

"How cold. I suppose it can't be helped. Go straight down this lane…" And so the otter gave him the directions.

Jint thanked it and took his leave. "It's over there!" he told Lafier, and together they once again trotted forward.

Suddenly, the rip of an explosion.

"They must've missed the emergency exit **controls**," said Jint.

"Who the!? Who's the idiot that…!?" cried Entryua inside the command car.

He thought some subordinate of his had been careless enough to jump the gun and start the attack. Then it dawned on him that no officers were equipped with explosive weapons. Or at the very least, his people weren't.

Then, could it have been the Abh? Was she trying to massacre officers who wielded only **needleguns**? But that didn't make sense, either. It hadn't come from the direction the Abh currently was thought to be.

At last, he remembered the other guys who were after the Abh. "Looks like your comrades are here," said Entryua, glancing at Keitt.

"Is that so?" The military police captain hung his head.

Entryua thought about calling it a day then and there. He'd been less than enthusiastic about this whole venture to begin with, and if the police did lay off, they'd be detained by the occupying army anyway. They were talking about one or two petty car thieves here. In the end, he could afford to forget about getting them under their custody…

No! We can't back down now! They'd come this far, come so close… or, more accurately, they'd put up a net around where those soldiers were chasing them toward, but in any case, he couldn't stand idly by and let perfect strangers take the credit while the suspects were so tantalizingly in reach.

"Hey, pedal to the metal!" he said, jabbing at the driver's back.

"There's nothing for it, Inspector," said the young officer. "These cutesy-wootsies don't seem to know traffic laws!" And even as they spoke, a blissful looking tanuki came very close to smashing into them.

"Because we're not on the road!" Entryua banged his right shoulder against the back of the seat. "If it was going to be like this, I should've taken a hoverboat!"

"Do we call for backup?"

"You think we've got that kind of time, dummy!?"

A big BOOM from behind. A patrol car was sticking out of a building from the front. Meanwhile, the tanuki peeped with evident concern.

Entryua heaved a sigh. This was turning into more of a laugh-and-cry procedural drama than he'd been anticipating.

"EMERGENCY, EMERGENCY!" shouted the speakers frantically. "Customers still within the premises, please hasten to the exits. We can't be held liable for your safety any longer. As for the parkgoers, no, the trespassers who blew up the emergency exit, we ask that you refrain from making a commotion on park grounds, and to exercise discretion with your acts of destruction! For heaven's sake, what could possibly warrant going to such extremes!?"

"Over there, Inspector!" Keitt pointed forward.

There stood a young pair, a boy and a girl. The girl's hair was black, but she had on an Abh **circlet**.

"Go, go, go!" Entryua roared. The sooner he was free of this farce of an errand, the better.

"They found us!" Jint froze in his tracks.

A row of **hovercars** crossed over toward them. Lafier tried to brandish her gun, but Jint had snapped to, and seized her hand. "No! Not here, at least! Let's go back to the market area!"

She cocked her head, doubtful, but soon she nodded assent. The pair turned on their heels.

"Wait right there! This is the police!" a menacing voice resounded through a megaphone.

Jint wondered how many people in the whole galaxy would actually stop when told to.

"Inspector, we can't go any farther!" The command vehicle came to a sudden stop. It was true that the "road" in front of their eyes could hardly be called a road at all. Not even three people could walk side-by-side down the lane safely, let alone a car. If they were to cut a swath through the shops, it would be a different matter, but an officer of the law beloved by the citizenry would never do that.

"Employees, evacuate as well!" continued the announcement. "Those with Level 3 or higher technician qualification, adjust as many animatronics as possible for automatic storage. If you're in either Area 6 or 7, evacuate regardless. Get a move on! C'mon, get! Bloody hell, what's it all come to!?"

"Everybody out!" said Entryua, commanding his officers to alight from the cars.

He took the initiative and issued the same order to the subsequent patrol cars as well. Not being able to use phones was frustrating.

A police squad of twenty formed a line on the street. The suspects weren't in plain view, having seemingly ducked into either a store or a side street somewhere.

"All hands, ready, aim."

The officers whipped out their **needleguns**, and switched off their safeties in unison. Keitt took that as his cue to do likewise and set his own weapon to fire.

"Now, after them!" Entryua rushed into the maze of alleyways.

Military Police Captain Keitt and the twenty-strong police squad followed in after him.

"Sorry, coming through!" said Jint as he climbed over the display case of a turtle's parlor.

The turtle simply shrugged without a word.

"You will forgive us," said Lafier, as she too climbed over it.

The turtle quickly made its way past the side of the horned owl sitting with its back to the turtle's.

"Bad children!" said the owl, whose merchandise they'd just rendered in disarray. "Bad children! You're being very bad!"

"Sorry!" said Jint, without looking back.

"May I draw your attention to something?" said Lafier through pants and gasps.

"What?"

"We're going down the same path as before."

"I mean, what else can we... oh." Jint remembered now. "The enemy soldiers are here, too, aren't they."

"You forgot? You are so easy-going it's impressive. You have my admiration."

"...Thanks..."

"Well if it isn't you! Weren't you going to leave?" said the otter from before. "Might as well have you buy something now, if you don't mind!"

"Got any hoverboats or spaceships?" Jint asked while rushing past storefronts.

"Of course we do!" answered the otter enthusiastically.

"Say what?" Before he knew it, Jint was looking over his shoulder.

The otter waved a toy spaceship in its hand. It probably had one or more otters on it, too. Behind the otter, the distant forms of police officers came peeking into view.

"Crap." Jint veered right, where there was a conveniently-placed side path. This time they wouldn't have to rough up any stores.

"Lafier, this way!"

"Huh? Where are you headed, sir!?" shouted the otter, rearing up.

"So you won't come quiet, huh!?" The officer's voice pelted them from behind.

That lane didn't connect to any lateral paths. Right in front of it sprawled a lawn, and beyond it they could make out a stone building. Jint was suffering from some mild agoraphobia, since in a wide-open space, he felt as though bullets and lasers could come flying from any direction. Yet this was the only option left to them.

Argh, give me a damned break, Entryua seethed. *Kids are reaching sexual awareness age, and here I am, dashing like mad chasing perps on foot like some caveman. Why's it gotta be this way? If the comms were online, I could've avoided this travesty. I could've laid back in the command car, split everyone into teams of two to search the maze, and then come running right when they'd been smoked out.*

He sized Keitt up beside him. Though he was technically older than him, bodily he was still young, so he wasn't breathing heavily. He was truly jealous in that moment, even rueful.

He swerved in his tracks by gripping a pillar of the store at the corner as he ran. He saw them. The backs of his quarry.

"Give it a rest!" Entryua took a knee and assumed firing stance. "Stop or I shoot!"

But by the time he heard his words of warning, Jint had already slipped away from the path. Naturally, they had no intention of stopping. They hid in an alleyway blind spot, but the moment they did, they snapped to a shout from their left.

A green-brown uniform. An enemy soldier. An adversary even more of a hassle to deal with than the police, but this soldier was alone.

Lafier took him down in a flowing martial arts throw before he could fire. "Jint, we must hurry. That soldier was one of many who have spread out to search for us. The others have been signaled."

"Don't need to tell me that…" Jint picked up into a run once again.

Their destination for the time being was the stone building. Though he had a bad feeling that its stone walls would serve as much protection as construction paper against the enemy's boulder-shattering crusher-bullets, it was probably more reliable than the marketplace.

However, they hadn't even made it halfway across the lawn before another enemy soldier appeared. Lafier didn't stop running as she mowed down the soldier brandishing their gun in a standing position.

Jint gripped a **lightgun cartridge** from his **pocket** and set it to grenade mode. He could feel it chirping its countdown in his hand. *CHEE CHEE CHEE CHEE…* He'd cultivated his pitching arm in many a match of *minchiu*, but given the distance, he couldn't be certain his lob would reach that far.

Which is why, when the soldier joined clods of dirt in the air, he reassessed the power of his throw. Unfortunately, these soldiers neither quailed nor flinched. Fresh infantry came out of the woodwork, one after the other.

Lafier, for her part, stayed a step ahead, firing her **lightgun** over her shoulder with her right hand while never taking her eyes away from their destination. Despite the fact that she wasn't even looking at her targets, her aim was always true, thanks to her *frocragh*. In this situation, her spatiosensory perception manifested like a feat of sorcery. An Abh with a **circlet** equipped had as good as 360 degree vision — she could sense motion in her surroundings through ultrahigh frequency waves. As such, she had no need to stop or turn to take aim.

Still, the bullets came hurtling their way, and with ever swelling intensity. A cloud of dust struck a mere five *dagh* away from Jint.

We're almost there...

Lafier stamped in through the wide-open entrance.

All right, my turn now.

He got within arm's reach of the entrance.

"What in the hell!?" Entryua reflexively ducked for cover, face-down on the ground.

It was when they'd almost cleared out of the alleyway in hot pursuit of the Abh that the firefight unfolded — a shoot-out the likes of which Clasbure had never before seen.

Guess that's the difference between a police force and a military. He knew it was pitiful, but he was too scared to even raise his head.

"Retreat!" ordered Entryua, plucking up his willpower. His voice, too, was nearly drowned out entirely by the gunfire. "We're heading back. This is no place for police."

"You can't be serious, Inspector!" Keitt objected. "You're giving up!?"

"What do you think!?" Entryua barked back. Though he was just as much lashing out against his own cowardice. "What exactly do you want us to do, huh, buddy!? 'Cause if you ask me, we'd just be a bunch of brats swearing we're strong to career boxers as they're slugging it out. I don't know what it's like on *your* world, but on this planet, police aren't trained or equipped to survive an active warzone. Now listen good, 'cause let me tell you, no matter how many cops you get killed in the line of duty, society won't value their capture any higher. And if you wanna catch the Abh that badly, I suggest you go join your little friends."

"Urgh..."

A round of crusher-bullets pierced through a handful of shops and flew inches beside Entryua, demolishing an animatronic.

"Your aim is goddamned terrible!" Entryua cursed them out, knowing full well they couldn't hear him. Then he faced his subordinates to address them. "What're you doing!? Fall back! Retreat to the cars. Keep your heads low and run. Damn it all to hell, coming to a place like this was a mistake!"

"Jint, come quickly!" Half of Lafier's body was poking out of the doorway, and she made ample use of her **lightgun** to defend him.

Jint slid in through the door hands first.

"Welcome!" It was a restaurant. The server rabbits flapped their ears in salutations. Needless to say, there were no customers, no other humans.

Jint swiftly scanned their surroundings. There was another entryway at the other side. It probably led to the kitchen.

Lafier was still returning fire.

"C'mon!" he said, dragging her by the sleeve.

"Okay." With three final barrages of gunfire, she ran deeper inside.

"Hello, how many in your party? I'll lead you to your seats," said one of the rabbits.

"Thank you, but there are many empty seats, so that's fine," he said, before heading for the kitchen.

"Sir, you can't go there!" The rabbit tried to deter him.

Meanwhile, the enemy was positioning themselves and making preparations outside. Jint noticed through the window and screamed: "GET DOWN!"

The only one that understood was Lafier, but that was to be expected, considering the designer of the animatronics' artificial intelligence could have never foreseen a gun battle.

It was a savage assault. The stone walls weren't as paper-thin as Jint had feared, but they weren't sturdy enough to withstand the attack. The walls came crumbling down while stone shards sprayed through the air. Crusher-bullets flew in from the where the walls collapsed, filling the restaurant with fiery death. Rabbit heads and parts tumbled across the floor.

"Warning!" Several rabbits looked out from the holes in the walls. "We are property of Guzonh Dream Park, and if you destroy us without cause, you will be committing vandalism, and be charged with indemnities for all damaged goods. Incidentally, the average price for one of us is—"

The roar of the enemy's firearms blew away the rabbits and their futile warnings.

"Lafier, are you okay!?"

"Of course I am, the **Kin of the Stars** would never…"

"Gotcha," Jint cut in. He started crawling along. "Now let's hurry!"

"Okay."

"Sir." A rabbit looked down at him. "It's dangerous here. We believe it may be in your best interest to evacuate."

"Thanks for the heads-up. I had a feeling the place wasn't the height of safety." It lifted Jint's spirits to exhibit the will to crack wise even during a nightmare like this.

Right after their exchange, the rabbit took a bullet and fell to ruin.

"Dammit!" Jint's high note proved brief, for now he was enraged. While he knew he'd been guilty of destroying a hyena, it was still a thing of woe to watch a being that traded some words with him get blasted apart.

The motion sensor door opened up for the two, and Lafier followed Jint into the kitchen. The kitchen was unscathed, practically a world removed, but they couldn't use it indefinitely. They got on their feet and ran between all of the cooking bots.

Another door, another room. They found themselves in a hallway, likely employee-use-only, with a number of doors on each side.

Suddenly, Lafier collapsed in a heap on the spot.

"What's wrong!? Are you hurt!?"

"No…" A weak smile, so weak as to ill fit an Abh. "How pathetic of me. It seems I'm exhausted."

"Wait, don't tell me you've got a *weakness*?" he said, though he commiserated. Abh bodies weren't used to running for long stretches, especially not at twice the gravity level of their everyday living environment.

This was Lafier, though. There was no question she'd pretend to be doing fine while burning through every last drop of energy in her.

How many hours had they been running? Three? Four? They'd stopped at points, and walked some stretches, but most of the time they'd jogged, and over the course of the last half hour, they'd been scampering with all of their might. Of course, Jint could hardly be described as a monster of stamina himself. He hadn't noticed earlier by dint of all the mortal peril, but he was so tired he could throw up at any moment.

"But we've still gotta go." Jint gulped down his nausea and fashioned a smile. "C'mon, I'll give you a shoulder."

"Thank you." Lafier offered a hand.

Jint helped her up and carried her arm on his shoulder. "Better yet, I'll give you a piggy-back ride."

"Don't mock me!"

"That's the Lafier I know," said Jint, relieved. Obviously, they couldn't sprint anymore. They were going as fast as they could, but that was no faster than normal walking speed, (or maybe slower).

"Hey, the enemy's gotta be pretty tuckered, too," said Jint, trying to cheer both himself and Lafier up.

The soldiers had chased after them on foot through that cave, and with all that heavy equipment weighing them down, at that. Of course, land wars were their expertise, and as such they must have undergone training to prepare them for lengthy foot marches while bearing heavy equipment, but he chose not to dwell on that inconvenient factoid.

Besides, when he focused on the sensation of Lafier's weight on his shoulders, his train of thought shifted tracks entirely.

She would never have leaned on his shoulders in the past, not this easily. She would've obstinately insisted Jint take the navigation log and go it alone.

His heart rejoiced.

Chapter 7: The *Üamh Gymehynr* (Horse of Dream Park)

They went through the closest door on the left. To neither's surprise, it was another kitchen, but more of a café's than a restaurant's. For one, it was much narrower than the other one, and secondly, the cooking bots were smaller models.

The building shook. Enemy gunfire pressed unrelenting. But they couldn't hope for better; what Jint feared most was them storming in. If the troops swarmed them, they'd have no leeway to fight back.

"Sit." There were no chairs, so he sat her down alongside the wall.

"What are you going to do?"

"I'm gonna play at burglar."

"We have no time."

"I know, but it's a necessary evil." Jint searched the place for a bottle of spring water, and handed one to Lafier. "We need to hydrate."

Still leaning against the wall, Lafier took the bottle in her hands and started drinking. Some of the pure spring water trickled out of her lips and wet her clothes.

Jint also drank about half a bottle's worth of the stuff. It was as though the water got sucked up before it even reached his stomach.

Lafier savored a moment. Then she said: "If the *üass béïcaiberér* (head chamberlain) were here to see this… It would cause a seizure."

Jint took two *sineucec* (cups) from the tableware washer as he asked: "Really particular about etiquette, I take it?"

"Yep. I got scolded constantly. However, seeing as I'm able to conduct myself with the utmost grace in a space-time that demands it, I think the chamberlains wouldn't fret too much."

"I'll take your word for it, though sadly, I still haven't come across the patch of space-time you speak of. In which reality do you conduct yourself with the utmost grace?" As they spoke, Jint inspected the niche-like depressions along the wall.

"Shut up, I'm always the picture of grace."

"Yeah?"

"Say one more word and I'll rip you to pieces."

"Well, I can't have that." Jint dared not defy her.

He placed a **cup** on the niche that read "GRAPE-FLAVORED CONCENTRATED SUGAR WATER" in Baronh. The liquid in question trickled into the glass.

He gave it a taste. It was grape-flavored concentrated sugar water all right. It smelled of grapes. Its texture felt viscous in the mouth. And it was so sweet it'd make an ant balk.

It was undiluted concentrate mixed with either booze or carbonated water. Normally, he'd have hated it, but right now, it tasted strangely good.

He filled the other **cup** and handed it to Lafier. "Drink."

Lafier took a sip. "In another time and place, I would've felt slighted by this."

"What our systems need right now is sugar."

"I know." Lafier gulped down the thick concoction in one go. Then she washed out the aftertaste with more spring water.

"Let's go," he said, offering a hand up.

"You needn't lend me your shoulder now. The sugar has had its effect." Yet she staggered on her feet, and she had to keep herself up by leaning against the hall with a hand.

"You can be the Abhest Abh ever, there's no way your metabolism's that fast. Don't push yourself so hard." Once again, he lent her a shoulder.

"Uh-huh..." She was still thirsty, so she started walking while drinking.

An explosion flared far too close for comfort, and the door into the hallway buckled.

There was no one in the café on the other side — neither animatronics, nor, of course, people. He was glad; nobody would be accosting them over something or other.

They exited the establishment, out onto a wide path of soft stone. Jint took Lafier's gun, and gave her spring water to hold instead.

Lafier took another sip, shook the remaining bottle, and pulled an inquisitive expression.

Jint shook his head.

Lafier threw it aside. The **plastick** bottle dropped to a useless little thud and rolled away.

"If that **chamberlain** saw you do that just now…"

"The consequences would be far graver than a mere seizure." Lafier squinted gleefully.

A horse approached them from in front: "It's naughty to litter."

"Sorry," Jint apologized in spite of himself.

"Are you tired?" The horse about-faced and began walking with them.

"Yes. Very," he confided.

"Would you like a ride?"

"You'd do that for us?" said Jint, startled. He looked the horse in its forehead, which sported a star.

"I would. It's my job, after all."

"Thank you so much. But we're more than just tired. We're also in a hurry."

"I can help with that, too."

"Sweet." Jint gave the **royal princess** a hitch up the horse's back, and handed back her gun. Then he straddled it behind her.

"You're quite heavy, little ones. You're actually grown-ups, aren't you?" it groused.

"We're just kids with weight problems."

"I sometimes give rides to pairs of smaller children, but two kids that're this big at the same time is a first."

"Can't hack it?"

"Oh, don't worry, I absolutely can."

"Great. Take us to the exit, if you don't mind."

"Without telling your mommy or daddy?"

"Daddy's at home. For us both." He had no idea how many hundreds of light-years away the **imperial capital** *Lacmhacarh* and the **Countdom of Hyde** were, but he spoke naught but the truth.

"Then we're off." It broke into a trot. Lafier held onto its neck, while Jint grabbed the reins. The horse's speed was on par with a dead sprinting human's, so they could probably gain quite some distance.

The building they'd hid inside was extensive, but soon its edge came into view. Lafier straightened her gun arm. They arrived in close proximity to the building. Ten or so soldiers were lying in wait, but it appeared the sight of the two cavaliers took them by surprise. They were a second slow to react. Invisible beams of light promptly burst from her muzzle. In the blink of an eye, they passed through a narrow gap, and a similar building obstructed them on the right hand side.

"Can you pick up the pace a bit!?" Jint asked their steed.

"It'd be no trouble for me, but it'd be dicey for you."

"We'll be fine, trust us."

"If you say so. Tell me if you ever think it's unsafe." With that, the horse sped up to about 500 *üésdagh* per hour.

Unsafe was right. Unlike a **hovercar** or a **conveyance ship**, a horseback ride came with a great share of shaking. Jint stuck his feet into the stirrups and struggled to stay mounted.

"Jint, you'd best lean back," said Lafier.

He gripped the reins for dear life and bent backward. He could swear he felt the laser graze past his chin.

Upside-down soldiers started firing at them from an upside-down world, shooting blindly from their cover behind buildings.

"Ahh!" His chest felt constricted. He could do nothing but hold on, and that powerlessness redoubled his terror.

Lafier's **lightgun** gouged at the corners of the buildings and took out enemy troops.

They passed by yet more buildings, and since the enemy fire died down, Jint exerted himself and sat back up.

A hemispherical facility greeted their eyes. The horse ran past it and turned right.

"Not there!" Jint panicked.

There were soldiers to the right. And while they were considerably far away, he had to suppose they were well within shooting range.

"How come? I'm taking a shortcut," the horse objected.

"Just not there!!"

While he bickered with a horse, one appeared from behind the hemisphere.

The space was akin to a plaza, with a fountain at its center, and surrounded by facilities of various shapes and configurations. To their right was a three-story town of pink coral, with an avenue as straight as an arrow. Meanwhile, soldiers lined up far down their current avenue, sending bullets their way all at once.

Lafier herself had already started shooting. Jint extended his own right arm (the fact that he hadn't dropped his gun deserved some credit, if he did say so himself) and pulled the trigger.

For a moment, the fruit of their deadly exchange was unclear, but the enemy had numbers on their side, and the horse was in any case exposed to a dense hail of fire. Luckily, they didn't score any direct hits, yet the vicinity bloomed with discharges and detonations. The stench of gun smoke curled across showers of soft stone shards.

"It's gotten harder to run. What's going on over there?" said the horse, not knowing just how valid its concern was.

"Faster!" Jint screamed, during a pause in the crossfire.

"Even faster? All right, here goes." The horse accelerated into a headlong gallop. In so doing, it cleared two thirds of the plaza space without sustaining any fire.

"Jint!" Lafier yelled in warning. "To your right, on that roof!" Thinking fast, Jint grabbed onto the saddle's cantle and leaned hard left. Lafier resumed fire just as a shot darted toward them. It grazed his sleeve, ripping it and leaving a welt.

"Crrhh!" Jint gritted his teeth.

"More from behind!"

Jint turned to look, to find three enemies in pursuit on horseback. They must have learned from their example and struck a deal with some wandering steeds.

"I can't manage all of them; you have my faith," said Lafier.

"You say that, but…"

The improvised cavalry clearly weren't trained for equine endeavors. Firing intermittent shots while also clinging so as not to get bucked off proved mostly ineffectual. That being said, they were closing the distance little by little.

Naturally, Jint too had no training to guide him, and even so much as bringing his gun to the ready was fumbly in this awkward position.

Jint tucked the gun into his armpit, and retrieved a **lightgun cartridge**.

"Lafier, close your eyes." He tossed it. Due in part to his unsteady position, it didn't come close to the enemy.

Right before it dropped, Jint shut his eyes and faced away.

A dazzling gleam.

When again his eyes opened, he caught sight of two of the enemies fallen from their mounts, rolling and clutching at their eyes.

"I told you, no littering!" the horse admonished.

"Sorry. I'm a rotten little brat."

The single remaining enemy ceased in their tracks.

"There, see it? The exit," said the horse. A row of about twenty glass doors lay open for them.

"I can't go any further from this point," it added, coming to a stop.

"Thank you!" Jint jumped off.

"C'mon, Jint!" Lafier launched into a sprint. It seemed as though this time, the sugar really had bestowed her the strength to go on.

"I look forward to seeing you ag—" Then the horse took a crusher-bullet right to the abdomen. Searing fumes shrouded its saddle while electric sparks charged through the air.

"Looks like I'm malfunctioning..." It slowly fell to its knees as its legs broke down.

"I'm so sorry!" Jint gripped at his chest.

"Hurry!" Lafier picked off the last of the makeshift cavalry.

"Yeah, I get the picture." Jint dashed for the exit.

They came to a small sort of hall. It housed some shops and guide maps, and there were ten stopped escalators before them. Needless to say, no other people were present. Jint searched the sides of the exit.

"What are you doing?" questioned Lafier, her voice severe, as she'd already stepped foot onto the escalator.

"Just give me five seconds."

There was no guarantee he'd come across what he hoped for, but there they were: three buttons, the **controls** under the words EMERGENCY SHUT-OFF DOOR. Next to them hung a notice reading, "WARNING: Activating without just cause will lead to criminal charges."

The controls were a tad difficult to work (probably in order to prevent mischief from prankster children). Jint followed the instructions and pressed Button 3, then 1, then 2. The buttons glowed when pressed, and then they started blinking on and off.

"Warning. Activating the shut-off door without need will hold you subject to criminal and civil affairs liability. Please confirm the situation is an emergency…" came the robo-voice, but Jint paid it no heed. There was no time. He slammed his hands against the buttons.

"Danger! The shut-off door will now close. Please get away from the door. Danger! The shut-off door will…" The glass doors closed shut at once. A steel door dropped down from above and caused the ground to quake with a THUD.

"All right, we're good to go!" Jint ran up to her.

The staircase was lengthy, with at least five stories' worth of height in all. They rushed up them without pause, and panted by the door.

"Are you okay?" asked Jint, concerned.

"Uh-huh." She was pale in the face, but she had enough left in her to give him a grin.

"Let's head into town again. We'll go back into hiding. I bet you anything the **Empire**'ll be back in no time."

The exit was unmanned. They stepped through it into the open. The daytime sky was without a cloud. Outside the exit, the ground slanted in a slight incline, shining hazily. The path stretched about as wide as the small plaza, and at its top, it divided in two. But they hadn't even reached that far before hovercars appeared from both ends to block their way.

"Police!" Jint looked back, and witnessed the darting figures of police officers.

"Don't move!" The officers fired warning shots.

Lafier's right hand made to move.

"No," said Jint, grabbing her by the wrist.

"Why!? You want to surrender here?"

"Yep, we're surrendering!"

They were flanked on both sides, and besides, the cops in front were hiding behind their cars. There could be no victory.

"**Landworld citizens** are better than the alternative," argued Jint. "Better than falling into enemy hands."

"But what if they hand us over!?"

"We'll cross that bridge when we get there. But if we fight here, we die. It's that simple."

Lafier bit her lower lip, and dropped her gun.

A man exited the hovercar at the center. A man with brown skin and a smoke in his mouth.

"Name's Entryua, and I'm an inspector with the Lune Beega Police. Now, I'd like to hear from you two about a grand theft auto incident that occurred some five days back."

"Are we under arrest!?" cried Jint, glowering at the inspector.

"Oh, so you speak Clasburian?" Entryua beamed. "That's a relief. Haven't studied Baronh since school, so I'm pleased as punch you and I can have a chat in Clasburian. And to answer your question, you're not under arrest. You'll be coming along with us voluntarily for a bit of questioning. We don't even know who you really are, so we can't issue warrants for your arrest, see. Though we probably *could* just arrest you on the spot for property damage and unauthorized possession of weapons."

"We plead self-defense."

"Thought you would, which is why I didn't throw murder on the list. In any case, I think it'd be in your best interest to take a ride with us."

"And we're NOT under arrest, right?" Jint pressed.

"Nope. Not as of now, anyway. So no cuffs, and no straightjackets."

"What about the property damage and unauthorized possession?"

"Well, to tell you the truth, we've got an arrangement or somesuch with the **Empire**, so it'll be the court that decides. I know your extenuating circumstances. So believe me when I say that at the moment, I've no desire to arrest. Now have we understood each other?"

Jint nodded slowly.

"Good, that's good. Can I get you to ditch the gun?" he said gently.

He let it go, dumping it on the ground alongside the single remaining **lightgun cartridge**.

Lafier still gripped hers.

"Now for the young Abh lady."

"You can do it, Lafier," Jint said in hushed tones.

"I shall trust your judgment," she told him, and she put it down.

Entryua, relieved, ordered a subordinate to take their firearms. "Now put your hands behind your head and come here. If you behave, we won't have to get rough."

Jint did as he was told. Lafier also complied, albeit grudgingly.

"Don't be naïve, Inspector!" Another man had exited the car, but this one was wearing a green-brown uniform. The uniform of a UH military officer.

"You tricked us!" Jint tried throwing himself at the cop they'd given the guns.

In that moment, the tension ran high.

"Wait! You've got the wrong idea!" said Entryua. "Calm down and let me explain!"

Jint froze in place.

"This is Military Police Captain Keitt. He's cooperating with us," he rattled on. "Listen, we aren't toadies of the occupiers. At the end of the day, I'm the one in charge here. So if you listen to what I say, there won't be any problems."

"Lunacy!" Keitt pressed a gun against the two. "There's absolutely a problem. We haven't even checked to see whether they're totally disarmed yet! How can you trust them so easily?"

"'Inspector *Entryac*,' was it?" said Lafier. "I don't know whether it means anything to the people of the land, but I swear upon *bar lepainec* (the honor of the Abh) that I have no other weapons on me."

"Yes, I trust you, I really trust you," said Entryua in clumsy Baronh.

"NO!" Keitt disheveled his blonde hair. "Look here, Abh, if you want us to believe you, then remove all of your clothes and lie on your back. We'll give you a thorough pat down."

Jint stepped in front of Lafier to defend her. "As if! We're not here to humor your stupid power play…"

"Out of the way, you idiot slave!" Keitt suddenly pulled the trigger.

"Augh!" Jint felt a searing heat in his left shoulder. His vision swam.

"JINT!" Lafier caught him in her arms.

Fortunately, Keitt's gun was a **lightgun**. It hadn't drawn much blood. However, he was assailed by intense pain, and beaded with greasy sweat. The light of the world dimmed for a moment.

"YOU WRETCH!" Lafier exploded with the wrath of a solar flare. "YOU SHALL PAY!!"

Chapter 8: The *Üadrhoth Sathotr* (Dance of Victory)

Entryua watched Keitt's scandalous behavior with speechless bafflement. The man had transformed before his very eyes. His timid personality had all but evaporated like a puddle under a blazing sun, and a sadistic smile turned his formerly handsome visage into an ugly perversion.

"And how do you propose to make me 'pay,' you Abh scum?" Keitt scoffed. "If you really care so much for your little pet, then why don't you get on with it and do as I say? It's not like you sub-humans have any scruples or shame. You're just a loathsome homunculus, you depraved scum Abh."

The Abh lass embraced the youth in her arms and stabbed at Keitt with a glare not unlike a **laser**. She didn't avert her baleful stare as she laid the lad down.

"N-No…" the young man could be heard mumbling.

Entryua was struck with admiration. *I don't believe it… The Abh girl means to scrap with Keitt bare-handed!*

The boy cottoned onto her intentions, and desperately attempted to keep her from going. He tottered over to cover her. The Abh girl's shield.

At that instant, Entryua had decided whose side to take. And it just so happened to be consistent with the mandates of Clasburian law.

Entryua pushed a **needlegun** to Keitt's temple. "Enough!"

"What are you doing?" Keitt panicked. "Are you afraid the Empire will retaliate? Then you needn't worry. Our fleet may have suffered a temporary defeat, but our invincible land war unit is unscathed. We shall continue to defend and maintain this surface world until, by the favor of the powers that be, we secure all of space once again. So stick by the side of justice without fear—"

"Oh, that's exactly what I'm doing," Entryua interrupted. "I don't give a rat's ass who rules space. But on this planet, it's Clasbure's law and justice system that ought to prevail, and your actions right now fly against them. It's a shame, too; I was starting to feel for you."

"I'm just dealing with a fraught situation with the proper rigor!"

"Now I know why the police on your world were so hated." Entryua then addressed his subordinates: "Hey, take this pinhead's gun, would you!?"

His order was executed by the closest officer.

"You've made a terrible mistake, Inspector! Our proud army will surely punish you!"

"Abh girl," said Entryua, ignoring Keitt's forewarning. "It's as you can see. I apologize for my mismanagement as the boss here, but I'm still going to ask you to come with me. That young man needs first aid."

Her shadow-black eyes regarded him.

Such a pretty young thing... Entryua marveled. She was covered in dirt, but that only highlighted her shining beauty all the more. The pride and dignity that kept her from taking a single step back even amidst a sea of strangers and hostiles were clear to see in the glint of her eyes. He'd previously pictured the Abh as lofty beings perched beyond the clouds, but at least with her, the stateliness with which she carried herself had kissed the surface as well.

Can't blame him at all for being so loyal, he mused, glancing at the boy who had been shot. For better or worse, he was the typical city boy that didn't exist among first-generation settlers. Which was to say, he had a weakling, vaguely unreliable air about him, which wasn't even dispelled by the fact that he'd come to this point by surviving a firefight that had the *police* too frightened to act.

Keitt's mad laughter rang through the scene. "You can cover for the Abh all you like, Inspector! I'll just have her dragged out of your detention center. Don't forget, the Abh is MINE. I'll be taking a whole host of soldiers straight to your doorstep, so don't think for a second you'll get away with this, Inspector!!"

Dammit, that rotter's right, he admitted to himself. *Aizan'll hand her over to the occupiers quicker than breathing. But wait — that might not necessarily be the case. After all, if he's got one good point, it's how quick he is to adapt, and now that the Abh've returned, he won't be quite so keen to butter up to this upstart army anymore. That said, by now the "liberation army" must've noticed they're not particularly welcome here, and so their manners've turned rougher as of late. They might just be willing to blow up a police force or two. But us guardians of the law could hardly sit idly by as these rabid mutts have their merry way.*

"Inspector *Entryac*," said the Abh. "I am choosing to believe you."

"Good. In that case…"

"However—"

Entryua was never to hear the rest of that sentence. Three streaks of white smoke traced arcs in the air and exploded at Entryua's feet. Entryua leapt back. "Who the!?"

"Mist shells!" shouted an officer, frantic.

Just before getting engulfed in the mist, Entryua spied a **hovercar** ride rushing over the embankment.

Jint had no idea what just happened; before he knew it, his surroundings were suffused by a thick fog.

Looks just like the scenery of the river in the realm of the dead, like Grandma used to say, Jint recalled. *Guess it's true after all, huh? Which means I've gone and snuffed it. Or have I? I can't even tell. I mean, I can still feel Lafier's warmth on my back… Is she dead, too? Or might I still be one for this world?*

"Abh! *Laimh*!" A voice from beyond the mist addressed him by the word for **imperial citizen.**

Jint started. It was Min's voice.

"Don't dawdle. Come! There's no time to waste!"

Jint slid an arm around Lafier's shoulders and pressed forward.

"Don't fire! We might shoot each other by accident!" Entryua yelled.

The hovercar began levitating within the fog. Jint stuck his head through its open door. In this situation, Lafier of course pushed Jint in and tried turning back.

"Where are you going!?" He grabbed her wrist in the nick of time.

"Let go of me." Lafier was on a tear.

"There's NO TIME." Malka, who was beside Jint, helped him pull her up into the car. "We're set, Bill!"

"Time to cheese it!" Bill exclaimed.

The hovercar got rolling. In the space of mere moments, it wove through the officers and sprinted down the road.

"Let go of me, Jint!" Lafier writhed in his right arm. "I have something I've yet to do!"

"Ow ow OW! Hey, I'm wounded here! A bit softer with me, please," he said, scowling from the pain in his shoulder. "Besides, what've you gotta do, anyway?"

"What do you think?" she said, her ire more than plain. "I'm going to take the man who harmed you, and turn him into fuel for the **plasma** winds of space! A poetic end for him, I should think!"

It wasn't a bad feeling, seeing her blow her top over him and him alone. But he couldn't exactly let her slake her thirst for revenge. "But we're not in the **vacuum of space**," said Jint, to calm her down. "He'd at most turn into a charred corpse smearing a decent length of the ground, which isn't the most poetic thing I've ever heard."

"Good. That would be the most fitting death for him."

"How would you even manage it unarmed?"

"I'd snatch a weapon!" she asserted categorically.

"So reckless," Undertaker sighed.

"Now now, be precise with your words," Min chided. "What he means by that particular choice of words is that you ought to take greater care in your deeds."

"You can take your time killing his ass later," Jint told the **royal princess**.

Lafier's eyes widened with shock. "You are a cruel and brutal man — I don't count 'taking my time to kill people' among my hobbies!"

"That's not what I meant!"

"Listen, you two," said Bill from the driver's seat, his voice weary and fed up. "I hate to butt in on your delightful little chat, but do you feel like closing the door for me? The Abh's footsy's stuck in it!"

"Feh! I suppose I must." And with that, Lafier corrected her posture in her seat. Then she looked at Jint's left shoulder, her expression turning concerned for the first time. "Are you okay, Jint?"

"It's just a scratch," he said, acting tough, while at the same time chagrined she didn't ask sooner.

"It's not just a scratch," said Malka, also glancing at the shoulder. "Your collar bone's popped clean off. If we don't treat it quickly, your whole left arm will need regenerating."

"Please," said Jint, scowling once again. "I don't need to hear the details. I feel like I could faint any second."

"You can faint. Daswani, dress it for him," said Malka, switching seats with the big lug.

Wordlessly, Daswani stopped the bleeding and applied local anesthesia to Jint's shoulder, then rubbed on some regeneration stimulant. Next, he wrapped his arm in bandages and sprayed it with a hardening agent, thereby holding it in place. Jint endured.

"I feel like you've got something to say," said Undertaker. "And if I had to guess, it'd maybe be words of thanks, or maybe words of thanks, or maybe even words of thanks."

"I thank you a millionfold," said Lafier.

"Thanks for treating my wound." Jint rubbed his shoulder, whose pain had dulled. "But you're still planning to hold us hostage, aren't you?"

"Of course we are. We still want our spaceships," said Malka, as though it'd been foolish to ask.

"Well I'm against it." A shudder went down Undertaker's frame. "I don't need any more misfortune in my life."

It was then Jint realized their unfavorable position. No weapons left.

"I don't get it. Why didn't you run?"

"We did run. But the situation changed."

"What do you mean?"

"A while after we left the caves and Bill picked us up, there started to be radio jamming," she explained. "Seems the soldiers at the checkpoints withdrew to the city center, too."

"Which'd mean..."

"Just look at that," she said, pointing out the window.

Six points of light left complex traces in the night sky as they repeatedly assembled and separated.

"Only the Abh do those kinds of meaningless maneuvers."

"They're not meaningless," said Lafier. "That's the **dance of victory**. A show of force to send the message that they've taken over the skies. That's how you learned of the **Star Forces'** return, is it not?"

"What an obnoxious custom. Very Abh-like," Bill remarked.

"Then the **Empire's** retaken the planet!" Jint rejoiced.

"Not yet on the surface, they haven't. But they'll be touching down any moment."

"Everybody together! All officers, get in your rides. We're going after them!" shouted Entryua.

Though much of the mist had cleared, they had to search for their vehicles by memory and blind fumbling. Suddenly, the ground rumbled, and the mist fluctuated.

"What now!?" Entryua was getting sick of this. "Is it *them*? No one else it could be, huh? All right people, hurry up, unless you're in for another headache."

But the sound of their disciplined march came slightly quicker than the cops could manage to depart. "Stop right there," rang a high-handed voice. "Move and we shoot."

"You're talking to the police!" Entryua barked right back. "We were about to tail the suspects. Don't get in our way!"

"We'll shoot, police or not." Green-brown uniforms appeared from within the fog, eyeing the convoy of cars. "I hear you have an officer of ours?"

Keitt saluted. "Military Police Captain Keitt speaking. And you are?"

"Captain Sleet. Where's the Abh? Didn't she come to this area?"

"She escaped." Keitt knitted his brows and frowned.

"Escaped? You mean to say she got the better of this place's police?"

"They're useless. Nothing more than the lapdog dupes of the slave democrats. I must say, though, that you let her slip away despite your regulation equipment."

"This is not regulation equipment. Due to needing to give chase through the caverns by foot, we had no choice but to stow all heavy weapons behind."

"So you say, but..." Then Keitt realized that the machine translator had been left on.

Afterward, both commissioned officers turned off their translation devices, so he couldn't understand the conversation from there on out. Of course, he had no interest in their game of blame-shifting anyway. That said, he couldn't shake his ominous feeling… which turned into reality in short order.

"Inspector," said Keitt, flashing a superficial smile, "we must chase and catch the Abh."

"We were about to until they stopped us!"

"No, WE will be chasing them. And commandeering your cars to do it."

"You'll WHAT!?"

"Our proud army has no means of transport," added Sleet. "That is why we're in need of you folk's vehicles. We'll take only the drivers among you, and have the rest stay here."

"And we don't get a say in this? By what authority do you—"

"By this authority." Sleet pressed a handgun to the tip of Entryua's nose. "We have no time. Make it snappy."

"You tell him!" Keitt was overjoyed by this turnabout. "Don't worry, we'll take you, too, Inspector. You can give us directions. Oh, and I'd like to have you hand me my weapon back, while we're at it."

"But how'd you know we were going to be there?" wondered Jint.

"The chances were fifty-fifty," shrugged Min. "But it would have been tougher to find you if you ended up exiting through the main cave system. Too many possible exits. That's why we put up a net for you on the Dream Park side. We knew we were right on the money when they started evacuating people from the park, and from there we could choose the perfect time to strike."

"Would've loved it if you kidnapped us before I got shot."

"Well aren't we the little prince," said Undertaker disgustedly. "I'll have you know we tread on some damn dangerous ground ourselves."

"Never mind that, there's something we'd like to ask the little Abh lady." Malka placed a hand on her forehead.

"What?" Lafier looked away from the glorious **dance of victory** unfolding in the night sky to face her.

"Earlier, before we entered the caves. I saw your ear. And it's been bugging me ever since, but it wasn't the right time to ask."

Jint's heart raced.

"It only came back to mind after we'd gotten separated. I can be a big ditz sometimes. But I still can't believe it. I just can't."

"What's the question?" Lafier egged her on.

"Here goes: Are the **Abliar ears** allowed outside the **Imperial Family**?"

"They are not," she replied guilelessly.

"I thought so. Then may I ask you your name, Honorable *Fïac*?"

"I am *Ablïarsec Néïc Dubreuscr Bœrh Parhynr Lamhirh*."

A solemn pall of silence.

The militants of the Clasbure Anti-Imperial Front were too busy processing this fresh revelation to make a sound. It was Jint who broke the silence, concluding that now that Lafier's social status had come to light, there would be no point keeping his own hidden.

"As for me..."

"Nobody asked for your name, **imperial citizen**," Bill butted in.

"All right then." Jint clammed up. On second thought, while it was true that keeping it hidden would be pointless, he realized revealing it would be just as much so.

"I did think it was strange," said Min. "I looked into it, and the **Marquessate of Sfagnoff** has two *ïarlymec* (noble princesses); the oldest of them is eight years old."

"Oh, things're strange, that's for damn sure," griped Undertaker. "The hell's a **royal princess** of the **Empire** doing in a place like this!?"

"Did you hear that, Jint?" Lafier's eyes sparkled. "Even **landworld citizens** know the difference between an **imperial princess** and a **royal princess**."

"Hold a grudge much? You're just that type, I guess. It's not like I meant anything by it, so whatever."

"'Whatever' is right; just answer the question," Undertaker grumbled.

"We were aboard a certain **patrol ship**," said Jint, taking it on himself to explain. "That patrol ship got attacked. I wasn't a **starpilot**, so..."

"Must've been an **NCC**," said Bill.

"Nope, not an **NCC**, either. I was just hitching a ride."

"Hitching a ride?" Malka cocked her head. "You can hitch a ride on a **patrol ship**?"

"*I* can. Just so happened to be of **noble rank**," he said nonchalantly. "And as I'm not a **soldier**, I was told to flee from the field of battle. But I can't work a **conveyance ship**'s controls, so Lafier was assigned to me. Aboard the **patrol ship**, she was just another **trainee starpilot**, you see."

"Hold on," said Malka, confused. "You're a **noble**, too?"

"Yep. Least, that's what I ended up becoming."

Bill whistled. "You really don't look like one."

"I get that all the time," he quipped. "Wonder why."

"Lots of questions today," said Malka. "But let's narrow question time down to what I'm more immediately interested in. Our hostages are a member of the **Imperials** and a **noble**. Plus, I'm fairly sure '*Néïc Dubreuscr*' is a surname associated with the **monarchy** to which the **Empress** belonged. Am I off the mark?"

"I am **Her Majesty the Empress**'s granddaughter, and Jint is the **noble prince of a countdom**," said Lafier. "We are not, however, your hostages."

"I assure you, you are," she said flatly. "How could we possibly let such valuable hostages go? Forget about exchanging you for spaceships; we might even be able to come by Min's ultimate dream — independence."

"I am grateful to all of you," said Lafier. "As such, I must tell you the truth. Misfortune has dogged all who have attempted to extort the **Empire** to the ends of their days. Referring, of course, to those few who survived to see another day."

"I don't doubt it." Yet another shudder ran down Undertaker. "I'm miserable enough as it is."

The windows gleamed. The peak of the mountain that towered over the horizon was brightly aglow. Lightning whipped the peak from the heavens above, sending rays of light out into a crazed dance each time.

"Must be the Abhs' above-surface assault..." muttered Min.

As though any one of them didn't already know.

"What could they be attacking, in a place like that?" Jint wondered aloud, spellbound by the sheer spectacle.

At last, the rumble of thunder reached them.

Something dawned on Malka. "Bill, is the jamming still in effect?"

White noise permeated the car.

"Still no good," said Bill, shaking his head.

"I see. And I thought for sure they were attacking the radio stations."

"No, you're probably right. There used to be a really strong signal source until a bit back, but now it's gone. Looks like they paid the wider-area station a visit."

"Any other places?"

"Dunno. Weak radio waves are coming in from all over the place. No clue how many sources."

"All likely the work of *daimbusec* (EM bugs)," Lafier conjectured. "The **Star Forces** possess similar devices."

"**EM bugs**? Bugs that generate EM waves?" said Min, curious.

"They're self-propagating nanomachines, and they're a pain to exterminate."

"Now I know. By the way, I wonder if the Abh will attack the capital?"

"I don't think they will."

"You don't 'think'?" Min had been expecting a more concrete reply.

"Full-scale land war is the endgame stage for the **Star Forces**. Before reaching that stage, they generally destroy means of communication and transport, or might send in the *byrec üacér* (airship fleet). I doubt they'd attack the capital so suddenly."

"Where do you plan to imprison us?" Jint asked, apprehensive. They could very well be exposed to **Star Forces** fire depending on the area.

"We plan on using Undertaker's place. You yourself must be well aware—"

"I told you, no way in hell," Undertaker protested.

"Then we'll have to make it where Undertaker works."

"Why's it always me!?"

"Where else could we? Besides, you want to go tell outside cells about a get this juicy?"

"I say Min's holiday home'd be way better."

"Are you nuts?"

"Think about it, they'd never suspect we'd choose to go back right after what happened…"

"It's just too much to hope for." And with that, Malka shot down the idea. "It's settled, Bill. We're headed for the funeral hall."

"I think for the time being, we'd maybe better focus on giving this place the slip," urged Bill. "It's the heat. They're on our tails."

"*Eh cohn! Eh cohn!*" barked Sleet.

After the large curves in the road drivers inevitably encountered upon leaving *Guzonh* Dream Park, the way to the streets of *Guzonh*-proper continued dead straight. Entering that unbending stretch, the hovercars zipping in the distance would then come into view.

"Do you not have vehicle-equipped weaponry?" asked Keitt.

"No, of course not." Entryua folded his arms and pressed a foot against the seat in front. "No need. The crime's not that serious 'round these parts."

"That's a shame." Keitt pushed the gun he'd regained to Entryua's head. "In any case, I do believe you ought to adjust your posture, Inspector. You're our prisoner."

"Is that right," he replied, cocking an eyebrow. "I thought you hired me to give directions."

"DON'T DEFY US!" Keitt shouted in his face. "Just do as we say, you mental slave."

Entryua concluded that open opposition was inadvisable. After all, he was dealing with an unstable child. If he was stupid enough to persist in stubbornness, then theirs would amount to no more than a spat between schoolboys. Only in this playground quarrel, one of the kids held a lethal weapon.

"As you wish, master." Entryua dropped the foot.

"*Eh brik!*" Sleet commanded.

At that cue, the occupation soldiers leaned out the windows and started firing.

"Those aren't police! The police don't pack that kind of weaponry!"

Incessantly, the bullets pelted. With explosive power despite their small caliber, the crusher-bullets gouged holes all over the shining roadway. Yet none reached their car. So far, the bullets were only hitting spaces of road that they'd already passed.

"Shouldn't we, I dunno, go off road or something!?" screamed Undertaker.

"There'd be no point," said Min calmly. "They must have detectors that allow them to take aim. Going off road would only hurt, by causing us to decelerate."

"But there's still that radio jamming!"

"You know nothing. Communications and detectors work over different bandwidths."

"'Fraid he's right," said Bill, who picked up speed. "Don't worry, Undertaker. I removed all of the safety mechanisms for a time like this."

"But driving straight ahead's basically ASKING them to snipe us off the road!"

"Aerodynamically speaking, we should be too far away for them to ever hit us," said Min, as composed as ever. "I don't know what their guns are capable of, but judging by the fact that we haven't gotten hit yet, I don't think I'm mistaken. In fact, the bullets haven't even reached that close to us."

"I'm praying you're not mistaken," said Malka, who had her hands clasped in front of her chest.

"Have you got anything to add, Lafier? You know, as an expert in war?" said Jint.

"I'm not an expert on *nahaineïocs* (landworld wars)." Lafier seemed wounded for some reason. "Regardless, I suggest you prepare your **lightguns**. At this distance, the damping is not enough."

"Do you have anything, Min?" asked Malka.

"I do. Should be able to make use of the smokescreen rounds. Former Republic of Camintale military issue, K211 model. It's made out to have the best EM wave absorption rate in cosmic history."

"Then why didn't you pull 'em out sooner!?" Undertaker blasted.

"Because they took a great deal of effort to acquire," said Min.

"Now's the time, if you don't mind," Malka ordered.

Min reluctantly drew the satchel closer, retrieved what looked like a can, and tossed it out the window. "I might as well throw these in for good measure." Min grabbed from the satchel ten-odd disks, each around three *dagh* in diameter, and scattered them over the road.

Bill looked back from the driver's seat. "What're those?"

"Sensor mines. They're designed with killing people in mind, but I don't see why they wouldn't work against cars."

"Holy hell, where the good goddamn did you get this stuff!? You're nuts for weapons, nuts!"

"Oh, those I made myself. Already tested them, too. They may seem small, but they're high-performance, and with extremely low incidence of mechanical error," he boasted. "But never mind that. Bill, can you shake them off?"

"Leave it to me. This baby's the fastest ground-crawler in Clasbure. And we've got a lead."

"Won't this thing go any faster!?" Sleet shouted at the officer driving.

"No can do," said Entryua, having the back of his cowering subordinate. "This is a command car. It's not built to be able to catch up to a speeding car. That's why we send the patrol cars first."

"Why didn't you say that before, dammit!?"

"You didn't ask," he said, unruffled.

That was met by a smack upside the mouth, delivered by Keitt with the handle of his gun.

Prick! He was dizzy with fury. He could list a number of things he hadn't much liked about how they'd treated him, but he never *hit* them. Entryua managed to swallow his rage, and wiped the blood from his mouth.

Suddenly, the car slowed. They looked up, and saw a wall of black approaching.

"Don't slow down, it's just a smokescreen!" said Sleet, nudging the driver in the head.

The command car ventured into the thick black brume, and the vapor, highly viscous, moved in through the windows kept open for firing. Entryua covered his face with his hands, hoping to protect his eyes and nose.

Suddenly, that instant, a merciless KAPOW!

We get hit!? Even as Entryua struggled to make heads or tails of the situation, the car lurched left.

"A mine! It blasted the electromagnet!" With the electromagnet at the hovercar's front left down for the count, all balance was lost. The horrid screech of metal scraping against the luminescent pavement of the road assailed their ears.

"All cars halt!" ordered Sleet.

"Don't stop, veer away!" Entryua leaned against the driver's seat. "We'd just be bumping right into the next ones, you dimwit!"

The driver chose Entryua to obey, and took the car into the field at the side of the road.

The patrol cars that had been following them also ran into disaster.

The one that punched the smokescreen right after the command vehicle got its anterior electromagnets destroyed, the frontal part that had been raised now swayed by wind pressure. It careened sideways and turned over, sliding across the road on its roof. The patrols cars after that one proceeded to collide into it.

To add to the list of woes, those cars that slammed on the brakes even more got hit by rear-end collisions, while others pitched forward above the cars that had stopped, and still others evaded those fates only to eat landmine blasts…

At last, the very last car in the line divined from the noise that something had happened beyond the mists, so its occupants released the wheels, rode into the fields, and thus became the sole car to avoid any damage.

"Quick, get away!" Entryua waved his hands in the air, forgetting the position he was in.

Soldiers and police officers alike came crawling out of their respective wrecks. Police cars had a reputation for sturdiness; regardless of the severity of the damage, there seemed to be next to no casualties to speak of. But they couldn't afford to dawdle.

The hydrogen fuel of the toppled cars had caught flame, and a blast rocked both soldiers and officers. The crops were also engulfed, and the smoke of the fires mixed with the smokescreen. Entryua coughed violently.

"Accident on the road," Undertaker solemnly informed the rest.

"Road safety. It's important," gloated Bill, his smile a mile wide.

"You're too right," said Min soberly.

"Is there jamming still?" asked Jint.

"Don't worry, **imperial citizen**. Oh wait, sorry, almost forgot, you're a **noble**," said Bill. "The jamming continues. They can't call for backup."

"But something is coming." Lafier shaded her eyes with her hand and looked into their travelling direction.

The sparkle of *Guzonh* lay right before them. Some object clad in flickering, twinkling lights was rising between the shining city-trees. Said object took along with it five smaller flying objects.

Then they passed overhead, soaring by without so much as sparing the gang a glance.

When the glowing crest emblazoned on the belly of the largest ship came into view, Malka's shoulders dropped with relief. "Phew, that had me wound up. It's just the fire department!"

"Well, that fire is pretty huge. They could probably see it from there," said Bill.

"Hold on…" said Jint. "That thing might be a plain old fire ship, but it's still flying."

"Duh. It's faster than over ground."

"But the enemy was riding in those cop cars just now, right?" said Jint.

"So it'd seem, but what're you getting at?" asked Min.

"I mean, if the enemy took to riding cop cars, what's to stop them from taking over the fire department?"

Chapter 9: *Robïach Saisera* (Space-Soaring Nuisances)

Must've fallen for me or something, Entryua thought as he looked askance at Keitt's emotionless mug, *'cause I can't seem to shake him.*

When the occupying forces commandeered the airborne fire ships and the airborne ambulance ships, he thought he'd finally be free of them, but he jumped the gun. Keitt insisted on accompanying Entryua, and Sleet gave him permission disinterestedly.

The fire ships that were made to land under duress proceeded to leave the firefighters, police officers, and soldiers who couldn't board in their wake. Consequently, the conflagration flared right back to full power. In addition to the single ambulance ship separated to act as a messenger, they established a light-wave communications system unaffected by radio wave jamming five *üésdagh* above the city of *Guzonh*, desperately scanning for a certain **hovercar**. A group of airborne vessels floated up from the central area of the range of city-trees below, exchanging information with the fire ships using the primitive means of blinking lights.

So over the top, Entryua scoffed. They were just wrestling with a bunch of lowlife radicals over two borderline children, and apparently willing to make use of all of the military power they had stationed in *Guzonh* to do it.

"Inspector," said Keitt, "do you know why I've taken you here?"

"No idea," said Entryua, his tone drenched with cold hostility.

"To give me directions."

"You're more than aware," Entryua sighed, "that I'm an officer of Lune Beega. Born and raised. *Guzonh* geography isn't—"

"Not *Guzonh*. You're going to take me to the Abh."

"Huh?"

A mocking, nihilistic smile. "You're going to take us straight to the pit of hell. I'll make the Abh watch as I kill you, then the mental slaves that obstructed her arrest, and then the boy she's made her little pet. If the Abh's

534

artificial pseudo-intelligence possesses the faintest trace of emotion, I'm sure she'll feign sorrow."

"I've got next to no ties with the Abh." *The bastard bond between you and me runs much deeper,* Entryua refrained from adding.

"That is why I will do you the service of simply shooting you. That being said, I rather think the people who more broadly supported the Abh shall face quite miserable deaths. Especially that boy. He'll be screaming for a whole night, I wager. As for the Abh herself, I will of course have a more elaborate farewell in store for her."

"And here I thought you were a tad more civilized."

"Oh yes, military law naturally forbids executing prisoners without trial, as well as cruel executions. Yet this is a time of crisis. We haven't even been told where the current location of Military Headquarters is. As such, we must have some room for discretion. Because here, the annoying, sanctimonious types in my country will never know what's happened."

Does he mean business? Or is he just trying to get me quaking in my boots as revenge? Entryua couldn't be sure.

Then he remembered: there was no way Keitt had the authority to decide such a thing. There had to be a commissioned officer higher in rank than captain in the unit stationed in *Guzonh*.

On the other hand, he didn't know the particulars of foreign military power's operations. And the fact of the matter was that madness is contagious.

A United Humankind Armored Air Mobile Personnel Transport Vessel landed right next to them.

"Over here!" Malka pulled Jint by the hand, and they hid behind a city-tree.

The hovercar was abandoned as soon as they entered the city proper. Otherwise they would have gotten blown up along with it.

They'd changed out of their dirty clothes; Malka had used her wallet to purchase new garb from the close-by automated clothing store. Their **wristgears** and **circlets** had been stowed away once again, and Lafier now had her *froch* hidden using a wide-brimmed hat.

"Let's go through the underground," proposed Min.

"Yes, let's," said Malka.

And so the five members of the *Guzonh* Cell of the Clasbure Anti-Imperial Front and their two hostages descended, stepping forth into a brightly illuminated undercity center. It was about the same width as one of the aboveground shine-roads, with automated stores situated 500 *dagh* apart from each other. People were standing alone, and drifting away at around jogging speed.

The seven got on the automated track.

"Things're really ramping up, huh?" said Jint.

"You sullied their names. Stomped all over their reputations. It's no wonder they're going all out," said Malka, looking back.

"Might it not be wise for you five to surrender?" suggested Lafier. "We're the ones that they're after. After all, I have no desire to embroil you in this."

"It's too late for that," said Min coldly. "At least for me, I'm already hopelessly embroiled. They know my name. And I've been worried sick about my family this entire time."

"Is that not all the more reason to surrender?"

"We can't let the sacrifices we've made go in vain. We want some kind of recompense," said Malka.

"Independence and **interstellar ships** are out of the question, but the **House of *Clybh*** will present you with tokens of its appreciation for your deeds thus far."

"So that's how the Abh repay their dues," Undertaker scoffed. "With gobs of gold and shinies."

"Sorry, but what we want are **interstellar ships**," said Malka.

A confounded look crossed Lafier's face. "I'm telling you that simply will not come to pass."

"What if they got them on loan?" piped up Jint. "I dunno what they wanna do with **interstellar ships**, but they probably aren't gonna pick a fight with the **Empire**, at least, not in the near future. So what's the problem?"

"You're right; we could perhaps do it that way," Lafier nodded.

"If that's our only choice… Shall we shake on it?" Malka looked at each of her comrades in turn.

"I wanted to try flying an **interstellar ship** myself… but oh well," said Bill. "Guess I'll just play a bit with the steering gear when I find the chance…"

"The ship's destination is based on where the borrower wishes to go, right?" Min asked. Lafier gestured affirmatively. "Excellent," he continued. "I take it detours are also allowed. I plan to shape an independent interplanetary conflict coalition."

Daswani nodded wordlessly.

"Might as well have them throw in the gobs of gold and shinies while we're at it," said Undertaker.

"That should be much easier compared to the **interstellar ships**," Lafier assured him.

"Then make us that promise, Your Highness," said Malka. "Promise us you'll lend us one or more **interstellar ships**. That is, without any fees or time limit."

"That is not the promise I can make." She furrowed her eyebrows. "I can only promise that I will ask **Her Majesty the Empress**."

"That's fine. The Empress is sure to humor the pleading of her adorable granddaughter."

"If I live to seek another audience with **Her Majesty**, I will ask her without fail." And with that, Lafier jumped into the automated track going in the opposite direction.

"Come, Jint!"

"Ah, right!" Jint took her lead.

Surprisingly, Malka followed them.

"I'm going to make sure you live to seek another audience with her," she whispered. "So I'm coming with you. We're the ones who can send you back into space."

"What do you mean?" asked Jint.

"Undertaker really is an undertaker," she answered enigmatically.

"Take a look at that signal, if you would." Keitt pointed out the window. "That's notification that the Transit Bureau has been seized. Soon the underground tracks will be stopped, and my army's battle troops will flood in. The Abh has nowhere to run."

Keitt kept Entryua abreast of all of the particulars of the progress of their manhunt, though likely only because he had nothing else to do. Every new bit of information would conclude with the words, *"The Abh has nowhere to run."*

As he listened to Keitt's rather dead monotone, Entryua felt fear creep across like ice. He knew for sure now. He knew that when they captured the Abh, he would die. It didn't matter whether Keitt had the authority to do so. There was no question: as soon as he heard news of the Abh's discovery, he'd take the fire ship to the scene and gun Entryua down with total glee.

He looked down; fires were raging all over the streets. The cars had been destroyed either because they looked somewhat similar to the one hovercar, or because they'd tried to ignore the checkpoint inspection. He could even see the flashes of gunfire.

"Civilians are hereby informed..." The air-mobile tanks were blaring their heavy-handed broadcast as they made their sweeping motions. "...That they are to aid in our search. You must answer any and all questions with the whole truth. In addition, if you spot suspicious persons, notify the nearest soldier. We are looking for an Abh. Civilians are hereby informed that they are to aid in our search..."

"Now look at that, sir." Keitt pointed to the top of a city-tree. The soldiers were sending coded signals by blinking their handheld lights. "They're messaging that they've searched all of the rooms in that city-tree. They're scouring every building with a fine-toothed comb... The Abh has nowhere to run."

"Searching premises without warrants, huh...? That's every officer's dream," said Entryua, trying his damnedest to serve up some sarcasm.

"You're the only ones to blame. If you had paid democracy and God's providence the respect they're due, we would've been able to act more gentlemanly. We aren't an occupying army. We're a liberation army," he added wistfully, as though speaking of some lost dream.

"We didn't ask you to come. Surely you acknowledge that?"

"It's such a shame, Inspector. I thought we'd come to understand one another." Keitt's eyes wandered around the scenery out the window. Then he pointed again. "Look over there..."

The city was in turmoil. The vast majority of the citizens had taken note of the Abhs' return. They couldn't help but doubt whether anything good would come of cooperating with the occupiers.

The larger part of the **landworld citizens** neither loved nor loathed the occupation forces, viewing them only as quirky guests that had paid Clasbure a momentary visit. Yes, the fact that important government figures had been taken away had wounded their pride. Yes, there were those who had been forced to shave their blue hair, and those whose family members had been sent to camps for "democracy reeducation." But this series of events was taken as nothing more than a transient natural disaster, with many even enjoying it, albeit as seeds of hatred were shut away in their hearts.

Yet over the past half-hour, those seeds of hatred were budding, and growing rapidly. The army was blocking roads, barging into homes, performing violent patdowns, even opening fire upon trivial misunderstandings… There was now no shortage of reasons to hate them.

"Good citizens, the Abh is to blame for all of this momentary chaos. Search for the Abh. If you can capture the Abh, the peace will be restored." The voice from above insisted, repeated this was the case, but the hatred of the people was firmly fixed on the green-brown army fatigues. After all, the soldiers with bloodshot eyes and guns at the ready weren't wearing the black **uniforms** of the Abh.

They had neither the weapons nor the organized bodies to revolt, yet unlucky and inattentive soldiers were frequently getting ganged up on by mobs and their weapons stolen all throughout town. As for the citizens who lacked confidence in their muscle power, and those who were wiser and more prudent, they instead exchanged information, trying to return home through paths where they wouldn't encounter any soldiers.

That was the course of events in which Jint's party was mired.

"Over there."

Malka was one of the five among them who had a grasp of *Guzonh*'s geography. Their sense for the places where the enemy was likely to be was impressive. When they did encounter soldiers, they either blended in with the crowd or went down empty paths. They ran down stopped automated tracks, ascended to the surface, and wove their way through the alleys. They even crossed over the open squares by using the sky-corridors that linked adjacent city-trees. One might think they would be running at top speed, but in fact, they walked with deliberate composure.

In areas devoid of other people, they split into two groups, with each pretending not to know the other. Even when they did enter a plaza, Jint was grouped with Malka and Daswani. Meanwhile, Lafier and the other three traversed the square one step ahead in their own group.

A coughing noise right above their heads — startled, Jint looked up, to find two enemy soldiers wearing jetpacks. They landed right in front of Lafier.

"Take that hat off, woman!" one demanded imperiously.

Something was pressed against Jint's hand. Malka was handing him a **stungun**.

"What're you two goin' on abou'?" said Undertaker, playing the drunk act. "Ya take a shine ta my niece'ssss *hat* or somefin?"

"Well it ain't yers ta take," said Bill, feigning drunkenness alongside him. "I's the one 'at bought it for 'er. You got a *problem* wizzat…"

"Aren't you being a little too rude to them?" said Min, "enraged."

Now all Lafier needed to do was look frightened, maybe even cling to Bill, and the ruse would be complete.

Needless to say, the Abh princess was far too prideful to put on such an act. All Jint could see of her was her back, but he could only imagine her eyes screamed *You're not fit to spit on.*

Jint and his group briskly slipped off to the side, cloaked in the act that they were simply loath to get wrapped up in this altercation.

"Just take it off! Or do you refuse?" One of the soldiers tried to lift it off her head by pushing against the brim with the gun's muzzle.

Malka and Daswani moved in tandem to either side. Jint, too, wasted no time turning right around and thrusting a **stungun** at the nape of a soldier's neck. His injured left shoulder throbbed with pain from the sudden exertion, but he endured it and pulled the trigger.

Lafier and the other three with her quickly hit the ground, causing her hat to dance in the air.

"Gwah!" the soldier groaned, emptying rounds fruitlessly into the sky. The other soldier collapsed without a single peep or shot. The band of seven ignored the weapons the soldiers had been wielding, since they would only make them stand out, and made haste to leave the scene.

"Remember that guy who jumped into a bed of thorns?" said Undertaker, upon reentering the underground from the plaza.

"You told us that story," said Malka impatiently.

"Well, there's more to it." Undertaker's voice grew vacant. "About a month after he left the hospital, he went and did it again. Obviously, he got hospitalized again. Then I went to see him again, and I asked him the same question. Then he said he couldn't remember much, but he couldn't think of it as having been a good idea."

"Uh-huh," she replied curtly. "We're almost to the place."

"We just have to hope no one is there," said Min, needlessly.

"They've found her," said Keitt, after reading the blinking signals with eyes entranced. "They've found the Abh."

"They capture her?" Entryua thought about the time he had left. *It was a short life. I never got to punch my daughter's marriage partner's lights out.*

"Not yet. It appears the report came from a pair of wounded soldiers, that have now been admitted. They found a girl who looked like an Abh. One testified that they saw her spatiosensory organ. I can't imagine they're mistaken." Keitt's smile was twisted like a revenant ghoul. "I'll be the one to capture her…"

He instructed the ship's pilot to do something. Then, the fire ship turned right around, heading for the northwest area of the city.

The group of spires appeared beyond the range of city-trees. "What are those?" said Keitt, puzzled.

Entryua immediately grasped the true identity of the spires, as well as what the Abh and the crowd working with her were up to.

"Beats me. I told you I'm not well acquainted with the geography of *Guzonh*," he lied.

"I'll find out easily enough just by looking it up."

"Then that's what you oughtta do. Don't lean on me for everything."

IN LIGHT OF A CONFLUENCE OF CIRCUMSTANCES, THE *GUZONH* MUNICIPAL FUNERAL MORTUARY WILL BE CLOSED FOR THE FORESEEABLE FUTURE.

Undertaker unlocked the lock with practiced hands; it opened without incident.

"When the occupiers touched down, the folks in the government got scared and closed the place off," said Undertaker, guiding the rest from in front. "So the army probably doesn't much care about it. They might not even know about it to begin with."

"But why close it?" asked Jint.

"They feared they might be mistaken for anti-orbital weaponry," Min explained. "And if they got bombed, *Guzonh* wouldn't come off unscathed."

"Weaponry?" Jint was more confused than ever.

When they exited the small building, the landscape opened up. Richly colored spires were lined up on a vast site. He remembered seeing them before, since he'd come to Guzonh while gazing askance at them.

"I've been wondering what they were ever since then," said Jint, viewing them once again as he quickly paced along the long corridor. "So they were giant graves, huh?"

"Don't mistake a funeral home for a cemetery," said Undertaker bitterly. "It's an inexcusable mistake."

"Sorry. But then, what are those?"

"They're caskets."

"They're what now?"

"And the cemetery's over there," he continued, pointing up at the sky.

"WHAT!?"

"I swear, kids like you are so ignorant of tradition it's scary."

"Well I understand," said Lafier, who gave Jint a reproachful glare. "You lack in common sense. It's a matter of course for the remains of the deceased to be set adrift into the **vacuum of space**."

"What she said. Though the Abh must do it directly from their spaceships, while we're forced to shoot them off because we're at the bottom of a gravity well."

"On my home planet, we either burn or bury our dead," said Jint feebly.

"When we touched down onto this planet, I thought it was rather riddled with dirt and dust, and surmised it was due to the war, but those are caskets, you say," said Lafier, satisfied she understood.

"But if you wanna shoot someone into **space**, wouldn't it be easier to do it from the **orbital tower**?" asked Jint.

"Have you no shred of emotion, young master?" Bill gestured dramatically. "A funeral's a sacred rite! You've gotta be flashy about it!"

"I'd thought of funerals as more quiet, dignified affairs…"

"That is what we call a preconceived notion," said Min. "This custom probably takes after Abh culture, but we settled this planet from space, too. We wouldn't be that off base."

"Don't get me wrong, it's not that I look down on the idea of setting dead bodies into **space**." Then Jint came to a hair-raising realization. "Don't tell me you're gonna 'send us back into space' *in these things*!?"

"What the hell're you saying!? You're backing down *now*!?" said Undertaker and Bill at the same time.

"But nobody told me anything!" Jint objected.

"I misjudged you, Jint." Lafier glowered at him scornfully. "I'd been under the impression that you had better discernment than that. As a fellow Abh, I am embarrassed."

"Sorry…" Jint had been battered into submission.

"There's a problem, though," said Lafier. Then she addressed Undertaker: "I'm not used to piloting this model of ship. Will I be able to steer it properly?"

Undertaker stared as though she couldn't be serious. "Not for nothing, Your Highness, but it's not *for* steering. There's no need; it just goes up and away. The end."

The blood drew away from Lafier's lovely countenance.

"I misjudged you, Lafier," said Jint, seizing on this chance. "I'd been under the impression that you had better…"

"Be quiet!"

Don't even know why I thought she'd do me the favor of letting me finish my sarcastic jab. While Jint questioned his own sanity, Lafier hit Undertaker with a follow-up question of her own.

"It is airtight, I hope?"

"'Course it is. I don't know what you believe, but rest assured us Landers do know a thing or two about what kind of beast the **vacuum of space** is. It's even got emergency oxygen in case somebody who's actually still alive is mistakenly placed inside. Twelve hours' worth."

A door lay at the end of the corridor, and a little past it, a staircase leading down into the basement, a small room furnished with several screens.

"Commence funeral preparations." Undertaker ran up to one of the screens.

"As per the orders of the municipal government, this mortuary is currently closed," responded the machine voice.

"Haven't you heard? The closure directive's been rescinded."

"Cannot confirm that statement's veracity."

"Never like it when machines get antagonistic." Undertaker looked behind him. "Daswani, if you could."

Daswani nodded, took out a *saigéth* (keyboard), and connected it to the **console**. His fat fingers pounded away at the small, compact keys at blinding speeds.

"I'm always telling him, it's faster by voice input, but Daswani's a man of few words," said Undertaker.

"This way, much faster," said Daswani.

"Holy moly," said Bill, astonished. "Have any of you ever heard him string together a sentence that long?"

"He must be feeling charged up," Min remarked.

"By the way, what's its propulsion source? The ship's, I mean?" Jint was cautious to avoid the word "casket."

"Hydrogen," said Undertaker.

"Hydrogen? As in nuclear fusion?"

"No," said Undertaker, his tone of voice strangely soft. "It's a chemical reaction. When hydrogen and oxygen are made to bond, heat and water are born. That's what it uses for propulsion. Put it simply, it burns hydrogen to fly."

"Jint," Lafier groaned. "Could you hold me up? I think I'm going to collapse."

"'Fraid I won't be much help," said Jint, dumbfounded. "I'm just as likely to faint."

"Don't fret," said Undertaker. "We haven't had any incidents in a while."

"In a while?" That was hardly much consolation.

"Sorry, that came out wrong. What I meant is that there hasn't been a single casualty since the establishment of civilization on the planet. There have been caskets that flew away, though."

"That's... awesome."

"By the way, there're two types, ones with self-destruct devices and ones without. Which would you prefer?"

"Self-destruct devices!?"

"Yeah, they come back down two hours after shooting them up. That's when we make them blow up in the air. It's for funerals where the mourners arrange to reminisce about the deceased yet again while watching them light up the sky as fireworks."

Jint paused.

"Give us one that can't self-destruct, please."

"Got it. Shame, though. The self-destruct device-equipped ones are the nicer ones."

"We appreciate the sentiment."

"Undertaker!" said Malka. "Quit teasing them already, would you?"

"I've got a right to settle a score, same as anybody," said Undertaker, clearly pleased with himself.

Daswani looked up from his **keyboard**.

"Commence funeral preparations," Undertaker ordered anew.

"Affirmative. Please input the name of the responsible funeral director." Undertaker slid his wallet into the **console**'s groove. "Please confirm your identity." He peered into the **console**'s small window for the retinal scan.

"Qualification to perform funeral service recognized. Please begin the necessary procedures. First, input the name of the defrayer of expenditures..."

"The funeral director will pay in their stead."

"Affirmative."

Undertaker gave Lafier a grin. "Be sure to pay me back, all right?"

"Okay," nodded Lafier.

"Next, please provide your interment authorization code." He inserted a string of numbers using a mobile terminal.

"From now on, you guys are one 'Bigg Tempill.' No doubt they're gonna throw a fit at the real Bigg's funeral, poor old bastard."

"Interment authorization code recognized. Next, please input the desired trajectory…"

"Malka, leave this to me, and take these two to the launcher for me. It's #3. You know where it is, right?"

"Sure do." Malka half-nodded to the two. "Let's go, *Fïac Lartnér*, Lonh-*ïarlucer Dreur*."

Inspector Entryua's cold eyes watched as Keitt fumbled with the unfamiliar Imperial-make computer terminal in his attempts to extract information. Entryua's unwillingness to help aside, the man could have asked the nearby firefighter to teach him how to use it, but it appeared Keitt could no longer trust any and all Clasburians.

When at last Keitt had translated the information he wanted using his own device, he looked stunned. "Why didn't you tell me about Clasbure-style funeral rites!?"

"You didn't ask." Entryua tensed and braced for impact.

Yet Keitt stopped at clenching his fist. Then, he burst into a howling fit of laughter. "As though she could escape that way! The Abh has nowhere to run."

He slapped the shoulder of a soldier aboard the ship and issued instructions. That soldier proceeded to flash a signal using the blinking light method.

A red light above the entombment door of Launcher #3 was on. "Fueling and servicing in progress. Please wait."

In front of the door lay an exquisite, brand-new coffin on a dolly tray. The launcher cylinder was below ground.

"It's to protect the city from the blast impact," explained Malka.

Bill, who'd come with them, had this to say: "When I was a kid, I watched a bunch launch from above ground. But then the city expanded, and they moved them underground. Weird spiel, but hey, Undertaker was the first to share a weird spiel."

"I just thought of something," said Jint, who'd stumbled across yet another seed of worry. "Is there a chance the **Star Forces** will mistake it for a weapon of attack?"

"A vessel that moves by burning hydrogen as fuel?" Lafier crinkled the gainly curve at the upper base of the bridge of her nose. "You may just make me die of laughter."

"Guess you've got a point..."

"You needn't guess. Besides, my **wristgear** will be emitting a friend-or-foe identifier signal. And there can't be any **EM bugs** above the stratosphere."

"Sounds good, then."

"You're such a worrywort, Jint."

"Careful, Lafier. You yourself were looking blue in the face earlier."

"I have now steeled myself. I trust these individuals."

"We're honored," Malka smiled.

"Hey, it's not like I don't trust them..."

"Malka!" Min shouted through the loudspeaker.

"They're here. But no need to worry. It's just the fire ship from before. We can prepare to launch within a minute's time."

"What're you guys gonna do after launching us? They might come for you."

"We've some leeway on that end," grinned Malka.

"So we'll be just fine. We were born and raised in *Guzonh*; we'll never fall into the hands of a bunch of bonehead interlopers. What you should be worrying about is the danger you'll face after you lift off. The thing isn't armored, after all. Be careful."

"Thank you. But how exactly are we supposed to be careful, when it can't be steered?"

"I've heard the Abh are areligious. Are you?" asked Malka.

"No." The abrupt question took Jint aback, but he answered honestly. "My family's been Presbyterian Christians for generations. Not that I'm that devout."

"Then there is something you can do." Malka put a hand on Jint's shoulder in encouragement. "Pray."

"Is backup still not here!?" Keitt snarled. By Entryua's count, this was the fifth time he'd asked.

"They're here," reported the soldier, relieved.

Five airships had reached the mortuary, swapping blinking light signals in a bustle of activity. "Only five?" Keitt seemed displeased. "But the area is so vast! And they're unarmed transport ships, are they not!?"

"They're asking where they should touch ground, sir," said the soldier.

"I don't know, either! We have no other option but to search for one that's readying for liftoff. Destroy it on sight!"

But since *Guzonh* Mortuary made use of underground launchers, the spires were essentially nothing more than casket-rockets: the bullets to be fired, as opposed to the shooters. Of course, Entryua knew this, but he chose to remain silent.

Come on, Abh, you've got to be quick. Get on out of here.

If he was going to be killed no matter what, he wanted to at least witness the occupiers get outwitted and outmaneuvered before he bit the dust.

The indicator light switched from red to blue. "Interment preparations complete."

"Hurry! Liftoff in thirty seconds!" Min announced through the loudspeaker.

"Don't forget about our **interstellar ships**," said Malka, pointing to the coffin.

"I won't. I promise I will ask." And so Lafier laid herself into it.

"You too, young master," urged Bill.

"Right. Thanks for everything…"

"You'd better return the favor."

Jint lay sprawled beside her.

The coffin got sucked into the door, and each of its three layers of hatches closed one after the other. The interior was pitch dark.

"The indignity," Lafier muttered. "To be forced to ride a ship with neither outboard *frocragh* nor a **control gauntlet**."

"It's not even a *ship*," said Jint, as a reality check. "It's a casket. A caaaskeeet."

A pause.

"You've taken a sudden turn for the repellent. Get back from me!"

"Don't be like that, it's so cramped in this thing. Ow! Hey, I'm wounded here!"

"It's just a scratch," she intoned ruthlessly.

"I lied. Don't you know that I do that sometimes? OWW! Stop!"

VHRRRRRR... The coffin began vibrating.

"THERE!" Keitt's eyes reeled wide, staring at the spire rising gradually from below ground. "What are you doing? Why aren't you shooting!? Don't you see it!?"

The five air-mobile military personnel transport vessels dispersed, alighted on the spire's threshold, and deployed their troops.

"A flash signal!"

The soldier in the assistant steerer's seat leaned over the **console** and began making the landing lights blink. But the casket-rocket's majestic climb continued unabated even as they maneuvered.

Finally, the empennage reached above ground. The blast winds sliced across the surface. Several soldiers could be witnessed hurtling through the air.

The casket-rocket steadily picked up speed as it rose. Eventually, the fire ship briefly came face to face with it.

"Smash into it! RAM IT!!" Keitt demanded madly.

However, it was a firefighter who'd been compulsorily conscripted that was steering. There was no way they'd comply with an order that meant certain suicide. Even a soldier in the occupying army might doubt the validity of the idea. Contrary to orders, the steerer caused the fire ship to withdraw for fear of getting caught up in the rocket's shock waves.

Keitt nearly slipped down and out of the window as he began opening fire himself. "Why isn't anyone calling for backup, dammit? What are the anti-aircraft units doing!? Bombard them! Shoot that flying nuisance down!"

VWOOOM...

Hot winds blew in through the open window, and the aerial fire ship shook. Entryua promptly braced his head against the back of the seat in front of him. Even Keitt wasn't so crazed that he neglected to block against the shock waves with his arms. When Entryua looked up, he saw the casket-rocket had already reached high into the sky, its propulsor flames like a flower blooming in the night.

"Dammit, DAMMIT!!" Keitt opened fire again.

At last, fire opened from the surface. But it was too late. The casket-rocket had already reached well into the stratosphere. Like a phoenix glaring down at the lowly lower realm, its propulsor flames made nothing of the fruitless gunfire.

"It's no use," said a soldier in a cold tone. "The 'flying nuisance' has become a space-soaring nuisance…"

As soon as Entryua heard those words, the urge to crack up rose from his insides and broke through to his lips. He threw his head back and roared with laughter. He hadn't felt this invigorated in quite some time. The fear he might get murdered did flit through his mind, but it couldn't suppress the primal need to laugh.

"Damn it to hell," Keitt cried tearfully. "WHY!? Why must everything always go their way? Does God not grant us divine commendation? Is God unwilling to serve us up a single sacrifice? Give me something to salve my heart!"

That was when it clicked for Entryua. Though the Abh and the Silesia Unaging were both born of genetic modification, the environments of their upbringing could scarcely be more different. He realized that Keitt's hatred stemmed not from anything personal, but from a severe, tribal sort of *envy*.

And while a faint measure of sympathy for the military police captain returned, it wasn't enough to restrain the Lune Beega City Police Inspector's gales of laughter — and Entryua didn't care to stop laughing for some time.

"The destruction of the materials depot at 38 degrees 11 minutes east longitude, 52 degrees 24 minutes south latitude, has been carried out to completion," reported Cfadiss. "Next…"

"Please, **Senior Staff Officer**," said **Associate Commodore** Sporr, **Commander** of the **recon sub-fleet** the *Ftunéc*. "Don't annoy me with such overly detailed reports."

"But **Commander…**"

"I'm leaving the cleanup campaign of all ground targets to you."

"But I must at least report to you after the fact."

"And I'm telling you, you don't need your **commandant**," said Sporr, looking away. "This isn't combat. It's closer to an extermination."

Can't argue with that.

Cfadiss, for his part, was beginning to regret having proposed this strategy. There were 15,000 people under the military command of the troops stationed in Clasbure on the transport vessels that they'd captured in **Sfagnoff Marquessate** astrospace, and the ships' memory drives hadn't had their information deleted.

That was why they had been releasing 300 million **EM bugs** across city centers. EM bugs were nanomachines that, upon receiving radio waves of a certain wavelength, emitted pure noise at the same wavelength. And though the generating power of each individual bug was weak, together they made for an energy output not to be underestimated. Once UH-made EM bugs were released, it was impossible to stamp them all out in a single swoop.

As such, the **Star Forces** couldn't stop the radio jamming with great ease, but nor could the enemy themselves. In other words, not only did the remaining 200,000 enemy troops on Clasbure's surface lack a unified military command, they also couldn't communicate with each other.

With the strike on the alpine radio station at the mountain's peak, the jamming had stopped being planetary in scale. In some remote areas, it was even possible to receive notifications from orbit. However, in the metropolitan areas, highly populous as they were, word from the Abh had not yet reached them.

So here the *Ftunéc*, which flashed through space like heavy cavalry, was stuck making the **airship fleet**'s job as easy as they could, striking units on the move and enemy bases that were removed from urban centers, among other targets.

To tell the truth, it felt empty. It harmed the soul to shoot down defenseless enemy remnants. To complicate matters, most of the enemy was in hiding within the planet's cities, out of the reach of orbital attack.

"Be a dear and ask me for approval only when it might cause harm to befall any **landworld citizens**. Apart from that, you can conduct this *work* as you please." When she uttered the word *work*, she visibly balked with a pronounced frown.

"Understood," said Cfadiss, head lowered.

"How many hours until the main unit arrives?" asked Sporr.

"They're scheduled to arrive in four hours and fifteen minutes by ship's time."

"I see." Sporr stood up from her seat. "Now I will take my leave and away to the *Chicrh Raichacer* (Commandant's Room)."

"Yes, ma'am." Cfadiss saluted.

"**Senior Staff Officer**, it's an urgent transmission," said the **communications staff officer**.

"Forward it."

"Yes, sir." The **wristgear** beeped, indicating that the information had been transferred.

"Please wait, **Commandamt**, said Cfadiss, calling her to a halt as soon as he perused the transmission's contents.

"What is it?" Sporr about-faced.

"It appears the *bodœmiac* (recon ship) of the *Lardbyrch* has rescued some drifters in orbit."

"So?"

"The drifters in question claim to be **Her Highness the Viscountess of Parhynh** and the **Honorable Noble Prince of the Countdom of Hyde**."

"*Fïac Bœrr Parhynr*?" Sporr repeated. "What's an Abliar princess doing in a place like this?" She cocked her head. "Is she running away from home?"

"I doubt it…"

"You can't be serious!" The **Associate Commodore**'s **long robe** waved as she strode back to the **Commandant's Chair**. "There's no elegance in keeping the company of a rebellious teen."

"That's not it, though," said Cfadiss. "If I recall, *Fïac Bœrr Parhynr* was on the **patrol ship** *Gothelauth* as a **trainee starpilot**, while Lonh-*Ïarlucer Dreur Haïder* was aboard for a ride. As such…"

"I know, **Senior Staff Officer**. I see you're another serious-minded type."

Cfadiss stood there for a second. "I apologize."

"Don't apologize over something so stupid."

"I apol— ...Yes, ma'am."

"In any case, it's a miracle she managed to survive on a **landworld**. How are they doing now?"

"They're still aboard the **recon ship**. The **captain** of the *Lardbyrch* is asking what we should do. I believe we should have them come to this vessel directly."

"We, the graceful Sporrs, have never gotten along with the unrefined Abliars..." So the Commander monologued, eyes cast down and arms folded.

"Then shall we have the *Lardbyrch* stay in place for the time being? To await handling by **Commodore** Tlife?"

"What are you saying?" Her red eyes stared into the **senior staff officer's** quizzically. "Have them come here, because it sounds like fun!"

Chapter 10: The *Saïrhoth Lothlotagh* (Return to Strange Skies)

The **recon ship** landed on the **take-off deck** of the **flagship** of the **recon sub-fleet** *Ftunéc*, the **patrol ship** *Hairbyrch*.

"We're here." While stroking his injured shoulder, Jint peered at Lafier's profile. She had her head in her hands. "What's up with you?"

"The **Archduchess of *Laitpanh*,**" she muttered as though delirious. "The **commander** of this **sub-fleet** is the Archduchess of *Laitpanh*. Why now, of all times…"

"Oh, you mean **Associate Commodore** Sporr? What about her?"

"We, the agreeable Abliars, have never gotten along with the sly and insidious Sporrs."

"Wow."

"Not only did I just get saved by a Sporr, I'm forced to meet one in such clothes!" she bemoaned, looking down at her garb. It was a Clasbure-style "one-piece."

"Boarding preparations complete. Please come this way, *Lonh*." The **ship commander** with the **rearguard starpilot** insignia proved a tad more tongue-tied when addressing Lafier, though. "**Trainee Starpilot** Abliar." Lafier stood up and saluted.

"Thank you very much." Jint saluted too, and headed for the **air lock room**.

Around ten **starpilots** were already waiting for them at the take-off deck.

The **starpilot** standing in the center was like a carnivorous butterfly: beguiling, yet fierce. Her rank insignia, **associate commodore**: she could be none other than Associate Commodore Sporr.

Upon descending from the recon ship, Lafier saluted, and Jint bowed his head.

Sporr glared at Lafier's saluting form as though to find fault, and bowed gracefully from the waist. The attendant starpilots emulated her gesture.

"Welcome, *Fïac*, welcome, *Lonh*. By the way, Your Highness, please conduct yourself as a member of the **Imperial Household** on this ship."

"But…"

"I have not received contact from a **trainee starpilot**."

"But **Associate Commodore**…" Lafier insisted.

"Besides, I can't think of you as a **trainee starpilot** even if I wanted to, with that attire," said Sporr, delivering the final blow.

"Very well then." She saluted with indignation. "It's been a while, **Archduchess**."

"It truly has. I haven't seen **Your Highness** since the banquet in celebration of your admission to the **academy**." Sporr bowed. "And I must say, I as the **Archduchess of *Laitpanh***, must too congratulate the healthy manner with which Your Highness is growing. Or at least, I *would* like to, but it looks as though there has been a gnarl in your eye for beauty. Do tell me, what has led to that choice of clothing?"

"It wasn't my idea." Lafier glowered at Jint askance. "It was Jint — I mean, the **Noble Prince of the Countdom of Hyde**'s idea."

"Oh my…" Sporr's eyes opened wide with surprise. "You mean to say *Ïarlucec Dreur* gave you that garb to wear, and had you dye your hair black?"

"These clothes are an improvement. The first set *Ïarlucec Dreur* bought me was gaudier still."

"My, my, my…" Speechless, her crimson eyes turned to Jint.

Jint was perplexed and embarrassed. If he explained that it was out of pure necessity, would this Lonh-*Nimr* understand and be reasonable about it?

"Please forgive me, *Lonh*." To his shock, she bowed her head deeply to him, despite his lower rank.

"Uhh, for what?" His confusion only intensified.

"When I heard *Fïac Lartr Barcœr* (His Highness the King of Barkeh) approved the founding of the **Countdom of Hyde**, I believed it to be the height of eccentricity. I wondered whether it was prudent to make someone ignorant of the ways of the Abh into a **noble**. I mean no disrespect, but the surface defense weapons of the planet *Martinh* were not enough to pose any threat."

"'Eccentric,' you say…" Jint didn't know what to make of all that.

"But I've changed my mind since then. Your achievements more than befit the rank of a **count**, *Lonh*."

"Th-Thank you..." What did he do that befitted the rank of **count**? Did she mean how he protected Lafier? But going by the flow of the conversation, he doubted that was it...

"The quickness with which Abliars fly into rage, and the intensity of their wrath once aroused, has echoed through all corners of the **Empire** as a legendary object of fear. Moreover, I've heard that *Fïac Lamhirr* of the **Royal House of *Clybh*** is an Abliar among Abliars, in that her fiery rage can be compared only to the first instants of the birth of the universe."

"**Archduchess**," said Lafier. She had something to say.

Sporr ignored her. "And to think that you would dye the hair of that selfsame *Fïac Lamhirr* black, and clothe her with such bizarre apparel. Though I see the evidence before my very eyes, I can still scarcely believe it. That's a feat for a *lœbec* (marquess), no, a *laicerec* (duke), let alone a **count**. You have my heartfelt admiration."

Jint cast his eyes down. He was unable to accept her words of praise as such. In fact, it seemed as though she was indirectly chastising him for dressing Lafier in peculiar garb.

"Don't let it get to you, Jint," Lafier said apologetically. "She's using you to make fun of me. It is in the nature of a Sporr to be as twisted as a molecule of nucleic acid. If I may borrow the **Archduchess**'s phrasing, Lonh-*Painaigr* of the *Nimïec Laitpanr* is a Sporr among Sporrs, in that she is renowned for having brought the technique of veiled disparagement the Sporr family has refined over a thousand years to the level of an artform."

"Hohhh ho ho ho!" Sporr threw back her pale white throat and laughed. Then she peered square into Jint's eyes for the first time. "But it's true that I like you, **noble prince**. I was told you will be a **quartermaster starpilot**. I invite you to fight under me."

"Before we discuss the future, there's a more important matter, **Archduchess**," Lafier cut in. She seemed flustered for some reason. "Could you lend me a **military uniform**? I'd also like to shed this hair dye."

"A **uniform** will be fetched for you on the double. As for your hair, how do we remove the dye? Might a hot bath be to your aid?"

"I tried. It didn't work."

"Then what is it we ought to do?"

"I don't know."

Lafier looked at Jint. Sporr looked at Jint. Jint looked bewildered.

"Now that you mention it, I feel like there was something about that in the product directions... Unfortunately, I threw it out..."

The two Abh females kept staring.

"Uhhh... There were plenty of those hair dye things on Clasbure, so if we touched down and asked somebody..."

"Just now, I heard somebody somewhere suggest a truly alarming idea." Sporr shuddered. "The idea goes that the **starpilots** of my glorious *Ftunéc* should descend onto a **landworld** still controlled by the enemy. That they should clear away enemy resistance, get their **uniforms** drenched in enemy blood, capture a frightened and quavering **landworld citizen**, and ask them: Hey, you know how to get rid of hair dye?' What a dreadful notion! The *Ftunéc*'s prestige would crash down to the ground."

Jint's shoulders drooped. "You're right." With the two of them safe and sound, the fact that enemy soldiers were still holding out on Clasbure's surface had slipped his mind.

"This is what I suggest we do: let's borrow a strand of *Fïac*'s hair. I'll send it to the *Cruriac* (Pharmaceutical Branch). Then we'll have them analyze it and formulate a drug to get the dye off. What do you say?"

"Please do so. There's also this." Lafier pulled the **memchip** up off her chest. "It's the navigation log of the **patrol ship** *Gothelauth*."

When Lafier held the **memchip** in hand, the starpilots saluted it.

After a moment of solemnity, Sporr gave a sign. "**Senior Staff Officer**, go take it off her hands."

"Yes." The starpilot with the emerald green hair and a mysteriously fatigued look on his otherwise arresting countenance stepped forward to receive the **memchip** with due reverence.

"Now then, *Fïac*, *Ïarlucec*, please follow me. I'll take you to your rooms. Actually, on second thought, it looks as though we should take the noble prince to the infirmary first," she said, eyes on his left shoulder. "I can't help but marvel at how it could even be possible: to get off with just an injured shoulder after fitting Her Highness with such *amusing* dress!"

"I'm not the one who shot him!" she snapped.

37 minutes later...

The *glagac byrec Tlaïmr* (flagship of the Tlife fleet), the **patrol ship** *Cairdigh*, reemerged into **3-space** from the **Sfagnoff Portal**. And as soon as it did, they received copious amounts of data in communications from the *Hairbyrch*, which they then began to greedily consume.

"*Lonh*," said **Kilo-Commander** Cahyoor.

"What?" **Commodore** Tlife looked up.

"Word has come in that *Fïac Bœrr Parhynr* and Lonh-Ïarlucer Dreur Haïder have been rescued."

Tlife grunted disbelievingly, mouth agape. It was just so implausible. He'd known them to have been on the **patrol ship** *Gothelauth*. What were they doing out here? "Is the *Gothelauth* actually intact?"

"I'm afraid not. It would seem the *Gothelauth* did fall in battle."

"Ah. I'm truly sorry to hear that. But if that's the case, then why is *Fïac Lartnér* here?"

"It appears she escaped as per the **ship commander**'s orders, and fled from danger to this **landworld**. However, the full report has yet to be composed, so I don't know the details."

"Hmm... Well, I can't blame you."

"*Fïac Lartnér* carried the *Gothelauth*'s navigation log back with her, and there is some information of especial interest recorded therein."

"Go on, then."

"I have ascertained whence they surfaced."

"Where was it?"

"**Portal 193 of *Céïch*.** According to the **ship commander**'s inference, they carried a portal from the area 4.1 light-years away to the Bascotton Star System."

"The ship commander being **Hecto-Commander** Lecsh... She was a fine **starpilot**," he said, pacing.

"Yes. Her reasoning process was fluid and unstrained, and I agree with the conclusion the **Hecto-Commander** reached. As for the analysis of the rest of the information stored in the captured ships, we have only just begun, but I assume it will corroborate her deductions."

The **map of planar space** rose back into view on the **Commander's Bridge**. Cahyoor indicated as he spoke: "Two **domains** exist between this point and **Portal 193 of *Céïch*.** They are the *Bœrscorh Gamtécr* (*Gamtéch* Viscountdom) and the **Febdash Barony.** I strongly suggest we split the **fleet** with all haste in order to allow the **lords** and the *gosuclach* (servant corps) to evacuate, if possible."

"Are we able to contact the **Vorlash Countdom?** Perhaps by skirting around **Portal 193 of *Céïch*?**" he pondered, back to standing still.

"We ought to try it. Shall we use the *Ftunéc?*"

"I think the *Ftunéc* might need to recuperate at the moment," Tlife feared.

"No other ships can bear to take up this mission," Cahyoor stated authoritatively.

"True..." Tlife nodded. "We need to carry on quickly. Let's drive the *Ftunéc* to the edge of exhaustion."

"Yes, sir. We mustn't, however, make those two accompany the ships there."

"Of course not. Why do you always insist on pointing out the obvious? Arrange for a ship to transfer them to at once."

"Understood."

"Surgery complete. But you received great first aid." The **army medic**, a genetic Lander, removed the *creurpaucec* (medical support machine) from Jint's shoulder. "So great we probably should've just left it as is. In any case, it'll be awkward for a bit, but by the time you reach *Lacmhacarh* your tissues will've totally regenerated." The medic bandaged Jint's left shoulder and made the dressing stiffen.

"Thanks." Jint stared at the shoulder. His new cast had hardened in place, running from his elbow up.

"Your clothes are here, by the way. Hope you like the design." The medic proffered the **jumpsuit.** Its left sleeve came out at around the hips. The rest of the outfit above the hips was seamless. It was tailored to match Jint's present figure.

"I like it a lot," he said, putting it on.

Then a **linewing starpilot** entered the infirmary with impeccable timing, as though they'd estimated Jint's surgery would be done at that moment.

"This **sub-fleet** has been tasked with a new mission," they stated. "We must have you depart the ship, *Lonh*."

"What, already?" said Jint, surprised.

"The **Commander** expresses her chagrin. She said she would've liked to ask you all about your adventures over a meal."

"Please give her my regards."

"Of course. Now, come with me, if you would."

Jint bade the **army medic** goodbye and exited the infirmary. The starpilot led him to the **take-off deck**.

"We'll be having *Lonh* and *Fïac* transfer to the **carrycraft** the *Aicrurh*. Since it will be taking you to the **imperial capital** without stopping, you should be home in around three days."

"I've never been to *Lacmhacarh*," admitted Jint.

"Is that so?" The **starpilot** looked a tad taken aback.

Upon embarking onto the **smallcraft**, he found Lafier waiting inside.

She was wearing a **military uniform** without any rank insignia, and her hair had turned bluish-black once again. "Hey, look at that, it's back to normal," he said jocundly. Though her black hair and "one piece" look had a charm all its own, seeing her now convinced him that her true hair color and a **military uniform** suited her the best.

"Do you really think it's back to normal?"

"Yeah, of course…" But Lafier's eyes and tone rang alarm bells in his head, and he lost all conviction.

"Look carefully." Lafier held some strands in hand. "It's lost color."

Now that she mentioned it, the color did look slightly lighter, closer to a primary shade of blue than before. "But this color's pretty, too," he said, trying to pacify her. He was about to defend himself, before realizing that there was no need.

The situation had demanded her hair be dyed. Besides, there was no reason she had to be in such a rush to remove the dye anyway. If more time had been spent analyzing it, it may even have proved possible to formulate a chemical capable of doing the job without damaging her hair.

"I'm not attacking you," said Lafier. "I'm simply disappointed in your faulty memory."

"C'mon, it's not *that* different!"

While Lafier hadn't been angry before, those words sealed his fate. The **royal princess** turned away pouting, and refused to speak until they sat down for breakfast the next day.

Chapter 11: The Imperial Capital of Lacmhacarh

It was the city without a map. The positions of structures that comprised it, unanchored by ground or land, rolled in a state of constant flux around the curves in space created by gravity. Only the *Spodéc Bilr Arocr* (Capital Traffic Bureau) had a grasp of their positions at any given moment, yet the next moment they would be somewhere else entirely anyway. That was why the city was called the *Birautec Cnaigena* (Turbulent Capital).

Another of its names was the *Sath Nocher* (Base of the Dragon's Necks), for the *Gaftnochec* on the **crest** of the **Empire** was also a metaphor for the Empire. The eight **monarchies** and the *bill* (routes) ran through them were often likened to the eight heads of the *nochec* (dragon). And no other place could be said to be where those heads were joined.

Yet another of the city's monikers was the decidedly more straightforward *Birautec Gasauder* (Capital of Eight Portals). There were multiple star systems with more than one portal, but only one with as many as eight in human-inhabited space. In the distant past, a millennium ago by the city's time, eight **closed portals** once scattered across the vast reaches of space were borne here by colossal starships, and summarily opened.

Further, it was dubbed the *Gyrsauge Frybarer* (Cradle of the Empire), for the greatest empire humankind had ever seen — an empire whose history would be tinged with blood and fire — traced its beginnings here.

It was through that ghastly history that the city earned the name *Daüatsariac* (The Unfelled). Many a time, the capital opened war with haughty arrogance, even in the face of likely defeat, and many a time, they watched the **propulsor flames** of enemy ships as they sailed away. But in the end, those enemies didn't undergo any infamous fall. Even the nations that made it all the way to invading the capital simply became the blood and bones of the empire, long-lived and triumphant.

Birautec Négr, another such sobriquet, meant "Capital of Love." Opportunities for brushes with romance were few and far between for a race that spent their days aboard **interstellar ships** and in **orbital estates**, and who were thinly scattered across a whopping range. As such, it was customary to spend half of one's life in this metropolis. In *Lacmhacarh*, open invitation banquets were always being held somewhere, and the Abh searched for a lover with whom the sparks reached supernova intensity.

Of course, more than a few simply referred to the city as *Murrautec* (Homespace). A majority of Abhs were the products of an explosive love triggered in the city. They were born here, scattered across the galaxy wide, and then one day returned.

The Turbulent Capital, and too, the **Root of the Dragon's Heads**. The **Capital of Eight Portals**, and too, the **Cradle of the Empire**, and too, the **Homespace,** and too, **The Unfelled**. These all were *Lacmhacarh*, and *Lacmhacarh* was all these.

The name of the **imperial capital**'s sun was Abliar. So too the city-ship their founding ancestors lived on, the surname of the **emperor**, and the star that illuminated their home were all called. When the group of people that birthed the Abh, (who could be called their indirect ancestors), lived off the land on their bow-shaped island chain, not yet having unraveled the secrets of the gene or the mysteries of the heavens above, the name of the sun goddess they worshiped, "Amaterasu," shifted drastically over the ages, ending up as "Abliar." This star system was therefore also known as the *Dreuhynh Abliarser* (Abliar Countdom). Incidentally, the **title** of *Dreuc Abliarser* (Count of Abliar) was always held by the current emperor.

As for Abliar the sun, those who drew closer could view the globular "basket" encompassing it. The spaces punctuating its trihexagonal tiling mesh were large, but the mesh itself was made of thin fibers. "Thin," that is, in comparison to the star itself; more precisely, the band-like structures spanned 500 *üésdagh* in width. The sides of the bands facing the sun were solar batteries, and the opposite sides contained countless linear accelerators which produced **antimatter fuel** without pause. It constituted the largest **antimatter fuel factory** in not just the **Empire**, but the known universe.

The **imperial capital** measured 300 *saidagh* in diameter, was shaped much like a sickle, and orbited at a distance of six *saidagh* from Abliar. The *Rüébéïc* (Imperial Palace), the **Royal Palaces**, the *garich arocr* (capital manors) of **grandees**, the *bach* (joined residences) of **gentry** and **imperial citizens**, the *débh* (space gardens), the *ilébh* (shopping halls), the **Star Forces** facilities, the *locrh* (warship construction sites)... It was a gathering of these kinds of artificial planetoids, and more. Innumerable **intrasystem ships**, as well as **interstellar ships** coming from **planar space**, soared through the city. Each facility possessed a measure of maneuverability, and avoided collision automatically.

The eight portals were evenly spaced in orbit 100 *saidagh* out from *Lacmhacarh*, each accompanying a *lonidec hoca* (mobile fort), and revolving in the opposite direction relative to the **capital**. Emerging now from one of those eight, the *Saudec Ilicr* (*Ilich* Portal), the **carrycraft** the *Aicrurh* carried Lafier and Jint into the **Abliar Countdom**.

Carrycrafts were different from **conveyance ships** in that they were constructed more like small-scale **cargo passenger ships**. Since they were meant to carry important guests and messengers in addition to information, the ship contained twelve rooms furnished with sanitary facilities, as well as a common room of modest size.

Jint, who was busy doing absolutely nothing in the living room, took a peek into the common room, to find Lafier there, much to his surprise. She was rarely there. "Hey-ya, report finished yet?"

"Yep." Lafier looked over her shoulder, pointing at the big screen in front. "What's your impression of *Lacmhacarh*?"

The **Homespace** was there to see. It was the first time Jint had laid eyes on such a cluster of lights. Splendorous and manifold of color, the array almost literally dazzled. With the ship and *Lacmhacarh*'s orbits coplanar with each other, it struck him as though he were viewing a galaxy from the side.

"It's even more amazing than I was expecting."

"I see!" said the **royal princess**, with a smile of unvarnished delight.

Jint grabbed himself some **coffee** and took the seat beside her. Regarding his first impressions of Lacmhacarh, Jint certainly hadn't lied. Yet a different emotion entirely was currently taking up his heart. Loneliness.

He'd taken quite the detour, but here at last he'd reached the **imperial capital** from the **Vorlash Countdom**. And now his journey was drawing to a close. This meant goodbye. He and Lafier would part, and there was no guarantee they'd ever see each other again.

On top of that, Lafier had holed herself up saying she needed to write the report, spending time with him almost only during meals. The feeling wasn't pleasant.

"Did the *Manoüass* (Captain) inform you?" asked Lafier.

"Of what?"

"We are proceeding toward the **Imperial Palace**."

"What, directly?" Jint was surprised.

"Yep. It appears **Her Majesty the Empress** wishes to speak of many things."

"Speak to you, you mean."

"Not just me. She wishes also to speak to you, it would seem."

"Whoa nelly," Jint tensed. "You're laying that on me like it's no big deal. Though I guess to you, she's your grandma."

"A year has passed since last I met Her Majesty."

"Yeah? Must be tons you wanna talk to her about, then."

"There is much to discuss, yes, but **Her Majesty** must be busy with all of her duties. In case you've forgotten, the **Empire** is currently at war."

"I know, I know. Heard anything about how the war's shaping up?"

"No, I'm out of the loop as well." She leaned her head in. "Worried?"

"'Course I am. Have *you* forgotten where my home planet is?"

Not far from the field of battle lay the **Countdom of Hyde**, whose residents continued to call Jint "heir to the traitor." The **Ilich Monarchy** was shaped like a ring, so contact wouldn't be severed immediately, but if it ever got annexed like the **Sfagnoff Marquessate** did, well, even just thinking about it chilled the nerves. The people of his homeland would probably be far more amenable to an occupying army than the **landworld citizens** of Sfagnoff were. He kept picturing, despite himself, what sort of treatment his father, the **Count of Hyde**, might receive at their hands. Though they hadn't met in years, and they'd never been very close, he was still his one and only blood relative.

"Ah. Right." Lafier's expression turned uncomfortable, embarrassed. "Forgive me my foolish question."

"It's all right. I myself forgot all about it while we were on Clasbure."

"We were fairly occupied."

"To say the least. You know, sometimes you really put things super mildly," said Jint, in admiration.

The lights of the **capital** approached, closer and closer, and the nearest structure came into focus. A set of spheres were stacked together, and they made a giant tube wriggle like a tentacle. It lent the appearance of a strange life form that had reached an evolutionary dead end.

"It's the *Locrh Baiturr* (*Baiturh* Warship Construction Site). The **patrol ship** *Gothelauth* was born there," said Lafier.

"Interesting."

"See that?" Lafier pointed at the spheroid beyond the site. "That's a *sodmronh* (babygarten). There are a few of them around Homespace. Inside, it's near weightless due to microgravity, the lining is soft, and foam stars are floating in the air. A while after birth, babies are given **circlets** and dropped there. That's how they learn the law of action and reaction, and how to use their circlets. If an Abh doesn't experience this during the developmental period, their brain's *rilbidoc* navigational area will never form..."

As Jint nodded and interjected to indicate to Lafier that he was listening as she began to describe the sites to see in the **capital**, he inwardly wondered whether she felt any sorrow over their imminent parting, and if she would express reluctance to leave him.

When they arrived at the **Imperial Palace, chamberlains** who were stern of feature pulled Jint away from her. Due to his experience in the **Febdash Barony**, he grew apprehensive, but his fears proved groundless. He was led to a grand and extensive **bathing room**, in whose warming waters he stretched out. After a thorough cleanse, he exited the **bathing room** to find a change of clothes already prepared for him.

Just as the **army medic** had predicted, his shoulder had completely healed. The hole had closed up with new skin, and the bones were devoid of pain.

He donned a **jumpsuit** with the hems of its sleeves at the shoulders, as well as a **long robe**, as usual. A **circlet** identical to the one that had been stolen from him at the **barony** and a **wristgear** to replace the one he'd borrowed from Sehrnye also lay for the taking. After putting on the full attire of an **Abh noble**, Jint gave the sign just as he'd been instructed.

"Please come with me," said a **chamberlain** who'd arrived at his summons, standing at attention to guide his way.

A **personal transporter** awaited him in the hallway. "You may get on."

"Okay." Jint stepped up onto it, and the chamberlain got on after him to input orders into its **console**. "Uhh, where are we going?" asked Jint timidly as the podium took off.

"To the waiting room of the **audience chamber**."

"The **audience chamber**!? But I thought it's only used for important events…"

"That is correct."

"So, uhh, what's on today?"

The chamberlain looked back, dark blue eyebrows raised. "Are you honestly unaware?"

"Know what, forget I said anything." He was happy so long as his astuteness level was deemed higher than that of a clump of blue-green algae.

"Quit your fidgeting, Jint," Lafier frowned. She'd arrived at the waiting room before him, and was sipping out of a glass.

"Sometimes you demand stuff that's easier said than done," said Jint, whose nerves were not so readily dispelled. "I've got no idea what the proper protocol is. Are there, like, special manners to this, or…?"

"It's not such a big deal. Just be at your most polite, as common sense dictates."

"C'mon, I can't have you forgetting that I'm not exactly an expert on Abh 'common sense.'"

"Then do as I do. We shall walk up to the **throne**, make a deep bow, and wait until we're greeted. It could hardly be simpler."

"Does sound pretty simple," Jint admitted.

"Because it is."

A **chamberlain** entered the room. "Thank you for waiting, *Fïac*, *Lonh*. All preparations have been made."

"Yes." Jint made to walk over to the chamberlain.

"Not there. Over here." Lafier pointed to the giant doors.

"Look at me, messing up before it's even begun," Jint muttered.

"Walk alongside me, and match my pace."

"Ah, right. Got it."

"You ought to hold your head up high. You're a hero, after all."

"Well that's the first I've heard of that."

"You're such an *onh*."

The big doors opened. The soft light of morning bathed the **audience chamber**. Basking directly in the rays of Abliar, it played across the room resplendent. A number of beams spanned the ceiling, but without a roof to support. Instead one could view the bright blue sky — for a *chnobézsiac* (scattering surface) splayed above them. From the beams hung **crest banners**, the flags of the **grandees** that made up the **Empire**. Jint noticed the brand-new crest banner of the **Countdom of Hyde** all the way in front.

Rows of *Sach Idarr* (Honor Guard NCCs), one to the left and one to the right, were standing straight with a dignified air. They trod across the black marble floor, approaching the **throne** as they did so.

Sach Arobhotr (Military Band NCCs) played the *Rüé Oll* (Imperial Anthem). The lyrics of the anthem weren't being sung, but Jint knew them. They heralded eternal prosperity for the **Empire**, and expressed its determination to live to be at the bedside of a dying cosmos. In its arrogance and temerity, it was a very Abh anthem indeed.

Since Jint hated the idea of bungling this like he had when he first met Lafier, he'd tried his best while still in the carrycraft to memorize the faces of the distinguished people he might encounter. Thanks to those efforts, he could distinguish the faces of the three people standing before them.

The one who stood up from the **Jade Throne** (its back to the **crest banners** of the **eight royal families**, which surrounded the still-larger **imperial flag**), was of course none other than **Her Majesty the Empress** *Lamagh*. The man with blue-grey hair, standing on the right and a step below the **throne**, was Lafier's father, *Larth Clybr Fïac Debeuser* (His Higness *Debeusec*, King of *Clybh*). Below him smiled a handsome indigo-haired boy. He could only be Lafier's younger brother, *Bœrh Üemdaiser Fïac Duhirr* (His Highness Duhier, Viscount of Wemdyse).

Jint felt disoriented. Though they were the **Empress** and the **King of Clybh**, he couldn't see them as anything but Lafier's siblings, so young they looked. At the same time, his brain categorized the *Clybh* King as being older than the Empress. On an intellectual level, he understood the Abh didn't physically age past a certain point, but seeing it in person threw him for a loop. How did the Abh themselves deal with this headache?

Lafier knelt upon the white carpet below the tiers leading to the **throne**. Jint hastened to follow her example.

"Stand, *Ïarlucec Dreur*," intoned a nearby voice.

When he looked up in surprise, he found *Lamagh* had descended from the **throne** to stand right in front of him. "On your feet," she prompted.

"Yes." Jint got back up.

"You will accept the thanks of the Abliars, *Ïarlucec*. This girl," she said, pointing to Lafier, "is nobody quite yet, but she holds much potential. And you are the one who safeguarded that potential, and brought it home safely. If it hadn't been for you, we would have never gotten another chance to see this hatchling alive."

Jint turned red. "But I... I didn't do anything. I was the one who got rescued, time after time..."

"Not so, *Ïarlucec*," said *Lamagh*, taking his hand. "Seeing as you may very well not have realized it, We do not think you are deliberately lying. Yet had you not rightfully told her to retreat when you did, she would have pressed on without ever ceasing, and fallen as a result. Though it may be in the nature of this clan of ours to misread when to withdraw, that disposition is particularly pronounced in this young one. Furthermore, you are an **Abh** that knows the ways of **landworlds**. Without that special and rare quality, it's not clear what fate she would have met."

She stared back at him at close quarters, her comely countenance so like Lafier's, her red-brown eyes radiating gratitude. While the **Empress**'s hands felt pleasantly cool, there was also, somehow, a warmth to them. Jint was disconcerted, abashed.

"Allow me to express my gratitude as well, *Ïarlucec*," said Dubeus. "To us who have first drawn breath in *Lacmhacarh*, **landworlds** are strange lands with strange skies. The majority of us were born in the Abh world, and die in the Abh world, without ever having so much as set foot on a planet's surface. I don't mean to offend you, but to state the unvarnished truth, we're afraid of surface worlds, Count Heir. I can't begin to express how thankful I am for bringing her back from one."

"Um…" Daringly, Jint rebutted. "There are people on **landworlds** with their hearts in the right place, and without their help, we would have gotten captured by the enemy."

"You misunderstand, *Ïarlucec*," Debeus smiled. "I'm not saying we think people on **landworlds** are typically wicked, or any such thing. In fact, when it comes to wickedness, we don't plan to be outdone by anybody. The fact is that Lander and Abh lifestyles are extremely different. And the clash of cultures can easily result in people slain. Moreover, that land was ruled over by people who detested us as vermin. If you weren't there to serve as a mediator, then my daughter wouldn't be standing here today."

"He speaks the truth, *Ïarlucec*," said *Lamagh*. "I have already read the **royal princess**'s report. As such, I know of the people who ended up saving you two on the **landworld**. They, too, have earned my everlasting thanks. However, now is the time for *you* to be acknowledged."

"But she saved me just as much. Especially when we were in **space**."

"That was the mission that Lecsh had entrusted to her." At her name, a brief flash of sorrow flitted across his flawless features. "*Ïarlucec*, you're unaccustomed to the **spacefaring world**. My daughter was ordered to help you cross that unfamiliar world. By that same token, no one ordered you to help her cross the **landworld**. You must credit yourself the venerableness of your deeds, *Ïarlucec*," said *Lamagh* firmly. "At least as of now, to us, there can be no nobler act."

"Please allow me to give you my thanks, too, Lonh-*Ïarlucer Dreur*," cut in *Duhirh*, his manner humble. "I'm so happy you've reunited me with my sister."

When Duhier offered his frank, unaffected vote of thanks, Jint's heart was finally soothed. The gratitude of the **Empress** and **King** was so lofty that try as he might, it didn't feel real or deserved. While their sentiments had come through, he felt so out of place that the back of his mind insisted they must be alluding to some other Jint.

"I am honored, *Fïac*," he said, bowing his head. "*Érumittonn, Fïac Lartr*, your praises are very generous, and I am most flattered and obliged."

"That's just how honorable you were, Jint," whispered Lafier. "Carry yourself bolder, more confidently."

"Am I coming across *that* nervous?" He thought he was already doing everything he could to uphold his dignity, so he was reluctant to go over the top.

"Yes. You're so blue in the face one would think you're being denounced."

"*Far frymec* (my daughter), my love, your report has a glaring omission," said Debeus, with an amused look. "You failed to mention how close you've become with *Ïarlucec Dreur Haïder.*"

"Can you blame me, after all the perils we faced, Father?" Lafier replied.

"No, I cannot," he said, though his devilish grin persisted. "What say you and I go on a walk, Lafier? It's been a while."

"Leave Us for the moment, Lafier," said *Lamagh*, her tone pensive. "It appears We have an unpleasant duty to attend to. You are to follow Us, *Ïarlucec Dreur.*"

"Yes... Uhh, what's this about an unpleasant duty?"

"We must be the bearer of bad news."

Lafier followed her father, treading across white sand. Pure, clear water formed a streamlet over the sand bed. Suffused with soft reflected light, the walls and ceiling also gleamed white, bereft of even a single blemish.

All over the handful of white columns, glyphs were written in miniscule text; since they weren't inlaid, they couldn't be read except up close. They were the names of those who had died for the sake of the **Empire**, engraved in order of passing without regard to social status (and, in the case of simultaneous death, in alphabetical order). Sufficiently close inspection would turn up people with the surname Abliar amongst the names of the various **gentry** and **imperial citizens**. In addition, one phrase was engraved at the top of each of the stone pillars: *Frybarec a dal fronédé*: The Empire shall not forget thee.

This was the *Graich Fronétara* (Hall of Remembrance), the most sacred room to the race that ridiculed all religions. Dubeus halted in front of one of the pillars.

"I forget, did I welcome you back yet?"

"No. You have not graced me with your words of welcome yet," she answered.

"Then welcome back, *dorfrymec* (prodigal daughter). I'm glad you made it home." Dubeus looked back. "Your flesh may remain young, but your mind and spirit will age with time. Even as an Abh, whose body will stay youthful to your dying day, your *true* youth will be over in the blink of an eye. And I'm wrestling with that reality as we speak. You've been through quite the valuable experience, and all during your true youth, at that."

Debeus looked back at the pillar, and stared at one name in particular. Lafier got closer to see it for herself.

Laicch Üémh Lobér Placïac

"There's something else I've neglected to tell you, *far négh* (my love). I didn't alter your genes. You're all natural. That is why your **Abliar ears** are so small."

Lafier looked up. "But why do such a thing?"

"Because there was no need to alter them, of course. *Placïac* just so happened to give me a wonderful gift, and with my level of talent, if I had adjusted your genes, there was no way I could make you even more beautiful than you already were."

"Father, I'm not sure I understand why," she said, confused by her own feelings, "but hearing that makes me happy."

Debeus laughed lightly. "Is that right? Then I'm glad. I'd been under the impression that you resented me about your ears."

"In truth, I did, somewhat," Lafier confessed.

"Well, I suppose that was inevitable, *noüonn* (beauteous one)." On that note, Dubeus fell silent, fixing his eyes on the name engraved on the pillar. Lafier too stood there, quietly gazing with her father.

"It was a glorious time," spoke Dubeus at last. "Right by a dying giant star... and also at the edge of an event horizon... and even in a nebula in the midst of becoming a star... *Placïac* and I loved each other, and we would use each other's privileges, and we'd annoy each other in grandiose fashion."

"'Privileges'? You mean to annoy the other?"

"No. To be annoyed." A faint little smile floated to his lips. "I'm relieved, *asaugec* (little child). You're still too young to fall in love."

"Am I really..." Lafier reacted sharply, but she couldn't issue a retort.

"When that marvelous time began to pull away from me, I couldn't believe it. But despite my disbelief, I could feel it in my bones. I could practically hear the sound of the footsteps as those days slipped away. That's why I, at the very least..."

"Father, don't tell me..." Doubt welled within her heart. "You aren't saying that you had me birthed me as a memento of *Cya Placér* (Dame Plakia), surely."

"Was that wrong of me?" Dubeus traced Lecsh's name with a finger. "Back then, *Placïac* was my everything. Tell me, *sériac* (shining one), is it not a matter of course to always want a keepsake on hand of such a splendid moment?"

"I am not a memento, Father. Nor am I a copy of *Cya Placér*!" Her doubt had turned to wrath.

"Of course, my little *loreucec isarhotr* (slave to fury). You are different from her. *Placïac* was bright. *She* would never raise her voice for no reason."

"FOR NO REASON!?" Lafier's anger only increased. "I am who I am! To think I thought you loved me for who I am..."

"I do love you. If I didn't, then why would I call you **my love**?" said Dubeus, unperturbed.

"You love me solely as an echo of *Cya Placér*."

"Wrong again. I love you for you, *gnac Ablïarser* (Abliar flower)."

"I don't believe you, Father."

"I didn't think you would, *clasononn noüa* (headstrong beauty). But know this: you were born as a *üabœdec Placér* (memento of Plakia), but grew into **my love**. As you are now, you look just like her, but inwardly you're totally different. I'll refrain from telling you how exactly you're different from her. It's true that in the past, my love passed through you and flew to Plakia, but I no longer see her behind you."

Lafier was far from convinced. She had respected **Hecto-Commander** Lecsh as a person and as a **starpilot**. She had looked up to her. Yet she wanted her father to acknowledge her as a person in her own right. And though he was telling her he did think of her as her own person, she couldn't think of that as anything other than a smokescreen.

"Please tell me: was it your idea that I be placed in **Dame Plakia**'s ship, Father?"

"I suppose calling it a coincidence would be too much. I wanted her to polish the treasure I raised, my *lamh* (ruby). I may be a reserve soldier, but I am technically an **associate commodore** in **rank**, so I do have some lobbying clout." Dubeus briefly became lost in thought. "Hmm... I suppose I won't be a reserve for much longer. War is upon us now... And I shudder to think that I might be placed under a certain laddie of the **royal family of Barkeh**."

"'Laddie'? But I thought you and *Fïac Lartr Barcœr* (His Highness the King of Barkeh) were the same age..." said Lafier, half without thinking.

"I was born from the **artificial womb** three months ahead of him. It makes a world of difference. When we were young, I would always win whenever we fought."

"Never mind that, Father." A fresh new seed of doubt had sprouted. "Were you behind Jint getting on the *Gothelauth*, too?"

"Yep. It was mostly coincidental, though. There were as many as 15 ships fit for *Ïarlucec Dreur* to ride, I pushed her ship to be the one from behind the scenes. I'd thought you ought to have at least one friend from a **landworld** — though I could never have imagined you'd grow that close."

"I'm beginning to think you were the force behind everything... even maybe the United Humankind's invasion."

"Then you overestimate me, **daughter of mine**. If I guided the enemy or somesuch, then your grandmother would rip me limb from limb."

"Perhaps so, but you're taking measures where I can't see in order to mold me..." Lafier didn't much care for that fact.

"Because I am your parent. I received half of Plakia and sired you, then raised you by myself. But that too is now over. You are already a *frymec Frybarer* (daughter of the Empire)."

"Is that so?" Lafier stared at Dubeus's profile with eyes of incertitude.

"She was a fantastic woman," said Dubeus, ignoring his beloved child's misgivings as he steeped himself back into reminiscence. "When I first met her, I was a **Deca-Commander** with a poor record, and she was a **linewing starpilot** with a bright future ahead of her. I can think of a hundred reasons she had me spellbound, but I still can't think of a single reason she fell for me."

"It must have been the royal *Fïac* in your **title**." Lafier surprised herself. She herself had little idea why she'd blurted something so mean. It was most likely her anger toward her father.

Dubeus looked back at her. The way his eyes were narrowed spoke volumes of his ire. Lafier's father stood out among his clan as a relatively calm and gentle sort, but even so, he was still an Abliar. "You've known Plakia since you were a baby. You've even been on her ship. Yet I see you would appraise the woman who is half of you as one blinded by social status, *Abliarsec Nëïc Dubreuscr Bœrh Parhynr Lamhirh*. Answer carefully."

"No." Lafier hung her head. "She was not that kind of person."

For a short while, Dubeus observed his daughter. He sensed her true remorse. "Very well, *onh*. See to it you don't spout such nonsense again."

"Yes…" Lafier couldn't bring herself to lift her face. "Please, just tell me one more thing. Do you know what **Dame Plakia** thought of me?"

"I do. She once wrote to me that she was proud of you."

"Proud of me…" The old days she spent with Plakia came flooding to mind. Vivid memories of the woman that held a position in her life that on most **landworlds** would be called "mother." Fun, happy memories… Suddenly, her vision turned blurry, and some warm liquid streaked down her cheeks.

"Are you weeping, Lafier?" noticed Dubeus.

"I'm not crying because you scolded me," she said through her convulsive sobbing. It was as though she'd regressed to her days as an infant.

"Then are you weeping over Plakia's death?"

Lafier couldn't speak, so frantic was she to curtail her sobbing fit. She simply nodded wordlessly.

"I'm disappointed in you. It seems I've raised you wrong." But his tone was full of affection "Come to think of it, this may be the first time you've cried since you were in nappies, *socrh ghainena* (steel heart)."

Dubeus pulled Lafier into his arms. "Listen, Lafier. Our clan has a reputation to protect. We Abliars are ruthless. We Abliars are callous. We Abliars wouldn't raise an eyebrow if death were to snatch away our closest friends and most intimate lovers. If it ever came out that an Abliar shed a tear or two, what would become of the infamy our ancestors carefully built? I don't care if you rage. You may even laugh and smile from time to time. However, no one born an Abliar has the right to weep. Even amongst fellow relatives, you cannot let your guard down. If you really must cry, do so in secret."

"It's not fair, Father!" Her tear-stained face looked at him from his breast.

"What isn't?"

"You never taught me how to cry without shedding tears!"

In the room to which the **Empress** accompanied Jint, a man in **military uniform** waited at attention.

She introduced him: "This is **Vice Hecto-Commander** *Birscuth* of the **Military Command HQ Information Bureau**. Vice Hecto-Commander, explain the current situation to *Ïarlucec Dreur Haïder*."

"Understood."

A **map of planar space** projected in the center of the room. It included all sectors as yet known to humanity. The vicinity of the **Sfagnoff Marquessate** suddenly turned red.

"This is where the engagement took place. I believe you're already aware, but the **Star Forces** prevailed, and recovered the **Sfagnoff Marquessate**."

Then, a red blip appeared between the **Sfagnoff Marquessate** and the **Vorlash Countdom**.

"This is **Portal 193** of *Céich*. It was the entry point of the invasion. The **recon sub-fleet** *Ftunéc* carried out reconnaissance-in-force…"

A red dotted line extended from **Portal 193**, dividing the *Ilich* **Monarchy** as it stretched. The portals that the dotted line intersected turned into red glints.

"The enemy has made the portals in the area into temporary military operation bases, totally blockading any and all passage. Of course, if that was all, the **Star Forces** would be able to break through with ease. The problem lies here…"

Now another area within the *Ilich* **Monarchy** (on the far side of the **Sfagnoff Portal** as viewed from *Lacmhacarh*) shifted red. Its borders were indistinct, but it included several portals. Then a red arrow emerged, advancing fiercely toward the *Saudec Ilicr* (*Ilich* Portal), the entrance to *Lacmhacarh*.

"The enemy aimed for the **capital** with 120 **sub-fleets**. Their actions on **Sfagnoff** must have been a diversion. While we surmised as much, we never dreamed they would make another place in the very same **monarchy** their invasion's point of entrance."

Now a blue arrow arose from the **Ilich Portal** to collide with its blue counterpart.

"We responded in kind, and under the command of *Fïac Glaharérr Rüé Byrer* (His Highness the Commander-in-Chief of the Imperial Fleet), counterattacked with 140 **sub-fleets**. And though we succeeded in repelling the invasion, it was not without a great number of casualties. We have lost many talented men and women, and many ships."

The **map** disappeared.

"That is all we have established as of this point in time. Earlier, it was reported that the **Imperial Fleet** is in pursuit, conducting reconnaissance around the entrance point. It must be said that the enemy cannot be failing to fortify their defenses in the area, however. Meanwhile, we don't have enough resources to initiate large-scale military action. That is because we must send troops to defend the remote regions and search with great care for other entrance points that may exist, all while planning the reconstruction of the **Star Forces**. It will take a minimum of three years to break down the two walls that now divide the **Ilich Monarchy**. Beyond those walls, there is only a single **sub-fleet** to contend with. Even then, it's only really a **sub-fleet** if they mobilize, as they are troops without a unified chain of command. They would be helpless before a full-fledged offensive."

Jint reflected on what it all meant. The **Countdom of Hyde**, too, lay beyond the walls...

"It is extremely unfortunate, *Ïarlucec Dreur*," said the Empress dolefully. "It's a shame that in exchange for the good news you brought us, We must give you such deplorable news. It was a failure on the part of the **Empire**, and now there are no words We can offer to rationalize it. Yet the facts are the facts, and We cannot expose the entire Empire to danger in order to save a part of it.

All contact with your **territory-nation** has been severed, and We do not see it being recovered in the near future."

Jint was stunned. Not only had all links to his birth planet of the **Countdom of Hyde** been taken from him, but also those to his second homeland, the **Countdom of Vorlash**. His entire past was now sectioned off. And yet, shockingly, he felt not an ounce of sorrow. Jint reacted to his lack of an emotional reaction with trepidation and confusion.

Chapter 12: Daughter of the Empire

On the day that Jint and Lafier arrived in *Lacmhacarh*, a meeting of the **Council of Abdicant Emperors** convened in the **Imperial Palace**.

The **council** was made up of one **abdicant emperor** chosen from each of the **eight royal families**. Its only functions were to oversee the promotion of, and reward or punish, **starpilots** that were **Imperial Family** members.

Under the principle, or perhaps pretense, that the most outstanding starpilot among a generation in the **Imperial Family** was to occupy the **Jade Throne**, it was the role of the **Council of Abdicant Emperors** to take their time in choosing the **Emperor** to be.

Needless to say, the topic of the session was to deliberate whether the **First Royal Princess** of the **Royal House of *Clybh*** was a worthy starpilot, and by that token, a worthy candidate for the **emperor**ship.

The meeting lasted for five days. In addition to Lafier's own report, they scrutinized the testimonies of the **former baron** and **servant vassals** that had been pulled out of the **Febdash Barony**.

Finally, on the last day, Lafier was called to the *Üabaiss Fanigalacr* (Chamber of the Abdicants), which was a spacious, circular room with the eight-headed *gaftnochec* dragon depicted on the floor's center, and a raised platform in front.

When Lafier identified herself, the holograms of the various **abdicants** appeared. They were the elders of the Abliar, old souls trapped in young flesh. Lafier bowed down.

"We are gathered to determine whether you, *Fïac Lamhirr* of the **Royal House of *Clybh***, are suitable to be appointed a **starpilot**. We have some questions for you, and so we shall be conducting a hearing," declared *speunaigh raica* (former emperor) *Nisoth Dugasr* (Their Eminence *Dugass*).

"Raise your face and look up, *Fïac Lamhirr*," spoke *Nisoth Dusumer* of the *Lartiéc Bargzedér* (Royal House of *Bargzedéc*), eldest of the **Imperials**.

"Yes," said Lafier.

All eight **abdicant emperors** were gazing down at her, including *Dugass* and *Dusumec*, who stood at the center. It appeared the two of them would be the driving force behind Lafier's hearing.

Dugass was among the youngest of the **abdicants**, but he too had already reached centenarian age — of course, his hundred plus years did not mar his youthful form. Physically, his aging had stopped halfway through adolescence, and so one could still see the sprightly boy in his especially juvenile visage.

On the other hand, *Dusumec* was well past two centuries in age. He had a poise all his own, his long flowing ringlets the light purple that came with occasional bleaching. For one reason or another, he relied on his *frocragh*, and was not wont to open his eyes. Even now, his eyes were screwed firmly shut.

Lafier was nervous. Though this was the first time she'd been the subject of the **Council**'s discussion, she had heard various things about it. Rumor had it that since the **abdicants**, who had retired from both war and commerce, had nothing else to do, they had honed their skills in ferreting out the faults of young Abliars.

"Usually, *radéüragh bucragr* (starpilot aptitude examinations) are boring affairs," said *Dugass*. "Most children may believe otherwise, but picking apart every little thing about a **trainee starpilot**'s conduct is not a very amusing pastime. One among us has commanded a **fleet** of 100,000 ships, and another among us has laid waste to a notorious interstellar power. Why, then, would we take delight in such trifling concerns?"

This was a nod to the achievements of *Nisoth Duradr*, who led the Shashyne Campaign one hundred years prior.

"However, your case was a fun one, *Fïac*," said *Lamlonh* of the *Lartiéc Üescor* (Royal House of *Üescoc*). Giving the **title** of *Fïac* a disdainful tang was a special skill of the elderly **Imperials**.

"Your actions were found to be unmindful in numerous ways. The atmospheric leakage incident in the **Febdash Barony** was particularly difficult to overlook," said *Dugass*.

"A petition was filed by the **former baron of Febdash**," spoke *Lamynh* of the *Lartiéc Scïrr* (Royal House of *Scirh*). "He asked that we refrain from censuring you for your behavior at the **barony**. However, he is operating under a false impression. It is not the task of the **Council of Abdicant Emperors** to call you to account. We are here solely to judge your aptitude to be a **starpilot**. As such, the **Empire** shall take responsibility for your impressive wake of destruction, deeming it collateral war damage."

Lafier had had no doubt otherwise, so she simply stood there.

"Regardless, the air leak is a serious matter. You can never know for certain what may happen in the midst of battle. And though we may have proclaimed ourselves the **Kin of the Stars**, I do believe you're aware that we cannot survive without air to breathe," quipped *Dugass* sarcastically.

"Yes." Naturally, this only heightened her unease. Nothing would be more humiliating than to be seen as incompetent despite her clear desire to fulfill her duties. If she was to be judged not worthy to be appointed starpilot, she would have rather not survived her ordeal.

"That being said, *Fïac*, the **Council** was unanimous in agreeing that that was a mistake any very young **trainee starpilot** could be guilty of," said *Dusumec*. "Every one of the people gathered here spent their trainee period uneventfully, but went on to make astonishing blunders after becoming **starpilots**. Do you remember, *Nisoth Ramlonr*, the day you stood here, and were demoted from **Commodore** to **Hecto-Commander**?"

"**Your Eminence**," objected a blushing *Lamlonh*, "I question the necessity to bring up things long since past."

Dusumec continued addressing Lafier: "Notwithstanding, *Fïac*, there are two issues even we cannot gloss over. We would like to hear your thoughts on those points."

"What might they be?" Resolutely, Lafier stared at the eldest of the Abliars. One could only wonder whether *Dusumec*, who had dispensed with his vision, was able to pick up on the ardent pride of younger Abliar. A faint smile played about his lips.

"*Fïac*," said *Dusumec*, "while in the **Febdash Barony**, did you or did you not make use of your status as an **Imperial** to incite a rebellion against the **baron**?"

Before she could answer, *Dugass* piped up: "*Fïac Lamhirr*, it is said we Abliars' souls blaze with imperial wrath. Reluctantly, I must agree. From time to time, I too lose myself to anger. Be that as it may, our **subjects** not only accept our rule, but harbor love and affection for us. Do you know why that is? It's because they can distinguish between fury as an individual, and fury as the **Empire**. Even when one is driven by wrath, if that wrath has nothing to do with the Empire, they do not use the bludgeon that is imperial authority, which no one ought to oppose, to strike one's personal enemy. And even if there were only one Abliar left, if a fool who would wield the *Rüé greuc* (Imperial Command Baton) as a cudgel impelled by personal passions were ever to accede to the **Jade Throne**, our subjects would lose faith in us. Ever since the **Founding Emperor**, the ultimate role of the **Council of Abdicant Emperors** has been to expel those who misunderstand the true meaning of pride from the path to the **emperorship**…"

"Please wait, *Nisoth*," Lafier interrupted.

"Speak, *Fïac*," *Dusumec* permitted.

"I did not abuse my social status, nor did I incite a rebellion. I merely asked for the aid of the *imperial citizens* as a **soldier** of the **Star Forces** to end the **Baron**'s meddling in my mission."

Dusumec crossed his arms. "I see. That does make some sense. However, *Fïac*, if you did not bear the Abliar **family name**, would it have played out as smoothly?"

"That is not something that has to do with me."

"What exactly do you mean by that?" said *Dugass*, brows knitted.

"It was battle, and in battle, luck is a factor. In that I happen to be an Abliar, fortune favored me. If ever I forget to acknowledge luck, and boast of my achievements to no effect, then you may call me haughty, but I did not forget."

"If you had been **gentry** by birth, what would you have done?"

"I would have acted no differently whatsoever," Lafier replied without delay. "Even now, I cannot think of a superior plan I could have adopted to ensure the mission succeeded."

Dusumec smiled. "You may yet be a baby bird, but I must admit, you did well to come through it all." Lafier couldn't tell whether by "come through it all" he meant the events at the **Febdash Barony**, or this hearing.

"Very well. Should you earn the sympathies of the **abdicants**, that will be the end of that matter. Have any of you any objections?" *Dugass* paused.

No objection was made.

"Then there's but a single issue left to discuss, *Fïac*," *Dugass* continued. "And it is this question that is the most significant by far. In fact, it involves the very foundation of the **Empire**. We hear you have promised to furnish **interstellar ships** to **landworld citizens** of the **Sfagnoff Marquessate**."

"That isn't true!" Lafier rebutted. "All I promised them was that I would beseech **Her Majesty the Empress** to lend them one or more **interstellar ships**."

"It's understandable, given how wet behind the ears you are, but you do not fully grasp the weight behind the words of the **Imperial Family**. Whenever an Abliar suggests something may be possible, people will assume it will definitely occur. And if it never materializes, they will consider it breaking a promise."

"Not only that," said *Lamynh*, "but they will then misconstrue it as having been a lie to save your own skin. It will manifest as a mark of shame."

Lafier found herself raising her voice: "**Your Eminences**, that statement is incredibly one-sided!"

"There is no way you will get your wish to begin with," said *Dugass* calmly. "According to the *darfass* (customs) of the **Empire**, a person below **gentry** in status cannot borrow an **interstellar ship**. Did you not know that?"

"I was not aware of that..." Lafier bit her lip. The customs of the **Empire** were wide-ranging, complicated, and arcane. And though she knew the basics, she'd never paid the trivial little details any attention.

"Now, how ought we to settle this?" *Dugass* shook his head. "That you didn't know the custom was an unavoidable development, but a moment's thought would have clued you in. The **Empire** and **landworld citizens** owe each other nothing, as the **Empire** hold **landworld governments** under their aegis, and those governments hold their citizens under their protection. **Landworld citizens** are, in a way, immaterial in the eyes of the Empire. Why, then, did you think **interstellar ships** could be lent to such people?"

"How heedless of you, *Fïac*," said *Lamlonh*.

Lafier didn't know what to say. She had not made any surefire guarantee. Anger against the Abliar elders flared within her. They were being unreasonable, irrational. Yet now that they had explained the weight behind the words of the **imperial family**, she realized there was truth in that idea.

After all, she remembered when the **servants** had misconstrued her promise at the **Febdash Barony**.

Suddenly, a ringing laugh. It was *Nisoth Dusemr* (His Eminence *Dusemh*) of the **Royal Family of Barkeh**.

"**Your Eminences**," said *Dusemh*, who spoke for the first time, "it is just as **His Eminence Dugass** stated earlier. It would be cruel to pillory a fledgling whose wings have not yet grown feathers. Besides, it is not as though the **royal princess** endeavored to tell some hideous lie. All she did was speak the truth."

Lafier was taken aback. She had not been expecting a helping hand.

"That is not good enough, *Nisoth*. Those **landworld citizens** will believe they were deliberately deceived by an Abliar. That is the problem," *Dugass* insisted.

"Then would it not be for the best to lend them the **interstellar ship**?" said *Dusemh* breezily.

"Not you, too!? Must I repeat the words of *Nisoth Duradr*..."

"In the end, those **landworld citizens** saved a **daughter of the Empire**," *Dusemh* cut in. "That is a deed worthy of appointment to **gentry** status. If they are appointed to gentry, and lent an **interstellar ship**, then the problem disappears."

"You would have **landworld citizens** be made **gentry** so abruptly? That would be unprecedented," protested *Duradh*.

"The **Count of Hyde** wasn't even a **landworld citizen** to start with. Compared to that, then..."

"It was your son that so readily set that precedent, *Larth Raica Barcœr* (Former King of Barkeh)," said *Duradh* bitterly.

Dusemh's face turned cool.

"Please hold on, *Nisoth*," said *Nisoth Lamodr* (Her Eminence Lamodh) of the *Lartiéc Ilicr* (Royal House of *Ilich*). "According to the report, they desire secession from the **Empire**. Would they take any joy in the prospect of being **gentry** of that empire?"

"It matters not whether or not they take joy in it. It is their right to turn down the offer. If they refuse to be **gentry**, then they cannot be lent **interstellar ships**, even by us. That is all."

"They may have gone underground," said *Dugass*.

"That is fine." The **abdicant** of the **Royal House of Barkeh** grinned mysteriously. "As luck would have it, the **airship fleet** is operating in the **Sfagnoff Marquessate**. If we were to send the rank and file to search for them, we can accompany them anywhere, by gunpoint if necessary. Let us inform the populace that they are to be appointed as **gentry**. They can then accept or refuse the offer, with the understanding that if they refuse, they will not be lent **interstellar ships**, but will be given some other reward as consolation."

"But the **Star Forces** aren't geared toward that sort of work," said *Lamodh*.

"If it proves beyond the **Star Forces**' powers, then that just means we should employ the **Institute of Crests**."

This is insane, thought Lafier, who had gone pale.

Much as the name suggested, the **Institute of Crests** was a government office that dealt in the safekeeping of the **crests** of **nobles** and **gentry**, and managed genealogical trees and family ranks. However, their operations expanded from there, and now they also administered covert investigations throughout the **domains** and **territory nations**, taking on the role of a kind of secret police.

"I thought we were talking about 'gratitude,'" said *Duradh* uncomfortably.

"Yes, this is of course an act of thanks. We don't wish to be called ungrateful." The fan-shaped sleeves of *Dusemh*'s *fécséic* (vestment) fluttered. "That is why we will hold a pomp-filled appointment ceremony on Clasbure's surface. Oh, and it would be wise as well to invite people known for being Secessionist Party members and extremists as the guests of honor."

"Why in tarnation would we do that...?" said *Dugass*, flashing *Dusemh* an extremely confused look.

"Those that yearn for independence disdain the **Empire**. I believe they are laughing at us and look down on the Empire as being unable to crack down on them."

"Are you saying we should clamp down on them, *Nisoth*?" Repulsed, *Dugass* hid his mouth with a sleeve. "That would be inelegant."

"Of course not. If we did that, the **Star Forces** and the **Institute of Crests** alike would swell to enormous size. It would indeed be far from the realm of the elegant." *Dusemh*'s smile turned yet ghastlier. "That said, we cannot tolerate their open contempt. To be hated is of no concern to us, but to be slighted is another matter. It is not that the **Empire** isn't capable of clamping down, it's that it elects not to. In other words, teaching the **landworld citizens** that the Empire can hunt down those who do not submit at any time if it so chooses might just prove an entertaining diversion. Their initial scheme is likely to threaten the Empire. Is it not necessary to give them a dose of reality?"

"You Sporr!" said *Lamynh* gleefully. "I've always thought the **family name** of the **Royal House of Barkeh** isn't Abliar, but Sporr. The way such devious ideas come to you."

Lafier couldn't stand it any longer. "**Your Eminences**, allow me to inform you that I am grateful to those people. I may even be rather fond of them. Their ways are different from our own, but they are proud folk in their own way. So, I implore you not to rebuke them..."

"This is a great example of how misunderstood we often are," said *Dusemh*, spreading his besleeved arms wide. "Even our own relatives can misunderstand us. Such is the fruit of our lack of discretion. *Fïac*, I am saying that we very much ought to thank them."

"Why do I get the feeling that tendency to be 'misunderstood,'" grumbled *Lamodh*, "is not so much the fruit of our indiscretions, but rather springs from what a certain **royal family** has assiduously built up?" But her derision fell on deaf ears.

"But *Nisoth*, we lack the authority to decide on such a plan," *Duradh* pointed out.

"Then we should ask **Her Majesty** *Lamagh* to decide. It wouldn't take much time at all, either. Kindly wait a moment, **Your Eminences**."

Dusemh's hologram disappeared. The projections of the other **abdicants** froze. Lafier could tell something was being discussed someplace she couldn't overhear, but she had no choice but to stand in place and wait to be addressed.

At last, *Dusemh* returned. The holograms of the rest of the **abdicants** resumed moving, as though returning to life.

"**Your Eminences**," *Lamagh* intoned. There was no hologram of her, only her audio. "We heard tell of the issue from *Nisoth Dusemr*. We had been racking Our mind over a suitable token of gratitude toward the **landworld citizens**. As such, We thank Your Eminences for your wise counsel. We shall adopt the measure at once; in My name, it shall be arranged."

"And so, with this, the matter is settled," said *Dusemh*.

"So it is," nodded *Dugass*, though his expression was fastidious. "Now the risk that the honor of the Abliars would be tarnished has cleared up."

"I wasn't aware patching up the mistakes of a **trainee starpilot** was a role of the **Council of Abdicants**," frowned *Duradh*.

"Is it not the duty of old birds to smooth over the little ones' blunders?" *Dusemh* retorted.

"In any case, we must make our final decision. We have been discussing for five days, and we have no more questions for *Fïac Lamhirr*," said *Dusumec*.

"Let us hear **Your Eminences**' opinions."

"I hereby acknowledge that *Fïac Lamhirr* has the aptitude to be a **starpilot**." With that, *Lamynh*'s hologram put her hands to her shoulders, and disappeared.

"I have no objections, either," said *Lamodh*, herself vanishing.

"Though I feel as though we've struck a tremendous blow to custom this day," said *Duradh*, shaking his head and putting his hands to his shoulders, "I suppose there's naught to be done about it."

"I'm looking forward to your future. I know you'll be able to overshadow my ignoble past," said *Lamlonh*. Then she, too, disappeared.

"It's as though I'm looking at my own daughter when she was small," spoke *Nisoth Lamaimer* (Her Eminence *Lamaimec*), Lafier's great-grandmother, for the first time in the meeting; perhaps she was not taking her position very seriously. "Be sure to pay me a visit before you receive another mission."

"You truly look just like **Her Majesty** *Lamagh*. You may just be the one to take the throne after my son." With that, *Dusemh* vanished.

"Let us meet again, little one. Though I hope that the next hearing will be easier on all of us," said *Dusumec*.

"Congratulations, **Linewing Starpilot** Abliar." To round out the meeting, *Dugass* saluted her (albeit his salute was a little off) and vanished.

To the Abh, the concept of seasons was not linked to the time of year, but to the mood in the air. The *Lartbéïc Clybr* (Royal Palace of *Clybh*) had a garden for spring, summer, autumn, and winter, each with their ecosystem and temperature adjusted accordingly. Seated on a wooden bench in the autumn garden, Jint counted the colored leaves dancing down.

"So that's where you were."

Jint looked toward the voice. There stood Lafier. She was not in her **military uniform**. Rather, she was wearing a bright golden **long robe** over a green **jumpsuit**, with the graceful and florid **circlet** of a **royal princess**. In her arms, she held a kitten.

"Yeah. It's the most calming place for me. *Fïac Lartr Clybr* told me to think of this place as my own home, but it's really a bit too big to square with the concept I have in my head of 'my own home.'"

Sure, it was small compared to the **Imperial Palace**, whose population once numbered over a million, but the **Royal Palace** of *Clybh* was an artificial planet in its own right. It was voluminous enough to house 50,000 people, and currently there were 10,000 who dwelt there in order to manage the *Saudec Clybr* (*Clybh* Portal) and the **Royal Palace**.

Lafier sat herself next to him. "Were you thinking about your **territory-nations?**"

"Nah…" He was surprised himself: "I didn't even look back at my home planets."

"Not even a little?" Lafier looked shocked.

"Not really. For some reason, hearing that I've lost contact with my home, I just don't feel sad at all. I'm actually relieved. Like a heavy burden's been lifted… I'm an awful person, aren't I?"

"I don't know," she said, confused. "Are you not worried about your father?"

"I thought I was worried about him, tried to convince myself I was, but I've come to realize that in my heart, I'm not… I mean, he's bound to be fine. He was born and raised in *Martinh*, and he's got experience and personal connections. If we survived Clasbure, he's sure to…"

But he realized at that moment that that was a lie. *Martinh*'s ecosystem had arisen independently of Earth's and was hostile to humans. Respect for the indigenous environment was drilled into Martinians from an early age. That meant that the only way his father could survive was by hiding in one of the planet's hybrid structure buildings, but any serious manhunt would turn him up given how limited the space was. And worst of all, the greater part of the Martinian populace despised him.

In all likelihood, the **Count of Hyde** was no longer of this world.

Jint changed the subject: "What's with the cat?"

"He's named '*Dïahoc*.' He's the son of Zaneria, the daughter of Horia. Here you are, Dyaho." Lafier let go of the kitten on the chaise. "He was born while I was out doing navigation drills."

Jint recalled what "Horia" referred to: it was the name of the cat that Lafier had believed, when she was a wee lass, to be her mother.

"So that'd make you this cat's aunt."

"You *onh!*" That epithet again.

Jint held his hand out, and Dyaho seized upon it, rubbing his head against it. Lafier looked vexed, and, for whatever reason, saw fit to apologize for Dyaho. "Despite being a cat, he hasn't a stoic bone in his body. Zaneria was much the same."

"It's adorable, if you ask me." Jint tickled his throat.

"Tomorrow, you'll be headed to the **Quartermaster Academy**, if I recall."

"Yeah. Somebody's coming to pick me up after breakfast. Since there's a war on now, a lot of kids got their date of entrance moved up, and it looks like I'll just be another in the crowd. Thanks to that, I don't have to worry about how I'll be starting late in the year. That said, I'll be living the life academic for three whole years. Please don't feel down over it." He transferred Dyaho to his lap and faced Lafier. "How about you?"

"It's still undecided which ship I'll be on." Lafier shook her head.

"Gotcha. Well, enjoy your moment of peace, I'd say. You'll be spending your every day on the battlefield for a good clip."

"Yeah." Lafier nodded. "Three years… In three years, you'll be a *faictodaïc sazoïr* (quartermaster linewing starpilot)."

"If everything goes smoothly, yeah."

"By three years' time, I will most likely have become a **Deca-Commander**, with the right to receive a small vessel, either a **defense ship** or an **assault ship**. Personally, I'd prefer an assault ship."

"Right, right." Jint caressed Dyaho's scruff, wondering what she was trying to say.

"Each **assault ship** requires a **quartermaster linewing starpilot** to serve as a **clerk**. And... as per **Star Forces** tradition, a ship's captain has some say in its personnel affairs. It's far from set in stone, but if the captain and the officer agree on it, then it should come to pass," she said, staring at him interrogatively.

Of course, Jint understood what she expected from him. "O future **Deca-Commander** Abliar," said Jint, putting on airs, "if at that time there should be a man named *Faictodaïc Sazoïr Linn*, you have but to call him by your side, and he will serve as your loyal clerk."

"Okay." Lafier's face shone bright. "If you put it that way, I suppose I have no other choice. I do have my misgivings, mind you. It's virtually set in stone that I will be a **Deca-Commander** in three years' time; that means it's up to you to be diligent and work your way up to being a **quartermaster linewing pilot**."

"Yeah, yeah, don't worry. I'll expend every effort, Lafier."

"All right, then, Jint, we'll see each other again at the supper table." Lafier stood up forcefully. "I'm rather busy at the moment."

"Hey! What about Dyaho?" Jint embraced the kitten in his arms.

"You've clearly taken a liking to him, so you ought to take him as your conversation partner. It's not as though you haven't the time."

"Can't say I'm as busy, no," he said resignedly, putting him back on his lap. "You're kind of a boring conversationalist, though." Dyaho responded by sniffing his fingers.

As he let the kitten entertain itself on his lap, Jint ruminated. *You're as terrible a liar as ever, Lafier. But I'm happy I can spend more time by your side. I'll age with time, and my lifespan is half yours at best. But I want to spend as much of my short life with you as possible. Whether you ascend to the **Jade Throne** or crumble to smithereens in a pocket of **planar space**, know that I'll be there with you. I'll see your destiny play out to the end, even if it displeases you. That is my will, the future I chose of my own volition. The value of one's life is bought and determined by offering the freedom they were born with for sale. Que Durin would probably wince and tell me it's too early to sell, but something tells me an opportunity this sweet won't come twice. After all, the buyer isn't* the **Empire**. *It's you, Lafier. You'll never taste the thrill, understand the joy of selling your freedom. Members of the* **Imperial Family** *aren't born with any.*

Memories of the planet Martin's Exotic Jungle floated to mind. It was the great new motherland of all Martinians. But now, he could only think of it as a foreign landscape, compared to the sea of *gereulach* (stars).

"Hey, Dyaho. Tell me: who am I? *What* am I?"

The kitty meowed.

Epilogue

At *Ralbrybh* **Astrobase**, on the **Commander's Bridge** of the **flagship** of the **recon sub-fleet** the *Ftunéc*, the **patrol ship** *Hairbyrch*…

"You're taking the *Ftunéc* away from me!?" Sporr cried.

"Somebody with the **rank** of **commodore** serving as a **sub-fleet commandant** is an exception to the norm to begin with," said the hologram of *Glaharérh Chtymer* (Astrobase Commander-in-Chief), *Spénec Laburer* (Star Forces Admiral) *Uneuch*, with an air of patience. "As you're aware, our ships were greatly depleted in number after the engagement three years ago. Now, the array of battle is finally in order. We will be having you head up a full **fleet**, under the wing of *Fofraudéc* (Grand Commodore) Tlife."

"And that **fleet** would be?" Sporr was not coy about her disaffection.

"It hasn't yet been organized. We will make you *Roïglaharérh Chtymer* (Astrobase Vice Commander-in-Chief) for the time being, but it won't be for long. That's because the time the enemy will be forced to recall the existence of the **Imperial Star Forces** fast approaches."

"Has the ship I'll be on been decided? I'm quite fond of the *Hairbyrch*, myself…"

"It won't be the *Hairbyrch*. That's the **flagship** of the *Ftunéc*. Assign it to a successor."

Her eyebrows of flowing scarlet-blue bristled.

"And that's that," said Uneuch, hastily. "Your appointment will come into effect in three days. I'd like you to set your personal affairs straight by then. I'm willing to discuss personnel matters at the new **Headquarters** as well. Now allow me to take my leave. And congratulations, **Commodore** Sporr."

Hurriedly, the **Commander-in-Chief**'s hologram vanished. Sporr continued to glare at a hologram that was no longer there.

"'Congratulations'!? Does he think I WANT a promotion? I'm already an **Archduchess**!"

Having overheard their exchange, Cfadiss was relieved. Sporr had been difficult to work for. He thought it'd take at most three years to grow used to it, but that had been wishful thinking. She was incorrigibly self-indulgent, capricious, and worst of all, an incredibly capable commander despite all that!

Cfadiss could see it now. A slightly more manageable **commandant** to take her place. That would be nice.

"And what do you look so happy about, **Senior Staff Officer**?" Cfadiss snapped to, to find Sporr staring daggers at him.

"Ah! I... I'm not," said Cfadiss, stiffening his face.

"Oh? But I'm *happy* that you're happy... so you'd better hurry and set your affairs in order, too."

"Huh? How come?" he said, dumbfounded.

"You heard what the man said. He'll hear me out with regard to the personnel affairs of the new **Headquarters**. And you're the new **Chief of Staff**!"

"Please, hold on," he said, dismayed. "I'm a **Hecto-Commander**. My **rank** isn't high enough."

"I think it's high time you get your promotion. In fact, I'll back your promotion. Why, I myself have just been promoted, so I simply must share this pleasure with my subordinates. Congratulations, **Kilo-Commander** Cfadiss."

"I'm beside myself with gratitude, but..."

"Does something about this *inconvenience* you?" she prodded, folding her arms.

"No, ma'am. It's a stupendous honor. Thank you very much," he said, his hand forced.

"You're welcome." She had an announcement for the other personnel on the bridge as well. "Everybody will rise up the ranks. I'm taking you all with me!"

Amidst the whole of the commander's bridge cheering with jubilation, Cfadiss alone heaved a deep sigh.

In **planar space**, in a room in an *isadh saura* (lightweight supply ship) named *Clasbyrh* in transit near *Saudec Matmatsocna Clohar* (Portal 229 of *Clohac*).

"This isn't the kind of aboard-ship lifestyle I had in mind," lamented Malka.

"No two ways about it," said Undertaker.

"Here I am, having left my beloved husband and child to see deep space, only to have to do the **Empire**'s bidding and help haul their cargo. Why, I ask you?"

"Can't be helped," said Undertaker.

"And it's not like we're actually the ones doing the hauling, either," said Bill, gulping down some booze. "It's an Abh who's piloting. Besides loading whatever cargo the **Empire** wants us to, all we can be said to be doing is drinking thusly, and watching our savings pile up."

"No other option," said Undertaker.

"Well, it helps to think of it as accumulating funds for the Clasbure Secession War to come." Min took another sip of drink. "And the **Empire**'s helping us do it. It amuses me."

"Oh, it amuses you, does it?" snapped Bill. "We can't even return to Clasbure. We're too famous there. I can hear the sarcasm now: '*Ceucec reucer* (honored gentry), I'm so terribly sorry to have to ask this of you, but could ya take 10 *üésboc* of pork shoulder into the next town over?'"

"Can't do a thing about it," said Undertaker.

"Well, I'm fairly satisfied with this arrangement. We can see different worlds. We can use these travels as reference for the independence effort. In any case, I say we should bide our time until the war's over. When it ends, this ship's destination will be freed up."

"You want us to wait until the war's over!?" Malka held her hands up in shock. "When's it going to end? It hasn't even really started yet!"

"It is what it is," said Undertaker.

"I swear..." Bill looked Daswani's way. "Hey, can you use your skills to take over this ship's **compucrystals**? Let's get this thing in human hands."

The hulking man shook his head silently.

"What the hell do we even do with ourselves!?"

"Oh well, nothing for it."

"Undertaker," said Malka, glaring at her comrade, "do you have *anything* else to add?"

Undertaker looked at her with eyes drowsy from drink. "Did I ever tell you about the guy who jumped into a bunch of thorns?"

"Oh yes, Undertaker. Hundreds of times."

In the **Sfagnoff Marquessate**, at the Lune Beega Municipal Police Agency building on the planet of Clasbure...

"The election results are in!" said a subordinate who came barging in.

Entryua looked up from the screen on his work desk. The officer didn't have to say a word; Entryua could tell from that look. Yet Entryua was forced to ask anyway.

"And?"

"Aizan's done!" Fists pumping, he was thoroughly delighted. "We're finally free from Commissioner Aizan's two-year reign!"

Entryua grinned. "Looks like cooperating with the occupiers blew up in his face."

"Aizan's backers are up in arms. They're saying that police officers passing damning information about the commissioner violated election law."

"All I told the press was the truth. They can hold my feet to the fire if I ever lied, but I didn't. What're they going to attack me for?"

"Too right, sir," replied the officer, smiling sweet revenge. "Though they're saying that you shouldn't have answered the press to begin with."

"They must be joking," said Entryua, cocking an eyebrow. "The people love us. We're cops the citizens respect! So how could we keep mum when the cameras and mics are on us?"

"Exactly, sir," said the subordinate, nodding gravely. "Now then, Inspector, allow me to make the rounds telling everybody the good news."

"I think everybody probably already knows."

"Probably. But I want to spread the message anyway — because there's no doubt in my mind they'd all like to hear this particular bit of news over and over again."

Entryua watched as he flew right back out of the office like a whirlwind, and then looked back at the screen, which displayed a letter. A letter from Military Police Captain Keitt, sent from *Loneucebhic Siturr* (*Siturh* Prison Camp) in the faraway *Faicec Üescor* (*Üescoc* Monarchy).

At the **Countdom of Abliar**, in the **airlock room** of the *radéüiac baicœcer* (antimatter fuel tank inspection ship) *Sérnaïc*, sailing via inertial navigation in an astrospace sector located between the sun of Abliar and a point three light-seconds from the **imperial capital** *Lacmhacarh*...

"That was quite the close call," said Sehrnye as she shed her **pressure suit**. "The magnetic flux density had dropped so low. But the **compucrystals** in the remote surveillance bot have degraded, so instead of the current situation, I was seeing the *memory drive*'s—"

"You don't need to lie to me, too," frowned Arsa, who helped her take off the **pressure suit**. "You've gone and done it again, haven't you, Sehrnye."

"Guess you found me out!" Sehrnye stuck out her tongue.

"Why on heaven are you pretending to have 'repaired' a **fuel tank** that's not broken?"

"C'mon, the money from just an inspection's nothing compared to inspection plus repair."

"Sure, but we have so much work coming in, there's no need. We just got word from Greda. The authorities think it's strange."

"Huh?" She frowned, a sense of foreboding in the air.

"They're asking why the **fuel tank** inspected by Sehrnye Ltd. was the only one with an unexpected anomaly spotted, and whether it's breaking new ground in the field of statistics or stems from some other cause entirely." Arsa took a breath. "Are you willing to gamble? Because I'd put all of my money on a new discipline of statistics NOT coming to be."

"Don't worry. We've the **Royal House of *Clybh*** backing us," she said, putting on a daring front.

"You can't be over-reliant on the good graces of the **royal family**. They've already funded this enterprise. Besides, how can you honestly ask them to be complicit in fraud? You're not unlikely to incur the wrath of the Abliars that way."

"But Sehrnye Ltd. still has so much room to grow!" she replied, pouting her lips.

"And if you keep at it, that potential will get nipped in the bud."

"Okay, okay…" Sehrnye hung her head. "I won't do it again."

"Sehrnye, do you have any idea how strange the authorities think this case is?" Arsa sighed.

"They're that suspicious?"

"It's worse than that," said Arsa, thrusting her face toward her. "They're not 'suspicious' at all! They *know* what you did. But they're willing to let past offenses slide, as long as you understand they won't overlook anymore."

"So, they're saying I can pretend this incident never happened, either!?" Sehrnye opened her arms.

"That's right. They'll forget it ever happened. Only, they'll be paying you solely for the inspection."

"But I repaired it, too!" said Sehrnye, displeased. "I DID replace the magnetic flux density meter with a new one, and I even refreshed the data on the **compucrystals**. I didn't NEED to, but I did."

"I'm going to tell Greda to dock your cut of the pay," resolved Arsa.

"But I'm the CEO!" said Sehrnye. That said, she had no true intention of wielding her position of authority. If Arsa or Greda abandoned her, it was obvious that the newly formed Sehrnye Ltd. would immediately tank, and to confound things further, it seemed the two of them knew that, too.

At the **imperial capital** *Lacmhacarh*, in the drawing room of the *Garich Arocr Lym Faibdacr* (Imperial Capital Manor House of the Baron of Febdash)…

"It's only been three years since then, eh? You've grown into a real man." The old man extended a hand.

"Thanks. You haven't changed, **Honorable Former Baron**." Jint gripped his hand. "How are you?"

"I'm holding up all right." The **former baron of Febdash** urged Jint to take a seat before setting himself down. "Seems you've inherited the *dreuragh* (rank of count)."

"Yep." Jint nodded and sat down.

According to a UH broadcast, the execution of the former **Count of Hyde**, Jint's father, had been carried out. Jint was thereupon made **count**. Though he hadn't yet gone through the military service that was a prerequisite of peerage, the **King of Barkeh** took him under his wardship, so it was no issue.

If the info was accurate, then a new head of government had been elected to lead the Hyde Star System, a man who was a solid member of the UH, and who had declared plans to fight against the **Empire**.

That new chancellor's name? Till Corint…

"I should probably be giving you my condolences, but instead I'll leave it at: congratulations, Lonh-*Dreur*," said Sroof.

"Thank you very much," smiled Jint, embracing the sentiment. He'd learned of his father's demise nearly a year prior. He'd seen it coming beforehand, and he'd long since worked out his feelings on the matter. "But don't call me '**Your Excellency the Count**.' I'm a count in name only, without a star-fief."

"You got it, **boy**."

"I mean, I'm not really a 'boy' anymore, either," said Jint, with a wry smile.

"'S'pose not. You're 20 years old, eh. A full-grown adult. But what should I call ya, then? '*Üanch* (young man) don't sound right."

"'Jint' is fine. But to be honest, it feels pretty ace to be called '**Quartermaster Linewing Starpilot**.'"

"Ah, makes sense. I oughta congratulate ya for your appointment. Congratulations."

"Thank you very much," Jint repeated.

"What would ya like to drink?" The **former baron** activated his **wristgear**. "Or would you rather an early meal?"

"Oh, uh, I'm sorry…" said Jint, scratching his head. "I actually don't have a lot of time."

"I see… Well, thanks for coming out of your way to visit me despite being busy."

"It's true, I swear," insisted Jint, noticing the melancholy look on Sroof's face. "I've been on holiday since finishing my training voyage, but one way or another…"

Sroof laughed. "I didn't think you were lying, **boy**... wouldn't ya know it, that's the name that fits you the most. And I think I'll be grateful if ya remember this doddering old fool, even if it's just one last time."

"One last time? I'd like to think I have to visit this place again, without fail."

"Thank you. I've got a lot of friends from way back in *Lacmhacarh*, but every time I see their still-young faces, I get on edge."

"I can't just let you lie like that."

Amusement crept on the **former baron**'s wrinkly visage. "Do ya remember when I told ya the same thing three years ago?"

"You did?" To tell the truth, he didn't recall.

"Good grief. Don't tell me your memory's lagging behind the memory of an old man like me. Do ya remember when I told ya I'd impart my wisdom on the Abh frame of mind?"

"Of course. And I'm looking forward to it; I just can't right now..."

"It's okay, I understand. I ain't gonna take any more time off the hands of a young adult with a future ahead of him. Youngsters finding the ramblings of the elderly boring's a law of nature."

"Boring? I'd never..."

"Do ya remember when I told ya? Blatant ego-salving's only gonna hurt people. You should've learned that fact by then, let alone three years later."

"Yeah, I remember," said Jint, red in the face. "But I really mean it. You're never boring."

"I find that doubtful, but I'm not gonna keep ya. Best be on your way, if you haven't got time."

"I've got a little time left."

Sroof waved a hand. "Don't strain yourself, **boy**. I'm looking forward to hearing about your exploits as a **quartermaster linewing starpilot**. Oh, hold on, there's something I need to know first. Where's your new post?"

"I've been appointed as a **clerk** on the **assault ship** *Basrogrh*."

"Haven't heard of that ship before. Guess it is an **assault ship**, though."

"And it's a new one, too. It'll become famous soon enough, of course."

"'Cause you'll be on it?"

"That won't hurt," nodded Jint, "but also because the **captain** happens to be named 'Abliar.'"

"Ho ho!" Sroof was thrilled. "You really did come pay me a visit at a busy time, **boy**. You have my gratitude. Now get your butt over to *Fïac Bœrr Parhynr*'s side."

"Got it." Jint stood up, albeit reluctantly. "I'm really sorry about the hurry."

"Don't worry about it. Just feel free to come here when you have got the time. I'll bore ya to tears."

"Of course. I'll be coming back. Please remain in good health, Lonh-*Lymr Raica*." Jint saluted.

"Oh, I will, **boy**," smiled Sroof mischievously.

In *Lacmhacarh*, on a **bridge** of the **assault ship** *Basrogrh* (presently in harbor)…

Everything was brand new. That wasn't surprising, considering it had just come fresh from its construction at the *Locrh Lespor* (*Lespoc* Warship Construction site). It hadn't even yet been taken for a familiarization-voyage whirl.

Lafier touched the brand-new equipment, and filled her lungs with the new-ship odor. Looking up at the **crest banner** of the *Basrogrh*, patterned after a *rogrh* (red-banded sand wasp, pronounced "royr"), her heart welled with pride and joy.

This was the very first ship she'd ever received. Over the past three years, the **Star Forces** had not been waging full-blown war. They couldn't afford to. Nor, it seemed, could the enemy. There had been no engagements apart from a handful of small skirmishes.

What was surprising were the developments in the Hania Federation. When Lafier brought back the navigation log of the **patrol ship** *Gothelauth* and the **Empire** went public with the evidence that the UH had attacked first, the Hania Federation condemned the UH for falsifying the reason they declared war, and opted for neutrality. Hania was a single nation among the **Four Nations Alliance**, and they hadn't joined in the assault on the **imperial capital**, so they lacked any incentive to aggravate the situation with regard to the Empire.

Of course, as the general public viewed it, the Hania Federation wouldn't place a premium on rendering justice. There was no doubt in their minds that if *Lacmhacarh* lay fallen, they'd instantly be there, pecking at its remains as a loyal member of the **FNA**. In short, they were waiting, observing from the sidelines. The other three nations of the **FNA** rebuked the Federation for its perfidy, but many Abhs also expressed consternation. They'd thought they could finally participate in the true war to end all wars.

Lafier felt likewise. That said, she knew they had to take care of the enemies before them. The front of battle was at a stalemate. Two thirds of the **Ilich** Monarchy (which was partitioned by two walls) had been annexed by the enemy and had yet to be retaken.

But this dreary, irritating reality would soon fall by the wayside. The empire was showing its warlike face, and an unprecedentedly large fleet, several times the size of that before the war, was emerging. The **Lespoc Warship Construction Site** was pumping out one *Rogrh*-class assault ship every ten minutes. Meanwhile, other **construction sites** were producing warships of all classes and varieties. The **Baiturh** Warship Construction Site was phasing out *Lauth* (Dragon) class patrol ships, now in the process of completing the leading-edge *Cau* patrol ships. The *Locrh Bhobinauter* (*Bhobinautec* Warship Construction Site) was producing *Saumh* class **battle-line warships**, the *Locrh Syrer* (*Syrec* Warship Construction Site) was building *Gammh* class assault ships and *Paigh* class **defense ships**, not to mention the *Locrh Gocrocr* (*Gocroch* Warship Construction Site)...

The vast majority of *lodaïrh cisaïna* (reserve starpilots) had been reconvened, with each **academy** swamped with the work of putting them through training once again. The numbers of new applicants had reached record highs. Across large numbers of **landworlds**, employment quotas for **NCCs** had greatly increased. Every warship needed to come with passengers to ride them, and so the fleet had to gather lives as the contents to fill the tin cans flying through space. The war proper would commence in the blink of an eye. Lafier and the ship she commanded would face the heat of battle.

She took a deep breath, attempting to quell the excitement bubbling inside.

There was nobody else aboard. The **NCCs** were busy getting ready for departure, while the **starpilots** were busy supervising them. Excluding Lafier, the capacity of starpilots was four. They were a pair of **Flight Branch starpilots**, a *lodaïrh scœmr* (mechanics starpilot) who served as **inspector supervisor**, and a certain **quartermaster starpilot** who served as **clerk**.

"**Captain**," reported the clerk who had entered, "we have finished loading the food and supplies."

Seeing his stuffy, ceremonious salute, she stifled a laugh. Was he holding a grudge for being called "**quartermaster linewing starpilot**"?

"You and I are the only ones here, Jint."

Jint beamed. "Ah, yeah, you're right. I missed you, you know."

"Listen, for I have a secret of great import to share: I missed you, too."

"Your secret's safe with me." Jint narrowed his eyes. "Man, though, you really haven't aged a day. You look exactly the same as three years ago."

"I'd hate to have visibly aged in just three years. You, on the other hand, you do look a little older."

"Aren't you gonna say I look more mature?"

"Feh."

"Did you just *scoff* at that, **Captain**."

"I told you, we're alone here," said Lafier pointedly.

"It's just, I can hardly seem too chummy when there are others around, right?"

"Right. It'd affect morale."

"What if I make an honest mistake? It might be smarter to start calling you **Captain** or **Deca-Commander Abliar**, you know, to make a habit of it."

"Is that what you WANT to do?" A mix of anxiety and rage welled up within her.

"Do you THINK that's what I want to do?" Jint smiled with his eyes.

"In that case…" Lafier threw out her chest. Her bluish-black hair swayed, as did the **functionality crystals** at the ends of her **access-cables**, not unlike a set of eccentric earrings.

"You will call me 'Lafier'!"

Appendix: Summary of the Formation of Baronh

Proto-Baronh had every mark of being a constructed language, as it was an "ancient language" reconstituted by dogmatic nationalists. For its vocabulary, they made a point of excising all historically "recent" loanwords originating from the various tongues of Europe, as well as those of Chinese origin that entered the language alongside the writing system.

Of course, such radical restructuring was bound to come with its fair share of problems. They may have pruned the language, but they had no intention of abandoning civilization. As such, they faced the need to rely on the vocabulary of ancestors who lived during the dawn of the age of metals to express the fruits of the science and technology that had made space travel a reality (though that technology was still in its infancy in the eyes of their descendants).

Similarly, when the nation of Israel was founded, Ancient Hebrew was revived by Jews; an arduous labor, to be sure, but the nationalists of our tale were forced to expend even more effort. Many of the twists and concessions they made were more than a stretch. They expanded the meanings of archaic, long-forgotten words, coined neologisms based on mimetic words, and employed many other means besides to resurrect an ancient language as a tongue capable of expressing concepts in a scientific world.

Due to the strained, arbitrary nature of this venture, Proto-Baronh yielded a handful of weak points. At the outset, this language was riddled with large numbers of syllables. The raft of Chinese-origin loanwords had tipped the actual historical language toward fewer syllables, but since those words were also abolished, syllable counts became more and more unwieldy.

That was the ungainly language that the first generation of Abhs lived using. It was only natural for Baronh vocabulary undergo a rapid and drastic phenomenon of abbreviation. Another reason for this is the fact that the original Abhs didn't have writing. The Abhs' creators never wanted them to develop a civilization of their own. They were to simply carry out the repetitive tasks they were taught, and make easy, uncomplicated decisions if ever an emergency arose. That was all that was desired of the Abh.

In accordance with the idea that the written word was not just unnecessary but an active hindrance, the first generation of Abhs were instructed without text or letters of any kind. The only forms of information storage bestowed to them were video and audio. They were not permitted the method of information transmission with a deeper pedigree. Letters, glyphs, text: all were banned.

It is well known that languages without orthographies shift at a quick pace, and Baronh is no exception. Yet another reason behind its rapid change must be that the Abhs numbered so few and coexisted in an enclosed environment. After all, whenever any one person affected a change, that change would immediately make it to the entire group and take root.

It follows, then, that the upheaval that laid waste to all of the phonological rules would progress at an extremely accelerated rate. Going by the precious little extant data left, it seems vowels were the first to shrink in number. That straightforward vowel reduction led, however, to the proliferation of homophones. They must have noted that was occurring, and in order to prevent it, the remaining vowels got tugged to different places by the vowels that had dropped out. Consequently, the variety of vowels had sprung back from its brief low point.

In addition, (though it's far from certain how exactly this relates to the vowel shifts), the transition of consonant pronunciation (such as the denasalization of certain formerly nasal sounds) also transpired, and it's reasonable to assume that that played a part in the fusion of word-ending inflections and case-marking particles.

Given the intensity of these changes, they must have taken place over an exceedingly short span of time — that is, within two or three generations. Afterward, the Abh declared independence, discarded the restrictions placed on them by the birth city, and designed letters for their own use.

Shifts in Baronh became much slower once a writing system was established. Moreover, the founding of the Empire accompanied the codification of the standard language. Not much of note changed after that, owing to their heightened awareness that, in order to keep communication between their brethren on separate ships or orbital cities smooth, they had to work to preserve a singular, "correct" Baronh.

As such, though the grammar of Baronh is more complex than its bygone parent language, it is kept the way it is. The most striking example of increased complexity would have to be the introduction of noun declension.

(Kindly refer to the declension tables included in the author's notes in Volume 1.)

Afterword

And with that, *CREST OF THE STARS* — the work that took three volumes despite being its no-name author's first longform — has come to an end. I wonder whether you enjoyed the read.

When I was concepting these books, I'd planned to write something pertaining to an interstellar war from the beginning. I soon realized, however, that simply taking nations that could exist or have existed on Earth and expanding them to a galactic scale wouldn't be engaging.

Instead, I thought I'd set up an interstellar empire that couldn't have arisen without the advancement of humanity to many different planets, and pit it against the countries that spread the political principles of Earth across the galaxy.

I created the *Humankind Empire of Abh* as a sovereign entity that could never exist on Earth, and the Abh race as a unifying element of that empire. I've fashioned a rather unique galactic superpower, if I do say so myself.

Meanwhile, I tasked young Jint with guiding the reader through the Empire. He knows just enough to need some but not all things explained to him from time to time, making him an ideal guide indeed. He is the indisputable protagonist of *CREST OF THE STARS*.

...As for why I felt the need to tell you that, I fear that the impression the guide's own guide, Lafier, left was so strong that it rather overshadowed his own. I can't help but laugh at that, but I assure you I do feel a little sorry for him.

Oh well. Nothing for it, really. With Lafier, I've never had that "I *crafted* her" feeling. I suppose that's also true of the other characters. There were even those who entered the fray in spite of the fact I never had any such plans, running roughshod over my plot. Then there were those characters I did plan on joining the fray that got zapped.

In any case, *CREST OF THE STARS* is hardly sufficient, on its own, to guide you through the Empire. It's particularly lacking in any depiction of the economic side of Abh life.

I don't feel too many misgivings over wrapping up *CREST OF THE STARS* here, because the plot naturally progressed to the "the war's going to start in earnest" point. (To you who already read Volumes I and II, there's no way you thought the war would be over in the space of three volumes, right?)

I actually found myself thinking *oh, I guess this phase of the story's complete.* Not even I know where exactly the Kin of the Stars are headed now. All I know is that if the Abh fall in battle, they can but suffer complete annihilation. An Abh bound to a surface world is an Abh no longer. Worse yet, if genetic modification is forbidden to them, they'd die out within a few generations anyway, due to their unstable genome.

I'd love to learn alongside all of you whether the Abh crumble to oblivion, or whether they bring the slumber that is "peace" to the galaxy. Yet at the same time, as embarrassing as it is to admit, I'd be lying if I said there wasn't a part of me that wants to leave them with an infinite future.

…But that makes it seem as though *CREST OF THE STARS* was penned with some grand and important idea behind it. In reality, as I confessed in the afterword to Volume I, I ended up creating the setting as I went along.

The actual impetus behind this series was all the murmuring that we were in "the Winter of SF." That made me want to write some light-reading SF that people might pick up precisely because it was the so-called "Winter of SF" (which doesn't seem to have abated, mind you), and so I started working on it, just like that.

Initially I was aiming for a piece of around 400 pages, thinking that'd make it easy to publish, but it dawned on me that was going to be impossible after the third day of writing. *All right, then, I'll get it done in 600 pages…* But it wasn't long before I was thinking, *800 pages and I'll have it published as one thick paperback.* I found myself constantly rethinking my initial conception.

I finally saw the light at the end of the tunnel at around page 550. I reckoned that turn of events would make for the best midpoint in terms of story balance. (Though I ended up writing 700 more pages before reaching the conclusion.)

I also altered the setting and terminology a great deal, retroactively. For instance, Lafier wasn't a Star Forces Trainee Starpilot, but rather a Space Army Cadet, and Ship Commander Lecsh was a colonel. After I'd written the series and waited a while before rereading it, those were the bits and bobs that felt "loose," strangely. The unique terms I came up with, such as "Star Forces" and "starpilot," were born then.

What had been created with relative care were the mechanics of planar space navigation and Baronh. I'm no august SF writer, of course; at the end of the day, the idea of "planar space navigation" is just a slight twist on the well-worn, hackneyed "warping" trope (evoking faster-than-light travel with one quick and easy word) that I wanted to avoid. With regard to the liberal sprinkling of Baronh all over the place, I had several reasons. To give you just one, I wanted to foster an alien atmosphere.

In terms of the feel of the setting, Jint hails from a society just 300 years from our present, so you can think of him as your stereotypical future human, but Lafier comes from more than 2,000 years in the future. For those of you who can't square that discrepancy, try looking up Lorentz contraction. Whatever you do, don't ask me to clarify, because then I'd have to give myself away! In truth, I just didn't want to go ham with too many foreign-origin words.

That said, "plasma" and "energy" were the words that had me stumped. Japanese just uses the English words for them for the most part. I was under the impression that a purely Japanese word whose characters combine to mean "ionized substance" was coined as a translation for the English word "plasma," but I couldn't find that word in the *Koujien* dictionary, so if I tried using that made-up word as the meaning of the Baronh for "plasma," readers wouldn't be able to understand what it was referring to. Obscuring the commonly used word with non-standard characters on top of piling on fictional vocabulary felt too unfriendly to the reader, so I gulped down the urge to overindulge in my little hobby.

Speaking of Baronh, its true origins became clear in Volume 2 — or at least, I hope I made them clear enough. In case you didn't buy that origin story ("How in sam heck did that become the language in the books!?"), I included an appendix in this volume that should help persuade you. If you've bought all three volumes at once and haven't read any of the story yet, I recommend not reading that appendix beforehand. It's a spoiler. (I see spoiler warnings from time to time, but I've never personally abided by that whole rule.)

Now then, seeing as this is the last volume, allow me to express my gratitude.

A hearty thank you to NODA Masahiro, who wasted a blurb on the likes of me. I only met him in person and greeted him once, but he introduced me to the sheer entertainment value of a good space opera through works published in SF magazines — works like "Heroic Figures of SF" (*SF Eiyuu Gunzou*). I'll never forget how, when I was in elementary school, I'd hole up in the tin-roof shed in the sizzling heat, browsing through back issues of SF magazines to read installments of "Heroic Figures."

I'd also like to thank one AKAI Takami, for decorating the covers with gorgeous illustrations despite how busy he always is. I'm sure the majority of people who picked these books up did so because they were captivated by the cover art (and I bet you did, too, dear reader).

In addition, I can't forget to thank all the people who put in the hours to slot in the Baronh. At first, I only added Baronh based on specific criteria, but then it ran away from me. I ended up laying down Baronh even where it wasn't really necessary; so much so, that to say I went mad with it would be an understatement. Making all of that Baronh play neatly with the rest of the text was largely on the shoulders of a certain someone in Editorial. Of course, that certain someone helped me with everything, not just with the Baronh text.

Moreover, all the work these books required must have been a nightmare to the proofreader(s) and overall production. Thank you so much! I do think less is more when it comes to auxiliary text, so I'll still be relying on their help from here on out.

Finally, I naturally need to thank you, the readers who followed along all this time, from the bottom of my heart. If you could send me your thoughts and feelings, I'd be even more grateful.

Writing *CREST OF THE STARS* was loads of fun, and if you experienced a tenth of the fun reading it as I did writing it, then I think you've thoroughly enjoyed it.

I sure hope we meet again, somewhere, some day. Until then!

May 10, 1996

Translating Baronh: On Rubi

If you'll indulge me for a moment, I, your humble translator, would like to take this page to show those of you who might be interested what the Baronh in the original Japanese text looks like.

バンゾール・ガリク
1 男爵館家政室

この年はフェブダーシュ男爵領歴で一三六年にあたる。といっても、男爵館の公転周期が短いため、男爵領の一年は標準の三分の一ほどしかない。

ごく新しい国家だといえる。

そう、住民がわずか五〇名ほどしかなくとも、フェブダーシュ男爵領はたしかにひとつの国家だった。

The small text that's hovering above a handful of the words in the above excerpt is called "rubi." Often (but not always), it's there to tell the reader how to pronounce a word that's tricky to read. To force an illustrative example:

cwire

choir.

In this series' case, the rubi is the Japanese transliteration of the Japanese word's equivalent Baronh word.

バンゾール・ガリク
1 男爵館家政室

Both the text on the bottom and at the top are Japanese. The characters at the bottom spell out what this word means (barony homemakers' office, *danshaku-kan kasei-shitsu* in Japanese). The very different-looking characters that comprise the rubi are purely phonetic, sounding out the equivalent Baronh word (BANZOHRU GARIKU).

As you may be aware, Japanese has a very small sound library compared to most other languages. Foreign words have to get squeezed into the hole of that sound library to be spoken in Japanese. For example, since there is no "see" sound in Japanese, any loanword that contains the syllable "see" gets

610

that syllable replaced with the closest extant sound in the Japanese sound library, which in this case is a "shee" sound. The English word "seat cover" is pronounced SHEETO KABAH.

MORIOKA created Baronh to sport a more robust sound library than Japanese, despite the limitations of getting those pronunciations across in the text itself. Through supplemental material and best-guessing, we know that the Baronh spelling of what in the text is spelled out as BANZOHRU GARIKU, is in fact *banzorh garicr*.

...Or is it *bandhorh garicr*? That would make it a voiced "th" sound instead of a "z" sound, but they're both pronounced "z" in Japanese. Another possibility is that it's pronounced with a "z," but it's spelled *banzzorh*.

There are official spellings for many of the words in the glossary, but others are truly best guesses based on the phonics and phonotactics of Baronh. As such, the glossary is *semi-official*. It's the official English rendition of Baronh, but is subject to change as more comes to light on the matter.

Selected Glossary

The following glossary is a curated version of the working document used throughout the translation process. As such, it is arranged topically rather than alphabetically; for example, *Fiac* directly precedes *Lonh* in spite of there certainly being Baronh words that could fall alphabetically between the two. The "complete" glossary is a substantially larger document, spanning many dozens of pages of Baronh words, their English translations, and explanatory translator's notes. Further selections from the glossary will be made available in the future, as the series progresses.

Note that true Baronh does not have capitalization, as it is written in the *ath* script.

Noble, Royal, and Imperial Ranks; Citizen Status; and Related Terms

- Flirich: court/palace
- Fasanzœrh: the Imperial Family; refers to all Abliars (the Emperor, Abdicant Emperors, and the eight royal families). I've opted to sometimes refer to them as "Imperials." They are the descendants of the Founding Emperor and his siblings. All are obligated to serve in the military.
- Scaimsorh (Rœnr): the (Jade) Throne
- Scaimsorragh: the Imperial Throne/Crown/the Emperorship
- Rüébéïc: Imperial Palace
- Rüéghéc: Imperial Household; none other than the Abliar clan.
- Rüénéc: Imperial Princess; what Jint mistakenly called Lafier (she is technically a Royal Rrincess).
- Rüébaugenéc: Imperial Granddaughter; a technically correct title for Lafier that no one actually uses.
- Bhoflic: Imperial Court
- Darmsath: hierarchy
- Darmsath bhoflir: Imperial Court Hierarchy

- Simh: noble/nobility; also what vassals call their lord in the third person (the English equivalent being "master"). During the City-Ship Era, this was the word used to denote the leaders of each of the clans. Note that there are also single-generation nobles, in which case instead of the name of a star-fief (which they don't have), their titles have an "imperial" tacked on the front (e.g., "imperial baron").
- Simfé: aristocracy/aristocratic society
- Bhodac: Grandee; specifically refers to particularly high-ranking nobles that possess inhabited planets, namely Dukes, Marquesses, Counts, and Archdukes.
- Bhodaghéc: grandee's house; "house" as in household/family.
- Fïac: Highness; used for royalty.
- Lonh: Excellency; note that the translations for these four titles are fairly arbitrary. There isn't actually a 1:1 correspondence to English titles. *Lonh* is used for nobles and ordained (i.e. higher-level) starpilots.
- Nisoth: Eminence; used for Abdicant Emperors.
- Érumitta, Érumittonn: Majesty; used for the Emperor.
- Speunaigh: Emperor/Empress
- Scurlaiteriac: Founding Emperor
- Cilugiac: Crown Prince(ss)
- Cilugéragh: the Crown Princeship
- Cilugragh: succession of the Emperorship
- Fanigac: Abdicant Emperor
- Fanigalach: Abdicant Emperors (plural)
- Luzœc Fanigalacr: Council of Abdicant Emperors; comprised of eight Abdicant Emperors, it is a council that administers penalties against, promotions for, and hearings with Imperial Family starpilots. Those hearings are harsher than what normal starpilots have to face.
- Larth: King/Queen/Monarch; there are always eight. Said to represent eight gods of the ancient mythical pantheon. The position is largely a formality; they are in charge of managing their region's portals, serving as proxies of the Emperor, and officiating various

ceremonies. Can only leave Royal Palaces on public business. The same word (larth) was used for the City-Ship Era's absolute authority, the so-called "Ship's Crown."

- (Ga) Lartïéc: the (Eight) Royal Families
- Lartbéic: Royal Palace
- Lartnéc: Royal Princess
- Lartragh: the Royal Throne/Crown of the Monarchy
- Lartsoc: Royal Prince
- Faicec: monarchy; faicec also means "a reason."
- Nimh: Archduke/Archduchess; non-Imperial Family clan leaders descended of the 28 founding families.
- Nimhynh: archduchy
- Nimïéc: archducal house
- Nimragh: the dukeship
- Laicerec: Duke/Duchess; the highest peerage a person of common blood can ascend to.
- Laicerhynh: duchy
- Lœbec: Marquess/Marchioness; a marquess's domain has an inhabited planet whose population exceeds one hundred million.
- Lœbeghéc: marquess's house
- Lœbehynh: marquessate
- Dreuc: count(ess); a count's domain has an inhabited planet.
- Dreughéc: count's house
- Dreuhynh: countdom
- Dreuragh: the countship
- Bœrh: Viscount(ess); a viscount's domain can be made habitable (like Lafier's).
- Bœriéc: viscount's house
- Bœrscorh: viscountdom; related to the word scorh, which I've rendered as "domain."
- Lymh: baron(ess); the lowest rank of nobility, a baron's domain lacks an inhabitable planet.
- Lymécth: baron's manor
- Lymeghéc: baron's house

- Lymragh: the baronship
- Lymscorh: barony
- Ïarlucec: noble prince; son of nobility.
- Ïarlymec: noble princess; daughter of nobility.
- Tlaïgac: title
- Sapainec: surnym; the portion of an Abh's full name that delineates their bloodline's status. They are Ssynec, Bautec, Baurgh, Araunn, and Nëïc. Check out the "surnyms" section of this glossary for more info.
- Snaic: imperial/royal/noble rank; in order to inherit a noble (or greater) rank, one must be born to a noble (or greater) house, and then spend ten years in the Star Forces as a starpilot.
- Snaironn: rank diploma; issued upon the conferral of a peerage, under the name of the Director Secretary.
- Lalasac: distinguished persons
- Raloch: knight first-class; held by those with designation as ship commander (sarérragh).
- Cizéc: knight second-class; held by those of rank equal to or higher than deca-Commander or vice hecto-Commander, but without designation as ship commander.
- Rufurh: knight third-class; rearguard and vanguard starpilots.
- Ainabh: knight fourth-class; linewing starpilots. Granted also to sach Landers upon working their way to linewing starpilot rank.
- Rihairh: knight fifth-class; those born as reucec gentry and who have grown of age without yet becoming a starpilot (includes trainee starpilots).
- Cya: sir/dame; a title of esteem for gentry (like Lecsh).
- Reucec: gentry; "gentry" in the sense that they're below nobility. They could also be classified as "loyal retainer families." This is the default Abh social status.
- Reuceragh: status as gentry
- Gosucec: vassal/servant; employees of certain Abh households.
- Gosuclach: vassal/servant corps

- Laimh: imperial citizen; refers to Landers who work for the Empire (as opposed to soss: landworld citizens). There is no gap in prestige between laimh and soss. Laimh can meritocratically rise in status.
- Bisarh: subject

Eight Royal Families and Their Monarchies

- Faicec Ilicr (Ilich): Ileesh Monarchy; located in the Twelfth Ring. The Empire expanded in both directions starting from the *Ilich* Portal, forming a shape often called the "Arms of the Abh," by which name the Ileesh Monarchy is also known. Housename: Néïc Dusirr.
- Faicec Üescor (Üescoc): Wesco Monarchy; located in a sector between the United Humankind and the People's Sovereign Stellar Union. Housename: Néïc Duairr.
- Faicec Clybr (Clybh): Clyoov Monarchy; surrounded by the Hania Federation. Housename: Néïc Dubreuscr.
- Faicec Scirr (Scirh): Skeer Monarchy; located in a sector between the Hania Federation and the People's Sovereign Stellar Union. Housename: Néïc Lamrer.
- Faicec Surgzedér (Surgzedéc): Soorgzedeh Monarchy; surrounded by the United Humankind. Housename: Néïc.
- Faicec Bargzedér (Bargzedé): Bargzedeh Monarchy; located in a sector between the Hania Federation and the Greater Alkont Republic. Housename: Néïc Düasecr.
- Faicec Barcœr (Barcœc): Barkeh Monarchy; located in a sector between the United Humankind and the People's Sovereign Stellar Union. Also borders Wesco. Housename: Néïc Lamsarr.
- Faicec Rasiser (Rasisec): Raseess Monarchy; located in a sector between the United Humankind and the Greater Alkont Republic. Housename: Néïc Lamryrer.

Surnyms (*Sapainec*)

Note: the "accessibility" spelling follows the Baronh spelling in the following section.

- Baurgh: Borzh; signifies one as a member of a gentry family line that became gentry after the founding of the Empire. That is to say, Landers who became Abh, and their descendants.
- Üémh: Wef; signifies one as a gentry descendant of one of the 29 Founding Families. Lecsh is one example.
- Ssynec: Syoon; signifies one as being a noble of a family line that received the surnym after the founding of the Empire. Jint is one example, albeit a rare one (his lineage having become a Ssynec without first being any other surnym).
- Aronn: Arohn; signifies a one as being a noble of a family line that became nobility starting with the founding of the Empire.
- Bautec: Both; signifies one as belonging to a house that used to be part of the Imperial Family, but has since separated. Considered of higher prestige than Aronn.
- Néïc: Nay; signifies one as a member of the Imperial Family, a so-called "Imperial." Lafier is one example.

Governmental Terms

- Agth: territory-nation; specifically, an imperial territory star system with one or more inhabited planets. Note that the spelling is strange, as it's pronounced A'EETH.
- Aroch: imperial capital; i.e., Lacmhacarh
- Arnaigh: orbital tower
- Bach: orbital city/joined residences (like a complex)
- Bandhorh: office
- Bandhorh Casobérlac: merchant ship headquarters
- bandhorh chtymer: astrobase headquarters; central facility of an army astrobase.
- Roïglaharérh Chtymer: Astrobase Vice Commander-in-Chief
- bandhorh garicr: homemakers' office; the post that deals with the affairs of orbital manors.

- bandhorh ludorhotr: recruiting office; compulsorily erected on each of the inhabited landworlds in the Empire. Solicits for emigrants, vassals, and NCCs. It's also where admittance exams for starpilot academies are held. Star Forces soldiers are stationed at a recruiting office by dint of force, but those are the only starpilots allowed on a landworld without the star-fief administration's permission.
- Bauchimh: Chancellor
- Bauchimïach: Chancellor's Office; the pinnacle of the Empire's bureaucracy, residing inside the Imperial Palace.
- Rüe Bauchimh: Imperial Chancellor; the person at the top of the Empire's bureaucracy. They receive the same treatment as nobility, and once they retire, they are conferred the title of baron (or of viscount if they were particularly accomplished). Relatively few Imperial Chancellors have been Abh since birth.
- Baulébh: administrative zone
- Béïc: (orbital) palace
- Bhorsorh: Financial Affairs Bureau
- Birautec: city
- Fapytec: lord/lady; this word has a feudalistic flavor to it, so I went with "star-fief" for ribeunec.
- Gahorh: Lord/Lady's Office; the room where the lord conducts their official duties.
- (Rüe) Casobérlach: (Imperial) Merchant Ship Company; the flotilla that oversees all interstellar ships in the Empire, lending them to companies and nobles with crews attached. The position of the chief executive, the Merchant Ship Dean, is always held by the current Emperor. Also refers to simple trading ship flotillas.
- Cfariac: lord/lady agent
- Roïcfariac: lord/lady agent's adjunct
- Ciïoth: star system
- Frybarec: Empire; alternately spelled "freubarec."
- Gaicec, gareurec: company/association
- Faziac diüimr: terraforming engineer
- Gareurec Fazér Diüimr: Terraforming Engineers' Association

- Gar glac: crest banner; refers to each clan, nation, and naval base's respective symbolic flag/coat of arms.
- Scass: (high) institute; high administrative organ of the Empire.
- Gar Scass: Institute of Imperial Crests; safekeeper of the crests of nobles and gentry, and the agency that administers family status and genealogies. At present, they also oversee internal investigations within territory-nations and domains, serving as a kind of secret police.
- Garich: (orbital) manor; sometimes not in orbit but on land. The residences of nobles and wealthy gentry. Many noble houses with short pedigrees use warships as their manors.
- garich arocr: capital manors; the manors in the capital, as opposed to ones in nobles' domains.
- Lusagac: representative
- Roïlusagac: secondary representative
- Nahainec/nahainelach: landworld(s); specifically refers to human-inhabited planets.
- Nahainudec: landworlder; as opposed to "Lander."
- Ribeunec: star-fief; a star system that is the territory of a fapytec. Ones with inhabited planets are agth territory-nations, and ones without are scorh domains.
- Razaimecoth: law
- Scorh: domain; ribeunec star-fiefs without inhabited planets, as opposed to agth territory-nations.
- Soss: landworld citizen
- Saiméic (sosr): landworld administration; often abbreviated to saiméic. Related to the word saimh (representative/director).
- Saimh: representative/director
- Saudonic: councilor; an administrative official at the Ambassadorial Agency (or elsewhere), helping the director while commanding and controlling the staff.
- Scass Lazassotr: Supreme Imperial Court Rules on punishments against nobles; possible sentences include monetary fines and divestiture of one's domain.

- Sozairh: Governor-General; the highest ranked in the government-general of a prison camp, as its commander, as well as a bureaucrat.
- Sozairïaic: government-general; the organization that oversees both the military and administration affairs of prison camps.
- Tosairh: magistrate; specifically, a person assigned to do a lord's work in their place.
- Tosairaüriac: magistrate agent; a temporary stopgap magistrate.

Star Forces Ranks and Terminology

- Laburec: The Star Forces
- Lodaïrh: starpilot; this is another fun little neologism of MORIOKA's. It translates to something like "flyer." I opted for a neologism of my own. The higher ranks of the Star Forces are all starpilots, and anyone who managed to become one is automatically considered an adult. Their minimum wage is 16 *scarh* a month.
- Lodaïrh cisaïna: reserve starpilot
- Alm Lodaïrh: Senior Starpilot; specifically the vice commander of a small-sized warship (such as an assault ship).
- Roïalm Lodaïrh: Deputy Starpilot; the position after *Alm Lodaïrh*.
- Bausnall: soldier; refers collectively to both starpilots and NCCs.
- Glaharérh (Byrer): (Fleet) Commander-in-Chief
- Glaharéribach: commander-in-chief's Seat
- Roïglaharérh: Vice Commander-in-Chief
- Luciac: adjutant; assistant to the Fleet Commander-in-Chief.
- Sairhinec: military uniform
- Rénsimesiac: rank insignia; borne on the breast of the military uniform. An isosceles triangle with curved sides. Contains a *silder gaftnochec* eight-headed dragon surrounded by silver bordering. The color of the base against which the dragon lies depends on the branch of the military (Flight Branch: scarlet; Mechanics Branch: green; Quartermasters Branch: white). The number of lines and stars displays one's rank.
- Buséspas: skipper's insignia
- Ptorahédésomh: commander's insignia

- Clapaimh: staff officer insignia
- Ctarœbh: bandolier sash; a belt for carrying gun holsters and grenades. Now that firearms aren't permitted onboard, it's mostly decorative, allowing ship commanders to display their designation as commander while also serving as holsters for their command batons.
- Üébh: waistsash; the ones starpilots wear are crimson red.
- Saputec: pressure helmet; as in "pressurized."
- Gonœc: pressure suit
- Creunoc: wristgear; multi-function device worn on the back of the left hand. Its color depends on one's family status (e.g., nouveau nobility like Jint have green wristgear).
- Clanh: lightgun; another neologism to indicate "laser," rendered in the Japanese characters for "compressed light." I went with lightgun due to its additional flashlight functionality.
- Clanragh: laser beam
- Ïapérh: (light)gun cartridge; acts as a low-power grenade in a pinch.
- Cénruc (lodaïrr): (starpilot) academy; three-year academy to train soldiers and drill reserve starpilots. Each branch of the Star Forces has at least one in the capital.
- Cénruc Sazoir: Quartermaster Academy; the academy Jint went to, in order to be a starpilot administrative official and clerk in the Budget Branch.
- Cénruc Scœmr: Mechanics Academy; for trainee pupils hoping to join the Artisans Branch of the Star Forces.
- Cénruc üacér: Airship Academy
- Cénruragh: academy admittance qualification(s)
- Cénruragh lordara: joint academy; an institution founded to gather and educate Abhs from their mid-teens to age 20, during the City-Ship Era. Back then, this was the age range between when a person's immediate family would give them preliminary basic education, and when a person's larger clan would educate them about their professional specialty. It was established by Abliar Duroïc, who feared a potential war between the clans, seven years before the

logbook's disappearance. Its educational course was comprised mostly of military training.

- Cénh (cénrur) (Laburer):(Star Forces) (academy) trainee pupils
- Sarérh: ship commander/unit commander; the captain of a large ship, such as a patrol or battle-line ship. Also the word for the commander of a unit (for squadrons and above, it's a *raichaicec* commandant). Also the word for the commanding officer of a spaceship in general, particularly an interstellar ship.
- Saréribach: ship commander's seat
- Sarérragh: designation as ship commander
- Sarérh doborr: encampment commander; the person in charge of the landworld training that trainee pupils go through at an encampment.
- Sobrelach Arocr: Imperial Defense Platoon; a standing unit composed of Imperials and nobles who have retired from military service, as well as other soldier applicants. It doesn't do much of consequence during peacetime, but if and when war comes to the capital, they are duty bound to fling themselves into the fray to buy time. The platoon commander is chosen from among the Abdicant Emperors.
- Sobriac arocr: Imperial Defense troop; a soldier in the Imperial Defense Platoon.
- Ruséc: vice commander; under a ship commander. A position that exists on mid-sized ships and above.
- Manoüass: captain; the captain of a small ship, such as an assault or escort ship.
- Paunoüass: skipper; the pilot of an onboard ship (*paunh*), such as a *pairriac* or *caricec*.
- Lonidec: (orbital) stronghold; for defending portals.
- Chtymec: (army) astrobase; a star system containing a number of facilities for military use, including for resupplying, for recreation, and for warship docking and maintenance. Each of the eight monarchies contains one such system, positioned close to the portal that leads to the imperial capital.

- Saucec: crewmember
- Greuc: command baton
- Slymecoth: military service
- Rénh: (military, court) rank
- Üanhirh: combat ration(s)
- Ïocsscurhoth: strategy
- Ïocsdozbhoth: war preparations
- Slachoth/tlachoth: battle
- Scoïcoth: mission
- Cimecoth: military secret
- Clabarhoth: battle formation
- Bhosecrac: military academy; for those who have already put in four and a half years of military service (or two years for Imperials), they may enlist here in order to be appointed Deca-Commanders.
- Bhosecrac Duner: Dunaic Academy; the most difficult of the bhosecrac military academies, and the one that Imperials attend.
- Glagamh: headquarters/command center; the division that commands each formation, for squadrons and above.
- Bhosorh: Military Administration Base; where military personnel matters are handled.
- Bhoboth: headquarters/home base
- Bhoboth Ménhotr: Warship Management Headquarters; handles the design and layout of warships, among other things.
- Catboth: command center soldiers; the "t" is silent. Soldiers besides command personnel that make up a given headquarters.
- Raichaicec: Commandant; the highest-level commanding officer of a corps, sub-fleet, or squadron. The commander of a sub-fleet is a separate position from a ship's captain in that they give their undivided attention to commanding.
- Raichaicibach: commandant's seat
- Rÿazonh: Military Command Headquarters; responsible for analyzing the war's progression. Directed by the Head of the Military Command Headquarters. Orders from Command carry the same weight as imperial decrees.

- Fsœtdoriac: ordained starpilot; the "f" is silent. Equivalent to a general officer, which is to say, ranks Kilo-Commander and up. They're allowed to decorate their seats at personal expense, and to wear things that display the family line they belong to.

Flight Department
- Rüéspénec (or Glaharérh Rüé Byrer): Imperial Admiral, aka Imperial Fleet Commander-in-Chief; note that this position only exists for the Flight Department. Once an Imperial has reached this rank, they have become Crown Prince(ss) as well as Imperial Fleet Commander-in-Chief. An Imperial Admiral is allowed to wear a special purple long robe as well.
- Spénec Laburer: Star Forces Admiral; this position is also Flight Department-only.
- Fofraudéc: Grand Commodore; the commander of a fleet.
- Fraudéc: Commodore; the commander of a fleet. Starpilots of this rank and above can wear twin-winged circlets.
- Roïfraudéc: associate commodore; the commander of a sub-fleet.
- Cheüass: kilo-commander; the commander of a squadron.

Field/Company Officers
- Bomoüass: hecto-commander
- Roïbomoüass: vice hecto-commander; starpilots of this rank and above can wear one-winged circlets.
- Loüass: deca-commander
- Raicléc: Vanguard Starpilot
- Rinhairh: Rearguard Starpilot
- Faictodaïc: Linewing Starpilot; the lowest rank of starpilot. Their salary is around 33 *scarh*.
- Bénaic/bénnaic: trainee
- Bénaic lodaïrr: trainee starpilot; equivalent to a military cadet.

Ranks of NCC

- Sach: NCC (Non-commissioned Crew); crew that rank below starpilot. (The Japanese word used for *sach* roughly means "follower.") Many are Landers. (A Lander that has managed to become a starpilot is treated as *reucec* gentry, and particularly outstanding high-ranking Landers can even become nobility.)
- Boalmüésach: most senior NCC leader
- Almüésach: Senior NCC Leader
- Üésach: NCC leader
- Sach Casna: NCC 1st-Class
- Sach Mata: NCC 2nd-Class
- Sach Bina: NCC 3rd-Class
- Sach Gona: NCC 4th-Class

Types of NCC

- Sach arobhotr: military band *sach*
- Sach idarr: honor guard NCC; elite NCCs chosen from among guard and airship NCCs, among other branches. They specialize in etiquette and security. In charge of patting down visitors and the like.
- Sach cnéïr: chef NCC
- Sach sazoir: quartermaster NCC; deals with accounting and sanitation.
- Sach satytr: mine NCC; manages the mines, which means many are on battle-line ships.
- Sach scœmr: mechanic NCC; deals with servicing the ship and with emergency measures.
- Sach scérr: accounting NCC; a quartermaster NCC that does office work such as checking the loading of replaceable parts and consumables.
- Sach sair: engine NCC; a mechanic NCC that services the space-time bubble generator engine(s).

- Sach lïalér: medic NCC; a quartermaster NCC that treats the wounded and the like.
- Sach laitefaicr: guard NCC; in charge of security and guarding, including surveilling prisoners.
- Sach üacér: airship NCC; an NCC on a landworld.

Ship Staff

- Casarhac Drochotr: Communiations Staff Division; in charge of analyzing the enemy's war potential.
- Casarelach: Staff Officers Division; an organization within the Imperial Fleet Headquarters consisting of staff officers. During large-scale drills and actual battle, they become the staff officers of the Commander-in-Chief, with the organization's Chief of Staff becoming the Chief of Staff of the fleet.
- Alm-: senior/lead (as in the top member of a work division); prefix. Related to almfac circlet (from root word "head"). The following words are also among the words that often take alm- as a prefix, as well as roï- and roïalm-.
- Roï-: associate; prefix.
- Roïalm-: deputy; prefix.
- Casariac: staff officer
- Drociac: communications officer; crew that's responsible for maintaining inter-ship communications, and for surveying planar space.
- Drociac raugrhothasairr: exploration communications officer
- Goneudec: homemakers' office
- Hymh: assemblage
- Rilbigac: navigator; specifically help with navigation in planar space. In 3d-space, they don't have much to do, so they tend to help any busy communications officers.
- Tlaciac: gunner; soldiers in charge of firing and of tactical analysis. Often also in charge of steering the ship when in the thick of battle.
- Tlaciac hocsathasairr: mine gunner

- Üigtec: clerk; on medium and larger-sized warships, clerks are senior quartermaster department starpilots in charge of office work, crewmember health management, purchasing and overseeing consumable supplies, cargo management, and the vessel's living environment (gravity control, air conditioning, pressurization, air and water purification, etc.). Can exercise a measure of budgetary discretion.
- Casariac drochotr: communications staff officer; staff officer who consolidates fleet information. In charge of inter-bubble communication.
- Casariac ïocsscurhotr: strategy staff officer; in charge of drafting strategies and calculating success rates.
- Casariac ragrhotr: exploration staff officer; staff officer who probes for space-time bubbles.
- Casariac rilbicotr: navigation staff officer; in charge of devising fleet formations and flight paths, as well as the steering of space-time bubbles.
- Casariac sair: engine staff officer; in charge of technical isues.
- Casariac sober: supply staff officer; in charge of supplying propellant and the loading and unloading of supply ships.
- Casariac tlachotr: gunnery staff officer
- Saidiac: steerer; the pilot of a small ship.

J-Novel Club Lineup

Ebook Releases Series List

Altina the Sword Princess
Amagi Brilliant Park
An Archdemon's Dilemma:
    How to Love Your Elf Bride
Arifureta Zero
Arifureta: From Commonplace
    to World's Strongest
Ascendance of a Bookworm
Bibliphile Princess
Bluesteel Blasphemer
By the Grace of the Gods
Campfire Cooking in Another World
    with My Absurd Skill
Cooking with Wild Game
Crest of the Stars
Demon King Daimaou
Demon Lord, Retry!
Der Werwolf: The Annals of Veight
From Truant to Anime Screenwriter: My
    Path to "Anohana" and "The Anthem of
    the Heart"
Full Metal Panic!
Grimgar of Fantasy and Ash
Her Majesty's Swarm
How a Realist Hero Rebuilt the Kingdom
How NOT to Summon a Demon Lord
I Refuse to Be Your Enemy
I Saved Too Many Girls and Caused the
    Apocalypse
I Shall Survive Using Potions!
If It's for My Daughter, I'd Even Defeat a
    Demon Lord
In Another World With My Smartphone
Infinite Dendrogram
Infinite Stratos
Invaders of the Rokujouma!?
Isekai Rebuilding Project
JK Haru is a Sex Worker in Another World
Kobold King
Kokoro Connect
Last and First Idol
Lazy Dungeon Master
Middle-Aged Businessman, Arise in Another
    World!
Mixed Bathing in Another Dimension
My Big Sister Lives in a Fantasy World
My Next Life as a Villainess: All Routes Lead
    to Doom!
Otherside Picnic
Outbreak Company
Outer Ragna
Paying to Win in a VRMMO

Record of Wortenia War
Seirei Gensouki: Spirit Chronicles
Seriously Seeking Sister! Ultimate Vampire
    Princess Just Wants Little Sister; Plenty of
    Service Will Be Provided!
Sexiled: My Sexist Party Leader Kicked
    Me Out, So I Teamed Up With a Mythical
    Sorceress!
Side-By-Side Dreamers
Sorcerous Stabber Orphen:
    The Wayward Journey
Tearmoon Empire
Togonia
The Economics of Prophecy
The Faraway Paladin
The Greatest Magicmaster's Retirement Plan
The Holy Knight's Dark Road
The Magic in this Other World is
    Too Far Behind!
The Master of Ragnarok & Blesser of Einherjar
The Tales of Marielle Clarac
The Underdog of the Eight Greater Tribes
The Unwanted Undead Adventurer
The World's Least Interesting Master Swordsman
There Was No Secret Evil-Fighting
    Organization (srsly?!), So I Made One
    MYSELF!
Welcome to Japan, Ms. Elf!

Manga Series:
A Very Fairy Apartment
An Archdemon's Dilemma:
    How to Love Your Elf Bride
Animeta!
Ascendance of a Bookworm
Cooking with Wild Game
Demon Lord, Retry!
Discommunication
How a Realist Hero Rebuilt the Kingdom
I Shall Survive Using Potions!
Infinite Dendrogram
Marginal Operation
Seirei Gensouki: Spirit Chronicles
Sorcerous Stabber Orphen:
    The Reckless Journey
Sweet Reincarnation
The Faraway Paladin
The Magic in this Other World is
    Too Far Behind!
The Master of Ragnarok & Blesser of Einherjar
The Unwanted Undead Adventurer